EVERYMAN,
I WILL GO WITH THEE,
AND BE THY GUIDE,
IN THY MOST NEED
TO GO BY THY SIDE

ALBERT CAMUS

THE PLAGUE
THE FALL
EXILE AND THE
KINGDOM
AND
SELECTED ESSAYS

WITH AN INTRODUCTION BY
DAVID BELLOS

EVERYMAN'S LIBRARY
Alfred A. Knopf New York London Toronto

278

THIS IS A BORZOI BOOK
PUBLISHED BY ALFRED A. KNOPF

First included in Everyman's Library, 2004

The Plague
Originally published in France as *La Peste* by Gallimard 1947.
US: Copyright 1947 by Editions Gallimard. Copyright renewed 1974 by Madame Albert Camus.
Translation Copyright 1948 by Stuart Gilbert. Copyright renewed 1975 by Stuart Gilbert.
UK: This translation first published in Great Britain by Hamish Hamilton 1948.
Published in Penguin Books 1960. Translation copyright © 1948 by Stuart Gilbert.

The Fall
Originally published in France as *La Chute* by Gallimard 1956.
US: Copyright 1956 by Librairie Gallimard. Translation Copyright 1956 by
Alfred A. Knopf, Inc. Copyright renewed 1984 by Alfred A. Knopf, Inc.
UK: This translation first published in Great Britain by Hamish Hamilton 1957.
Published in Penguin Books 1963. Translation copyright © 1957 by Justin O'Brien.

Exile and the Kingdom
Originally published in France as *L'Exil et le royaume* by Gallimard 1957.
US: Copyright 1957 by Librairie Gallimard. Translation Copyright 1957, 1958
by Alfred A. Knopf, Inc. Copyright renewed 1985 and 1986 by Alfred A. Knopf, Inc.
UK: This translation first published in Great Britain by Hamish Hamilton 1958.
Published in Penguin Books 1962. Translation Copyright © 1958 by Justin O'Brien.

The Myth of Sisyphus
Originally published in France as *Le Mythe de Sisyphe* by Gallimard 1942.
US: Copyright 1942 by Librairie Gallimard. Translation Copyright © 1955 by
Alfred A. Knopf, Inc. Copyright renewed 1983 by Alfred A. Knopf, Inc.
UK: This translation first published in Great Britain by Hamish Hamilton 1955.
Published in Penguin Books 1975. Translation Copyright © 1955 by Justin O'Brien.

Reflections on the Guillotine
Originally published in France as *Réflexions sur la peine capitale* (with Arthur Koestler),
Calmann-Lévy, 1957.
US: Copyright © 1957 by Calmann-Lévy. Translation Copyright © 1960 by
Alfred A. Knopf, Inc. Copyright renewed 1988 by Alfred A. Knopf, Inc.
UK: © Editions Gallimard, Paris, 2002. Translation first published in Great Britain by Hamish
Hamilton 1961, in a selection of essays by Camus entitled *Resistance, Rebellion and Death*.

In the UK, all the above published by arrangement with Hamish Hamilton Ltd.

Introduction Copyright © 2004 by David Bellos
Bibliography and Chronology Copyright © 2004 by Everyman's Library
Typography by Peter B. Willberg
Seventh printing (US)

All rights reserved. Published in the United States by Alfred A. Knopf, a division of Random
House, Inc., New York, and in Canada by Random House of Canada Limited, Toronto.
Distributed by Random House, Inc., New York. Published in the United Kingdom by
Everyman's Library, Northburgh House, 10 Northburgh Street, London EC1V 0AT,
and distributed by Random House (UK) Ltd.

US website: www.randomhouse/everymans

ISBN: 978-1-4000-4255-5 (US)
978-1-85715-278-4 (UK)

A CIP catalogue reference for this book is available from the British Library

Book design by Barbara de Wilde and Carol Devine Carson
Printed and bound in Germany by GGP Media GmbH, Pössneck

33090014430187

ALBERT CAMUS

—

CONTENTS

The Sun, the Sea...

Albert Camus was born on 1 November 1913 at Mondovi, a small town in the eastern part of Algeria, which was then an integral part of the French state. His early life was harsh and poor, but a boy doesn't need to be rich to relish the best things about Mediterranean life: sun, sea, soccer ... and girls. Though much of Camus's work as a writer tackles tough moral issues from a perspective that is bleak at best, it is also shot through with the joy of physical life. Many of Camus's characters share their author's delight in the sea. In *The Plague*, for example, Tarrou and Rieux, the two stalwart defenders of the human race in its struggle against evil and oppression, cement their friendship by going for a swim in the warm, star-lit sea. Similarly, in all Camus's works the sun represents not just warmth and pleasure, but life itself. Soccer, which occupied much of Camus's energy as a boy, figures more rarely in the work, but it remained a fundamental part of Camus's sense of self:

Only in team sports played in my youth have I ever known that overpowering sense of hope and solidarity that goes with long periods of training leading up to victory or defeat on the day of the match. Really, the little moral philosophy I know I learned on the soccer pitch and on the stage; those were my two real universities.

(From a television interview, 1959)

The main part of Camus's life that is almost entirely omitted from his works is the subject of women and sexual love. Camus was from his teens a handsome and energetic charmer of the opposite sex. His conquests were legion, ranging from one-night stands after a beach encounter to a drawn-out, stormy romance with the great actress Maria Casarès. But save for an oblique confession in the pages on Don Juan in *The Myth of Sisyphus*, Camus did not write about desire, love or sex. His are novels of ideas, not novels of adultery in the manner of Balzac or Tolstoy; they are novels of moral and topical import, not stories of amorous intrigue or psychological analysis. It is true that Meursault, the central figure of Camus's first novel, *The Outsider*, picks up a girl and spends the night with her – but the episode is narrated as a matter of routine, as something so unexceptional as to require no explanation or analysis. The beach, the sea, and the body are as it were equal partners in the immaculate sensuality of Mediterranean life.

Camus was both deeply attached to heliotropic physicality and irremediably cut off from it. At the age of seventeen he contracted tuberculosis, and remained a more or less sick man, requiring periods of convalescence and care, for the rest of his life. From then on, however much he liked to kick a ball around, Camus did not have enough wind to last a match, and he had to fall back on flag-waving for his old club, *Racing Universitaire d'Alger*, for which he had briefly played goal. Illness, though, had many more serious and fruitful consequences. At that time an incurable as well as a contagious and infectious disease, tuberculosis debarred Camus from teaching at school or university. Without the infection Camus would almost certainly have been a teacher as well as a writer. If at times his essays sound a little schoolmasterly, it is out of frustration, not out of habit or routine. Tuberculosis also exempted Camus from military service, and furthermore prevented him enlisting in wartime. Passionately opposed to Franco's Fascist rebellion in Spain, passionately opposed to Nazism and to German aggression against Poland and then France, Camus could only ever fight evil with words. But chronic illness never stopped Camus from loving the outdoor life or from chasing every good-looking woman who crossed his path. He was a man of his time in this as in many other respects: his colleagues and rivals Jean-Paul Sartre, Arthur Koestler, even Romain Gary were equally voracious in their sexual appetites; and with the exception of Gary, they all drank and smoked – in blind disregard of tuberculosis or any other condition – to a degree that would today have that whole bunch of Parisian intellectuals dispatched to a rehab clinic for multiple substance abuse.

INTRODUCTION

Scholarship Boy

Camus had the good fortune to be a bright boy in the heyday of the French education system. Scholarships were available to ensure that he pursued the curriculum through to the baccalaureate at age eighteen. He also had the good fortune to encounter first-rate teachers who awoke his interest in philosophy, literature and politics. The curriculum in Algeria was of course identical to the one pursued in every other part of the French Empire, from Brittany to Indo-China. The curriculum in literature and philosophy, with their associated exercises of *explication de texte* and *dissertation*, constituted the mortar which held France's far-flung communities together and made the 'civilizing mission' of the colonial project self-evident. Camus proved very good at subjects held to sit at the very pinnacle of the system. Schooling in Latin, in literature, and in philosophy made a proud and self-confident Frenchman out of a poor boy from the back of beyond.

He went on to the University of Algiers, which similarly taught the standard French curriculum, obtained a first degree in letters and then a master's in philosophy, with a dissertation entitled *Christian Metaphysics and Neo-Platonism: Plotinus and Saint Augustine* (1936). Camus's dissertation supervisor, Jean Grenier, a humanist philosopher with an interest in Eastern religions, had immense influence on the younger man, who became and remained a close friend and companion.

There were no scholarships for university studies, so Camus supported himself through all kinds of odd jobs, collecting experience of varied worlds which he would use now and again in his later work (for example, the strike at the coopers' yard which forms the subject of 'The Silent Ones' in *Exile and the Kingdom*). As a student, Camus also discovered amateur dramatics, which became a real passion. He founded his own theatrical troupe, acted and directed, adapted novels for the stage, and ended up writing his own plays too. Although Camus is now best known for his fiction and essays, he himself always felt most at home in the theatre. He loved the collaborative aspect of play production, the process of putting different skills together, the atmosphere and the illusory reality of the stage. Though not all his plays and productions were well received, Camus never stopped being involved in theatricals all his life long. Indeed, the last and perhaps the most completely successful of all his novels, *The Fall* (1958), is a dramatic monologue almost ready to be staged as it stands in book form.

There is in all Camus's writing a quite noticeable aspiration towards the elegance and abstraction that gets high marks in French schools. It would perhaps be unflattering but it is not unfair to say that Camus's concept of good style rests on what he had learned by the age of eighteen or twenty. The only way out of poverty and provinciality for Albert Camus was the education system, and he had every reason to believe that the values that it was built on as well as the techniques that it taught him held universal, even magical power. The system had already proved its worth in raising him from the very bottom of the pile.

White Trash

Camus's father was vineyard labourer. Though he did not toil in the field but in the vinification process, his position was barely a rung above that of peasant. He was conscripted at the outbreak of the First World War and fell on the fields of Flanders. Camus never knew him. His mother, Catherine Sintès, had to earn her own living thenceforth: illiterate and unqualified, she became a cleaner. The family had other relatives in French Algeria who were moderately successful, but Camus's personal background is one of such poverty as can hardly be imagined nowadays. It did not make Camus a bitter or jealous man. But it has profound importance for the ways in which we should try to understand his moral and political attitudes.

Camus lived in Algeria for all his formative years, and all his fictional works save for *The Fall* are set there. Yet as Conor Cruise O'Brien acutely observed thirty years ago, not a single Arab speaks in the entire *œuvre*. In the story called 'The Guest', the Arab prisoner's comrades leave a message on the blackboard – but still not a word is spoken aloud. In *The Outsider*, an Arab is shot – but has not a single word attributed to him in direct speech. The Oran of *The Plague* is an entirely European city. The native population is alluded to here and there, but Arab Algerians are never seen and never heard in the text, as if only Europeans could even catch bubonic plague. The deafening silence of the Arabs is not a cynical ploy on Camus's part, and it is probably a quite unconscious aspect of the novel. In failing to give any place to the vast majority of the population of Algeria, Camus reproduces the mindset not of the wealthy colonialists who employed (and thus en-countered) the Arab population, but of the *petits Blancs* ('white trash') whose Frenchness was their only asset.

Alongside theatre, Camus's main activity in his young manhood in Algiers was in journalism, and he spoke out courageously against the abuses of colonial rule. But it did not occur to him that the colonial project itself was flawed, even if he came to fear that it was doomed. After he moved to France in 1940, and long after that, as the situation in Algeria became ever more fraught, he remained unable to comprehend the true drama of his native land. He was a man of his time, not a far-sighted prophet, and he remained loyal to his own people and class, the European population of Algeria. He deplored settler violence but he felt more threatened by the violence of the nationalists. In reply to a question from the floor after his acceptance speech for the Nobel Prize in Literature in 1957, Camus said:

I must also denounce a terrorism which is exercised blindly, in the streets of Algiers for example, and which some day could strike my mother or my family. I believe in justice, but I shall defend my mother above justice.

Camus certainly did his best to promote the cause of justice in the European theatre and the world at large, and he was not insensitive to the plight of the Arab population of Algeria. It's just that he could not connect to them as people: and how could he? Like all the settlers save those who actually managed farms or factories with Arab employees, Camus never acquired a single word of Arabic. What we can see in his fiction is an accurate and sensitive reproduction of the *blank stare at the other* that lies at the heart of the historical tragedy of the *petits Blancs*.

ALBERT CAMUS

The Work Ahead

Camus is one of those rare writers who worked out what he had to say early on, and proceeded along a plan laid out in advance. As he said in Stockholm in 1957:

> I had a precise plan when I began my work. What I wanted to express first was negation. In three ways: in novel form (which produced *The Outsider*); in theatrical form (which produced *Caligula* and *Cross Purposes*); and in essay form (*The Myth of Sisyphus*). Then I foresaw three more works expressing positive values: in the form of a novel (*The Plague*); as theatre (*State of Siege* and *Les Justes*); and in an essay (*Rebellion and Revolt*). I also dimly projected a third layer of writing, on the theme of love.

This is not a retrospective imposition of order on a life as full as any other of unforeseen events. Camus really did have a plan at the start: 'I'm twenty-five, I have a life ahead of me, and I know what I want,' Camus wrote in his notebook around the outbreak of the Second World War, and in its tripartite form Camus's grand plan reminds us once again of the influence of his French *lycée* training. He summed it up in three key words: *The Absurd – Revolt – Love.* Of these three terms, the first is the one most lastingly associated with the work of Albert Camus. He became first and foremost the 'novelist of the absurd'. But as his plan makes clear, the absurd is only the first panel of the triptych Camus envisaged as his lifework. Nowadays, looking back on a life and on novels profoundly moulded by a particular place and time, we may not think the absurd the most important of Camus's ideas. But it cannot be avoided, as it forms the first pillar in a moral and literary edifice of lasting beauty and value.

The absurd is the state of being in the absence of religious faith. Camus held no religious beliefs, of course. But he held his non-belief with a kind of moral fervour and intellectual intensity that has become very rare – and perhaps rather naïve – in a world more secularized than the one in which Camus grew up. In the absence of faith or belief in an order transcending the murky mess of human existence, death is an end that undermines the value of anything that precedes it. At least, that's what Camus argued, not just for the sake of it,

xiv

but because he felt it deeply. Only a god could make human actions meaningful in an absolute sense, and as there was no god, actions and states in the world have no 'ultimate' meaning. From this Camus drew the conclusion that life was 'absurd'. As he often explained, there is no credible argument that can justify the existence of evil; there is no sophistry that can ever make sense of why bad things happen to nice people and to innocent babes. So what can you do? Camus's first project was simply to describe the true state of our being, to make us see, in fiction, on stage, and in ideas, just what it is to be alive in a world that is, in his special sense, absurd. That is the sole real purpose of Camus's first and still most widely read novel, *The Outsider*. The second part of his plan was to investigate the kinds of response such a realization should prompt: broadly labelled 'revolt', this phase of Camus's work is devoted to ways of making a human sense of an inhumanly meaningless world. Most of the texts grouped in the present selection of Camus's writing belong to the second part of the overall project.

It has often been pointed out that Camus's concept of the absurd is itself rather absurd. Why should anyone find it at all remarkable – or even more strangely, lamentable – that there is no transcendent meaning to human acts? Things would surely be far worse if the opposite were the case. If the world were not at all absurd, in Camus's sense, then things in general and acts in particular would be endowed irrevocably with 'meaning'. And that would make the world a very strange and inhuman place indeed. Every cup of tea, broken shoelace, premature death, and outbreak of slaughter would be 'meaningful', that is to say fully explicable in terms of a higher order, and thus necessary. Under such conditions, human life, which characteristically involves imponderable choices, rough guesses, effort, and surprise, would surely seem quite futile, since no matter what a person did, it would fit in with a higher scheme by the very fact of having been done. A necessary world thus seems to many readers (myself included) as rather more absurd than one in which meanings are not given. Indeed, by the time *The Outsider* was completed, Camus himself lost his conviction in the importance of his own 'absurdist' premise:

The greatest timesaving device there is in the realm of thought is to accept the non-intelligibility of the world – and to get down to worrying about humankind.

(From Camus's *Notebooks*)

All the same, the absence of 'ultimate' meaning, even if it is what makes life possible in practice, was felt by Camus, and by millions of people of his generation, as a palpable gap, as an emotional void in the place previously occupied by religious faith. For that reason Camus's work belongs not just to the history of literature, but also to the history of European consciousness. Camus gives us access to one important aspect of what it was like to be alive and to be thinking in a world which, although barely more than half a century away from us now, really had a different set of collective fears, regrets and aspirations.

'Revolt', on the other hand, continues to have great purchase. The point that Camus makes in *The Myth of Sisyphus* is that the fact that life is absurd is not a reason for ending it; on the contrary, 'man' should rejoice in the struggle to overcome absurdity by giving his own life a human, not a transcendental sense. The best way to cope with the absurdity of existence, Camus argues, is to treat it with contempt – by behaving as if every aspect of human life really mattered. That is all that Camus really meant by 'revolt'. *The Plague* is Camus's principal lesson in 'revolt', and it is therefore a novel of vague but persuasive optimism about the possibility for achieving a meaningful life in the struggle against the incomprehensible and the oppressive.

The third cycle of work that Camus intended, focused on 'love', is in a sense broached by *The Fall* and perhaps by the unfinished novel Camus left at his death, *The First Man*. But Camus did not have time to develop this 'third layer' of his work. He died in 1960, not of tuberculosis or of the consequences of a difficult and hard-drinking life – but from a banal road accident. He was not yet forty-seven years of age.

INTRODUCTION

Days and Nights

Journalism was Camus's first career and the only one in which he could be called a professional. At the age of twenty-five he was taken on to the staff of a left-wing daily, *Alger républicain*, when it was founded in October 1938, and wrote copiously for it as reporter, book-reviewer, and editorialist until it folded under political pressure in its second incarnation as *Le Soir républicain* in early 1941. In 1943, when *The Outsider* and *The Myth of Sisyphus*, both published in 1942, had begun to make Camus a well-known figure in Occupied France, he joined the clandestine newspaper *Combat*, and emerged as its editor-in-chief when the paper appeared legitimately on the Liberation of Paris in August 1944. For the following four years Camus ran France's most prestigious if not most popular daily paper, and wrote a huge number of editorials on the many burning political and moral questions of post-war France. Working for *Alger républicain* had taught Camus how to transform his facility for academic prose into plain-speaking and pointed fluency. But the obligation to give leadership to public opinion in the fluid, fractious world of liberation France got Camus into numerous political dog-fights which pushed him ever forward in the search for abstract and general principles of justice in human affairs.

Camus, like so many French intellectuals of his generation, but more briefly than most, had flirted with Communism in his youth. Even after the war, he continued to feel it was wrong to attack the Party, for fear of giving comfort to the 'forces of reaction'. *Combat* itself proclaimed on its post-war masthead that it would take France 'from Resistance to Revolution'. But from one crisis to another, Camus's view of the Soviet Union and of the French Communist Party grew ever more negative, and he emerged by the late 1940s as the leading anti-Communist intellectual in France. Jean-Paul Sartre moved in the opposite direction, coming ever closer to the Party, and acting in effect, from about 1952 to 1956, though without declaring any formal allegiance, as what was then called a 'fellow-traveller'. Though it had numerous other personal, intellectual and cultural determinants, the split between Sartre and Camus can most easily be understood as a parting of the ways over the question of support for Communism in France. This clash of the Titans caused vast amounts of ink to be spilled, and it still does today, though its importance to us is far from obvious. But it led to at least one important clarification, as it prompted Camus to declare unambiguously that he was not an existentialist. That much was unquestionably true.

One of the most difficult issues for Camus the journalist was the question of violence. In 1944, the victorious French Resistance sought to punish those who had collaborated with the Nazi occupiers, and a wave of reprisals, kangaroo courts and summary justice nearly engulfed France in civil war. Initially Camus led *Combat* to take the side of the 'purifiers'. But when he realized what that meant in practice – shaving heads, expropriating owners, imprisonments and executions – he started to take his distance from 'revolutionary justice'. In stages Camus came to preach non-violence as a mode of action, and to denounce the use of violence wherever it occurred, but more often in Eastern Europe than elsewhere, such as in the French colonies. He reserved his strongest language and effort for a campaign against the death penalty, a campaign inherited from his literary forebear Victor Hugo, and carried forward by the French Socialist Party until it was finally enacted into law in 1981. The essay on capital punishment in the present selection was originally published in 1957 in a jointly authored volume alongside a piece on the same subject by Arthur Koestler.

Camus's collected journalism makes up the bulk of all he ever wrote (by volume, it outweighs the fiction, drama and essayistic work rolled into one). Much of it has aged, as is only to be expected; but what is most striking about even the best editorials now is their stylistic resemblance to lay sermons. It's a tone that doesn't only belong to its epoch, but to Camus quite especially; it might best be thought of as the moral earnestness of a resolutely secular but still surreptitiously Christian preacher.

Camus and the Church

The Fall presents in the form of a dramatic monologue the paradox of moral responsibility in a world without God. The speaker-hero Clamence has left an easy life in Paris to serve the dregs of human society in the rough quarters of Amsterdam, because he has come to realize that thieves, pimps and thugs are just as human as anyone else, himself included – or rather, that he, the successful and narcissistic lawyer, is in no fundamental way morally superior to an offender. In imitation of a Dostoevskian set-piece scene, Clamence's self-abasement is also a moral apotheosis, since he now lives in accordance with the self-evident moral truth that no man can be an island and that, as Simone de Beauvoir claimed in the epigraph to *The Blood of Others*, 'we must all answer for everything to the world at large' (an epigraph attributed by poetic licence to Dostoevsky himself). In what sense then is *The Fall* the story of a fall? The 'fall' from Paris to Amsterdam, from the *beaux quartiers* to the red-light district, only makes sense if you fail to adopt Clamence's moral perspective (and remain snobbishly Parisian and/or heliocentric as well). The real 'fall' to which the title of Camus's novel-drama alludes is far more general. It is the fall from grace. And it is not Clamence who falls, as an individual. His fall is our fall, for what Camus has to tell us is that we all live in a fallen world in which salvation can come only from human effort, not from providence. *The Fall* is not a Christian tract, of course. It is nonetheless couched in the language of the church and it is only really comprehensible as a vigorous contribution to a moral debate set by the church. As a work of moral philosophy it is no doubt more passionately interesting to readers attempting to free themselves from a Christian perspective than it is to those from a different religious or cultural background; but the underlying questions that it tackles concern every human being, irrespective of religious views.

The Plague is similarly an argument with the church conducted in part in the language of the sermon. Indeed, Father Paneloux gives two extensive sermons in the novel, and Camus has no difficulty whatsoever in making his pastiches sound like the real thing. In the first sermon Paneloux argues, in sum, that the plague has been sent by God to try man's faith. In the second, he preaches that maybe God is not involved so directly in a scourge that has caused the deaths of innocent children. Of course Camus believes and wants us to believe, from the evidence he presents so authentically, that Paneloux is plain wrong on both counts. It is neither original nor sophisticated to argue that the existence of plague proves the non-existence of God (Voltaire had pursued the same argument with respect to the Lisbon earthquake two hundred years earlier, and with greater anti-theological punch.) You might even think that only a very recently dechristianized preacher could possibly imagine that such an abstract issue might be morally or practically relevant to dealing with an outbreak of plague.

There's no point doubting Camus's agnosticism. At the same time, we do have to recognize that Camus's fiction is built on premises and couched in language that constantly imply the presence, not the absence, of Christian discourse and of its religious presuppositions. This is not just because of Camus's initial training in Christian theology, in his master's thesis on St Augustine; it is also because it spoke eloquently to Camus's first audience, large sections of which were still, in mid-twentieth century, straining to free themselves from the mental and moral authority of the church.

Parables and Code

Camus began to sketch out his second novel, *The Plague*, around 1942, when France was under German military occupation, but did not finish it until after the end of the war. It is set in the Algerian coastal city of Oran, which Camus knew well, and it purports to narrate an outbreak of bubonic plague at an unspecified time which is clearly intended to be the reader's 'now'. The authorities put the whole city under quarantine, so that the inhabitants live a long period in an effective state of siege. (When Camus transposed the underlying theme of the novel to the stage in 1948, he titled the play *State of Siege*.) The purely symbolic nature of the epidemic in the novel could hardly be more clearly indicated than by the measures taken to contain it.

As a matter of fact, the plague bacillus, *Yersinia pestis*, is a disease of rats transmitted to humans by a specific flea, *Nosopsyllus fasciatus*. Infected humans are neither infectious nor contagious, so they cannot pass the disease on to anyone else. Quarantine thus serves no purpose whatsoever. The bacillus and the flea were identified correctly in the late nineteenth century – by French scientists, moreover – and the outbreaks of plague in Paris in 1920, in Casablanca in the 1940s and in the very last epidemic in Europe, at Ajaccio (Corsica) in 1945, were quickly eradicated by modern medical approaches utterly unlike those used in Camus's novel.

Camus was neither a scientist nor a medical doctor: his 'plague' is a literary device, and its sources are clear enough: Daniel Defoe's *Journal of the Plague Year* (1722), a largely fictional account of the outbreak of the Great Plague in London in 1666; and folk memories of the Plague of Marseille (1722), when the whole area around the city was not only quarantined, but shut off from the rest of the world by a huge wall, the *mur de Provence*, remnants of which still stand not far from Lourmarin, Camus's summer retreat in the south of France. What makes *The Plague* such a powerful novel is what might be called its *constructed authenticity*, a literary effect built not on factual accuracy but on echoes of ancient nightmares, on recourse to literary reminiscences, and on a barely perceptible play on words. In French as in English we flee evil-doers *like the plague*. Camus's novel tackles the obvious question of what we might or should do when we're *plagued* by something we cannot flee.

The symbolic nature of the setting of Camus's third novel, *The Fall*, is similarly obvious. It is set in the bars of the seedier district of Amsterdam, a city Camus knew only from a 48-hour stop-over there, on 5 and 6 October 1954, which he spent in the city's art museums, not in its bars or brothels. The city where Clamence confesses himself is simply the opposite of Algiers: dark, wet and cold, 'Amsterdam' symbolizes Camus's personal idea of hell on earth, and the (sharp-angled) canals of the city are for him like the nine circles of Dante's underworld. The name Clamence, too, is not an actual name in French or any other language, but it echoes directly the French pronunciation of the Latin version of the Gospel according to St Mark, where John the Baptist appears as 'The voice of one crying in the wilderness, Prepare ye the way of the Lord, make his paths straight' (Mark 1.3). 'Crying in the wilderness' is *clamans in desertò*, and Clamence/*clamans*, though he may not be John the Baptist and may have no transcendent truth to announce, is 'crying in the wilderness' (of Amsterdam, which is hell, into which he has – as we have – 'fallen') to tell us at least something we should attend to.

Works like *The Plague* and *The Fall* are of course inexhaustible in the meanings that they suggest. Much of the planning for the first of these novels was done at a place called Le Panelier, in the Auvergne, where Camus had been sent for health reasons (it has particularly dry, clean mountain air). What is almost never said is that the nearby village of Le Chambon-sur-Lignon was then the centre of a network of Protestant (Darbyist) priests devoted to saving Jewish children from deportation to the Nazi death-camps. Was Camus aware that he was living amongst those extremely discreet heroes of the Resistance, whose courage saved several thousand lives? He had the intuitions of an artist more than the nose of a detective. *The Plague* would be an even more remarkable novel if it were a parable of Le Chambon-sur-Lignon written by a man who only guessed what was going on all around him.

The Message of Albert Camus

The Myth of Sisyphus, which belongs to the first phase of Camus's three-layered lifework, tells us simply that life is worth living because it is all that we have. As an essay on suicide, which it purports to be at the start, it is seriously deficient. It seems to have been written without extensive knowledge of actual suicides or of the medical, social or psychoanalytical literature about them. As an essay on the relative importance of human issues and metaphysical ones, however, it is entirely persuasive. Living a life and living it well is more important, Camus demonstrates, than knowing what it means.

INTRODUCTION

The Plague is most easily approached as a parable about the German Occupation of France. The 'state of siege' under which the residents of Oran are put is easily decoded as the situation of a subject population under foreign military rule. Paneloux's sermons are certainly intended to mimic the spineless response of many Frenchmen (including large sections of the established church and the implicitly pro-Nazi regime that ruled the so-called 'Free Zone' of wartime France). Rambert's desperate attempts to flee 'Oran' might also be read as referring to an attempt to escape to Britain to join the Free French Forces under Charles de Gaulle. And the steady, devoted efforts of Tarrou, Rieux and their helpers to bring what succour they can to the besieged population offer a parable of 'practical resistance', not to defeat the enemy in battle, but to preserve human dignity and to last the course, and in so doing to develop and to promote those virtues which misfortune can call forth: co-operation, solidarity, and the art of small kindnesses.

The parallels should not be pushed too far, however. The obsessive collection of statistical data for dealing with the outbreak of plague, even if it is meant to suggest that knowing the truth is always better than burying your head in the sand, is technically far more reminiscent of the bureaucratic efficiency of the Nazi occupiers than of the behaviour of the occupied French. Furthermore, the novel's silence about the majority population of the besieged city – assuming that we take the novel's Oran to represent the real Oran – simply has no meaning that can be transferred straightforwardly to the plight of Occupied France. Similarly, Cottard's struggle to find the right opening sentence for his novel belongs to a quite different layer of fiction, one that can't be read simply as a parable for resistance or oppression in the immediate context of France in the Second World War.

The Plague, for all its manifest encoding of the very recent past, is best read as a parable of a more general kind. It is a novel not so much about the Nazi Occupation, as about occupation, oppression, isolation and trial. It shows what it means to resist, not just a foreign invader, but incomprehensible evil in whatever form it may manifest itself. And it says:

good men – just men – do what they can, and they can do a great deal. In a story called 'The Wall', which Camus reviewed for *Alger républicain*, Sartre had argued forcefully that even in the direst confrontation with death, a man can always make a choice. *The Plague* can best be thought of as a brilliant transposition, expansion and modification of Sartre's schematic demonstration of the inalienability of human freedom, and thus as a work of bleak but profound optimism about human nature.

The Fall is much the most complex of the texts included in this selection. Beyond parable, beyond metaphor, it seeks to bring to life the contradictory, self-ironizing and painfully sensitive mind of a man who is not Albert Camus, but who shares with his creator a passion for justice in a world where it is far from easy to know where justice lies. It has no single argument, but it juggles with a whole set of arguments which contradict and complement each other, and yet constantly return to the question that plagues anyone who seeks to know how to live: what is justice? What is injustice? What, in a world without transcendental meaning, makes us able to tell 'good' from 'bad'? It is to Camus's credit as a thinker and artist that *The Fall* gives no final answers. What it does magnificently is to make these long-debated problems seem fresh, urgent, and difficult to solve.

Reading, Writing

Camus was a voracious reader in his youth, and a professional reader for much of his adult life. However, a relatively small set of important books formed Camus's ideas of what writing was for, and how it could best be done. Many of these 'master texts' were not part of the canon of French literature as it was taught at school and university. It is true that Camus's first novel, *The Outsider*, can be seen as a modern reply to Victor Hugo's *Last Day of a Condemned Man* (1828), which influenced Camus deeply in other respects too. There are other instances where Camus is, so to speak, in close dialogue with well-known works in the French school canon: 'The Artist at Work', for example, reads like an answer to Balzac's 'Unknown

Masterpiece' (1837). It is also true that Camus's idea of literary style owes much to the specifically French preference for brevity, abstraction and harmoniousness. However, the three greatest influences on Camus's writerly career come from outside the standard curriculum, and mostly from outside of France: Fyodor Dostoevsky, André Malraux and Franz Kafka. The first showed how to use the novel form to conduct philosophical argument and exercise moral suasion (*The Fall*, in its form as well as its moral content, could almost be an updated chapter from *The Brothers Karamazov*). The second offered a brilliant, seductive, utterly modern model for making fiction a form of thinking aloud about 'man's estate', as Malraux's *The Human Condition* is often titled in English translation. As for Kafka, Camus probably misread him (the essay appended to *The Myth of Sisyphus* would hardly pass muster with most Kafka scholars today), but he most certainly tried to imitate Kafka's blending of the fantastic and the real in stories like 'The Renegade' and 'The Growing Stone' (in *Exile and the Kingdom*).

The Art of Albert Camus

Because Albert Camus cast his first novel, *The Outsider*, in a very special variety of French – short declarative sentences rarely involving subordination, simple vocabulary, and verb forms more characteristic of the spoken than of the written language – he obtained, and seems to have retained, a reputation as a master of blunt plain speaking. And because of its special language, over the last fifty years *The Outsider* has often been the first book that foreign-language learners manage to read through to the end in French. Deeply-felt gratitude to the author of the first book read in a foreign tongue should not be allowed to obscure the fact that only *The Outsider* was written in that way. Camus uses language appropriate to the moral, philosophical and artistic aim of the work in hand, and his style varies considerably amongst his different novels, stories and essays.

Like any experienced journalist, Camus could be long-winded, vague, pompous, funny and sharp, as the matter –

and the situation – required. In his fiction, he is long-winded in *The Fall* (for Clamence can never quite get to the point of his lament, or to the bottom of his self-disgust) and sober in *The Plague*; insanely incoherent in 'The Renegade' (for the narrator is more than a little mad) and magnificently restrained in 'The Guest', which must be one of Camus's most finely crafted pieces of all. (It perches on an even sharper knife-edge of ambiguity in French because the title-word, 'L'Hôte', means both 'guest' and 'host'.) Camus is in fact much more varied as a writer and craftsman of language than he is as a moralist or thinker, in which domain, naturally enough, he tends to say much the same thing.

Some critics have expressed reservations about the narrative form of *The Plague*, regretting the turn in the tale where we learn that the narrator is in fact Dr Rieux (whose name suggests 'smiling'). It is true that re-reading the novel knowing that the narrative is in Rieux's own voice runs up against insoluble problems of narrative plausibility: there are episodes – Rambert's rendez-vous with smugglers in the docks, for example – to which Rieux is not a witness; and there is the larger question of when such a busy and exhausted man could have taken time out to write it all down. The only answer to such criticism is to say that on first reading you really don't notice. The art of Camus *as a novelist* – what he has in common with all great novelists – is the ability to create an irresistibly convincing fiction in conditions of logical impossibility. What might turn out to be an embarrassing flaw in a film script is, in the realm of fiction, part and parcel of the enchantment of art. Many of Camus's own commentaries about the meaning of his works make it seem as though art was for him but the sugar coating the pill of moral inquiry. He should not have sold himself so short. *The Plague*, *The Fall* and the stories of *Exile and the Kingdom* are amongst the most crafted and polished pieces of story-telling in all of modern literature.

David Bellos

SELECT BIBLIOGRAPHY

CONOR CRUISE O'BRIEN, *Albert Camus*, Collins, London, 1970. Fontana Modern Masters. A lively, intelligent polemic which focuses attention on the role of Camus's background in Algeria in the construction and meaning of his work.

ROGER GRENIER, *Album Camus*, Gallimard (Bibliothèque de la Pléïade), Paris, 1982. An outstandingly intelligent and sympathetic illustrated biography by a man who knew Camus well.

PATRICK MCCARTHY, *Camus*, Random House, New York, 1982. A readable 'life and works' of manageable dimensions.

PHILIP THODY, *Albert Camus*, Macmillan, London, 1989. Macmillan Modern Novelists. Informative and commonsensical, from a resolutely British point of view. Not especially sensitive to Camus's philosophical position, but quite acute on his art of writing.

OLIVIER TODD, *Albert Camus*, Gallimard, Paris, 1996. The standard narrative biography; a very long book, for specialists.

PHILIP HALLIE, *Lest Innocent Blood be Shed: The Story of the Village of Le Chambon and How Goodness Happened There*, Harper and Row, New York, 1979. An exhaustive narrative and moral account of the events taking place at and around Le Chambon-sur-Lignon when Camus was drafting *The Plague* at Le Panelier in 1942.

DAVID BELLOS is Professor of French and Comparative Literature at Princeton University. He is the author of *Georges Perec. A Life in Words* and *Jacques Tati. His Life and Art*.

CHRONOLOGY

DATE	AUTHOR'S LIFE	LITERARY CONTEXT
1913	Born in Mondovi, Algeria.	Proust: *Swann's Way*. Gide: *The Vatican Swindle*.
1914	Father mortally wounded at Battle of the Marne, awarded Croix de Guerre and Médaille Militaire. Trauma of his mother, Catherine Camus.	
1919		Gide: *The Pastoral Symphony*.
1925		Kafka: *The Trial*. Gide: *The Counterfeiters*.
1926		Hemingway: *The Sun Also Rises*. Malraux: *The Temptation of the West*. Kafka: *The Castle*.
1928		Malraux: *The Conquerors*.
1929	Discovers the work of André Gide.	
1930	First attack of tuberculosis.	Malraux: *The Royal Way*.
1932	Articles in *Sud*.	Céline: *Journey to the End of the Night*.
1933	Student, University of Algiers.	Malraux: *The Human Condition*. J. Grenier: *Islands*. Faulkner: French trans. of *Sanctuary*.
1934	Marries Simone Hié. Job at the Algiers Préfecture as a clerk. First art reviews for *Alger-Etudiant*.	
1935	Joins Communist Party.	
1936	*Licence*. Starts theatre group. First play: adaptation of Malraux's *Days of Wrath*. Actor with Radio-Alger. Divorce.	Céline: *Death on the Instalment Plan*.
1937	Leaves Communist Party. *The Right Side and the Wrong Side*.	Caldwell: French trans. of *Tobacco Road*. Malraux: *Man's Hope*.
1938	Journalist: *Alger républicain*.	Sartre: *Nausea*. Beckett: *Murphy*.

Outbreak of World War I.

Treaty of Versailles.

Centenary of the conquest of Algeria.

Hitler appointed Chancellor.

Anti-parliamentary riots by right-wing groups in an attempt to block the confidence vote for Daladier's Radical-Socialist government.

Abyssinia invaded. Franco-Soviet Pact. Malraux addresses the Algiers section of the Comité de Vigilance des Intellectuels Antifascistes. Popular Front government in France. Spanish Civil War.

Munich Agreement.

DATE	AUTHOR'S LIFE	LITERARY CONTEXT
1939	Articles on Kabylia. *Nuptials*.	Sartre: *The Wall*. Steinbeck: French trans. of *Of Mice and Men*.
1940	*Alger républicain* banned. Marries Françine Faure.	
1941	Returns to Oran. Finishes *Sisyphus*. The three absurds are now complete.	Koestler: *Darkness at Noon*.
1942	Convalescent in the Massif Central. *The Outsider* (also translated as *The Stranger*). *The Myth of Sisyphus*.	Ponge: *The Voice of Things*. Sartre: *The Flies*.
1943	Moves to Paris and works for Editions Gallimard. Joins staff of *Combat*.	Sartre: *Being and Nothingness*.
1944	*Cross Purpose*.	Sartre: *No Exit*.
1945	*Caligula. Letters to a German Friend*.	Sartre: *The Age of Reason*. Gary: *A European Education*.
1947	Leaves *Combat*. *The Plague*.	
1948	*State of Siege*.	Sartre: *Dirty Hands* and *What is Literature?*
1949	*The Just*.	
1950	*Actuelles I*.	
1951	*The Rebel*. 'First series: Absurd ... Second series: Revolt.'	Death of André Gide.
1952	Quarrel with Sartre and the Surrealists.	Beckett: *Waiting for Godot*.
1953	*Actuelles II*.	Robbe-Grillet: *The Erasers*.
1954	*Summer*.	
1955	Writes for *L'Express*.	
1956	Separation from wife. Leaves *L'Express*. *The Fall*.	Sarraute: *The Age of Suspicion*.
1957	*Exile and the Kingdom*. Nobel Prize for Literature. 'Reflections on the Guillotine'.	Butor: *La Modification*. Beckett: *Endgame*. Céline: *Castle to Castle*. Tati: *Mon Oncle*.
1958	Brings together articles on Algeria: *Actuelles III. The Right Side and the Wrong Side* republished with preface.	
1959	Adaptation of Dostoevsky's *The Possessed*.	Queneau: *Zazie dans le métro*. Schwartz-Bart: *The Last of the Just*.
1960	Killed in car crash at Villeblevin, 4 January. Unfinished novel: *Le Premier homme*.	

C H R O N O L O G Y

Germany invades Czechoslovakia. Spain falls to Franco. Germany invades Poland.

Germany invades France. Assemblée Nationale votes full powers to Pétain.

Germany invades the Soviet Union.

Allied invasion of North Africa. The southern French 'Free Zone' occupied by the Germans. Comité National des Ecrivains set up to promote intellectual resistance.

Italy surrenders.

Allied landings in Normandy. Liberation of Paris.
Fall of Berlin. Hiroshima. Germany and Japan surrender. Massacre in Sétif, Algeria.
Rebellion against French rule in Madagascar.

Outbreak of the Algerian War of Independence.

Franco-British invasion of Suez. Budapest uprising.

OAS action in Algeria. General de Gaulle returns to power. Fifth Republic founded.

THE PLAGUE

TRANSLATED FROM THE FRENCH BY
STUART GILBERT

It is as reasonable to represent one kind of imprisonment by another, as it is to represent anything that really exists by that which exists not!

    'Robinson Crusoe's Preface' to the third volume of *Robinson Crusoe*

DANIEL DEFOE

PART ONE

I

THE UNUSUAL EVENTS described in this chronicle occurred in 194..., at Oran. Everyone agreed that, considering their somewhat extraordinary character, they were out of place there. For its ordinariness is what strikes one first about the town of Oran, which is merely a large French port on the Algerian coast, headquarters of the Prefect of a French 'Department'.

The town itself, let us admit, is ugly. It has a smug, placid air and you need time to discover what it is that makes it different from so many business centres in other parts of the world. How conjure up a picture, for instance, of a town without pigeons, without any trees or gardens, where you never hear the beat of wings or the rustle of leaves — a thoroughly negative place in short? The seasons are discriminated only in the sky. All that tells you of spring's coming is the feel of the air, or the baskets of flowers brought in from the suburbs by hawkers; it's a spring cried in the market-places. During the summer the sun bakes the houses bone-dry, sprinkles our walls with greyish dust, and you have no option but to survive those days of fire indoors, behind closed shutters. In autumn, on the other hand, we have deluges of mud. Only winter brings really pleasant weather.

Perhaps the easiest way of making a town's acquaintance is to ascertain how the people in it work, how they love, and how they die. In our little town (is this, one wonders, an effect of the climate?) all three are done on much the same lines, with the same feverish yet casual air. The truth is that everyone is bored, and devotes himself to cultivating habits. Our citizens work hard, but solely with the object of getting rich. Their chief interest is in commerce, and their chief aim in life is, as they call it, 'doing business'. Naturally they don't eschew such simpler pleasures as love-making, sea-bathing, going to the pictures. But, very sensibly, they reserve these pastimes for Saturday afternoons and Sundays, and employ the rest of the week in making money, as much as possible. In the evening, on leaving the office, they forgather, at an hour that never varies, in the cafés, stroll the same boulevard, or take the air on their balconies. The passions of the young are violent and short-lived; the vices of older men seldom range beyond an addiction to games of bowls, to banquets and 'socials', or clubs where large sums change hands on the fall of a card.

It will be said, no doubt, that these habits are not peculiar to our town; really all our contemporaries are much the same. Certainly nothing is commoner nowadays than to see people working from morn till night and then proceeding to fritter away at card-tables, in cafés and in small-talk what time is left for living. Nevertheless, there still exist towns and countries where people have now and again an inkling of something different. In general it doesn't change their lives. Still, they have had an intimation, and that's so much to the good. Oran, however, seems to be a town without intimations; in other words, completely modern. Hence I see no need to dwell on the manner of loving in our town. The men and women consume each other rapidly in what is called 'the act of love', or else settle down to a mild habit of conjugality. We seldom find a mean between these extremes. That, too, is not exceptional. At Oran, as elsewhere, for lack of time and thinking, people have to love each other without knowing much about it.

What is more exceptional in our town is the difficulty one may experience there in dying. 'Difficulty', perhaps, is not the right word; 'discomfort' would come nearer. Being ill is never agreeable, but there are towns which stand by you, so to speak, when you are sick; in which you can, after a fashion, let yourself go. An invalid needs small attentions, he likes to have something to rely on, and that's natural enough. But at Oran the violent extremes of temperature, the exigencies of business, the uninspiring surroundings, the sudden nightfalls, and the very nature of its pleasures call for good health. An invalid feels out of it there. Think what it must be for a dying man, trapped behind hundreds of walls all sizzling with heat, while the whole population, sitting in cafés or hanging on the telephone, is discussing shipments, bills of lading, discounts! It will then be obvious what discomfort attends death, even modern death, when it waylays you under such conditions in a dry place.

These somewhat haphazard observations may give a fair idea of what our town is like. However, we must not exaggerate. Really, all that was to be conveyed was the banality of the town's appearance and of life in it. But you can get through the days there without trouble, once you have formed habits. And since habits are precisely what our town encourages, all is for the best. Viewed from this angle, its life is not particularly exciting; that must be admitted. But, at least, social unrest is quite unknown amongst us. And our frank-spoken, amiable and industrious citizens have always inspired a reasonable esteem in visitors. Treeless, glamourless, soulless, the town of Oran ends by seeming restful and, after a while, you go complacently to sleep there.

It is only fair to add that Oran is grafted on to a unique landscape, in the centre of a bare plateau, ringed with luminous hills and above a perfectly shaped bay. All we may regret is the town's being so disposed that it turns its back on the bay, with the result that it's impossible to see the sea, you always have to go to look for it.

Such being the normal life of Oran, it will be easily understood that our fellow-citizens had not the faintest reason to apprehend the incidents which took place in the spring of the year in question and were (as we subsequently realized) premonitory signs of the grave events we are to chronicle. To some, these events will seem quite natural; to others, all but incredible. But, obviously, a narrator cannot take account of these differences of outlook. His business is only to say, 'This is what happened,' when he knows that it actually did happen, that it closely affected the life of a whole populace, and that there are thousands of eyewitnesses who can appraise in their hearts the truth of what he writes.

In any case the narrator (whose identity will be made known in due course) would have little claim to competence for a task like this, had not chance put him in the way of gathering much information, and had he not been, by the force of things, closely involved in all that he proposes to narrate. This is his justification for playing the part of an historian. Naturally an historian, even an amateur, always has data, personal or at second hand, to guide him. The present narrator has three kinds of data, first, what he saw himself; secondly, the accounts of other eyewitnesses (thanks to the part he played, he was enabled to learn their personal impressions from all those figuring in this chronicle); and, lastly, documents which subsequently came into his hands. He proposes to draw on these records whenever this seems desirable, and to employ them as he thinks best. He also proposes . . .

But perhaps the time has come to drop preliminaries and cautionary remarks, and to launch into the narrative proper. The account of the first days needs giving in some detail.

II

WHEN LEAVING HIS surgery on the morning of April 16, Dr Bernard Rieux felt something soft under his foot. It was a dead rat lying in the middle of the landing. On the spur of the moment he kicked it to one side and, without giving it further thought, continued on his way downstairs. Only when he was stepping forth into the street did it occur to him that a dead rat had no business to be on his landing, and he turned back to ask the door-porter of the building to see to its removal. It was not until he noticed old M. Michel's reaction to the news that he realized the peculiar nature of his discovery. Personally, he had thought the presence of the dead rat rather odd, no more than that; the door-porter, however, was genuinely outraged. On one point he was categorical; 'There weren't no rats here.' In vain the doctor assured him that there *was* a rat, presumably dead, on the first-floor landing; M. Michel's conviction wasn't to be shaken. There 'weren't no rats in the building', he repeated, so someone must have brought this one from outside. Some youngster trying to be funny, most likely.

That evening, when Dr Rieux was standing in the entrance, feeling for the latch-key in his pocket before starting up the stairs to his flat, he saw a big rat coming towards him from the dark end of the passage. It moved uncertainly, and its fur was sopping wet. The animal stopped and seemed to be trying to get its balance, moved forward again towards the doctor, halted again, then spun round on itself with a little squeal and fell on its side. Its mouth was slightly open and blood was spurting from it. After gazing at it for a moment the doctor went upstairs.

He wasn't thinking about the rat. That glimpse of spurting blood had switched his thoughts back to something that had been on his mind all day. His wife, who had been ill for a year now, was due to leave next day for a sanatorium in the mountains. He found her lying down in the bedroom, resting, as he had asked her to do, in view of the exhausting journey before her. She gave him a smile.

'Do you know, I'm feeling ever so much better!'

The doctor gazed down at the face that turned towards him, in the glow of the bedside lamp. His wife was thirty, and the long illness had left its mark on her face. Yet the thought that came to Rieux's mind as he gazed at her was, How young she looks, almost like a little girl! But perhaps that was because of the smile, which effaced all else.

'Now try to sleep,' he counselled. 'The nurse is coming at eleven, you know, and you have to catch the midday train.'

He kissed the slightly moist forehead. The smile escorted him to the door.

Next day, April 17, at eight o'clock the porter buttonholed the doctor as he was going out. Some young scallywags, he said, had dumped three dead rats in the hall. They'd obviously been caught in traps with very strong springs as they were bleeding profusely. The porter had lingered in the doorway for quite a while, holding the rats by their legs, and keeping a sharp eye on the passers-by, on the off-chance that the miscreants would give themselves away by grinning, or by some facetious remark. His watch had been in vain.

'But I'll nab 'em all right,' said M. Michel hopefully.

Much puzzled, Rieux decided to begin his round in the outskirts of the town, where his poorer patients lived. The scavenging in these districts was done late in the morning and, as he drove his car along the straight, dusty streets, he cast glances at the garbage-bins aligned along the pavement's edge. In one street alone the doctor counted as many as a dozen rats deposited on the vegetable and other refuse in the bins.

He found his first patient, an asthma case of long-standing, in bed, in a room which served both as dining-room and bedroom and overlooked the street. The invalid was an old Spaniard with a hard, rugged face. Placed on the coverlet in front of him were two cooking-pots containing dried peas. When the doctor entered the old man was sitting up, bending his neck back, gasping and wheezing in his efforts to recover his breath. His wife brought a bowl of water.

'Well, doctor,' he said, while the injection was being made, 'they're coming out good and proper, have you noticed?'

'The rats, he means,' his wife explained. 'The man next door found three on his doorstep.'

'Aye, they're coming out, you can see them in the dustbins by dozens. It's hunger, that's what it is, driving them out.'

Rieux soon discovered that the rats were the great topic of conversation in that part of the town. After his round of visits he drove home.

'There's a telegram for you, sir, upstairs,' M. Michel informed him.

The doctor asked him if he'd seen any more rats.

'No,' the porter replied, 'there ain't been no more. I'm keeping a sharp look-out, you know. Those youngsters wouldn't dare, not when I'm about.'

The telegram informed Rieux that his mother would be arriving next day. She was going to keep house for her son during his wife's absence. When the doctor entered his flat he found the nurse already there. He looked at his wife. She was in a tailor-made suit, and he noticed that she had used colour. He smiled to her.

'That's splendid,' he said. 'You're looking very nice.'

A few minutes later he was seeing her into the sleeping-car. She glanced round the compartment.

'It's too dear for us really, isn't it?'

'Don't worry about that,' Rieux replied. 'It had to be done.'

'I say, what's this story about rats that's going round?'

'I can't explain it. It certainly is queer...but it'll pass.'

Then hurriedly he begged her to forgive him; he felt he should have looked after her better, he'd been most remiss. When she shook her head, as if to make him stop, he added: 'Anyhow, once you're back everything will be better. We'll make a fresh start, you and I, dear.'

'That's it!' Her eyes were sparkling. 'Let's make a fresh start.'

But then she turned her head and seemed to be gazing through the carriage window at the people on the platform, jostling each other in their haste. The hissing of the locomotive reached their ears. Gently he called his wife's first name; when she looked round he saw her face wet with tears.

'Don't,' he murmured. Behind the tears the smile returned, a little tense. She drew a deep breath.

'Now, off you go! Everything will be quite all right.'

He took her in his arms, then stepped back on to the platform. Now he could only see her smile across the window.

'Please, dear,' he said, 'take great care of yourself.'

But she could not hear him.

As he was leaving the platform, near the exit he met M. Othon, the police magistrate, holding his small boy by the hand. The doctor asked him if he was going away.

Tall and dark, M. Othon had something of the air of what used to be called 'a man of the world', and something of an undertaker's mute.

'No,' the magistrate replied, 'I've come to meet Madame Othon, who's been to present her respects to my family.'

The engine whistled.

'These rats, now...' the magistrate began.

Rieux made a brief movement in the direction of the train, then turned back towards the exit.

'The rats?' he said. 'It's nothing....'

The only impression of that moment which, afterwards, he could recall was the passing of a railwayman with a box full of dead rats under his arm.

Early in the afternoon of that day, when his consultations were beginning, a young man called on Rieux. The doctor gathered that he had called before, in the morning, and was a journalist by profession. His name was Raymond Rambert. Short, square-shouldered, with a determined-looking face and keen, intelligent eyes, he gave the impression of someone who could keep his end up in any circumstances. He affected a sporting type of dress. He came straight to the point. His newspaper, one of the leading Paris dailies, had commissioned him to make a report on the living conditions prevailing amongst the Arab population, and especially on the sanitary conditions.

Rieux replied that these conditions were not good. But, before he said any more, he wanted to know if the journalist would be allowed to tell the truth.

'Certainly I shall,' Rambert replied.

'I mean,' Rieux explained, 'would you be allowed to publish an unqualified condemnation of the present state of things?'

'Unqualified? Well, I must own I couldn't go that far. But surely things aren't quite so bad as that?'

'No,' Rieux said quietly, they weren't so bad as that. He had put the question solely to find out if Rambert could or couldn't state the facts without paltering with the truth.

'I've no use for statements in which something is kept back,' he added. 'And that is why I shall not furnish information in support of yours.'

The journalist smiled. 'You talk the language of St Just.'

Without raising his voice Rieux said he knew nothing about that. The language he used was that of a man who was sick and tired of the world he lived in – though he had much liking for his fellow-men – and had resolved, for his part, to have no truck with injustice and compromises with the truth.

His shoulders hunched, Rambert gazed at the doctor for some moments without speaking. Then, 'I think I understand you,' he said, getting up from his chair.

The doctor accompanied him to the door.

'It's good of you to take it like that,' he said.

'Yes, yes, I understand,' Rambert repeated, with what seemed a hint of impatience in his voice. 'Sorry to have troubled you.'

When shaking hands with him, Rieux suggested that if he was out for curious 'stories' for his paper, he might say something about the extraordinary number of dead rats that were being found in the town just now.

'Ah!' Rambert exclaimed. 'That certainly interests me.'

On his way out at five for another round of visits, the doctor passed on the staircase a stocky, youngish man, with a big, deeply furrowed face and bushy eyebrows. He had met him once or twice in the top-floor flat, which was occupied by some male Spanish dancers. Puffing a cigarette, Jean Tarrou was gazing down at the convulsions of a rat dying on the step in front of him. He looked up, and his grey eyes remained fixed on the doctor for some moments; then, after wishing him good day, he remarked that it was rather odd, the way all these rats were coming out of their holes to die.

'Very odd,' Rieux agreed. 'And it ends by getting on one's nerves.'

'In a way, doctor, only in a way. We've not seen anything of the sort before, that's all. Personally I find it interesting, yes, definitely interesting.'

Tarrou ran his fingers through his hair to brush it off his forehead, looked again at the rat that had now stopped moving, then smiled towards Rieux.

'But really, doctor, it's the porter's headache, isn't it?'

As it so happened the porter was the next person Rieux encountered. He was leaning against the wall, beside the street door; he was looking tired and his normally rubicund face had lost its colour.

'Yes, I know,' the old man told Rieux, who had informed him of the latest casualty amongst the rats. 'I keep finding 'em by twos and threes. But it's the same thing in the other houses in the street.'

He seemed depressed and worried, and was scratching his neck absent-mindedly. Rieux asked him how he felt. The porter wouldn't go so far as to say he was feeling ill. Still he wasn't quite up to the mark. In his opinion it was just due to worry; these damned rats had given him 'a shock, like'. It would be a relief when they stopped coming out and dying all over the place.

Next morning – it was April 18 – when the doctor was bringing back his mother from the station, he found M. Michel looking still more out of sorts. The staircase from the cellar to the attics was strewn with dead rats, ten or a dozen of them. The garbage-bins of all the houses in the street were full of rats.

The doctor's mother took it quite calmly.

'It's like that sometimes,' she said vaguely. She was a small woman with silver hair and dark, gentle eyes. 'I'm so glad to be with you again, Bernard,' she added. 'The rats can't change *that*, anyhow.'

He nodded. It was a fact that everything seemed easy when she was there.

However, he rang up the Municipal Office. He knew the man in charge of the department concerned with the extermination of vermin and he asked him if he'd heard about all the rats that were coming out to die in the open. Yes, Mercier knew all about it; in fact, fifty rats had been found in his offices, which were near the harbour. To tell the truth, he was rather perturbed; did the doctor think it meant anything serious? Rieux couldn't give a definite opinion, but he thought the sanitary service should take action of some kind.

Mercier agreed. 'And, if you think it's really worth the trouble, I'll get an order issued as well.'

'It certainly is worth the trouble,' Rieux replied.

His charwoman had just told him that several hundred dead rats had been collected in the big factory where her husband worked.

It was about this time that our townsfolk began to show signs of uneasiness. For, from April 18 onwards, quantities of dead or dying rats were found in factories and warehouses. In some cases the animals were killed to put an end to their agony. From the outer suburbs to the centre of the town, in all the byways where the doctor's duties took him, in every thoroughfare, rats were piled up in garbage-bins or lying in long lines in the gutters. The evening papers that day took up the matter and inquired whether or not the city fathers were going to take steps, and what emergency measures were contemplated, to abate this particularly disgusting nuisance. Actually the Municipality had not contemplated doing anything at all; but now a meeting was convened to discuss the situation. An order was transmitted to the sanitary service to collect the dead rats at daybreak every morning. When the rats had been collected two municipal vans were to take them to be burnt in the town incinerator.

But the situation worsened in the following days. There were more and more dead vermin in the streets and the scavengers had bigger vanloads every morning. On the fourth day the rats began to come out and die in batches. From basements, cellars and sewers they emerged in long wavering files into the light of day, swayed helplessly, then did a sort of pirouette and fell dead at the feet of the horrified onlookers. At night, in passages and alleys, their shrill little death-cries could be clearly heard. In the mornings the bodies were found lining the gutters, each with a gout of blood, like a red flower, on its tapering muzzle; some were bloated and already beginning to rot, others rigid, with their whiskers still erect. Even in the busy heart of the town you found them piled in little heaps on landings and in backyards. Some stole forth to die singly in the halls of public offices, in school playgrounds, and even on café terraces. Our townsfolk were amazed to find such busy centres as the Place d'Armes, the boulevards, the Strand, dotted with repulsive little corpses. After the daily clean-up of the town, which took place at sunrise, there was a brief respite; then gradually the rats began to appear again in numbers that went on increasing throughout the day. People out at night would often feel underfoot the squelchy roundness of a still warm body. It was as if the earth on which our houses stood were being purged of its secreted humours – thrusting up to the surface the abscesses and pus-clots that had been forming in its entrails. You must picture the consternation of our little town, hitherto so tranquil, and now, out of the blue, shaken to its core, like a quite healthy man who all of a sudden feels his temperature shoot up and the blood seething like wildfire in his veins.

Things went so far that the Ransdoc Information Bureau (Inquiries on all Subjects Promptly and Accurately Answered), which ran a Free Information talk on the wireless, by way of publicity, began its talk by announcing that no fewer than 6,231 rats had been collected and burnt in a single day, April 25. Giving as it did an ampler, more precise view of the scene daily enacted before our eyes, this amazing figure administered a jolt to the public nerves. Hitherto people had merely grumbled at a stupid, rather obnoxious visitation; they now realized that this strange phenomenon, whose scope could not be measured and whose origins escaped detection, had something vaguely menacing about it. Only the old Spaniard whom Dr Rieux was treating for asthma went on rubbing his hands and chuckling, 'They're coming out, they're coming out,' with senile glee.

On April 28, when the Ransdoc Bureau announced that 8,000 rats had been collected, a wave of something like panic swept the town. There was a demand for drastic measures, the authorities were accused of slackness, and people who had houses on the coast spoke of moving there, early in the year though it was. But next day the Bureau informed them that the phenomenon had abruptly ended and the sanitary service had collected only a trifling number of rats. And everyone breathed more freely.

It was, however, on this same day, at noon, that Dr Rieux, when parking his car in front of the block of flats where he lived, noticed the door-porter coming towards him from the end of the street. He was dragging himself along, his head bent, arms and legs curiously splayed out, with the jerky movements of a clockwork doll. The old man was leaning on the arm of a priest, whom the doctor knew. It was Father Paneloux, a learned and militant Jesuit, whom he had met occasionally and who was very highly thought of in our town, even in circles quite indifferent to religion. Rieux sat in his car, waiting for the two men to draw level with him. He noticed that M. Michel's eyes were fever-bright and he was breathing wheezily. The old man explained that, feeling 'a bit off colour', he had gone out to take the air. But he had started feeling pains in all sorts of places – in his neck, armpits and groin – and had been obliged to turn back and ask Father Paneloux to give him an arm.

'It's just swellings, but they hurt cruel,' he said. 'I must have strained myself somehow.'

Leaning out of the window of the car, the doctor ran his hand over the base of Michel's neck; a hard lump, like a knot in wood, had formed there.

'Go to bed at once, and take your temperature. I'll come to see you this afternoon.'

When the old man had gone, Rieux asked Father Paneloux what he made of this queer business about the rats.

'Oh, I suppose it's an epidemic they've been having.' The Father's eyes were smiling behind his big round glasses.

While Rieux was reading for the second time the telegram his wife had sent him from the sanatorium, announcing her arrival, the phone rang. It was one of his former patients, a clerk in the Municipal Office, ringing him up. He had suffered for a long time from a constriction of the aorta, and, as he was poor, Rieux had charged no fee.

'Thanks, doctor, for remembering me. But this time it's somebody else. The man next door has had an accident. Please come at once, it's urgent.' He sounded out of breath.

Rieux thought quickly; yes, he could see the porter afterwards. A few minutes later he was entering a small house in the Rue Faidherbe, on the outskirts of the town. Half-way up the draughty, foul-smelling stairs, he saw Joseph Grand, the municipal clerk, hurrying down to meet him. He was a man of about fifty years of age, tall and drooping, with narrow shoulders, thin limbs and a yellowish moustache.

'He looks better now,' he told Rieux, 'but I really thought his number was up.' He blew his nose vigorously.

On the top floor, the second, Rieux noticed something scrawled in red chalk on a door on the left. *Come in, I've hanged myself.*

They entered the room. A rope dangled from a hanging-lamp above a chair lying on its side. The dining-room table had been pushed into a corner. But the rope hung empty.

'I got him down just in time.' Grand seemed always to have trouble in finding his words, though he expressed himself in the simplest possible way. 'I was going out and I heard a noise. When I saw that writing on the door, I thought it was a . . . a leg-pull. Only, then I heard a funny sort of groan; it made my blood run cold, as they say.' He scratched his head. 'That must be a painful way of . . . of doing it, I should think. So naturally I went in.'

Grand had opened a door and they were standing on the threshold of a bright, but scantily furnished bedroom. There was a brass bedstead against one of the walls and a plump little man was lying there, breathing heavily. He gazed at them with bloodshot eyes. Abruptly Rieux stopped short. In the intervals of the man's breathing he seemed to hear the little squeals of rats. But he couldn't see anything moving in the corners of the room. Then he went to the bedside. Evidently the man had not fallen from a sufficient height, or very quickly, for the collar-bone had held. Naturally there was some asphyxia. An X-ray photograph would be needed. Meanwhile the doctor gave him a camphor injection and assured him he would be all right in a few days.

'Thanks, doctor,' the man mumbled.

When Rieux asked Grand if he had notified the police, he hung his head.

'Well, as a matter of fact, I haven't. The first thing, I thought, was to . . .'

'Quite so,' Rieux cut in. 'I'll see to it.'

But the invalid made a fretful gesture and sat up in bed. He felt much better, he explained; really it wasn't worth the trouble.

'Don't feel alarmed,' Rieux said. 'It's little more than a formality. Anyhow, I have no option; I have to report this to the police.'

'Oh!' The man slumped back on the bed, and started sobbing weakly.

Grand, who had been twiddling his moustache while they were speaking, went up to the bed.

'Come, Monsieur Cottard. Try to understand. People could say the doctor was to blame, if you took it into your head to have another shot at it.'

Cottard assured him tearfully that there wasn't the least risk of that; he'd had a sort of crazy fit, but it had passed and all he wanted now was to be left in peace. Rieux was writing a prescription.

'Very well,' he said. 'We'll say no more about it for the present. I'll come and see you again in a day or two. But mind you don't do anything silly.'

On the landing he told Grand that he was obliged to make a report, but would ask the police inspector to hold up the inquiry for a couple of days.

'But somebody should watch Cottard tonight,' he added. 'Has he any relations?'

'Not that I know of. But I can very well stay with him. I can't say I really know him, but one's got to help a neighbour, hasn't one?'

As he walked down the stairs Rieux caught himself glancing into the darker corners, and he asked Grand if the rats had quite disappeared in his part of the town.

Grand had no idea. True he'd heard some talk about rats, but he never paid much attention to gossip like that. 'I've other things to think about,' he added.

Rieux, who was in a hurry to get away, was already shaking his hand. There was a letter to write to his wife, and he wanted to see the porter first.

Newspaper-vendors were shouting the latest news – that the rats had disappeared. But Rieux found his patient leaning over the edge of the bed, one hand pressed to his belly and the other to his neck, vomiting pinkish bile into a slop-pail. After retching for some moments, the man lay back again, gasping. His temperature was 103, the ganglions of his neck and limbs were swollen, and two black patches were developing on his thighs. He now complained of internal pains.

'It's like fire,' he whimpered. 'The bastard's burning me inside.'

He could hardly get the words through his fever-crusted lips and he gazed at the doctor with bulging eyes that his headache had suffused with tears. His wife cast an anxious look at Rieux, who said nothing.

'Please, doctor, what is it?'

'It might be – almost anything. There's nothing definite as yet. Keep him on a light diet and give him plenty to drink.'

The sick man had been complaining of a raging thirst.

On returning to his flat Rieux rang up his colleague Richard, one of the leading practitioners in the town.

'No,' Richard said, 'I can't say I've noticed anything exceptional.'

'No cases of fever with local inflammation?'

'Wait a bit! I have two cases with inflamed ganglions.'

'Abnormally so?'

'Well,' Richard said, 'that depends on what you mean by "normal".'

Anyhow, that night the porter was running a temperature of 104 and in delirium, always babbling about 'them rats'. Rieux tried a fixation abscess. When he felt the sting of the turpentine, the old man yelled 'The bastards!'

The ganglions had become still larger and felt like lumps of solid fibrous matter embedded in the flesh. Mme Michel had completely broken down.

'Sit up with him,' the doctor said, 'and call me, if necessary.'

Next day, April 30, the sky was blue and slightly misty. A warm, gentle breeze was blowing, bringing with it a smell of flowers from the outlying suburbs. The morning noises of the streets sounded louder, gayer than usual. For everyone in our little town this day brought the promise of a new lease of life, now that the shadow of fear under which they had been living for a week had lifted. Rieux, too, was in an optimistic mood when he went down to see the door-porter; he had been cheered up by a letter from his wife that had come with the first post.

Old M. Michel's temperature had gone down to 99 and, though he still looked very weak, he was smiling.

'He's better, doctor, isn't he?' his wife inquired.

'Well, it's a bit too early to say.'

At noon the sick man's temperature shot up abruptly to 104, he was in constant delirium and had started vomiting again. The ganglions in the neck were painful to the touch, and the old man seemed to be straining to hold his head as far as possible from his body. His wife sat at the bottom of the bed, her hands on the counterpane, gently clasping his feet. She gazed at Rieux imploringly.

'Listen,' he said. 'We'll have to move him to hospital and try a special treatment. I'll ring up for the ambulance.'

Two hours later the doctor and Mme Michel were in the ambulance bending over the sick man. Rambling words were issuing from the gaping mouth, thickly coated now with sordes. He kept on repeating, 'Them rats! Them blasted rats!' His face had gone livid, a greyish green, his lips were bloodless, his breath came in sudden gasps. His limbs spread out by the ganglions, embedded in the berth as if he were trying to bury himself in it or a voice from the depths of the earth were summoning him below, the unhappy man seemed to be stifling under some unseen pressure. His wife was sobbing. . . .

'Isn't there any hope left, doctor?'

'He's dead.'

III

M. MICHEL'S DEATH MARKED, one might say, the end of the first period, that of bewildering portents, and the beginning of another, relatively more trying, in which the perplexity of the early days gradually gave place to panic. Reviewing that first phase in the light of subsequent events, our townsfolk realized that they had never dreamt it possible that our little town should be chosen out for the scene of such grotesque happenings as the wholesale death of rats in broad daylight or the decease of door-porters through exotic maladies. In this respect they were wrong, and their views obviously called for revision. Still, if things had gone thus far and no farther, force of habit would doubtless have gained the day, as usual. But other members of our community, not in all cases menials or poor people, were to follow the path down which M. Michel had led the way. And it was then that fear, and with fear serious reflection, began.

However, before entering on a detailed account of the next phase, the narrator proposes to give the opinion of another witness on the period which has been described. Jean Tarrou, whose acquaintance we have already made, at the beginning of this narrative, had come to Oran some weeks before and was staying in a big hotel in the centre of the town. Apparently he had private means and was not engaged in business. But though he gradually became a familiar figure in our midst, no one knew where he hailed from or what had brought him to Oran. He was often to be seen in public and at the beginning of the spring patronized one or other of the beaches almost every day; obviously he was fond of swimming. Good-humoured, always ready with a smile, he seemed an addict of all normal pleasures without being their slave. In fact, the only habit he was known to have was that of cultivating the society of the Spanish dancers and musicians who abound in our town.

His notebooks comprise a sort of chronicle of those strange early days we all lived through. But an unusual type of chronicle, since the writer seems to make a point of understatement, and at first sight we might almost imagine that Tarrou had a habit of observing events and people through the wrong end of a telescope. In those chaotic times he set himself to recording the history of what the normal historian passes over. Obviously we may deplore this curious kink in his character and suspect in him a lack of proper feeling. All the same it is undeniable that these notebooks, which form a sort of discursive diary, supply the chronicler of the period with a host of seeming-trivial details which yet have their importance, and whose very oddity should be enough to prevent the reader from passing hasty judgment on this singular man.

The earliest entries made by Jean Tarrou synchronize with his coming to Oran. From the outset they reveal a paradoxical satisfaction at the discovery of a town so intrinsically ugly. We find in them a minute description of the two bronze lions adorning the Town Hall, and appropriate comments on the lack of trees, the hideousness of the houses and the absurd layout of the town. Tarrou sprinkles his descriptions with bits of conversation overheard in trams and in the streets, never adding a comment on them except – this comes somewhat later – in the report of a dialogue concerning a man named Camps. It was a chat between two tram-conductors.

'You knew Camps, didn't you?' asked one of them.

'Camps? A tall chap with a black moustache?'

'That's him. A pointsman.'

'Ah yes, I remember now.'

'Well, he's dead.'

'Oh? When did he die?'

'After that business about the rats.'

'You don't say so! What did he die of?'

'I couldn't say exactly. Some kind of fever. Of course, he never was what you might call fit. He got abscesses under the arms, and they did him in, it seems.'

'Still, he didn't look that different from other people.'

'I wouldn't say that. He had a weak chest and he used to play the trombone in the Town Band. It's hard on the lungs, blowing down a trombone.'

'Aye, if you've got weak lungs, it don't do you no good, blowing down a big instrument like that.'

After jotting down this dialogue Tarrou went on to speculate why Camps had joined a band when it was so clearly unadvisable, and what obscure motive had led him to risk his life for the sake of parading the streets on Sunday mornings.

We gather that Tarrou was agreeably impressed by a little scene that took place daily on the balcony of a house facing his window. His room at the hotel looked on to a small side street and there were always several cats sleeping in the shadow of the walls. Every day, soon after lunch, at a time when most people stayed indoors, enjoying a siesta, a dapper little old man stepped out on to the balcony on the other side of the street. He had a soldierly bearing, very erect, and affected a military style of dressing; his snow-white hair was always brushed to perfect smoothness. Leaning over the balcony he would call 'Pussy! Pussy!' in a voice at once haughty and endearing. The cats blinked up at him with sleep-pale eyes, but made no move as yet. He then proceeded to tear some paper into scraps, and let them fall into the street; interested by the fluttering shower of white butterflies, the cats came forward, lifting tentative paws towards the last scraps of paper. Then, taking careful aim, the old man would spit vigorously at the cats and whenever a liquid missile hit the quarry would beam with delight.

Lastly, Tarrou seemed to have been quite fascinated by the commercial character of the town, whose aspect, activities and even pleasures all seemed to be dictated by considerations of business. This idiosyncrasy – the term he uses in his diary – was warmly approved of by Tarrou; indeed, one of his appreciative comments ends on the exclamation 'At last!'

These are the only passages in which our visitor's record, at this period, strikes a seemingly personal note. Its significance and the earnestness behind it might escape the reader, on a casual perusal. For example, after describing how the discovery of a dead rat led the hotel cashier to make an error in his bill, Tarrou added: '*Query*: How contrive not to waste one's time? *Answer*: By being fully aware of it all the while. *Ways in which this can be done*: By spending one's days on an uneasy chair in a dentist's waiting-room; by remaining on one's balcony all a Sunday afternoon; by listening to lectures in a language one doesn't know; by travelling by the longest and least convenient train routes, and of course standing all the way; by queueing at the box-office of theatres and then not booking a seat. And so forth.'

Then, immediately following these eccentricities of thought and expression, we come on a detailed description of the tram-service in the town, the structure of the cars, their indeterminate colour, their unvarying dirtiness – and he concludes his observations with a 'Very odd', which explains nothing.

So much by way of introduction to Tarrou's comments on 'the phenomenon' of the rats.

'The little old fellow opposite is quite disconsolate today. There are no more cats. The sight of all those dead rats strewn about the street may have excited their hunting instinct; anyhow, they all have vanished. To my thinking, there's no question of their eating the dead rats. Mine, I remember, turned up their noses at dead things. All the same, they're probably busy hunting in the cellars – hence the old boy's plight. His hair isn't as well brushed as usual, and he looks less alert, less military. You can see he is worried. After a few moments he went back into the room. But, first, he spat once – on emptiness.

'In town today a tram was stopped because a dead rat had been found in it. (*Query*: How did it get there?) Two or three women promptly alighted. The rat was thrown out. The tram went on.

'The night-porter at the hotel, a level-headed man, assured me that all these rats meant trouble coming. "You know what they say, sir? When the rats leave a ship . . ." I replied that this held good for ships, but, for towns, it hadn't yet been demonstrated. But he stuck to his point. I asked what sort of "trouble" we might expect. That he couldn't say; disasters always come out of the blue. But he wouldn't be surprised if there were an earthquake brewing. I admitted that was possible, and then he asked if the prospect didn't alarm me.

' "The only thing I'm interested in," I told him, "is acquiring peace of mind."

'He understood me perfectly.

'I find a family which has its meals in this hotel quite interesting. The paterfamilias is a tall, thin man, always dressed in black and wearing a starched collar. The top of his head is bald, with two tufts of grey hair on each side. His small beady eyes, narrow nose, and hard, straight mouth make him look like a well-brought-up owl. He is always first at the door of the restaurant, stands aside to let his wife – a tiny woman, like a black mouse – go in, and then comes in himself with a small boy and girl, dressed like performing poodles, at his heels. When they are at the table he remains standing till his wife is seated and only then the two "poodles" can perch themselves on their chairs. He uses no terms of endearment to his family, addresses politely spiteful remarks to his wife, and bluntly tells the kids what he thinks of them.

' "Nicole, you're behaving quite disgracefully."

'The little girl is on the brink of tears – which is as it should be.

27

'This morning the small boy was all excitement about the rats, and started saying something on the subject.

' "Philippe, one doesn't talk of rats at table. For the future I forbid you to use the word. Do you understand?"

' "Your father's right," approved the mouse.

'The two poodles buried their noses in their plates, and the owl acknowledged thanks by a curt, perfunctory nod.

'This excellent example notwithstanding, everybody in town is talking about the rats, and the local newspaper has taken a hand. The town topics column, usually very varied, is now devoted exclusively to a campaign against the local authorities. "Are our City Fathers aware that the decaying bodies of these rodents constitute a grave danger to the population?" The manager of the hotel can talk of nothing else. But he has a personal grievance, too; that dead rats should be found in the lift of a three-star hotel seems to him the end of all things. To console him I said, "But, you know, everybody's in the same boat."

' "That's just it," he replied. "Now we're like everybody else."

'He was the first to tell me about the outbreak of this queer kind of fever, which is causing much alarm. One of his chambermaids has got it.

' "But I feel sure it's not infectious," he hastened to assure me.

'I told him it was all the same to me.

' "Ah, I understand, sir. You're like me, you're a fatalist."

'I had said nothing of the kind, and, what's more, am not a fatalist. I told him so. . . . '

From this point onwards Tarrou's entries deal in some detail with the curious fever that was causing much anxiety amongst the public. When noting that the little old man, now that the rats had ceased appearing, had regained his target-cats and was studiously perfecting his 'shooting', Tarrou adds that a dozen or so cases of this fever were known to have occurred and most had ended fatally.

For the light it may throw on the narrative that follows, Tarrou's description of Dr Rieux may be suitably inserted here. So far as the narrator can judge, it is fairly accurate.

'Looks about thirty-five. Moderate height. Broad shoulders. Almost rectangular face. Dark, steady eyes, but prominent jaws. A biggish, well-modelled nose. Black hair, cropped very close. A curving mouth with thick, usually tight-set lips. With his tanned skin, the black down on his hands and arms, the dark but becoming suits he always wears, he reminds one of a Sicilian peasant.

'He walks quickly. When crossing a street, he steps off the pavement without changing his pace, but two out of three times makes a little hop when he steps on to the pavement on the other side. He is absent-minded and when driving his car often leaves his side-signals on after he has turned a corner. Always bare-headed. Looks knowledgeable.'

IV

TARROU'S FIGURES WERE correct. Dr Rieux was only too well aware of the serious turn things had taken. After seeing to the isolation of the porter's body, he had rung up Richard and asked what he made of these inguinal fever cases.

'I can make nothing of them,' Richard confessed. 'There have been two deaths, one in forty-eight hours, the other in three days. And the second patient showed all the signs of convalescence when I visited him on the second day.'

'Please let me know if you have other cases,' Rieux said.

He rang up some other colleagues. As a result of these inquiries he gathered that there had been some twenty cases of the same type within the last few days. Almost all had ended fatally. He then advised Richard, who was chairman of the local Medical Association, to have any fresh cases put into isolation wards.

'Sorry,' Richard said, 'but I can't do anything about it. An order to that effect can be issued only by the Prefect. Anyhow, what grounds have you for supposing there's danger of contagion?'

'No definite grounds. But the symptoms are definitely alarming.'

Richard, however, repeated that 'such measures were outside his province'. The most he could do was to put the matter up to the Prefect.

But while these talks were going on the weather changed for the worse. On the day following old Michel's death the sky clouded up and there were brief torrential downpours, each of which was followed by some hours of muggy heat. The aspect of the sea, too, changed; its dark blue translucency had gone and, under the lowering sky, it had steely or silvery glints that hurt the eyes to look at. The damp heat of the spring made everyone long for the coming of the dry, clean summer heat. On the town, humped snailwise on its plateau and shut off almost everywhere from the sea, a mood of listlessness descended. Hemmed in by lines and lines of whitewashed walls, walking between rows of dusty shops, or riding in the dingy yellow trams, you felt as it were trapped by the climate. This, however, was not the case with Rieux's old Spanish patient, who welcomed this weather with enthusiasm.

'It cooks you,' he said. 'Just the thing for asthma.'

Certainly it 'cooked you' – but exactly like a fever. Indeed, the whole town was running a temperature; such anyhow was the impression Dr Rieux could not shake off as he drove to the Rue Faidherbe for the inquiry into Cottard's attempted suicide. That this impression was unreasonable, he knew, and he attributed it to nervous exhaustion; he had certainly his full share of worries just at present. In fact, it was high time to put the brakes on and try to get his nerves into some sort of order.

On reaching his destination he found that the police inspector hadn't turned up yet. Grand, who met him on the landing, suggested they should wait in his place, leaving the door open. The municipal clerk had two rooms, both very sparsely funished. The only objects to catch the eye were a book-shelf on which lay two or three dictionaries and a small blackboard on which one could just read two half-obliterated words, 'flowery avenues'.

Grand announced that Cottard had had a good night. But he'd woken up this morning with pains in his head and feeling very low. Grand, too, looked tired and overwrought; he kept pacing up and down the room, opening and closing a portfolio crammed with sheets of manuscript that lay on the table.

Meanwhile, however, he informed the doctor that he really knew very little about Cottard, but believed him to have private means in a small way. Cottard was 'a rum bird'. For a long while their relations went no further than wishing each other 'good day' when they met on the stairs.

'I've only had two conversations with him. Some days ago I upset a box of coloured chalks I was bringing home, on the landing. They were red and blue chalks. Just then Cottard came out of his room and he helped to pick them up. He asked me what I wanted coloured chalks for.'

Grand had then explained to him that he was trying to brush up his Latin. He'd learnt it at school, of course, but his memory had grown blurred.

'You see, doctor, I've been told that a knowledge of Latin gives one a better understanding of the real meaning of French words.'

So he wrote Latin words on his blackboard, then copied out again in blue chalk the part of each word that changed in conjugation or declension, and in red chalk the part of the word that never varied.

'I'm not sure if Cottard followed this very clearly, but he seemed interested, and asked me for a red chalk. That rather surprised me, but after all . . . Of course I couldn't guess the use he'd put it to.'

Rieux asked what was the subject of their second conversation. But just then the inspector came, accompanied by a clerk, and said he wished to begin by hearing Grand's statement. The doctor noticed that Grand, when referring to Cottard, always called him 'the unfortunate man', and at one moment used even the expression 'his grim resolve'.

When discussing the possible motives for the attempted suicide, Grand showed an almost finical anxiety over his choice of words. Finally he elected for the expression 'a secret grief'. The inspector asked if there had been anything in Cottard's manner which suggested what he called his 'intent to felo-de-se'.

'He knocked at my door yesterday,' Grand said, 'and asked me for a match. I gave him a box. He said he was sorry to disturb me but that, as we were neighbours, he hoped I wouldn't mind. He assured me he'd bring back my box, but I told him to keep it.'

The inspector asked Grand if he'd noticed anything queer about Cottard.

'What struck me as queer was that he always seemed to want to start a conversation. But he should have seen I was busy with my work.' Grand turned to Rieux, and added rather shyly, 'Some private work I'm engaged on.'

The inspector now said that he must see the invalid and hear what he had to say. Rieux thought it would be wiser to prepare Cottard for the visit. When he entered the bedroom he found Cottard, who was wearing a grey flannel nightshirt, sitting up in bed and gazing at the door with a scared expression on his face.

'It's the police, isn't it?'

'Yes,' Rieux said, 'but don't get flustered. There are only some formalities to be gone through, and then you'll be left in peace.'

Cottard replied that all this was quite needless, to his thinking, and anyhow he didn't like the police.

Rieux showed some irritation.

'I don't love them either. It's only a matter of answering a few questions as briefly and correctly as you can, and then you'll be through with it.'

Cottard said nothing and Rieux began to move to the door. He had hardly taken a step when the little man called him back and, as soon as he was at the bedside, gripped his hands.

'They can't be rough with an invalid, a man who's hanged himself, can they, doctor?'

Rieux gazed down at him for a moment, then assured him that there was no question of anything like that, and in any case he was here to protect his patient. At which Cottard seemed relieved, and Rieux went out to fetch the inspector.

After Grand's deposition had been read out, Cottard was asked to state the exact motive of his act. He merely replied, without looking at the police officer, that 'a secret grief' described it well enough. The inspector then asked him peremptorily if he intended to 'have another go at it'. Showing more animation, Cottard said, 'Certainly not,' his one wish was to be left in peace.

'Allow me to point out, my man,' the police officer rejoined with asperity, 'that just now it's you who're troubling the peace of others.' Rieux signed to him not to continue, and he left it at that.

'A good hour wasted!' the inspector sighed when the door closed behind them. 'As you can guess, we've other things to think about what with this fever everybody's talking of.'

He then asked the doctor if there was any serious danger to the town; Rieux answered that he couldn't say.

'It must be the weather,' the police officer decided. 'That's what it is.'

No doubt it was the weather. As the day wore on, everything grew sticky to the touch, and Rieux felt his anxiety increasing after each visit. That evening a neighbour of his old patient in the suburbs started vomiting, pressing his hand to his groin, and running a high fever accompanied by delirium. The ganglions were much bigger than M. Michel's. One of them was beginning to suppurate, and presently split open like an overripe fruit. On returning to his flat, Rieux rang up the medical stores depot for the district. In his professional diary for the day the only entry was 'Negative reply'. Already he was receiving calls for similar cases from various parts of the town. Obviously the abscesses had to be lanced. Two criss-cross strokes, and the ganglion disgorged a mixture of blood and pus. Their limbs stretched out as far as they could manage, the sick men went on bleeding. Dark patches appeared on their legs and stomachs; sometimes a ganglion would stop suppurating, then suddenly swell again. Usually the sick man died, in a stench of corruption.

The local Press, so lavish of news about the rats, now had nothing to say. For rats die in the street; men in their homes. And newspapers are concerned only with the street. Meanwhile, Government and municipal officials were putting their heads together. So long as each individual doctor had come across only two or three cases, no one had thought of taking action. But it was merely a matter of adding up the figures and, once this had been done, the total was startling. In a very few days the number of cases had risen by leaps and bounds, and it became evident to all observers of this strange malady that a real epidemic had set in. This was the state of affairs when Castel, one of Rieux's colleagues and a much older man than he, came to see him.

'Naturally,' he said to Rieux, 'you know what it is.'

'I'm waiting for the result of the post-mortems.'

'Well, *I* know. And I don't need any post-mortems. I was in China for a good part of my career, and I saw some cases in Paris twenty years ago. Only no one dared to call them by their name on that occasion. The usual taboo, of course; the public mustn't be alarmed, that wouldn't do at all. And then, as one of my colleagues said, "It's unthinkable. Everyone knows it's ceased to appear in Western Europe." Yes, everyone knew that – except the dead men. Come now, Rieux, you know as well as I do what it is.'

Rieux pondered. He was looking out of the window of his surgery, at the tall cliff that closed the half-circle of the bay on the far horizon. Though blue, the sky had a dull sheen that was softening as the light declined.

'Yes, Castel,' he replied. 'It's hardly credible. But everything points to its being plague.'

Castel got up and began walking towards the door.

'You know,' the old doctor said, 'what they're going to tell us? That it vanished from temperate countries long ago.'

'"Vanished"? What does that word really mean?' Rieux shrugged his shoulders.

'Yes. And don't forget. Just under twenty years ago, in Paris too. . . .'

'Right. Let's hope it won't prove any worse this time than it did then. But really it's . . . incredible.'

v

THE WORD 'PLAGUE' had just been uttered for the first time. At this stage of the narrative, with Dr Bernard Rieux standing at his window, the narrator may, perhaps, be allowed to justify the doctor's uncertainty and surprise – since, with very slight differences, his reaction was the same as that of the great majority of our townsfolk. Everybody knows that pestilences have a way of recurring in the world; yet somehow we find it hard to believe in ones that crash down on our heads from a blue sky. There have been as many plagues as wars in history; yet always plagues and wars take people equally by surprise.

In fact, like all our fellow-citizens, Rieux was caught off his guard, and we should understand his hesitations in the light of this fact; and similarly understand how he was torn between conflicting fears and confidence. When a war breaks out people say, 'It's too stupid; it can't last long.' But though a war may well be 'too stupid', that doesn't prevent its lasting. Stupidity has a knack of getting its way; as we should see if we were not always so much wrapped up in ourselves.

In this respect our townsfolk were like everybody else, wrapped up in themselves; in other words they were humanists; they disbelieved in pestilences. A pestilence isn't a thing made to man's measure; therefore we tell ourselves that pestilence is a mere bogy of the mind, a bad dream that will pass away. But it doesn't always pass away and, from one bad dream to another, it is men who pass away, and the humanists first of all, because they haven't taken their precautions. Our townsfolk were not more to blame than others, they forgot to be modest — that was all — and thought that everything still was possible for them; which presupposed that pestilences were impossible. They went on doing business, arranged for journeys, and formed views. How should they have given a thought to anything like plague, which rules out any future, cancels journeys, silences the exchange of views. They fancied themselves free, and no one will ever be free so long as there are pestilences.

Indeed, even after Dr Rieux had admitted in his friend's company that a handful of persons, scattered about the town, had without warning died of plague, the danger still remained fantastically unreal. For the simple reason that, when a man is a doctor, he comes to have his own ideas of physical suffering, and to acquire somewhat more imagination than the average. Looking from his window at the town, outwardly quite unchanged, the doctor felt little more than a faint qualm for the future, a vague unease.

He tried to recall what he had read about the disease. Figures floated across his memory, and he recalled that some thirty or so great plagues known to history had accounted for nearly a hundred million deaths. But what are a hundred million deaths? When one has served in a war, one hardly knows what a dead man is, after a while. And since a dead man has no substance unless one has actually seen him dead, a hundred million corpses broadcast through history are no more than a puff of smoke in the imagination. The doctor remembered the plague at Constantinople which, according to Procopius, caused ten thousand deaths in a single day. Ten thousand dead made about five times the audience in a biggish cinema. Yes, that was how it should be done. You should collect the people at the exits of five picture-houses, you should lead them to a city square and make them die in heaps, if you wanted to get a clear notion of what it means. Then at least you could add some familiar faces to the anonymous mass. But naturally that was impossible to put into practice; moreover, what man knows ten thousand faces? In any case the figures of those old historians, like Procopius, weren't to be relied on; that was common knowledge. Seventy years ago, at Canton, forty thousand rats died of plague before the disease spread to the inhabitants. But, again, in the Canton epidemic there was no reliable way of counting up the rats. A very rough estimate was all that could be made, with, obviously, a wide margin for error. 'Let's see,' the doctor murmured to himself, 'supposing the length of a rat to be ten inches, forty thousand rats placed end to end would make a line of . . . '

He pulled himself up sharply. He was letting his imagination play pranks – the last thing wanted just now. A few cases, he told himself, don't make an epidemic; they merely call for serious precautions. He must fix his mind, first of all, on the observed facts: stupor and extreme prostration, buboes, intense thirst, delirium, dark blotches on the body, internal dilatation, and, in conclusion . . . In conclusion, some words came back to the doctor's mind; aptly enough, the concluding sentence of the description of the symptoms given in his Medical Handbook. 'The pulse becomes fluttering, dicrotic and intermittent, and death ensues as the result of the slightest movement.' Yes, in conclusion, the patient's life hung on a thread, and three people out of four (he remembered the exact figures) were too impatient not to make the very slight movement that snapped the thread.

The doctor was still looking out of the window. Beyond it lay the tranquil radiance of a cool spring sky; inside the room a word was echoing still, the word 'plague'. A word that conjured up in the doctor's mind not only what science chose to put into it, but a whole series of fantastic possibilities utterly out of keeping with that grey-and-yellow town under his eyes, from which were rising the sounds of mild activity characteristic of the hour; a drone rather than a bustling, the noises of a happy town, in short, if it's possible to be at once so dull and happy. A tranquillity so casual and thoughtless seemed almost effortlessly to give the lie to those old pictures of the plague: Athens, a charnel-house reeking to heaven and deserted even by the birds; Chinese towns cluttered up with victims silent in their agony; the convicts at Marseilles piling rotting corpses into pits; the building of the Great Wall in Provence to fend off the furious plague-wind; the damp, putrefying pallets stuck to the mud floor at the Constantinople lazar-house, where the patients were hauled up from their beds with hooks; the carnival of masked doctors at the Black Death; men and women copulating in the cemeteries of Milan; cartloads of dead bodies rumbling through London's ghoul-haunted darkness – nights and days filled always, everywhere, with the eternal cry of human pain. No, all those horrors were not near enough as yet even to ruffle the equanimity of that spring afternoon. The clang of an unseen tram came through the window, briskly refuting cruelty and pain. Only the sea, murmurous behind the dingy chequerboard of houses, told of the unrest, the precariousness of all things in this world. And, gazing in the direction of the bay, Dr Rieux called to mind the plague-fires of which Lucretius tells, which the Athenians kindled on the seashore. The dead were brought there after nightfall, but there was not room enough, and the living fought each other with torches for a space where to lay those who had been dear to them; for they had rather engage in bloody conflicts than abandon their dead to the waves. A picture rose before him of the red glow of the pyres mirrored on a wine-dark, slumbrous sea, battling torches whirling sparks across the darkness, and thick, fetid smoke rising towards the watchful sky. Yes, it was not beyond the bounds of possibility. . . .

But these extravagant forebodings dwindled in the light of reason. True, the word 'plague' had been uttered; true, at this very moment one or two victims were being seized and laid low by the disease. Still, that could stop, or be stopped. It was only a matter of lucidly recognizing what had to be recognized; of dispelling extraneous shadows and doing what needed to be done. Then the plague would come to an end, because it was unthinkable, or, rather, because one thought of it on misleading lines. If, as was most likely, it died out, all would be well. If not, one would know it anyhow for what it was and what steps should be taken for coping with, and finally overcoming, it.

The doctor opened the window, and at once the noises of the town grew louder. The brief, intermittent sibilance of a machine-saw came from a near-by workshop. Rieux pulled himself together. There lay certitude; there, in the daily round. All the rest hung on mere threads and trivial contingencies; you couldn't waste your time on it. The thing was to do your job as it should be done.

VI

THE DOCTOR'S MUSINGS had reached this point when the visit of Joseph Grand was announced. Grand's duties as clerk in the Municipal Office were varied, and he was sometimes employed in the Statistical Department on compiling the figures of births, marriages and deaths. Thus it had fallen to him to add up the number of deaths during the last few days and, being of an obliging disposition, he had volunteered to bring a copy of the latest figures to the doctor.

Grand, who was waving a sheet of paper, was accompanied by his neighbour, Cottard.

'The figures are going up, doctor. Eleven deaths in forty-eight hours.'

Rieux shook hands with Cottard and asked him how he was feeling. Grand put in a word explaining that Cottard had thought it up to him to thank the doctor and apologize for the trouble he had given. But Rieux was gazing frowningly at the figures on the sheet of paper.

'Well,' he said, 'perhaps we'd better make up our minds to call this disease by its name. So far we've been only shilly-shallying. Look here, I'm off to the laboratory; like to come with me?'

'Quite so, quite so,' Grand said as he went down the stairs at the doctor's heels. 'I, too, believe in calling things by their name. . . . But what's the name in this case?'

'That I shan't say; and anyhow you wouldn't gain anything by knowing.'

'You see,' Grand smiled. 'It's not so easy after all!'

They started off towards the Place d'Armes. Cottard still kept silent. The streets were beginning to fill up. The brief dusk of our town was already giving place to night and the first stars glimmered above the still clearly marked horizon. A few moments later all the street-lamps went on, dimming the sky, and the voices in the street seemed to rise a tone.

'Excuse me,' Grand said at the corner of the Place d'Armes, 'but I must catch my tram now. My evenings are . . . sacred. As we say in my part of the world. "Never put off to tomorrow . . . "'

Rieux had already noticed Grand's trick of professing to quote some turn of speech from 'his part of the world' (he hailed from Montélimar), and following up with some such hackneyed expression as 'lost in dreams', or 'pretty as a picture'.

'That's so,' Cottard put in. 'You can never budge him from his den after dinner.'

Rieux asked Grand if he was doing extra work for the municipality. Grand said 'No', he was working on his own account.

'Really?' Rieux said, to keep the conversation going. 'And are you getting on well with it?'

'Considering I've been at it for years, it would be surprising if I wasn't. Though, in one sense, there hasn't been much progress.'

'May one know' – the doctor halted – 'what it is that you're engaged on?'

Grand put a hand up to his hat and tugged it down upon his big, protruding ears, then murmured some half-inaudible remark from which Rieux seemed to gather that Grand's work was connected with 'the growth of a personality'. Then he turned rather hastily and a moment later was hurrying, with short, quick steps, under the fig-trees lining the Boulevard de la Marne.

When they were at the laboratory gate Cottard told the doctor that he would greatly like to see him and ask his advice about something. Rieux, who was fingering in his pocket the sheet of paper with the figures on it, said he'd better call during his consulting-hours; then, changing his mind, told him he would be in his part of the town next day and would drop in to see him at the end of the afternoon.

On leaving Cottard the doctor noticed that he was thinking of Grand, trying to picture him in the midst of an outbreak of plague – not an outbreak like the present one, which would probably not prove serious, but like one of the great visitations of the past. 'He's the kind of man who always escapes in such cases.' Rieux remembered having read somewhere that the plague spared weak constitutions and chose its victims chiefly amongst the robust. Still thinking of Grand, he decided that he was something of a 'mystery man' in his small way.

True, at first sight, Grand manifested both the outward signs and typical manner of a humble employee in the local administration. Tall and thin, he seemed lost in garments that he always chose a size too large, under the illusion that they would wear longer. Though he still had most of the teeth in his lower jaw, all the upper ones were gone, with the result that when he smiled, raising his upper lip – the lower scarcely moved – his mouth looked like a small black hole let into his face. Also he had the walk of a shy young priest, sidling along walls and slipping mouse-like into doorways, and he exuded a faint odour of smoke and basement-rooms; in short, he had all the attributes of insignificance. Indeed, it cost an effort to picture him otherwise than bent over a desk, studiously revising the tariff of the Town Baths or gathering, for a junior secretary, the materials of a report on the new scavenging tax. Even before you knew what his employment was you had a feeling that he'd been brought into the world for the sole purpose of performing the discreet but needful duties of a temporary assistant municipal clerk on a salary of 62 francs, 30 centimes *per diem*.

This was, in fact, the entry that he made each month in the Staff Register at the Town Hall, in the column *Post in Which Employed*. When twenty-two years previously – after obtaining a matriculation certificate beyond which, for lack of money, he was unable to progress – he was given this temporary post, he had been led to expect, or so he said, speedy 'confirmation' in it. It was only a matter of proving his ability to cope with the delicate problems raised by the administration of our city. Once confirmed, they had assured him, he couldn't fail to be promoted to a grade which would enable him to live quite comfortably. Ambition, certainly, was not the spur that activated Joseph Grand; that he would swear to, wryly smiling. All he desired was the prospect of a life suitably insured on the

42

material side by honest work, enabling him to devote his leisure to his hobbies. If he'd accepted the post offered him, it was from honourable motives and, if he might say so, loyalty to an ideal.

But this 'temporary' state of things had gone on and on, the cost of living rose by leaps and bounds, and Grand's pay, in spite of some statutory rises, was still a mere pittance. He had confided this to Rieux, but nobody else seemed aware of his position. And here lies Grand's originality or, anyhow, an indication of it. He could certainly have brought to official notice, if not his rights – of which he wasn't sure – at least the promises given him when he joined his post. But, for one thing, the departmental head who made them had been dead for some time and, furthermore, Grand no longer remembered their exact terms. And lastly – this was the real trouble – Joseph Grand couldn't find his words.

This peculiarity, as Rieux had noticed, was really the key to the personality of our worthy fellow-citizen. And this it was which always prevented him from writing the mildly protesting letter he had in mind, or taking the steps the situation called for. According to him, he felt a particular aversion from talking about his 'rights' – the word was one which gave him pause – and likewise from mentioning a 'promise' – which would have implied that he was claiming his due and thus bespeak an audacity incompatible with the humble post he filled. On the other hand, he refused to use expressions such as 'your kindness', 'gratitude', or even 'solicit', which, to his thinking, were incompatible with his personal dignity. Thus, owing to his inability to find the right words, he had gone on performing his obscure, ill-paid duties until a somewhat advanced age. Also – this, anyhow, was what he told Dr Rieux – he had come, after long experience, to realize that he could always count on living within his means; all he had to do was to scale down his needs to his income. Thus he confirmed the wisdom of an opinion often voiced by our mayor, a business magnate of the town, when he insisted vehemently that in the last analysis (he emphasized this choice expression, which indeed clinched his argument) there was no reason to believe that anyone had ever died of hunger in the town. In any case, the austere, not to say ascetic life of Joseph Grand was, in the last analysis, a guarantee against any anxiety in this respect.... He went on looking for his words.

In a certain sense it might well be said that his was an exemplary life. He was one of those rare people, rare in our town as elsewhere, who have the courage of their good feelings. What little he told of his personal life vouched for acts of kindness and a capacity for affection which no one in our times dares to own to. Without a blush he confessed to dearly loving his nephews and sister, his only surviving near relation, whom he went to France to visit every other year. He admitted that the thought of his parents, whom he lost when he was very young, often gave him a pang. He did not conceal the fact that he had a special affection for a church-bell in his part of the town which started pealing very melodiously at about five every afternoon. Yet to express such emotions, simple as they were, the least word cost him a terrible effort. And this difficulty in finding his words had come to be the bane of his life. 'Oh doctor,' he would exclaim, 'how I'd like to learn to express myself!' He brought the subject up each time he met Rieux.

That evening, as he watched Grand's receding form, it flashed on the doctor what it was that Grand was trying to convey; he was evidently writing a book or something of the sort. And quaintly enough, as he made his way to the laboratory, this thought reassured him. He realized how absurd it was, but he simply couldn't believe that a pestilence on the great scale could befall a town where people like Grand were to be found, obscure functionaries cultivating harmless eccentricities. To be precise, he couldn't picture such eccentricities existing in a plague-stricken community, and he concluded that the chances were all against the plague's making any headway amongst our fellow-citizens.

NEXT DAY, BY dint of a persistence which many thought ill-advised, Rieux persuaded the authorities to convene a 'health committee' at the Prefect's office.

'People in town are getting nervous, that's a fact,' Dr Richard admitted. 'And of course all sorts of wild rumours are going round. The Prefect said to me, "Take prompt action if you like, but don't attract attention." He personally is convinced that it's a false alarm.'

Rieux gave Castel a lift to the Prefect's office.

'Do you know,' Castel said when they were in the car, 'that we haven't a gramme of serum in the whole district?'

'I know. I rang up the depot. The director seemed quite startled. It'll have to be sent from Paris.'

'Let's hope they're quick about it.'

'I sent a wire yesterday,' Rieux said.

The Prefect greeted them amiably enough, but one could see his nerves were on edge.

'Let's make a start, gentlemen,' he said. 'Need I review the situation?'

Richard thought that wasn't necessary. He and his colleagues were acquainted with the facts. The only question was what measures should be adopted.

'The question,' old Castel cut in almost rudely, 'is to know whether it's plague or not.'

Two or three of the doctors present protested. The others seemed to hesitate. The Prefect gave a start and hurriedly glanced towards the door to make sure it had prevented this outrageous remark from being overheard in the passage. Richard said that in his opinion the great thing was not to take an alarmist view. All that could be said at present was that we had to deal with a special type of fever, with inguinal complications; in medical science, as in daily life, it was unwise to jump to conclusions. Old Castel, who was placidly chewing his draggled yellow moustache, raised his pale, bright eyes and gazed at Rieux. Then, after sweeping the other members of the committee with a friendly glance, he said that he knew quite well that it was plague and, needless to say, he also knew that, were this to be officially admitted, the authorities would be compelled to take very drastic steps. This was, of course, the explanation of his colleagues' reluctance to face the facts and, if it would ease their minds, he was quite prepared to say it wasn't plague. The Prefect seemed ruffled and remarked that, in any case, this line of argument seemed to him unsound.

'The important thing,' Castel replied, 'isn't the soundness or otherwise of the argument – but for it to make you think.'

Rieux, who had said nothing so far, was asked for his opinion.

'We are dealing,' he said, 'with a fever of a typhoidal nature, accompanied by vomiting and buboes. I have incised these buboes and had the pus analysed; our laboratory analyst believes he has identified the plague bacillus. But I am bound to add that there are specific modifications which don't quite tally with the classical description of the plague bacillus.'

Richard pointed out that this justified a policy of wait-and-see; anyhow, it would be wise to await the statistical report on the series of analyses that had been going on for several days.

'When a microbe,' Rieux said, 'after a short intermission can quadruple in three days' time the volume of the spleen, can swell the mesenteric ganglions to the size of an orange and give them the consistence of gruel, a policy of wait-and-see is, to say the least of it, unwise. The foci of infection are steadily extending. Judging by the rapidity with which the disease is spreading, it may well, unless we can stop it, kill off half the town before two months are out. That being so, it has small importance whether you call it plague or some rare kind of fever. The important thing is to prevent its killing off half the population of this town.'

Richard said it was a mistake to paint too gloomy a picture, and, moreover, the disease hadn't been proved to be contagious; indeed, relatives of his patients, living under the same roof, had escaped it.

'But others have died,' Rieux observed. 'And obviously contagion is never absolute; otherwise you'd have a constant mathematical progression and the death-rate would rocket up catastrophically. It's not a question of painting too black a picture. It's a question of taking precautions.'

Richard, however, summing up the situation as he saw it, pointed out that, if the epidemic did not cease spontaneously, it would be necessary to apply the rigorous prophylactic measures laid down in the Code. And, to do this, it would be necessary to admit officially that plague had broken out. But of this there was no absolute certainty; therefore any hasty action was to be deprecated.

Rieux stuck to his guns. 'The point isn't whether the measures provided for in the Code are rigorous, but whether they are needful to prevent the death of half the population. All the rest is a matter of administrative action, and I needn't remind you that our constitution has provided for such emergencies by empowering Prefects to issue the necessary orders.'

'Quite true,' the Prefect assented. 'But I shall need your professional declaration that the epidemic is one of plague.'

'If we don't make that declaration,' Rieux said, 'there's a risk that half the population may be wiped out.'

Richard cut in with some impatience.

'The truth is that our colleague is convinced it's plague; his description of the syndrome proved it.'

Rieux replied that he had not described a 'syndrome' – but merely what he'd seen with his own eyes. And what he'd seen was buboes, and high fever accompanied by delirium, ending fatally within forty-eight hours. Could Dr Richard take the responsibility of declaring that the epidemic would die out without the imposition of rigorous prophylactic measures?

Richard hesitated, then fixed his eyes on Rieux.

'Please answer me quite frankly. Are you absolutely convinced it's plague?'

'You're stating the problem wrongly. It's not a question of the term I use; it's a question of time.'

'Your view, I take it,' the Prefect put in, 'is this. Even if it isn't plague, the prophylactic measures enjoined by law for coping with a state of plague should be put into force immediately?'

'If you insist on my having a "view", that conveys it accurately enough.'

The doctors confabulated. Richard was their spokesman.

'It comes to this. We are to take the responsibility of acting as though the epidemic were plague?'

This way of putting it met with general approval.

'It doesn't matter to me,' Rieux said, 'how you phrase it. My point is that we should not act as if there were no likelihood that half the population wouldn't be wiped out; for then it would be.'

Followed by scowls and protestations, Rieux left the committee-room. Some minutes later, as he was driving down a back street redolent of fried fish and urine, a woman screaming in agony, her groin dripping blood, stretched out her arms towards him.

VIII

ON THE DAY after the committee meeting the fever notched another small advance. It even found its way into the papers, but discreetly; only a few brief references to it were made. On the following day, however, Rieux observed that small official notices had been just put up about the town, though in places where they would not attract much attention. It was hard to find in these notices any indication that the authorities were facing the situation squarely. The measures enjoined were far from Draconian and one had the feeling that many concessions had been made to a desire not to alarm the public. The instructions began with a bald statement that a few cases of a malignant fever had been reported in Oran; it was not possible as yet to say if this fever was contagious. The symptoms were not so marked as to be really perturbing and the authorities felt sure they could rely on the townspeople to treat the situation with composure. None the less, guided by a spirit of prudence which all would appreciate, the Prefect was putting into force some precautionary measures. If these measures were carefully studied and properly applied, they would obviate any risk of an epidemic. This being so, the Prefect felt no doubt that everybody in his jurisdiction would wholeheartedly second his personal efforts.

The notice outlined the general programme that the authorities had drawn up. It included a systematic extermination of the rat population by injecting poison gas into the sewers, and a strict supervision of the water-supply. The townspeople were advised to practise extreme cleanliness, and any who found fleas on their persons were directed to call at the municipal dispensaries. Also, heads of households were ordered promptly to report any fever case diagnosed by their doctors and to permit the isolation of sick members of their families in special wards at the hospital. These wards, it was explained, were equipped to provide patients with immediate treatment and ensure the maximum prospect of recovery. Some supplementary regulations enjoined compulsory disinfection of the sick-room and of the vehicle in which the patient travelled. For the rest, the Prefect confined himself to advising all who had been in contact with the patient to consult the sanitary inspector and strictly to follow his advice.

Dr Rieux swung round brusquely from the poster and started back to his surgery. Grand, who was awaiting him there, raised his arms dramatically when the doctor entered.

'Yes,' Rieux said, 'I know. The figures are rising.'

On the previous day ten deaths had been reported. The doctor told Grand that he might be seeing him in the evening, as he had promised to visit Cottard.

'An excellent idea,' Grand said. 'You'll do him good. As a matter of fact, I find him greatly changed.'

'In what way?'

'He's become amiable.'

'Wasn't he amiable before?'

Grand seemed at a loss. He couldn't say that Cottard used to be unamiable; the term wouldn't have been correct. But Cottard was a silent, secretive man, with something about him that made Grand think of a wild boar. His bedroom, meals at a cheap restaurant, some rather mysterious comings and goings – these were the sum of Cottard's days. He described himself as a traveller in wines and spirits. Now and again he was visited by two or three men, presumably customers. Sometimes in the evening he would go to a cinema across the way. In this connexion Grand mentioned a detail he had noticed – that Cottard seemed to have a preference for gangster films. But the thing that had struck him most about the man was his aloofness, not to say his mistrust of everyone he met.

And now, so Grand said, there had been a complete change.

'I don't quite know how to put it, but I must say I've an impression that he is trying to make himself agreeable to all and sundry, to be in everybody's good books. Nowadays he often talks to me, he suggests we should go out together, and I can't bring myself to refuse. What's more, he interests me, and of course I saved his life.'

Since his attempt at suicide Cottard had had no more visitors. In the streets, in shops, he was always trying to strike up friendships. To the grocer he was all affability; no one could take more pains than he to show his interest in the tobacconist's gossip.

'This particular tobacconist – a woman, by the way –,' Grand explained, 'is a holy terror. I told Cottard so, but he replied that I was prejudiced and she had plenty of good points, only one had to find them out.'

On two or three occasions Cottard had invited Grand to come with him to the luxury restaurants and cafés of the town – which he had recently taken to patronizing.

'There's a pleasant atmosphere in them,' he explained, 'and then one's in good company.'

Grand noticed that the staff made much of Cottard and he soon discovered why, when he saw the lavish tips his companion gave. The commercial traveller seemed greatly to appreciate the amiability shown him in return for his largesse. One day when the head waiter had escorted him to the door and helped him into his overcoat, Cottard said to Grand:

'He's a nice fellow, and he'd make a good witness.'

'A witness? I don't follow.'

Cottard hesitated before answering.

'Well, he could say I'm not really a bad kind of man.'

But his humour had its ups and downs. One day when the grocer had shown less affability, he came home in a tearing rage.

'He's siding with the others, the swine!'

'With what others?'

'The whole damned lot of them.'

Grand had personally witnessed an odd scene that took place at the tobacconist's. An animated conversation was in progress and the woman behind the counter started airing her views about a murder case which had created some stir in Algiers. A young commercial employee had killed an Algerian on a beach.

'I always say,' the woman began, 'if they clapped all that scum in jail, decent folks could breathe more freely.'

She was too much startled by Cottard's reaction – he dashed out of the shop without a word of excuse – to continue. Grand and the woman gazed after him, dumbfounded.

Subsequently Grand reported to the doctor other changes in Cottard's character. Cottard had always professed very liberal ideas, as his pet dictum on economic questions, 'Big fish eat little fish', implied. But now the only Oran newspaper he bought was the conservative organ, and one could hardly help suspecting that he made a point of reading it in public places. Somewhat of the same order was a request he made to Grand shortly before he left his sick-bed; Grand mentioned he was going to the post office and Cottard asked him to be kind enough to dispatch a money-order for a hundred francs to a sister living at a distance, mentioning that he sent her this sum every month. Then, just when Grand was leaving the room, he called him back.

'No, send her two hundred francs. That'll be a nice surprise for her. She believes I never give her a thought. But, actually, I'm devoted to her.'

Not long after this he made some curious remarks to Grand in the course of conversation. He had badgered Grand into telling him about the somewhat mysterious 'private work' to which Grand gave his evenings.

'I know!' Cottard exclaimed. 'You're writing a book, aren't you?'

'Something of the kind. But it's not so simple as that.'

'Ah!' Cottard sighed. 'I only wish I had a knack for writing.'

When Grand showed his surprise, Cottard explained with some embarrassment that being a literary man 'must make things easier in lots of ways'.

'Why?' Grand asked.

'Why, because an author has more rights than ordinary folk, as everybody knows. People will stand much more from him.'

'It looks,' said Rieux to Grand on the morning when the official notices were posted, 'as if this business of the rats had addled his brain, as it has done for so many other people. That's all it is. Or perhaps he's scared of the "fever".'

'I doubt it, doctor. If you want to know my opinion, he . . .'

He paused; with a machine-gun rattle from its exhaust the 'deratization' van was clattering by. Rieux kept silent until it was possible to make himself audible, then asked, without much interest, what Grand's opinion was.

'He's a man with something pretty serious on his conscience,' Grand said gravely.

The doctor shrugged his shoulders. As the inspector had said, he'd other fish to fry.

That afternoon Rieux had another talk with Castel. The serum had not yet come.

'In any case,' Rieux said, 'I wonder if it will be much use. This bacillus is such a queer one. . . . '

'There,' Castel said, 'I don't agree with you. These little brutes always have an air of originality. But, at bottom, it's always the same thing.'

'That's *your* theory, anyhow. Actually, of course, we know next to nothing on the subject.'

'I grant you, it's only my theory. Still, in a sense, that goes for everybody.'

Throughout the day the doctor was conscious that the slightly dazed feeling which came over him whenever he thought about the plague was growing more pronounced. Finally, he realized what it meant; simply that he was afraid! On two occasions he entered crowded cafés. Like Cottard he felt a need for friendly contacts, human warmth. A stupid instinct, Rieux told himself; still it served to remind him that he'd promised to visit the commercial traveller.

Cottard was standing beside the dining-table when the doctor entered his room that evening. A detective story lay open on the tablecloth. But the night was closing in and it would have been difficult to read in the growing darkness. Most likely Cottard had been sitting, musing in the twilight, until he heard the ring at his door. Rieux asked how he was feeling. Cottard sat down and replied rather grumpily that he was feeling tolerably well, adding that he'd feel better if only he could be sure of being left in peace. Rieux remarked that one couldn't always be alone.

'That's not what I meant. I was thinking of people who take an interest in you only to make trouble for you.' When Rieux said nothing, he went on: 'Mind you, that's not my case. Only I've been reading that detective story. It's about a poor devil who's arrested one fine morning, all of a sudden. People had been taking an interest in him and he knew nothing about it. They were talking about him in offices, entering his name on card-indexes. Now do you think that's fair? Do you think people have a right to treat a man like that?'

'Well,' Rieux said, 'that depends. In one sense I agree, nobody has the right. But all that's beside the mark. What's important is for you to go out a bit. It's a mistake staying indoors too much.'

Cottard seemed vexed, and said that on the contrary he was always going out and, if need arose, all the people in the street could vouch for him. What's more, he knew lots of people in other parts of the town.

'Do you know Monsieur Rigaud, the architect? He's a friend of mine.'

The room was in almost complete darkness. Outside, the street was growing noisier and a sort of murmur of relief greeted the moment when all the street-lamps lit up, all together. Rieux went out on to the balcony, and Cottard followed him. From the outlying districts – as happens every evening in our town – a gentle breeze wafted a murmur of voices, smells of roasting meat, a gay, perfumed tide of freedom sounding on its ways, as the streets filled up with noisy young people released from shops and offices. Nightfall with its deep, remote baying of unseen ships, the rumour rising from the sea, and the happy tumult of the crowd – that first hour of darkness which in the past had always had a special charm for Rieux – seemed today charged with menace, because of all he knew.

'How about turning on the lights?' he suggested when they went back into the room.

After this had been done the little man gazed at him, blinking his eyes.

'Tell me, doctor. Suppose I feel ill, would you put me in your ward at the hospital?'

'Why not?'

Cottard then inquired if it ever happened that a person in a hospital or a nursing-home was arrested. Rieux said it had been known to happen, but all depended on the invalid's condition.

'You know, doctor,' Cottard said, 'I've confidence in you.' Then he asked the doctor if he'd be kind enough to give him a lift, as he was going into town.

In the centre of the town the streets were already growing less crowded and the lights fewer. Children were playing in front of the doorways. At Cottard's request the doctor stopped his car beside one of the groups of children. They were playing hopscotch, and making a great deal of noise. One of them, a boy with sleek, neatly parted hair and a grubby face, stared hard at Rieux with bright, bold eyes. The doctor looked away. Standing on the pavement Cottard shook his head. He then said in a hoarse, rather laboured voice, casting uneasy glances over his shoulder:

'Everybody's talking about an epidemic. Is there anything in it, doctor?'

'People always talk,' Rieux replied. 'That's only to be expected.'

'You're right. And if we have ten deaths they'll think it's the end of the world. But it's not that we need here.'

The engine was ticking over. Rieux had his hand on the gear lever. But he was looking again at the boy who was still watching him with an oddly grave intentness. Suddenly, unexpectedly, the child smiled, showing all his teeth.

'Yes? And what do we need here?' Rieux asked, returning the child's smile.

Abruptly Cottard gripped the door of the car and, as he turned to go, almost shouted in a rageful, passionate voice:

'An earthquake! A big one – to smash everything up!'

There was no earthquake, and the whole of the following day was spent, so far as Rieux was concerned, in long drives to every corner of the town, in parleyings with the families of the sick and arguments with the invalids themselves. Never had Rieux known his profession weigh on him so heavily. Hitherto his patients had helped to lighten his task; they gladly put themselves into his hands. For the first time the doctor felt they were keeping aloof, wrapping themselves up in their malady with a sort of bemused hostility. It was a struggle to which he wasn't yet accustomed. And when, at ten that evening, he parked his car outside the home of his old asthma patient – his last visit of the day – it was an effort for Rieux to drag himself from his seat. For some moments he lingered, gazing up the dark street, watching the stars appear and disappear in the blackness of the sky.

When Rieux entered the room, the old man was sitting up in bed, at his usual occupation, counting out dried peas from one pan to another. On seeing his visitor he looked up, beaming with delight.

'Well, doctor? It's cholera, isn't it?'

'Where on earth did you get that idea from?'

'It's in the paper, and the radio said it, too.'

'No, it's not cholera.'

'Anyhow,' the old man chuckled excitedly, 'the big bugs are laying it on thick. Got the jitters, haven't they?'

'Don't you believe a word of it,' the doctor said.

He had examined the old man, and now was sitting in the middle of the dingy little dining-room. Yes, despite what he had said, he was afraid. He knew that in this suburb alone eight or ten unhappy people, cowering over their buboes, would be awaiting his visit next morning. In only two or three cases had incision of the buboes caused any improvement. For most of them it would mean going to hospital, and he knew how poor people feel about hospitals. 'I don't want them trying their experiments on him,' had said the wife of one of his patients. But he wouldn't be experimented on; he would die, that was all. That the regulations now in force were inadequate was lamentably clear. As for the 'specially equipped' wards, he knew what they amounted to: two outbuildings from which the other patients had been hastily evacuated; whose windows had been hermetically sealed; and round which a sanitary cordon had been set. The only hope was that the outbreak would die a natural death; it certainly wouldn't be arrested by the measures the authorities had so far devised.

Nevertheless, that night, the official communiqué was still optimistic. On the following day 'Ransdoc' announced that the rules laid down by the local administration had won general approval and already thirty sick persons had reported. Castel rang up Rieux.

'How many beds are there in the special wards?'

'Eighty.'

'Surely there are far more than thirty cases in the town?'

'Don't forget there are two sorts of cases; those who take fright, and those – they're the majority – who don't have time to do so.'

'I see. Are they checking up on the burials?'

'No. I told Richard over the phone that energetic measures were needed, not just words; we'd got to set up a real barrier against the disease, otherwise we might just as well do nothing.'

'Yes? And what did he say?'

'Nothing doing. He hadn't the powers. And so forth. In my opinion it's going to get worse.'

That was so. Within three days both wards were full. According to Richard there was talk of requisitioning a school and opening an auxiliary hospital. Meanwhile, Rieux continued incising buboes and waiting for the anti-plague serum.

Castel went back to his old books, and spent long hours in the Public Library.

'Those rats died of plague,' was his conclusion. 'Or of something extremely like it. And they've loosed on the town tens of thousands of fleas which will spread the infection in geometrical progression unless it's checked in time.'

Rieux said nothing.

About this time the weather appeared set fair, and the sun had drawn up the last puddles left by the recent rain. There was a serene blue sky flooded with golden light each morning, with sometimes a drone of planes in the rising heat – all seemed well with the world. And yet within four days the fever had made four startling strides; sixteen deaths, twenty-four, twenty-eight and thirty-two. On the fourth day the opening of the auxiliary hospital in the premises of an infant school was officially announced. The local population, who so far had made a point of masking their anxiety by facetious comments, now seemed tongue-tied and went their ways with gloomy faces.

Rieux decided to ring up the Prefect.

'The regulations don't go anything like far enough, considering how things are.'

'Yes,' the Prefect replied. 'I've seen the statistics and, as you say, they're most perturbing.'

'They're more than perturbing; they're conclusive.'

'I'll ask Government for orders.'

When Rieux next met Castel, the Prefect's remark was still rankling.

'"Orders"!' he said scornfully. 'When what's needed is imagination.'

'Any news of the serum?'

'It'll come this week.'

The Prefect sent instructions to Rieux, through Richard, asking him to draw up a minute to be transmitted for orders to the central administration of the Colony. Rieux included in it a clinical diagnosis and statistics of the epidemic. On that day forty deaths were reported. The Prefect took the responsibility, as he put it, of tightening up the new regulations. Compulsory declaration of all cases of fever and their isolation were to be strictly enforced. The residences of sick people were to be shut up and disinfected; persons living in the same house were to go into quarantine; burials were to be supervised by the local authorities – in a manner which will be described later on. Next day the serum arrived by plane. There was enough for immediate requirements, but not enough if the epidemic were to spread. In reply to his telegram Rieux was informed that the emergency reserve stock was exhausted, but that a new supply was in preparation.

Meanwhile, from all the outlying districts, spring was making its progress into the town. Thousands of roses wilted in the flower-vendors' baskets in the market-places and along the streets, and the air was heavy with their cloying perfume. Outwardly, indeed, this spring was like any other. The trams were always packed at the rush-hours, empty and untidy during the rest of the day. Tarrou watched the little old man, and the little old man spat on the cats. Grand hurried home every evening to his mysterious literary activities. Cottard went his usual desultory ways, and M. Othon, the magistrate, continued to parade his menagerie. The old Spaniard decanted his dried peas from pan to pan, and sometimes you encountered Rambert, the journalist, looking interested as ever in all he saw. In the evening the usual crowd thronged the streets and the queues lengthened outside the picture-houses. Moreover, the epidemic seemed to be on the wane; on some days only ten or so deaths were notified. Then, all of a sudden, the figure shot up again, vertically. On the day when the death-roll touched thirty, Dr Rieux read an official telegram which the Prefect had just handed him, remarking, 'So they've got alarmed – at last.' The telegram ran: *Proclaim a state of plague stop Close the town.*

PART TWO

I

FROM NOW ON it can be said that plague was the concern of all of us. Hitherto, surprised as he may have been by the strange things happening around him, each individual citizen had gone about his business as usual, so far as this was possible. And, no doubt, he would have continued doing so. But once the town gates were shut, every one of us realized that all, the narrator included, were, so to speak, in the same boat, and each would have to adapt himself to the new conditions of life. Thus, for example a feeling normally as individual as the ache of separation from those one loves suddenly became a feeling in which all shared alike and – together with fear – the greatest affliction of the long period of exile that lay ahead.

One of the most striking consequences of the closing of the gates was, in fact, this sudden deprivation befalling people who were completely unprepared for it. Mothers and children, lovers, husbands and wives, who had a few days previously taken it for granted that their parting would be a short one, who had kissed each other good-bye on the platform and exchanged a few trivial remarks, sure as they were of seeing each other again after a few days or, at most, a few weeks, duped by our blind human faith in the near future and little if at all diverted from their normal interests by this leave-taking – all these people found themselves, without the least warning, hopelessly cut off, prevented from seeing each other again, or even communicating with each other. For actually the closing of the gates took place some hours before the official order was made known to the public, and, naturally enough, it was impossible to take individual cases of hardship into account.

It might indeed be said that the first effect of this brutal visitation was to compel our townsfolk to act as if they had no feelings as individuals. During the first part of the day on which the prohibition to leave the town came into force the Prefect's office was besieged by a crowd of applicants advancing pleas of equal cogency but equally impossible to take into consideration. Indeed, it needed several days for us to realize that we were completely cornered; that words like 'special arrangements', 'favour', and 'priority' had lost all effective meaning.

Even the small satisfaction of writing letters was denied us. It came to this: not only had the town ceased to be in touch with the rest of the world by normal means of communication, but also – according to a second notification – all correspondence was forbidden, to obviate the risk of letters' carrying infection outside the town. In the early days a favoured few managed to persuade the sentries at the gates to allow them to get messages through to the outside world. But that was only at the beginning of the epidemic, when the sentries found it natural to obey their feelings of humanity. Later on, when these same sentries had had the gravity of the situation drummed into them, they flatly refused to take responsibilities whose possible after-effects they could not foresee. At first, telephone-calls to other towns were allowed, but this led to much crowding of the telephone-booths and delays on the lines so that for some days they also were prohibited, and thereafter limited to what were called 'urgent cases', such as deaths, marriages and births. So we had to fall back on telegrams. People linked together by close friendship, affection, or physical love, found themselves reduced to hunting for tokens of their past communion within the compass of a ten-word telegram. And since, in practice, the phrases one can use in a telegram are quickly exhausted, long lives passed side by side, or passionate yearnings, soon declined on the exchange of such trite formulas as, 'Am fit. Always thinking of you. Love.'

Some few of us, however, persisted in writing letters, and gave much time to hatching plans for corresponding with the outside world; but almost always these plans came to nothing. Even on the rare occasions when they succeeded, we could not know this, since we received no answer. For weeks on end we were reduced to starting the same letter over and over again, recopying the same scraps of news and the same personal appeals, with the result that after a certain time the living words, into which we had as it were transfused our hearts' blood, were drained of any meaning. Thereafter we went on copying them mechanically, trying, through the dead phrases, to convey some notion of our ordeal. And, in the long run, to these sterile, reiterated monologues, these futile colloquies with a blank wall, even the banal formulas of a telegram came to seem preferable.

Also, after some days – when it was clear that no one had the least hope of being able to leave our town – inquiries began to be made whether the return of people who had gone away before the outbreak would be permitted. After some days' consideration of the matter the authorities replied affirmatively. They pointed out, however, that in no case would persons who returned be allowed to leave the town again; once here, they would have to stay, whatever happened. Some families – actually very few – refused to take the position seriously and in their eagerness to have the absent members of the family with them again, cast prudence to the winds and wired to them to take this opportunity of returning. But very soon those who were prisoners of the plague realized the terrible danger to which this would expose their relatives, and sadly resigned themselves to their absence. At the height of the epidemic we saw only one case in which natural emotions overcame the fear of death in a particularly painful form. It was not, as might be expected, the case of two young people, whose passion made them yearn for each other's nearness at whatever cost of pain. The two were old Dr Castel and his wife, and they had been married for very many years. Mme Castel had gone on a visit to a neighbouring town some days before the epidemic started. They weren't one of those exemplary married couples of the Darby-and-Joan pattern; on the contrary, the narrator has grounds for saying that, in all probability, neither partner felt quite sure the marriage was all that could have been desired. But this ruthless, protracted separation enabled them to realize that they could not live apart, and in the sudden glow of this discovery the risk of plague seemed insignificant.

That was an exception. For most people it was obvious that the separation must last until the end of the epidemic. And for every one of us the ruling emotion of his life – which he had imagined he knew through and through (the people of Oran, as has been said, have simple passions) – took on a new aspect. Husbands who had had complete faith in their wives found, to their surprise, that they were jealous; and lovers had the same experience. Men who had pictured themselves as Don Juans became models of fidelity. Sons who had lived beside their mothers hardly giving them a glance fell to picturing with poignant regret each wrinkle in the absent face that memory cast upon the screen. This drastic, clean-cut deprivation and our complete ignorance of what the future held in store had taken us unawares; we were unable to react against the mute appeal of presences, still so near and already so far, which haunted us daylong. In fact, our suffering was twofold; our own to start with, and then the imagined suffering of the absent one, son, mother, wife or mistress.

Under other circumstances our townsfolk would probably have found an outlet in increased activity, a more sociable life. But the plague forced inactivity on them, limiting their movements to the same dull round inside the town, and throwing them, day after day, on the illusive solace of their memories. For in their aimless walks they kept on coming back to the same streets and usually, owing to the smallness of the town, these were streets in which, in happier days, they had walked with those who now were absent.

Thus the first thing that plague brought to our town was exile. And the narrator is convinced that he can set down here, as holding good for all, the feeling he personally had and to which many of his friends confessed. It was undoubtedly the feeling of exile – that sensation of a void within which never left us, that irrational longing to hark back to the past or else to speed up the march of time, and those keen shafts of memory that stung like fire. Sometimes we toyed with our imagination, composing ourselves to wait for a ring at the bell announcing somebody's return, or for the sound of a familiar footstep on the stairs; but, though we might deliberately stay at home at the hour when a traveller coming by the evening train would normally have arrived, and though we might contrive to forget for the moment that no trains were running, that game of make-believe, for obvious reasons, could not last. Always a moment came when we had to face the fact that no trains were coming in. And then we realized that the separation was destined to continue, we had no choice but to come to terms with the days ahead. In short, we returned to our prison-house, we had nothing left us but the past, and even if some were tempted to live in the future, they had speedily to abandon the idea – anyhow, as soon as could be – once they felt the wounds that the imagination inflicts on those who yield themselves to it.

It is noteworthy that our townspeople very quickly desisted, even in public, from a habit one might have expected them to form; that of trying to figure out the probable duration of their exile. The reason was this. When the most pessimistic had fixed it at, say six months; when they had drunk in advance the dregs of bitterness of those six black months, and painfully screwed up their courage to the sticking-place, straining all their remaining energy to endure valiantly the long ordeal of all those weeks and days – when they had done this, some friend they met, an article in a newspaper, a vague suspicion or a flash of foresight would suggest that, after all, there was no reason why the epidemic shouldn't last more than six months; why not a year, or even more?

At such moments the collapse of their courage, will-power and endurance was so abrupt that they felt they could never drag themselves out of the pit of despond into which they had fallen. Therefore they forced themselves never to think about the problematic day of escape, to cease looking to the future, and always to keep, so to speak, their eyes fixed on the ground at their feet. But, naturally enough, this prudence, this habit of feinting with their predicament and refusing to put up a fight were ill rewarded. For, while averting that revulsion which they found so unbearable, they also deprived themselves of those redeeming moments, frequent enough when all is told, when by conjuring up pictures of a reunion to be, they could forget about the plague. Thus, in a middle course between these heights and depths, they drifted through life rather than lived, the prey of aimless days and sterile memories, like wandering shadows that could have acquired substance only by consenting to root themselves in the solid earth of their distress.

Thus, too, they came to know the incorrigible sorrow of all prisoners and exiles, which is to live in company with a memory that serves no purpose. Even the past, of which they thought incessantly, had a savour only of regret. For they would have wished to add to it all that they regretted having left undone, while they might yet have done it, with the man or woman whose return they now awaited; just as in all the activities, even the relatively happy ones, of their life as pris-oners they kept vainly trying to include the absent one. And thus there was always something missing in their lives. Hostile to the past, impatient of the present, and cheated of the future, we were much like those whom men's justice, or hatred, forces to live behind prison bars. Thus the only way of escaping from that intolerable leisure was to set the trains running again in one's imagination and in filling the silence with the fancied tinkle of a door-bell, in practice obstinately mute.

Still, if it was an exile, it was, for most of us, exile in one's own home. And, though the narrator experienced only the common form of exile, he cannot forget the case of those who, like Rambert the journalist and a good many others, had to endure an aggravated deprivation, since, being travellers caught by the plague and forced to stay where they were, they were cut off both from the person with whom they wanted to be and from their homes as well. In the general exile they were the most exiled; since while time gave rise for them, as for us all, to the suffering appropriate to it, there was also for them the space factor; they were obsessed by it and at every moment knocked their heads against the walls of this huge and alien lazar-house secluding them from their lost homes. These were the people, no doubt, whom one often saw wandering forlornly in the dusty town at all hours of the day, silently invoking nightfalls known to them alone and the daysprings of their happier land. And they fed their despondency with fleeting intimations, messages as disconcerting as a flight of swallows, a dew-fall at sun-down, or those queer glints the sun sometimes dapples on empty streets. As for that outside world, which can always offer an escape from everything, they shut their eyes to it, bent as they were on cherishing the all-too-real phantoms of their imagination and conjuring up with all their might pictures of a land where a special play of light, two or three hills, a favourite tree, a woman's smile, composed for them a world that nothing could replace.

To come at last, and more specifically, to the case of parted lovers who present the greatest interest and of whom the narrator is, perhaps, better qualified to speak – their minds were the prey of different emotions, notably remorse. For their present position enabled them to take stock of their feelings with a sort of feverish objectivity. And, in these conditions, it was rare for them not to detect their own shortcomings. What first brought these home to them was the trouble they experienced in summoning up any clear picture of what the absent one was doing. They came to deplore their ignorance of the way in which that person used to spend his or her days, and reproached themselves for having troubled too little about this in the past, and for having affected to think that, for a lover, the occupations of the loved one when they are not together could be a matter of indifference and not a source of joy. Once this had been brought home to them, they could retrace the course of their love and see where it had fallen short. In normal times all of us know, whether consciously or not, that there is no love which can't be bettered; nevertheless, we reconcile ourselves more or less easily to the fact that ours has never risen above the average. But memory is less disposed to compromise. And, in a very definite way, this misfortune which had come from outside and befallen a whole town did more than inflict on us an unmerited distress with which we might well be indignant. It also incited us to create our own suffering and thus to accept frustration as a natural state. This was one of the tricks the pestilence had of diverting attention and confounding issues.

Thus each of us had to be content to live only for the day, alone under the vast indifference of the sky. This sense of being abandoned, which might in time have given characters a finer temper, began, however, by sapping them to the point of futility. For instance, some of our fellow-citizens became subject to a curious kind of servitude, which put them at the mercy of the sun and the rain. Looking at them, you had an impression that for the first time in their lives they were becoming, as some would say, weather-conscious. A burst of sunshine was enough to make them seem delighted with the world, while rainy days gave a dark cast to their faces and their mood. A few weeks before they had been free of this absurd subservience to the weather, because they had not to face life alone; the person they were living with held, to some extent, the foreground of their little world. But from now on it was different; they seemed at the mercy of the sky's caprices, in other words, suffered and hoped irrationally.

Moreover, in this extremity of solitude none could count on any help from his neighbour; each had to bear the load of his troubles alone. If, by some chance, one of us tried to unburden himself or to say something about his feelings, the reply he got, whatever it might be, usually wounded him. And then it dawned on him that he and the man with him weren't talking about the same thing. For while he himself spoke from the depths of long days of brooding upon his personal distress, and the image he had tried to impart had been slowly shaped and proved in the fires of passion and regret, this meant nothing to the man to whom he was speaking, and who pictured a conventional emotion, a grief that is traded on the market-place, mass-produced. Whether friendly or hostile, the reply always missed fire, and the attempt to communicate had to be given up. This was true of those at least for whom silence was unbearable, and since the others could not find the truly expressive word, they resigned themselves to using the current coin of language, the commonplaces of plain narrative, of anecdote and of their daily paper. So, in these cases, too, even the sincerest grief had to make do with the set phrases of ordinary conversation. Only on these terms could the prisoners of the plague ensure the sympathy of their door-porter and the interest of their hearers.

Nevertheless – and this point is important – however bitter their distress and however heavy their hearts, for all their emptiness, it can be truly said of these exiles that in the early period of the plague they could account themselves privileged. For at the precise moment when the residents of the town began to panic, their thoughts were wholly fixed on the person whom they longed to meet again. The egoism of love made them immune to the general distress and, if they thought of the plague, it was only in so far as it might threaten to make their separation eternal. Thus in the very heart of the epidemic they maintained a saving indifference, which one was tempted to take for composure. Their despair saved them from panic, thus their misfortune had a good side. For instance, if it happened that one of them was carried off by the disease, it was almost always without his having had time to realize it. Snatched suddenly from his long, silent communion with a wraith of memory, he was plunged straightway into the densest silence of all. He'd had no time for anything.

II

WHILE OUR TOWNSFOLK were trying to come to terms with their sudden isolation, the plague was posting sentries at the gates and turning away ships bound for Oran. No vehicle had entered the town since the gates were closed. From that day onwards one had the impression that all cars were moving in circles. The harbour, too, presented a strange appearance to those who looked down on it from the top of the boulevards. The commercial activity which hitherto made it one of the chief ports on the coast had ceased abruptly. Only a few ships, detained in quarantine, were anchored in the bay. But the gaunt, idle cranes on the wharves, tip-wagons lying on their sides, neglected heaps of sacks and barrels – all testified that commerce, too, had died of plague.

In spite of such unusual sights our townsfolk apparently found it hard to grasp what was happening to them. There were feelings all could share, such as fear and separation, but personal interests, too, continued to occupy the foreground of their thoughts. Nobody as yet had really acknowledged to himself what the disease connoted. Most people were chiefly aware of what ruffled the normal tenor of their lives or affected their interests. They were worried and irritated – but these are not feelings with which to confront plague. Their first reaction, for instance, was to abuse the authorities. The Prefect's riposte to criticisms echoed by the Press – Could not the regulations be modified and made less stringent? – was somewhat unexpected. Hitherto neither the newspapers nor the Ransdoc Information Bureau had been given any official statistics relating to the epidemic. Now the Prefect supplied them daily to the Bureau, with the request that they should be broadcast once a week.

In this, too, the reaction of the public was slower than might have been expected. Thus the bare statement that three hundred and two deaths had taken place in the third week of plague failed to strike their imagination. For one thing, all the three hundred and two deaths might not have been due to plague. Also, no one in the town had any idea of the average weekly death-rate in ordinary times. The population of the town was about two hundred thousand. There was no knowing if the present death-rate were really so abnormal. This is, in fact, the kind of statistic that nobody ever troubles much about – nothwithstanding that its interest is obvious. The public lacked, in short, standards of comparison. It was only as time passed and the steady rise in the death-rate could not be ignored, that public opinion became alive to the truth. For in the fifth week there were three hundred and twenty-one deaths, and three hundred and forty-five in the sixth. These figures, anyhow, spoke for themselves. Yet they were still not sensational enough to prevent our townsfolk, perturbed though they were, from persisting in the idea that what was happening was a sort of accident, disagreeable enough, but certainly of a temporary order.

So they went on strolling about the town as usual and sitting at the tables on café terraces. Generally speaking, they did not lack courage, bandied more jokes than lamentations, and made a show of accepting cheerfully unpleasantnesses which obviously could be only passing. In short, they kept up appearances. However, towards the end of the month, about the time of the

Week of Prayer which will be described later on, there were more serious developments, altering the whole aspect of the town. To begin with, the Prefect took measures controlling the traffic and the food supply. Petrol was rationed and restrictions were placed on the sale of foodstuffs. Reductions were ordered in the use of electricity. Only necessaries were brought by road or air to Oran. Thus the traffic thinned out progressively until hardly any private cars were on the roads; luxury shops closed overnight, and others began to put up '*Sold Out*' notices while crowds of buyers stood waiting at their doors.

Oran assumed a novel appearance. You saw more pedestrians, and in the slack hours numbers of people, reduced to idleness because shops and a good many offices were closed, crowded the streets and cafés. For the present they were not unemployed; merely on holiday. So it was that on fine days, towards three in the afternoon, Oran brought to mind a city where public rejoicings are in progress, shops are shut, and traffic is stopped to give a merry-making populace the freedom of the streets.

Naturally the picture-houses benefited by the situation and made money hand over fist. They had one difficulty, however – to provide a change of programme, since the circulation of films in the region had been suspended. After a fortnight the various cinemas were obliged to exchange films and, after a further lapse of time, to show always the same programme. In spite of this their takings did not fall off.

The cafés, thanks to the big stocks accumulated in a town where the wine-and-spirit trade holds pride of place, were equally able to cater for their patrons. And, to tell the truth, there was much heavy drinking. One of the cafés had the brilliant idea of putting up a slogan: 'The best protection against infection is a bottle of good wine', which confirmed an already prevalent opinion that alcohol is a safeguard against infectious disease. Every night towards 2 a.m., quite a number of drunk men, ejected from the cafés, staggered down the streets, vociferating optimism.

Yet all these changes were, in one sense, so fantastic and had been made so precipitately that it wasn't easy to regard them as likely to have any permanence. With the result that we went on focusing our attention on our personal feelings.

When leaving the hospital two days after the gates were closed, Dr Rieux met Cottard in the street. The little man was beaming with satisfaction. Rieux congratulated him on his appearance.

'Yes,' Cottard said, 'I'm feeling very fit. Never was fitter in my life. But tell me, doctor. This blasted plague, what about it? Getting to look mighty serious, isn't it?' When the doctor nodded, he continued exuberantly: 'And there's no reason for it to stop, now. This town's going to be in an unholy mess, by the look of things.'

They walked a little way together. Cottard told the story of a grocer in his street who had laid by masses of tinned provisions with the idea of selling them later on at a big profit. When the ambulance men came to fetch him he had several dozen tins of meat under his bed. 'He died in hospital. There's no money in plague, that's sure.' Cottard was a mine of stories of this kind, true or false, about the epidemic. One of them was about a man with all the symptoms and running a high fever who dashed out into the street, flung himself on the first woman he met and embraced her, yelling that he'd 'got it'.

'Good for him!' was Cottard's comment. But his next remark seemed to belie his gleeful exclamation. 'Anyhow, we'll all be nuts before long, unless I'm much mistaken.'

It was on the afternoon of the same day that Grand at last unburdened himself to Rieux. Noticing Mme Rieux's photograph on the desk, he looked at the doctor inquiringly. Rieux told him that his wife was under treatment in a sanatorium some distance from the town. 'In one way,' Grand said, 'that's lucky.' The doctor agreed that it was lucky in a sense; but, he added, the great thing was that his wife should recover.

'Yes,' Grand said, 'I understand.'

And then, for the first time since Rieux had made his acquaintance, he became quite voluble. Though he still had trouble over his words he succeeded nearly always in finding them; indeed, it was as if he'd been thinking over what he now said, for years.

When in his 'teens he had married a very young girl, one of a poor family living near-by. It was, in fact, in order to marry that he'd abandoned his studies and taken up his present job. Neither he nor Jeanne ever stirred from their part of the town. In his courting days he used to go to see her at her home and the family were inclined to make fun of her bashful, silent admirer. Her father was a railwayman. When off duty, he spent most of the time seated in a corner beside the window gazing meditatively at the passers-by, his enormous hands splayed out on his thighs. His wife was always busy with domestic duties, in which Jeanne gave her a hand. Jeanne was so tiny that it always made Grand nervous to see her crossing a street; the vehicles bearing down on her looked so gigantic. Then one day shortly before Christmas they went out for a short walk together and stopped to admire a gaily decorated shop-window. After gazing ecstatically at it for some moments, Jeanne turned to him. 'Oh, isn't it lovely!' He squeezed her wrist. It was thus that the marriage had come about.

The rest of the story, to Grand's thinking, was very simple. The common lot of married couples. You get married, you go on loving a bit longer, you work. And you work so hard that it makes you forget to love. As the head of the office where Grand was employed hadn't kept his promise, Jeanne, too, had to work outside. At this point a little imagination was needed to grasp what Grand was trying to convey. Owing largely to fatigue he gradually lost grip of himself, had less and less to say, and failed to keep alive the feeling in his wife that she was loved. An overworked husband, poverty, the gradual loss of hope in a better future, silent evenings at home – what chance had any passion of surviving such conditions? Probably Jeanne had suffered. And yet she'd stayed; of course one may often suffer a long time without knowing it. Thus years went by. Then, one day, she left him. Naturally she hadn't gone alone. 'I was *very* fond of you, but now I'm so, so tired. I'm not happy to go, but one needn't be happy to make another start.' That, more or less, was what she'd said in her letter.

Grand, too, had suffered. And he, too, might – as Rieux pointed out – have made a fresh start. But, no, he had lost faith. . . . Only, he couldn't stop thinking about her. What he'd have liked to do was to write her a letter justifying himself.

'But it's not easy,' he told Rieux. 'I've been thinking it over for years. While we loved each other we didn't need words to make ourselves understood. But people don't love for ever. A time came when I should have found the words to keep her with me – only I couldn't.' Grand produced from his pocket something that looked like a check duster and blew his nose noisily. Then he wiped his moustache. Rieux gazed at him in silence. 'Forgive me, doctor,' Grand added hastily, 'but – how shall I put it? – I feel you're to be trusted. That's why I can talk to you about these things. And then, you see, I get all worked up.'

Obviously Grand's thoughts were leagues away from the plague.

That evening Rieux sent a telegram to his wife, telling her that the town was closed, that she must go on taking great care of herself, and that she was in his thoughts.

One evening when he was leaving the hospital – it was about three weeks after the closing of the gates – Rieux found a young man waiting for him in the street.

'You remember me, don't you?'

Rieux believed he did, but couldn't quite 'place' him.

'I called on you just before this trouble started,' the young man said, 'for information about the living conditions in the Arab quarter. My name is Raymond Rambert.'

'Ah yes, of course. Well, you've now the makings of a good story for your paper.'

Rambert, who gave the impression of being much less self-assured than he had seemed on the first occasion when they met, said it wasn't that he'd come about. He wanted to know if the doctor would kindly give him some help.

'I must apologize,' he continued, 'but really I don't know a soul here, and the local representative of my paper is a complete dud.'

Rieux said he had to go to a dispensary in the centre of the town and suggested they should walk there together. Their way lay through the narrow streets of the negro district. Evening was coming on, but the town, once so noisy at this hour, was strangely still. The only sounds were some bugle-calls echoing through the air still golden with the end of daylight; the army, anyhow, was making a show of carrying on as usual. Meanwhile, as they walked down the steep little streets flanked by blue, mauve and saffron-yellow walls, Rambert talked incessantly, as if his nerves were out of hand.

He had left his wife in Paris, he said. Well, she wasn't actually his wife, but it came to the same thing. The moment the town was put into quarantine he had sent her a wire. His impression then was that this state of things was quite temporary, and all he'd tried to do was to get a letter through to her. But the post-office officials had vetoed this, his colleagues of the local Press said they could do nothing for him, and a clerk in the Prefect's office had laughed in his face. It was only after waiting in a queue for a couple of hours that he had managed to get a telegram accepted: '*All goes well. Hope to see you soon.*'

But next morning, when he woke up, it had dawned on him that, after all, there was absolutely no knowing how long this business was going to last. So he'd decided to leave the

75

town at once. Being able, thanks to his professional status, to pull some strings, he had secured an interview with a high official in the Prefect's office. He had explained that his presence in Oran was purely accidental, he had no connexion with the town, and no reasons for staying in it; that being so, he surely was entitled to leave, even if, once outside the town, he had to undergo a spell of quarantine. The official told him he quite appreciated his position, but no exceptions could be made. He would, however, see if anything could be done, though he could hold out little hope of a quick decision, as the authorities were taking a very serious view of the situation.

'But, confound it,' Rambert exclaimed, 'I don't belong here!'

'Quite so. . . . Anyhow, let's hope the epidemic will soon be over.' Finally, he had tried to console Rambert by pointing out that, as a journalist, he had an excellent subject to his hand in Oran; indeed, when one came to think of it, no event, however disagreeable in some ways, but had its bright side. Whereat Rambert had shrugged his shoulders petulantly and walked out.

They had come to the centre of the town.

'It's so damn' silly, doctor, isn't it? The truth is, I wasn't brought into the world to write newspaper articles. But it's quite likely I was brought into the world to live with a woman. That's reasonable enough, isn't it?'

Rieux replied cautiously that there might be something in what he said.

The central boulevards were not so crowded as usual. The few people about were hurrying to distant homes. Not a smile was to be seen on any face. Rieux guessed that this was a result of the latest Ransdoc announcement. After twenty-four hours our townspeople would begin to hope again. But on the days when they were announced the statistics were too fresh in everybody's memory.

'The truth,' Rambert remarked abruptly, 'is that she and I have been together only a short time, and we suit each other perfectly.' When Rieux said nothing, he continued: 'I can see I'm boring you. Sorry. All I wanted to know was whether you couldn't possibly give me a certificate stating that I haven't got this damned disease. It might make things easier, I think.'

Rieux nodded. A small boy had just run against his legs, and fallen; he set him on his feet again. Walking on, they came to the Place d'Armes. Grey with dust, the palms and fig-trees drooped despondently around a statue of the Republic, which too was coated with grime and dust. They stopped beside the statue. Rieux stamped his feet on the flagstones to shake off the coat of white dust that had gathered on them. His hat pushed slightly back, his shirt-collar gaping under a loosely knotted tie, his cheeks ill-shaven, the journalist had the sulky, stubborn look of a young man who feels himself deeply injured.

'Please don't doubt I understand you,' Rieux said, 'but you must see your argument doesn't hold water. I can't give you that certificate because I don't know whether you have the disease or not, and, even if I did, how could I certify that between the moment of leaving my consulting-room and your arrival at the Prefect's office you wouldn't be infected? And even if I did . . . '

'And even if you did . . . ?'

'Even if I gave you a certificate, it wouldn't help.'

'Why not?'

'Because there are thousands of people placed as you are in this town and there can't be any question of allowing them to leave it.'

'Even supposing they haven't got plague?'

'That's not a sufficient reason. Oh, I know it's an absurd situation, but we're all involved in it, and we've got to accept it as it is.'

'But I don't belong here.'

'Unfortunately from now on you'll belong here, like everybody else.'

Rambert raised his voice a little.

'But, damn it, doctor, can't you see, it's a matter of common human feeling? Or don't you realize what this sort of separation means to people who ... who are fond of each other?'

Rieux was silent for a moment, then said he understood it perfectly. He wished nothing better than that Rambert should be allowed to return to his wife and that all who loved each other and were parted should come together again. Only the law was the law, plague had broken out, and he could only do what had to be done.

'No,' Rambert said bitterly, 'you can't understand. You're using the language of reason, not of the heart; you live in a world of ... of abstractions.'

The doctor glanced up at the statue of the Republic, then said he did not know if he was using the language of reason, but he knew he was using the language of the facts as everybody could see them – which wasn't necessarily the same thing.

The journalist tugged at his tie to straighten it.

'So, I take it, I can't count on help from you. Very good. But' – his tone was challenging – 'leave this town I shall.'

The doctor repeated that he quite understood, but all that was none of his business.

'Excuse me, but it *is* your business,' Rambert raised his voice again. 'I approached you because I'd been told you played a large part in drawing up the orders that have been issued. So I thought that in one case anyhow you could unmake what you'd helped to make. But you don't care; you never gave a thought to anybody, you didn't take the case of people who are separated into account.'

Rieux admitted this was true up to a point; he'd preferred not to take such cases into account.

'Ah, I see now!' Rambert exclaimed. 'You'll soon be talking about the interests of the general public. But public welfare is merely the sum total of the private welfares of each of us.'

The doctor seemed abruptly to come out of a dream.

'Oh, come!' he said. 'There's that, but there's much more to it than that. It doesn't do to rush to conclusions, you know. . . . But you've no reason to feel angered. I assure you that if you find a way out of your quandary, I shall be extremely pleased. Only, there are things which my official position debars me from doing.'

Rambert tossed his head petulantly.

'Yes, yes. I was wrong to show annoyance. And I've taken up too much of your time already.'

Rieux asked him to let him know how he got on with his project, and not to bear him a grudge for not having been more amenable. He was sure, he added, that there was some common ground on which they could meet. Rambert looked perplexed.

Then, 'Yes,' he said after a short silence, 'I rather think so, too – in spite of myself, and of all you've just been saying.' He paused. 'Still, I can't agree with you.'

Pulling down his hat over his eyes, he walked quickly away. Rieux saw him enter the hotel where Tarrou was staying.

After a moment the doctor gave a slight nod, as if approving of some thought that had crossed his mind. Yes, the journalist was right in refusing to be baulked of happiness. But was he right in reproaching him, Rieux, with living in a world of abstractions? Could that term 'abstraction' really apply to these days he spent in his hospital while the plague was battening on the town, raising its death-toll to five hundred victims a week? Yes, an element of abstraction, of a divorce from reality, entered into such calamities. Still, when abstraction sets to killing you, you've got to get busy with it. And so much Rieux knew: that this wasn't the easiest course. Running this auxiliary hospital, for instance, of which he was in charge – there were now three such hospitals – was no light task.

He had had an anteroom, giving on his surgery, installed, equipped for dealing with patients on arrival. The floor had been excavated and replaced by a shallow lake of water and cresylic acid, in the centre of which was a sort of island made of bricks. The patient was carried to the island, rapidly undressed, and his clothes dropped into the disinfectant water. After being washed, dried and dressed in one of the coarse hospital night-shirts, he was taken to Rieux for examination, then carried to one of the wards. This hospital, a requisitioned schoolhouse, now contained five hundred beds, almost all of which were occupied. After the reception of the patients, which he personally supervised, Rieux injected serum, lanced buboes, checked the statistics again, and returned for his afternoon consultations. Only when night was setting in did he start on his round of visits, and he never got home till a very late hour. On the previous night his mother, when handing him a telegram from his wife, had remarked that his hands were shaking.

'Yes,' he said. 'But it's only a matter of sticking to it, and my nerves will steady down, you'll see.'

He had a robust constitution and, as yet, wasn't really tired. Still his visits, for one thing, were beginning to put a great strain on his endurance. Once the epidemic was diagnosed, the patient had to be evacuated forthwith. Then indeed began 'abstraction' and a tussle with the family who knew they would not see the sick man again until he was dead or cured. 'Have some pity, doctor!' It was Mme Loret, mother of the chambermaid at Tarrou's hotel, who made the appeal. An unnecessary appeal; of course he had pity. But what purpose could it serve? He *had* to telephone, and soon the ambulance could be heard clanging down the street. (At first the neighbours used to open widows and watch. Later, they promptly shut them.) Then came a second phase of conflict, tears and pleadings – abstraction, in a word. In those fever-hot, nerve-ridden sickrooms crazy scenes took place. But the issue was always the same. The patient was removed. Then Rieux, too, could leave.

In the early days he had merely telephoned, then rushed off to see other patients, without waiting for the ambulance. But no sooner was he gone than the family locked and barred their doors, preferring contact with the plague to a parting whose issue they now knew only too well. There followed objurgations, screams, batterings on the door, action by the police and, later, armed force; the patient was taken by storm. Thus, during the first few weeks, Rieux was compelled to stay with the patient till the ambulance came. Later, when each doctor was accompanied by a volunteer police-officer, Rieux could hurry away to the next patient.

But, to begin with, every evening was like that evening when he was called in for Mme Loret's daughter. He was shown into a small flat decorated with fans and artificial flowers. The mother greeted him with a faltering smile.

'Oh, I do hope it's not the fever everyone's talking about.'

Lifting the coverlet and chemise, he gazed in silence at the red blotches on the girl's thighs and stomach, the swollen ganglions. After one glance, the mother broke into shrill, uncontrollable cries of grief. And every evening mothers wailed thus, with a distraught abstraction, as their eyes fell on those fatal stigmata on limbs and bellies; every evening hands gripped Rieux's arms, there was a rush of useless words, promises and tears; every evening the nearing tocsin of the ambulance provoked scenes as vain as every form of grief. Rieux had nothing to look forward to but a long sequence of such scenes, renewed again and again. Yes, plague, like abstraction, was monotonous; perhaps only one factor changed, and that was Rieux himself. Standing at the foot of the statue of the Republic that evening, he felt it; all he was conscious of was a bleak indifference steadily gaining on him, as he gazed at the door of the hotel Rambert had just entered.

After these wearing weeks, after all those nightfalls when the townsfolk poured into the streets to roam them aimlessly, Rieux had learnt that he need no longer steel himself against pity. One grows out of pity when it's useless. And in this feeling that his heart had slowly closed in on itself, the doctor found a solace, his only solace, for the almost unendurable burden of his days. This, he knew, would make his task easier, and therefore he was glad of it. When he came home at two in the morning and his mother was shocked at the blank look he gave her, she was deploring precisely the sole alleviation Rieux could then experience. To fight abstraction you must have something of it in your own make-up. But how could Rambert be expected to grasp that? Abstraction for him was all that stood in the way of his happiness. Indeed, Rieux had to admit the journalist was right, in one sense. But he knew, too, that abstraction sometimes proves itself stronger than happiness; and then, if only then, it has to be taken into account. And this was what was going to happen to Rambert as the doctor was to learn when, much later, Rambert told him more about himself. Thus he was enabled to follow, and on a different plane, the dreary struggle in progress between each man's happiness and the abstractions of the plague – which constituted the whole life of our town over a long period of time.

III

BUT WHERE SOME saw abstraction others saw the truth. The first month of the plague ended gloomily, with a violent recrudescence of the epidemic and a dramatic sermon preached by Father Paneloux, the Jesuit priest who had given an arm to old Michel when he was tottering home at the start of his illness. Father Paneloux had already made his mark with frequent contributions to the Oran Geographical Society; these dealt chiefly with ancient inscriptions, on which he was an authority. But he had also reached a wider, non-specialist public with a series of lectures on present-day individualism. In these he had shown himself a stalwart champion of Christian doctrine at its most precise and purest, equally remote from modern laxity and the obscurantism of the past. On these occasions he had not shrunk from trouncing his hearers with some vigorous home-truths. Hence his local celebrity.

Towards the end of the month the ecclesiastical authorities in our town resolved to do battle against the plague with the weapons appropriate to them, and organized a Week of Prayer. These manifestations of public piety were to be concluded on Sunday by a High Mass celebrated under the auspices of St Roch, the plague-stricken saint, and Father Paneloux was asked to preach the sermon. For a fortnight he desisted from the research-work on St Augustine and the African Church which had won for him a high place in his Order. A man of a passionate, fiery temperament, he flung himself whole-heartedly into the task assigned him. The sermon was a topic of conversation long before it was delivered and, in its way, it marks an important date in the history of the period.

There were large attendances at the services of the Week of Prayer. It must not, however, be assumed that in normal times the townsfolk of Oran are particularly devout. On Sunday mornings, for instance, sea-bathing competes seriously with church-going. Nor must it be thought that they had seen a great light, and had a sudden change of heart. But, for one thing, now that the town was closed and the harbour out of bounds, there was no question of sea-bathing; moreover, they were in a quite exceptional frame of mind and, though in their heart of hearts they were far from recognizing the enormity of what had come on them, they couldn't help feeling, for obvious reasons, that decidedly something had changed. Nevertheless, many continued hoping that the epidemic would soon die out and they and their families be spared. Thus they felt under no obligation to make any change in their habits, as yet. Plague was for them an unwelcome visitant, bound to take its leave one day as unexpectedly as it had come. Alarmed, but far from desperate, they hadn't yet reached the phase when plague would seem to them the very tissue of their existence; when they forgot the lives which until now it had been given them to lead. In short, they were waiting for the turn of events. With regard to religion – as to many other problems – plague had induced in them a curious frame of mind, as remote from indifference as from fervour; the best name to give it, perhaps, might be 'objectivity'. Most of those who took part in the Week of Prayer would have echoed a remark made by one of the church-goers in Dr Rieux's hearing. 'Anyhow, it can't do any harm.' Even Tarrou, after recording in his notebook that in such cases the Chinese fall to playing tambourines before the Genius of Plague, observed that there was no means of telling whether, in practice, tambourines proved more efficacious than prophylactic measures. He merely added that, to decide the point, we should need first to ascertain if a Genius of Plague actually existed, and our ignorance on this point nullified any opinions we might form.

In any case the Cathedral was practically always full of worshippers throughout the Week of Prayer. For the first two or three days many stayed outside, under the palms and pomegranate-trees in the garden in front of the porch, and listened from a distance to the swelling tide of prayers and invocations whose backwash filled the neighbouring streets. But, once an example had been given, they began to enter the Cathedral and join timidly in the responses. And on the Sunday of the sermon a huge congregation filled the nave, overflowing on to the steps and precincts. The sky had clouded up on the previous day, and now it was raining heavily. Those in the open unfurled umbrellas. The air inside the Cathedral was heavy with fumes of incense and the smell of wet clothes when Father Paneloux stepped into the pulpit.

He was a stockily built man, of medium height. When he leant on the edge of the pulpit, grasping the woodwork with his big hands, all one saw was a black, massive torso and, above it, two rosy cheeks overhung by steel-rimmed spectacles. He had a powerful, rather emotional delivery which carried to a great distance, and when he launched at the congregation his opening phrase in clear, emphatic tones – 'Calamity has come on you, my brethren, and, my brethren, you deserved it' – there was a flutter of aghast surprise that extended to the crowd massed in the rain outside the porch.

In strict logic what came next did not seem to follow from this dramatic opening. Only as the sermon proceeded did it become apparent to the congregation that, by a skilful oratorical device, Father Paneloux had launched at them, like a fisticuff, the gist of his whole discourse. After launching it he went on at once to quote a text from Exodus relating to the plague of Egypt, and said: 'The first time this scourge appears in history, it was wielded to strike down the enemies of God. Pharaoh set himself up against the divine will, and the plague beat him to his knees. Thus from the dawn of recorded history the scourge of God has humbled the proud of heart and laid low those who hardened themselves against Him. Ponder this well, my friends, and fall on your knees.'

The downpour had increased in violence and these words, striking through a silence intensified by the drumming of raindrops on the chancel windows, carried such conviction that, after a momentary hesitation, some of the worshippers slipped forwards from their seats on to their knees. Others felt it right to follow their example and the movement gradually spread, until presently everyone was kneeling, from end to end of the Cathedral. No sound, except an occasional creak of chairs, accompanied the movement. Then Paneloux drew himself up to his full height, took a deep breath, and continued his sermon in a voice that gathered strength as it proceeded.

'If today the plague is in your midst, that is because the hour has struck for taking thought. The just man need have no fear, but the evil-doer has good cause to tremble. For plague is the flail of God and the world His threshing-floor, and implacably He will thresh out His harvest until the wheat is separated from the chaff. There will be more chaff than wheat, few chosen of the many called. Yet this calamity was not willed by God. Too long this world of ours has connived at evil, too long has it counted on the divine mercy, on God's forgiveness. Repentance was enough, men thought; nothing was forbidden. Everyone felt comfortably assured; when the day came he would surely turn from his sins and repent. Pending that day, the easiest course was to surrender all along the line; divine compassion would do the rest. For a long while God gazed down on this town with eyes of compassion; but He grew weary of waiting, His eternal hope was too long deferred, and now He has turned His face away from us. And so, God's light withdrawn, we walk in darkness, in the thick darkness of this plague.'

Someone in the congregation gave a little snort, like that of a restive horse. After a short silence the preacher continued in a lower tone.

'We read in the Golden Legend that in the time of King Umberto Italy was swept by plague and its greatest ravages took place in Rome and Pavia. So dreadful were these that the living hardly sufficed to bury the dead. And a good angel was made visible to human eyes, giving his orders to an evil angel who bore a great hunting-spear, and bidding him strike the houses; and, as many strokes as he dealt a house, so many dead were carried out of it.'

Here Paneloux stretched forth his two short arms towards the open porch, as if pointing to something behind the tumbling curtain of the rain.

'My brothers,' he cried, 'that fatal hunt is up, and harrying our streets today. See him there, that angel of the pestilence, comely as Lucifer, shining like Evil's very self! He is hovering above your roofs with his great spear in his right hand, poised to strike, while his left hand is stretched towards one or other of your houses. Maybe at this very moment his finger is pointing to your door, the red spear crashing on its panels, and even now the plague is entering your home and settling down in your bedroom to await your return. Patient and watchful, ineluctable as the order of the scheme of things, it bides its time. No earthly power, nay, not even – mark me well – the vaunted might of human science can avail you to avert that hand once it is stretched towards you. And winnowed like corn on the bloodstained threshing-floor of suffering, you will be cast away with the chaff.'

At this point the Father reverted with heightened eloquence to the symbol of the flail. He bade his hearers picture a huge wooden bar whirling above the town, striking at random, swinging up again in a shower of drops of blood, and spreading carnage and suffering on earth, 'for the seed-time that shall prepare the harvest of the truth'.

At the end of this long phrase Father Paneloux paused; his hair was straggling over his forehead, his body shaken by tremors that his hands communicated to the pulpit. When he spoke again his voice was lower, but vibrant with accusation.

'Yes, the hour has come for serious thought. You fondly imagined it was enough to visit God on Sundays, and thus you could make free of your weekdays. You believed some brief formalities, some bendings of the knee, would recompense Him well enough for your criminal indifference. But God is not mocked. These brief encounters could not sate the fierce hunger of His love. He wished to see you longer and more often; that is His manner of loving and, indeed, it is the only manner of loving. And this is why, wearied of waiting for you to come to Him, He loosed on you this visitation; as He has visited all the cities that offended against Him, since the dawn of history. Now you are learning your lesson, the lesson that was learnt by Cain and his offspring, by the people of Sodom and Gomorrah, by Job and Pharaoh, by all that hardened their hearts against Him. And like them you have been beholding mankind and all creation with new eyes, since the gates of this city closed on you and on the pestilence. Now, at last, you know the hour has struck to bend your thoughts to first and last things.'

A wet wind was sweeping up the nave, making the candle-flames bend and flicker. The pungency of burning wax, coughs, a stifled sneeze, rose towards Father Paneloux who, reverting to his exordium, with a subtlety that was much appreciated, went on in a calm, almost matter-of-fact voice. 'Many of you are wondering, I know, what I am leading up to. I wish to lead you to the truth and teach you to rejoice, yes, rejoice – in spite of all that I have been telling you. For the time is past when a helping hand or mere words of good advice could set you on the right path. Today the truth is a command. It is a red spear sternly pointing to the narrow path, the one way of salvation. And thus, my brothers, at last it is revealed to you, the divine compassion which has ordained good and evil in everything; wrath and pity; the plague and your salvation. This same pestilence which is slaying you works for your good and points your path.

'Many centuries ago the Christians of Abyssinia saw in the plague a sure and God-sent means of winning eternal life. Those who were not yet stricken wrapped round them sheets in which men had died of plague, so as to make sure of their death. I grant you such a frenzied quest of salvation was not to be commended. It shows an overhaste, indeed a presumptu-ousness, which we can but deplore. No man should seek to force God's hand or to hurry on the appointed hour, and from a practice that aims at speeding up the order of events, which God has ordained unalterably from all time, it is but a step to heresy. Yet we can learn a salutary lesson from the zeal, excessive though it was, of those Abyssinian Christians. Much of it is alien to our more enlightened spirits, and yet it gives us a glimpse of that radiant eternal light which glows, a small still flame, in the dark core of human suffering. And this light, too, illuminates the shadowed paths that lead towards deliverance. It reveals the will of God in action, unfailingly transforming evil into good. And once again today it is leading us through the dark valley of fears and groans towards the holy silence, the well-spring of all life. This, my friends, is the vast consolation I would hold out to you, so that when you leave this House of God you will carry away with you not only words of wrath, but a message, too, of comfort for your hearts.'

Everyone supposed that the sermon had ended. Outside, the rain had ceased and watery sunshine was yellowing the Cathedral Square. Vague sounds of voices came from the streets, and a low hum of traffic; the speech of an awakening town. Discreetly, with a subdued rustling, the congregation gathered together their belongings. However, the Father had a few more words to say. He told them that after having made it clear that this plague came from God, for the punishment of their sins, he would not have recourse, in concluding, to an eloquence which, considering the tragic nature of the occasion, would be out of keeping. He hoped and believed that all of them now saw their position in its true light. But, before leaving the pulpit, he would like to tell them of something he had been reading in an old chronicle of the Black Death at Marseilles. In it Mathieu Marais, the chronicler, laments his lot; he says he has been cast into hell to languish without succour and without hope. Well! Mathieu Marais was blind! Never more intensely than today had he, Father Paneloux, felt the immanence of divine succour and Christian hope, granted to all alike. He hoped against hope that, despite all the horrors of these dark days, despite the groans of men and women in agony, our fellow-citizens would offer up to heaven that one prayer which is truly Christian, a prayer of love. And God would see to the rest.

IV

IT IS HARD to say if this sermon had any effect on our townsfolk. M. Othon, the magistrate, assured Dr Rieux that he had found the preacher's arguments 'absolutely irrefutable'. But not everyone took so unqualified a view. To some the sermon simply brought home the fact that they had been sentenced, for an unknown crime, to an indeterminate period of punishment. And while a good many people adapted themselves to confinement and carried on their humdrum lives as before, there were others who rebelled, and whose one idea now was to break loose from the prison-house.

At first the fact of being cut off from the outside world was accepted with a more or less good grace; much as people would have put up with any other temporary inconvenience that interfered with only a few of their habits. But, now they had abruptly become aware that they were undergoing a sort of incarceration under that blue dome of sky, already beginning to sizzle in the fires of summer, they had a vague sensation that their whole lives were threatened by the present turn of events, and in the evening, when the cooler air revived their energy, this feeling of being locked in like criminals prompted them sometimes to foolhardy acts.

It is noteworthy – this may or may not have been due to mere coincidence – that this Sunday of the sermon marked the beginning of something like a widespread panic in the town, and it took so deep a hold as to lead one to suspect that only now had the true nature of their situation dawned on our townsfolk. Seen from this angle, the atmosphere of the town was somewhat changed. But, actually, it was a problem whether the change was in the atmosphere or in their hearts.

A few days after the sermon, when Rieux, on his way to one of the outlying districts of the town, was discussing the change with Grand, he collided in the darkness with a man who was standing in the middle of the pavement swaying from side to side without trying to advance. At the same moment the street-lamps, which were being lit later and later in the evening, went on suddenly, and a lamp just behind Rieux and his companion threw its light full on the man's face. His eyes were shut and he was laughing soundlessly. Big drops of sweat were rolling down the face convulsed with silent merriment.

'A lunatic at large,' Grand observed.

Rieux took his arm and was shepherding him on, when he noticed that Grand was trembling violently.

'If things go on as they are going,' Rieux remarked, 'the whole town will be a madhouse.' He felt exhausted, his throat was parched. 'Let's have a drink.'

They turned into a small café. The only light came from a lamp over the bar, the heavy air had a curious reddish tinge, and for no apparent reason everyone was speaking in undertones.

To the doctor's surprise Grand asked for a small glass of neat spirits, which he drank off at a gulp. 'Fiery stuff!' he observed; then, a moment later, suggested making a move.

Out in the street it seemed to Rieux that the night was full of whispers. Somewhere in the black depths above the street-lamps there was a low soughing that brought to his mind that unseen flail threshing incessantly the languid air of which Paneloux had spoken.

'Happily, happily . . .' Grand muttered; then paused.

Rieux asked him what he had been going to say.

'Happily, I've my work.'

'Ah yes,' Rieux said. 'That's something, anyhow.' Then, so as not to hear that eerie whistling in the air, he asked Grand if he was getting good results.

'Well, yes. I think I'm making headway.'

'Have you much more to do?'

Grand began to show an animation unlike his usual self; and his voice took ardour from the spirits he had drunk.

'I don't know. But that's not the point, doctor; yes, I can assure you that's not the point.'

It was too dark to see clearly, but Rieux had the impression that he was waving his arms. He seemed to be working himself up to say something, and when he spoke the words came with a rush.

'What I really want, doctor, is this. On the day when the manuscript reaches the publisher, I want him to stand up – after he's read it through, of course – and say to his staff, "Gentlemen, hats off!" '

Rieux was dumbfounded, and, to add to his amazement, he saw, or seemed to see, the man beside him making as if to take off his hat with a sweeping gesture, bringing his hand to his head, then holding his arm out straight in front of him. That queer whistling overhead seemed to gather force.

'So you see,' Grand added, 'it's got to be . . . flawless.'

Though he knew little of the literary world, Rieux had a suspicion that things didn't happen in it quite so picturesquely – that, for instance, publishers do not keep their hats on in their offices. But, of course, one never can tell, and Rieux preferred to hold his peace. Try as he might to shut his ears to it, he still was listening to that eerie sound above, the whispering of the plague. They had reached the part of the town where Grand lived and, as it was on a slight eminence, they felt the cool night breeze fanning their cheeks and at the same time carrying away from them the noises of the town.

Grand went on talking, but Rieux failed to follow all the worthy man was saying. All he gathered was that the work he was engaged on ran to a great many pages, and he was at almost excruciating pains to bring it to perfection. 'Evenings, whole weeks, spent on one word, just think! Sometimes on a mere conjunction!'

Grand stopped abruptly and seized the doctor by a button of his coat. The words came stumbling out of his almost toothless mouth.

'I'd like you to understand, doctor. I grant you it's easy enough to choose between a "but" and an "and". It's a bit more difficult to decide between "and" and "then". But definitely the hardest thing may be to know whether one should put an "and" or leave it out.'

'Yes,' Rieux said, 'I see your point.'

He started walking again. Grand looked abashed, then stepped forward and drew level.

'Sorry,' he said awkwardly. 'I don't know what's come over me this evening.'

Rieux patted his shoulder encouragingly, saying he'd been much interested in what Grand had said and would like to help him. This seemed to reassure Grand and when they reached his place he suggested, after some slight hesitation, that the doctor should come in for a bit. Rieux agreed.

They entered the dining-room and Grand gave him a chair beside a table strewn with sheets of paper covered with writing in a microscopic hand, criss-crossed with corrections.

'Yes, that's it,' he said in answer to the doctor's questioning glance. 'But won't you drink something? I've some wine.'

Rieux declined. He was bending over the manuscript.

'No, don't look,' Grand said. 'It's my opening phrase – and it's giving trouble, no end of trouble.'

He too was gazing at the sheets of paper on the table, and his hand seemed irresistibly drawn to one of them. Finally he picked it up and held it to the shadeless electric bulb so that the light shone through. The paper shook in his hand and Rieux noticed that his forehead was moist with sweat.

'Sit down,' he said, 'and read it to me.'

'Yes.' There was a timid gratitude in Grand's eyes and smile. 'I think I'd like you to hear it.'

He waited for a while, still gazing at the writing; then sat down. Meanwhile Rieux was listening to the curious buzzing sound that was rising from the streets as if in answer to the soughings of the plague. At that moment he had a preternaturally vivid awareness of the town stretched out below, a victim world secluded and apart, and of the groans of agony stifled in its darkness. Then, pitched low but clear, Grand's voice came to his ears.

'One fine morning in the month of May an elegant young horsewoman might have been seen riding a handsome sorrel mare along the flowery avenues of the Bois de Boulogne.'

Silence returned, and with it the vague murmur of the prostrate town. Grand had put down the sheet and was still staring at it. After a while he looked up.

'What do you think of it?'

Rieux replied that this opening phrase had whetted his curiosity; he'd like to hear what followed. Whereat Grand told him he'd got it all wrong. He seemed excited and slapped the papers on the table with the flat of his hand.

'That's only a rough draft. Once I've succeeded in rendering perfectly the picture in my mind's eye, once my words have the exact *tempo* of this ride – the horse is trotting, one-two-three, one-two-three, see what I mean? – the rest will come more easily and, what's even more important, the illusion will be such that from the very first words it will be possible to say, "Hats off!"'

But, before that, he admitted, there was lots of hard work to be done. He'd never dream of handing that sentence to the printer in its present form. For though it sometimes satisfied him, he was fully aware it didn't quite hit the mark as yet, and also that to some extent it had a facility of tone approximating, remotely perhaps but recognizably, to the commonplace. That was more or less what he was saying when they heard the sound of people running in the street below the window. Rieux stood up.

'Just wait and see what I make of it,' Grand said, and, glancing towards the window, added: 'When all this is over.'

But then the sound of hurried footsteps came again. Rieux was already half-way down the stairs, and when he stepped out into the street two men brushed past him. They seemed to be on their way to one of the town gates. In fact, what with the heat and the plague, some of our fellow-citizens were losing their heads; there had already been some scenes of violence and nightly attempts were made to elude the sentries and escape to the outside world.

V

OTHERS, TOO, RAMBERT for example, were trying to escape from this atmosphere of growing panic, but with more skill and persistence, if not with greater success. For a while Rambert had gone on struggling with officialdom. If he was to be believed, he had always thought that perseverance would win through, inevitably, and, as he pointed out, resourcefulness in emergency was 'up his street', in a manner of speaking. So he plodded away, calling on all sorts of officials and others whose influence would have had weight in normal conditions. But, as things were, such influence was unavailing. For the most part they were men with well-defined and sound ideas on everything concerning exports, banking, the fruit or wine trade; men of proved ability in handling problems relating to insurance, the interpretation of ill-drawn contracts and the like; of high qualifications and evident good intentions. That, in fact, was what struck one most – the excellence of their intentions. But as regards plague their competence was practically nil.

However, whenever opportunity arose, Rambert had tackled each of them and pleaded his cause. The gist of his argument was always the same; that he was a stranger to our town and, that being so, his case deserved special consideration. Mostly, the men he talked to conceded this point readily enough. But usually they added that a good number of other people were in a like case, and thus his position was not so exceptional as he seemed to suppose. To this Rambert could reply that this did not affect the substance of his argument in any way. He was then told that it did affect the position, already difficult, of the authorities, who were against showing any favouritism and thus running the risk of creating what, with obvious repugnance, they called 'a precedent'.

In conversation with Dr Rieux, Rambert classified the people whom he had approached in various categories. Those who used the arguments mentioned above he called the sticklers. Besides these there were the consolers, who assured him that the present state of things couldn't possibly last and, when asked for definite suggestions, fobbed him off by telling him he was making too much fuss about a passing inconvenience. Then there were the very-important-persons who asked the visitor to leave a brief note of his case and informed him they would decide on it in due course; the triflers, who offered him billeting warrants or gave the addresses of lodgings; the red-tape-merchants who made him fill up a form and promptly interred it in a file; overworked officials who raised their arms to heaven, and much-harassed officials who simply looked away; and, finally, the traditionalists – these were by far the greatest number – who referred Rambert to another office or recommended some new method of approach.

These fruitless interviews had thoroughly worn out the journalist; on the credit side, he had obtained much insight into the inner workings of a municipal office and a Prefect's headquarters, by dint of sitting for hours on imitation-leather sofas, confronted by posters urging him to invest in Savings Bonds exempt from income-tax, or to enlist in the Colonial Army; and by dint of entering offices where human faces were as blank as the filing-cabinets and the dusty records on the shelves behind them. The only thing gained by all this expenditure of energy, Rambert told Rieux with a hint of bitterness, was that it served to keep his mind off his predicament. In fact, the rapid progress of the plague practically escaped his notice.

Also, it made the days pass more quickly and, given the situation in which the whole town was placed, it might be said that every day lived through brought everyone, provided he survived, twenty-four hours nearer the end of his ordeal. Rieux could but admit the truth of this reasoning, but to his mind its truth was of rather too general an order.

At one moment Rambert had a gleam of hope. A form was sent him from the Prefect's office with instructions that he was to fill in carefully all the blanks. It included questions concerning his identity, his family, his present and former sources of income; in fact he was to give what is known as a *curriculum vitae*. He got an impression that inquiries were on foot with a view to drawing up a list of persons who might be instructed to leave the town and return to their homes. Some vague information gleaned from an employee in one of the offices confirmed this impression. But on going further into the matter and finally discovering the office from which the form had emanated, he was told that this information was being collected with a view to certain contingencies.

'What contingencies?' he asked.

He then learnt that the contingency was the possibility of his falling ill and dying of plague; the data supplied would enable the authorities to notify his family and also to decide if the hospital expenses should be borne by the Municipality or if, in due course, they could be recovered from his relatives. On the face of it this implied that he was not completely cut off from the woman who was awaiting his return, since the powers-that-be were obviously giving heed to both of them. But that was no consolation. The really remarkable thing, and Rambert was greatly struck by this, was the way in which, in the very midst of catastrophe, offices could go on functioning serenely, and take initiatives of no immediate relevance, and often unknown to the highest authority, purely and simply because they had been created originally for this purpose.

The next phase was at once the easiest and the hardest for Rambert. It was a period of sheer lethargy. He had gone the round of offices, taken every step that could be taken, and realized that for the present all avenues of that kind were closed to him. So now he drifted aimlessly from café to café. In the mornings he would sit on the terrace of one of them, and read a newspaper in the hope of finding some indication that the epidemic was on the wane. He would gaze at the faces of the passers-by, often turning away disgustedly from their look of unrelieved gloom, and after reading for the nth time the shop-signs on the other side of the street, the advertisements of popular drinks that were no longer procurable, would rise and walk again at random in the yellow streets. Thus he killed time till nightfall, moving about the town and stopping now and again at a café or restaurant. One evening Rieux noticed him hovering round the door of a café, unable to make up his mind to enter. At last he decided to go in, and sat down at a table at the back of the room. It was the time when, acting under orders, café-proprietors deferred as long as possible turning on their lights. Grey dusk was seeping into the room, the pink of sunset glowed in the wall-mirrors, and the marble-topped tables glimmered white in the gathering darkness. Seated in the empty café, Rambert looked pathetically 'lost', a mere shade amongst the shadows, and Rieux guessed this was the hour when he felt most derelict. It was, indeed, the hour of day when all the prisoners of the town realized their dere-liction and each was thinking that something, no matter what, must be done to hasten their deliverance. Rieux turned hurriedly away.

Rambert also spent a certain amount of time at the railway-station. No one was allowed on the platforms. But the waiting-rooms, which could be entered from outside, remained open and, being cool and dark, were often patronized by beggars on very hot days. Rambert spent much time studying the time-tables, reading the prohibitions against spitting, and the Passengers' Regulations. After that he sat down in a corner. An old cast-iron stove, that had been stone-cold for months, rose like a sort of landmark in the middle of the room, surrounded by figure-of-eight patterns on the floor, the traceries of long-past sprinklings. Posters on the walls gaily invited tourists to a care-free holiday at Cannes or Bandol. And in his corner Rambert savoured that bitter sense of freedom which comes of total deprivation. The evocations which at that time he found most poignant were – anyhow according to what he told Rieux – those of Paris. There rose before his eyes, unsummoned, vistas of old stones and riverbanks, the pigeons of the Palais-Royal, the Gare du Nord, quiet old streets round the Panthéon and many another scene of the city he'd never known he loved so much, and these mental pictures killed all desire for any form of action. Rieux felt fairly sure he was identifying these scenes with memories of his love. And when one day Rambert told him that he liked waking up at four in the morning and thinking of his beloved Paris, the doctor guessed easily enough, basing this on his own experience, that that was his favourite time for conjuring up pictures of the woman from whom he now was parted. This was, indeed, the hour when he could feel surest she was wholly his. Till four in the morning one is seldom doing anything and at that hour, even if the night has been a night of betrayal, one is asleep. Yes, everyone sleeps at that hour, and this is reassuring, since the great longing of an unquiet heart is to possess constantly and consciously the loved one, or, failing that, to be able to plunge the loved one, when a time of absence intervenes, into a dreamless sleep timed to last unbroken until the day they meet again.

VI

SHORTLY AFTER FATHER Paneloux's sermon the hot weather set in with a vengeance. On the day following the unseasonable downpour of that Sunday, summer blazed out above the housetops. First a strong, scorching wind blew steadily for a whole day, drying up the walls. And then the sun took charge, incessant waves of heat and light swept the town daylong, and, but for arcaded streets and the interiors of houses, everything lay naked to the dazzling impact of the light. The sun stalked our townsfolk along every byway, into every nook, and when they paused it struck.

Since this first onslaught of the heat synchronized with a startling increase in the number of victims — there were now nearly seven hundred deaths a week — a mood of profound discouragement settled on the town. In the suburbs little was left of the wonted animation between the long flat streets and the terraced houses; ordinarily people living in these districts used to spend the best part of the day on their doorsteps, but now every door was shut, nobody was to be seen, even the venetian blinds stayed down, and there was no knowing if it was the heat or the plague that they were trying to shut out. In some houses groans could be heard. At first, when that happened, people often gathered outside and listened, prompted by curiosity or compassion. But under the pro-longed strain, it seemed that hearts had toughened; people lived beside those groans or walked past them as though they had become the normal speech of men.

As a result of the fighting at the gates, in the course of which the police had had to use their revolvers, a spirit of lawlessness was abroad. Some had certainly been wounded in these brushes with the police, but in the town where, owing to the combined influences of heat and terror, everything was exag-gerated, there was talk of deaths. One thing, anyhow, was certain; discontent was on the increase and, fearing worse to come, the local officials debated lengthily on the measures to be taken if the populace, goaded to frenzy by the epidemic, got completely out of hand. The newspapers published new regu-lations reiterating the orders against attempting to leave the town and warning those who infringed them that they were liable to long terms of imprisonment.

A system of patrols was instituted and often in the empty, sweltering streets, heralded by the clatter of horse-hoofs on the cobbles, a detachment of mounted police would make its way between the parallel lines of close-shut windows. Now and again a gunshot was heard; the special brigade recently detailed to destroy cats and dogs, as possible carriers of infection, was at work. And these whipcrack sounds startling the silence increased the nervous tension already existing in the town.

For, in the heat, and stillness, and for the troubled hearts of our townsfolk, anything, even the least sound, had a heightened significance. The varying aspects of the sky, the very smells rising from the soil that mark each change of season, were taken notice of for the first time. Everyone realized with dismay that hot weather would favour the epidemic, and it was clear that summer was setting in. The cries of swifts in the evening air above the housetops were growing shriller. And the sky, too, had lost the spaciousness of those June twilights when our horizons seem infinitely remote. In the markets the flowers no longer came in buds; they were already in full bloom and, after the morning's marketing, the dusty pavements were littered with trampled petals. It was plain to see that spring had spent itself, lavished its ardour on the myriads of flowers that were bursting everywhere into bloom, and now was being crushed out by the twofold onslaught of heat and plague. For our fellow-citizens that summer sky, and the streets thick in dust, grey as their present lives, had the same ominous import as the hundred deaths now weighing daily on the town. That incessant sunlight and those bright hours associated with siesta or with holidays no longer invited, as in the past, to frolics and flirtation on the beaches. Now they rang hollow in the silence of the closed town, they had lost the golden spell of happier summers. Plague had killed all colours, vetoed pleasure.

That, indeed, was one of the great changes brought by the epidemic. Hitherto all of us welcomed summer in with pleasant anticipation. The town was open to the sea and its young folk made free of the beaches. But this summer, for all its nearness, the sea was out of bounds; young limbs had no longer the run of its delights. What could we do under these conditions? It is Tarrou once again who paints the most faithful picture of our life in those days. Needless to say, he outlines the progress of the plague and he, too, notes that a new phase of the epidemic was ushered in when the wireless announced no longer weekly totals, but ninety-two, a hundred and seven, and a hundred and thirty deaths in a day. 'The newspapers and the authorities are playing ball with the plague. They fancy they're scoring off it because a hundred and thirty is a smaller figure than nine hundred and ten.' He also records such striking or moving incidents of the epidemic as came under his notice; that, for instance, of the woman in a lonely street who abruptly opened a shuttered window just above his head, and gave two loud shrieks before closing the shutters again on the dark interior of a third-floor bedroom. But he also noted that peppermint lozenges had vanished from the chemists' shops, because there was a popular belief that when sucking them you were proof against contagion.

He went on watching his pet specimen on the opposite balcony. It seemed that tragedy had come to the ancient small-game hunter as well. One morning there had been gunshots in the street and, as Tarrou put it, 'some gobs of lead' had killed off most of the cats and scared away the others; anyhow they were no longer about. That day the little old man went on to his balcony at the usual hour, showed some surprise and, leaning on the rail, closely scanned the corners of the street. Then he settled down to wait, fretfully tapping the balustrade with his right hand. After staying there for some time he tore up a few sheets of paper, went back into his room, and came out again. After another longish wait he retreated again into the room, slamming the french windows behind him. He followed the same procedure daily during the rest of the week, and the sadness and bewilderment on the old face deepened as the days went by. On the eighth day Tarrou waited in vain for his appearance; the windows stayed resolutely closed on an all-too-comprehensible distress. This entry ends with Tarrou's summing up. 'It is forbidden to spit on cats in plague-time.'

In another context Tarrou notes that, on coming home in the evenings, he invariably saw the night-porter pacing the hall, like a sentry on his beat. The man never failed to remind everyone he met that he'd foreseen what was happening. Tarrou agreed that he'd predicted a disaster, but reminded him that the event predicted by him was an earthquake. To which the old fellow replied: 'Ah, if only it had been an earthquake! A good bad shock, and there you are! You count the dead and living, and that's an end of it. But this here blasted disease – even them as haven't got it can't think of anything else.'

The manager of the hotel was equally downhearted. In the early days travellers, unable to leave the town, had kept on their rooms. But one by one, seeing that the epidemic showed no sign of abating, they moved out to stay with friends. And the same cause that had led to all the rooms' being occupied now kept them empty, since there were no new-comers to the town. Tarrou was one of the very few remaining guests, and the manager never lost an opportunity of informing him that, were he not reluctant to put these gentlemen to inconvenience, he would have closed the hotel long ago. He often asked Tarrou to say how long he thought the epidemic would last. 'They say,' Tarrou informed him, 'that cold weather stamps out diseases of this type.' The manager looked aghast. 'But, my dear sir, it's never really cold in these parts. And, anyhow, that would mean it's going to last many months more.' Moreover, he was sure that for a long while to come travellers would give the town a wide berth. This epidemic spelt the ruin of the tourist trade, in fact.

After a short absence, M. Othon, the owlish paterfamilias, made a reappearance in the restaurant, but accompanied only by the two 'performing poodles', his offspring. On inquiry it came out that Mme Othon was in quarantine; she had been nursing her mother who had succumbed to plague.

'I don't like it a bit,' the manager told Tarrou. 'Quarantine or not, she's under suspicion, which means that they are, too.'

Tarrou pointed out that, if it came to that, everyone was 'under suspicion'. But the manager had his own ideas, and was not to be shaken out of them.

'No, sir. You and I, we're not under suspicion. But they certainly are.'

However, M. Othon was impervious to such considerations, and would not let the plague change his habits. He entered the restaurant with his wonted dignity, sat down in front of his children, and addressed to them at intervals the same nicely worded, unamiable remarks. Only the small boy looked somewhat different; dressed in black like his sister, a little more shrunken than before, he now seemed a miniature replica of his father. The night-porter, who had no liking for M. Othon, had said of him to Tarrou:

'That fine gentleman will pass out with his clothes on. All dressed up and ready to go. So he won't need no laying-out.'

Tarrou has some comments on the sermon preached by Paneloux. 'I can understand that type of fervour and find it not displeasing. At the beginning of a pestilence and when it ends, there's always a propensity for rhetoric. In the first case, habits have not yet been lost; in the second, they're returning. It is in the thick of a calamity that one gets hardened to the truth, in other words to silence. So – let's wait.'

Tarrou also records that he had a long talk with Dr Rieux; all he remembered was that it had 'good results'. In this connexion he notes the colour of Mme Rieux, the doctor's mother's eyes, a limpid brown, and makes the odd observation that a gaze revealing so much goodness of heart would always triumph over plague.

He has also a good deal to say about Rieux's asthma patient. He went with the doctor to see him, immediately after their conversation. The old man greeted Tarrou with a chuckle, and rubbed his hands cheerfully. He was sitting up in bed with the usual two pans of dried peas in front of him. 'Ah, here's another of 'em!' he exclaimed when he saw Tarrou. 'It's a topsy-turvy world all right, more doctors than patients. Because it's mowing them down, ain't it, more and more. That priest's right; we were asking for it.' Next day Tarrou came to see him, without warning.

From Tarrou's notes we gather that the old man, a draper by occupation, decided at the age of fifty that he'd done enough work for a lifetime. He took to his bed and never left it again – but not because of his asthma, which would not have prevented his getting about. A small fixed income had seen him through to his present age, seventy-five, and the years had not damped his cheerfulness. He couldn't bear the sight of a watch, and indeed there wasn't one in the whole house. 'Watches,' he said, 'are silly gadgets, and dear at that.' He worked out the time – that is to say, the time for meals – with his two saucepans, one of which was always full of peas when he woke in the morning. He filled the other, pea by pea, at a constant, carefully regulated speed. Thus time for him was reckoned by these pans and he could take his bearings in it at any moment of the day. 'Every fifteen pans,' he said, 'it's feeding-time. What could be simpler?'

If his wife was to be trusted, he had given signs of his vocation at a very early age. Nothing, in fact, had ever interested him; his work, friendship, cafés, music, women, outings – to all he was indifferent. He had never left his home town except once when he had been called to Algiers for family affairs, and even then he had alighted from the train at the first station after Oran, incapable of continuing the adventure. He took the first train back.

To Tarrou, who had shown surprise at the secluded life he led, he had given the following explanation, more or less. According to religion, the first half of a man's life is an up-grade; the second goes downhill. On the descending days he has no claim, they may be snatched from him at any moment; thus he can do nothing with them and the best thing, precisely, is to do nothing with them. He obviously had no compunction about contradicting himself, for a few minutes later he told Tarrou that God did not exist, since otherwise there would be no need for priests. But, from some observations which followed, Tarrou realized that the old fellow's philosophy was closely involved with the irritation caused by the house-to-house collections in aid of charities, which took place almost incessantly in that part of the town. What completed the picture of the old man was a desire he expressed several times, and which seemed deeply rooted; the desire to die at a very advanced age.

'Is he a saint?' Tarrou asked himself, and answered, 'Yes, if saintliness is an aggregate of habits.'

Meanwhile Tarrou was compiling a longish description of a day in the plague-stricken town; it was to give a full and accurate picture of the life of our fellow-citizens during that summer. 'Nobody laughs,' Tarrou observes, 'except the drunks, and they laugh too much.' After which he embarks on his description.

'At daybreak light breaths of air fan the still empty streets. At this hour, between the night's victims and the death-agonies of the coming day, it is as if for a while plague stays its hand and takes breath. All shops are shut. But on some a notice, *Closed owing to plague*, shows that when the others open presently these will not. Still half-asleep, the newsboys do not yet cry the news but, lounging at street-corners, offer their wares to the lamp-posts, with the vague gestures of sleepwalkers. Soon, awakened by the early trams, they will fan out through the town, holding at arm's length sheets on which the word *PLAGUE* looms large. Will there be a plague autumn? Professor B. says, "No." Toll of the 94th Day of Plague: 124 deaths.

'In spite of the growing shortage of paper, which has compelled some dailies to reduce their pages, a new paper has been launched, *The Plague Chronicle*, which sets out "to inform our townspeople, with scrupulous veracity, of the daily progress or recession of the disease; to supply them with the most authoritative opinions available as to its future course; to offer the hospitality of its columns to all, in whatever walk of life, who wish to join in combating the epidemic; to keep up the morale of the populace, to publish the latest orders issued by the authorities, and to centralize the efforts of all who desire to give active and whole-hearted help in the present emergency". Actually this newspaper very soon came to devote its columns to advertisements of new, "infallible" antidotes against plague.

'Towards six in the morning all these papers are being sold to the queues that begin to form outside the shops over an hour before they open; then to the passengers alighting from the trams coming in, packed to capacity, from the suburbs. The trams are now the only means of transport, and they have much difficulty in progressing, what with people standing on the footboards and hanging in clusters from the handrails. A queer thing is how the passengers all try to keep their backs turned to their neighbours, twisting themselves into grotesque attitudes in the attempt – the idea being, of course, to avoid contagion. At every stop a cataract of men and women is disgorged, each in haste to put a safe distance between himself or herself and the rest.

'When the first trams have gone by, the town gradually wakes up, early cafés open their doors, and you see an array of cards on the counter, *No Coffee, Bring Your Own Sugar*, and the like. Next the shops open and the streets grow livelier. And meanwhile the light is swelling and the sky, even at this early hour, beginning to grow leaden-hued with heat. This is the time when those who have nothing to do venture out on the boulevards. Most of them seem determined to counter-act the plague by a lavish display of luxury. Daily, round about eleven, you see a sort of dress parade of youths and girls, who make you realize the frantic desire for life that thrives in the heart of every great calamity. If the epidemic spreads, morals too will broaden, and we may see again the Saturnalia of Milan, men and women dancing round the graves.

'At noon, in a flash, all the restaurants fill up. Very quickly small groups of people unable to find a seat form at the doors. Because of the intense heat the sky is losing its brightness. Under big awnings the aspirants to food wait their turn, aligned along the kerbs of streets gaping and sizzling in the fires of noon. The reason for the restaurants' being so crowded is that they solve for many the feeding problem. But they do nothing to allay the fear of contagion. Many of the customers spend several minutes methodically wiping their plates. Not long ago some restaurants put up notices, *Certified that our plates, knives and forks are sterilized*. But gradually they discon-tinued publicity of this order, since their customers came in any case. People, moreover, spend very freely. Choice wines, or wines alleged to be such, the costliest extras – a mood of reckless extravagance is setting in. It seems that there was something like a panic in a restaurant because a customer suddenly felt ill, went very white, and staggered precipitately to the door.

'Towards two the town slowly empties; it is the time when silence, sunlight, dust and plague have the streets to them-selves. Wave after wave of heat flows over the frontage of the tall grey houses, during these long, languid hours. Thus the afternoon wears on, slowly merging into an evening that settles down like a red winding-sheet on the serried tumult of the town. At the start of the great heat, for some unascertained reason, the evenings found the streets almost empty. But now the least ripple of cooler air brings an easing of the strain, if not a flutter of hope. Then all stream out into the open, drug themselves with talking, start arguing or love-making, and in the last glow of sunset the town, freighted with lovers two by two and loud with voices, drifts like a helmless ship into the throbbing darkness. In vain a zealous evangelist with a felt hat and flowing tie threads his way through the crowd, crying without cease, "God is great and good. Come unto Him." On the contrary, they all make haste towards some trivial objective that seems of more immediate interest than God.

'In the early days, when they thought this epidemic was much like other epidemics, religion held its ground. But, once these people realized their instant peril, they gave their thoughts to pleasure. And all the hideous fears which stamp their faces in the daytime are transformed in the fiery, dusty nightfall into a sort of hectic exaltation, an unkempt freedom fevering their blood.

'And I, too, I'm no different. But what matter? Death means nothing to men like me. It's the event that proves them right.'

VII

IT WAS TARROU who had asked Rieux for the interview he refers to in his diary. On that evening, as it happened, just before Tarrou arrived, the doctor had gazed for some moments at his mother, who was sitting very still in a corner of the dining-room. Once her household tasks were over, she spent most of her time in that chair. Her hands folded in her lap, she sat there waiting. Rieux wasn't even sure it was for him she waited. However, something always changed in his mother's face when he came in. The silent resignation that a laborious life had given it seemed to light up with a sudden glow. Then she returned to her tranquillity. That evening she was gazing out of the window at the now empty street. The street-lighting had been reduced by two-thirds and only at long intervals a lamp cast flickering gleams through the thick darkness of the town.

'Will they keep to the reduced lighting as long as the plague lasts?' Mme Rieux asked.

'I expect so.'

'Let's hope it doesn't last till winter. It would be terribly depressing.'

'Yes,' Rieux said.

He saw his mother's gaze settle on his forehead. He knew that the worry and overwork of the last few days had scored their traces there.

'Didn't things go well today?' his mother asked.

'Oh, much as usual.'

As usual! That was to say, the new consignment of serum sent from Paris seemed less effective than the first, and the death-rate was rising. It was still impossible to administer prophylactic inoculations elsewhere than in families already attacked; if its use was to be generalized, very large quantities of the vaccine would have been needed. Most of the buboes refused to burst – it was as if they underwent a seasonal hardening – and the victims suffered horribly. During the last twenty-four hours there had been two cases of a new form of the epidemic; the plague was becoming pneumonic. On this very day, in the course of a meeting, the much-harassed doctors had pressed the Prefect – the unfortunate man seemed quite at his wits' end – to issue new regulations to prevent contagion being carried from mouth to mouth, as happens in pneumonic plague. The Prefect had done as they wished, but as usual they were groping, more or less, in the dark.

Looking at his mother, he felt an uprush of a half-forgotten emotion, the love of his boyhood, at the sight of her soft brown gaze intent on him.

'Don't you ever feel alarmed, Mother?'

'Oh, at my age there isn't much left to fear.'

'The days are very long, and just now I'm hardly ever at home.'

'I don't mind waiting, if I know you're going to come back. And when you aren't here, I think of what you're doing. . . . Have you any news?'

'Yes, if I'm to believe the last telegram, everything's going as well as could be expected. But I know she says that to prevent my worrying.'

The door-bell rang. The doctor gave his mother a smile, and went to open the door. In the dim light on the landing Tarrou looked like a big grey bear. Rieux gave his visitor a seat facing his desk, while he himself remained standing behind the desk-chair. Between them was the only light in the room, a desk-lamp.

Tarrou came straight to the point.

'I know,' he said, 'that I can talk to you quite frankly.'

Rieux nodded.

'In a fortnight or a month at most,' Tarrou continued, 'you'll serve no purpose here. Things will have got out of hand.'

'I agree.'

'The sanitary department is inefficient – understaffed, for one thing – and you're worked off your feet.'

Rieux admitted this was so.

'Well,' Tarrou said, 'I've heard that the authorities are thinking of a sort of conscription of the population, and all men in good health will be required to help in fighting the plague.'

'Your information was correct. But the authorities are in none too good odour as it is, and the Prefect can't make up his mind.'

'If he daren't risk compulsion, why not call for voluntary help?'

'It's been done. The response was poor.'

'It was done through official channels, and half-heartedly. What they're short of is imagination. Officialdom can never cope with something really catastrophic. And the remedial measures they think up are hardly adequate for a common cold. If we let them carry on like this they'll soon be dead – and so shall we.'

'That's more than likely,' Rieux said. 'I should tell you, however, that they're thinking of using the prisoners in the jails for what we call the "heavy work".'

'I'd rather free men were employed.'

'So would I. . . . But might I ask why you feel like that?'

'I loathe men's being condemned to death.'

Rieux looked Tarrou in the eyes.

'So . . . what?' he asked.

'It's this I have to say. I've drawn up a plan for voluntary groups of helpers. Get me empowered to try out my plan, and then let's sidetrack officialdom. In any case the authorities have their hands more than full already. I have friends in many walks of life; they'll form a nucleus to start from. And, of course, I'll take part in it myself.'

'I need hardly tell you,' Rieux replied, 'that I accept your suggestion most gladly. One can't have too many helpers, especially in a job like mine under present conditions. I undertake to get your plan approved by the authorities. Anyhow, they've no choice. But . . . ' Rieux pondered. 'But I take it you know that work of this kind may prove fatal to the worker. And I feel I should ask you this; have you weighed the dangers?'

Tarrou's grey eyes met the doctor's gaze serenely.

'What did you think of Paneloux's sermon, doctor?'

The question was asked in a quite ordinary tone, and Rieux answered in the same tone.

'I've seen too much of hospitals to relish any idea of collective punishment. But, as you know, Christians sometimes say that sort of thing without really thinking it. They're better than they seem.'

'However, you think, like Paneloux, that the plague has its good side; it opens men's eyes and forces them to take thought?'

The doctor tossed his head impatiently.

'So does every ill that flesh is heir to. What's true of all the evils in the world is true of plague as well. It helps men to rise above themselves. All the same, when you see the misery it brings, you'd need to be a madman, or a coward, or stone blind, to give in tamely to the plague.'

Rieux had hardly raised his voice at all; but Tarrou made a slight gesture as if to calm him. He was smiling.

'Yes,' Rieux shrugged his shoulders. 'But you haven't answered my question yet. Have you weighed the consequences?'

Tarrou squared his shoulders against the back of the chair, then moved his head forward into the light.

'Do you believe in God, doctor?'

Again the question was put in an ordinary tone. But this time Rieux took longer to find his answer.

'No – but what does that really mean? I'm fumbling in the dark, struggling to make something out. But I've long ceased finding that original. . . . '

'Isn't that it – the gulf between Paneloux and you?'

'I doubt it. Paneloux is a man of learning, a scholar. He hasn't come in contact with death; that's why he can speak with such assurance of the truth – with a capital T. But every country priest who visits his parishioners, and has heard a man gasping for breath on his death-bed, thinks as I do. He'd try to relieve human suffering before trying to point out its excellence.' Rieux stood up: his face was now in shadow. 'Let's drop the subject,' he said, 'as you won't answer.'

Tarrou remained seated in his chair; he was smiling again.

'Suppose I answer with a question?'

The doctor now smiled, too.

'You like being mysterious, don't you? . . . Yes, fire away.'

'My question's this,' said Tarrou. 'Why do you yourself show such devotion, considering you don't believe in God? I suspect your answer may help me to mine.'

His face still in shadow, Rieux said that he'd already answered: that if he believed in an all-powerful God he would cease curing the sick and leave that to Him. But no one in the world believed in a God of that sort; no, not even Paneloux, who believed that he believed in such a God. And this was proved by the fact that no one ever threw himself on Providence completely. Anyhow, in this respect Rieux believed himself to be on the right road – in fighting against creation as he found it.

'Ah,' Tarrou remarked. 'So that's the idea you have of your profession?'

'More or less.' The doctor came back into the light.

Tarrou made a faint whistling noise with his lips, and the doctor gazed at him.

'Yes, you're thinking it calls for pride to feel that way. But I assure you I've no more than the pride that's needed to keep me going. I have no idea what's awaiting me, or what will happen when all this ends. For the moment I know this: there are sick people and they need curing. Later on, perhaps, they'll think things over; and so shall I. But what's wanted now is to make them well. I defend them as best I can, that's all.'

'Against whom?'

Rieux turned to the window. A shadow-line on the horizon told of the presence of the sea. He was conscious only of his exhaustion, and at the same time was struggling against a sudden, irrational impulse to unburden himself a little more to his companion; an eccentric, perhaps, but who, he guessed, was one of his own kind.

'I haven't a notion, Tarrou; I assure you I haven't a notion. When I entered this profession, I did it "abstractedly", so to speak; because I had a desire for it, because it meant a career like another, one that young men often aspire to. Perhaps, too, because it was particularly difficult for a workman's son, like myself.... And then I had to see people die. Did you know that there are some who *refuse* to die? Have you ever heard a woman scream "Never!" with her last gasp? Well, I have. And then I saw that I could never get hardened to it. I was young then, and I was outraged by the whole scheme of things, or so I thought. Subsequently, I grew more modest. Only, I've never managed to get used to seeing people die. That's all I know. Yet after all . . . '

Rieux fell silent, and sat down. He felt his mouth dry.

'After all . . . ?' Tarrou prompted softly.

'After all,' the doctor repeated, then hesitated again, fixing his eyes on Tarrou, 'it's something that a man of your sort can understand most likely, but, since the order of the world is shaped by death, mightn't it be better for God if we refuse to believe in Him, and struggle with all our might against death, without raising our eyes towards the heaven where He sits in silence?'

Tarrou nodded.

'Yes. But your victories will never be lasting; that's all.'

Rieux's face darkened.

'Yes, I know that. But it's no reason for giving up the struggle.'

'No reason, I agree.... Only, I now can picture what this plague must mean for you.'

'Yes. A never-ending defeat.'

Tarrou stared at the doctor for a moment, then turned and tramped heavily towards the door. Rieux followed him and was almost at his side when Tarrou, who was staring at the floor, suddenly said:

'Who taught you all this, doctor?'

The reply came promptly.

'Suffering.'

Rieux opened the door of his surgery and told Tarrou that he, too, was going out; he had a patient to visit in the suburbs.

Tarrou suggested they should go together and he agreed. In the hall they encountered Mme Rieux and the doctor introduced Tarrou to her.

'A friend of mine,' he said.

'Indeed,' said Mme Rieux, 'I'm very pleased to make your acquaintance.'

When she left them Tarrou turned to gaze after her. On the landing the doctor pressed a switch to turn on the lights along the stairs. But the stairs remained in darkness. Possibly some new light-saving order had come into force. Really, however, there was no knowing; for some time past, in the streets no less than in private houses, everything had been going out of order. It might be only that the door-porter, like everyone in the town, was ceasing to bother about his duties. The doctor had no time to follow up his thoughts; Tarrou's voice came from behind him.

'Just one word more, doctor, even if it sounds to you a bit nonsensical. You are perfectly right.'

The doctor merely gave a little shrug, unseen in the darkness.

'To tell the truth, all that's outside my range. But you – what do *you* know about it?'

'Ah,' Tarrou replied quite coolly, 'I've little left to learn.'

Rieux paused and, behind him, Tarrou's foot slipped on a step. He steadied himself by gripping the doctor's shoulder.

'Do you really imagine you know everything about life?'

The answer came through the darkness in the same cool, confident tone.

'Yes.'

Once in the street, they realized it must be quite late, eleven perhaps. All was silence in the town, except for some vague rustlings. An ambulance bell clanged faintly in the distance. They stepped into the car and Rieux started the engine.

'You must come to the hospital tomorrow,' he said, 'for an injection. But, before embarking on this . . . adventure, you'd better know your chances of coming out of it alive; they're one in three.'

'That sort of reckoning doesn't hold water; you know it, doctor, as well as I. A hundred years ago plague wiped out the entire population of a town in Persia, with one exception. And the sole survivor was precisely the man whose job it was to wash the dead bodies, and who carried on throughout the epidemic.'

'He pulled off his one-in-three chance, that's all.' Rieux had lowered his voice. 'But you're right; we know next to nothing on the subject.'

They were entering the suburbs. The headlights lit up empty streets. The car stopped. Standing in front of it, Rieux asked Tarrou if he'd like to come in. Tarrou said, 'Yes.' A glimmer of light from the sky lit up their faces. Suddenly Rieux gave a short laugh, and there was much friendliness in it.

'Out with it, Tarrou! What on earth prompted you to take a hand in this?'

'I don't know. My . . . my code of morals, perhaps.'

'Your code of morals. What code, if I may ask?'

'Comprehension.'

Tarrou turned towards the house and Rieux did not see his face again until they were in the old asthma patient's room.

VIII

NEXT DAY TARROU set to work and enrolled a first team of workers, soon to be followed by many others.

However, it is not the narrator's intention to ascribe to these sanitary groups more importance than their due. Doubtless today many of our fellow-citizens are apt to yield to the temptation of exaggerating the services they rendered. But the narrator is inclined to think that by attributing over-importance to praiseworthy action one may, by implication, be paying indirect but potent homage to the worst side of human nature. For this attitude implies that such actions shine out as rare exceptions, while callousness and apathy are the general rule. The narrator does not share that view. The evil that is in the world always comes of ignorance, and good intentions may do as much harm as malevolence, if they lack understanding. On the whole men are more good than bad; that, however, isn't the real point. But they are more or less ignorant, and it is this that we call vice or virtue; the most incorrigible vice being that of an ignorance which fancies it knows everything and therefore claims for itself the right to kill. The soul of the murderer is blind; and there can be no true goodness nor true love without the utmost clear-sightedness.

Hence the sanitary groups, whose creation was entirely Tarrou's work, should be considered with objectivity as well as with approval. And this is why the narrator declines to vaunt in over-glowing terms a courage and a devotion to which he attributes only a relative and reasonable importance. But he will continue being the chronicler of the troubled, rebellious hearts of our townsfolk under the impact of the plague.

Those who enrolled in the 'sanitary squads' as they were called had, indeed, no such great merit in doing as they did, since they knew it was the only thing to do, and the unthinkable thing would then have been not to have brought themselves to do it. These groups enabled our townsfolk to come to grips with the disease, and convinced them that, now that plague was amongst us, it was up to them to do whatever could be done to fight it. Since plague became in this way some men's duty, it revealed itself as what it really was; that is, the concern of all.

So far, so good. But we do not congratulate a schoolmaster on teaching that two and two make four, though we may, perhaps, congratulate him on having chosen his laudable vocation. Let us then say it was praiseworthy that Tarrou and so many others should have elected to prove that two and two make four, rather than the contrary; but let us add that this goodwill of theirs was one that is shared by the schoolmaster and by all who have the same feelings as the schoolmaster and, be it said to the credit of mankind, are more numerous than one would think – such, anyhow, is the narrator's conviction. Needless to say, he can see quite clearly a point that could be made against him; which is that these men were risking their lives. But again and again there comes a time in history when the man who dares to say that two and two make four is punished with death. The schoolteacher is well aware of this. And the question is not one of knowing what punishment or reward attends the making of this calculation. The question is that of knowing whether two and two do make four. For those of our townsfolk who risked their lives in this predicament the issue was whether or not plague was in their midst and whether or not they must fight against it.

Many fledgling moralists in those days were going about our town proclaiming there was nothing to be done about it and we should bow to the inevitable. And Tarrou, Rieux and their friends might give one answer or another, but its conclusion was always the same, their certitude that a fight must be put up, in this way or that, and there must be no bowing down. The essential thing was to save the greatest possible number of persons from dying and being doomed to unending separation. And to do this there was only one resource; to fight the plague. There was nothing admirable about this attitude; it was merely logical.

Thus it was only natural that old Dr Castel should plod away with unshaken confidence, never sparing himself, at making anti-plague serum on the spot with the makeshift equipment at his disposal. Rieux shared his hope that a vaccine made with cultures of the bacilli obtained locally would take effect more actively than serum coming from outside, since the local bacillus differed slightly from the normal plague bacillus as defined in textbooks of tropical diseases. And Castel expected to have his first supply ready within a surprisingly short period.

That, too, is why it was natural that Grand, who had nothing of the hero about him, should now be acting as a sort of general secretary to the sanitary squads. A certain number of the groups organized by Tarrou were working in the congested areas of the town, with a view to improving the sanitary conditions there. Their duties were to see that houses were kept in a proper hygienic state, and to list attics and cellars that had not been disinfected by the official sanitary service. Other teams of volunteers accompanied the doctors on their house-to-house visits, saw to the evacuation of infected persons and subsequently, owing to the shortage of drivers, even drove the vehicles conveying sick persons and dead bodies. All this involved the upkeep of registers and statistics, and Grand undertook the task.

From this angle, the narrator holds that, more than Rieux or Tarrou, Grand was the true embodiment of the quiet courage that inspired the sanitary groups. He had said 'Yes' without a moment's hesitation and with the large-heartedness that was a second nature with him. All he had asked was to be allotted light duties: he was too old for anything else. He could give his time from six to eight every evening. When Rieux thanked him with some warmth he seemed surprised. 'Why, *that's* not difficult! Plague is here and we've got to make a stand, that's obvious. Ah, I only wish everything were as simple!' And he went back to his phrase. Sometimes in the evening, when he had filed his reports and worked out his statistics, Grand and Rieux would have a chat. Soon they formed the habit of including Tarrou in their talks and Grand unburdened himself with increasingly apparent pleasure to his two companions. They began to take a genuine interest in the laborious literary task to which he was applying himself while plague raged around him. Indeed, they, too, found in it a relaxation of the strain.

'How's your young lady on horseback progressing?' Tarrou would ask. And invariably Grand would answer with a wry smile, 'Trotting along, trotting along!' One evening Grand announced that he had definitely discarded the adjective 'elegant' for his horsewoman. From now on it was replaced by 'slim'. 'That's more concrete,' he explained. Soon after, he read out to his two friends the new version of the sentence.

'One fine morning in May a slim young horsewoman might have been seen riding a handsome sorrel mare along the flowery avenues of the Bois de Boulogne.

'Don't you agree with me one sees her better that way? And I've put "one fine morning in May" because "in the month of May" tended rather to drag out the trot, if you see what I mean.'

Next, he showed some anxiety about the adjective 'handsome'. In his opinion it didn't convey enough, and he set to looking for an epithet that would promptly and clearly 'photograph' the superb animal he saw with his mind's eye. 'Plump' wouldn't do; though concrete enough, it sounded perhaps a little disparaging, also a shade vulgar. 'Beautifully groomed' had tempted him for a moment, but it was cumbrous and made the rhythm limp somewhat. Then one evening he announced triumphantly that he had 'got it!' 'A black sorrel mare.' To his thinking, he explained, 'black' conveyed a hint of elegance and opulence.

'It won't do,' Rieux said.

'Why not?'

'Because "sorrel" doesn't mean a breed of horse; it's a colour.'

'What colour?'

'Well – er – a colour that, anyhow, isn't black.'

Grand seemed greatly troubled.

'Thank you,' he said warmly. 'How fortunate you're here to help me! But you see how difficult it is.'

'How about "glossy"?' Tarrou suggested.

Grand gazed at him meditatively, then 'Yes!' he exclaimed. 'That's good.' And slowly his lips parted in a smile.

Some days later he confessed that the word 'flowery' was bothering him considerably. As the only towns he knew were Oran and Montélimar, he sometimes asked his friends to tell him about the avenues of the Bois de Boulogne, what sort of flowers grew in them and how they were disposed. Actually neither Rieux nor Tarrou had ever gathered the impression that those avenues were 'flowery', but Grand's conviction on the subject shook their confidence in their memories. He was amazed at their uncertainty. 'It's only artists who know how to use their eyes,' was his conclusion. But one evening the doctor found him in a state of much excitement. For 'flowery' he had substituted 'flower-strewn'. He was rubbing his hands. 'At last one can see them, smell them! Hats off, gentlemen!' Triumphantly he read out the sentence.

'One fine morning in May a slim young horsewoman might have been seen riding a glossy sorrel mare along the flower-strewn avenues of the Bois de Boulogne.'

But, spoken aloud, the numerous 's' sounds had a disagreeable effect and Grand stumbled over them, lisping here and there. He sat down, crestfallen; then asked the doctor if he might go. Some hard thinking lay ahead of him.

It was about this time, as was subsequently learnt, that he began to display signs of absent-mindedness in office. A serious view was taken of these lapses of attention, as the Municipality was not only working at high pressure with a reduced staff, but was constantly having new duties thrust upon it. His department suffered, and his Chief took him severely to task, pointing out that he was paid to do certain work and was failing to do it as it should be done. 'I am told that you are acting as a voluntary helper in the sanitary groups. You do this out of office hours, so it's no concern of mine. But the best way of making yourself useful in a terrible time like this is to do your work well. Otherwise all the rest is useless.'

'He's right,' Grand said to Rieux.

'Yes, he's right,' the doctor agreed.

'But I can't steady my thoughts; it's the end of my phrase that's worrying me, I don't seem able to sort it out.'

The plethora of sibilants in the sentence still offended his ear but he saw no way of amending them without using what were, to his mind, inferior synonyms. And that 'flower-strewn' which had rejoiced him when he first lit on it now seemed unsatisfactory. How could one say the flowers were 'strewn' when presumably they had been planted along the avenues, or else grew there naturally? On some evenings, indeed, he looked more tired than Rieux.

Indeed this unavailing quest which never left his mind had worn him out; none the less, he went on adding up the figures and compiling the statistics needed for the sanitary groups. Patiently every evening he brought his totals up to date, illustrated them with graphs, and racked his brains to present his data in the most exact, clearest form. Quite often he went to see Rieux at one of the hospitals and asked to be given a table in an office or the dispensary. He would settle down at it with his papers, exactly as he settled down at his desk in the Municipal Office, and wave each completed sheet to dry the ink in the warm air, noisome with disinfectants and the disease itself. At these times he made honest efforts not to think about his 'horsewoman', and concentrate on what he had to do.

Yes, if it is a fact that people like to have examples given them, men of the type they call heroic, and if it is absolutely necessary that this narrative should include a 'hero', the narrator commends to his readers, with, to his thinking, perfect justice, this insignificant and obscure hero who had to his credit only a little goodness of heart and a seemingly absurd ideal. This will render to the truth its due, to the addition of two and two its sum of four, and to heroism the secondary place which rightly falls to it, just after, never before, the noble claim of happiness. It will also give this chronicle its character, which is intended to be that of a narrative made with good feelings, that is to say feelings which are neither demonstrably bad nor overcharged with emotion in the ugly manner of a stage-play.

Such at least was Dr Rieux's opinion when he read in newspapers or heard on the wireless the messages and encouragement the outer world transmitted to the plague-ridden populace. Besides the comforts sent by air or overland, compassionate or admiring comments were lavished on the henceforth isolated town, by way of newspaper articles or broadcast talks. And invariably their epical or prize-speech verbiage jarred on the doctor. Needless to say, he knew the sympathy was genuine enough. But it could be expressed only in the conventional language with which men try to express what unites them with mankind in general; a vocabulary quite unsuited, for example, to Grand's small daily effort, and incapable of describing what Grand stood for under plague conditions.

Sometimes at midnight, in the great silence of the sleep-bound town, the doctor turned on his wireless before going to bed for the few hours' sleep he allowed himself. And from the ends of the earth, across thousands of miles of land and sea, kindly, well-meaning speakers tried to voice their fellow-feeling, and indeed did so, but at the same time proved the utter incapacity of every man truly to share in suffering which he cannot see. 'Oran! Oran!' In vain the call rang over oceans, in vain Rieux listened hopefully; always the tide of eloquence began to flow, bringing home still more the unbridgeable gulf that lay between Grand and the speaker. 'Oran, we're with you!' they called emotionally. But not, the doctor told himself, to love or to die together – and that's the only way. They're too remote.

IX

AND, AS IT so happens, what has yet to be recorded before coming to the culmination, during the period when the plague was gathering all its forces to fling them at the town and lay it waste, is the long, heartrendingly monotonous struggle put up by some obstinate people like Rambert to recover their lost happiness, and to balk the plague of that part of themselves which they were ready to defend in the last ditch. This was their way of resisting the bondage closing in upon them, and while their resistance lacked the active virtues of the other, it had (to the narrator's thinking) its point, and moreover it bore witness, even in its futility and incoherences, to a salutary pride.

Rambert fought to prevent the plague from besting him. Once assured that there was no way of getting out of the town by lawful methods, he decided, as he told Rieux, to have recourse to others. He began by sounding café waiters. A waiter usually knows much of what's going on behind the scenes. But the first he spoke to knew only of the very heavy penalties imposed on such attempts at evasion. In one of the cafés he visited he was actually taken for a stool-pigeon and curtly sent about his business. It was not until he happened to meet Cottard at Rieux's place that he made a little headway. On that day he and Rieux had been talking again about his unsuccessful efforts to interest the authorities in his case, and Cottard heard the tail-end of the conversation.

Some days later, Cottard met him in the street and greeted him with the hail-fellow-well-met manner that he now used on all occasions.

'Hullo, Rambert! Still no luck?'

'None whatever.'

'It's no good counting on the red-tape merchants. They couldn't understand if they tried.'

'I know that, and I'm trying to find some other way. But it's damned difficult.'

'Yes,' Cottard replied. 'It certainly is. However...'

He, however, knew a way to go about it, and he explained to Rambert, who was much surprised to learn this, that for some time past he had been going the rounds of the cafés, had made a number of acquaintances, and had learnt of the exist-ence of an 'organization' handling this sort of business. The truth was that Cottard, who had been beginning to live above his means, was now involved in smuggling ventures concerned with rationed goods. Selling contraband cigarettes and inferior spirits at steadily rising prices, he was on the way to building up a small fortune.

'Are you quite sure of this?' Rambert asked.

'Quite. I had a proposal of the sort made to me the other day.'

'But you didn't accept it.'

'Oh, come, there's no need to be suspicious.' Cottard's tone was genial. 'I didn't accept it because, personally, I've no wish to leave. I have my reasons.' After a short silence he added: 'You don't ask me what my reasons are, I notice.'

'I take it,' Rambert replied, 'that they're none of my business.'

'That's so, in a way, of course. But from another angle . . . Well, let's put it like this; I've been feeling much more at ease here since plague settled in.'

Rambert made no comment. Then he asked:

'And how does one approach this organization as you call it?'

'Ah,' Cottard replied, 'that's none too easy . . . Come with me.'

It was four in the afternoon. The town was warming up to boiling-point under a sultry sky. Nobody was about, all shops were shuttered. Cottard and Rambert walked some distance without speaking, under the arcades. This was an hour of the day when the plague lay low, so to speak; the silence, the extinction of all colour and movement might have been due as much to the fierce sunlight as to the epidemic, and there was no telling if the air was heavy with menace or merely with dust and heat. You had to look closely and take thought, to realize that plague was here. For it betrayed its presence only by negative signs. Thus Cottard, who had affinities with it, drew Rambert's attention to the absence of the dogs which in normal times would have been seen sprawling in the shadow of the doorways, panting, trying to find a non-existent patch of coolness.

They went along the Boulevard des Palmiers, crossed the Place d'Armes, and then turned down towards the dockyard. On the left was a café painted green, with a wide awning of coarse yellow canvas projecting over the pavement. Cottard and Rambert wiped their brows on entering. There were some small iron tables also painted green, and folding chairs. The room was empty, the air humming with flies; in a yellow cage on the bar-counter a parrot squatted on its perch, all its feathers drooping. Some old pictures of military scenes, covered with grime and cobwebs, adorned the walls. On the tables, including that at which Rambert was sitting, bird-droppings were drying, and he was puzzled whence they came until, after some wing-flappings, a handsome cock came hopping out of his retreat in a dark corner.

Just then the heat seemed to rise several degrees more. Cottard took off his coat and banged on the table-top. A very small man wearing a long blue apron that came nearly to his neck emerged from a doorway at the back, shouted a greeting to Cottard and, vigorously kicking the cock out of his way, came up to the table. Raising his voice to drown the cock's indignant cacklings, he asked what the gentleman would like. Cottard ordered white wine and asked 'Where's Garcia?' The dwarf replied that he'd not shown up at the café for several days.

'Think he'll come this evening?'

'Well, I ain't in his secrets – but you know when he usually comes, don't you?'

'Yes. Really, it's nothing very urgent; I only want him to know this friend of mine.'

The bar-keeper rubbed his moist hands on the front of his apron.

'Ah, so this gentleman's in business, too?'

'Yes,' Cottard said.

The little man made a snuffling noise.

'All right. Come back this evening. I'll send the kid to warn him.'

After they had left Rambert asked what the business in question might be.

'Why, smuggling, of course. They get the stuff in past the sentries at the gates. There's plenty of money in it.'

'I see.' Rambert paused for a moment, then asked: 'And, I take it, they've friends in court?'

'You've said it!'

In the evening the awning was rolled up, the parrot squawking in its cage, and the small tables were surrounded by men in their shirt-sleeves. When Cottard entered, one man, with a white shirt gaping on a brick-red chest and a straw hat planted well back on his head, rose to his feet. He had a sun-tanned face, regular features, small black eyes, very white teeth, and two or three rings on his fingers. He looked about thirty.

'Cheer-o!' he said to Cottard, ignoring Rambert. 'Let's have one at the bar.'

They drank three rounds in silence.

'How about a stroll?' Garcia suggested.

They walked towards the harbour. Garcia asked what he was wanted to do. Cottard explained that it wasn't really for a deal that he wanted to introduce his friend, Monsieur Rambert, but only for what he called a 'get-away'. Puffing at his cigarette, Garcia walked straight ahead. He asked some questions, always referring to Rambert as 'he', and appearing not to notice his presence.

'Why does he want to go?'

'His wife is in France.'

'Ah!' After a short pause he added: 'What's his job?'

'He's a journalist.'

'Is he now? Journalists have long tongues.'

'I told you he's a friend of mine,' Cottard replied.

They walked on in silence until they were near the wharves, which were now railed off. Then they turned in the direction of a small tavern from which came a smell of fried sardines.

'In any case,' Garcia said finally, 'it's not up my street. Raoul's your man, and I'll have to get in touch with him. It's none too easy.'

'That so?' Cottard sounded interested. 'He's lying low, is he?'

Garcia made no answer. At the door of the tavern he halted, and for the first time addressed Rambert directly.

'The day after tomorrow, at eleven, at the corner of the Customs Barracks in the Upper Town.' He made as if to go, then seemed to have an afterthought. 'It's going to cost something, you know.' He made the observation in a quite casual tone.

Rambert nodded. 'Naturally.'

On the way back the journalist thanked Cottard.

'Don't mention it, old chap. I'm only too glad to help you. And then, you're a journalist, I dare say you'll put in a word for me one day or another.'

Two days later Rambert and Cottard climbed the wide shadeless street leading to the upper part of the town. The barracks occupied by the Customs Officers had been partially transformed into a hospital, and a number of people were standing outside the main entrance, some of them hoping to be allowed to visit a patient – a futile hope, since such visits were strictly prohibited – and others to glean some news of an invalid, news which in the course of an hour would have ceased to count. For these reasons there were always a number of people and a certain amount of movement at this spot; a fact which probably accounted for its choice by Garcia for his meeting with Rambert.

'It puzzles me,' Cottard remarked, 'why you're so keen on going. Really, what's happening here is extremely interesting.'

'Not to me,' Rambert replied.

'Well, yes, one's running some risks, I grant you. All the same, when you come to think of it, one ran quite as much risk in the old days, crossing a busy street.'

Just then Rieux's car drew up level with them. Tarrou was at the wheel, and Rieux seemed half-asleep. He roused himself to make the introductions.

'We know each other,' Tarrou said. 'We're at the same hotel.' He then offered to drive Rambert back to the centre.

'No, thanks. We've an appointment here.'

Rieux looked hard at Rambert.

'Yes,' Rambert said.

'What's that?' Cottard sounded surprised. 'The doctor knows about it?'

'There's the magistrate.' Tarrou gave Cottard a warning glance.

Cottard's look changed. M. Othon was striding down the street towards them, briskly yet with dignity. He took off his hat as he came level with them.

'Good morning, Monsieur Othon,' said Tarrou.

The magistrate returned the greeting of the men in the car, and, turning to Rambert and Cottard who were in the background, gave them a quiet nod. Tarrou introduced Cottard and the journalist. The magistrate gazed at the sky for a moment, sighed, and remarked that these were indeed sad times.

'I've been told, Monsieur Tarrou,' he continued, 'that you are helping to enforce the prophylactic measures. I need hardly say how commendable that is, a fine example....Do you think, Doctor Rieux, that the epidemic will get worse?'

Rieux replied that one could only hope it wouldn't, and the magistrate replied that one must never lose hope, the ways of Providence were inscrutable.

Tarrou asked if his work had increased as the result of present conditions.

'Quite the contrary. Criminal cases of what we call the first instance are growing rarer. In fact, almost my only work just now is holding inquiries into more serious breaches of the new regulations. Our ordinary laws have never been so well respected.'

'That's because, by contrast, they necessarily appear good ones,' Tarrou observed.

The magistrate, who seemed unable to take his gaze off the sky, abruptly dropped his mildly meditative air, and stared at Tarrou.

'What does that matter? It's not the law that counts, it's the sentence. . . . And that is something we must all accept.'

'That fellow,' said Cottard when the magistrate was out of hearing, 'is Enemy Number One.'

Tarrou pressed the starter.

Some minutes later Rambert and Cottard saw Garcia approaching. Without making any sign of recognition he came straight up to them, and by way of greeting said, 'You'll have to wait a bit.'

There was complete silence in the crowd around them, most of whom were women. Nearly all were carrying parcels; they had the vain hope of somehow smuggling these in to their sick kinsfolk, and the even crazier idea that the latter could eat the food they'd brought. The gate was guarded by armed sentries and, now and again, an eerie cry resounded in the courtyard between the barrack-rooms and the entrance. Whenever this happened anxious eyes turned towards the sick-wards.

The three men were watching the scene when a brisk 'Good morning' from behind them made them swing round. In spite of the heat Raoul was wearing a well-cut dark suit and a felt hat with rolled-up brim. He was tall and strongly built; his face rather pale. Hardly moving his lips, he said quickly and clearly:

'Let's walk down to the centre.... You, Garcia, needn't come.'

Garcia lit a cigarette and remained there while they walked away. Placing himself between Rambert and Cottard, Raoul set the pace, a fast one.

'Garcia's explained the situation,' he said. 'We can fix it. But I must warn you it'll cost you a cool ten thousand.'

Rambert said he agreed to these terms.

'Lunch with me tomorrow at the Spanish restaurant near the docks.'

Rambert said 'Right,' and Raoul shook his hand, smiling for the first time. After he had gone Cottard said he wouldn't be able to come to luncheon next day, as he had an engagement, but anyhow Rambert didn't need him any more.

When next day Rambert entered the Spanish restaurant everyone turned and stared at him. The dark, cellar-like room, below the level of the small, yellow street, was patronized only by men, mostly Spaniards, judging by their looks. Raoul was sitting at a table at the back of the room. Once he had beckoned to the journalist and Rambert started to go towards him, the curiosity left the faces of others and they bent over their plates again. Raoul had beside him a tall, thin, ill-shaven man, with enormously wide shoulders, an equine face and thinning hair. His shirt-sleeves were rolled up, displaying long, skinny arms covered with black hair. When Rambert was introduced he gave three slow nods. His own name, however, was not announced and Raoul, when referring to him, always said 'our friend'.

'Our friend here thinks he may be able to help you. He is going...' Raoul broke off, as the waitress had just come to take Rambert's order. 'He is going to put you in touch with two of our friends who will introduce you to some sentries whom we've squared. But that doesn't mean you can start right away. You'll have to leave it to the sentries to decide on the best moment. The simplest thing will be for you to stay some nights with one of them; his home is quite near the gate. The first thing is for our friend here to give you the contacts needed; then when everything's set, you'll settle with him for the expenses.'

Again the 'friend' slowly moved his equine head up and down, without ceasing to munch the tomato and pimento salad he was shovelling into his mouth. After which, he began to speak, with a slight Spanish accent. He asked Rambert to meet him, the next day but one, at eight in the morning, in the Cathedral porch.

'Another two days' wait,' Rambert observed.

'It ain't so easy as all that, you see,' Raoul said. 'Them boys take some finding.'

Horse-face nodded slow approval once more. Some time was spent looking for a subject of conversation. The problem was solved easily enough when Rambert discovered that horse-face was an ardent football-player. He, too, had been very keen on Association football. They discussed the French championship, the merits of professional English teams, and the technique of passing. By the end of the meal horse-face was in high good humour, was calling Rambert 'old boy', and trying to convince him that the most sporting place by far on the football field was that of centre-half. 'You see, old boy, it's the centre-half that does the placing. And that's the whole art of the game, isn't it?' Rambert was inclined to agree, though he, personally, had always played centre-forward. The discussion proceeded peacefully until a wireless was turned on and, after at first emitting a series of sentimental songs, broke into the announcement that there had been a hundred and thirty-seven plague deaths on the previous day. No one present betrayed the least emotion. Horse-face merely shrugged and stood up. Raoul and Rambert followed his example.

133

As they were going out the centre-half shook Rambert's hand vigorously. 'My name's Gonzales,' he said.

To Rambert the next two days seemed endless. He looked up Rieux and described to him the latest developments, then accompanied the doctor on one of his calls. He took leave of him on the doorstep of a house where a patient, suspected to have plague, was awaiting him. There was a sound of footsteps and voices in the hall; the family were being warned of the doctor's visit.

'I hope Tarrou will be up to time,' Rieux murmured. He looked worn out.

'Is the epidemic getting out of hand?' Rambert asked.

Rieux said it wasn't that; indeed the death-graph was rising less steeply. Only they lacked adequate means of coping with the disease.

'We're short of equipment. In all the armies of the world a shortage of equipment is usually compensated for by man-power. But we're short of man-power, too.'

'Haven't doctors and trained assistants been sent from other towns?'

'Yes,' Rieux said. 'Ten doctors and a hundred helpers. That sounds a lot, no doubt. But it's barely enough to cope with the present state of affairs. And it will be quite inadequate if things get worse.'

Rambert, who had been listening to the sounds within the house, turned to Rieux with a friendly smile.

'Yes,' he said, 'you'd better make haste to win your battle.' Then a shadow crossed his face. 'You know,' he added, in a low tone, 'it's not because of *that* I'm leaving.'

Rieux replied that he knew it very well, but Rambert went on to say:

'I don't think I'm a coward – not as a rule, anyhow. And I've had opportunities of putting it to the test. Only, there are some thoughts I simply cannot endure.'

The doctor looked him in the eyes.

'You'll see her again,' he said.

'Maybe. But I just can't stomach the thought that it may last on and on, and all the time she'll be growing older. At thirty one's beginning to age, and one's got to squeeze all one can out of life. . . . But I doubt if you can understand.'

Rieux was replying that he thought he could, when Tarrou came up, obviously much excited.

'I've just asked Paneloux to join us.'

'Well?'

'He thought it over, then said "Yes."'

'That's good,' the doctor said. 'I'm glad to know he's better than his sermon.'

'Most people are like that,' Tarrou replied. 'It's only a matter of giving them the chance.' He smiled and winked at Rieux. 'That's my job in life – giving people chances.'

'Excuse me,' Rambert said, 'I've got to be off.'

On Thursday, the day of the appointment, Rambert entered the Cathedral porch at five minutes to eight. The air was still relatively cool. Small fleecy clouds, which presently the sun would swallow at a gulp, were drifting across the sky. A faint smell of moisture rose from the lawns, parched though they were. Still masked by the eastward houses, the sun was warming up Joan of Arc's helmet only, and it made a solitary patch of brightness in the Cathedral Square. A clock struck eight. Rambert took some steps in the empty porch. From inside came a low sound of intoning voices, together with stale wafts of incense and dank air. Then the voices ceased. Ten small black forms came out of the building, and hastened away towards the centre of the town. Rambert grew impatient. Other black forms climbed the steps and entered the porch. He was about to light a cigarette when it struck him that smoking might be frowned on here.

At eight-fifteen the organ began to play, very softly. Rambert entered. At first he could see nothing in the dim light of the aisle; after a moment he made out the small black forms that had preceded him in the nave. They were all grouped in a corner, in front of a makeshift altar on which stood the statue of St Roch, carved in haste by one of our local sculptors. Kneeling, they looked even smaller than before, blobs of clotted darkness hardly more opaque than the grey, smoky haze in which they seemed to float. Above them the organ was playing endless variations.

When Rambert stepped out of the Cathedral, he saw Gonzales already going down the steps on his way back to the town.

'I thought you'd cleared off, old boy,' he said to the journalist. 'Considering how late it is.'

He proceeded to explain that he'd gone to meet his friends at the place agreed on – which was quite near-by – at ten to eight, the time they'd fixed, and waited twenty minutes without seeing them.

'Something must have held them up. There's lots of snags, you know, in our line of business.'

He suggested another meeting at the same time on the following day, beside the War Memorial. Rambert sighed and pushed his hat back on his head.

'Don't take it so hard,' Gonzales laughed. 'Why, think of all the swerves and runs and passes you got to make to score a goal.'

'Quite so,' Rambert agreed. 'But the game lasts only an hour and a half.'

The War Memorial at Oran stands at the one place where one has a glimpse of the sea, a sort of esplanade following for a short distance the brow of the cliff overlooking the harbour. Next day, being again the first to arrive at the meeting-place, Rambert whiled away the time reading the list of names of those who had died for their country. Some minutes later two men strolled up, gave him a casual glance, then, resting their elbows on the parapet of the esplanade, gazed down intently at the empty, lifeless harbour. Both wore short-sleeved jerseys and blue trousers, and were of much the same height. The journalist moved away and, seated on a stone bench, studied their appearance at leisure. They were obviously youngsters, not more than twenty. Just then he saw Gonzales coming up.

'Those are our friends,' he said, after apologizing for being late. Then he led Rambert to the two youths, whom he introduced as Marcel and Louis. They looked so much alike that Rambert had no doubt they were brothers.

'Right,' said Gonzales. 'Now you know each other, you can get down to business.'

Marcel, or Louis, said that their turn of sentry duty began in two days' time and lasted a week; they'd have to watch out for the night when there was the best chance of bringing it off. The trouble was that there were two other sentries, regular soldiers, besides themselves, at the West Gate. These two men had better be kept out of the business; one couldn't depend on them, and anyhow it would pile up expenses unnecessarily. Some evenings, however, these two sentries spent several hours in the back room of a near-by bar. Marcel, or Louis, said that the best thing he could do would be to stay at their place, which was only a few minutes' walk from the gate, and wait till one of them came to tell him the coast was clear. It should then be quite easy for him to 'make his getaway'. But there was no time to lose; there had been talk about setting up duplicate sentry-posts a little farther out.

Rambert agreed and handed some of his few remaining cigarettes to the young men. The one who had not yet spoken asked Gonzales if the question of expenses had been settled and whether an advance would be given.

'No,' Gonzales said, 'and you needn't bother about that; he's a pal of mine. He'll pay when he leaves.'

Another meeting was arranged. Gonzales suggested their dining together on the next day but one, at the Spanish restaurant. It was at easy walking distance from where the young men lived. 'For the first night,' he added, 'I'll keep you company, old boy.'

Next day on his way to his bedroom Rambert met Tarrou coming down the stairs at the hotel.

'Like to come with me?' he asked. 'I'm just off to see Rieux.'

Rambert hesitated.

'Well, I never feel sure I'm not disturbing him.'

'I don't think you need worry about that; he's talked about you quite a lot.'

The journalist pondered. Then, 'Look here,' he said. 'If you've any time to spare after dinner, never mind how late, why not come to the hotel, both of you, and have a drink with me?'

'That will depend on Rieux.' Tarrou sounded doubtful. 'And on the plague.'

At eleven o'clock that night, however, Rieux and Tarrou entered the small, narrow bar of the hotel. Some thirty people were crowded into it, all talking at the top of their voices. Coming from the silence of the plague-bound town, the two new-comers were startled by the sudden burst of noise, and halted in the doorway. They understood the reason for it when they saw that spirits were still to be had here. Rambert, who was perched on a stool at a corner of the bar, beckoned to them. With complete coolness he elbowed away a noisy customer beside him to make room for his friends.

'You've no objection to a spot of something strong?'

'No,' Tarrou replied. 'Quite the contrary.'

Rieux sniffed the pungency of bitter herbs in the drink that Rambert handed him. It was hard to make oneself heard in the din of voices, but Rambert seemed chiefly concerned with drinking. The doctor couldn't make up his mind whether he was drunk yet. At one of the two tables which occupied all the remaining space beyond the half-circle round the bar, a naval officer, with a girl on each side of him, was describing to a fat, red-faced man a typhus epidemic at Cairo. 'They had camps, you know,' he was saying, 'for the natives, with tents for the sick ones and a ring of sentries all round. If a member of the family came along and tried to smuggle in one of those damn-fool native remedies, they fired at sight. A bit tough, I grant you, but it was the only thing to do.' At the other table, round which sat a bevy of bright young people, the talk was incomprehensible, half-drowned by the stridency of 'St James' Infirmary' coming from a loudspeaker just above their heads.

'Any luck?' Rieux had to raise his voice.

'I'm getting on,' Rambert replied. 'In the course of the week, perhaps.'

'A pity!' Tarrou shouted.

'Why?'

'Oh,' Rieux put in, 'Tarrou said that because he thinks you might be useful to us here. But, personally, I understand your wish to get away only too well.'

Tarrou stood the next round of drinks.

Rambert got off his stool and looked him in the eyes for the first time.

'How could I be useful?'

'Why, of course,' Tarrou replied, slowly reaching towards his glass, 'in one of our sanitary squads.'

The look of brooding obstinacy that Rambert so often had came back to his face, and he climbed again on to his stool.

'Don't you think these squads of ours do any good?' Tarrou had just taken a sip of his glass and was gazing hard at Rambert.

'I'm sure they do,' the journalist replied, and drank off his glass.

Rieux noticed that his hand was shaking, and he decided, definitely, that the man was far gone in drink.

Next day when, for the second time, Rambert entered the Spanish restaurant he had to make his way through a group of men who had taken chairs out on to the pavement and were sitting in the green-gold evening light, enjoying the first breaths of cooler air. They were smoking an acrid-smelling tobacco. The restaurant itself was almost empty. Rambert went to the table at the back at which Gonzales had sat when they met for the first time. He told the waitress he would wait a bit. It was seven-thirty.

In twos and threes, the men from outside began to dribble in and seated themselves at the tables. The waitresses started serving and a tinkle of knives and forks, a hum of conversation, began to fill the cellar-like room. At eight Rambert was still waiting. The lights were turned on. A new set of people took the other chairs at his table. He ordered dinner. At half-past eight he had finished without having seen either Gonzales or the two young men. The restaurant was gradually emptying, and, outside, night was falling rapidly. The curtains hung across the doorway were billowing in a warm breeze from the sea. At nine Rambert realized that the restaurant was quite empty and the waitress eyeing him curiously. He paid, went out and, noticing that a café across the road was open, settled down there at a place from which he could keep an eye on the entrance of the restaurant. At half-past nine he walked slowly back to his hotel, racking his brains for some method of tracking down Gonzales, whose address he did not know, and bitterly discouraged by the not unlikely prospect of having to start the tiresome business all over again.

It was at this moment, as he walked in the dark streets along which ambulances were speeding, that it suddenly struck him − as he informed Dr Rieux subsequently − that all this time he'd practically forgotten the woman he loved, so absorbed had he been in trying to find a rift in the walls that cut him off from her. But at this same moment, now that once more all ways of escape were sealed against him, he felt his longing for her blaze up again, with a violence so sudden, so intense that he started running to his hotel, as if to escape the burning pain that none the less pervaded him, racing like wildfire in his blood.

Very early next day, however, he called on Rieux, to ask him where he could find Cottard.

'The only thing to do is to pick up the thread again where I dropped it.'

'Come tomorrow night,' Rieux said. 'Tarrou asked me to invite Cottard here – I don't know why. He's due to come at ten. Come at half-past ten.'

When Cottard visited the doctor next day Tarrou and Rieux were discussing the case of one of Rieux's patients who against all expectation had recovered.

'It was ten to one against,' Tarrou commented. 'He was in luck.'

'Oh, come now,' Cottard said. 'It can't have been plague, that's all.'

They assured him there was no doubt it was a case of plague.

'That's impossible, since he recovered. You know as well as I do, once you have plague your number's up.'

'True enough, as a general rule,' Rieux replied. 'But, if you refuse to be beaten, you have some pleasant surprises.'

Cottard laughed.

'Precious few, anyhow. You saw the number of deaths this evening?'

Tarrou, who was gazing amiably at Cottard, said he knew the latest figures, and that the position was extremely serious. But what did that prove? Only that still more stringent measures should be applied.

'How? You can't make more stringent ones than those we have now.'

'No. But every person in the town must apply them to himself.'

Cottard stared at him in a puzzled manner, and Tarrou went on to say that there were far too many slackers, that this plague was everybody's business, and everyone should do his duty. For instance, any able-bodied man was welcome in the sanitary squads.

'That's an idea,' Cottard smiled. 'But it won't get you anywhere. The plague has the whiphand of you and there's nothing to be done about it.'

'We shall know whether that is so' – Tarrou's voice was carefully controlled – 'only when we've tried everything.'

Meanwhile Rieux had been sitting at his desk, copying out reports. Tarrou was still gazing at the little business man, who was stirring uneasily in his chair.

'Look here, Monsieur Cottard, why don't you join us?'

Picking up his bowler hat, Cottard rose from his chair with an offended expression.

'It's not my job,' he said. Then, with an air of bravado, added: 'What's more, the plague suits me quite well and I see no reason why I should bother about trying to stop it.'

As if a new idea had just waylaid him, Tarrou struck his forehead.

'Why, of course, I was forgetting. If it wasn't for your good friend, the plague, you'd be arrested.'

Cottard gave a start and gripped the back of the chair, as if he were about to fall. Rieux had stopped writing and was observing him with grave interest.

'Who told you that?' Cottard almost screamed.

'Why, you yourself!' Tarrou looked surprised. 'At least that's what the doctor and I have gathered from the way you speak.'

Losing all control of himself, Cottard let out a volley of oaths.

'Don't get excited,' Tarrou said quietly. 'Neither I nor the doctor would dream of reporting you to the police. What you may have done is no business of ours. And, anyhow, we've never had much use for the police. Come now! Sit down again.'

Cottard looked at the chair, then hesitantly lowered himself into it. He heaved a deep sigh.

'It's something that happened ages ago,' he began. 'Somehow they've dug it up. I thought it had all been forgotten. But somebody started talking, blast him! They sent for me and told me not to budge till the inquiry was finished. And I felt pretty sure they'd end up by arresting me.'

'Was it anything serious?' Tarrou asked.

'That depends on what you mean by "serious". It wasn't murder, anyhow.'

'Imprisonment or penal servitude?'

Cottard was looking almost abject.

'Well, imprisonment – if I'm lucky.' But after a moment he grew excited again. 'It was all a mistake. Everybody makes mistakes, don't they? And I can't bear the idea of being pulled in for that, of being torn from my home and habits and everyone I know.'

'And is that the reason,' Tarrou asked, 'why you had the bright idea of hanging yourself?'

'Yes. It was a damn-fool thing to do, I admit.'

For the first time Rieux spoke. He told Cottard that he quite understood his anxiety, but perhaps everything would come right in the end.

'Oh, for the moment I've nothing to fear.'

'I can see,' Tarrou said, 'that you're not going to join in our effort.'

Twiddling his hat uneasily, Cottard gazed at Tarrou with shifty eyes.

'I hope you won't bear me a grudge, Monsieur Tarrou . . .'

'Certainly not. But,' Tarrou smiled, 'do try at least not to propagate the microbe deliberately.'

Cottard protested that he'd never wanted the plague, it was pure chance that it had broken out, and he wasn't to blame if it happened to make things easier for him just now. Then he seemed to pluck up courage again, and when Rambert entered was shouting almost aggressively:

'What's more, I'm pretty sure you won't get anywhere.'

Rambert learnt to his chagrin that Cottard didn't know where Gonzales lived; he suggested that they'd better pay another visit to the small café. They made an appointment for the following day. When Rieux gave him to understand that he'd like to be kept posted as to his success or otherwise, Rambert proposed that he and Tarrou should look him up one night at the end of the week. They could come as late as they liked and would be sure to find him in his room.

Next morning Cottard and Rambert went to the café and left a message for Garcia, asking him to come that evening, or if this could not be managed, next day. They waited for him in vain that evening. Next day, Garcia turned up. He listened in silence to what Rambert had to say; then informed him he had no idea what had happened, but knew that several districts of the town had been isolated for twenty-four hours, for a house-to-house inspection. Quite possibly Gonzales and the two youngsters hadn't been able to get through the cordon. All he could do was to put them in touch once more with Raoul. Naturally this couldn't be done before the next day but one.

'I see,' Rambert said. 'I'll have to start it all over again, from scratch.'

On the next day but one Raoul, whom Rambert met at a street-corner, confirmed Garcia's surmise; the low-lying districts had, in fact, been isolated and a cordon put round them. The next thing was to get in contact with Gonzales. Two days later Rambert was lunching with the footballer.

'It's too damn' silly,' Gonzales said. 'Of course you should have arranged some way of seeing each other.'

Rambert heartily agreed.

'Tomorrow morning,' Gonzales continued, 'we'll look up the kids and try to get a real move on.'

When they called next day, however, the youngsters were out. A note was left fixing a meeting for the following day at noon, outside the High School. When Rambert came back to his hotel Tarrou was struck by the look on his face.

'Not feeling well?' he asked.

'It's having to start it all again that's got me down.' Then he added: 'You'll come tonight, won't you?'

When the two friends entered Rambert's room that night, they found him lying on the bed. He got up at once and filled the glasses he had ready. Before lifting his to his lips, Rieux asked him if he was making progress. The journalist replied that he'd started the same round again and got to the same point as before; in a day or two he was to have his last appointment. Then he took a sip of his drink, and added gloomily: 'Needless to say, they won't turn up.'

'Oh come! That doesn't follow because they let you down last time.'

'So you haven't understood yet?' Rambert shrugged his shoulders almost scornfully.

'Understood what?'

'The plague.'

'Ah!' Rieux exclaimed.

'No, you haven't understood that it means exactly that – the same thing over and over and over again.'

He went to a corner of the room and started a small gramophone.

'What's that record?' Tarrou asked. 'I've heard it before.'

'It's "St James' Infirmary".'

While the gramophone was playing two shots rang out in the distance.

'A dog or a getaway,' Tarrou remarked.

When, some moments later, the record ended, an ambulance-bell could be heard clanging past under the window, and receding into silence.

'Rather a boring record,' Rambert remarked. 'And this must be the tenth time I've put it on today.'

'Are you really so fond of it?'

'No, but it's the only one I have.' And after a moment he added: 'That's what I said "it" was – the same thing over and over again.'

He asked Rieux how the sanitary groups were functioning. Five teams were now at work, and it was hoped to form others. Sitting on the bed, the journalist seemed to be studying his finger-nails. Rieux was gazing at his squat, powerfully built form, hunched up on the edge of the bed. Suddenly he realized that Rambert was returning his gaze.

'You know, doctor, I've given a lot of thought to your campaign. And if I'm not with you, I have my reasons. . . . No, I don't think it's that I'm afraid to risk my skin again. I took part in the Spanish civil war.'

'On which side?' Tarrou asked.

'The losing side. But since then I've done a bit of thinking.'

'About what?'

'Courage. I know now that man is capable of great deeds. But if he isn't capable of a great emotion, well, he leaves me cold.'

'One had the idea that he is capable of everything,' Tarrou remarked.

'I can't agree; he's incapable of suffering for a long time, or being happy for a long time. Which means that he's incapable of anything really worth while.' He looked at the two men in turn, then asked: 'Tell me, Tarrou, are you capable of dying for love?'

'I couldn't say, but I hardly think so – as I am now.'

'You see. But you're capable of dying for an idea; one can see that right away. Well, personally, I've seen enough of people who die for an idea. I don't believe in heroism; I know it's easy and I've learnt it can be murderous. What interests me is living and dying for what one loves.'

Rieux had been watching the journalist attentively. With his eyes still on him, he said quietly:

'Man isn't an idea, Rambert.'

Rambert sprang off the bed, his face ablaze with passion.

'Man *is* an idea, and a precious small idea, once he turns his back on love. And that's my point; we – mankind – have lost the capacity for love. We must face that fact, doctor. Let's wait to acquire that capacity or, if really it's beyond us, wait for the deliverance that will come to each of us anyway, without his playing the hero. Personally, I look no further.'

Rieux rose. He suddenly appeared very tired.

'You're right, Rambert, quite right, and for nothing in the world would I try to dissuade you from what you're going to do; it seems to me absolutely right and proper. However, there's one thing I must tell you; there's no question of heroism in all this. It's a matter of common decency. That's an idea which may make some people smile, but the only means of fighting a plague is – common decency.'

'What do you mean by "common decency"?' Rambert's tone was grave.

'I don't know what it means for other people. But in my case I know that it consists in doing my job.'

'Your job! I only wish I were sure what my job is!' There was a mordant edge to Rambert's voice. 'Maybe I'm all wrong in putting love first.'

Rieux looked him in the eyes.

'No,' he said vehemently. 'You are *not* wrong.'

Rambert gazed thoughtfully at them.

'You two,' he said, 'I suppose you've nothing to lose in all this. It's easier, that way, to be on the side of the angels.'

Rieux drained his glass.

'Come along,' he said to Tarrou. 'We've work to do.'

He went out.

Tarrou followed, but seemed to change his mind when he reached the door. He stopped and looked at the journalist.

'I suppose you don't know that Rieux's wife is in a sanatorium, a hundred miles or so away.'

Rambert showed surprise, and began to say something; but Tarrou had already left the room.

At a very early hour next day Rambert rang up the doctor.

'Would you agree to my working with you until I find some way of getting out of the town?'

There was a moment's silence before the reply came.

'Certainly, Rambert. Thanks.'

PART THREE

I

THUS WEEK BY week the prisoners of plague put up what fight they could. Some, like Rambert, even contrived to fancy they were still behaving as free men and had the power of choice. But actually it would have been truer to say that by this time, mid-August, the plague had swallowed up everything and everyone. No longer were there individual destinies; only a collective destiny, made of plague and the emotions shared by all. Strongest of these emotions was the sense of exile and of deprivation, with all the cross-currents of revolt and fear set up by these. That is why the narrator thinks this moment, registering the climax of the summer heat and the disease, the best for describing, on general lines and by way of illustration, the excesses of the living, burials of the dead, and the plight of parted lovers.

It was at this time that a high wind rose and blew for several days through the plague-stricken city. Wind is particularly dreaded by the inhabitants of Oran, since the plateau on which the town is built presents no natural obstacle, and it can sweep our streets with unimpeded violence. During the months when not a drop of rain had refreshed the town, a grey crust had formed on everything, and this flaked off under the wind, disintegrating into dust-clouds. What with the dust and scraps of paper whirled against people's legs, the streets grew emptier. Those few who went out could be seen hurrying along, bent forward, with handkerchiefs or their hands pressed to their mouths. At nightfall, instead of the usual throng of people, each trying to prolong a day which might well be his last, you met only small groups hastening home or to a favourite café. With the result that for several days when twilight came – it fell much quicker at this time of the year – the streets were almost empty, and silent but for the long-drawn stridency of the wind. A smell of brine and seaweed came from the unseen, storm-tossed sea. And in the growing darkness the almost empty town, palled in dust, swept by bitter sea-spray, and loud with the shrilling of the wind, seemed a lost island of the damned.

Hitherto the plague had found far more victims in the more thickly populated and less well-appointed outer districts than in the heart of the town. Quite suddenly, however, it launched a new attack and established itself in the business centre. Residents accused the wind of carrying infection, 'broadcasting germs', as the hotel manager put it. Whatever the reason might be, people living in the central districts realized that their turn had come when each night they heard oftener and oftener the ambulances clanging past, sounding the plague's dismal, passionless tocsin under their windows.

The authorities had the idea of segregating certain particularly affected central areas and permitting only those whose services were indispensable to cross the cordon. Dwellers in these areas could not help regarding these regulations as a sort of taboo specially directed at themselves, and thus they came, by contrast, to envy residents in other districts their freedom. And the latter, to cheer themselves up in despondent moments, fell to picturing the lot of those others less free than themselves. 'Anyhow there's some worse off than I' was a remark that voiced the only solace to be had in those days.

About the same time we had a recrudescence of outbreaks of fire, especially in the residential area near the West Gate. It was found, after inquiry, that people who had returned from quarantine were responsible for these fires. Thrown off their balance by bereavement and anxiety, they were burning their houses under the odd delusion that they were killing off the plague in the holocaust. Great difficulty was experienced in fighting these fires, whose numbers and frequency exposed whole districts to constant danger, owing to the high wind. When the attempts made by the authorities to convince these well-meaning fire-raisers that the official fumigation of their houses effectively removed any risk of infection, had proved unavailing, it became necessary to decree very heavy penalties for this type of arson. And most likely it was not the prospect of mere imprisonment that deterred these unhappy people, but the common belief that a sentence of imprisonment was tantamount to a death-sentence, owing to the very high mortality prevailing in the town jail. It must be admitted that there was some foundation for this belief. It seemed that, for obvious reasons, the plague launched its most virulent attacks on those who lived, by choice or by necessity, in groups; soldiers, prisoners, monks and nuns. For though some prisoners are kept solitary, a prison forms a sort of community, as is proved by the fact that in our town jail the warders died of plague in the same proportion as the prisoners. The plague was no respecter of persons and under its despotic rule everyone, from the Governor down to the humblest delinquent, was under sentence and, perhaps for the first time, impartial justice reigned in the prison.

Attempts made by the authorities to redress this levelling-out by some sort of hierarchy – the idea was to confer a decoration on warders who died in the exercise of their duties – came to nothing. Since martial law had been declared and the warders might, from a certain angle, be regarded as on active service, they were awarded posthumously the Military Medal. But though the prisoners raised no protest, strong exception was taken in military circles, and it was pointed out, logically enough, that a most regrettable confusion in the public mind would certainly ensue. The civil authority conceded the point, and decided that the simplest solution was to bestow on warders who died at their post a 'Plague Medal'. Even so, since as regards the first recipients of the Military Medal the harm had been done and there was no question of withdrawing the decoration from them, the military were still dissatisfied. Moreover, the Plague Medal had the disadvantage of having far less moral effect than that attaching to a military award – since in time of pestilence a decoration of this sort is too easily acquired. Thus nobody was satisfied.

Another difficulty was that the jail administration could not follow the procedure adopted by the religious and, in a less degree, the military authorities. The monks in the two monasteries of the town had been evacuated and lodged for the time being with religious-minded families. In the same way, whenever possible, small bodies of men had been moved out of barracks and billeted in schools or public buildings. Thus the disease, which, apparently, had forced on us the solidarity of a beleaguered town, disrupted at the same time long-established communities and sent men out to live, as individuals, in relative isolation. This, too, added to the general feeling of unrest.

Indeed it can easily be imagined that these changes, combined with the high wind, also had an incendiary effect on certain minds. There were frequent attacks on the gates of the town, and the men who made them now were armed. Shots were exchanged, there were casualties, and some few got away. Then the sentry-posts were reinforced, and such attempts quickly ceased. None the less, they sufficed to start a wave of revolutionary violence, though only on a small scale. Houses which had been burnt or closed by the sanitary control were looted. However, it seemed unlikely that these excesses were premeditated. Usually it was some chance incentive that led normally well-behaved people to acts which promptly had their imitators. Thus you sometimes saw a man, acting on some crazy impulse, dash into a blazing house under the eyes of its owner, who was standing by, dazed with grief, watching the flames. Seeing his indifference, many of the onlookers would follow the lead given by the first man, and presently the dark street was full of running men, changed to hunched, misshapen gnomes by the flickering glow from the dying flames and the ornaments or furniture they carried on their shoulders. It was incidents of this sort that compelled the authorities to declare Martial Law and enforce the regulations deriving from it. Two looters were shot, but we may doubt if this made much impression on the others; with so many deaths taking place every day, these two executions went unheeded – a mere drop in the ocean. Actually scenes of this kind continued to take place fairly often, without the authorities' making even a show of intervening. The only regulation that seemed to have some effect on the populace was the establishment of a curfew hour. From eleven onwards, plunged in complete darkness, Oran seemed a huge necropolis.

On moonlight nights the long, straight streets and dirty white walls, nowhere darkened by the shadow of a tree, their peace untroubled by footsteps or a dog's bark, glimmered in pale recession. The silent city was no more than an assemblage of huge, inert cubes, between which only the mute effigies of great men, carapaced in bronze, with their blank stone or metal faces, conjured up a sorry semblance of what the man had been. In lifeless squares and avenues these tawdry idols lorded it under the lowering sky; stolid monsters that might have personified the rule of immobility imposed on us, or, anyhow, its final aspect, that of a defunct city in which plague, stone and darkness had effectively silenced every voice.

But there was darkness also in men's hearts, and the true facts were as little calculated to reassure our townsfolk as the wild stories going round about the burials. The narrator cannot help talking about these burials, and a word of excuse is here in place. For he is well aware of the reproach that might be made him in this respect; his justification is that funerals were taking place throughout this period and in a way he was compelled, as indeed everybody was compelled, to give heed to them. In any case it should not be assumed that he has a morbid taste for such ceremonies; quite the contrary, he much prefers the society of the living and – to give a concrete illustration – sea-bathing. But the bathing beaches were out of bounds and the company of the living ran a risk, increasing as the days went by, of being perforce converted into the company of the dead. That was, indeed, self-evident. True, one could always refuse to face this disagreeable fact, shut one's eyes to it or thrust it out of mind, but there is a terrible cogency in the self-evident; ultimately it breaks down all defences. How, for instance, continue to ignore the funerals on the day when somebody you loved needed one?

Actually the most striking feature of our funerals was their speed. Formalities had been whittled down, and, generally speaking, all elaborate ceremonial suppressed. The plague victim died away from his family and the customary vigil beside the dead body was forbidden, with the result that a person dying in the evening spent the night alone, and those who died in the daytime were promptly buried. Needless to say the family was notified, but, in most cases, since the deceased had lived with them, its members were in quarantine and thus immobilized. When, however, the deceased had not lived with his family, they were asked to attend at a fixed time; after, that is to say, the body had been washed and put in the coffin, and when the journey to the cemetery was about to begin.

Let us suppose that these formalities were taking place at the auxiliary hospital of which Dr Rieux was in charge. This converted school had an exit at the back of the main building. A large storeroom giving on the passage contained the coffins. On arrival, the family found a coffin already nailed up in the passage. Then came the most important part of the business, the signing of official forms by the head of the family. Next the coffin was loaded on to a motor-vehicle: a real hearse or a large converted ambulance. The mourners stepped into one of the few taxis still allowed to ply and the vehicles drove hell-for-leather to the cemetery by a route avoiding the centre of the town. There was a halt at the Gate, where police-officers applied a rubber stamp to the official exit permit, without which it was impossible for our citizens to have what they called a last resting-place. The policeman stood back and the cars drew up near a plot of ground where a number of graves stood open, waiting for inmates. A priest came to meet the mourners, since church services at funerals were now prohibited. To an accompaniment of prayers the coffin was dragged from the hearse, roped up and carried to the graveside; the ropes were slipped and it came heavily to rest at the bottom of the grave. No sooner had the priest begun to sprinkle holy water than the first sod rebounded from the lid. The ambulance had already left and was being sprayed with disinfectant, and while spadefuls of clay thudded more and more dully on the rising layer of earth, the family were bundling into the taxi. A quarter of an hour later they were back at home.

The whole process was put through with the maximum of speed and minimum of risk. It cannot be denied that, anyhow in the early days, the natural feelings of the family were somewhat outraged by these lightning funerals. But obviously in time of plague such sentiments can't be taken into account, and all was sacrificed to efficiency. And though, to start with, the morale of the population was shaken by this summary procedure – for the desire to have a 'proper funeral' is more widespread than is generally believed – as time went on, fortunately enough, the food problem became more urgent, and the thoughts of our townsfolk were diverted to more instant needs. So much energy was expended on filling up forms, hunting round for supplies and queueing up, that people had no time to think of the manner in which others were dying around them and they themselves would die one day. Thus the growing complications of our everyday life, which might have been an affliction, proved to be a blessing in disguise. Indeed, had not the epidemic, as already mentioned, spread its ravages, all would have been for the best.

For then coffins became scarcer; also there was a shortage of winding-sheets, and of space in the cemetery. Something had to be done about this, and one obvious step, justified by its practical convenience, was to combine funerals and, when necessary, multiply the trips between the hospital and the burial-place. At one moment the stock of coffins in Rieux's hospital was reduced to five. Once filled, all five were loaded together in the ambulance. At the cemetery they were emptied out and the iron-grey corpses put on stretchers and deposited in a shed reserved for that purpose, to wait their turn. Meanwhile, the empty coffins, after being sprayed with antiseptic fluid, were rushed back to the hospital, and the process was repeated as often as necessary. This system worked excellently and won the approval of the Prefect. He even told Rieux that it was really a great improvement on the death-carts driven by negroes, of which one reads in accounts of former visitations of this sort.

'Yes,' Rieux said. 'And, though the burials are much the same, we keep careful records of them. That, you will agree, is Progress.'

Successful, however, as the system proved itself in practice, there was something so distasteful in the last rites as now performed, that the Prefect felt constrained to forbid relations of the deceased being present at the actual interment. They were allowed to come only as far as the cemetery gates – and even that was not authorized officially. For things had somewhat changed as regards the last stage of the ceremony. In a patch of open ground dotted with lentisk-trees at the far end of the cemetery, two big pits had been dug. One was reserved for the men, the other for the women. Thus, in this respect, the authorities still gave thought to propriety and it was only later that, by the force of things, this last remnant of decorum went by the board, and men and women were flung into the death-pits indiscriminately. Happily this ultimate indignity synchronized with the plague's last ravages.

In the period we are now concerned with, the separation of the sexes was still in force and the authorities set great store by it. At the bottom of each pit a deep layer of quicklime steamed and seethed. On the lips of the pit a low ridge of quicklime threw up bubbles that burst in the air above it. When the ambulance had done its trips, the stretchers were carried to the pits in Indian file. The naked, somewhat contorted bodies were slid off into the pit almost side by side, then covered with a layer of quicklime and another of earth, the latter only a few inches deep, so as to leave space for subsequent consignments. On the following day the next of kin were asked to sign in the Register of Burials – which showed the distinction that can be made between men and, for example, dogs; men's deaths are checked and entered up.

Obviously all these activities called for a considerable staff, and Rieux was often on the brink of a shortage. Many of the gravediggers, stretcher-bearers and the like, public servants to begin with, and later volunteers, died of plague. However stringent the precautions, sooner or later contagion did its work. Still, when all is said and done, the really amazing thing is that, so long as the epidemic lasted, there was never any lack of men for these duties. The critical moment came just before the outbreak touched high-water mark, and the doctor had good reason for feeling anxious. There was then a real shortage of man-power both for the higher posts and for the rough work, as Rieux called it. But, paradoxically enough, once the whole town was in the grip of the disease, its very prevalence tended to make things easier, since the disorganization of the town's economic life threw a great number of persons out of work. Few of the workers thus made available were qualified for administrative posts, but the recruiting of men for the 'rough work' became much easier. From now on, indeed, poverty showed itself a stronger stimulus than fear, especially as, owing to its risks, such work was highly paid. The sanitary authorities always had a waiting-list of applicants for work; whenever there was a vacancy the men at the top of the list were notified and, unless they too had laid off work for good, they never failed to appear when summoned. Thus the Prefect, who had always been reluctant to employ the prisoners in the jail, whether short-term men or lifers, was able to avoid recourse to this distasteful measure. As long, he said, as there were unemployed, we could afford to wait.

Thus until the end of August our fellow-citizens could be conveyed to their last resting-place, if not under very decorous conditions, at least in a manner orderly enough for the authorities to feel that they were doing their duty by the dead and the bereaved. However, we may here anticipate a little, and describe the pass to which we came in the final phase. From August onwards the plague mortality was and continued such as to far exceed the capacity of our small cemetery. Such expedients as knocking down walls and letting the dead encroach on neighbouring land proved inadequate; some new method had to be evolved without delay. The first step taken was to bury the dead by night, which obviously permitted a more summary procedure. The bodies were piled into ambulances in larger and larger numbers. And the few belated wayfarers who, in defiance of the regulations, were abroad in the outlying districts after curfew hour, or whose duties took them there, often saw the long white ambulances hurtling past, making the nightbound streets reverberate with the dull clangour of their bells. The corpses were tipped pell-mell into the pits and had hardly settled into place when spadefuls of quicklime began to sear their faces and the earth covered them indistinctively, in holes dug steadily deeper as time went on.

Shortly afterwards, however, it became necessary to find new space and to strike out in a new direction. By a special urgency measure the denizens of grants in perpetuity were evicted from their graves and the exhumed remains dispatched to the crematorium. And soon the plague-victims likewise had to go to a fiery end. This meant that the old crematorium east of the town, outside the gates, had to be utilized. Accordingly the East Gate sentry-post was moved farther out. Then a municipal employee had an idea which greatly helped the harassed authorities; he advised them to employ the tramline running along the coastal road, which was now unused. So the interiors of tramcars and trailers were adapted to this new purpose, and a branch-line was laid down to the crematorium, which thus became a terminus.

During all the late summer and throughout the autumn there could daily be seen moving along the road skirting the cliffs above the sea, a strange procession of passengerless trams swaying against the skyline. The residents in this area soon learnt what was going on. And, though the cliffs were patrolled day and night, little groups of people contrived to thread their way unseen between the rocks and would toss flowers into the open trailers as the trams went by. And in the warm darkness of the summer nights the cars could be heard clanking on their way, laden with flowers and corpses.

During the first few days an oily, foul-smelling cloud of smoke hung low upon the eastern districts of the town. These effluvia, all the doctors agreed, though unpleasant, were not in the least harmful. However, the residents of this part of the town threatened to migrate in a body, convinced that germs were raining down on them from the sky, with the result that an elaborate apparatus for diverting the smoke had to be installed, to appease them. Thereafter, only when a strong wind was blowing did a faint, sickly odour coming from the east remind them that they were living under a new order and the plague fires took their nightly toll.

Such were the consequences of the epidemic at its culminating point. Happily it grew no worse, for otherwise, it may well be believed, the resourcefulness of our administration, the competence of our officials, not to mention the burning capacity of our crematorium, would have proved unequal to their tasks. Rieux knew that desperate solutions had been mooted, such as throwing the corpses into the sea, and a picture had risen before him of hideous jetsam lolling in the shallows under the cliffs. He knew, too, that if there was another rise in the death-rate, no organization, however efficient, could stand up to it; that men would die in heaps and corpses rot in the street, whatever the authorities might do, and the town would see, in public squares, the dying embrace the living in the frenzies of an all-too-comprehensible hatred or some crazy hope.

Such were the sights and apprehensions that kept alive in our townsfolk their feeling of exile and separation. In this connexion the narrator is well aware how regrettable is his inability to record at this point something of a really spectacular order; some heroic feat, or memorable deed like those that thrill us in the chronicles of the past. The truth is that nothing is less sensational than pestilence and by reason of their very duration great misfortunes are monotonous. In the memories of those who lived through them, the grim days of plague do not stand out like lived flames, ravenous and inextinguishable, beaconing a troubled sky, but rather like the slow, deliberate progress of some monstrous thing crushing out all upon its path.

No, the real plague had nothing in common with the grandiose imaginings that had haunted Rieux's mind at its outbreak. It was, above all, a shrewd, unflagging adversary; a skilled organizer, doing his work thoroughly and well. That, it may be said in passing, is why, so as not to play false to the facts, and, still more, so as not to play false to himself, the narrator has aimed at objectivity. He has made hardly any changes for the sake of artistic effect, except those elementary adjustments needed to present his narrative in a more or less coherent form. And in deference to this scruple he is constrained to admit that, though the chief source of distress, the deepest as well as the most widespread, was separation – and it is his duty to say more about it, as it existed in the later stages of the plague – it cannot be denied that even this distress was coming to lose something of its poignancy.

Was it that our fellow-citizens, even those who had felt the parting from their loved ones most keenly, were getting used to doing without them? To assume this would fall somewhat short of the truth. It would be more correct to say that they were wasting away emotionally as well as physically. At the beginning of the plague they had a vivid recollection of the absent ones, and bitterly felt their loss. But, though they could clearly recall the face, the smile and voice of the beloved, and this or that occasion when (as they now saw in retrospect) they had been supremely happy, they had trouble in picturing what he or she might be doing at the moment when they conjured up these memories, in a setting so hopelessly remote. In short, at these moments, memory played its part, but their imagination failed them. During the second phase of the plague, their memory failed them, too. Not that they had forgotten the face itself, but – what came to the same thing – it had lost fleshly substance, and they no longer saw it in memory's mirror.

Thus, while during the first weeks they were apt to complain that only shadows remained to them of what their love had been and meant, they now came to learn that even shadows can waste away, losing the faint hues of life that memory may give. And by the end of their long sundering they had also lost the power of imagining the intimacy that once was theirs, or understanding what it can be to live with someone whose life is wrapped up in yours.

In this respect they had adapted themselves to the very condition of the plague, all the more potent for its mediocrity. None of us was capable any longer of an exalted emotion; all had trite, monotonous feelings. 'It's high time it stopped,' people would say, because in time of calamity the obvious thing is to desire its end, and, in fact, they wanted it to end. But, when making such remarks, we felt none of the passionate yearning or fierce resentment of the early phase; we merely voiced one of the few clear ideas that lingered in the twilight of our minds. The furious revolt of the first weeks had given place to a vast despondency, not to be taken for resignation, though it was none the less a sort of passive and provisional acquiescence.

Our fellow-citizens had fallen into line, adapted themselves, as people say, to the situation, because there was no way of doing otherwise. Naturally they retained the attitudes of sadness and suffering, but they had ceased to feel their sting. Indeed to some, Dr Rieux amongst them, this precisely was the most disheartening thing; that the habit of despair is worse than despair itself. Hitherto those who were parted had not been utterly unhappy, there was always a gleam of hope in the night of their distress, but that gleam had now died out. You could see them at street-corners, in cafés or friends' houses, listless, indifferent, and looking so bored that, because of them, the whole town seemed like a railway waiting-room. Those who had jobs went about them at the exact tempo of the plague, with dreary perseverance. Everyone was modest. For the first time exiles from those they loved had no reluctance to talking freely about them, using the same words as everybody else, and regarding their deprivation from the same angle as that from which they viewed the latest statistics of the epidemic. This change was striking since, until now, they had jealously withheld their personal grief from the common stock of suffering; now they accepted its inclusion. Without memories, without hope, they lived for the moment only. Indeed the Here and Now had come to mean everything to them. For there is no denying that the plague had gradually killed off in all of us the faculty not of love only but even of friendship. Naturally enough, since love asks something of the future, and nothing was left us but a series of present moments.

However, this account of our predicament gives only the broad lines. Thus, while it is true that all who were parted came ultimately to this state, we must add that all did not attain it simultaneously; moreover, once this utter apathy had fallen on them, there were still flashes of lucidity, broken lights of memory that rekindled in the exiles a younger, keener sensibility. This happened when, for instance, they fell to making plans implying that the plague had ended. Or when, quite unexpectedly, by some kindly chance, they felt a twinge of jealousy, none the less acute for its objectlessness. Others, again, had sudden accesses of energy and shook off their languor on certain days of the week — for obvious reasons, on Sundays and Saturday afternoons, because these had been devoted to certain ritual pleasures in the days when the loved ones were still accessible. Sometimes the mood of melancholy that descended on them with the nightfall acted as a sort of warning, not always fulfilled, however, that old memories were floating up to the surface. That evening hour, which for believers is the time to look into their consciences, is hardest of all hours on the prisoner or exile who has nothing to look into but the void. For a moment it held them in suspense; then they sank back into their lethargy, the prison door had closed on them once again.

Obviously all this meant giving up what was most personal in their lives. Whereas in the early days of the plague they had been struck by the host of small details that, while meaning absolutely nothing to others, meant so much to them, personally, and thus had realized, perhaps for the first time, the uniqueness of each man's life; now, on the other hand, they took an interest only in what interested everyone else, they had only general ideas, and even their tenderest affections now seemed abstract, items of the common stock. So completely were they dominated by the plague that sometimes the one thing they aspired to was the long sleep it brought, and they caught themselves thinking, 'A good thing if I get plague, and have done with it!' But, really, they were asleep already; this whole period was, for them, no more than a long night's slumber. The town was peopled with sleep-walkers, whose trance was broken only on the rare occasions when at night their wounds, to all appearance closed, suddenly reopened. Then, waking with a start, they would run their fingers over the wounds with a sort of absent-minded curiosity, twisting their lips, and in a flash their grief blazed up again, and abruptly there rose before them the mournful visage of their love. In the morning they harked back to normal conditions, in other words, the plague.

What impression, it may be asked, did these exiles of the plague make on the observer? The answer is simple; they made none. Or, to put it differently, they looked like everybody else; nondescript. They shared in the torpor of the town and in its puerile agitations. They lost every trace of a critical spirit, while gaining an air of sang-froid. You could see, for instance, even the most intelligent amongst them, making a show like all the rest of studying the newspapers or listening to the wireless, in the hope apparently of finding some reason to believe the plague would shortly end. They seemed to derive fantastic hopes or equally exaggerated fears from reading the lines that some journalist had scribbled at random, yawning with boredom at his desk. Meanwhile they drank their beer, nursed their sick, idled or doped themselves with work, filed documents in offices, or played the gramophone at home, without betraying any difference from the rest of us. In other words, they had ceased to choose for themselves; plague had levelled out discrimination. This could be seen by the way nobody troubled about the quality of the clothes or food he bought. Everything was taken as it came.

And, finally, it is worth noting that those who were parted ceased to enjoy the curious privilege which had been theirs at the outset. They had lost love's egoism and the benefit they derived from it. Now, at least, the position was clear; this calamity was everybody's business. What with the gunshots echoing at the gates, the punctual thuds of rubber stamps marking the rhythm of lives and deaths, the files and fires, the panics and formalities, all alike were pledged to an ugly but recorded death, and, amidst noxious fumes and the muted clang of ambulances, all of us ate the same sour bread of exile, unconsciously waiting for the same reunion, the same miracle of peace regained. No doubt, our love persisted, but in practice it served nothing; it was an inert mass within us, sterile as crime or a life sentence. It had declined on a patience that led nowhere, a dogged expectation. Viewed from this angle, the attitude of some of our fellow-citizens resembled that of the long queues one saw outside the food-shops. There was the same resignation, the same long-sufferance, inexhaustible and without illusions. The only difference was that the mental state of the food-seekers would need to be raised to a vastly higher power to make it comparable with the gnawing pain of separation: since this latter came from a hunger fierce to the point of insatiability.

In any case, if the reader would have a correct idea of the mood of these exiles, we must conjure up once more those dreary evenings, sifting down through a haze of dust and golden light upon the treeless streets filled with teeming crowds of men and women. For, characteristically, the sound that rose towards the terraces still bathed in the last glow of daylight, now that the noises of vehicles and motors – the sole voice of cities in ordinary times – had ceased, was but one vast rumour of low voices and incessant footfalls, the drumming of innumerable soles timed to the eerie whistling of the plague in the sultry air above, the sound of a huge concourse of people marking time, a never-ending, stifling drone that, gradually swelling, filled the town from end to end, and evening after evening gave its truest, mournfullest expression to the blind endurance which had ousted love from all our hearts.

PART FOUR

I

THROUGHOUT SEPTEMBER AND October the town lay prostrate, at the mercy of the plague, there was nothing to do but to 'mark time', and some hundreds of thousands of men and women went on doing this, through weeks that seemed interminable. Mist, heat and rain rang their changes in our streets. From the south came silent coveys of starlings and thrushes, flying very high, but always giving the town a wide berth, as though the strange implement of the plague described by Paneloux, the giant flail whirling and shrilling over the housetops, warned them off us. At the beginning of October torrents of rain swept the streets clean. And all the time nothing more important befell us than that multitudinous marking time.

It was now that Rieux and his friends came to realize how exhausted they were. Indeed, the workers in the sanitary squads had given up trying to cope with their fatigue. Rieux noticed the change coming over his associates, and himself as well, and it took the form of a strange indifference to everything. Men, for instance, who hitherto had shown a keen interest in every scrap of news concerning the plague now displayed none at all. Rambert, who had been temporarily put in charge of a quarantine station – his hotel had been taken over for this purpose – could state at any moment the exact number of persons under his observation, and every detail of the procedure he had laid down for the prompt evacuation of those who suddenly developed symptoms of the disease was firmly fixed in his mind. The same was true of the statistics of the effects of anti-plague inoculations on the persons in his quarantine station. Nevertheless, he could not have told you the week's total of plague deaths, and he could not even have said if the figure was rising or falling. And meanwhile, in spite of everything, he had not lost hope of being able to 'make his getaway' from one day to another.

As for the others, working themselves almost to a standstill throughout the day and far into the night, they never bothered to read a newspaper or listen to the wireless. When told of some unlooked-for recovery, they made a show of interest but actually received the news with the stolid indifference which we may imagine the fighting man in a great war to feel, who, worn out by the incessant strain and mindful only of the duties daily assigned to him, has ceased even to hope for the decisive battle or the bugle-call of armistice.

Though he still worked out methodically the figures relating to the plague, Grand would certainly have been quite unable to say to what they pointed. Unlike Rieux, Rambert and Tarrou, who obviously had great powers of endurance, he had never had good health. And now, in addition to his duties in the Municipal Office, he had his night work and his secretarial post under Rieux. One could see that the strain was telling on him and, if he managed to keep going, it was thanks to two or three fixed ideas, one of which was to take, the moment the plague ended, a complete holiday of a week at least which he would devote 'hats off' to his work in progress. He was also becoming subject to excesses of sentimentality and at such times would unburden himself to Rieux, about Jeanne. Where was she now? he wondered; did her thoughts sometimes turn to him when she read the papers? It was Grand to whom one day Rieux caught himself talking – much to his own surprise – about his wife, and in the most commonplace terms – something he had never done as yet to anyone.

Doubtful how far he could trust his wife's telegrams – their tone was always reassuring – he had decided to wire the House

Physician of the sanatorium. The reply informed him that her condition had worsened, but everything was being done to arrest further progress of the disease. He had kept the news to himself so far, and could only put it down to his nervous exhaustion that he passed it on to Grand. After talking to the doctor about Jeanne, Grand had put some questions about Mme Rieux and, on hearing Rieux's reply, said, 'You know, it's wonderful, the cures they bring off nowadays.' Rieux agreed, merely adding that the long separation was beginning to tell on him, and, what was more, he might have helped his wife to make a good recovery; whereas, as things were, she must be feeling terribly lonely. After which he fell silent, and gave only evasive answers to Grand's further questions.

The others were in much the same state. Tarrou held his own better, but the entries in his diary show that while his curiosity had kept its depth it had lost its diversity. Indeed, throughout this period, the only person, apparently, who really interested him was Cottard. In the evening, at Rieux's flat, where he had come to live now that the hotel was requisitioned as a quarantine centre, he paid little or no attention to Grand and the doctor when they read over the day's statistics. At the earliest opportunity, he switched the conversation over to his pet subject, small details of the daily life at Oran.

More perhaps than any of them, Dr Castel showed signs of wear and tear. On the day when he came to tell Rieux that the anti-plague serum was ready, and they decided to try it for the first time on M. Othon's small son, whose case seemed all but hopeless, Rieux suddenly noticed, while he was announcing the latest statistics, that Castel was slumped in his chair, sound asleep. The difference in his old friend's face shocked him. The smile of benevolent irony that always played on it had seemed to endow it with perpetual youth; now, abruptly left out of control, with a trickle of saliva between the slightly parted lips, it betrayed its age and the wastage of the years. And, seeing this, Rieux felt a lump come to his throat.

It was by such lapses that Rieux could gauge his exhaustion. His sensibility was getting out of hand. Kept under all the time, it had grown hard and brittle and seemed to snap completely now and then, leaving him the prey of his emotions. No resource was left him but to tighten the stranglehold on his feelings and harden his heart protectively. For he knew this was the only way of carrying on. In any case, he had few illusions left, and fatigue was robbing him of even these remaining few. He knew that, over a period whose end he could not glimpse, his task was no longer to cure but to diagnose. To detect, to see, to describe, to register, and then condemn – that was his present function. Sometimes a woman would clutch his sleeve, crying shrilly, 'Doctor, you'll save him, won't you?' But he wasn't there for saving life; he was there to order a sick man's evacuation. How futile was the hatred he saw on faces then! 'You haven't a heart!' a woman told him on one occasion. She was wrong; he had one. It saw him through his twenty-hour day, when he hourly watched men dying who were meant to live. It enabled him to start anew each morning. He had just enough heart for that, as things were now. How could that heart have sufficed for saving life?

No, it wasn't medical aid that he dispensed in those crowded days: only information. Obviously that could hardly be reckoned a man's job. Yet, when all was said and done, who, in that terror-stricken, decimated populace, had scope for any activity worthy of his manhood? Indeed, for Rieux his exhaustion was a blessing in disguise. Had he been less tired, his senses more alert, that all-pervading odour of death might have made him sentimental. But, when a man has had only four hours' sleep, he isn't sentimental. He sees things as they are: that is to say, he sees them in the garish light of justice; hideous, witless justice. And those others, the men and women under sentence of death, shared his bleak enlightenment. Before the plague, he was welcomed as a saviour. He was going to make them right with a couple of pills or an injection, and people took him by the arm on his way to the sickroom. Flattering, but dangerous. Now, on the contrary, he came accompanied by soldiers, and they had to hammer on the door with rifle-butts before the family would open it. They'd have liked to drag him, drag the whole human race, with them to the grave. Yes, it was quite true that men can't do without their fellow-men; that he was as helpless as these unhappy people and he, too, deserved the same faint thrill of pity that he allowed himself once he had left them.

Such, anyhow, were the thoughts that in those endless-seeming weeks ran in the doctor's mind, along with thoughts about his severance from his wife. And such, too, were his friends' thoughts, judging by the look he saw on their faces. But the most dangerous effect of the exhaustion steadily gaining on all engaged in the fight against the epidemic did not consist in their relative indifference to outside events and the feelings of others, but in the slackness and supineness which they allowed to invade their personal lives. They developed a tendency to shirk every movement that didn't seem absolutely necessary, or called for efforts that seemed too great to be worth while. Thus these men were led to break, oftener and oftener, the rules of hygiene they themselves had instituted, to omit some of the numerous disinfections they should have practised, and sometimes to visit the homes of people suffering from pneumonic plague without taking steps to safeguard themselves against infection, because they had been notified only at the last moment and could not be bothered with returning to a sanitary service station, sometimes a considerable distance away, to have the necessary instillations. There lay the real danger; for the energy they devoted to fighting the disease made them all the more liable to it. In short, they were gambling on their luck, and luck is not to be coerced.

There was, however, one man in the town who seemed neither exhausted nor discouraged; indeed, the living image of contentment. It was Cottard. Though maintaining contact with Rieux and Rambert, he still kept rather aloof, whereas he deliberately cultivated Tarrou, seeing him as often as Tarrou's scanty leisure permitted. He had two reasons for this; one that Tarrou knew all about his case, and the other that he always gave him a cordial welcome and made him feel at ease. That was one of the remarkable things about Tarrou; no matter how much work he had put in, he was always a ready listener and an agreeable companion. Even when, some evenings, he seemed completely worn out, the next day brought him a new lease of energy. 'Old Tarrou's a fellow one can talk to,' Cottard once told Rambert, 'because he's really human, if you see what I mean. He always understands.'

This may explain why the entries in Tarrou's diary of this period tend to converge on Cottard's personality. It is obvious that Tarrou was attempting to give a full-length picture of the man, and noted all his reactions and reflections, whether as conveyed to him by Cottard or interpreted by himself. Under the heading 'Cottard and his Relations with the Plague', we find a series of notes covering several pages and, in the narrator's opinion, these are well worth summarizing here.

One of the first entries gives Tarrou's general impression of Cottard at this time. 'He is blossoming out. Expanding in geniality and good humour.' For Cottard was anything but upset by the turn events were taking. Sometimes, in Tarrou's company, he voiced his true feelings in remarks of this order: 'Getting worse every day, isn't it? Well, anyhow, everyone's in the same boat.'

'Obviously,' Tarrou comments, 'he's in the same peril of death as everyone else, but that's just the point; he's in it *with the others*. And then I'm pretty sure he doesn't seriously think he runs much personal risk. He has got the idea into his head, apparently – and perhaps it's not so far-fetched as it seems – that a man suffering from a dangerous ailment or grave anxiety is allergic to other ailments and anxieties. "Have you noticed," he asked me, "that no one ever runs two diseases at once? Let's suppose you have an incurable disease like cancer or a galloping consumption, well, you'll never get plague or typhus; it's a physical impossibility. In fact, one might go further; have you ever heard of a man with cancer being killed in a motor smash?" This theory, for what it's worth, keeps Cottard cheerful. The thing he'd most detest is being cut off from others; he'd rather be one of a beleaguered crowd than a prisoner alone. The plague has put an effective stop to police inquiries, sleuthings, warrants of arrest, and so forth. Come to that, we have no police nowadays; no crimes past or present, no more criminals – only condemned men hoping for the most capricious of pardons; and amongst these are the police themselves.'

Thus Cottard (if we may trust Tarrou's diagnosis) had good grounds for viewing the symptoms of mental confusion and distress in those around him with an understanding and an indulgent satisfaction which might have found expression in the remark, 'Prate away, my friends – but I had it first!'

'When I suggested to him,' Tarrou continues, 'that the surest way of not being cut off from others was having a clean conscience, he frowned. "If that is so, everyone's always cut off from everyone else." And a moment later he added: "Say what you like, Tarrou, but let me tell you this: the one way of making people hang together is to give 'em a spell of plague. You've only got to look around you." Of course I see his point, and I understand how congenial our present mode of life must be to him. How could he fail to recognize at every turn reactions that were his; the efforts everyone makes to "keep on the right side" of other people; the obligingness sometimes shown in helping someone who has lost his way, and the ill humour shown at other times; the way people flock to the luxury restaurants, their pleasure at being there and their reluctance to leave; the crowds queueing up daily at the picture-houses, filling theatres and music-halls and even dance-halls, and flooding boisterously out into the squares and avenues; the shrinking from every contact and, notwith-standing, the craving for human warmth that urges people to each other, body to body, sex to sex? Cottard has been through all that obviously − with one exception; we may rule out women in his case. With that mug of his . . . ! And I should say that when tempted to visit a brothel he refrains; it might give him a bad name and be held up against him one day.

'In short, this epidemic has done him proud. Of a lonely man who hated loneliness it has made an accomplice. Yes, "accomplice" is the word that fits, and doesn't he relish his complicity! He is happily at one with all around him, with their superstitions, their groundless panics, the susceptibilities of people whose nerves are always on the stretch; with their fixed idea of talking the least possible about plague and, never-theless, talking of it all the time; with their abject terror at the slightest headache, now they know headache to be an early symptom of the disease; and, lastly, with their frayed, irritable sensibility that takes offence at trifling oversights and brings tears to their eyes over the loss of a trouser-button.'

Tarrou often went out with Cottard in the evening, and he describes how they would plunge together into the dark crowds filling the streets at nightfall; how they mingled, shoul-der to shoulder, in the black-and-white moving mass lit here and there by the fitful gleam of a street-lamp; and how they let themselves be swept along with the human herd towards resorts of pleasure whose companionable warmth seemed a safeguard from the plague's cold breath. What Cottard had some months previously been looking for in public places, luxury and the lavish life, the frenzied orgies he had dreamt of without being able to procure them − these were now the quest of a whole populace. Though prices soared inevitably, never had so much money been squandered, and whilst bare necessities were often lacking, never had so much been spent on superfluities. All the recreations of leisure, due though it now was to unemployment, multiplied a hundredfold.

Sometimes Tarrou and Cottard would follow for some minutes one of those amorous couples who in the past would have tried to hide the passion drawing them to each other, but now, pressed closely to each other's side, paraded the streets amongst the crowd, with the trance-like self-absorption of great lovers, oblivious of the people round them. Cottard watched them gloatingly. 'Good work, my dears!' he'd exclaim. 'Go to it!' Even his voice had changed, grown louder; as Tarrou wrote, he was 'blossoming out' in the congenial atmosphere of mass excitement, fantastically large tips clinking on café-tables, love-affairs shaping under his eyes.

However, Tarrou seemed to detect little if any spitefulness in Cottard's attitude. His 'I've been through the mill myself' had more pity than triumph in it. 'I suspect,' Tarrou wrote, 'that he's getting quite fond of these people shut up under their little patch of sky within their city walls. For instance, he'd like to explain to them, if he had a chance, that it isn't so terrible as all that. "You hear them saying," he told me, " 'After the plague I'll do this or that.' ... They're eating their hearts out instead of staying put. And they don't even realize their privileges. Take my case: could I say 'After my arrest I'll do this or that...?' Arrest's a beginning, not an end. Whereas plague... Do you know what I think? They're fretting simply because they won't let themselves go. And I know what I'm talking about."

'Yes, he knows what he's talking about,' Tarrou added. 'He has an insight into the anomalies in the lives of the people here who, though they have an instinctive craving for human contacts, can't bring themselves to yield to it, because of the mistrust that keeps them apart. For it's common knowledge that you can't trust your neighbour; he may pass the disease to you without your knowing it, and take advantage of a moment of inadvertence on your part to infect you. When one has spent one's days, as Cottard has, seeing a possible police-spy in everyone, even in persons he feels drawn to, it's easy to understand this reaction. One can have fellow-feelings towards people who are haunted by the idea that when they least expect it plague may lay its cold hand on their shoulders, and is, perhaps, about to do so at the very moment when one is congratulating oneself on being safe and sound. So far as this is possible, he is at ease under a reign of terror. But I suspect that, just because he has been through it before them, he can't wholly share with them the agony of this feeling of uncertainty that never leaves them. It comes to this. Like all of us who have not yet died of plague he fully realizes that his freedom and his life may be snatched from him at any moment. But since he, personally, has learnt what it is to live in a state of constant fear, he finds it normal that others should come to know this state. Or, perhaps, it should be put like this: fear seems to him more bearable under these conditions than it was when he had to bear its burden alone. In this respect he's wrong, and this makes him harder to understand than other people. Still, after all, that's why he is worth a greater effort to understand.'

Tarrou's notes end with a story illustrating the curious state of mind arrived at no less by Cottard than by other dwellers in the plague-stricken town. The story re-creates as nearly as may be the curiously feverish atmosphere of this period, and that is why the narrator attaches importance to it.

One evening Cottard and Tarrou went to the Municipal Theatre and Opera House, where Gluck's *Orpheus* was being given. Cottard had invited Tarrou. A touring operatic company had come to Oran in the spring for a short series of performances of this opera. Marooned there by the outbreak of plague and finding themselves in difficulties, the company had come to an agreement with the management of the Opera House, under which they were to give one performance a week until further notice. Thus for several months our theatre had been resounding every Friday evening with the melodious laments of Orpheus, and Eurydice's vain appeals. None the less, the opera continued in high favour and played regularly to full houses. From their seats, the most expensive, Cottard and Tarrou could look down at the stalls filled to capacity with the cream of Oran society. It was interesting to see how careful they were, as they went to their places, to make an elegant entrance. While the orchestra was discreetly tuning up, men in evening dress could be seen moving from one row to another, bowing gracefully to friends, under the flood of light bathing the proscenium. In the soft hum of well-mannered conversation they regained the confidence denied them when they walked the dark streets of the town; evening dress was a sure charm against plague.

Throughout the first act Orpheus lamented suavely his lost Eurydice, with women in Grecian tunics singing melodious comments on his plight, and love was hymned in alternating arias. The audience showed their appreciation in discreet applause. Only a few people noticed that in his song of the Second Act Orpheus introduced some tremolos not in the score, and voiced an almost exaggerated emotion when begging the Lord of the Shades to be moved by his tears. Some rather jerky movements he indulged in gave our connoisseurs of stagecraft an impression of clever, if slightly overdone, effects, intended to bring out the emotion of the words he sang.

Not until the big duet between Orpheus and Eurydice in the Third Act — at the precise moment when Eurydice was being torn from her lover — did a flutter of surprise run through the house. And, as though the singer had been waiting for this cue, or, more likely, because the faint sounds that came to him from stalls and pit confirmed what he was feeling, he chose this moment to stagger grotesquely to the footlights, his arms and legs splayed out under his antique robe, and fall down in the middle of the property sheepfold, always anachronistic, but now in the eyes of the spectators, significantly, appallingly so. For at the same moment the orchestra stopped playing, the audience rose and began to leave the auditorium, slowly and

silently at first, like worshippers leaving church when the
service ends, or a death-chamber after a farewell visit to the
dead, women lifting their skirts and moving with bowed
heads, men steering the ladies by the elbow to prevent their
brushing against the tip-up seats at the ends of the rows. But
gradually their movements quickened, whispers rose to exclamations, and finally the crowd stampeded towards the exits,
wedged together in the bottlenecks, and poured out into the
street in a confused mass, with shrill cries of dismay.

Cottard and Tarrou, who had merely risen from their seats,
gazed down at what was a dramatic picture of their life in those
days: plague on the stage in the guise of a disarticulated
mummer and, in the stalls, the toys of luxury, so futile now,
forgotten fans and lace shawls derelict on the red plush seats.

II

DURING THE FIRST part of September Rambert had worked
conscientiously at Rieux's side. He had merely asked for a few
hours' leave on the day he was due to meet Gonzales and the
two youngsters outside the Boys' School.

Gonzales kept the appointment and, while he and the
journalist were talking, they saw the two boys coming towards
them, laughing. They said they'd had no luck last time, but that
was only to be expected. Anyhow, it wasn't their turn for
sentry-go this week. Rambert must have patience till next
week; then they'd have another shot at it. Rambert observed
that 'patience' certainly was needed in this business. Gonzales
suggested they should all meet again on the following Monday
and, this time, Rambert had better move in to stay with Marcel
and Louis. 'We'll make a date, you and I. If I don't turn up, go
straight to their place. I'll give you the address.' But Marcel or
Louis told him that the safest thing was to take his 'pal' there
right away, then he'd be sure of finding it. If he wasn't too
particular, there was enough grub for the four of them. That

way he'd 'get the hang of things, like'. Gonzales agreed it was a good idea, and the four of them set off towards the harbour.

Marcel and Louis lived on the outskirts of the dockyard, near the Gate giving on the cliff road. It was a small Spanish house with gaily painted shutters and bare, dark rooms. The boys' mother, a wrinkled old Spanish woman with a smiling face, produced a dish of which the chief ingredient was rice. Gonzales showed surprise, as rice had been unprocurable for some time in the town. 'We fix it up at the Gate,' Marcel explained. Rambert ate and drank heartily, and Gonzales informed him he was 'a damned good sort'. Actually the journalist was thinking solely of the coming week.

It turned out that he had a fortnight to wait, as the periods of sentry-duty were extended to two weeks, to reduce the number of shifts. During that fortnight Rambert worked indefatigably, getting every ounce out of himself, with his eyes shut, as it were, from dawn till night. He went to bed very late and always slept like a log. This abrupt transition from a life of idleness to one of constant work had left him almost void of thoughts or energy. He talked little about his impending escape. Only one incident is worth noting; after a week he confessed to the doctor that for the first time he'd got really drunk. It was the evening before; on leaving the bar he had an impression that his groin was swollen and he had pains in his armpits when he moved his arms. I'm for it! he thought. And his only reaction – an absurd one, as he frankly admitted to Rieux – had been to start running to the Upper Town and when he reached a small square, from which if not the sea, a fairly big patch of open sky could be seen, to call to his wife with a great cry, over the walls of the town. On returning home and failing to discover any symptoms of plague on his body, he had felt far from proud of having given way like that. Rieux, however, said he could well understand one's being moved to act thus. 'Or, anyhow, one may easily feel inclined that way.'

'Monsieur Othon was talking to me about you this morning,' Rieux suddenly remarked, when Rambert was bidding him good night. 'He asked me if I knew you, and I told him I did. Then he said, "If he's a friend of yours, advise him not to associate with smugglers. It's bound to attract attention."'

'Meaning – what?'

'It means you'd better hurry up.'

'Thanks.' Rambert shook the doctor's hand.

In the doorway he suddenly swung round. Rieux noticed that, for the first time since the outbreak of plague, he was smiling.

'But why don't you stop my going? You could easily manage it.'

Rieux shook his head with his usual deliberateness. It was none of his business, he said. Rambert had elected for happiness, and he, Rieux, had no argument to put up against him. Personally he felt incapable of deciding which was the right course and which the wrong in such a case as Rambert's.

'If that's so, why tell me to hurry up?'

It was Rieux who now smiled.

'Perhaps because I, too, would like to do my bit for happiness.'

Next day, though they were working together most of the time, neither referred to the subject. On the following Sunday Rambert moved into the little Spanish house. He was given a bed in the living-room. As the brothers did not come home for meals and he'd been told to go out as little as possible, he was always alone, but for occasional meetings with the boys' mother. She was a dried-up little wisp of a woman, always dressed in black, busy as a bee, and had a nut-brown, wrinkled face and immaculately white hair. No great talker, she merely smiled genially when her eyes fell on Rambert.

On one of the few occasions when she spoke it was to ask him if he wasn't afraid of infecting his wife with plague. He replied that there might be some risk of that, but only a very slight one; while if he stayed in the town there was a fair chance of their never seeing each other again.

The old woman smiled. 'Is she nice?'

'Very nice.'

'Pretty?'

'I think so.'

'Ah,' she nodded, 'that explains it.'

She went to Mass every morning. 'Don't you believe in God?' she asked him one morning, on her return.

On Rambert's admitting he did not, she said again that 'that explained it'.

'Yes,' she added, 'you're right. You must go back to her. Or else – what would be left you?'

Rambert spent most of the day prowling round the room, gazing vaguely at the distempered walls, idly fingering the fans which were their only decoration, or counting the woollen balls on the tablecloth fringe. In the evening the youngsters came home; they hadn't much to say, except that the time hadn't come yet. After dinner Marcel played the guitar, and they drank an anise-flavoured liqueur. Rambert seemed lost in thought.

On Wednesday Marcel announced: 'It's for tomorrow night, at midnight. Mind you're ready on time.' Of the two men sharing the sentry-post with them, he explained, one had got plague and the other, who had slept in the same room, was now under observation. Thus for two or three days Marcel and Louis would be alone at the post. They'd fix up the final details in the course of the night, and he could count on them to see it through. Rambert thanked them.

'Pleased?' the old woman asked.

He said 'Yes,' but his thoughts were elsewhere.

The next day was very hot and muggy and a heat-mist veiled the sun. The total of deaths had jumped up. But the old Spanish woman lost nothing of her serenity. 'There's so much wicked-ness in the world,' she said. 'So what can you expect?'

Like Marcel and Louis, Rambert was stripped to the waist. But, even so, sweat was trickling down his chest and between his shoulder-blades. In the dim light of the shuttered room, their torsos glowed like highly polished mahogany. Rambert kept prowling round like a caged animal, without speaking. Abruptly, at four in the afternoon, he announced that he was going out.

'Don't forget,' Marcel said. 'At midnight sharp. Everything's set.'

Rambert went to the doctor's flat. Rieux's mother told him he would find the doctor at the hospital in the Upper Town. As before, a crowd was circling in front of the entrance gates. 'Move on, there!' a police-sergeant with bulging eyes bawled every few minutes. And the crowd kept moving, but always in a circle. 'No use hanging round here. Why don't you go home?' The sergeant's coat was soaked in sweat. They knew it was 'no use', but they stayed on, despite the devastating heat. Rambert showed his pass to the sergeant, who told him to go to Tarrou's office. Its door gave on the courtyard. He passed Father Paneloux, who was coming out of the office.

Tarrou was sitting at a black-wood desk, with his sleeves rolled up, mopping up with his handkerchief a trickle of sweat in the bend of his arm. The office, a small, white-painted room, smelt of drugs and damp cloth.

'Still here?' Tarrou seemed surprised.

'Yes. I'd like to have a word with Rieux.'

'He's in the ward. Look here! Don't you think you could fix up whatever you've come for, without seeing him?'

'Why?'

'He's overdoing it. I try to spare him as much as I can.'

Rambert gazed thoughtfully at Tarrou. He'd grown thinner, his eyes and features were blurred with fatigue, his broad shoulders sagged. There was a knock at the door. A male attendant, wearing a white mask, entered. He laid a little sheaf of cards on Tarrou's desk and, his voice coming thickly through the cloth, said 'Six,' then went out. Tarrou looked at the journalist, and showed him the cards, spreading them fanwise.

'Neat little gadgets, aren't they? Well, they're deaths. Last night's takings.' Frowning, he slipped the cards together. 'The only thing that's left us is – accountancy!'

Taking his purchase on the table, Tarrou rose slowly to his feet.

'You're off quite soon, I take it?'

'Tonight, at midnight.'

Tarrou said he was glad to hear it, and Rambert had better look after himself for a bit.

'Did you say that . . . sincerely?'

Tarrou shrugged his shoulders.

'At my age one's got to be sincere. Lying's too much effort.'

'Excuse me, Tarrou,' the journalist said, 'but I'd greatly like to see the doctor.'

'I know. He's more human than I. All right, come along.'

'It's not that . . . ' Rambert stumbled over his words, and broke off in mid-phrase.

Tarrou stared at him; then, unexpectedly, his face broke into a smile.

They walked down a narrow passage; the walls were painted pale green, and the light was glaucous, like that in an aquarium. Before they reached the two-leaved glazed door at the end of the passage, behind which shadowy forms could be seen moving, Tarrou took Rambert into a small room, all the wall-space of which was occupied by cupboards. Opening one of these, he took from a sterilizer two masks of cotton-wool enclosed in muslin, handed one to Rambert and told him to put it on.

The journalist asked if it was really any use. Tarrou said 'No,' but it inspired confidence in others.

They opened the glazed door. It led into an enormous room all the windows of which were shut, in spite of the great heat.

Electric fans buzzed near the ceiling, churning up the stagnant, overheated air above two long rows of grey beds. Groans shrill or stifled rose on all sides, blending in a monotonous dirge-like refrain. Men in white moved slowly from bed to bed under the garish light flooding in from high, barred windows. The appalling heat in the ward made Rambert ill at ease, and he had difficulty in recognizing Rieux, who was bending over a groaning form. The doctor was lancing the patient's groin, while two nurses, one on each side, held his legs apart. Presently Rieux straightened up, dropped his instruments into a tray that an attendant held out to him, and remained without moving for some moments, gazing down at the man, whose wound was now being dressed.

'Any news?' he asked Tarrou, who had come beside him.

'Paneloux is prepared to replace Rambert at the quarantine station. He has put in a lot of useful work already. All that remains is to reorganize Number Three Group, now that Rambert's going.'

Rieux nodded.

'Castel has his first lot of the vaccine ready now,' Tarrou continued. 'He's in favour of its being tried at once.'

'Good,' Rieux said. 'That's good news.'

'And Rambert's come.'

Rieux looked round. His eyes narrowed above the mask when he saw the journalist.

'Why have you come?' he asked. 'Surely you should be elsewhere?'

Tarrou explained that 'it' was fixed for midnight. To which Rambert added: 'That's the idea, anyhow.'

Whenever any of them spoke through the mask the muslin bulged and grew moist over the lips. This gave a sort of unreality to the conversation; it was like a colloquy of statues.

'I'd like to have a word with you,' Rambert said.

'Right. I'm just going. Wait for me in Tarrou's office.'

A minute or so later Rambert and Rieux were sitting at the back of the doctor's car.

Tarrou, who was at the wheel, looked round as he let in the gear.

'Petrol's running out,' he said. 'We'll have to foot-slog it tomorrow.'

'Doctor,' Rambert said, 'I'm not going. I want to stay with you.'

Tarrou made no movement; he went on driving. Rieux seemed unable to shake off his fatigue.

'And – what about *her*?' His voice was hardly audible.

Rambert said he'd thought it over very carefully, and his views hadn't changed, but, if he went away, he would feel ashamed of himself, and that would embarrass his relations with the woman he loved.

Showing more animation, Rieux told him that was sheer nonsense; there was nothing shameful in preferring happiness.

'Certainly,' Rambert replied. 'But it may be shameful to be happy by oneself.'

Tarrou, who had not spoken so far, now remarked, without turning his head, that if Rambert wished to take a share in other people's unhappiness, he'd have no time left for happiness. So the choice had to be made.

'That's not it,' Rambert rejoined. 'Until now I always felt a stranger in this town, and that I'd no concern with you people. But now that I've seen what I have seen, I know that I belong here whether I want it or not. This business is everybody's business.' When there was no reply from either of the others, Rambert seemed to grow annoyed. 'But you know that as well as I do, damn it! Or else – what are you up to in that hospital of yours? Have *you* made a definite choice, and turned down happiness?'

Rieux and Tarrou still said nothing, and the silence lasted until they were nearing the doctor's home. Then Rambert repeated his last question in a yet more emphatic tone.

Only then Rieux turned towards him, raising himself with an effort from the cushion.

'Forgive me, Rambert, only – well, I simply don't know. But stay with us if you want to.' A swerve of the car made him break off for a moment. Then, looking straight in front of him, he said: 'For nothing in the world is it worth turning one's back on what one loves. Yet that is what I'm doing – though *why* I do not know.' He sank back on the cushion. 'That's how it is,' he added wearily, 'and there's nothing to be done about it. So let's recognize the fact, and draw the conclusions.'

'What conclusions?'

'Ah,' Rieux said, 'a man can't cure and *know* at the same time. So let's cure as quickly as we can. That's the more urgent job.'

At midnight Tarrou and Rieux were giving Rambert the map of the district he was to keep under surveillance. Tarrou glanced at his watch. Looking up, he met Rambert's gaze.

'Have you let them know?' he asked.

The journalist looked away.

'I'd sent them a note' – he spoke with an effort – 'before coming to see you.'

III

TOWARDS THE CLOSE of October Castel's anti-plague serum was tried for the first time. Practically speaking, it was Rieux's last card. If it failed, the doctor was convinced the whole town would be at the mercy of the epidemic, which would either continue its ravages for an unpredictable period, or perhaps die out abruptly of its own accord.

The day before Castel called on Rieux, M. Othon's son had fallen ill and all the family had to go into quarantine. Thus the mother, who had only recently come out of it, found herself isolated once again. In deference to the official regulations, the magistrate had promptly sent for Dr Rieux the moment he saw symptoms of the disease in his little boy. Mother and father were standing at the bedside when Rieux entered the room. The boy was in the phase of extreme prostration and submitted without a whimper to the doctor's examination. When Rieux raised his eyes he saw the magistrate's gaze intent on him, and, behind, the mother's pale face. She was holding a handkerchief to her mouth, and her big, dilated eyes followed each of the doctor's movements.

'He has it, I suppose?' the magistrate asked in a tone-less voice.

'Yes.' Rieux gazed down at the child again.

The mother's eyes widened yet more but she still said nothing. M. Othon, too, kept silent for a while before saying in an even lower tone:

'Well, doctor, we must do as we are told to do.'

Rieux avoided looking at Mme Othon, who was still holding her handkerchief to her mouth.

'It needn't take long,' he said rather awkwardly, 'if you'll let me use your phone.'

The magistrate said he would take him to the telephone. But, before going, the doctor turned towards Mme Othon.

'I regret very much indeed, but I'm afraid you'll have to get your things ready. You know how it is.'

Mme Othon seemed disconcerted. She was staring at the floor.

Then, 'I understand,' she murmured, slowly nodding her head. 'I'll set about it at once.'

Before leaving, Rieux on a sudden impulse asked the Othons if there wasn't anything they'd like him to do for them. The mother gazed at him in silence. And now the magistrate averted his eyes.

'No,' he said; then swallowed hard. 'But . . . save my son.'

In the early days a mere formality, quarantine had now been reorganized by Rieux and Rambert on very strict lines. In particular they insisted on having members of the family of a patient kept apart. If, unawares, one of them had been infected, the risks of an extension of the infection must not be multiplied. Rieux explained this to the magistrate, who signified his approval of the procedure. Nevertheless, he and his wife exchanged a glance which made it clear to Rieux how keenly they both felt the separation thus imposed on them. Mme Othon and her little girl could be given rooms in the quarantine hospital under Rambert's charge. For the magistrate, however, no accommodation was available except in an isolation camp the authorities were now installing in the Municipal Sports Ground, using tents supplied by the Highways Department. When Rieux apologized for the poor accommodation, M. Othon replied that there was one rule for all alike, and it was only proper to abide by it.

The boy was taken to the Auxiliary Hospital and put in a small ward, which had formerly been a junior classroom. After some twenty hours Rieux became convinced that the case was hopeless. The infection was steadily spreading, and the boy's body putting up no resistance. Tiny, half-formed, but acutely painful buboes were clogging the joints of the child's puny limbs. Obviously it was a losing fight.

Under the circumstances Rieux had no qualms about testing Castel's serum on the boy. That night, after dinner, they performed the inoculation, a lengthy process, without getting the slightest reaction. At daybreak on the following day they gathered round the bed to observe the effects of this test inoculation on which so much hung.

The child had come out of his extreme prostration and was tossing about convulsively on the bed. From four in the morning Dr Castel and Tarrou had been keeping watch and noting, stage by stage, the progress and remissions of the malady. Tarrou's bulky form was slightly drooping at the head of the bed, while at its foot, with Rieux standing beside him, Castel was seated, reading, with every appearance of calm, an old leather-bound book. One by one, as the light increased in the former classroom, the others arrived. Pane-loux, the first to come, leant against the wall on the opposite side of the bed to Tarrou. His face was drawn with grief, and the accumulated weariness of many weeks, during which he had never spared himself, had deeply seamed his somewhat prominent forehead. Grand came next. It was seven o'clock, and he apologized for being out of breath; he could only stay a moment, but wanted to know if any definite results had been observed. Without speaking, Rieux pointed to the child. His eyes shut, his teeth clenched, his features frozen in an agonized grimace, he was rolling his head from side to side on the bolster. When there was just light enough to make out the half-obliterated figures of an equation chalked on a blackboard that still hung on the wall at the far end of the room, Rambert entered. Posting himself at the foot of the next bed, he took a packet of cigarettes from his pocket. But after his first glance at the child's face he put it back.

From his chair Castel looked at Rieux, over his spectacles. 'Any news of his father?'

'No. He's in the Isolation Camp.'

The doctor's hands were gripping the rail of the bed, his eyes fixed on the small tortured body. Suddenly it stiffened, and seemed to give a little at the waist, as slowly the arms and legs spread out X-wise. From the body, naked under an army blanket, rose a smell of damp wool and stale sweat. The boy had gritted his teeth again. Then very gradually he relaxed, bringing his arms and legs back towards the centre of the bed, still without speaking or opening his eyes, and his breathing seemed to quicken. Rieux looked at Tarrou, who hastily lowered his eyes.

They had already seen children die – for many months now death had shown no favouritism – but they had never yet watched a child's agony minute by minute, as they had now been doing since daybreak. Needless to say, the pain inflicted on these innocent victims had always seemed to them to be what in fact it was: an abominable thing. But hitherto they had felt its abomination in, so to speak, an abstract way; they had never had to witness over so long a period the death-throes of an innocent child.

And, just then, the boy had a sudden spasm, as if something had bitten him in the stomach, and uttered a long, shrill wail. For moments that seemed endless he stayed in a queer, contorted position, his body racked by convulsive tremors; it was as if his frail frame were bending before the fierce breath of the plague, breaking under the reiterated gusts of fever. Then the storm-wind passed, there came a lull and he relaxed a little; the fever seemed to recede, leaving him gasping for breath on a dank, pestilential shore, lost in a languor that already looked like death. When for the third time the fiery wave broke on him, lifting him a little, the child curled himself up and shrank away to the edge of the bed, as if in terror of the flames advancing on him, licking his limbs. A moment later, after tossing his head wildly to and fro, he flung off the blanket. From between the inflamed eyelids big tears welled up and trickled down the sunken, leaden-hued cheeks. When the spasm had passed, utterly exhausted, tensing his thin legs and arms on which, within forty-eight hours, the flesh had wasted to the bone, the child lay flat, racked on the tumbled bed, in a grotesque parody of crucifixion.

Bending, Tarrou gently stroked with his big paw the small face stained with tears and sweat. Castel had closed his book a few moments before, and his eyes were now fixed on the child. He began to speak, but had to give a cough before continuing, because his voice rang out so harshly.

'There wasn't any remission this morning, was there, Rieux?'

Rieux shook his head, adding, however, that the child was putting up more resistance than one would have expected. Paneloux, who was slumped against the wall, said in a low voice:

'So, if he is to die, he will have suffered longer.'

Light was increasing in the ward. The occupants of the other nine beds were tossing about and groaning, but in tones that seemed deliberately subdued. Only one – at the far end of the ward – was screaming, or, rather, uttering little exclamations at regular intervals, which seemed to convey surprise more than pain. Indeed one had the impression that even for the sufferers the frantic terror of the early phase had passed, and there was a sort of mournful resignation in their present attitude towards the disease. Only the child went on fighting with all his little might. Now and again Rieux took his pulse – less because this served any purpose than as an escape from his utter helplessness – and, when he closed his eyes, he seemed to feel its tumult mingling with the fever of his own blood. And then, at one with the tortured child, he struggled to sustain him with all the remaining strength of his own body. But, linked for a few moments, the rhythms of their heart-beats soon fell apart, the child escaped him, and again he knew his impotence. Then he released the small, thin wrist and moved back to his place.

The light on the whitewashed walls was changing from pink to yellow. The first waves of another day of heat were beating on the windows. They hardly heard Grand saying he would come back, as he turned to go. All were waiting. The child, his eyes still closed, seemed to grow a little calmer. His clawlike fingers were feebly plucking at the sides of the bed. Then they rose, scratched at the blanket over his knees and suddenly he doubled up his limbs, bringing his thighs above his stomach, and remained quite still. For the first time he opened his eyes, and gazed at Rieux, who was standing immediately in front of him. In the small face, rigid as a mask of greyish clay, slowly the lips parted and from them rose a long, incessant scream, hardly varying with his respiration, and filling the ward with a fierce, indignant protest, so little childish that it seemed like a collective voice issuing from all the sufferers there. Rieux clenched his jaws, Tarrou looked away. Rambert went and stood beside Castel, whose closed book was lying on his knees. Paneloux gazed down at the small mouth, fouled with the sordes of the plague and pouring out the angry death-cry that has sounded through the ages of mankind. He sank on to his knees, and all present found it natural to hear him say in a voice hoarse but clearly audible across that nameless, never-ending wail:

'My God, spare this child...!'

But the wail continued without cease and the other sufferers began to grow restless. The patient at the far end of the ward, whose little broken cries had gone on without a break, now quickened their tempo so that they flowed together in one unbroken cry, while the others' groans grew louder. A gust of sobs swept through the room, drowning Paneloux's prayer, and Rieux, who was still tightly gripping the rail of the bed, shut his eyes, dazed with exhaustion and disgust.

When he opened them again, Tarrou was at his side.

'I must go,' Rieux said. 'I can't bear to hear them any longer.'

But then, suddenly, the other sufferers fell silent. And now the doctor grew aware that the child's wail, after weakening more and more, had fluttered out into silence. Round him the groans began again, but more faintly, like a far echo of the fight that now was over. For it was over. Castel had moved round to the other side of the bed and said the end had come. His mouth still gaping, but silent now, the child was lying amongst the tumbled blankets, a small, shrunken form, with the tears still wet on his cheeks.

Paneloux went up to the bed, and made the sign of benediction. Then gathering up his cassock, he walked out by the passage between the beds.

'Will you have to start it all over again?' Tarrou asked Castel.

The old doctor nodded slowly, with a twisted smile.

'Perhaps. After all, he put up a surprisingly long resistance.'

Rieux was already on his way out, walking so quickly and with such a strange look on his face that Paneloux put out an arm to check him when he was about to pass him in the doorway.

'Come, doctor . . . ' he began.

Rieux swung round on him fiercely.

'Ah! That child, anyhow, was innocent – and you know it as well as I do!'

He strode on, brushing past Paneloux, and walked across the school playground. Sitting on a wooden bench under the dingy, stunted trees, he wiped off the sweat which was beginning to run into his eyes. He felt like shouting imprecations – anything to loosen the stranglehold lashing his heart with steel! Heat was flooding down between the branches of the fig-trees. A white haze, spreading rapidly over the blue of the morning sky, made the air yet more stifling. Rieux lay back wearily on the bench. Gazing up at the ragged branches, the shimmering sky, he slowly got back his breath and fought down his fatigue.

He heard a voice behind him.

'Why was there that anger in your voice just now? What we'd been seeing was as unbearable to me as it was to you.'

Rieux turned towards Paneloux.

'I know. I'm sorry. But weariness is a kind of madness. And there are times when the only feeling I have is one of mad revolt.'

'I understand,' Paneloux said in a low voice. 'That sort of thing is revolting because it passes our human understanding. But perhaps we should love what we cannot understand.'

Rieux straightened up slowly. He gazed at Paneloux, summoning to his gaze all the strength and fervour he could muster against his weariness. Then he shook his head.

'No, Father. I've a very different idea of love. And until my dying day I shall refuse to love a scheme of things in which children are put to torture.'

A shade of disquietude crossed the priest's face. He was silent for a moment. Then, 'Ah, doctor,' he said sadly, 'I've just realized what is meant by "grace".'

Rieux had sunk back again on the bench. His lassitude had returned and from its depths he spoke, more gently.

'It's something I haven't got; that I know. But I'd rather not discuss that with you. We're working side by side for something that unites us – beyond blasphemy and prayers. And it's the only thing that matters.'

Paneloux sat down beside Rieux. It was obvious that he was deeply moved.

'Yes, yes,' he said, 'you, too, are working for man's salvation.'

Rieux tried to smile.

'Salvation's much too big a word for me. I don't aim so high. I'm concerned with man's health; and for me his health comes first.'

Paneloux seemed to hesitate. 'Doctor...' he began, then fell silent. Down his face, too, sweat was trickling. Murmuring, 'Good-bye for the present,' he rose. His eyes were moist. When he turned to go, Rieux, who had seemed lost in thought, suddenly rose and took a step towards him.

'Again, please forgive me. I can promise there won't be another outburst of that kind.'

Paneloux held out his hand, saying regretfully:

'And yet – I haven't convinced you!'

'What does it matter? What I hate is death and disease – as you well know. And whether you wish it or not, we're allies, facing them and fighting them together.' Rieux was still holding Paneloux's hand. 'So you see' – but he refrained from meeting the priest's eyes – 'God Himself can't part us now.'

IV

SINCE JOINING RIEUX'S band of workers Paneloux had spent his entire time in hospitals and places where he came in contact with plague. He had elected for the place amongst his fellow-workers that he judged incumbent on him – in the forefront of the fight. And constantly since then he had rubbed shoulders with death. Though theoretically immunized by periodical inoculations, he was well aware that at any moment death might claim him too, and he had given thought to this. Outwardly he had lost nothing of his serenity. But, from the day on which he saw a child die, something seemed to change in him. And his face bore traces of the rising tension of his thoughts. When one day he told Rieux with a smile that he was working on a short essay entitled *Is a Priest Justified in Consulting a Doctor?* Rieux had gathered that something graver lay behind the question than the priest's tone seemed to imply. On the doctor's saying he would greatly like to have a look at the essay, Paneloux informed him that he would shortly be preaching at a Mass for men, and his sermon would convey some at least of his considered opinions on the question.

'I hope you'll come, doctor. The subject will interest you.'

A high wind was blowing on the day Father Paneloux preached his second sermon. The congregation, it must be admitted, was sparser than on the first occasion; partly because this kind of performance had lost its novelty for our townsfolk. Indeed, considering the abnormal conditions they were up against, the very word 'novelty' had lost all meaning. More-over, most people, assuming they had not altogether aban-doned religious observances, or did not combine them naïvely with a thoroughly immoral way of living, had replaced normal religious practice by more or less extravagant superstitions. Thus they were readier to wear prophylactic medals of St Roch than to go to Mass.

An illustration may be found in the remarkable interest shown in prophecies of all descriptions. True, in the spring, when the epidemic was expected to end abruptly at any moment, no one troubled to take another's opinion as to its probable duration; since everyone had persuaded himself that it would have none. But as the days went by, a fear grew up that the calamity might last indefinitely, and then the ending of the plague became the target of all hopes. As a result copies of predictions attributed to soothsayers or saints of the Catholic Church circulated freely from hand to hand. The local printing firms were quick to realize the profit to be made by pandering to this new craze and printed large numbers of the prophecies that had been going round in manuscript. Finding that the public appetite for this type of literature was still unsated, they had researches made in the municipal libraries for all the mental pabulum of the kind available in old chronicles, memoirs and the like. And when this source ran dry, they commissioned journalists to write up forecasts and, in this respect at least, the journalists proved themselves equal to their prototypes of earlier ages.

Some of these prophetic writings were actually serialized in our newspapers and read with as much avidity as the love-stories which had occupied these columns in the piping times of health. Some predictions were based on far-fetched arith-metical calculations, involving the figures of the year, the total of deaths, and the number of months the plague had so far lasted. Others made comparisons with the great pestilences of former times, drew parallels (which the forecasters called 'con-stants'), and claimed to deduce conclusions bearing on the present calamity. But our most popular prophets were un-doubtedly those who in an apocalyptic jargon had announced sequences of events, any one of which might be construed as applicable to the present state of affairs, and was abstruse enough to admit of almost any interpretation. Thus Nostrada-mus and St Odilia were consulted daily, and always with happy results. Indeed the one thing these prophecies had in common was that, ultimately, all were reassuring. Unfortunately, though, the plague was not.

Thus superstition had usurped the place of religion in the life of our town, and this is why the church in which Paneloux preached his sermon was only three-quarters full. That evening, when Rieux arrived, the wind was pouring in great gusts through the swing-doors and filling the aisles with sudden draughts. And it was in a cold, silent church, surrounded by a congregation of men exclusively, that Rieux watched the Father climb into the pulpit. He spoke in a gentler, more thoughtful tone than on the previous occasion, and several times was noticed to be stumbling over his words. A yet more noteworthy change was that instead of saying 'You' he now said 'We'.

However, his voice grew gradually firmer as he proceeded. He started by recalling that for many a long month plague had been in our midst, and we now knew it better, after having seen it often and often seated at our tables or at the bedsides of those we loved. We had seen it walking at our side, or waiting for our coming at the places where we worked. Thus we were now, perhaps, better able to comprehend what it was telling us unceasingly; a message to which, in the first shock of the visitation, we might not have listened with due heed. What he, Father Paneloux, had said in his first sermon still held good – such, anyhow, was his belief. And yet, perhaps, as may befall any one of us (here he struck his breast) his words and thoughts had lacked in charity. However this might be, one thing was not to be gainsaid; a fact which always, under all circumstances, we should bear in mind. Appearances notwithstanding, all trials, however cruel, worked together for good to the Christian. And, indeed, what a Christian should always seek in his hour of trial was to discern that good, in what it consisted and how best he could turn it to account.

At this stage the people near Rieux seemed to settle in against the armrests of their pews, and make themselves as comfortable as they could. One of the big padded entrance doors was softly thudding in the wind, and someone got up to secure it. As a result, Rieux's attention wandered and he did not follow well what Paneloux now went on to say.

Apparently it came to this: we might try to explain the phenomenon of the plague, but, above all, should learn what it had to teach us. Rieux gathered that, to the Father's thinking, there was really nothing to explain.

His interest quickened when, in a more emphatic tone, the preacher said that there were some things we could grasp as touching God, and others we could not. There was no doubt as to the existence of Good and Evil and, as a rule, it was easy to see the difference between them. The difficulty began when we looked into the nature of Evil, and amongst things evil he included human suffering. Thus we had apparently needful pain, and apparently needless pain; we had Don Juan cast into hell, and a child's death. For while it is right that a libertine should be struck down, we see no reason for a child's suffering. And, truth to tell, nothing was more important on earth than a child's suffering, the horror it inspires in us, and the reasons we must find to account for it. In other manifestations of life God made things easy for us and, thus far, our religion had no merit. But, in this respect, He put us, so to speak, with our backs to the wall. Indeed we all were up against the wall that plague had built around us, and in its lethal shadow we must work out our salvation. He, Father Paneloux, refused to have recourse to simple devices enabling him to scale that wall. Thus he might easily have assured them that the child's sufferings would be compensated for by an eternity of bliss awaiting him. But how could he give that assurance when, to tell the truth, he knew nothing about it? For who would dare to assert that eternal happiness can compensate for a single moment's human suffering? He who asserted that would not be a true Christian, a follower of the Master who knew all the pangs of suffering in His body and His soul. No, he, Father Paneloux, would keep faith with that great symbol of all suffering, the tortured body on the Cross; he would stand fast, his back to the wall, and face honestly the terrible problem of a child's agony. And he would boldly say to those who listened to his words today: 'My brothers, a time of testing has come for us all. We must believe everything or deny everything. And who, I ask, amongst you would dare to deny everything?'

It crossed Rieux's mind that Father Paneloux was dallying with heresy in speaking thus, but he had no time to follow up the thought. The preacher was declaring vehemently that 'this uncompromising duty laid on the Christian was at once his ruling virtue and his privilege'. He was well aware that certain minds, schooled to a more indulgent and conventional morality, might well be dismayed, not to say outraged, by the seemingly excessive standard of Christian virtue about which he was going to speak. But religion in a time of plague could not be the religion of every day. While God might accept and even desire that the soul should take its ease and rejoice in happier times, in periods of extreme calamity He laid extreme demands on it. Thus today God had vouchsafed to His creatures an ordeal such that they must acquire and practise the greatest of all virtues: that of the All or Nothing.

Many centuries previously a profane writer had claimed to reveal a secret of the Church by declaring that Purgatory did not exist. He wished to convey that there could be no half-measures, there was only the alternative between Heaven and Hell; you were either saved or damned. That, according to Paneloux, was a heresy that could spring only from a blind, disordered soul. Nevertheless, there may well have been periods of history when Purgatory could not be hoped for; periods when it was impossible to speak of venial sin. Every sin was deadly, and any indifference criminal. It was All or it was Nothing.

The preacher paused, and Rieux heard more clearly the whistling of the wind outside; judging by the sounds that came in below the closed doors, it had risen to storm-pitch. Then he heard Father Paneloux's voice again. He was saying that the total acceptance of which he had been speaking was not to be taken in the limited sense usually given to the words;

he was not thinking of mere resignation or even of that harder virtue, humility. It involved humiliation, but a humiliation to which the person humiliated gave full assent. True, the agony of a child was humiliating to the heart and to the mind. But that was why we had to come to terms with it. And that, too, was why — and here Paneloux assured those present that it was not easy to say what he was about to say — since it was God's will, we, too, should will it. Thus and thus only the Christian could face the problem squarely and, scorning subterfuge, pierce to the heart of the supreme issue, the essential choice. And his choice would be to believe everything, so as not to be forced into denying everything. Like those worthy women who, after learning that buboes were the natural issues through which the body cast out infection, went to their church and prayed, 'Please, God, give him buboes,' thus the Christian should yield himself wholly to the divine will, even though it passed his understanding. It was wrong to say, '*This* I understand, but *that* I cannot accept'; we must go straight to the heart of that which is unacceptable, precisely because it is thus that we are constrained to make our choice. The sufferings of children were our bread of affliction, but without this bread our souls would die of spiritual hunger.

The shuffling sounds which usually followed the moment when the preacher paused were beginning to make themselves heard when, unexpectedly, he raised his voice, making as if to put himself in his hearers' place and were asking what then was the proper course to follow. He made no doubt that the ugly word 'fatalism' would be applied to what he said. Well, he would not boggle at the word, provided he were allowed to qualify it with the adjective 'active'. Needless to say, there was no question of imitating the Abyssinian Christians of whom he had spoken previously. Nor should one even think of acting like those Persians who, in time of plague, threw their infected garments on the Christian sanitary workers, and loudly called on heaven to give the plague to these infidels who were trying to avert a pestilence sent by God. But, on the other hand, it would be no less wrong to imitate the monks at Cairo who, when plague was raging in the town, distributed the Host with pincers at the Mass, so as to avoid contact with wet, warm mouths in which infection might be latent. The plague-stricken Persians and the monks were equally at fault. For the former a child's agony did not count; with the latter on the contrary the natural dread of suffering ranked highest in their conduct. In both cases the real problem had been shirked; they had closed their ears to God's voice.

But, Paneloux continued, there were other precedents of which he would now remind them. If the chronicles of the Black Death at Marseilles were to be trusted, only four of the eighty-one monks in the Mercy Monastery survived the epidemic, and of these four three took to flight. Thus far the chronicler, and it was not his task to tell us more than the bare facts. But when he read that chronicle, Father Paneloux had found his thoughts fixed on that monk who stayed on by himself, despite the death of his seventy-seven companions, and, above all, despite the example of his three brothers who had fled. And, bringing down his fist on the edge of the pulpit, Father Paneloux cried in a ringing voice: 'My brothers, each one of us must be the one who stays!'

There was no question of not taking precautions or failing to comply with the orders wisely promulgated for the public weal in the disorders of a pestilence. Nor should we listen to certain moralists who told us to sink on our knees and give up the struggle. No, we should go forward, groping our way through the darkness, stumbling perhaps at whiles, and try to do what good lay in our power. As for the rest, we must hold fast, trusting in the divine goodness, even as to the deaths of little children, and not seeking personal respite.

At this point Father Paneloux evoked the august figure of Bishop Belzunce during the Marseilles plague. He reminded his hearers how, towards the close of the epidemic, the Bishop, having done all that it behoved him, shut himself up in his palace, behind high walls, after laying in a stock of food and drink. With a sudden revulsion of feeling, such as often comes in times of extreme tribulation, the inhabitants of Marseilles, who had idolized him hitherto, now turned against him, piled up corpses round his house in order to infect it, and even flung bodies over the walls to make sure of his death. Thus in a moment of weakness the Bishop had proposed to isolate himself from the outside world – and lo and behold, corpses rained down on his head! This had a lesson for us all; we must convince ourselves that there is no island of escape in time of plague. No, there was no middle course. We must accept the dilemma; and choose either to hate God or to love God. And who would dare to choose to hate Him?

'My brothers' – the preacher's tone showed he was nearing the conclusion of his sermon – 'the love of God is a hard love. It demands total self-surrender, disdain of our human personality. And yet it alone can reconcile us to suffering and the deaths of children, it alone can justify them, since we cannot understand them, and we can only make God's will ours. That is the hard lesson I would share with you today. That is the faith, cruel in men's eyes, and crucial in God's, which we must ever strive to compass. We must aspire beyond ourselves towards that high and fearful vision. And on that lofty plane all will fall into place, all discords be resolved, and truth flash forth from the dark cloud of seeming injustice. Thus in some churches of the South of France plague victims have lain sleeping many a century under the flagstones of the chancel, and priests now speak above their tombs, and the divine message they bring to men rises from that charnel, to which, nevertheless, children have contributed their share.'

When Rieux was preparing to leave the church a violent gust swept up the nave through the half-open doors and buffeted the faces of the departing congregation. It brought with it a smell of rain, a tang of drenched pavements, warning them of the weather they would encounter outside. An old priest and a young deacon, who were walking immediately in front of Rieux, had much difficulty in keeping their head-dress from blowing away. But this did not prevent the elder of the two from discussing the sermon they had heard. He paid tribute to the preacher's eloquence, but the boldness of thought Paneloux had shown gave him pause. In his opinion the sermon had displayed more uneasiness than real power, and at Paneloux's age a priest had no business to feel uneasy. The young deacon, his head bowed to protect his face from the wind, replied that he saw much of the Father, had followed the evolution of his views, and believed his forthcoming pamphlet would be bolder still; indeed it might well be refused the *Imprimatur.*

'You don't mean to say so! What's the main idea?'

They were now in the Cathedral Square and for some moments the roar of the wind made it impossible for the younger man to speak. When there was a slight lull, he said briefly to his companion:

'That it's illogical for a priest to call in a doctor.'

Tarrou, when told by Rieux what Paneloux had said, remarked that he'd known a priest who had lost his faith during the war, as the result of seeing a young man's face with both eyes destroyed.

'Paneloux is right,' Tarrou continued. 'When an innocent youth can have his eyes destroyed, a Christian should either lose his faith or consent to having his eyes destroyed. Paneloux declines to lose his faith, and he will go through with it to the end. That's what he meant to say.'

It may be that this remark of Tarrou's throws some light on the regrettable events which followed, in the course of which the priest's conduct seemed inexplicable to his friends. The reader will judge for himself.

A few days after the sermon Paneloux had to move out of his rooms. It was a time when many people were obliged to change their residence owing to the new conditions created by the plague. Thus Tarrou, when his hotel was requisitioned, had gone to live with Rieux, and now the Father had to vacate the lodgings provided for him by his Order and stay in the house of a pious old lady who had so far escaped the epidemic. During the process of house-moving Paneloux had been feeling more run down than ever, mentally as well as physically. And it was this that put him in the bad books of his hostess. One evening when she was enthusiastically vaunting the merits of St Odilia's prophecies, the priest betrayed a slight impatience, due probably to fatigue. All his subsequent efforts to bring the good lady round to, anyhow, a state of benevolent neutrality came to nothing. He had made a bad impression and it went on rankling. So each night on his way to his bedroom, where almost all the furniture was dotted with crochet-covers, he had to contemplate the back of his hostess seated in her drawing-room and carry away with him a memory of the sour 'Good night, Father,' she flung at him over her shoulder. It was on one such evening that he felt, like a flood bursting the dykes, the turbulent onrush in his wrists and temples of the fever latent in his blood for several days past.

The only available account of what followed comes from the lips of the old lady. Next morning she rose early, as was her wont. After an hour or so, puzzled at not seeing the Father leave his room, she brought herself, not without some hesitation, to knock at his door. She found him still in bed after a sleepless night. He had difficulty in breathing and looked more flushed than usual. She had suggested most politely (as she put it) that a doctor should be called in, but her suggestion had been brushed aside with a curtness that she described as 'quite unmannerly'. So she had no alternative but to leave the room. Later in the morning the Father rang for the maid and sent a message asking if he could see her. He apologized for his lack of courtesy and assured her that what he was suffering from could not be plague, as he had none of the symptoms; it was no more than a passing indisposition. The lady replied with dignity that her suggestion had not been prompted by any apprehension of that sort – she took no thought for her personal security, which was in God's hands – but that she felt a certain measure of responsibility for the Father's welfare while he was under her roof. When he said nothing, his hostess, wishing (according to her account) to do her duty by him, offered to send for her doctor. Father Paneloux told her not to trouble, adding some explanations which seemed to the old lady incoherent, not to say nonsensical. The only thing she gathered, and it was precisely this that appeared to her so incomprehensible, was that the Father refused to hear of a doctor's visit because it was against his principles. Her impression was that her guest's mind had been unhinged by fever, and she confined herself to bringing him a cup of tea.

Resolutely mindful of the obligations imposed on her by the situation, she visited the invalid regularly every two hours. What struck her most about him was his restlessness, which continued throughout the day. He would throw off the blankets, then pull them back, and he kept running his hand over his forehead which was glistening with sweat. Every now and then he sat up in bed and tried to clear his throat with a thick, grating cough, which sounded almost like retching. At these moments he seemed to be vainly struggling to force up from his lungs a clot of some semi-solid substance that was choking him. After each unavailing effort, he sank back, utterly exhausted, on the pillow. Then he would raise himself again a little and stare straight in front of him with a fixity even more dismaying than the paroxysms which had preceded it. Even now the old lady was reluctant to annoy her guest by calling in the doctor. After all, it might be no more than an attack of fever, spectacular as were its manifestations.

However, in the afternoon she made another attempt to talk to the priest, but she could get out of him no more than a few rambling phrases. She renewed her proposal to call in the doctor. Whereat Paneloux sat up and in a stifled voice emphatically declined to see a doctor. Under these circumstances it seemed best to the old lady to wait till the following morning; if the Father's condition showed no more improvement she would ring up the number announced ten times daily on the wireless by the Ransdoc Information Bureau. Still conscious of her obligations, she resolved to visit the invalid from time to time in the course of the night, and give him any attention he might need. But, after bringing him a decoction of herbal tea at about eleven, she felt so tired that she decided to lie down on a sofa for half an hour or so. Only at daybreak did she wake up, and then her first act was to go to the priest's room.

Father Paneloux was lying quite still; his face had lost its deep flush of the previous day and had now a deathly pallor, all the more impressive because the cheeks had kept their fullness. He was gazing up at the bead fringe of a lamp hanging above the bed. When the old lady came in he turned his head. As she quaintly put it, he looked as if he'd been severely thrashed all the night long, and more dead than alive. She was greatly struck by the apathy of his voice when, on her asking how he was feeling, he replied that he was in a bad way, he did not need a doctor and all he wished was to be taken to hospital, so as to comply with the regulations. Panic-stricken, she hurried to the telephone.

Rieux came at noon. After hearing what the old lady had to say he replied briefly that Paneloux was right, but it was probably too late. The Father welcomed him with the same air of complete indifference. Rieux examined him and was surprised to find none of the characteristic symptoms of bubonic or pneumonic plague, except congestion and obstruction of the lungs. But his pulse was so weak and his general state so alarming that there was little hope of saving him.

'You have none of the specific symptoms of the disease,' Rieux told him. 'But I admit one can't be sure, and I must isolate you.'

The Father smiled queerly, as if for politeness' sake, but said nothing. Rieux left the room to telephone, then came back and looked at the priest.

'I'll stay with you,' he said gently.

Paneloux showed a little more animation and a sort of warmth came back to his eyes when he looked up at the doctor. Then, speaking with such difficulty that it was impossible to tell if there was sadness in his voice, he said:

'Thanks. But priests can have no friends. They have given their all to God.'

He asked for the crucifix which hung above the head of the bed; when given it, he turned away to gaze at it.

At the hospital Paneloux did not utter a word. He submitted passively to the treatment given him, but never let go of the crucifix. However, his case continued doubtful, and Rieux could not feel sure how to diagnose it. For several weeks, indeed, the disease had seemed to make a point of confounding diagnoses. In the case of Paneloux, what followed was to show that this uncertainty had no consequence.

His temperature rose. Throughout the day the cough grew louder, racking the enfeebled body. At last, at nightfall, Father Paneloux brought up the clot of matter that was choking him; it was red. Even at the height of his fever Paneloux's eyes kept their blank serenity and when, next morning, he was found dead, his body drooping over the bedside, they betrayed nothing. Against his name the index-card recorded: 'Doubtful case.'

V

ALL SOULS' DAY that year was very different from what it had been in former years. True, the weather was seasonable; there had been a sudden change, and the great heat had given place to mild autumnal air. As in other years a cool wind blew all day, and big clouds raced from one horizon to the other, trailing shadows over the houses upon which fell again, when they had passed, the pale gold light of a November sky.

The first waterproofs made their appearance. Indeed, one was struck by the number of glossy, rubberized garments to be seen. The reason was that our newspapers had informed us that two hundred years previously, during the great pestilences of Southern Europe, the doctors wore oiled clothing as a safeguard against infection. The shops had seized this opportunity of unloading their stock of out-of-fashion waterproofs, which their purchasers fondly hoped would guarantee immunity from 'germs'.

But these familiar aspects of All Souls' Day could not make us forget that the cemeteries were left unvisited. In previous years the rather sickly smell of chrysanthemums had filled the trams, while long lines of women could be seen making pilgrimage to the places where members of the family were buried, to lay flowers on the graves. This was the day when they made amends for the oblivion and dereliction in which their dead had slept for many a long month. But in the plague year people no longer wished to be reminded of their dead. Because, indeed, they were thinking all too much about them, as it was. There was no more question of revisiting them with a shade of regret and much melancholy. They were no longer the forsaken to whom, one day in the year, you came to justify yourself. They were intruders whom you would rather forget. That is why the Day of the Dead this year was tacitly but wilfully ignored. As Cottard dryly remarked – Tarrou noted that the habit of irony was growing on him more and more – each day was for us a Day of the Dead.

And, in fact, the bale-fires of the pestilence were blazing ever more merrily in the crematorium. It is true that the actual number of deaths showed no increase. But it seemed that plague had settled in for good at its most virulent, and it took its daily toll of deaths with the punctual zeal of a good civil servant. Theoretically, and in the view of the authorities, this was a hopeful sign. The fact that the graph after its long rising curve had flattened out seemed to many, Dr Richard for example, reassuring. 'The graph's good today,' he would remark, rubbing his hands. To his mind the disease had reached what he called high-water mark. Thereafter it could but ebb. He gave the credit of this to Dr Castel's new serum which, indeed, had brought off some quite unlooked-for recoveries. While not dissenting, the old doctor reminded him that the future remained uncertain; history proved that epidemics had a way of recrudescing when least expected. The authorities, who had long been desirous of giving a fillip to the morale of the populace, but had so far been prevented by the plague from doing so, now proposed to convene a meeting of the medical corps and ask for an announcement on the subject. Unfortunately, just before the meeting was due to take place, Dr Richard, too, was carried off by the plague, then precisely at 'high-water mark'.

The effect of this regrettable event, which, sensational as it was, actually proved nothing, was to make our authorities swing back to pessimism as inconsequently as they had previously indulged in optimism. As for Castel, he confined himself to preparing his serums with the maximum of care. By this time no public place or building had escaped conversion into a hospital or quarantine camp, with the exception of the Prefect's offices, which were needed for administrative purposes and committee-meetings. In a general way, however, owing to the relative stability of the epidemic at this time, Rieux's organizations were still able to cope with the situation. Though working constantly at high pressure, the doctors and their helpers were not forced to contemplate still greater efforts. All they had to do was to carry on automatically, so to speak, their all-but-superhuman task. The pneumonic type of infection, cases of which had already been detected, was now spreading all over the town; one could almost believe that the high winds were kindling and fanning its flames in people's chests. The victims of pneumonic plague succumbed much more quickly, after coughing up bloodstained sputum. This new form of the epidemic looked like being more contagious as well as even more fatal. However, the opinions of experts had always been divided on this matter. For greater safety all sanitary workers wore masks of sterilized three-ply muslin. On the face of it, the disease should have extended its ravages. But, the cases of bubonic plague showing a decrease, the death-rate remained constant.

Meanwhile the authorities had another cause for anxiety in the difficulty of maintaining the food-supply. Profiteers were taking a hand and purveying at enormous prices essential foodstuffs not available in the shops. The result was that poor families were in great straits, while the rich went short of practically nothing. Thus, whereas plague by its impartial ministrations should have promoted equality amongst our townsfolk, it now had the opposite effect and, thanks to the habitual conflict of cupidities, exacerbated the sense of injustice rankling in men's hearts. They were assured, of course, of the inerrable equality of death – but nobody wanted that kind of equality. Poor people who were feeling the pinch thought still more nostalgically of towns and villages in the near-by countryside, where bread was cheap and life without restrictions. Indeed, they had a natural if illogical feeling that they should have been permitted to move out to these happier places. The feeling was embodied in a slogan shouted in the streets and chalked up on walls: 'Bread – or fresh air!' This half-ironical battle-cry was the signal for some demonstrations which, though easily repressed, made everyone aware that an ugly mood was developing amongst us.

The newspapers, needless to say, complied with the instructions given them; optimism at all costs. If one was to believe what one read in them, our populace was giving 'a fine example of courage and composure'. But in a town thrown back upon itself, in which nothing could be kept secret, no one had illusions about the 'example' given by the public. To form a correct idea about the courage and composure talked about by our journalists you had only to visit one of the quarantine depots or isolation camps established by our authorities. As it so happens, the narrator, being fully occupied elsewhere, had no occasion to visit any of them, and must fall back on Tarrou's Diary for a description of the conditions in these places.

Tarrou gives an account of a visit he made, accompanied by Rambert, to the camp located in the Municipal Sports Ground. The Sports Ground lies on the outskirts of the town, between a street along which runs a tramline and a stretch of waste land extending to the extreme edge of the plateau on which Oran is built. It was already surrounded by high concrete walls and all that was needed to make escape practically impossible was to post sentries at the four entrance-gates. The walls served another purpose; they screened the unfortunates in quarantine from the view of people on the road. Against this advantage may be set the fact that the inmates could hear all day – though they could not see them – the passing trams, and recognize by the increased volume of sound coming from the road the hours when people had knocked off work or were going to it. And this brought home to them that the life from which they were debarred was going on as before, within a few yards of them, and that those high walls parted two worlds as alien to each other as two different planets.

Tarrou and Rambert chose a Sunday afternoon for their visit to the Sports Ground. They were accompanied by Gonzales, the football-player, with whom Rambert had kept in contact, and who had let himself be persuaded into undertaking, in rotation with others, the surveillance of the camp. This visit was to enable Rambert to introduce Gonzales to the Camp Commandant. When they met that afternoon Gonzales' first remark was that this was exactly the time when, before the plague, he used to start getting into his football togs. Now that the playing-fields had been requisitioned, all that was of the past, and Gonzales was feeling – and showed it – at a loose end. This was one of the reasons why he had accepted the post proposed by Rambert, but he made it a condition that he was to be on duty during week-ends only.

The sky was overcast and, glancing up at it, Gonzales observed regretfully that a day like this, neither too hot nor rainy, would have been perfect for a match. And then he fell to conjuring up, as best he could, the once familiar smell of embrocation in the dressing-rooms, the stands crowded with people, the coloured shirts of the players, showing up brightly against the tawny soil, the half-time lemons or bottled lemon-ade that titillated parched throats with a thousand refreshing pin-pricks. Tarrou also records how on the way, as they walked the shabby outer streets, the footballer gave kicks to all the small loose stones. His object was to shoot them into the vent-holes of the gutters, and whenever he did this, he would shout 'Bravo! Goal!' When he had finished his cigarette he spat the stub in front of him and tried to catch it on his toe before it touched the ground. Some children were playing near the Sports Ground, and when one of them sent a ball towards the three men, Gonzales went out of his way to 'return' it neatly.

On entering the ground they found the stands full of people. The playing-field was dotted with tents inside which one had glimpses of bedding and bundles of clothes or rugs. The stands had been kept open for the use of the internees in hot or rainy weather. But it was a rule of the camp that everyone must be in his tent at sunset. Shower-baths had been installed under the stands, and what used to be the players' dressing-rooms converted into offices and infirmaries. The majority of the inmates of the camp were sitting about on the stands. Some, however, were strolling on the touchlines, and a few, squatting at the entrances of their tents, were listlessly contemplating the scene around them. In the stands, many of those slumped on the wooden tiers had a look of vague expectancy.

'What do they do with themselves all day?' Tarrou asked Rambert.

'Nothing.'

Almost all, indeed, had empty hands and idly dangling arms. Another curious thing about this multitude of derelicts was its silence.

'When they first came there was such a din you couldn't hear yourself speak,' Rambert said. 'But as the days went by they grew quieter and quieter.'

In his notes Tarrou gives what to his mind would explain this change. He pictures them in the early days bundled together in the tents, listening to the buzz of flies, scratching themselves, and whenever they found an obliging listener shrilly voicing their fear or indignation. But when the camp grew overcrowded, fewer and fewer people were inclined to play the part of sympathetic listener. So they had no choice but to hold their peace and nurse their mistrust of everything and everyone. One had, indeed, a feeling that suspicion was falling, dewlike, from the greyly shining sky over the brick-red camp.

Yes, there was suspicion in the eyes of all. Obviously, they were thinking, there must be some good reason for the isolation inflicted on them, and they had the air of people who are puzzling over their problem and are afraid. Everyone Tarrou set eyes on had that vacant gaze, and was visibly suffering from the complete break with all that life had meant to him. And since they could not be thinking of their death all the time, they thought of nothing. They were on holiday. 'But worst of all,' Tarrou writes, 'is that they're forgotten, and they know it. Their friends have forgotten them because they have other things to think about, naturally enough. And those they love have forgotten them because all their energies are devoted to making schemes and taking steps to get them out of the camp.

And by dint of always thinking about these schemes and steps they have ceased thinking about those whose release they're trying to secure. And that, too, is natural enough. In fact, it comes to this: nobody is capable of really thinking about anyone, even in the worst calamity. For really to think about someone means thinking about that person every minute of the day, without letting one's thoughts be diverted by any-thing; by meals, by a fly that settles on one's cheek, by house-hold duties, or by a sudden itch somewhere. But there are always flies and itches. That's why life is difficult to live. And these people know it only too well.'

The Camp President came up; a gentleman named Othon, he said, would like to see them. Leaving Gonzales in the office, he led the others to a corner of the grandstand, where they saw M. Othon sitting by himself. He rose as they approached. The magistrate was dressed exactly as in the past and still wore a stiff collar. The only changes Tarrou noted were that the tufts of hair over his temples were not brushed back and that one of his shoelaces was undone. M. Othon appeared very tired and not once did he look his visitors in the face. He said he was glad to see them and requested them to thank Dr Rieux for all he had done.

Some moments of silence ensued, then with an effort the magistrate spoke again.

'I hope Jacques did not suffer too much.'

This was the first time Tarrou heard him utter his son's name, and he realized that something had changed. The sun was setting and, flooding through a rift in the clouds, the level rays raked the stands, tingeing their faces with a yellow glow.

'No,' Tarrou said. 'No, I couldn't really say he suffered.'

When they took their leave, the magistrate was still gazing towards the light.

They called in at the office to say good-bye to Gonzales, whom they found studying the duty roster. The footballer was laughing when he shook hands with them.

'Anyhow, I'm back in the good old dressing-room,' he chuckled. 'That's something to go on with.'

Soon after, when the Camp President was seeing Tarrou and Rambert out, they heard a crackling noise coming from the stands. A moment later the loudspeakers, which in happier times served to announce the results of matches or to introduce the teams, informed the inmates of the camp that they were to go back to their tents for the evening meal. Slowly everyone filed off the stands and shuffled towards the tents. After all were under canvas two small electric trucks, of the kind used for transporting luggage on railway platforms, began to wend their way between the tents. While the occupants held forth their arms, two ladles plunged into the two big cauldrons on each truck, and neatly tipped their contents into the waiting dixies. Then the truck moved on to the next tent.

'Very efficient,' Tarrou remarked.

The Camp President beamed, as he shook hands.

'Yes, isn't it? We're great believers in efficiency in this camp.'

Dusk was falling. The sky had cleared and the camp was bathed in cool, soft light. Through the hush of evening came a faint tinkle of spoons and plates. Above the tents bats were circling, vanishing abruptly into the darkness. A tramcar squealed on the points outside the walls.

'Poor Monsieur Othon!' Tarrou murmured as the gate closed behind them. 'One would like to do something to help him. But how can you help a judge?'

VI

THERE WERE OTHER camps of much the same kind in the town, but the narrator, for lack of first-hand information and in deference to veracity, has nothing to add about them. This much, however, he can say: the mere existence of these camps, the smell of crowded humanity coming from them, the baying of their loudspeakers in the dusk, the air of mystery that clung about them and the dread these forbidden places inspired told seriously on our fellow-citizens' morale and added to the general nervousness and apprehension. Breaches of the peace and minor riots became more frequent.

As November drew to a close the mornings turned much colder. Heavy downpours had scoured the streets and washed the sky clean of clouds. In the mornings a weak sunlight bathed the town in a cold, sparkling sheen. The air warmed up, however, as night approached. It was such a night that Tarrou chose for telling something of himself to Rieux.

After a particularly tiring day, Tarrou proposed to the doctor that they should go together for the evening visit to Rieux's old asthma patient. There was a soft glow above the housetops in the Old Town and a light breeze fanned their faces at the street-crossings. Coming from the silent streets, they found the old man's loquacity rather irksome at first. He launched into a long harangue to the effect that 'some folks were getting fed up', that it was always the same people had all the jam, and things couldn't go on like that indefinitely, one day there'd be – he rubbed his hands – 'a fine old dust-up'. He continued expatiating on this theme all the time the doctor was attending to him.

They heard footsteps overhead. Noticing Tarrou's upward glance, the old woman explained that it was the girls from next door walking on the terrace. She added that one had a lovely view up there, and that as the terraces in this part of the town often joined up with the next one on one side, the women could visit their neighbours without having to go into the street.

'Why not go up and have a look?' the old man suggested. 'You'll get a breath of nice fresh air.'

They found nobody on the terrace; only three empty chairs. On one side, as far as eye could reach, was a row of terraces, the most remote of which abutted on a dark, rugged mass which they recognized as the hill nearest the town. On the other side, spanning some streets and the unseen harbour, their gaze came to rest on the horizon, where sea and sky merged in a dim, vibrant greyness. Beyond a black patch which they knew to be the cliffs a sudden glow, whose source they could not see, sprang up at regular intervals; the light at the entrance of the fairway was still functioning for the benefit of ships that, passing Oran's unused harbour, went on to other ports along the coast. In a sky swept crystal-clear by the night wind, the stars showed like silver flakes, tarnished now and again by the yellow gleam of the revolving light. Perfumes of spice and warm stone were wafted on the breeze. Everything was very still.

'A pleasant spot,' said Rieux, as he lowered himself into a chair. 'You'd think that plague had never found its way up here.'

Tarrou was gazing seawards, his back to the doctor.

'Yes,' he replied, after a moment's silence. 'It's good to be here.'

Then, settling into the chair beside Rieux, he fixed his eyes on his face. Three times the glow spread up the sky and died away. A faint clatter of crockery rose from a room giving on the street below. A door banged somewhere in the house.

'Rieux,' Tarrou said in a quite ordinary tone, 'do you realize that you've never tried to find out anything about me – the man I am? Can I regard you as a friend?'

'Yes. Of course we're friends; only, so far we haven't had much time to show it.'

'Good. That gives me confidence. Suppose we now take an hour off – for friendship?'

Rieux smiled by way of answer.

'Well . . . Here goes!'

There was a long faint hiss some streets off, the sound of a car speeding on the wet roadway. It died away; then some vague shouts a long way off broke the stillness again. Then, like a dense veil slowly falling from the starry sky on the two men, silence returned. Tarrou had moved and now was sitting on the parapet, facing Rieux, who was slumped back in his chair. All that could be seen of him was a dark, bulky form outlined against the glimmering sky. He had much to tell; what follows gives it more or less in his own words.

'To make things simpler, Rieux, let me begin by saying I had plague already, long before I came to this town and encountered it here. Which is tantamount to saying I'm like everybody else. Only there are some people who don't know it, or feel at ease in that condition; others know, and want to get out of it. Personally, I've always wanted to get out of it.

'When I was young I lived with the idea of my innocence; that is to say, with no idea at all. I'm not the self-tormenting kind of person, and I made a suitable start in life. I brought off everything I set my hand to, I moved at ease in the field of the intellect, I got on excellently with women and, if I had occasional qualms, they passed as lightly as they came. Then one day I started thinking. And now . . .

'I should tell you I wasn't poor in my young days, as you were. My father had an important post – he was Director of Public Prosecutions; but to look at him, you'd never have guessed it, he appeared, and was, a kindly, good-natured man. My mother was a simple, rather shy woman, and I've always loved her greatly; but I'd rather not talk about her. My father was always very kind to me, and I even think he tried to understand me. He wasn't a model husband, I know that now, but I can't say it shocks me particularly. Even in his infidelities he behaved as one could count on his behaving and never gave rise to scandal. In short, he wasn't at all original and, now he's dead, I realize that, while no plaster saint, he was a very decent man as men go. He kept the middle way, that's all: he was the type of man for whom one has an affection of the mild but steady order – which is the kind that wears best.

'My father had one peculiarity; the big Railway Directory was his bedside book. Not that he often took a train; almost his only journeys were to Brittany, where he had a small country house to which we went every summer. But he was a walking time-table; he could tell you the exact times of departure and arrival of the Paris–Berlin expresses; how to get from Lyon to Warsaw, which trains to take and at what hours; the precise distance between any two capital cities you might mention. Could you tell me, offhand, how to get from Briançon to Chamonix? Even a station-master would scratch his head, I should say. Well, my father had the answer pat. Almost every evening he enlarged his knowledge of the subject, and he prided himself on it. This hobby of his much amused me; I would put complicated travel problems to him and check his answers afterwards by the Railway Directory. They were invariably correct. My father and I got on together excellently, thanks largely to these railway games we played in the evenings; I was exactly the audience he needed, attentive and appreciative. Personally I regarded this accomplishment of his as quite as admirable in its way as most accomplishments.

'But I'm letting my tongue run away with me, and attributing too much importance to that worthy man, my father. Actually he played only an indirect role in the great change of heart about which I want to tell you. The most he did to me was to touch off a train of thoughts. When I was seventeen my father asked me to come to hear him speak in Court. There was a big case on at the Assizes, and probably he thought I'd see him to his best advantage. Also I suspect he hoped I'd be duly impressed by the pomp and ceremony of the Law, and encouraged to take up his profession. I could tell he was keen on my going, and the prospect of seeing a side of my father's character so different from that we saw at home appealed to me. Those were absolutely the only reasons I had for going to the trial. What happened in a Court had always seemed to me as natural, as much in the order of things, as a military parade on the

Fourteenth of July or a school Speech Day. My notions on the subject were purely abstract, and I'd never given it serious thought.

'The only picture I carried away with me of that day's proceedings was a picture of the criminal. I have little doubt he was guilty – of what crime is no great matter. That little man of about thirty, with sparse, sandy hair, seemed so eager to confess everything, so genuinely horrified at what he'd done and what was going to be done with him, that after a few minutes I had eyes for nothing and nobody else. He looked like a yellow owl scared blind by too much light. His tie was slightly awry, he kept biting his nails, those of one hand only, his right. . . . I needn't go on, need I? You've understood – he was a living human being.

'As for me, it came on me suddenly, in a flash of understanding; until then I'd thought of him only under his commonplace official designation, as "the defendant". And though I can't say I quite forgot my father, something seemed to grip my vitals at that moment, and riveted all my attention on the little man in the dock. I hardly heard what was being said; I only knew that they were set on killing that living man and an uprush of some elemental instinct, like a wave, had swept me to his side. And I did not really wake up until my father rose to address the Court.

'In his red gown he was another man, no longer genial or good-natured; his mouth spewed out long, turgid phrases like an endless stream of snakes. I realized he was clamouring for the prisoner's death, telling the jury that they owed it to society to find him guilty; he went so far as to demand that the man should have his head cut off. Not exactly in those words, I admit. "He must pay the supreme penalty" was the formula. But the difference, really, was slight, and the result the same. He had the head he asked for. Only of course it wasn't he who did the actual job. I, who saw the whole business through to its conclusion, felt a far closer, far more terrifying intimacy with that wretched man than my father can ever have felt. Never-theless, it fell to him, in the course of his duties, to be present at what's politely termed the prisoner's last moments – but what would be better called murder in its most despicable form.

'From that day on I couldn't even see the Railway Direc-tory without a shudder of disgust. I took a horrified interest in legal proceedings, death-sentences, executions, and I realized with dismay that my father must have often witnessed those brutal murders – on the days when, as I'd noticed without guessing what it meant, he rose very early in the morning. I remembered he used to wind his alarm-clock on those occasions, to make sure. I didn't dare to broach the subject with my mother, but I watched her now more closely and saw that their life in common had ceased to mean anything, she had abandoned hope. That helped me to "forgive her", as I put it to myself at the time. Later on, I learnt that there'd been nothing to forgive; she'd been quite poor until her marriage and pov-erty had taught her resignation.

'Probably you're expecting me to tell you that I left home at once. No, I stayed on many months, nearly a year, in fact. Then one evening my father asked for the alarm-clock as he had to get up early. I couldn't sleep that night. Next day, when he came home, I'd gone.

'To cut a long story short, I had a letter from my father, who had set inquiries on foot to find me. I went to see him, and, without explaining my reasons, told him quite calmly that I'd kill myself if he forced me to return. He wound up by letting me have my way – he was, as I've said, a kindly man at bottom – gave me a lecture on the silliness of wanting to "live my life" (that was how he accounted for my conduct and I didn't undeceive him), and plenty of good advice. I could see he really felt it deeply and it was an effort for him to keep back his tears. Subsequently – but quite a long time after that – I formed a habit of visiting my mother periodically, and I always saw him on these occasions. I imagine these infrequent meetings satisfied my father. Personally, I hadn't the least antipathy to him, only a little sadness of heart. When he died I had my mother come to live with me, and she'd still be with me if she were alive.

'I've had to dwell on my start in life, since for me it really was the start of... everything. I came to grips with poverty when I was eighteen, after an easy life till then. I tried all sorts of jobs, and I didn't do too badly. But my real interest in life was the death penalty; I wanted to square accounts with that poor blind "owl" in the dock. So I became an agitator as they say. I didn't want to be pestiferous, that's all. To my mind the social order round me was based on the death-sentence, and by fighting the established order I'd be fighting against murder. That was my view, others had told me so, and I still think that this belief of mine was substantially true. I joined forces with a group of people I then liked, and indeed have never ceased to like. I spent many years in close co-operation with them, and there's not a country in Europe in whose struggles I haven't played a part. But that's another story.

'Needless to say, I knew that we, too, on occasion, passed sentences of death. But I was told that these few deaths were inevitable for the building up of a new world in which murder would cease to be. That also was true up to a point – and maybe I'm not capable of standing fast where that order of truths is concerned. Whatever the explanation, I hesitated. But then I remembered that miserable "owl" in the dock, and it enabled me to keep on. Until the day when I was present at an execution – it was in Hungary – and exactly the same dazed horror that I'd experienced as a youngster made everything reel before my eyes.

'Have you ever seen a man shot by a firing-squad? No, of course not; the spectators are hand-picked and it's like a private party, you need an invitation. The result is that you've gleaned your ideas about it from books and pictures. A post, a blindfolded man, some soldiers in the offing. But the real thing isn't a bit like that. Do you know that the firing-squad stands only a yard and a half from the condemned man? Do you know that if the victim took two steps forward his chest would touch the rifles? Do you know that, at this short range, the soldiers concentrate their fire on the region of the heart and their big bullets make a hole into which you could thrust your fist? No, you didn't know all that; those are things that are never spoken of. For the plague-stricken their peace of mind is more important than a human life. Decent folks must be allowed to sleep easy o' nights, mustn't they? Really it would be shockingly bad taste to linger on such details, that's common knowledge. But personally I've never been able to sleep well since then. The bad taste remained in my mouth and I've kept lingering on the details, brooding over them.

'And thus I came to understand that I, anyhow, had had plague through all those long years in which, paradoxically enough, I'd believed with all my soul that I was fighting it. I learned that I had had an indirect hand in the deaths of thousands of people; that I'd even brought about their deaths by approving of acts and principles which could only end that way. Others did not seem embarrassed by such thoughts, or anyhow never voiced them of their own accord. But I was different; what I'd come to know stuck in my gorge. I was with them and yet I was alone. When I spoke of these matters they told me not to be so squeamish; I should remember what great issues were at stake. And they advanced arguments, often quite impressive ones, to make me swallow what none the less I couldn't bring myself to stomach. I replied that the most eminent of the plague-stricken, the men who wear red robes, also have excellent arguments to justify what they do, and once I admitted the arguments of necessity and *force majeure* put forward by the less eminent, I couldn't reject those of the eminent. To which they retorted that the surest way of playing the game of the red robes was to leave to them the monopoly of the death penalty. My reply to this was that, if you gave in once, there was no reason for not continuing to give in. It seems to me that history has borne me out; today there's a sort of competition who will kill the most. They're all mad-crazy over murder and they couldn't stop killing men even if they wanted to.

'In any case, my concern was not with arguments. It was with the poor "owl"; with that foul procedure whereby dirty mouths stinking of plague told a fettered man that he was going to die, and scientifically arranged things so that he should die, after nights and nights of mental torture while he waited to be murdered in cold blood. My concern was with that hole, big as a fist, in a man's chest. And I told myself that meanwhile, so far anyhow as I was concerned, nothing in the world would induce me to accept any argument that justified such butcheries. Yes, I chose to be blindly obstinate, pending the day when I could see my way more clearly.

'I'm still of the same mind. For many years I've been ashamed, mortally ashamed, of having been, even with the best intentions, even at many removes, a murderer in my turn. As time went on I merely learned that even those who were better than the rest could not keep themselves nowadays from killing or letting others kill, because such is the logic by which they live; and that we can't stir a finger in this world without the risk of bringing death to somebody. Yes, I've been ashamed ever since; I have realized that we all have plague, and I have lost my peace. And today I am still trying to find it; still trying to understand all those others and not to be the mortal enemy of anyone. I only know that one must do what one can to cease being plague-stricken, and that's the only way in which we can hope for some peace or, failing that, a decent death. This, and only this, can bring relief to men and, if not save them, at least do them the least harm possible and even, sometimes, a little good. So that is why I resolved to have no truck with anything which, directly or indirectly, for good reasons or for bad, brings death to anyone, or justifies others' putting him to death.

'That, too, is why this epidemic has taught me nothing new, except that I must fight it at your side. I know positively – yes, Rieux, I can say I know the world inside out, as you may see – that each of us has the plague within him; no one, no one on earth, is free from it. And I know, too, that we must keep endless watch on ourselves lest in a careless moment we breathe in somebody's face and fasten the infection on him. What's natural is the microbe. All the rest – health, integrity, purity (if you like) – is a product of the human will, of a vigilance that must never falter. The good man, the man who infects hardly anyone, is the man who has the fewest lapses of attention. And it needs tremendous will-power, a never-ending tension of the mind, to avoid such lapses. Yes, Rieux, it's a wearying business, being plague-stricken. But it's still more wearying to refuse to be it. That's why everybody in the world today looks so tired; everyone is more or less sick of plague. But that is also why some of us, those who want to get the plague out of their systems, feel such desperate weariness, a weariness from which nothing remains to set us free, except death.

'Pending that release, I know I have no place in the world of today; once I'd definitely refused to kill, I doomed myself to an exile that can never end. I leave it to others to "make history". I know, too, that I'm not qualified to pass judgment on those others. There's something lacking in my mental make-up, and its lack prevents me from being a rational murderer. So it's a deficiency, not a superiority. But, as things are, I'm willing to be as I am; I've learnt modesty. All I maintain is that on this earth there are pestilences and there are victims, and it's up to us, so far as possible, not to join forces with the pestilences. That may sound simple to the point of childishness; I can't judge if it's simple, but I know it's true. You see, I'd heard such quantities of arguments, which very nearly turned my head,

and turned other people's heads enough to make them approve
of murder; and I'd come to realize that all our troubles spring
from our failure to use plain, clean-cut language. So I resolved
always to speak – and to act – quite clearly, as this was the only
way of setting myself on the right track. That's why I say there
are pestilences and there are victims; no more than that. If, by
making that statement, I, too, become a carrier of the plague-
germ, at least I don't do it wilfully. I try, in short, to be an
innocent murderer. You see, I've no great ambitions.

'I grant we should add a third category: that of the true
healers. But it's a fact one doesn't come across many of them,
and anyhow it must be a hard vocation. That's why I decided
to take, in every predicament, the victims' side – so as to
reduce the damage done. Amongst them I can at least try to
discover how one attains to the third category; in other words,
to peace.'

Tarrou was swinging his leg, tapping the terrace lightly with
his heel, as he concluded. After a short silence the doctor raised
himself a little in his chair and asked if Tarrou had an idea of the
path to follow for attaining peace.

'Yes,' he replied. 'The path of sympathy.'

Two ambulances were clanging in the distance. The dis-
persed shouts they had been hearing off and on drew together
on the outskirts of the town, near the stony hill, and presently
there was a sound like a gun-shot. Then silence fell again.
Rieux counted two flashes of the revolving light. The breeze
freshened and a gust coming from the sea filled the air for a
moment with the smell of brine. And at the same time they
clearly heard the low sound of waves lapping the foot of
the cliffs.

'It comes to this,' Tarrou said almost casually, 'what interests
me is learning how to become a saint.'

'But you don't believe in God.'

'Exactly! Can one be a saint without God? – that's the
problem, in fact the only problem, I'm up against today.'

A sudden blaze sprang up above the place the shouts had come from and, stemming the wind-stream, a rumour of many voices came to their ears. The blaze died down almost at once, leaving behind it only a dull red glow. Then in a break of the wind they distinctly heard some strident yells and the discharge of a gun, followed by the roar of an angry crowd. Tarrou stood up and listened, but nothing more could be heard.

'Another skirmish at the gates, I suppose.'

'Well, it's over now,' Rieux said.

Tarrou said in a low voice that it was never over, and there would be more victims, because that was in the order of things.

'Perhaps,' the doctor answered. 'But, you know, I feel more fellowship with the defeated than with saints. Heroism and sanctity don't really appeal to me, I imagine. What interests me is – being a man.'

'Yes, we're both after the same thing, but I'm less ambitious.'

Rieux supposed Tarrou was jesting and turned to him with a smile. But, faintly lit by the dim radiance falling from the sky, the face he saw was sad and earnest. There was another gust of wind and Rieux felt it warm on his skin. Tarrou gave himself a little shake.

'Do you know,' he said, 'what we now should do for friendship's sake?'

'Anything you like, Tarrou.'

'Go for a swim. It's one of these harmless pleasures that even a saint-to-be can indulge in, don't you agree?' Rieux smiled again, and Tarrou continued: 'Really it's too damn' silly living only in and for the plague. Of course a man should fight for the victims, but, if he ceases caring for anything outside that, what's the use of his fighting?

'Right,' Rieux said. 'Let's go.'

Some minutes later the car drew up at the harbour gates. The moon had risen and a milk-white radiance, dappled with shadows, lay around them. Behind them rose the town, tier on tier, and from it came warm, fetid breaths of air that urged them towards the sea. After showing their passes to a sentry, who inspected them minutely, they crossed some open ground littered with casks, and headed towards the jetty. The air here reeked of stale wine and fish. Just before they reached the jetty a smell of iodine and seaweed announced the nearness of the sea and they clearly heard the sound of waves breaking gently on the big stone blocks. Once they were on the jetty they saw the sea spread out before them, a gently heaving expanse of deep-piled velvet, supple and sleek as a creature of the wild. They sat down on a boulder facing the open. Slowly the waters rose and sank, and with their tranquil breathing sudden oily glints formed and flickered over the surface in a haze of broken lights. Before them the darkness stretched out into infinity. Rieux could feel under his hand the gnarled, weather-worn visage of the rocks, and a strange happiness possessed him. Turning to Tarrou, he caught a glimpse on his friend's face of the same happiness, a happiness that forgot nothing, not even murder.

They undressed, and Rieux dived in first. After the first shock of cold had passed and he came back to the surface the water seemed tepid. When he had taken a few strokes he found that the sea was warm that night with the warmth of autumn seas that borrow from the shore the accumulated heat of the long days of summer. The movement of his feet left a foaming wake as he swam steadily ahead, and the water slipped along his arms to close in tightly on his legs. A loud splash told him that Tarrou had dived. Rieux lay on his back and stayed motionless, gazing up at the dome of sky lit by the stars and moon. He drew a deep breath. Then he heard a sound of beaten water, louder and louder, amazingly clear in the hollow silence of the night. Tarrou was coming up with him, he now could hear his breathing.

Rieux turned and swam level with his friend, timing his stroke to his. But Tarrou was the stronger swimmer and Rieux had to put on speed to keep up with him. For some minutes they swam side by side, with the same zest, in the same rhythm, isolated from the world, at last free of the town and of the plague. Rieux was the first to stop and they swam back slowly, except at one point, where unexpectedly they found themselves caught in an ice-cold current. Their energy whipped up by this trap the sea had sprung on them, both struck out more vigorously.

They dressed and started back. Neither had said a word, but they were conscious of being perfectly at one, and that the memory of this night would be cherished by them both. When they caught sight of the plague watchman, Rieux guessed that Tarrou, like himself, was thinking that the disease had given them a respite, and this was good, but now they must set their shoulders to the wheel again.

VII

YES, THE PLAGUE gave short shrift indeed, and they must set their shoulders to the wheel again. Throughout December it smouldered in the chests of our townsfolk, fed the fires in the crematorium, and peopled the camps with human jetsam. In short, it never ceased progressing with its characteristically jerky, but unfaltering stride. The authorities had optimistically reckoned on the coming of winter to halt its progress, but it lasted through the first cold spells without the least remission. So the only thing for us to do was to go on waiting, and since after a too long waiting one gives up waiting, the whole town lived as if it had no future.

As for Dr Rieux, that brief hour of peace and friendship which had been granted him was not, and could not be, repeated. Yet another hospital had been opened, and his only converse was with his patients. However, he noticed a change at this stage of the epidemic, now that the plague was assuming more and more the pneumonic form; the patients seemed, after their fashion, to be seconding the doctor. Instead of giving way to the prostration or the frenzies of the early period, they appeared to have a clearer idea of where their interests lay and on their own initiative asked for what might be most beneficial. Thus they were always clamouring for something to drink and insisted on being kept as warm as possible. And though the demands on him were as exhausting as before, Rieux no longer had the impression of putting up a solitary fight; the patients were co-operating.

Towards the end of December he received a letter from M. Othon, who was still in quarantine. The magistrate stated that his quarantine period was over; unfortunately the date of his admission to camp seemed to have been mislaid by the secretariat, and if he was still detained it was certainly due to a mistake. His wife, recently released from quarantine, had gone to the Prefect's office to protest, and been rudely treated; they had told her that the office never made mistakes. Rieux asked Rambert to look into the matter and, a few days later, M. Othon called on him. There had, in fact, been a mistake, and Rieux showed some indignation. But M. Othon, who had grown thinner, raised a limp, deprecating hand; weighing his words, he said that everyone could make mistakes. And the doctor thought to himself that decidedly something had changed.

'What will you do now, Monsieur Othon?' Rieux asked. 'I suppose you have a pile of work awaiting you.'

'Well, as a matter of fact, I'm putting in for some leave.'

'I quite understand. You need a rest.'

'It's not that. I want to go back to the camp.'

Rieux couldn't believe his ears.

'But you've only just come out of it!'

'I'm afraid I did not make myself clear. I'm told there are some voluntary workers from government offices in that camp.' The magistrate rolled his round eyes a little and tried to smooth down a tuft of hair. 'It would keep me busy, you see.

And also – I know it may sound absurd, but I'd feel less separated from my little boy.'

Rieux stared at him. Could it be that a sudden gentleness showed in those hard, inexpressive eyes? Yes, they had grown misted, lost their steely glitter.

'Certainly,' Rieux said. 'Since that's your wish, I'll fix it up for you.'

The doctor kept his word, and the life of the plague-ridden town resumed its course until Christmas. Tarrou continued to bring his quiet efficiency to bear on every problem. Rambert confided in the doctor that, with the connivance of the two young sentries, he was sending letters to his wife and, now and again, receiving an answer. He suggested to Rieux that he should avail himself of this clandestine channel, and Rieux agreed to do so. For the first time for many months he sat down to write a letter. He found it a laborious business, as if he were manipulating a language that he had forgotten. The letter was dispatched. The reply was slow in coming. As for Cottard, he was prospering, making money hand over fist, in small, somewhat shady transactions. With Grand, however, it was otherwise; the Christmas season did not seem to agree with him.

Indeed, Christmas that year had none of its old-time associations; it smacked of hell rather than of heaven. Empty, unlighted shops, dummy sweets or empty boxes in the confectioners' windows, trams laden with listless, dispirited passengers – all was as unlike previous Christmastides as it well could be. In the past all the townsfolk, rich and poor alike, indulged in seasonable festivity; now only a privileged few, those with money to burn, could do so, and they caroused in shamefast solitude in a dingy back-shop or a private room. In the churches there were more supplications than carols. You saw a few children, too young to realize what threatened them, playing in the frosty, cheerless streets. But no one dared to bid them welcome-in the God of former days, bringer of gifts, and old as human sorrow yet new as the hopes of youth. There was no room in any heart but for the very old, grey hope, that hope which keeps men from letting themselves drift into death and is nothing but a dogged will to live.

Grand had failed to show up as usual on the previous evening. Feeling somewhat anxious, Rieux called at his place early in the morning, but he wasn't at home. His friends were asked to keep a look-out for him. At about eleven Rambert came to the hospital with the news that he'd had a distant glimpse of Grand, who seemed to be wandering aimlessly, 'looking very queer'. Unfortunately he had lost sight of him almost at once. Tarrou and the doctor set out in the car to hunt for Grand.

At noon Rieux stepped out of his car into the frozen air; he had just caught sight of Grand some distance away, his face glued to a shop-window, full of crudely carved wooden toys. Tears were steadily flowing down the old fellow's cheeks and they wrung the doctor's heart, for he could understand them, and he felt his own tears welling up in sympathy. A picture rose before him of that scene of long ago – the youngster standing in front of another shop-window, like this one dressed for Christmas, and Jeanne turning towards him in a sudden access of emotion and saying how happy she was. He could guess that through the mists of the past years, from the depth of his fond despair, Jeanne's young voice was rising, echoing in Grand's ears. And he knew, also, what the old man was thinking as his tears flowed, and he, Rieux, thought it too: that a loveless world is a dead world, and always there comes an hour when one is weary of prisons, of one's work and of devotion to duty, and all one craves for is a loved face, the warmth and wonder of a loving heart.

Grand saw the doctor's reflection in the window. Still weeping, he turned and, leaning against the shop-front, watched Rieux approach.

'Oh, doctor, doctor . . . !' He could say no more.

Rieux, too, couldn't speak; he made a vague, understanding gesture. At this moment he suffered with Grand's sorrow, and what filled his breast was the passionate indignation we feel when confronted by the anguish all men share.

'Yes, Grand,' he murmured.

'Oh, if only I could have time to write to her! To let her know . . . and to let her be happy without remorse!'

Almost roughly Rieux took Grand's arm and drew him forward. Grand did not resist, and went on muttering broken phrases.

'Too long! It's lasted too long. All the time one's wanting to let oneself go, and then one day one has to. . . . Oh, doctor, I know I look a quiet sort, just like anybody else. But it's always been a terrible effort – only to be . . . just normal. And now, well, even that's too much for me.'

He stopped dead. He was trembling violently, his eyes were fever-bright. Rieux took his hand; it was burning hot.

'You must go home.'

But Grand wrenched himself free and started running. After a few steps he halted, and stretched out his arms, swaying to and fro. Then he spun round on himself and fell flat on the pavement, his face stained with the tears that went on flowing. Some people who were approaching stopped abruptly and watched the scene from a little way off, not daring to come nearer. Rieux had to carry the old man to the car.

Grand lay in bed, gasping for breath; his lungs were congested. Rieux pondered. The old fellow hadn't any family. What would be the point of having him evacuated? He and Tarrou could look after him.

Grand's head was buried in the pillow, his cheeks were a greenish grey, his eyes had gone dull, opaque. He seemed to be gazing fixedly at the scanty fire Tarrou was kindling with the remains of an old packing-case. 'I'm in a bad way,' he muttered. A queer crackling sound came from his flame-seared lungs whenever he tried to speak. Rieux told him not to talk and promised to come back. The sick man's lips parted in a curious smile, and a look of humorous complicity flickered across the haggard face. 'If I pull through, doctor – hats off!' A moment later he sank into extreme prostration.

Visiting him again some hours later, they found him half sitting up in bed, and Rieux was horrified by the rapid change that had come over his face, ravaged by the fires of the disease consuming him. However, he seemed more lucid, and almost immediately asked them to fetch his manuscript from the drawer where he always kept it. When Tarrou handed him the sheets he pressed them to his chest without looking at them, then held them out to the doctor, indicating by a gesture that he was to read them. There were some fifty pages of manuscript. Glancing through them, Rieux saw that the bulk of the writing consisted of the same sentence written again and again with small variants, simplifications or elaborations. Persistently the month of May, the lady on horseback, the avenues of the Bois recurred, regrouped in different patterns. There were, besides, explanatory notes, some exceedingly long, and lists of alternatives. But at the foot of the last page was written in a studiously clear hand: '*My dearest Jeanne, Today is Christmas Day and . . .*' Eight words only. Above it, in copper-plate script, was the latest version of the famous phrase. 'Read it,' Grand whispered. And Rieux read:

'One fine morning in May, a slim young horsewoman might have been seen riding a glossy sorrel mare along the avenues of the Bois, amongst the flowers. . . .'

'Is that *it*?' There was a feverish quaver in the old voice. Rieux refrained from looking at him, and he began to toss about in the bed. 'Yes, I know. I know what you're thinking. "Fine" isn't the word. It's . . .'

Rieux clasped his hand under the coverlet.

'No, doctor. It's too late . . . no time . . .' His breast heaved painfully, then suddenly he said in a loud, shrill voice: 'Burn it!'

The doctor hesitated, but Grand repeated his injunction in so violent a tone and with such agony in his voice that Rieux walked across to the fireplace and dropped the sheets on the dying fire. It blazed up, and there was a sudden flood of light, a fleeting warmth, in the room. When the doctor came back to the bed, Grand had his back turned, his face almost touching the wall. After injecting the serum Rieux whispered to his friend that Grand wouldn't last the night, and Tarrou volunteered to stay with him. The doctor approved.

All night Rieux was haunted by the idea of Grand's death. But next morning he found his patient sitting up in bed, talking to Tarrou. His temperature was down to normal and there were no symptoms other than a generalized prostration.

'Yes, doctor,' Grand said. 'I was over-hasty. But I'll make another start. You'll see, I can remember every word.'

Rieux looked at Tarrou dubiously. 'We must wait,' he said.

But at noon there was no change. By nightfall Grand could be considered out of danger. Rieux was completely baffled by this 'resurrection'.

Other surprises were in store for him. About the same time a girl was brought to hospital, whose case Rieux diagnosed as hopeless, and he had her sent immediately to the isolation ward. She was delirious and had all the symptoms of pneumonic plague. Next morning, however, the temperature had fallen. As in Grand's case the doctor assumed this was the ordinary morning fall which his experience had taught him to regard as a bad sign. But at noon her temperature still showed no rise and at night it went up only a few degrees. Next morning it was down to normal. Though very exhausted, the girl was breathing freely. Rieux remarked to Tarrou that her recovery was 'against all the rules!' But in the course of the next week four similar cases came to his notice.

The old asthma patient was bubbling over with excitement when Rieux and Tarrou visited him at the end of the week.

'Would you ever have believed it! They're coming out again.'

'Who?'

'Why, the rats!'

Not one dead or living rat had been seen in the town since April. Tarrou looked anxiously at Rieux.

'Does that mean it's starting all over again?'

The old man was rubbing his hands.

'You should see 'em running, doctor! It's a fair treat, that it is!'

He himself had seen two rats slipping into the house by the street door, and some neighbours, too, had told him they'd seen rats in their basements. In some houses people had heard those once familiar scratchings and rustlings behind the woodwork. Rieux awaited with much interest the mortality figures which were announced every Monday. They showed a decrease.

PART FIVE

I

THOUGH THIS SUDDEN setback of the plague was as welcome as it was unlooked-for, our townsfolk were in no hurry
to jubilate. While intensifying their desire to be set free, the
terrible months they had lived through had taught them prudence, and they had come to count less and less on a speedy
end of the epidemic. All the same, this new development was
the talk of the town and people began to nurse hopes none the
less heartfelt for being unavowed. All else took a back place;
that daily there were new victims counted for little beside that
staggering fact: the weekly total showed a decrease. One of the
signs that a return to the golden age of health was secrctly
awaited was that our fellow-citizens, careful though they were
not to voice their hope, now began to talk – in, it is true, a
carefully detached tone – of the new order of life that would
set in after the plague.

All agreed that the amenities of the past couldn't be restored
at once; destruction is an easier, speedier process than recon-
struction. However, it was thought that a slight improvement
in the food-supply could safely be counted on, and this would
relieve what was just now the acutest worry of every house-
hold. But, in reality, behind these mild aspirations lurked wild,
extravagant hopes, and often one of us, becoming aware of
this, would hastily add that, even on the rosiest view, you
couldn't expect the plague to stop from one day to another.

Actually, while the epidemic did not stop 'from one day to
another', it declined more rapidly than we could reasonably
have expected. With the first week of January an unusually
persistent spell of very cold weather settled in and seemed to

crystallize above the town. Yet never before had the sky been so blue; day after day its icy radiance flooded the town with brilliant light, and in the frost-cleansed air the epidemic seemed to lose its virulence, and in each of three consecutive weeks a big drop in the death-roll was announced. Thus over a relatively brief period the disease lost practically all the gains piled up over many months. Its setbacks with seemingly pre-destined victims, like Grand and Rieux's girl-patient, its bursts of activity for two or three days in some districts synchronizing with its total disappearance from others, its new practice of multiplying its victims on, say, a Monday, and on Wednesday letting almost all escape, in short its accesses of violence followed by spells of complete inactivity – all these gave an impression that its energy was flagging, out of exhaustion and exasperation, and it was losing, with its self-command, the ruthless, almost mathematical efficiency that had been its trump-card hitherto. Of a sudden Castel's anti-plague injec-tions scored frequent successes, denied it until now. Indeed all the treatments the doctors had tentatively employed, without definite results, now seemed almost uniformly efficacious. It was as if the plague had been hounded down and cornered, and its sudden weakness lent new strength to the blunted weapons so far used against it. Only at rare moments did the disease brace itself and make as it were a blind and fatal leap at three or four patients whose recovery had been expected – a truly ill-starred few, killed off when hope ran highest. Such was the case of M. Othon, the magistrate, evacuated from the quarantine camp; Tarrou said of him that 'he'd had no luck', but one couldn't tell if he had in mind the life or the death of M. Othon.

But, generally speaking, the epidemic was in retreat all along the line; the official communiqués, which had at first encouraged no more than shadowy, half-hearted hopes, now confirmed the popular belief that the victory was won and the enemy abandoning his positions. Really, however, it is doubt-ful if this could be called a victory. All that could be said was that the disease seemed to be leaving as unaccountably as it had come. Our strategy had not changed, but whereas yesterday it had obviously failed, today it seemed triumphant. Indeed, one's chief impression was that the epidemic had called a retreat after reaching all its objectives; it had, so to speak, achieved its purpose.

Nevertheless, it seemed as if nothing had changed in the town. Silent as ever by day, the streets filled up at nightfall with the usual crowds of people, now wearing overcoats and scarves. Cafés and picture-houses did as much business as before. But on a closer view you might notice that people looked less strained, and occasionally smiled. And this brought home the fact that since the outbreak of plague no one had hitherto been seen to smile in public. The truth was that for many months the town had been stifling under an airless shroud, in which a rent had now been made, and every Monday when he turned on the wireless, each of us learnt that the rift was widening; soon he would be able to breathe freely. It was at best a negative solace, with no immediate impact on men's lives. Still, had anyone been told a month earlier that a train had just left or a boat put in, or that cars were to be allowed on the streets again, the news would have been received with looks of incredulity; whereas in mid-January an announcement of this kind would have caused no surprise. The change, no doubt, was slight. Yet, however slight, it proved what a vast forward stride our townsfolk had made in the way of hope. And indeed it could be said that once the faintest stirring of hope became possible, the dominion of the plague was ended.

It must, however, be admitted that our fellow-citizens' reactions during that month were diverse to the point of incoherence. More precisely, they fluctuated between high optimism and extreme depression. Hence the odd circumstance that several more attempts to escape took place at the very moment when the statistics were most encouraging. This took the authorities by surprise, and, apparently, the sentries too – since most of the 'escapists' brought it off. But, looking into it, one saw that people who tried to escape at this time were prompted by quite understandable motives. Some of them plague had imbued with a scepticism so thorough that it was now a second nature; they had become allergic to hope in any form. Thus even when the plague had run its course, they went on living by its standards. They were, in short, behind the times. In the case of others – chiefly those who had been living until now in forced separation from those they loved – the rising wind of hope, after all these months of durance and depression, had fanned impatience to a blaze and swept away their self-control. They were seized with a sort of panic at the thought that they might die so near the goal and never see again the ones they loved, and their long priva-tion have no recompense. Thus, though for weary months and months they had endured their long ordeal with dogged per-severance, the first thrill of hope had been enough to shatter what fear and hopelessness had failed to impair. And in the frenzy of their haste they tried to outstrip the plague, incapable of keeping pace with it up to the end.

Meanwhile, there were various symptoms of the growing optimism. Prices, for instance, fell sharply. This fall was un-accountable from the purely economic viewpoint. Our diffi-culties were as great as ever, the gates were kept rigorously closed and the food situation was far from showing any im-provement. Thus it was a purely psychological reaction – as if the dwindling of the plague must have repercussions in all fields. Others to profit by the spread of optimism were those who used to live in groups and had been forced to live apart. The two convents reopened and their communal life was resumed. The troops, too, were regrouped in such barracks as had not been requisitioned, and settled down to the garrison life of the past. Minor details, but significant.

This state of subdued yet active ferment prevailed until January 25, when the weekly total showed so striking a decline that, after consulting the Medical Board, the authorities announced that the epidemic could be regarded as definitely stemmed. True, the communiqué went on to say that, acting with a prudence of which the population would certainly approve, the Prefect had decided that the gates of the town were to remain closed for two weeks more, and the prophylactic measures to remain in force for another month. During this period, at the least sign of danger 'the standing orders would be strictly enforced and, if necessary, prolonged thereafter for such a period as might be deemed desirable'. All, however, concurred in regarding these phrases as mere official verbiage, and the night of January 25 was the occasion of much festivity. To associate himself with the popular rejoicings, the Prefect gave orders for the street lighting to be resumed as in the past. And the townspeople paraded the brilliantly lighted streets in boisterous groups, laughing and singing.

True, in some houses the shutters remained closed, and those within listened in silence to the joyful shouts outside. Yet even in these houses of mourning a feeling of deep relief prevailed; whether because at last the fear of seeing other members of the household taken from them was calmed or because the shadow of personal anxiety was lifted from their hearts. The families which perforce withdrew themselves the most from the general jubilation were those who at this hour had one of their members down with plague in hospital and, whether in a quarantine camp or at home, waited in enforced seclusion for the epidemic to have done with them as it had done with the others. No doubt these families had hopes, but they hoarded them, and forbade themselves to draw on them before feeling quite sure they were justified. And this time of waiting in silence and exile, in a limbo between joy and grief, seemed still crueller for the gladness all around them.

But these exceptions did not diminish the satisfaction of the great majority. No doubt the plague was not yet ended – a fact of which they were to be reminded; still in imagination they could already hear, weeks in advance, trains whistling on their ways to an outside world that had no limit, and steamers hooting as they put out from the harbour across shining seas. Next day these fancies would have passed and qualms of doubt return. But for the moment the whole town was on the move, quitting the dark, lugubrious confines where it had struck its roots of stone, and setting forth at last, like a shipload of survivors, towards a land of promise.

That night Tarrou, Rieux, Rambert and their colleagues joined for a while the marching crowds and they, too, felt as if they trod on air. Long after they had turned off the main streets, even when in empty byways they walked past shuttered houses, the joyful clamour followed them up, and because of their fatigue somehow they could not discriminate the sorrow behind those closed shutters from the joy filling the central streets. Thus the coming liberation had a twofold aspect, of happiness and tears.

At one moment, when the cries of exultation in the distance were swelling to a roar, Tarrou stopped abruptly. A small, sleek form was scampering along the roadway; a cat, the first cat any of them had seen since the spring. It stopped in the middle of the road, hesitated, licked a paw and quickly passed it behind its right ear; then it started forward again and vanished into the darkness. Tarrou smiled to himself; the little old man on the balcony, too, would be pleased.

II

BUT IN THOSE days when the plague seemed to be retreating, slinking back to the obscure lair from which it had stealthily emerged, one person at least in the town viewed this retreat with consternation, if Tarrou's notes are to be trusted; and that man was Cottard.

To tell the truth, these diary notes take a rather curious turn from the date on which the death returns began to drop. The handwriting becomes much harder to read – this may have been due to fatigue – and the diarist jumps from one topic to another without transition. What is more, these later notes lack the objectivity of the earlier ones; personal considerations creep in. Thus, sandwiched between long passages dealing with the case of Cottard, we find a brief account of the old man and the cats. Tarrou conveys to us that the plague had in no wise lessened his appreciation of the old fellow, who continued equally to interest him after the epidemic had run its course; unfortunately, he could not go on interesting him, and this through no lack of good intentions on Tarrou's part. He had done his best to see him again. Some days after that memorable twenty-fifth of January he stationed himself at the corner of the little street. The cats were back at their usual places, basking in the patches of sunlight. But at the ritual hour the shutters stayed closed. And never once did Tarrou see them open on the following days. He drew the rather odd conclusion that the old fellow was either dead or vexed – if vexed, the reason being that he had thought that he was right and the plague had put him in the wrong; if dead, the question was (as in the case of the old asthmatic), had he been a saint? Tarrou hardly thought so, but he found in the old man's case 'a pointer'. 'Perhaps', he wrote, 'we can only reach approximations of sainthood. In which case we must make shift with a mild, benevolent diabolism.'

Interspersed with observations relating to Cottard are remarks, scattered here and there, about Grand – he was now convalescent and had gone back to work as if nothing had happened – and about Rieux's mother. The occasional conversations he had with her, when living under the same roof, the old lady's attitudes, her opinions on the plague, are all recorded in detail in the Diary. Tarrou lays stress above all on Mme Rieux's self-effacement, her way of explaining things in the simplest possible words, her predilection for a special window at which she always sat in the early evenings, holding herself rather straight, her hands at rest, her eyes fixed on the quiet street below, until twilight filled the room and she showed amongst the gathering shadows as a motionless black form, which gradually merged into the darkness. He remarks on the 'lightness' with which she moved from one room to the other; on her kindness – though no precise instances had come to his notice he discerned its gentle glow in all she said and did; on the gift she had of knowing everything without (apparently) taking thought; and, lastly, that dim and silent though she was, she quailed before no light, even the garish light of the plague. At this point Tarrou's handwriting began to fall off oddly; indeed the following lines were almost illegible. And, as if in confirmation of this loss of grip upon himself, the last lines of the entry deal – for the first time in the Diary – with his personal life. 'She reminds me of my mother; what I loved most in mother was her self-effacement, her "dimness", as they say, and it's her I've always wanted to get back to. It happened eight years ago; but I can't say she died. She only effaced herself a trifle more than usual, and when I looked round she was no longer there.'

But, to return to Cottard. When the weekly totals began to show a decline, he visited Rieux several times on various pretexts. But obviously what he really wanted was to get from Rieux his opinion on the probable course of the epidemic. 'Do you really think it can stop like that, all-of-a-sudden, like?' He was sceptical about this, or anyhow professed to be. But the fact that he kept on asking the question seemed to imply he was less sure than he professed to be. From the middle of January Rieux gave him fairly optimistic answers. But these were not to Cottard's liking, and his reactions varied on each occasion, from mere petulance to great despondency. One day the doctor was moved to tell him that, though the statistics were highly promising, it was too soon to say definitely that we were out of the wood.

'In other words,' Cottard said promptly, 'there's no knowing. It may start again at any moment.'

'Quite so. Just as it's equally possible the improvement may speed up.'

Distressing to everyone else, this state of uncertainty seemed to agree with Cottard. Tarrou observed that he would enter into conversations with shop-keepers in his part of the town, with the obvious desire of propagating the opinion expressed by Rieux. Indeed, he had no trouble in doing this. After the first exhilaration following the announcement of the plague's decline had worn off, doubts had returned to many minds. And the sight of their anxiety reassured Cottard. Just as at other times he yielded to discouragement. 'Yes,' he said gloomily to Tarrou, 'one of these days the gates will be opened. And then, you'll see, they'll drop me like a live coal.'

Everyone was struck by his abrupt changes of mood during the first three weeks of January. Though normally he spared no pains to make himself liked by neighbours and acquaintances, now, for whole days, he deliberately cold-shouldered them. On these occasions, so Tarrou gathered, he abruptly cut off outside contacts and retired morosely into his shell. He was no more to be seen in restaurants or at the theatre or in his favourite cafés. However, he seemed unable to resume the obscure, humdrum life he had led before the epidemic. He stayed in his room and had his meals sent up from a near-by restaurant. Only at nightfall did he venture forth to make some small purchases, and on leaving the shop he would roam furtively the darker, less-frequented streets. Once or twice Tarrou ran into him on these occasions, but failed to elicit more than a few gruff monosyllables. Then, from one day to another, he became sociable again, talked volubly about the plague, asking everyone for his views on it, and mingled in the crowd with evident pleasure.

On January 25, the day of the official announcement, Cottard went to cover again. Two days later Tarrou came across him loitering in a side-street. When Cottard suggested he should accompany him home, Tarrou demurred; he'd had a particularly tiring day. But Cottard wouldn't hear of a refusal. He seemed much agitated, gesticulated freely, spoke very rapidly and in a very loud tone. He began by asking Tarrou if he really thought the official communiqué meant an end of the plague. Tarrou replied that obviously a mere official announcement couldn't stop an epidemic, but it certainly looked as if, barring accidents, it would shortly cease.

'Yes,' Cottard said. 'Barring accidents. And accidents *will* happen, won't they?'

Tarrou pointed out that the authorities had allowed for that possibility by refusing to open the gates for another fortnight.

'And very wise they were!' Cottard exclaimed in the same excited tone. 'By the way things are going, I should say they'll have to eat their words.'

Tarrou agreed this might be so; still he thought it wiser to count on the opening of the gates and a return to normal life in the near future.

'Granted!' Cottard rejoined. 'But what do you mean by "a return to normal life"?'

Tarrou smiled. 'New films at the picture-houses.'

But Cottard didn't smile. Was it supposed, he asked, that the plague wouldn't have changed anything and the life of the town would go on as before, exactly as if nothing had happened? Tarrou thought that the plague would have changed things and not changed them; naturally our fellow-citizens' strongest desire was, and would be, to behave as if nothing had changed and for that reason nothing would be changed, in a sense. But — to look at it from another angle — one can't forget everything, however great one's wish to do so; the plague was bound to leave traces, anyhow, in people's hearts.

To this Cottard rejoined curtly that he wasn't interested in hearts; indeed they were the last thing he bothered about. What interested him was knowing whether the whole administration wouldn't be changed, lock, stock and barrel; whether, for instance, the public services would function as before. Tarrou had to admit he had no inside knowledge on the matter; his personal theory was that after the upheaval caused by the epidemic there would be some delay in getting these services under way again. Also, it seemed likely that all sorts of new problems would arise and necessitate at least some re-organization of the administrative system.

Cottard nodded. 'Yes, that's quite on the cards; in fact everyone will have to make a fresh start.'

They were nearing Cottard's house. He now seemed more cheerful, determined to take a rosier view of the future. Obviously he was picturing the town entering on a new lease of life, blotting out its past and starting again with a clean sheet.

'So that's that,' Tarrou smiled. 'Quite likely things will pan out all right for you, too – who can say? It'll be a new life for all of us, in a manner of speaking.'

They were shaking hands at the door of the apartment house where Cottard lived.

'Quite right!' Cottard was growing more and more excited. 'That would be a great idea, starting again with a clean sheet.'

Suddenly from the lightless hall two men emerged. Tarrou had hardly time to hear his companion mutter, 'Now what do they want, those chaps?' when the men in question, who looked like subordinate government employees in their best clothes, cut in with an inquiry if his name was Cottard. With a stifled exclamation Cottard swung round and dashed off into the darkness. Taken by surprise, Tarrou and the two men gazed blankly at each other for some moments. Then Tarrou asked them what they wanted. In non-committal tones they informed him that they wanted 'some information', and walked away, unhurrying, in the direction Cottard had taken.

On his return home Tarrou wrote out an account of this peculiar incident, following it up with a 'Feeling very tired tonight' – which is confirmed by his handwriting in this entry.

He added that he had still much to do, but that was no reason for not 'holding himself in readiness', and he questioned if he were ready. As a sort of postscript — and, in fact, it is here that Tarrou's Diary ends — he noted that there is always a certain hour of the day and of the night when a man's courage is at its lowest ebb, and it was that hour only which he feared.

III

WHEN NEXT DAY, a few days before the date fixed for the opening of the gates, Dr Rieux came home at noon, he was wondering if the telegram he was expecting had arrived. Though his days were no less strenuous than at the height of the epidemic, the prospect of imminent release had obliterated his fatigue. Hope had returned and with it a new zest for life. No man can live on the stretch all the time, with his energy and will-power strained to the breaking-point, and it is a joy to be able to relax at last, and loosen nerves and muscles that were braced for the struggle. If the telegram, too, that he awaited brought good news, Rieux would be able to make a fresh start. Indeed, he had a feeling that everyone, in those days, was making a fresh start.

He walked past the door-porter's room in the hall. The new man, old Michel's successor, his face pressed to the window looking on the hall, gave him a smile. As he went up the stairs, the man's face, pale with exhaustion and privation, but smiling, hovered before his eyes.

Yes, he'd make a fresh start, once the period of 'abstractions' was over, and with any luck . . . He was opening the door with these thoughts in his mind when he saw his mother coming down the hall to meet him. Monsieur Tarrou, she told him, wasn't well. He had risen at the usual time, but did not feel up to going out, and had returned to bed. Mme Rieux felt worried about him.

'Quite likely it's nothing serious,' her son said.

Tarrou was lying on his back, his heavy head deeply indenting the pillow, the coverlet bulging above his massive chest. His head was aching and his temperature up. The symptoms weren't very definite, he told Rieux, but they might well be those of plague.

After examining him Rieux said, 'No, there's nothing definite as yet.'

But Tarrou also suffered from a raging thirst, and in the passage the doctor told his mother that it might be plague.

'Oh!' she exclaimed. 'Surely that's not possible, not now!' And after a moment added: 'Let's keep him here, Bernard.'

Rieux pondered. 'Strictly speaking, I've no right to do that,' he said doubtfully. 'Still, the gates will be opened quite soon. If you weren't here, I think I'd take it on myself. . . .'

'Bernard, let him stay, and let me stay too. You know, I've just had another inoculation.'

The doctor pointed out that Tarrou, too, had had inoculations, though it was possible, tired as he was, he'd overlooked the last one or omitted to take the necessary precautions.

Rieux was going to the surgery as he spoke, and when he returned to the bedroom Tarrou noticed that he had a box of the big ampoules containing the serum.

'Ah, so it *is* that,' he said.

'Not necessarily; but we mustn't run any risks.'

Without replying Tarrou extended his arm and submitted to the prolonged injections he himself had so often administered to others.

'We'll judge better this evening.' Rieux looked Tarrou in the eyes.

'But – what about isolating me?'

'It's by no means certain that you have plague.'

Tarrou smiled, with an effort.

'Well, it's the first time I've known you do the injection without ordering the patient off to the isolation ward.'

Rieux looked away.

'You'll be better here. My mother and I will look after you.'

Tarrou said nothing and the doctor, who was putting away the ampoules in the box, waited for him to speak before looking round. But still Tarrou said nothing, and finally Rieux went up to the bed. The sick man was gazing at him steadily and though his face was drawn, the grey eyes were calm. Rieux smiled down on him.

'Now try to sleep. I'll be back presently.'

As he was going out he heard Tarrou calling, and turned back. Tarrou's manner had an odd effect, as though he were at once trying to keep back what he had to say and forcing himself to say it.

'Rieux,' he said at last, 'you must tell me the whole truth. I count on that.'

'I promise it.'

Tarrou's heavy face relaxed in a brief smile.

'Thanks. I don't want to die, and I shall put up a fight. But if I lose the match, I want to make a good end of it.'

Bending forward, Rieux pressed his shoulder.

'No. To become a saint you need to live. So – fight away!'

In the course of that day the weather, which after being very cold had grown slightly milder, broke in a series of violent hailstorms followed by rain. At sunset the sky cleared a little, and it was bitterly cold again. Rieux came home in the evening. His overcoat still on, he entered his friend's bedroom. Tarrou did not seem to have moved, but his set lips, drained white by fever, told of the effort he was keeping up.

'Well?' Rieux asked.

Tarrou raised his broad shoulders a little out of the bed-clothes.

'Well,' he said, 'I'm losing the match.'

The doctor bent over him. Ganglions had formed under the burning skin and there was a rumbling in his chest, like the sound of a hidden forge. The strange thing was that Tarrou showed symptoms of both varieties of plague at once.

Rieux straightened up and said the serum hadn't yet had time to take effect. An uprush of fever in his throat drowned the few words that Tarrou tried to utter.

After dinner Rieux and his mother took up their posts at the sick man's bedside. The night began with a struggle, and Rieux knew that this grim wrestling with the angel of plague was to last until dawn. In this struggle Tarrou's robust shoulders and chest were not his greatest assets; rather, the blood which had spurted under Rieux's needle and, in this blood, that something more vital than the soul, which no human skill can bring to light. The doctor's task could be only to watch his friend's struggle. As to what he was about to do, the stimulants to inject, the abscesses to stimulate – many months' repeated failures had taught him to appreciate such expedients at their true value. Indeed, the only way in which he might help was to provide opportunities for the beneficence of chance, which too often stays dormant unless roused to action. Luck was an ally he could not dispense with. For Rieux was confronted by an aspect of the plague that baffled him. Yet again it was doing all it could to confound the tactics used against it; it launched attacks in unexpected places and retreated from those where it seemed definitely lodged. Once more it was out to darken counsel.

Tarrou struggled without moving. Not once in the course of the night did he counter the enemy's attacks by restless agitation; only with all his stolid bulk, with silence, did he carry on the fight. Nor did he even try to speak, thus intimating, after his fashion, that he could no longer let his attention stray. Rieux could follow the vicissitudes of the struggle only in his friend's eyes, now open and now shut; in the eyelids now more closely welded to the eyeball, now distended; and in his gaze fixed on some object in the room or brought back to the doctor and his mother. And each time it met the doctor's gaze, with a great effort Tarrou smiled.

At one moment there came a sound of hurrying footsteps in the street. They were in flight before a distant throbbing which gradually approached until the street was loud with the clamour of the downpour; another rain-squall was sweeping the town, mingled presently with hailstones that clattered on the pavement. Window awnings were flapping wildly. Rieux, whose attention had been diverted momentarily by the noises of the squall, looked again across the shadows at Tarrou's face, on which fell the light of a small bedside lamp. His mother was knitting, raising her eyes now and again from her work to gaze at the sick man. The doctor had done everything that could be done. When the squall had passed the silence in the room grew denser, filled only by the silent turmoil of the unseen battle. His nerves overwrought by sleeplessness, the doctor fancied he could hear, on the edge of the silence, that faint eerie sibilance which had haunted his ears ever since the beginning of the epidemic. He made a sign to his mother, indicating she should go to bed. She shook her head, and her eyes grew brighter; then she examined carefully, at her needle-tips, a stitch of which she was unsure. Rieux got up, gave the sick man a drink, and sat down again.

Footsteps rang on the pavement, nearing, then receding; people were taking advantage of the lull to hurry home. For the first time the doctor realized that this night, without the clang of ambulances and full of belated wayfarers, was just like a night of the past; a plague-free night. It was as if the pestilence, hounded away by cold, the street-lamps and the crowd, had fled from the depths of the town and taken shelter in this warm room, and was launching its last offensive at Tarrou's inert body. No longer did it thresh the air above the houses with its flail. But it was whistling softly in the stagnant air of the sick-room, and this it was that Rieux had been hearing since the long vigil began. And now it was for him to wait and watch until that strange sound ceased here too, and here as well the plague confessed defeat.

A little before dawn Rieux leaned towards his mother and whispered:

'You'd better have some rest now, as you'll have to relieve me at eight. Mind you take your drops before going to bed.'

Mme Rieux rose, folded her knitting and went to the bedside. Tarrou had had his eyes shut for some time. Sweat had plastered his hair on his stubborn forehead. Mme Rieux sighed, and he opened his eyes. He saw the gentle face bent over him and, athwart the surge of fever, that steadfast smile took form again. But at once the eyes closed. Left to himself, Rieux moved into the chair his mother had just left. The street was silent and no sound came from the sleeping town. The chill of daybreak was beginning to make itself felt.

The doctor dozed off, but very soon an early cart rattling down the street awakened him. Shivering a little, he looked at Tarrou and saw that a lull had come; he, too, was sleeping. The iron-shod wheels rumbled away into the distance. Darkness still was pressing on the window-panes. When the doctor came beside the bed, Tarrou gazed at him with expressionless eyes, like a man still on the frontier of sleep.

'You slept, didn't you?' Rieux asked.

'Yes.'

'Breathing better?'

'A bit. Does that mean anything?'

Rieux kept silent for some moments; then he said:

'No, Tarrou, it doesn't mean anything. You know as well as I that there's often a remission in the morning.'

'Thanks.' Tarrou nodded his approval. 'Always tell me the exact truth.'

Rieux was sitting on the side of the bed. Beside him he could feel the sick man's legs, stiff and hard as the limbs of an effigy on a tomb. Tarrou was breathing with more difficulty.

'The fever'll come back, won't it, Rieux?' he gasped.

'Yes. But at noon we shall know where we stand.'

Tarrou shut his eyes; he seemed to be mustering up his strength. There was a look of utter weariness on his face. He was waiting for the fever to rise and already it was stirring somewhere in the depths of his being. When he opened his eyes, his gaze was misted. It brightened only when he saw Rieux bending over him, a tumbler in his hand.

'Drink.'

Tarrou drank, then slowly lowered his head on to the pillow.

'It's a long business,' he murmured.

Rieux clasped his arm but Tarrou, whose head was averted, showed no reaction. Then suddenly, as if some inner dyke had given way without warning, the fever surged back, dyeing his cheeks and forehead. Tarrou's eyes came back to the doctor who, bending again, gave him a look of affectionate encouragement. Tarrou tried to shape a smile, but it could not force its way through the set jaws and lips welded by dry saliva. In the rigid face only the eyes lived still, glowing with courage.

At seven Mme Rieux returned to the bedroom. The doctor went to the surgery to ring up the hospital and arrange for a substitute. He also decided to put back his consultations; then lay down for some moments on the surgery couch. Five minutes later he went back to the bedroom. Tarrou's face was turned towards Mme Rieux, who was sitting close beside the bed, her hands folded on her lap; in the dim light of the room she seemed no more than a darker patch of shadow. Tarrou was gazing at her so intently that, putting a finger to her lips, Mme Rieux rose and switched off the bedside lamp. Behind the curtains the light was growing and presently, when the sick man's face grew visible, Mme Rieux could see his eyes still intent on her. Bending above the bed, she smoothed out the counterpane and, as she straightened up, laid her hand for a moment on his moist, tangled hair. Then she heard a muffled voice, that seemed to come from very far away, murmur, 'Thank you,' and that all was well now. By the time she was back in her chair Tarrou had shut his eyes, and, despite the sealed mouth, a faint smile seemed to hover on the wasted face.

At noon the fever reached its climax. A visceral cough racked the sick man's body and he now was spitting blood. The ganglions had ceased swelling, but they were still there, like lumps of iron embedded in the joints. Rieux decided that lancing them was impracticable. Now and again, in the intervals between bouts of fever and coughing fits, Tarrou still gazed at his friends. But soon his eyes opened less and less often and the glow that shone out from the ravaged face in the brief moments of recognition grew steadily fainter. The storm, lashing his body into convulsive movement, lit it up with ever rarer flashes, and in the heart of the tempest he was slowly drifting, derelict. And now Rieux had before him only a mask-like face, inert, from which the smile had gone for ever. This human form, his friend's, lacerated by the spear-thrusts of the plague, consumed by searing, superhuman fires, buffeted by all the raging winds of heaven, was foundering under his eyes in the dark flood of the pestilence, and he could do nothing to avert the wreck. He could only stand, unavailing, on the shore, empty-handed and sick at heart, unarmed and helpless yet again under the onset of calamity. And thus, when the end came, the tears that blinded Rieux's eyes were tears of impotence; and he did not see Tarrou roll over, face to the wall, and die with a short, hollow groan as if somewhere within him an essential cord had snapped. . . .

The next night was not one of struggle but of silence. In the tranquil death-chamber, beside the dead body now in everyday clothing – here, too, Rieux felt it brooding, that elemental peace which, when he was sitting many nights before on the terrace high above the plague, had followed the brief foray at the gates. Then, already, it had brought to his mind the silence brooding over the beds in which he had let men die. There as here it was the same solemn pause, the lull that follows battle;

the silence of defeat. But the silence now enveloping his dead friend, so dense, so much akin to the nocturnal silence of the streets and of the town set free at last, made Rieux cruelly aware that this defeat was final, the last disastrous battle that ends a war and makes peace itself an ill beyond all remedy. The doctor could not tell if Tarrou had found peace, now that all was over, but for himself he had a feeling that no peace was possible to him henceforth, any more than there can be an armistice for a mother bereaved of her son or for a man who buries his friend.

The night was cold again, with frosty stars sparkling in a clear, wintry sky. And in the dimly lit room they felt the cold pressing itself to the window-panes and heard the long, silvery suspiration of a polar night. Mme Rieux sat near the bed in her usual attitude, her right side lit up by the bedside lamp. In the centre of the room, outside the little zone of light, Rieux sat, waiting. Now and again thoughts of his wife waylaid him, but he brushed them aside each time.

When the night began the heels of passers-by had rung briskly in the frozen air.

'Have you attended to everything?' Mme Rieux had asked.

'Yes. I've telephoned.'

Then they had resumed their silent vigil. From time to time Mme Rieux stole a glance at her son and, whenever he caught her doing this, he smiled. Out in the street the usual night-time sounds bridged the long silences. A good many cars were on the road again, though officially this was not yet permitted; they sped past with a long hiss of tyres on the roadway, receded and returned. Voices, distant calls, silence again, a clatter of horse-hoofs, the squeal of trams rounding a curve, vague murmurs – then once more the quiet breathing of the night.

'Bernard?'

'Yes?'

'Not too tired?'

'No.'

At that moment he knew what his mother was thinking, and that she loved him. But he knew, too, that to love someone means relatively little; or, rather, that love is never strong enough to find the words befitting it. Thus he and his mother would always love each other silently. And one day she – or he – would die, without ever, all their lives long, having gone further than this by way of making their affection known. Thus, too, he had lived at Tarrou's side and Tarrou had died this evening without their friendship's having had time to enter fully into the life of either. Tarrou had 'lost the match', as he put it. But what had he, Rieux, won? No more than the experience of having known plague and remembering it, of having known friendship and remembering it, of knowing affection and being destined one day to remember it. So all a man could win in the conflict between plague and life was knowledge and memories. But Tarrou, perhaps, would have called that winning the match.

Another car passed, and Mme Rieux stirred slightly. Rieux smiled towards her. She assured him she wasn't tired and immediately added:

'You must go and have a good long rest in the mountains, over there.'

'Yes, Mother.'

Certainly he'd take a rest 'over there'. It, too, would be a pretext for memory. But if that was what it meant, winning the match – how hard it must be to live only with what one knows and what one remembers, cut off from what one hopes for! It was thus, most probably, that Tarrou had lived, and he realized the bleak sterility of a life without illusions. There can be no peace without hope, and Tarrou, denying as he did the right to condemn anyone whomsoever – though he knew well that no one can help condemning and it befalls even the victim sometimes to turn executioner – Tarrou had lived a life riddled with contradictions, and had never known hope's solace. Did that explain his aspiration towards saintliness, his quest of peace by service in the cause of others? Actually Rieux had no idea of the answer to that question, and it mattered little. The only picture of Tarrou he would always have would be the picture of a man who firmly gripped the steering-wheel of his car when driving, or else the picture of that stalwart body, now lying motionless. Knowing meant that: a living warmth, and a picture of death.

That, no doubt, explains Dr Rieux's composure on receiving next morning the news of his wife's death. He was in the surgery. His mother came in, almost running, and handed him a telegram; then went back to the hall to give the telegraph-boy a tip. When she returned, her son was holding the telegram open in his hand. She looked at him, but his eyes were resolutely fixed on the window; it was flooded with the effulgence of the morning sun rising above the harbour.

'Bernard,' she said gently.

The doctor turned and looked at her almost as if she were a stranger.

'The telegram?'

'Yes,' he said. 'That's it. . . . A week ago.'

Mme Rieux turned her face towards the window. Rieux kept silent for a while. Then he told his mother not to cry, he'd been expecting it, but it was hard all the same. And he knew, in saying this, that this suffering was nothing new. For many months, and for the last two days, it was the self-same suffering going on and on.

IV

AT LAST, AT daybreak on a fine February morning, the ceremonial opening of the gates took place, acclaimed by the populace, the newspapers, the wireless and official communiqués. It only remains for the narrator to give what account he can of the rejoicings that followed, though he himself was one of those debarred from sharing in them wholeheartedly.

Elaborate day and night fêtes were organized, and at the same time smoke began to rise from locomotives in the station and ships were already heading for our harbour – reminders in their divers ways that this was the long-awaited day of reuniting, and the end of tears for all who had been parted.

We can easily picture, at this stage, the consequences of that feeling of separation which had so long rankled in the hearts of so many of our townsfolk. Trains coming in were as crowded as those that left the town in the course of the day. Every passenger had reserved his seat long in advance and had been on tenterhooks during the past fortnight lest at the last moment the authorities should go back on their decision. Some of these incoming travellers were still somewhat nervous; though as a rule they knew the lot of those nearest and dearest to them, they were still in the dark about the others and the town itself – of which their imagination painted a grim and terrifying picture. But this applies only to people who had not been eating their hearts out during the long months of exile, and not to parted lovers.

The lovers, indeed, were wholly wrapped up in their fixed idea, and for them one thing only had changed. Whereas during those months of separation time had never gone quickly enough for their liking and they were always wanting to speed its flight; now that they were in sight of the town they would have liked to slow it down and to hold each moment in suspense once the brakes went on and the train was entering the station. For the sensation, confused perhaps but none the less poignant for that, of all those days and weeks and months of life lost to their love made them vaguely feel they were entitled to some compensation; this present hour of joy should run at half the speed of those long hours of waiting. And the people who awaited them at home or on the platform – amongst the latter, Rambert, whose wife, warned in good time, had got busy at once and was coming by the first train – were likewise fretting with impatience and quivering with anxiety. For even

Rambert felt a nervous tremor at the thought that soon he would have to confront a love and a devotion, that the plague months had slowly refined to a pale abstraction, with the flesh-and-blood woman who had given rise to them.

If only he could put the clock back and be once more the man who, at the outbreak of the epidemic, had had only one thought and one desire: to escape and return to the woman he loved! But that, he knew, was out of the question now; he had changed too greatly. The plague had forced on him a detach-ment which, try as he might, he couldn't think away, and which like a formless fear haunted his mind. Almost he thought the plague had ended too abruptly, he hadn't had time to pull himself together. Happiness was bearing down on him, full speed; the event outrunning expectation. Ram-bert understood that all would be restored to him in a flash, and joy break on him like a flame with which there is no dallying.

Everyone indeed, more or less consciously, felt as he did, and it is of all those people on the platform that we wish to speak. Each was returning to his personal life, yet the sense of comradeship persisted and they were exchanging smiles and cheerful glances amongst themselves. But the moment they saw the smoke of the approaching engine, the feeling of exile vanished before an uprush of overpowering, bewildering joy. And, when the train stopped, all those interminable-seeming separations that often had begun on this same platform came to an end in one ecstatic moment, when arms closed with hungry possessiveness on bodies whose living shape they had forgot-ten. As for Rambert, he hadn't time to see her running towards him; already she had flung herself upon his breast. And with his arms locked round her, pressing to his shoulder the head of which he saw only the familiar hair, he let his tears flow freely, unknowing if they rose from present joy or from sorrow too long repressed; aware only that they would prevent his making sure if the face buried in the hollow of his shoulder were the face of which he had dreamed so often and so often, or, instead, a stranger's face. For the moment, he wished to behave like all those others round him who believed, or made believe, that plague can come and go without changing anything in men's hearts.

Nestling to each other, they went to their homes, blind to the outside world and seemingly triumphant over the plague, forgetting every sadness and the plight of those who had come by the same train and found no one awaiting them, and were bracing themselves to hear in their homes a confirmation of the fear which the long silence had already implanted in their hearts. For these last, who had now for company only their newborn grief, for those who at this moment were dedicating themselves to a lifelong memory of bereavement – for these unhappy people matters were very different, the pangs of separation had touched their climax. For the mothers, husbands, wives and lovers who had lost all joy, now that the loved one lay under a layer of quicklime in a death-pit, or was a mere handful of indistinctive ashes in a grey mound, the plague had not yet ended.

But who gave a thought to these lonely mourners? Routing the cold flaws that had been threshing the air since early morning, the sun was pouring on the town a steady flood of tranquil light. In the forts, on the hills, under a sky of pure, unwavering blue, guns were thundering, without a break. And everyone was out and about to celebrate those crowded moments when the time of ordeal ended and the time of forgetting had not yet begun.

In streets and squares people were dancing. Within twenty-four hours the motor traffic had doubled and the ever more numerous cars were held up at every turn by merry-making crowds. Every church-bell was in full peal throughout the afternoon, and the bells filled the blue and gold sky with their reverberations. Indeed, in all the churches thanksgiving services were being held. But, at the same time, the places of entertainment were packed, and the cafés, caring nothing for the morrow, were producing their last bottles of spirits. A noisy concourse surged round every bar, including loving couples who fondled each other without a thought for appearances. All were laughing or shouting. The reserves of emotion pent up during those many months when for everybody the flame of life burnt low were being recklessly squandered to celebrate this, the red-letter day of their survival. Tomorrow real life would begin again, with its restrictions. But for the moment people in very different walks of life were rubbing shoulders, fraternizing. The levelling-out that death's imminence had failed in practice to accomplish was realized at last, for a few gay hours, in the rapture of escape.

But this rather tawdry exuberance was only one aspect of the town that day; not a few of those filling the streets at sundown, amongst them Rambert and his wife, hid under an air of calm satisfaction subtler forms of happiness. Many couples, indeed, and many families, looked like people out for a casual stroll, no more than that; in reality most of them were making sentimental pilgrimages to places where they had gone to school with suffering. The new-comers were being shown the striking or obscurer tokens of the plague, relics of its passage. In some cases the survivor merely played the part of guide, the eyewitness who has 'been through it', and talked freely of the danger without mentioning his fear. These were the milder forms of pleasure, little more than recreation. In other cases, however, there was more emotion to these walks about the town, as when a man, pointing to some place charged for him with sad yet tender associations, would say to the girl or woman beside him, 'This is where one evening just like this, I longed for you so desperately – and you weren't there!' These passionate pilgrims could readily be distinguished; they formed oases of whispers, aloof, self-centred, in the turbulence of the crowd. Far more effectively than the bands playing in the squares they vouched for the vast joy of liberation. These ecstatic couples, locked together, hardly speaking, proclaimed in the midst of the tumult of rejoicing, with the proud egoism and injustice of happy people, that the plague was over, the reign of terror ended. Calmly they denied, in the teeth of the evidence, that we had ever known a crazy world in which men were killed off like flies, or that precise savagery, that calculated frenzy of the plague, which instilled an odious freedom as to all that was not the Here and Now; or those charnel-house stenches which stupefied whom they did not kill. In short, they denied that we had ever been that hag-ridden populace a part of which was daily fed into a furnace and went up in oily fumes, while the rest, in shackled impotence, waited their turn.

That, anyhow, was what seemed evident to Rieux when towards the close of the afternoon, on his way to the outskirts of the town, he walked alone in an uproar of bells, guns, bands and deafening shouts. There was no question of his taking a day off; sick men have no holidays. Through the cool, clear light bathing the town rose the familiar smells of roasting meat and anise-flavoured spirit. All round him happy faces were turned towards the shining sky, men and women with flushed cheeks embraced each other, with low, tense cries of desire. Yes, the plague had ended with the terror, and those passionately straining arms told what it had meant: exile and deprivation in the profoundest meaning of the words.

For the first time Rieux found that he could give a name to the family likeness which for several months he had detected in the faces in the streets. He had only to look around him, now. At the end of the plague, with its misery and privations, these men and women had come to wear the aspect of the part they had been playing for so long; the part of emigrants whose faces first, and now their clothes, told of long banishment from a distant homeland. Once plague had shut the gates of the town, they had settled down to a life of separation, debarred from the living warmth that gives forgetfulness of all. In different degrees, in every part of the town, men and women had been yearning for a reunion, not of the same kind for all, but for all alike ruled out. Most of them had longed intensely for an absent one, for the warmth of a body, for love, or merely for a life that habit had endeared. Some, often without knowing it, suffered from being deprived of the company of friends and from their inability to get in touch with them through the usual channels of friendship – letters, trains and boats. Others, fewer these – Tarrou may have been one of them – had desired reunion with something they couldn't have defined, but which seemed to them the only desirable thing on earth. For want of a better name, they sometimes called it peace.

Rieux walked on. As he progressed, the crowds grew thicker, the din multiplied, and he had a feeling that his destination was receding as he advanced. Gradually he found himself drawn into the seething, clamorous mass, and understanding more and more the cry that went up from it, a cry that, for some part at least, was his. Yes, they had suffered together, in body no less than in soul, from a cruel leisure, exile without redress, thirst that was never slaked. Amongst the heaps of corpses, the clanging bells of ambulances, the warnings of what goes by the name of Fate, amongst unremitting waves of fear and agonized revolt, the horror that such things could be, always a great voice had been ringing in the ears of these forlorn, panicked people, a voice calling them back to the land of their desire, a homeland. It lay outside the walls of the stifled, strangled town, in the fragrant brushwood of the hills, in the waves of the sea, under free skies, and in the custody of love. And it was to this, their lost home, towards happiness, they longed to return, turning their backs disgustedly on all else.

As to what that exile and that longing for reunion meant, Rieux had no idea. But as he walked ahead, jostled on all sides, accosted now and then, and gradually made his way into less crowded streets, he was thinking it has no importance whether such things have or have not a meaning; all we need consider is the answer given to men's hope.

Henceforth he knew the answer, and he perceived it better now he was in the outskirts of the town, in almost empty streets. Those who, clinging to their little own, had set their hearts solely on returning to the home of their love, had sometimes their reward – though some of them were still walking the streets alone, without the one they had awaited. Then, again, those were happy who had not suffered a twofold separation, like some of us who, in the days before the epidemic, had failed to build their love on a solid basis at the outset, and had spent years blindly groping for the pact, so slow and hard to come by, that in the long run binds together ill-assorted lovers. Such people had had, like Rieux himself, the rashness of counting overmuch on time; and now they were parted for ever. But others – like Rambert, to whom the doctor had said early that morning, 'Courage! It's up to you *now* to prove you're right' – had, without faltering, welcomed back the loved one who they thought was lost to them. And for some time, anyhow, they would be happy. They knew now that if there is one thing one can always yearn for, and sometimes attain, it is human love.

But for those others, who aspired beyond and above the human individual towards something they could not even imagine, there had been no answer. Tarrou might seem to have won through to that hardly-come-by peace of which he used to speak; but he had found it only in death, too late to turn it to account. If others, however – Rieux could see them in the doorways of houses, passionately embracing and gazing hungrily at each other in the failing sunset glow – had got what they wanted, this was because they had asked for the one thing that depended on them solely. And, as he turned the corner of the street where Grand and Cottard lived, Rieux was thinking it was only right that those whose desires are limited to man and his humble yet formidable love, should enter, if only now and again, into their reward.

V

THIS CHRONICLE IS drawing to an end, and this seems to be the moment for Dr Bernard Rieux to confess that he is the narrator. But, before describing the closing scenes, he would wish anyhow to justify his undertaking and to set it down that he expressly made a point of adopting the tone of an impartial observer. His profession put him in touch with a great many of our townsfolk while plague was raging, and he had opportunities of hearing their various opinions. Thus he was well placed for giving a true account of all he saw and heard. But in so doing he has tried to keep within the limits that seemed desirable. For instance, in a general way he has confined himself to describing only such things as he was enabled to see for himself, and refrained from attributing to his fellow-sufferers thoughts that, when all is said and done, they were not bound to have. And, as for documents, he has used only such as chance, or mischance, put in his way.

Summoned to give evidence regarding what was a sort of crime, he has exercised the restraint that behoves a conscientious witness. All the same, following the dictates of his heart, he has deliberately taken the victims' side and tried to share with his fellow-citizens the only certitudes they had in common — love, exile and suffering. Thus he can truly say there was not one of their anxieties in which he did not share, no predicament of theirs that was not his.

To be an honest witness, it was for him to confine himself mainly to what people did or said and what could be gleaned from documents. Regarding his personal troubles and his long suspense, his duty was to hold his peace. When now and again he refers to such matters, it is only for the light they may throw on his fellow-citizens and in order to give a picture, as well-defined as possible, of what most of the time they felt confusedly. Actually, this self-imposed reticence cost him little effort. Whenever tempted to add his personal note to the myriad voices of the plague-stricken, he was deterred by the thought that not one of his sufferings but was common to all the others and that in a world where sorrow is so often lonely this was an advantage. Thus, decidedly, it was up to him to speak for all.

But there was at least one of our townsfolk for whom Dr Rieux could not speak, the man of whom Tarrou said one day to Rieux, 'His only real crime is that of having in his heart approved of something that killed off men, women and children. I can understand the rest, but for *that* I am obliged to pardon him.' It is fitting that this chronicle should end with some reference to that man, who had an ignorant, that is to say lonely, heart.

On turning out of the main thoroughfares where the rejoicings were in full swing, and entering the street where Grand and Cottard lived, Dr Rieux was held up by a police cordon. Nothing could have surprised him more. This quiet part of the town seemed all the quieter for the sounds of festivity in the distance, and the doctor pictured it as deserted as it was tranquil.

'Sorry, doctor,' a policeman said, 'but I can't let you through. There's a crazy fellow with a gun, shooting at everybody. But you'd better stay; we may need you.'

Just then Rieux saw Grand coming towards him. Grand, too, had no idea what was happening and the police had stopped him, too. He had been told that the shots came from the house where he lived. They could see, some way down the street, the frontage of the house, bathed in cool evening light. Farther down the street was another line of policemen like the one which had prevented Rieux and Grand from advancing, and behind the line some of the local residents could be seen crossing and recrossing the street hastily. The roadway immediately in front of the house was quite empty and in the middle of the hollow square lay a hat and a piece of dirty cloth. Looking more carefully, they saw more policemen, revolver in hand, sheltering in doorways facing the house. All the shutters in Grand's house were closed, except one on the second floor which seemed to be hanging loose, on one hinge only. Not a sound could be heard in the street, but for occasional snatches of music coming from the centre of the town.

Suddenly two revolver shots rang out; they came from one of the buildings opposite and some splinters flew off the dismantled shutter. Then silence came again. Seen from a distance, after the tumult of the day, the whole business seemed to Rieux fantastically unreal, like something in a dream.

'That's Cottard's window,' Grand suddenly exclaimed. 'I can't make it out. I thought he'd disappeared.'

'Why are they shooting?' Rieux asked the policeman.

'Oh, just to keep him busy. We're waiting for a van to come with the stuff that's needed. He looses off at anyone who tries to get in by the front door. He got one of our men just now.'

'But why did he fire?'

'Ask me another! Some folks were larking about in the street, and he let off at them. They couldn't make it out at first. When he fired again they started yelling, one man was wounded and the rest took to their heels. Some fellow gone off his rocker, I should say.'

The minutes seemed interminable, in the silence that had returned. Then they noticed a dog, the first dog Rieux had seen for many months, emerging on the other side of the street; a draggled-looking spaniel which its owners had, presumably, kept in hiding. It ambled along the wall, stopped in the doorway and began to flea itself. Some of the policemen whistled for it to come away. It raised its head, then walked out into the road and was sniffing at the hat when a revolver barked from the second-floor window. The dog did a somersault like a tossed pancake, lashed the air with its legs and floundered on to its side, its body writhing in long convulsions. As if by way of reprisal five or six shots from the opposite house knocked more splinters off the shutter. Then silence fell again. The sun had moved a little and the shadow-line was nearing Cottard's window. There was a low squeal of brakes in the street, behind the doctor.

'Here they are,' the policeman said.

A number of police-officers jumped out of the van and unloaded coils of rope, a ladder and two big oblong packages wrapped in oilcloth. Then they turned into a street behind the row of houses facing Grand's. A minute or so later there were signs of movement, though little could be seen, in the doorways of the houses. Then came a short spell of waiting. The dog had ceased moving; it now was lying in a small, dark, glistening pool.

Suddenly from the window of one of the houses which the police-officers had entered from behind there came a burst of machine-gun fire. They were still aiming at the shutter, which literally shredded itself away, disclosing a dark gap into which neither Grand nor Rieux could see from where they stood. When the first machine-gun stopped firing, another opened up from a different angle, in a house a little farther up the street. The shots were evidently directed into the window space and a fragment of the brickwork clattered down upon the pavement. At the same moment three police-officers charged across the road and disappeared into the doorway. The machine-gun ceased fire. Then came another wait. Two muffled detonations sounded inside the house, followed by a confused hubbub growing steadily louder until they saw a small man in his shirt-sleeves, screaming at the top of his voice, being carried more than dragged out by the doorway.

As if at an expected signal all the shutters in the street flew open and excited faces lined the windows, while people streamed out of the houses and jostled the lines of police. Rieux had a brief glimpse of the small man, on his feet now, in the middle of the road, his arms pinioned behind him by two police-officers. He was still screaming. A policeman went up and dealt him two hard blows with his fists, quite calmly, with a sort of conscientious thoroughness.

'It's Cottard!' Grand's voice was shrill with excitement. 'He's gone mad!'

Cottard had fallen backwards, and the policeman launched a vigorous kick into the crumpled mass sprawling on the ground. Then a small, surging group began to move towards the doctor and his old friend.

'Stand clear!' the policeman bawled.

Rieux looked away when the group, Cottard and his captors, passed him . . .

The dusk was thickening into night when Grand and the doctor made a move at last. The Cottard incident seemed to have shaken the neighbourhood out of its normal lethargy and even these remote streets were becoming crowded with noisy merry-makers. On his doorstep Grand bade the doctor good night; he was going to put in an evening's work, he said. Just as he was starting up the stairs he added that he'd written to Jeanne, and was feeling much happier. Also he'd made a fresh start with his phrase. 'I've cut out all the adjectives.'

And, with a twinkle in his eye, he took his hat off, bringing it low in a courtly sweep. But Rieux was thinking of Cottard, and the dull thud of fists belabouring the wretched man's face haunted him as he went to visit his old asthma patient. Perhaps it was more painful to think of a guilty man than of a dead man.

It was quite dark by the time he reached his patient's house. In the bedroom the distant clamour of a populace rejoicing in its new-won freedom could be faintly heard, and the old fellow was as usual transposing peas from one pan to another.

'They're quite right to amuse themselves,' he said. 'It takes all sorts to make a world, as they say. . . . And your colleague, doctor, how's he getting on?'

'He's dead.' Rieux was listening to his patient's rumbling chest.

'Ah . . . really?' The old fellow sounded embarrassed.

'Of plague,' Rieux added.

'Yes,' the old man said, after a moment's silence, 'it's always the best who go. That's how life is. But he was a man who knew what he wanted.'

'Why do you say that?' The doctor was putting back his stethoscope.

'Oh, for no particular reason. Only . . . well, he never talked just for talking's sake. I'd rather cottoned on to him. But there you are! All those folks are saying, "It was plague. We've had the plague here." You'd almost think they expected to be given medals for it. But what does that mean – "plague"? Just life, no more than that.'

'Mind you do your inhalations regularly.'

'Don't worry about me, doctor! There's lots of life in the old dog yet, and I'll see 'em all into their graves.' He chuckled. 'That's where I have 'em beat; *I* know how to live.'

A burst of joyful shouts in the distance seemed an echo of his boast. Half-way across the room the doctor halted.

'Would you mind if I go up on to the terrace?'

'Of course not. You'd like to have a look at 'em – that it? But they're just the same as ever, really.' When Rieux was leaving the room a new thought crossed the old man's mind. 'I say, doctor. Is it a fact they're going to put up a memorial to the people who died of plague?'

'So the papers say. A monument, or just a tablet.'

'I could have sworn it! And there'll be speeches.' Again he chuckled throatily. 'I can almost hear them saying, "Our dear departed . . . " And then they'll go off and have a good tuck-in.'

Rieux was already half-way up the stairs. Cold, fathomless depths of sky glimmered overhead, and near the hilltops stars shone hard as flint. It was much like the night when he and Tarrou had come to the terrace to forget the plague. Only, tonight the sea was breaking on the cliffs more loudly and the air was calm and limpid, free of the tang of brine the autumn wind had brought. The noises of the town were still beating like waves at the foot of the long line of terraces, but tonight they told not of revolt, but of deliverance. In the distance a reddish glow hung above the big central streets and squares. In this night of newborn freedom desires knew no limits, and it was their clamour that reached Rieux's ears.

From the dark harbour soared the first rocket of the fire-work display organized by the municipality, and the town acclaimed it with a long-drawn sigh of delight. Cottard, Tar-rou, the men and the woman Rieux had loved and lost — all alike, dead or guilty, were forgotten. Yes, the old fellow had been right; these people were 'just the same as ever'. But this was at once their strength and their innocence, and it was on this level, beyond all grief, that Rieux could feel himself at one with them. And it was in the midst of shouts rolling against the terrace wall in massive waves that waxed in volume and duration while cataracts of coloured fire fell thicker through the darkness, that Dr Rieux resolved to compile this chronicle, so that he should not be one of those who hold their peace but should bear witness in favour of those plague-stricken people; so that some memorial of the injustice and outrage done them might endure; and to state quite simply what we learn in a time of pestilence: that there are more things to admire in men than to despise.

None the less, he knew that the tale he had to tell could not be one of a final victory. It could be only the record of what had had to be done, and what assuredly would have to be done again in the never-ending fight against terror and its relentless onslaughts, despite their personal afflictions, by all who, while unable to be saints but refusing to bow down to pestilences, strive their utmost to be healers.

And, indeed, as he listened to the cries of joy rising from the town, Rieux remembered that such joy is always imperilled.

He knew what those jubilant crowds did not know but could have learned from books: that the plague bacillus never dies or disappears for good; that it can lie dormant for years and years in furniture and linen-chests; that it bides its time in bedrooms, cellars, trunks and book-shelves; and that perhaps the day would come when, for the bane and the enlightening of men, it roused up its rats again and sent them forth to die in a happy city.

THE FALL

TRANSLATED FROM THE FRENCH BY
JUSTIN O'BRIEN

Some were dreadfully insulted, and
quite seriously, to have held up as
a model such an immoral character as
A Hero of Our Time; others shrewdly
noticed that the author had portrayed
himself and his acquaintances. . . .
A Hero of Our Time, gentlemen, is in
fact a portrait but not of an individual;
it is the aggregate of the vices of
our whole generation in their fullest
expression.

LERMONTOV

MAY I, MONSIEUR, offer my services without running the risk of intruding? I fear you may not be able to make yourself understood by the worthy gorilla who presides over the fate of this establishment. In fact, he speaks nothing but Dutch. Unless you authorize me to plead your case, he will not guess that you want gin. There, I dare hope he understood me; that nod must mean that he yields to my arguments. He's on the move; indeed, he is making haste with a sort of careful deliberateness. You are lucky; he didn't grunt. When he refuses to serve someone, he merely grunts. No one insists. Being master of one's moods is the privilege of the larger animals. Now I shall withdraw, Monsieur, happy to have been of help to you. Thank you; I'd accept if I were sure of not being a nuisance. You are too kind. Then I shall bring my glass over beside yours.

You are right. His dumbness is deafening. It's the silence of the primeval forest, heavy with menaces. At times I am amazed by his obstinacy in snubbing civilized languages. His business consists in entertaining sailors of all nationalities in this Amsterdam bar, which he happens to have named – no one knows why – *Mexico City*. With such duties wouldn't you think there might be some fear that his ignorance would be uncomfortable? Fancy the Cro-Magnon man lodged in the Tower of Babel! He would certainly feel out of his element. Yet this one is not aware of his exile; he goes his own sweet way and nothing touches him. One of the rare sentences I have ever heard from his mouth proclaimed that you could take it or leave it. What did one have to take or leave? Doubtless our friend himself. I confess I am drawn by such creatures who are all of a piece. Anyone who has meditated a good deal on man, by profession or vocation, is led to feel nostalgia for the primates. They at least don't have any ulterior motives.

Our host, to tell the truth, has some, although he harbours them deep within him. As a result of not understanding what is said in his presence, he has taken on a distrustful character. Hence that look of touchy dignity as if he suspected, at least, that all is not perfect among men. That disposition makes it less easy to discuss anything with him which doesn't concern his business. Notice, for instance, on the back wall above his head that empty rectangle marking the place where a picture has been taken down. Indeed, there *was* a picture there, a particularly interesting one, a real masterpiece. Well, I was present when the master of the house received it and when he parted with it. In both cases he did so after weeks of rumination, with the same distrust. In that respect society has somewhat spoiled, you must admit, the frank simplicity of his nature.

Mind you, I'm not judging him. I consider his distrust justified and should be inclined to share it if, as you see, my communicative nature were not opposed to this. I am talkative, alas, and make friends easily. Although I know how to keep my distance, I seize any and every opportunity. When I used to live in France, were I to meet an intelligent man I immediately sought his company. If that be foolish . . . Ah, I see you smile at that use of the subjunctive. I confess my weakness for that mood and for fine speech in general. A weakness that I criticize in myself, believe me. I am well aware that an addiction to silk underwear does not necessarily imply that one's feet are dirty. None the less, style, like sheer silk, too often hides eczema. My consolation is to tell myself that, after all, those who murder the language are not pure either. Why yes, let's have another gin.

Are you staying long in Amsterdam? A beautiful city, isn't it? Fascinating? There's an adjective I haven't heard for some time. Not since leaving Paris in fact, years ago. But the heart has its own memory and I have forgotten nothing of our beautiful capital, nor of its quays. Paris is a real *trompe-l'œil*, a magnificent dummy setting inhabited by four million silhouettes. Nearly five million at the last census? Why, they must have multiplied. And that wouldn't surprise me. It always seemed to me that our fellow-citizens had two passions: ideas and fornication. Without rhyme or reason, so to speak. Still, let us take care not to condemn them; they are not the only ones, for all Europe is in the same boat. I sometimes think of what future historians will say of us. A single sentence will suffice for modern man: he fornicated and read the papers. After that vigorous definition, the subject will be, if I may say so, exhausted.

Oh, not the Dutch; they are much less modern! They have time – just look at them. What do they do? Well, these gentlemen over here live off the labours of those ladies over there. All of them, moreover, both male and female, are very middle-class creatures who have come here, as usual, out of mythomania or stupidity. Through too much or too little imagination, in other words. From time to time, these gentlemen indulge in a little knife- or revolver-play, but don't get the idea that they're keen on it. The role calls for it, that's all, and they are dying of fright as they shoot it out. Nevertheless, I find them more moral than the others, those who kill in the bosom of the family by a process of attrition. Haven't you noticed that our society is organized for this kind of liquidation? You have heard, of course, of those tiny fish in the rivers of Brazil that attack the unwary swimmer by thousands and with swift little nibbles clean him up in a few minutes, leaving only an immaculate skeleton? Well, that's what their organization is. 'Do you want a good clean life? Like everybody else?' You say yes, of course. How can one say no? 'OK. You'll be cleaned up. Here's a job, a family, and organized leisure.' And the little teeth attack the flesh, right down to the bone. But I am unjust.

I shouldn't say *their* organization. It is *ours*, after all: it's a question of which will clean up the other.

Here is our gin at last. To your prosperity. Yes, the gorilla opened his mouth to call me doctor. In these countries everyone is a doctor, or a professor. They like showing respect, partly out of kindness, partly out of modesty. With these people, at least, spitefulness is not a national institution. Besides, I am not a doctor. If you want to know, I was a lawyer before coming here. Now, I am a judge-penitent.

But allow me to introduce myself: Jean-Baptiste Clamence, at your service. Pleased to know you. You are in business, no doubt? In a way? Excellent reply! Judicious too: in all things we are merely 'in a way'. Now, allow me to play the detective. You are my age in a way, with the sophisticated eye of the man in his forties who has seen everything, in a way; you are well dressed in a way, that is as people are in our country; and your hands are smooth. Hence a bourgeois, in a way! But a cultured bourgeois! Smiling at the use of the subjunctive, in fact, proves your culture twice over because you recognize it to begin with and then because you feel superior to it. Lastly, I amuse you. And be it said without vanity, this implies in you a certain open-mindedness. Consequently you are in a way . . . But no matter. Professions interest me less than sects. Allow me to ask you two questions and don't answer if you consider them indiscreet. Do you have any possessions? Some? Good. Have you shared them with the poor? No? Then you are what I call a Sadducee. If you are not familiar with the Scriptures, I admit that this won't help you. But it does help you? So you know the Scriptures? Decidedly, you interest me.

As for me . . . Well, judge for yourself. By my stature, my shoulders, and this face that I have often been told was shy, I look rather like a football-player, don't I? But if I am judged by my conversation it must be allowed I have a little subtlety. The camel that provided the hair for my overcoat may have been mangy; instead, my nails are manicured. I, too, am sophisticated, and yet I confide in you without caution on the sole basis of your looks. Finally, despite my good manners and my fine speech, I frequent sailors' bars on the Zeedijk. Come on, give up. My profession is double, that's all, like the human being. I have already told you, I am a judge–penitent. Only one thing is simple in my case: I possess nothing. Yes, I was rich. No, I shared nothing with the poor. What does that prove? That I, too, was a Sadducee . . . Oh, do you hear the fog-horns in the harbour? There'll be fog tonight on the Zuyderzee.

You're leaving already? Forgive me for having perhaps detained you. No, I beg you; I won't let you pay. I am at home at *Mexico City* and have been particularly pleased to receive you here. I shall certainly be here tomorrow, as I am every evening, and I shall be glad to accept your invitation. Your way back? . . . Well . . . But if you don't have any objection, the easiest thing would be for me to accompany you as far as the harbour. Thence, by going around the Jewish quarter you'll come to those handsome avenues with the trams loaded with flowers and noisy as thunder trooping down them. Your hotel is on one of them, the Damrak. You first, please. I live in the Jewish quarter or what was called so until our Hitlerian brethren spaced it out a bit. What a clean-up! Seventy-five thousand Jews deported or assassinated; that's real vacuum-cleaning. I admire that diligence, that methodical patience! When one has no character one *has* to apply a method. Here it did wonders, no one can deny it, and I am living on the site of one of the greatest crimes in history. Perhaps that's what helps me to understand the gorilla and his mistrustfulness. Thus I can struggle against my natural inclination carrying me towards what I like. When I see a new face, something inside me sounds the alarm. 'Slow! Danger!' Even when the attraction is strongest, I am on my guard.

Do you know that in my little village, during a reprisal operation, a German officer courteously asked an old woman to please choose which of her two sons would be shot as a hostage? Choose! – can you imagine that? That one? No, this one. And see him go. Let's not dwell on it, but believe me, Monsieur, any sort of surprise is possible. I knew one pure heart who rejected distrust. He was a pacifist and a libertarian and loved all humanity and the animals with an equal love. An exceptional soul, that's certain. Well, during the last wars of religion in Europe he had retired to the country. He had written on his threshold: 'Wherever you come from, come in and be welcome.' Who do you think answered that noble invitation? The militia, who entered and made themselves at home, and disembowelled him.

Oh, pardon, Madame! But she didn't understand a word of it anyway. All these people, eh? out so late despite the rain which hasn't let up for days. Fortunately there is gin, the sole glimmer in this darkness. Do you feel the golden, copper-coloured light it kindles in you? I like walking through the city of an evening in the warmth of gin. I walk for nights on end, I dream or talk to myself interminably. Yes, like this evening – and I fear making your head swim somewhat. Thank you, you are most courteous. But it's my overflow; as soon as I open my mouth, sentences pour out. Besides, this country inspires me. I like this crowd of people swarming on the pavements, wedged into a little space of houses and canals, hemmed in by fogs, cold lands, and the sea steaming like wet washing. I like it, for it is double. It is here and elsewhere.

Yes, indeed! From hearing their heavy tread on the damp pavement, from seeing them move ponderously in and out of their shops full of gilded herrings and jewels the colour of dead leaves, you probably think they are here this evening? You are like everybody else; you take these good people for a tribe of syndics and merchants counting up their gold crowns together with their chances of eternal life, whose only lyricism consists in occasionally, without doffing their broad-brimmed hats, taking anatomy lessons? You are wrong. They walk along with us, to be sure, and yet see where their heads are: in that fog compounded of neon, gin, and peppermint emanating from the red and green shop-signs above them. Holland is a dream, Monsieur, a dream of gold and smoke — smokier by day, more gilded by night. And night and day that dream is peopled with Lohengrins like these, dreamily riding their black bicycles with high handlebars, funereal swans constantly drifting throughout the whole country, around the seas, along the canals. Their heads in their copper-coloured clouds, they dream; they ride in circles; they pray, sleep-walking in the fog's gilded incense; they have ceased to be here. They have gone thousands of miles away, towards Java, the distant isle. They pray to those grimacing gods of Indonesia with which they have decorated all their shop-windows and which at this moment are floating aimlessly above us before alighting, like gorgeous monkeys, on the signs and stepped roofs, to remind these homesick colonials that Holland is not only the Europe of merchants but also the sea, the sea that leads to Cipango and to those islands where men die mad and happy.

But I am letting myself go! I am pleading a case! Forgive me. Habit, Monsieur, vocation, also the desire to make you fully understand this city, and the heart of things! For we are at the heart of things here. Have you noticed that Amsterdam's concentric canals resemble the circles of hell? The middle-class hell, of course, peopled with bad dreams. When one comes from the outside, as one gradually goes through those circles, life — and hence its crimes — becomes denser, darker. Here, we are in the last circle. The circle of the ... Ah, you know that? By heaven, you become harder to classify. But you understand then why I can say that the centre of things is here although we stand at the tip of the continent. A sensitive man grasps such oddities. In any case the newspaper-readers and the fornicators can go no farther. They come from the four corners of Europe and stop facing the inland sea, on the drab strand. They listen to the fog-horns, vainly try to make out the silhouettes of boats in the fog, then turn back over the canals and go home through the rain. Chilled to the bone, they come and ask in all languages for gin at *Mexico City*. That's where I wait for them.

Till tomorrow, then, Monsieur *et cher compatriote*. No, you will easily find your way now; I'll leave you near this bridge. I never cross a bridge at night. It's because of a vow. Suppose, after all, that someone should jump in the water. One of two things – either you follow suit to fish him out and, in cold weather, that's taking a great risk! Or you forsake him there and to suppress a dive sometimes leaves one strangely aching. Good night. What? Those ladies behind those windows? Dream, Monsieur, cheap dream, a trip to the Indies! Those persons perfume themselves with spices. You go in, they draw the curtains and the navigation begins. The gods come down on to the naked bodies and the islands are set adrift, lost souls crowned with the tousled hair of palm trees in the wind. Try it.

What is a judge-penitent? Ah, I intrigued you with that little matter. I meant no harm by it, believe me, and I can explain myself more clearly. In a manner of speaking, it's really one of my official duties. But first I must set forth a certain number of facts that will help you to understand my story.

A few years ago I was a lawyer in Paris and, indeed, a rather well-known lawyer. Of course, I didn't tell you my real name. I used to specialize in noble cases. The widow and orphan, as the saying goes – I don't know why, because there are widows who cheat and orphans who are quite savage. Yet it was enough for me to sniff the slightest scent of victim on a defendant for me to swing into action. And what action! A real tempest! My heart was on my sleeve. You really might have thought that justice slept with me every night. I am sure you would have admired the accuracy of my tone, the appropriateness of my emotion, the persuasion and warmth, the restrained indignation of my speeches before the court. Nature has favoured me as to my physique, and the noble attitude comes effortlessly. Furthermore, I was buoyed up by two sincere feelings: the satisfaction of being on the right side of the bar and an instinctive scorn for judges in general. That scorn, after all, wasn't perhaps so instinctive. I know now that it had its reasons. But, seen from the outside, it appeared to be more like a passion. It can't be denied that, for the moment at least, we have to have judges, don't we? I could not understand, however, how a man could set himself up to perform such a surprising function. I accepted the fact because I saw it, but rather as I accepted locusts. With this difference that the invasions of those orthoptera never brought me a sou whereas I earned my living by carrying on dialogues with people I scorned.

But after all, I was on the right side; that was enough to assure my peace of conscience. The feeling of the law, the satisfaction of being right, the joy of self-esteem, *cher* Monsieur, are powerful incentives to keep us upright or make us move forward. On the other hand, if you deprive men of them, you transform them into dogs frothing with rage. How many crimes committed merely because their authors could not endure being wrong! I once knew a businessman who had a perfect wife, admired by all, and yet he deceived her. That man was literally enraged to be in the wrong, to be cut off from receiving, or granting himself, a certificate of virtue. The more virtues his wife displayed, the more vexed he became. Eventually, living in the wrong became unbearable to him. What do you think he did then? He gave up deceiving her? Not at all. He killed her. That is how I came to have dealings with him.

My situation was more enviable. Not only did I run no risk of joining the criminal camp (in particular I had no chance of killing my wife, being a bachelor), but I even took up their defence, on the sole condition that they should be noble murderers, just as others are noble savages. The very manner in which I conducted that defence gave me great satisfactions.

I was truly above reproach in my professional life. I never accepted a bribe, it goes without saying, nor again did I ever stoop to any shady proceedings. And – this is even rarer – I never deigned to flatter any journalist to get him on my side nor any civil servant whose friendship might be useful to me. I even had the luck to see the Legion of Honour offered to me two or three times and be able to refuse it with a discreet dignity, in which I found my true reward. Finally, I never charged the poor and never boasted of it. Don't think for a moment, *cher* Monsieur, that I am bragging. I take no credit for this. The avidity which in our society is a substitute for ambition has always made me laugh. I was aiming higher; you will see that the expression is exact in my case.

But you can already imagine my satisfaction. I enjoyed my own nature to the fullest and we all know that therein lies happiness, although, to soothe one another mutually, we occasionally pretend to condemn such joys as selfishness. At least I enjoyed that part of my nature which reacted so appropriately to the widow and the orphan that eventually, through exercise, it came to dominate my whole life. For instance, I loved to help blind people cross streets. From as far away as I could see a cane hesitating on the edge of a pavement, I would rush forward, sometimes only a second ahead of another charitable hand already outstretched, snatch the blind person from any solicitude but mine, and lead him gently but firmly over the pedestrian crossing amidst the hazards of the traffic towards the quiet haven of the other pavement, where we would separate with a mutual emotion. In the same way, I always enjoyed telling people the way in the street, giving a light, lending a hand with heavy barrows, pushing a stranded car, buying a paper from the Salvation Army girl or flowers from the old woman pedlar though I knew she stole them from the Montparnasse cemetery. I also liked – and this is harder to say – I liked to give alms. A very Christian friend of mine admitted that one's initial feeling on seeing a beggar approach one's house is unpleasant. Well, with me it was worse: I used to exult. But let's say no more about it.

Let us speak rather of my courtesy. It was famous and yet beyond question. Indeed, good manners provided me with great delights. If I had the luck, on certain mornings, to give up my seat in the bus or the underground to someone who obviously deserved it, to pick up some object an old lady had dropped and return it to her with a smile I knew well, or merely to forfeit my taxi to someone in a greater hurry than I, it was a red-letter day. I even rejoiced, I must admit, on those days when, because the public transport was on strike, I had a chance to load into my car at the bus-stops some of my unfortunate fellow-citizens unable to get home. Giving up my seat in the theatre to allow a couple to sit together, lifting a girl's suitcases on to the rack in a train – these were all deeds I performed more often than others because I paid more attention to the opportunities and was better able to relish the pleasure they gave.

Consequently I was considered generous, and so I was. I gave a great deal in public and in private. But far from suffering when I had to part with an object or a sum of money, I derived constant pleasures from this – among them a sort of melancholy which occasionally rose within me at the thought of the sterility of these gifts and the probable ingratitude that would follow. I even took such pleasure in giving that I hated to be obliged to do so. Exactitude in money matters bored me to death and I conformed ungraciously. I had to be the master of my liberalities.

These are just little touches but they will help you to grasp the constant delights I experienced in my life, and especially in my profession. Being stopped in the corridor of the law-courts by the wife of a defendant you represented for the sake of justice or pity alone – I mean without charging a fee – hearing that woman whisper that nothing, no nothing could ever repay what you had done for them, replying that it was quite natural, that anyone would have done as much, even offering some financial help to tide over the bad days ahead, then – in order to cut the effusions short and preserve their proper resonance – kissing the hand of the poor woman and breaking away – believe me, *cher* Monsieur, this is achieving more than the vulgar ambitious man and rising to that supreme summit where virtue is its own reward.

Let's pause on these heights. Now you understand what I meant when I spoke of aiming higher. I was talking, it so happens, of those supreme summits, the only places I can really live. Yes, I have never felt comfortable except in lofty sur-roundings. Even in the details of daily life, I needed to feel *above*. I preferred the bus to the underground, open carriages to taxis, terraces to being indoors. I was an amateur pilot in planes in which one's head is in the open. While on boats I was the eternal pacer of the top deck. In the mountains I used to flee the deep valleys for the passes and plateaux; at the very least, I was a man of the uplands. If fate had forced me to choose between manual labour at a lathe or as a roofer, don't worry, I'd have chosen the roofs and become acquainted with dizzi-ness. Coal-bunkers, ship-holds, subways, grottoes, pits were repulsive to me. I had even developed a special loathing for speleologists, who had the nerve to fill the front page of our newspapers, and whose activities nauseated me. Striving to descend two thousand feet at the risk of getting one's head caught in a rocky funnel (a siphon as those fools say!) seemed to me the exploit of perverted or traumatized characters. There was something criminal underlying it.

A natural balcony fifteen hundred feet above a sea still visible bathed in sunlight was, on the other hand, the place where I could breathe most freely, especially if I were alone, well above the human ants. I could readily understand why sermons, decisive preachings, and fire-miracles took place on accessible heights. In my opinion no one meditated in cellars or prison cells (unless they were situated in a tower with a broad view); one just became mouldy. And I could understand that man who, having entered holy orders, gave up the frock because his cell, instead of overlooking a vast landscape as he expected, looked out on a wall. Rest assured that as far as I was concerned I did not grow mouldy. At every hour of the day, within myself and among others, I would scale the heights and light conspicuous fires, and a joyful greeting would rise towards me. Thus at least I took pleasure in life and in my own excellence.

My profession satisfied most happily that vocation for summits. It cleansed me of all bitterness towards my neighbour, whom I always obliged without ever owing him anything. It set me above the judge whom I judged in turn, above the defendant whom I forced to gratitude. Just consider this, *cher* Monsieur, I lived with impunity. I was concerned in no judgment; I was not on the floor of the courtroom but somewhere in the flies like those gods that are brought down by machinery from time to time to transfigure the action and give it its meaning. After all, living aloft is still the only way of being seen and hailed by the largest number.

Some of my good criminals, besides, had killed in obedience to the same feeling. Reading the newspapers afterwards in the sorry condition in which they then were, doubtless brought them a sort of unhappy compensation. Like many men, they had no longer been able to endure anonymity, and that impatience had contributed to leading them to unfortunate extremes. To achieve notoriety it is enough, after all, to kill one's concierge. Unhappily, this is usually an ephemeral reputation, so many concierges are there who deserve and receive the knife. Crime constantly monopolizes the headlines but the criminal appears there only fugitively, to be replaced at once. In short, such brief triumphs cost too dear. Defending our unfortunate aspirants after a reputation amounted, on the other hand, to becoming really well known, at the same time and in the same places, but by more economical means.

Consequently this encouraged me to making more meritorious efforts so that they should pay as little as possible. They were paying their due to some extent in my place. The indignation, talent, and emotion I expended on them washed away, in return, any debt I might feel towards them. The judges punished and the defendants expiated, while I, free of any duty, shielded equally from judgment as from penalty, I freely held sway bathed in a light as of Eden.

Indeed, wasn't that Eden, *cher* Monsieur – no intermediary between life and me? Such was my life. I never had to learn how to live. In that respect, I already knew everything at birth. Some people's problem is to protect themselves from men or at least to come to terms with them. In my case, the understanding was already established. Familiar when it was appropriate, silent when necessary, capable of a free and easy manner as readily as of dignity, I was always in harmony. Hence my popularity was great and my successes in society innumerable. I was acceptable in appearance; I revealed myself to be both a tireless dancer and an unobtrusively learned man; I managed to love simultaneously – and this is not easy – women and justice; I indulged in sports and the fine arts – but enough, I'll not go on for fear you might suspect me of self-flattery. But just imagine, I beg you, a man at the height of his powers, in perfect health, generously gifted, skilled in bodily exercises as in those of the mind, neither rich nor poor, sleeping well and fundamentally pleased with himself without showing this otherwise than by a happy sociability. You will readily see how I can speak, without immodesty, of a successful life.

Yes, few creatures were more natural than I. I was altogether in harmony with life, fitting into it from top to bottom without rejecting any of its ironies, its grandeur or its servitude. In particular the flesh, matter, the physical in short, which disconcerts or discourages so many men in love or in solitude, without enslaving me, brought me steady joys. I was made to have a body. Whence that harmony in me, that relaxed mastery that people felt, even to telling me sometimes that it helped them in life. Thereby my company was in demand. Often, for instance, people thought they had met me before. Life, its creatures and its gifts, offered themselves to me and I accepted such marks of homage with a kindly pride. To tell the truth, just from being so fully and simply a man, I looked upon myself as something of a superman.

I was of respectable but humble birth (my father was an officer), and yet, on certain mornings, let me confess it humbly, I felt like a king's son, or a burning bush. It was not a matter, mind you, of the certainty I had of being more intelligent than everyone else. Besides, such certainty is of no consequence because so many imbeciles share it. No, as a result of being showered with blessings, I felt, I hesitate to admit, marked out. Personally marked out, among all, for that long and uninterrupted success. This, after all, was a result of my modesty. I refused to attribute that success to my own merits and could not believe that the conjunction in a single person of such different and such extreme virtues was the result of chance alone. This is why in my happy life I felt somehow that that happiness was authorized by some higher decree. When I add that I had no religion you can see even better how extraordinary that conviction was. Whether ordinary or not, it served for some time to raise me above the daily routine and I literally soared for a period of years, for which, to tell the truth, I still long in my heart of hearts. I soared until the evening when . . . But no, that's another matter and it must be forgotten. Anyway, I am perhaps exaggerating. I was at ease in everything, to be sure, but at the same time satisfied with nothing. Each joy made me desire another. I went from festivity to festivity. On occasion I danced for nights on end, ever madder about people and life. At times, late on those nights when the dancing, the slight intoxication, my wild enthusiasm, everyone's violent unrestraint would fill me with a tired and overwhelmed rapture, it would seem to me – at the breaking-point of fatigue and for a second's flash – that at last I understood the secret of creatures and of the world. But my fatigue would disappear the next day, and with it the secret; I would rush forth anew. I ran on like that, always heaped with favours, never satiated, without knowing where to stop, until the day – until the evening rather when the music stopped and the lights went out. The gay party at which I had been so happy . . . But allow me to call on our friend the primate. Nod your head to thank him and, above all, drink up with me, I need your understanding.

I see that this declaration amazes you. Have you never suddenly needed understanding, help, friendship? Yes, of course. I have learned to be satisfied with understanding. It is found more readily and, besides, it's not binding. 'I beg you to believe in my sympathetic understanding' in the inner discourse always precedes immediately 'and now, let's turn to other matters'. It's a board-chairman's emotion; it comes cheap, after catastrophes. Friendship is less simple. It is long and hard to obtain but when one has it there's no getting rid of it; one simply has to cope with it. Don't think for a minute that your friends will telephone you every evening, as they ought to, in order to find out if this doesn't happen to be the evening when you are deciding to commit suicide, or simply whether you don't need company, whether you are not in the mood to go out. No, don't worry, they'll ring up the evening you are not alone, when life is beautiful. As for suicide, they would be more likely to push you to it, by virtue of what you owe to yourself, according to them. May heaven protect us, *cher* Monsieur, from being set on a pedestal by our friends! Those whose duty is to love us – I mean relatives and connexions (what an expression!) – are another matter. They find the right word, of course, and it hits the bull's-eye; they ring up as if shooting a rifle. And they know how to aim. Oh, the Bazaines!

What? What evening? I'll get to it, be patient with me. In a certain way I *am* sticking to my subject with all that about friends and connexions. You see, I've heard of a man whose friend had been imprisoned and who slept on the floor of his room every night in order not to enjoy a comfort of which his friend had been deprived. Who, *cher* Monsieur, will sleep on the floor for us? Am I capable of it myself? Look, I'd like to be and I shall be. Yes, we shall all be capable of it one day, and that will be salvation. But it's not easy, for friendship is absent-minded or at least unavailing. It is incapable of achieving what it wants. Maybe, after all, it doesn't want it enough? Maybe we don't love life enough? Have you noticed that death alone awakens our feelings? How we love the friends who have just left us? How we admire those of our teachers who have ceased to speak, their mouths filled with earth? Then the expression of admiration springs forth naturally, that admiration they were perhaps expecting from us all life long. But do you know why we are always more just and more generous towards the dead? The reason is simple. With them there is no obligation. They leave us free and we can take our time, fit the testimonial in between a cocktail-party and a nice little mistress, in our spare time, in short. If they forced us to anything, it would be to remembering, and we have a short memory. No, it is the recently dead we love among our friends, the painful dead, our emotion, ourselves after all!

For instance, I had a friend I generally avoided. He rather bored me, and, besides, he was something of a moralist. But when he was on his death-bed, I was there – don't worry. I never missed a day. He died satisfied with me, holding both my hands. A woman who used to chase after me, and in vain, had the good sense to die young. What room in my heart at once! And when, in addition, it's a suicide! Lord, what a delightful commotion! One's telephone rings, one's heart overflows, and the sentences intentionally short yet heavy with implications, one's restrained suffering and even, yes, a bit of self-accusation!

That's the way man is, *cher* Monsieur. He has two faces: he can't love without self-love. Notice your neighbours if perchance a death takes place in the building. They were asleep in their little routine and suddenly, for example, the concierge dies. At once they awake, bestir themselves, get the details, commiserate. A newly dead man and the show begins at last. They need tragedy, don't you know; it's their little transcendence, their *apéritif*. Actually, is it mere chance that I should speak of a concierge? I had one, really ill-favoured, malice incarnate, a monster of insignificance and rancour, who would have discouraged a Franciscan. I had even given up speaking to him, but by his mere existence he compromised my customary contentedness. He died and I went to his funeral. Can you tell me why?

Anyway, the two days preceding the ceremony were full of interest. The concierge's wife was ill, lying in the single room, and near her the coffin had been set on trestles. Everyone had to collect his own letters. You opened the door, said '*Bonjour, Madame*', listened to her praise of the dear departed as she pointed to him, and took your letters. Nothing very amusing about that. And yet the whole building passed through her room which stank of carbolic. And the tenants didn't send their servants either; they came themselves to take advantage of the unexpected attraction. The servants too, of course, but on the sly. The day of the funeral, the coffin was too big for the door. 'O my dearie,' the wife said from her bed with a surprise at once delighted and grieved, 'how big he was!' 'Don't worry, Madame,' replied the undertaker, 'we'll get him through edgewise, and upright.' He was got through upright and then laid down again, and I was the only one (with a former cabaret doorman who, I gathered, used to drink his Pernod every evening with the departed) to go as far as the cemetery and strew flowers on a coffin which astounded me with its sumptuousness. Then I paid a visit to the concierge's wife to receive her thanks which she expressed like a great tragedienne. Tell me, what was the reason for all that? None, except the *apéritif*.

I likewise buried an old fellow-member of the Bar Association. A clerk to whom no one paid any attention, though I always shook his hand. Where I worked I used to shake everyone's hand, anyway, most of them twice over. It didn't cost me anything, and that sort of cordial simplicity won me the popularity so necessary to my contentment. The President of the Bar had not put himself out over the funeral of our clerk. But I did so, and on the eve of a journey, at that, as was amply pointed out. It so happened that I knew my presence would be noticed and favourably commented on. Hence, you see, not even the snow that was falling that day made me withdraw.

What? I'm getting to it, never fear; besides, I have never left it. But let me first point out that my concierge's wife, who had gone to such expense for the crucifix, and the heavy oak and silver handles for the coffin in order to get the most out of her emotion, took up a month later with an overdressed dandy who had a fine voice. He used to beat her; frightful screams could be heard and immediately afterward he would open the window and give cry with his favourite song: 'Women, how pretty you are!' 'All the *same*!' the neighbours would say. All the same what? I ask you. All right, appearances were against the baritone, and against the concierge's wife too. But nothing proves that they were not in love. And nothing proves either that she did not love her husband. Moreover, when the dandy took flight, exhausted in voice and arm, she – that faithful wife – resumed her praises of the departed! After all, I know of others who have appearances on their side and are no more faithful or sincere. I knew a man who gave twenty years of his life to a scatterbrained woman, sacrificing everything to her, his friendships, his work, the very respectability of his life, and who one evening realized that he had never loved her. He had been bored, that's all, bored like most people. Hence he had made himself out of whole cloth a life full of complications and drama. Something must happen – and that explains most human commitments. Something must happen, even loveless slavery, even war or death. Hurrah then for funerals!

But I at least didn't have that excuse. I was not bored because I was riding on the crest of the wave. On the evening I am speaking about I can say that I was even less bored than ever. And yet . . . You see, *cher* Monsieur, it was a fine autumn evening, still warm in town and already damp over the Seine. Night was falling; the sky, still bright in the west, was darkening; the street-lamps were glowing dimly. I was walking up the quays of the Left Bank towards the Pont des Arts. The river was gleaming between the stalls of the second-hand booksellers. There were but few people on the quays; Paris was already at dinner. I was trampling the dusty yellow leaves that still recalled summer. Gradually the sky was filling with stars that could be seen for a moment after leaving one street-lamp and moving on towards another. I enjoyed the return of silence, the evening's mildness, the emptiness of Paris. I was happy. The day had been good: a blind man, the reduced sentence I had hoped for, a cordial handclasp from my client, a few generous actions and, in the afternoon, a brilliant improvisation in the company of several friends on the hard-heartedness of our governing class and the hypocrisy of our leaders.

I had gone up on to the Pont des Arts, deserted at that hour, to look at the river that could hardly be made out now night had come. Facing the statue of the Vert-Galant, I dominated the island. I felt rising within me a vast feeling of power and – I don't know how to express it – of completion, which cheered my heart. I straightened up and was about to light a cigarette, the cigarette of satisfaction, when, at that very moment, a laugh burst out behind me. Taken by surprise, I suddenly wheeled round; there was no one there. I stepped to the railing; no barge or boat. I turned back towards the island and, again, heard the laughter behind me, a little farther off as if it were going downstream. I stood there motionless. The sound of the laughter was decreasing, but I could still hear it distinctly behind me, coming from nowhere unless from the water. At the same time I was aware of the rapid beating of my heart. Please don't misunderstand me; there was nothing mysterious about that laugh; it was a good, hearty, almost friendly laugh, which put everything properly in its place. Soon I could hear nothing more, anyway. I returned to the quays, went up the Rue Dauphine, bought some cigarettes which I didn't need. I was dazed and was breathing fast. That evening I rang up a friend who wasn't at home. I was hesitating about going out when, suddenly, I heard laughter under my windows. I opened them. On the pavement, in fact, some youths were noisily saying good night. I shrugged my shoulders as I closed the windows; after all, I had a brief to study. I went into the bathroom to drink a glass of water. My reflection was smiling in the mirror, but it seemed to me that my smile was double . . .

What? Forgive me, I was thinking of something else. I'll see you again tomorrow, probably. Tomorrow, yes, that's right. No, no, I can't stay. Besides, I'm being called for a consultation by the brown bear you see over there. A decent fellow, to be sure, whom the police are meanly persecuting out of sheer perversity. You think he looks like a killer? Rest assured that his actions conform to his looks. He burgles likewise, and you will be surprised to learn that that caveman specializes in the art-trade. In Holland everyone is a specialist in paintings and in tulips. This one, with his modest look, is the author of the most famous theft of a painting. Which one? I may tell you one day. Don't be surprised at my knowledge. Although I am a judge-penitent, I have my sideline here: I am the legal counsellor of these good people. I studied the laws of the country and built up a clientele in this quarter where diplomas are not required. It wasn't easy, but I inspire confidence, don't I? I have a good, hearty laugh and an energetic handshake, and those are trump-cards. Besides, I settled a few difficult cases, out of self-interest to begin with and later out of conviction. If pimps and thieves were invariably sentenced, all decent people would get to thinking they themselves were constantly innocent, *cher* Monsieur. And in my opinion — all right, all right, I'm coming! — that's what must be avoided at all costs. Otherwise, everything would be just a joke.

I am indeed grateful to you, *mon cher compatriote*, for your curiosity. However, there is nothing extraordinary about my story. Since you are interested, I'll tell you that I thought a little about that laugh, for a few days, then forgot about it. Once in a great while, I seemed to hear it within me. But most of the time, without making any effort, I thought of other things.

Yet I must admit that I ceased to walk along the Paris quays. Whenever I travelled along them in a car or bus, a sort of silence would descend on me. I was waiting, I believe. But I would cross the Seine, nothing would happen, and I would breathe again. I also had some trouble with my health at that time. Nothing definite, a dejection perhaps, a sort of difficulty in recovering my good spirits. I saw doctors, who gave me stimulants. I was alternately stimulated and depressed. Life became less easy for me: when the body is sad the heart languishes. It seemed to me that I was half unlearning what I had never learned and yet knew so well — how to live. Yes, I think it was probably then that everything began.

But this evening I don't feel quite up to the mark either. I even find trouble expressing myself. I'm not talking so well, it seems to me, and my words are less assured. Probably the weather. It's hard to breathe; the air is so heavy it weighs on one's chest. Would you object, *mon cher compatriote*, to going out and walking in the town a little? Thank you.

How beautiful the canals are this evening! I like the breath of stagnant waters, the smell of dead leaves soaking in the canal and the funereal scent rising from the barges loaded with flowers. No, no, there's nothing morbid about such a taste, I assure you. On the contrary, it's a deliberate act on my part. The truth is that I force myself to admire these canals. What

I like most in the world is Sicily, you see, and especially from the top of Etna, in the sunlight, provided I dominate the island and the sea. Java too, but at the time of the trade-winds. Yes, I went there in my youth. In a general way, I like all islands. It is easier to dominate them.

Charming house, isn't it? The two heads you see up there are heads of negro slaves. A shop-sign. The house belonged to a slave-dealer. Oh, they weren't squeamish in those days! They were self-assured; they announced: 'You see, I'm a man of substance; I'm in the slave-trade; I deal in black flesh.' Can you imagine anyone today making it known publicly that such is his business? What a scandal! I can hear my Parisian colleagues right now. They are adamant on the subject; they wouldn't hesitate to launch two or three manifestoes, maybe even more! And on reflection, I'd add my signature to theirs. Slavery? – certainly not, we are against it! That we should be forced to have it in our homes or in our factories – well, that's natural; but boasting about it, that's the limit!

I am well aware that one can't get along without dominating or being served. Every man needs slaves as he needs fresh air. Commanding is breathing – you agree with me? And even the most destitute manage to breathe. The lowest man in the social scale still has his wife or his child. If he's unmarried, a dog. The essential thing, after all, is being able to get angry with someone who has no right to answer back. 'One doesn't answer back to one's father' – you know the expression? In one way it is very odd. To whom should one answer back in this world if not to what one loves? In another way, it is convincing. Somebody has to have the last word. Otherwise, every reason can be met with another one and there would never be an end to it. Power, on the other hand, settles everything. It took time, but we finally realized that. For instance, you must have noticed that our old Europe at last philosophizes in the right way. We no longer say as in simple times: 'This is my opinion. What are your objections?' We have become lucid. For the dialogue we have substituted the communiqué. 'This is the truth,' we say. 'You can discuss it as much as you want; we aren't interested. But in a few years there'll be the police to show you I'm right.'

Ah, this dear old planet! All is clear now. We know ourselves; we now know of what we are capable. Just take me, to change examples if not subjects. I have always wanted to be served with a smile. If the maid looked sad, she poisoned my days. She had a right not to be cheerful, to be sure. But I told myself that it was better for her to perform her service with a laugh than with tears. In fact, it was better for me. Yet, without boasting, my reasoning was not altogether idiotic. Likewise, I always refused to eat in Chinese restaurants. Why? Because when they are silent and in the presence of whites, Orientals often look scornful. Naturally they keep that look when serving. How then can you enjoy the lacquered chicken? And, above all, how can you look at them and think you are right?

Just between ourselves, slavery, preferably smiling, is therefore inevitable. But we must not admit it. Isn't it better that whoever cannot do without having slaves should call them free men? As a matter of principle to begin with, and, secondly, not to drive them to despair. We owe them that compensation, don't we? In that way, they will continue to smile and we shall maintain our good conscience. Otherwise, we'd be obliged to reconsider our opinion of ourselves; we'd go mad with suffering, or even become modest – for anything might happen. Consequently no shop-signs, and this one is shocking. Besides, if everyone told all, displayed his true profession and identity, we shouldn't know which way to turn! Just fancy visiting-cards: Dupont, jittery philosopher, or Christian land-owner, or adulterous humanist – indeed, there's a wide choice. But it would be hell! Yes, hell must be like that: streets filled with shop-signs and no way of explaining oneself. One is classified once and for all.

You, for instance, *mon cher compatriote*, stop and think of what your sign would be. You are silent? Well, you'll tell me later on. I know mine in any case: a double face, a charming Janus, and above it the motto of the house: 'Don't rely on it.' On my cards: 'Jean-Baptiste Clamence, play-actor.' Why, shortly after the evening I told you about, I discovered something. Whenever I left a blind man on the pavement to which I had convoyed him, I used to touch my hat to him. Obviously the hat-touching wasn't intended for him since he couldn't see it. To whom was it addressed? To the public. After playing my part, I would take my bow. Not bad, eh? Another day during the same period, when a motorist thanked me for helping him, I replied that no one would have done as much. I meant, of course, anyone. But that unfortunate slip weighed heavy on me. At modesty I really was a champion.

I have to admit it humbly, *mon cher compatriote*, I was always bursting with vanity. I, I, I is the refrain of my whole life and it could be heard in everything I said. I could never speak without boasting, especially if I did so with that shattering discretion of which I was a master. It is quite true that I always lived free and powerful. I simply felt released in my relations with everyone else for the excellent reason that I recognized no equals. I always considered myself more intelligent than anyone else, as I've told you, but also more sensitive and more skilful, a crack shot, an incomparable driver, a better lover. Even in the fields in which it was easy for me to verify my inferiority – like tennis for instance in which I was but a passable partner – it was hard for me not to think that, with a little time for practice, I would surpass the best players. I found nothing but superiorities in myself and this explained my goodwill and serenity. When I was concerned with others, it was out of pure condescension, in utter freedom, and all the credit went to me: my self-esteem would go up a degree.

Along with a few other truths, I discovered these facts little by little in the period following the evening I told you about.

Not all at once nor very clearly. First I had to recover my memory. By gradual degrees I saw more clearly, I learned a little of what I knew. Until then I had always been aided by an extraordinary ability to forget. I used to forget everything, beginning with my resolutions. Fundamentally, nothing mattered. War, suicide, love, poverty got my attention, of course, when circumstances forced me, but a courteous, superficial attention. At times, I would pretend to get excited about some cause foreign to my daily life. But basically I didn't really take part in it except, of course, when my freedom was thwarted. How can I express it? Everything slid off – yes, just rolled off me.

Let's be fair to myself: sometimes my forgetfulness was praiseworthy. You have noticed that there are people whose religion consists in forgiving all offences, and who do in fact forgive them but never forget them? I wasn't good enough to forgive offences, but eventually I always forgot them. And the man who thought I hated him couldn't get over seeing me touch my hat to him with a smile. According to his nature, he would then admire my nobility of character or scorn my ill-breeding without realizing that my reason was simpler: I had forgotten his very name. The same infirmity that often made me indifferent or ungrateful made me magnanimous in such cases.

I lived consequently without any other continuity than that, from day to day, of I, I, I. Without thought for the morrow with women, without thought for the morrow in virtue or vice, each day for itself, just like dogs – but every day myself secure at my post. Thus I progressed on the surface of life, in the realm of words as it were, never in reality. All those books barely read, those friends barely loved, those cities barely visited, those women barely possessed! I went through the gestures out of boredom or absent-mindedness. Then came human beings; they wanted to cling but there was nothing to cling to, and that was unfortunate. For them. As for me, I forgot. I never remembered anything but myself.

Gradually, however, my memory returned. Or rather, I returned to it, and in it I found the recollection that was awaiting me. But before telling you of it, allow me, *mon cher compatriote*, to give you a few examples (they will be useful to you, I am sure) of what I discovered in the course of my exploration.

One day in my car when I was slow in making a get-away at the green light while our patient fellow-citizens immediately began honking furiously behind me, I suddenly remembered another occasion set in similar circumstances. A motor-cycle ridden by a spare little man wearing spectacles and plus-fours had gone around me and planted itself in front of me at the red light. As he came to a stop the little man had stalled his motor and was vainly striving to revive it. When the light changed, I asked him with my usual courtesy to take his motor-cycle out of the way so that I might pass. The little man was getting irritable over his wheezy motor. Hence he replied, according to the rules of Parisian courtesy, that I could go and climb a tree. I insisted, still polite but with a slight shade of impatience in my voice. I was immediately told in no uncertain terms that I could go to hell. Meanwhile several horns began noisily behind me. With greater firmness I begged my interlocutor to be polite and to realize that he was blocking the traffic. The irascible character, probably exasperated by the now evident ill-temper of his motor, informed me that if I wanted what he called a thorough dusting off he would gladly give it to me. Such cynicism filled me with a healthy rage and I got out of my car with the intention of thrashing this foul-mouthed individual. I don't think I am cowardly (but what doesn't one think!); I was a head taller than my adversary and my muscles have always been sound. I still believe the dusting off would have been received rather than given. But I had hardly set foot on the pavement when from the gathering crowd a man stepped forth, rushed at me, informed me that I was the scum of the earth and that he would not allow me to strike a man who had a motor-cycle between his legs and hence was at a disadvantage. I turned towards this musketeer and, in truth, didn't even see him. Indeed, hardly had I turned my head when, almost simultaneously, I heard the motor-cycle begin popping again and received a violent blow on the ear. Before I had time to register what had happened, the motor-cycle drove away. Dazed, I mechanically walked towards D'Artagnan when, at the same moment, an exasperated concert of horns rose from the now considerable line of vehicles. The light was changing to green. Then, still somewhat bewildered, instead of giving a drubbing to the idiot who had addressed me, I docilely returned to my car and started up, while as I passed the idiot greeted me with a 'Silly ass!' that I still recall.

A totally insignificant story, in your opinion? Probably. Still it took me some time to forget it, and that's the point. Yet I had excuses. I had let myself be beaten without replying, but I could not be accused of cowardice. Taken by surprise, addressed from both sides, I had mixed everything up and the motor horns had put the finishing touch to my embarrassment. Yet I was unhappy about this as if I had violated the code of honour. I could see myself getting back into my car without any reaction, under the ironic gaze of a crowd especially delighted because, as I recall, I was wearing a very elegant blue suit. I could hear the 'Silly ass!' which, in spite of everything, struck me as justified. In short, I had collapsed in public. As a result of a series of circumstances, to be sure, but there are always circumstances. As an afterthought I clearly saw what I should have done. I saw myself felling D'Artagnan with a good hook to the jaw, getting back into my car, pursuing the monkey who had struck me, overtaking him, jamming his machine against the kerb, taking him aside and giving him the licking he had fully deserved. With a few variants, I ran off this little film a hundred times in my imagination. But it was too late, and for several days I gnawed on a feeling of bitter resentment.

Why, it's raining again. Let's stop, shall we, under this portico? Good. Where was I? Oh yes, honour! Well, when I recovered the recollection of that episode, I realized what it meant. After all, my dream had not stood up to facts. I had dreamed – this was now clear – of being a complete man who managed to make himself respected in his person as well as in his profession. Half Cerdan, half de Gaulle, if you will. In short, I wanted to dominate in all things. This is why I put on airs, made a particular point of displaying my physical skill rather than my intellectual gifts. But after having been struck in public without reacting, it was no longer possible for me to cherish that fine picture of myself. If I had been the friend of truth and intelligence I claimed to be, what would that episode have mattered to me? It was already forgotten by those who had witnessed it. I'd have barely accused myself of having got angry over nothing and also, having got angry, of not having managed to face up to the consequences of my anger, for want of presence of mind. Instead of that, I was eager to get my revenge, to strike and conquer. As if my true desire were not to be the most intelligent or most generous creature on earth, but only to beat anyone I wanted, to be the stronger, in fact, and in the most elementary way. The truth is that every intelligent man, as you know, dreams of being a gangster and of ruling over society by force alone. As it is not so easy as the detective novels might lead one to believe, one generally relies on politics and rushes to join the cruellest party. What does it matter, after all, if by humiliating one's mind one succeeds in dominating everyone? I discovered in myself sweet dreams of oppression.

I learned at least that I was on the side of the guilty, the accused, only exactly in so far as their crime caused me no harm. Their guilt made me eloquent because I was not its victim. When I was threatened, I became not only a judge in turn but even more: an irascible master who wanted, regardless of all laws, to strike down the offender and get him on his knees. After that, *mon cher compatriote*, it is very hard to continue seriously believing one has a vocation for justice and is the predestined defender of the widow and orphan.

Since the rain is coming down harder and we have the time, may I share with you another discovery I made, soon after, in my memory? Let's sit down on this bench out of the rain. For centuries pipe-smokers have been watching the same rain falling on the same canal. What I have to tell you is a bit more difficult. This time it concerns a woman. To begin with, you must know that I always succeeded with women – and without much effort. I don't say succeed in making them happy or even in making myself happy through them. No, simply succeed. I used to achieve my ends just about whenever I wanted. I was considered to have charm. Fancy that! You know what charm is: a way of getting the answer yes without having asked any clear question. And that was true of me at the time. Does that surprise you? Come now, don't deny it. With the face I now have, that's quite natural. Alas, after a certain age every man is responsible for his face. Mine . . . But what matter? It's a fact – I was considered to have charm and I took advantage of it.

Without calculation, however; I acted in good faith, or almost. My relationship with women was natural, free, easy as the saying goes. No guile in it except that obvious guile which they look upon as a homage. I loved them, according to the hallowed expression, which amounts to saying that I never loved any of them. I always considered misogyny vulgar and stupid, and almost all the women I have known seemed to me better than I. Nevertheless, setting them so high, I made use of them more often than I served them. How can one make it out?

Of course, true love is exceptional, two or three times a century, more or less. The rest of the time there is vanity or boredom. As for me, in any case I was no Portuguese Nun. I am not hard-hearted; far from it – full of pity, on the contrary, and with a ready tear to boot. Only, my emotional impulses always turn towards me, my feelings of pity concern me. It is not true, after all, that I never loved. I conceived at least one great love in my life, of which I was always the object. From that point of view, after the inevitable hardships of youth, I had settled down early on: sensuality alone dominated my love-life. I looked merely for objects of pleasure and conquest. Moreover, I was aided in this by my looks: nature had been generous with me. I was considerably proud of this and derived many satisfactions therefrom – without my knowing now whether they were due to physical pleasure or to prestige. Of course you will say that I am boasting again. I shan't deny it and I am hardly proud of doing so, for here I am boasting of what is true.

In any case, my sensuality (to limit myself to it) was so real that even for a ten-minute adventure I'd have disowned father and mother, even were I to regret it bitterly. Nay – *especially* for a ten-minute adventure and even more so if I were sure it was to have no sequel. I had principles, to be sure, such as that the wife of a friend is sacred. But I simply ceased quite sincerely, a few days before, to feel any friendship for the husband. Maybe I ought not to call this sensuality? Sensuality is not repulsive. Let's be indulgent and use the word infirmity, a sort of con-genital inability to see in love anything but the physical. That infirmity, after all, was convenient. Combined with my faculty for forgetting, it favoured my freedom. At the same time, through a certain appearance of inaccessibility and unshakeable independence it gave me, it provided the opportunity for new successes. As a result of not being romantic, I gave romance something to work on. Our feminine friends have this in common with Bonaparte, that they always think they can succeed where everyone else has failed.

In this exchange, moreover, I satisfied something in add-ition to my sensuality: my passion for gambling. Amongst women I loved those who would be my partners in a sort of game, which has at least the taste of innocence. You see, I can't endure being bored and appreciate only the diversions of life. Any society, however brilliant, soon crushes me, whereas I have never been bored with the women I liked. It hurts me to confess it, but I'd have given ten conversations with Einstein for a first meeting with a pretty chorus-girl. It's true that at the tenth meeting I was longing for Einstein or a serious book. In short, I was never concerned with the major problems except in the intervals between my little excesses. And how often, standing on the pavement involved in a passionate discussion with friends, I lost the thread of the argument being developed because a devastating woman was crossing the street at that very moment.

Hence I played the game. I knew they didn't like one to reveal one's purpose too quickly. First, there had to be conversation, fond attentions as they say. I wasn't worried about speeches, being a lawyer, nor about glances, having been an amateur actor during my military service. I often changed parts, but it was always the same play. For instance, the little act of incomprehensible attraction, of the 'mysterious something', of the 'it's unreasonable, I certainly didn't want to be attracted, I was even tired of love, etc. . . . ' always worked, though it is one of the oldest in the repertory. There was also the one of the mysterious happiness no other woman has ever given you; it may be a blind alley perhaps – indeed, it surely is (for one cannot cover oneself too much) – but it just happens to be unique. Above all, I had perfected a little speech which was always well received and which, I am sure, you will applaud. The essential part of that act lay in the assertion, painful and resigned, that I was nothing, that it was not worth getting involved with me, that my life was elsewhere and not related to everyday happiness – a happiness that maybe I should have preferred to anything, but there you were, it was too late. As to the reasons behind this decisive lateness, I maintained secrecy, knowing that it is always better to go to bed with a mystery. In a way, moreover, I believed what I said; I was living my part. It is not surprising that my partners likewise began to tread the boards enthusiastically. The most sensitive among them tried to understand me, and that effort led them to a sort of abandoned melancholy. The others, satisfied to note that I was respecting the rules of the game and had the tactfulness to talk before acting, progressed without delay to the realities. This meant I had won – and twice over, since, besides the desire I felt for them, I was satisfying the love I bore myself by proving my special powers on each occasion.

This was so much so that even if some among them provided but slight pleasure, I nevertheless tried to resume relations with them, at long intervals, helped doubtless by that strange desire which absence fosters, when it is followed by the sudden rediscovery of an involvement, but also to verify the fact that our ties still held and that it was my privilege alone to tighten them. Sometimes I went so far as to make them swear not to give themselves to any other man, in order to quiet my worries once and for all on that score. My heart, however, played no part in that worry, nor even my imagination. A certain type of pretension was in fact so personified in me that it was hard for me to imagine, despite the facts, that a woman who had once been mine could ever belong to another. But the oath they swore to me liberated me while it bound them. As soon as I knew they would never belong to anyone else, I could make up my mind to break off – which otherwise was almost always impossible for me. As far as they were concerned, I had proved my point once and for all and assured my power for a long time. Strange, isn't it? But that's the way it was, *mon cher compatriote*. Some cry: 'Love me!' Others: 'Don't love me!' But a certain genus, the worst and most unhappy, cries: 'Don't love me and be faithful to me!'

Except that the proof is never definitive, after all; one has to begin again with each new person. As a result of beginning over and over again, one gets in the habit. Soon the speech comes without thinking and the reflex follows; and one day you find yourself taking without really desiring. Believe me, for certain men at least, not taking what one doesn't desire is the hardest thing in the world.

This is what happened eventually and there's no point in telling you who she was except that, without really stirring me, she had attracted me by her passive, avid manner. Frankly, it was a shabby experience, as I should have expected. But I never had any complexes and soon forgot a person whom I didn't see again. I thought she hadn't noticed anything and didn't even imagine she could have an opinion. Besides, her passive manner cut her off from the world in my eyes. A few weeks later, however, I learned that she had related my deficiencies to a third person. At once I felt as if I had been somewhat deceived; she wasn't so passive as I had thought and she didn't lack judgment. Then I shrugged my shoulders and pretended to laugh. I even laughed outright; clearly the incident was unimportant. If there is any realm in which modesty ought to be the rule, isn't it sex with all the unforeseeable there is in it? But no, each of us tries to show up to advantage, even in solitude. Despite having shrugged my shoulders, what was my behaviour in fact? I saw that woman again a little later and did everything necessary to charm her and really take her back. It was not very difficult, for *they* don't like, either, to end on a failure. From that moment onwards, without really intending it, I began, in fact, to mortify her in every way. I would give her up and take her back, force her to give herself at inappropriate times and in inappropriate places, treat her so brutally, in every respect, that eventually I attached myself to her as I imagine the jailer is bound to his prisoner. And this kept up till the day when, in the violent disorder of painful and constrained pleasure, she paid a tribute aloud to what was enslaving her. That very day I began to move away from her. I have forgotten her since.

I'll agree with you, though you politely haven't said a word, that that adventure is not a very pretty one. But just think of your life, *mon cher compatriote*! Search your memory and perhaps you will find some similar story that you'll tell me later on. As for me, when that little matter came to mind, I again began to laugh. But it was another kind of laugh, rather like the one I had heard on the Pont des Arts. I was laughing at my speeches and my pleadings in court. Even more at my pleading in court than at my speeches to women. To them, at least, I did not lie much. Instinct spoke clearly, without subterfuges, in my attitude. The act of love, for instance, is a confession. Selfishness screams aloud, vanity shows off, or else true generosity reveals itself. Ultimately in that regrettable story, even more than in my other affairs, I had been more outspoken than I thought; I had declared who I was and how I could live. Despite appearances, I was therefore more worthy in my private life – even and especially when I behaved as I have told you – than in my great professional flights about innocence and justice. At least, seeing myself act with others, I couldn't deceive myself as to the truth of my nature. No man is a hypocrite in his pleasures – I read that or did I think it myself, *mon cher compatriote*?

When I examined thus the trouble I had in separating once and for all from a woman – a trouble which involved me in so many simultaneous liaisons – I didn't blame my soft-heartedness. That was not what impelled me when one of my mistresses tired of waiting for the Austerlitz of our passion and spoke of leaving me. At once I was the one who made a step forward, who yielded, who became eloquent. As for the affection and soft-heartedness, I aroused these in her, experiencing merely the appearance of them myself – simply a little excited by this refusal, alarmed also by the possible loss of an affection. At times I truly thought I was suffering, to be sure. But the rebellious one had merely to leave me in fact for me to forget her without effort, just as I forgot her at my side when, on the contrary, she had decided to return. No, it was not love or generosity that aroused me when I was in danger of being forsaken, but merely the desire to be loved and to receive what, in my opinion, was my due. The moment I was loved and my partner again forgotten, I shone, I was at the top of my form, I became likeable.

Be it said, moreover, that as soon as I had re-won that affection I became aware of its weight. In my moments of irritation I told myself that the ideal solution would have been the death of the person I was interested in. Her death would, on the one hand, have fixed our relationship once and for all and, on the other, removed its constraint. But one cannot long for the death of everyone or, to go to extremes, depopulate the planet in order to enjoy a freedom that is unthinkable otherwise. My sensibility was opposed to this, and my love of mankind.

The only deep emotion I occasionally felt in these affairs was gratitude, when all was going well and I was left, not only peace, but freedom to come and go – never kinder and gayer with one than when I had just left another's bed, as if I extended to all other women the debt I had just contracted towards one of them. In any case, however apparently confused my feelings were, the result I achieved was clear: I kept all my affections within reach to make use of them when I wanted. On my own admission, I could live happily only on condition that all the individuals on earth, or the greatest possible number, were turned towards me, eternally unattached, deprived of any separate existence and ready to answer my call at any moment, doomed in short to sterility until the day I should deign to favour them. In short, for me to live happily it was essential for the individuals I chose not to live at all. They must receive their life, sporadically, only at my bidding.

Oh, I don't feel any self-satisfaction, believe me, in telling you this. Upon thinking of that time when I used to ask for everything without paying anything myself, when I used to mobilize so many people in my service, when I used to put them in the refrigerator, so to speak, in order to have them at hand some day when it would suit me, I don't know how to name the odd feeling that comes over me. Isn't it shame, perhaps? Tell me, *mon cher compatriote*, doesn't shame sting a little? It does? Well, it's probably shame, then, or one of those silly emotions to do with honour. It seems to me in any case that that emotion has never left me since the adventure I found at the heart of my memory, which I cannot any longer put off relating, despite my digressions and the inventive efforts for which, I hope, you give me credit.

Look, the rain has stopped! Be kind enough to walk home with me. I am strangely tired, not from having talked so much but at the mere thought of what I still have to say. Oh well, a few words will suffice to relate my essential discovery. What's the use of saying more, anyway? For the statue to stand bare the fine speeches must take flight. So here goes. That particular night in November, two or three years before the evening when I thought I heard laughter behind me, I was returning to the Left Bank and to my home by way of the Pont Royal. It was an hour past midnight, a fine rain was falling, a drizzle rather, that scattered the few people on the streets. I had just left a mistress, who was surely already asleep. I was enjoying that walk, a little numbed, my body calmed and irrigated by a flow of blood rather like the falling rain. On the bridge I passed behind a figure leaning over the railing and seeming to stare at the river. On closer view, I made out a slim young woman dressed in black. Between her dark hair and coat collar could be seen the back of her neck, cool and damp, which stirred me. But I went on, after a moment's hesitation. At the end of the bridge I followed the quay towards Saint-Michel, where I lived. I had already gone some fifty yards when I heard the sound – which, despite the distance, seemed dreadfully loud in the midnight silence – of a body striking the water. I stopped short but without turning round. Almost at once I heard a cry, repeated several times, which was going downstream; then it abruptly ceased. The silence that followed, as the night suddenly stood still, seemed interminable. I wanted to run and yet didn't move an inch. I was trembling, I believe from cold and shock. I told myself that I had to be quick and I felt an irresistible weakness steal over me. I have forgotten what I thought then. 'Too late, too far...' or something of the sort. I was still listening as I stood motionless. Then, slowly, in the rain, I went away. I told no one.

But here we are; here's my house, my refuge! Tomorrow? Yes, if you wish. I'd like to take you to the island of Marken so that you can see the Zuyderzee. Let's meet at eleven at *Mexico City*. What? That woman? Oh, I don't know. Really I don't know. The next day and the days following, I didn't read the papers.

A dolls' village, isn't it? No shortage of quaintness here! But I didn't bring you to this island for quaintness, *cher ami*. Anyone can show you peasant head-dresses, wooden shoes and ornamented houses with fishermen smoking choice tobacco surrounded by the smell of furniture-polish. I am one of the few people, on the other hand, who can show you what really matters here.

We are reaching the dyke. We'll have to follow it to get as far as possible from these too charming houses. Please, let's sit down. Well, what do you think of it? Isn't it the most beautiful negative landscape? Just see on the left that pile of ashes they call a dune here, the grey dyke on the left, the livid beach at our feet and, in front of us, the sea looking like a weak lye-solution with the vast sky reflecting the colourless waters. A flabby hell, indeed! Everything horizontal, no relief; space is colourless and life dead. Is it not universal obliteration, everlasting nothingness made visible? No human beings, above all, no human beings! You and I alone facing the planet at last deserted! The sky is alive? You are right, *cher ami*. It thickens, becomes concave, opens up air shafts and closes cloudy doors. Those are the doves. Haven't you noticed that the sky of Holland is filled with millions of doves, invisible because of their altitude, which flap their wings, rise or fall in unison, filling the heavenly space with dense multitudes of greyish feathers carried hither and thither by the wind. The doves wait up there all year round. They wheel above the earth, look down, and would like to come down. But there is nothing but the sea and the canals, roofs covered with shop-signs, and never a head on which to alight.

You don't understand what I mean? I'll grant you I'm tired. I lose the thread of what I am saying; I've lost that lucidity to which my friends used to enjoy paying respects. I say 'my friends', moreover, as a matter of principle. I have no more friends; I have nothing but accomplices. To make up for this, their number has increased; they are the whole human race. And within the human race, you first of all. Whoever is at hand is always the first. How do I know I have no friends? It's very easy: I discovered it the day I thought of killing myself to play a trick on them, to punish them, in a way. But punish whom? Some would be surprised; no one would feel punished. I realized I had no friends. Besides, even if I had I shouldn't be any better off. If I'd been able to commit suicide and then see their reaction, why, then the game would have been worth the candle. But the earth is dark, *cher ami*, the coffin thick, and the shroud opaque. The eyes of the soul – to be sure – if there is a soul and it has eyes! But you see, we're not sure, we can't be sure. Otherwise, there would be a solution; at least one could get oneself taken seriously. Men are never convinced of your reasons, of your sincerity, of the seriousness of your sufferings, except by your death. So long as you are alive, your case is doubtful; you have a right only to their scepticism. So if there were the least certainty that one could enjoy the show, it would be worth proving to them what they are unwilling to believe and thus amazing them. But you kill yourself and what does it matter whether or not they believe you? You are not there to see their amazement and their contrition (fleeting at best), to witness – such is every man's dream – your own funeral. In order to cease being a doubtful case, one has to cease being, that's all.

Besides, isn't it better thus? We'd suffer too much from their indifference. 'You'll pay for this!' a daughter said to her father who had prevented her from marrying too smart a suitor. And she killed herself. But the father paid for nothing. He loved fly-fishing. Three Sundays later he went back to the river – to forget, as he said. He was right; he forgot. To tell the truth, the contrary would have been surprising. You think you are dying to punish your wife and actually you are freeing her. It's better not to see that. Apart from the fact that you might hear the reasons they give for your action. As far as I'm concerned, I can hear them now: 'He killed himself because he couldn't bear . . . ' Ah, *cher ami*, how poor in invention men are! They always think one commits suicide for a reason. But it's quite possible to commit suicide for two reasons. No, that never occurs to them. So what's the good of dying intentionally, of sacrificing yourself to the idea you want people to have of you? Once you are dead, they will take advantage of it to attribute idiotic or vulgar motives to your action. Martyrs, *cher ami*, must choose between being forgotten, mocked, or made use of. As for being understood – never!

Besides, let's not beat about the bush; I love life – that's my real weakness. I love it so much that I am incapable of imagining what is not life. Such avidity has something plebeian about it, don't you think? Aristocracy cannot imagine itself without a little distance surrounding itself and its own life. One dies if necessary, one breaks rather than bends. But I bend, because I continue to love myself. For example, after all I have told you, what do you think I developed? An aversion for myself? Come, come, it was mostly with others that I was fed up. To be sure, I knew my failings and regretted them. Yet

I continued to forget them with a rather meritorious obstinacy. The prosecution of others, on the contrary, went on constantly in my heart. Of course – does that shock you? Maybe you think it's not logical? But the question is not how to remain logical. The question is how to slip through and, above all – yes, above all, the question is how to elude judgment. I'm not saying to avoid punishment, for punishment without judgment is bearable. It has a name, besides, that guarantees our innocence: it is called misfortune. No, on the contrary, it's a matter of dodging judgment, of avoiding being for ever judged without ever having a sentence pronounced.

But one can't dodge it so easily. Today we are always as ready to judge as we are to fornicate. With this difference that there are no inadequacies to fear. If you doubt this, just listen to the table-conversation during August in those summer hotels where our charitable fellow-citizens take their cure for boredom. If you still hesitate to come to a conclusion, read the writings of our great men of the moment. Or else observe your own family; you will learn a thing or two. *Mon cher ami*, let's not give them any pretext, no matter how small, for judging us! Otherwise, we'll be left in shreds. We are forced to take the same precautions as the lion-tamer. If, before going into the cage, he has the misfortune to cut himself while shaving, what a feast for the animals! I realized this all of a sudden the day I began to suspect that maybe I wasn't so admirable. From then on, I became mistrustful. Since I was bleeding slightly, there was no escape for me; they would devour me.

My relations with my contemporaries were apparently the same and yet subtly out of tune. My friends hadn't changed. On occasion, they still extolled the harmony and security they found in my company. But I was aware only of the dissonances and disorder that filled me; I felt vulnerable and as if I were handed over to public accusation. In my eyes my fellows ceased to be the respectful public to which I was accustomed. The circle of which I was the centre broke and they lined up in a row as on the judges' bench. The moment I grasped that there was something to judge in me, I realized that, in fact, they had an irresistible vocation for judgment. Yes, they were there as before, but they were laughing. Or rather it seemed to me that every one of them that I met was looking at me with a hidden smile. I even had the impression, at that time, that people were tripping me up. Two or three times, in fact, I stumbled as I entered public places. Once, even, I went sprawling on the floor. The Cartesian Frenchman in me didn't take long to catch hold of himself and attribute those accidents to the only reasonable divinity – that is, chance. None the less, my distrust remained.

Once my attention was aroused, it was not hard for me to discover that I had enemies. In my profession, to begin with, and also in my social life. Some among them I had obliged. Others I should have obliged. All that, after all, was natural, and I discovered it without too much grief. It was harder and more painful, on the other hand, to admit that I had enemies among people I hardly knew or didn't know at all. I had always thought, with the ingenuousness I have already illustrated to you, that those who didn't know me couldn't resist liking me if they came to know me. Not at all! I encountered hostility especially among those who knew me only at a distance without my knowing them myself. Doubtless they suspected me of living fully and being given up completely to happiness; and that cannot be forgiven. The look of success, when it is worn in a certain way, would infuriate a jackass. Then again, my life was full to bursting and, for lack of time, I used to refuse many advances. Then I would forget my refusals, for the same reason. But those advances had been made me by people whose life was not full and who, for that very reason, would remember my refusals.

Thus it is that, to take but one example, women, in the end, cost me dear. The time I used to devote to them I couldn't give to men, who didn't always forgive me this. Is there any way out? Your successes and happiness are forgiven you only if you generously consent to share them. But to be happy it is essential not to be too concerned with others. Consequently, there is no escape. Happy and judged or absolved and wretched. As for me, the injustice was even greater: I was condemned for past successes. For a long time I had lived in the illusion of a general agreement, whereas, from all sides, judgments, arrows, mockeries rained upon me, inattentive and smiling. The day I was alerted I became lucid; I received all the wounds at the same time and lost my strength all at once. The whole universe then began to laugh at me.

That is what no man (except those who are not really alive – in other words, wise men) can endure. Spitefulness is the only possible ostentation.

People hasten to judge in order not to be judged themselves. What do you expect? The idea that comes most naturally to man, as if from his very nature, is the idea of his innocence. From this point of view, we are all like that little Frenchman at Buchenwald who insisted on registering a complaint with the clerk, himself a prisoner, who was recording his arrival. A complaint? The clerk and his comrades laughed: 'Useless, old man. You don't lodge complaints here.' 'But you see, sir,' said the little Frenchman, 'my case is exceptional. I am innocent!'

We are all exceptional cases. We all want to appeal against something! Each of us insists on being innocent at all costs, even if he has to accuse the whole human race and heaven itself. You won't delight a man by complimenting him on the efforts by which he has become intelligent or generous. On the other hand, he will beam if you admire his natural generosity. Inversely, if you tell a criminal that his crime is not due to his nature or his character but to unfortunate circumstances, he will be extravagantly grateful to you. During the counsel's speech, this is the moment he will choose to weep. Yet there is no credit in being honest or intelligent by birth. Just as one is surely no more responsible for being a criminal by nature than for being a criminal by force of circumstance. But those rascals want grace, that is irresponsibility, and they shamelessly allege the justifications of nature or the excuses of circumstances, even if they are contradictory. The essential thing is that they should be innocent, that their virtues, by grace of birth, should not be in question and that their misdeeds, born of a momentary misfortune, should never be more than temporary. As I told you, it's a matter of dodging judgment. Since it is hard to dodge it, tricky to get one's nature simultaneously admired and excused, they all strive to be rich. Why? Did you ever ask yourself? For power, of course. But especially because wealth shields from immediate judgment, takes you out of the subway crowd to enclose you in a chromium-plated automobile, isolates you in huge protected lawns, Pullman cars, first-class cabins. Wealth, *cher ami*, is not quite acquittal but reprieve, and that's always worth taking.

Above all, don't believe your friends when they ask you to be sincere with them. They merely hope you will encourage them in the good opinion they have of themselves by providing them with the additional assurance they find in your promise of sincerity. How could sincerity be a condition of friendship? A liking for truth at any cost is a passion that spares nothing and that nothing resists. It's a vice, at times a comfort, or a selfishness. Therefore, if you are in that situation, don't hesitate: promise to tell the truth and lie as best you can. You will satisfy their hidden desire and doubly prove your affection.

This is so true that we rarely confide in those who are better than ourselves. Rather, we are more inclined to flee their society. Most often, on the other hand, we confess to those who are like us and who share our weaknesses. Hence we don't want to improve ourselves or be bettered, for we should first be bound to be judged in default. We merely wish to be pitied and encouraged in the course we have chosen. In short, we should like, at the same time, to cease being guilty and yet not to make the effort of cleansing ourselves. Not enough cynicism and not enough virtue. We lack the energy required for evil as well as that required for good. Do you know Dante? Really? Well, I'll be damned! Then you know that Dante accepts the idea of neutral angels in the quarrel between God and Satan. And he puts them in Limbo, a sort of vestibule of his Hell. We are in the vestibule, *cher ami*.

Patience? You are probably right. It would take patience to wait for the Last Judgment. But there you are, we're in a hurry. So much in a hurry, indeed, that I was obliged to make myself a judge-penitent. First, however, I had to make shift with my discoveries and put myself right with my contemporaries' laughter. From the evening when I was called – for I was really called – I had to answer or at least seek an answer. It wasn't easy; for some time I floundered. To begin with, that perpetual laugh and the laughers had to teach me to see clearly within me and to discover at last that I was not simple. Don't smile; that truth is not so fundamental as it seems. What we call fundamental truths are simply the ones we discover after all the others.

However that may be, after prolonged research on myself, I brought out the basic duplicity of the human being. Then I realized, as a result of delving in my memory, that modesty helped me to shine, humility to conquer, and virtue to oppress. I used to wage war by peaceful means and eventually used to achieve, through disinterested means, everything I desired. For instance, I never complained that my birthday was overlooked; people were even surprised, with a touch of admiration, by my discretion on this subject. But the reason for my disinterestedness was even more discreet: I longed to be forgotten in order to be able to complain to myself. Several days before the famous date (which I knew very well) I was on the alert, eager to let nothing slip that might arouse the attention and memory of those on whose lapse I was counting (didn't I once go so far as to consider falsifying a friend's calendar?). Once my solitude was thoroughly proved, I could surrender to the charms of a virile self-pity.

Thus the surface of all my virtues had a less imposing reverse side. It is true that, in another sense, my shortcomings turned to my advantage. The obligation I felt to hide the vicious part of my life gave me, for example, a cold look that was confused with the look of virtue; my indifference made me loved; my selfishness culminated in my generosities. I stop there, for too great a symmetry would upset my argument. But after all, I presented a harsh exterior and yet could never resist the offer of a glass or of a woman! I was considered active, energetic, and my kingdom was the bed. I used to advertise my loyalty and I don't believe there is a single person I loved that I didn't eventually betray. Of course, my betrayals didn't stand in the way of my fidelity; I used to knock off a considerable pile of work through successive periods of idleness; and I had never ceased aiding my neighbour, thanks to my enjoyment in so doing. But however much I repeated such facts to myself, they gave me but superficial consolations. On certain mornings, I would get up the case against myself most thoroughly, coming to the conclusion that I excelled above all in scorn. The very people I helped most often were the most scorned. Courteously, with a solidarity charged with emotion, I used to spit daily in the face of all the blind.

Tell me frankly, is there any excuse for that? There is one, but so wretched that I cannot dream of advancing it. In any case, here it is: I have never been really able to believe that human affairs were serious matters. I had no idea where the serious might lie, except that it was not in all this I saw around me — which seemed to me merely an amusing game, or tiresome. There are really efforts and convictions I have never been able to understand. I always looked with amazement, and a certain suspicion, on those strange creatures who died for money, fell into despair over the loss of a 'position', or sacrificed themselves with a high-and-mighty manner for the prosperity of their family. I could better understand that friend who had made up his mind to stop smoking and through sheer will-power had succeeded. One morning he opened the paper, read that the first H-bomb had been exploded, learned about its wonderful effects, and hastened to a tobacco-shop.

To be sure, I occasionally pretended to take life seriously. But very soon the frivolity of seriousness struck me and I merely went on playing my role as well as I could. I played at being efficient, intelligent, virtuous, a good citizen, shocked, indulgent, responsible, high-minded... In short, there's no need to go on, you have already grasped that I was like my Dutchmen who are here without being here: I was absent at the moment when I took up most space. I have never been really sincere and enthusiastic except when I used to indulge in sports and, in the army, when I used to act in plays we put on for our own amusement. In both cases there was a rule of the game which was not serious but which we enjoyed taking as if it were. Even now, the Sunday games in an overflowing stadium and the theatre, which I loved with an unparalleled devotion, are the only places in the world where I feel innocent.

But who would consider such an attitude legitimate in the face of love, death, and the wages of the poor? Yet what can be done about it? I could imagine the love of Isolde only in novels or on the stage. At times people on their death-beds seemed to me convinced of their roles. The lines spoken by my poor clients always struck me as fitting the same pattern. Hence, living among men without sharing their interests, I could not manage to believe in the commitments I made. I was courteous and indolent enough to live up to what was expected of me in my profession, my family, or my life as a citizen, but each time with a sort of indifference that spoiled everything. I lived my whole life under a double code, and my most serious acts were often the ones in which I was the least involved. Wasn't it this, after all, for which, on top of my blunders, I could not forgive myself, which made me revolt most violently against the judgment I felt forming, in me and around me, and that forced me to seek an escape?

For some time, in appearances my life continued as if nothing had changed. I was on rails and speeding ahead. As if purposely, people's praises increased. And that's just where the trouble came from. You remember the remark: 'Woe to you when all men speak well of you!' Ah, the one who said that spoke words of wisdom! Woe to me! Consequently, the engine began to have whims, inexplicable breakdowns.

Then it was that the thought of death burst into my daily life. I would measure the years separating me from my end. I would look for examples of men of my age who were already dead. And I was tormented by the thought that I might not have time to accomplish my task. What task? I had no idea. Frankly, was what I was doing worth continuing? But that was not quite it. A ridiculous fear pursued me, in fact: one could not die without having confessed all one's lies. Not to God or to one of his representatives; I was above that, as you well imagine. No, it was a matter of confessing to men, to a friend, to a beloved woman, for example. Otherwise, even if there were only one lie hidden in a life, death made it definitive. No one, ever again, would know the truth on this point since the only one to know it was precisely the dead man sleeping on his secret. That absolute murder of a truth used to make me dizzy. Today, by the way, it would cause me, instead, subtle joys. The idea, for instance, that I am the only one to know what everyone is looking for and that I have at home an object which has kept the police of three countries on the run to no avail is a sheer delight. But let's not go into that. At the time, I had not yet found the recipe and I was fretting.

I pulled myself together, of course. What did one man's lie matter in the history of generations? And what presumption to want to drag out into the full light of truth a paltry fraud, lost in the sea of ages like a grain of sand in the ocean! I also told myself that the body's death, to judge from those I had seen, was in itself sufficient punishment and that it absolved all. Salvation was won (that is, the right to disappear for good) in the sweat of the death-agony. None the less the discomfort grew; death was faithful at my bedside; I used to get up with it every morning, and compliments became more and more unbearable to me. It seemed to me that the falsehood increased with them so inordinately that never again could I put myself right.

A day came when I could bear it no longer. My first reaction was excessive. Since I was a liar, I would reveal this and hurl my duplicity in the face of all those imbeciles, even before they discovered it. Provoked to truth, I would accept the challenge. In order to forestall the laughter, I dreamed of hurling myself into the general derision. In fact, it was still a question of dodging judgment. I wanted to put the laughers on my side, or at least to put myself on their side. I contemplated, for instance, jostling the blind on the street; and from the secret, unexpected joy this gave me I recognized how much a part of my soul loathed them; I planned to puncture the tyres of wheelchairs, to go and shout 'lousy proletarian' under the scaffoldings on which labourers were working, to smack infants in the subway. I dreamed of all that and did none of it, or if I did something of the sort, I have forgotten it. In any case, the very word 'justice' gave me strange fits of rage. I continued, of necessity, to use it in my speeches to the court. But I took my revenge by publicly inveighing against the humanitarian spirit; I announced the publication of a manifesto exposing the oppression that the oppressed inflict on decent people. One day while I was eating lobster at a terrace restaurant and a beggar bothered me, I called the proprietor to drive him away and loudly approved the words of that administrator of justice: 'You are embarrassing people,' he said. 'Just put yourself in the place of these ladies and gents, after all!' Finally, I used to express, to whoever would listen, my regret that it was no longer possible to act like a certain Russian landowner whose character I admired. He would have a beating administered both to his peasants who bowed to him and to those who didn't bow to him in order to punish a boldness he considered equally impudent in both cases.

However, I recall more serious excesses. I began to write an *Ode to the Police* and an *Apotheosis of the Guillotine*. Above all, I used to force myself to visit regularly the special cafés where our professional humanitarian free-thinkers gathered. My good past record assured me of a welcome. There, without seeming to, I would let fly a forbidden expression: 'Thank God...' I would say, or more simply: 'My God...' You know what shy little children our café atheists are. A moment of amazement would follow that outrageous expression, they would look at one another dumbfounded, then the tumult would burst forth. Some would flee the café, others would gabble indignantly without listening to anything, and all would writhe in convulsions like the devil in holy water.

You must find all that childish. Yet maybe there was a more serious reason for those little jokes. I wanted to upset the game and above all to destroy that flattering reputation, the thought of which threw me into a rage. 'A man like you...' people would say sweetly, and I would blanch. I didn't want their esteem because it wasn't general, and how could it be general when I couldn't share in it? Hence it was better to cover everything, judgment and esteem, with a cloak of ridicule. I had to liberate at all costs the feeling that was stifling me. In order to reveal to all eyes what he was made of, I wanted to break open the handsome wax-figure I presented everywhere. For instance, I recall an informal lecture I had to give to a group of young fledgling lawyers. Irritated by the fantastic praises of the President of the Bar who had introduced me, I couldn't resist long. I had begun with the enthusiasm and emotion expected of me, which I had no trouble in summoning up to order. But I suddenly began to advise alliance as a system of defence. Not, I said, the alliance perfected by modern inquisitions which judge simultaneously a thief and an honest man in order to crush the second under the crimes of the first. On the contrary, I meant to defend the thief by exposing the crimes of the honest man, the lawyer in this instance. I explained myself very clearly on this point:

'Let us suppose that I have accepted the defence of some pitiable citizen, a murderer through jealousy. Gentlemen of the Jury, consider (I should say) how venial it is to get angry when one sees one's natural goodness put to the test by the malignity of the fair sex. Is it not more serious, on the contrary, to be on this side of the bar, on my own bench, without ever having been good or suffered from being duped? I am free, shielded from your severities, yet who am I? A Louis XIV in pride, a billy-goat for lust, a Pharaoh for wrath, a king of laziness. I haven't killed anyone? Not yet, to be sure! But have I not let deserving creatures die? Maybe. And maybe I am ready to do so again. Whereas this man – just look at him – will not do so again. He is still quite amazed to have accomplished what he has.' This speech rather upset my young colleagues. After a moment, they made up their minds to laugh at it. They became completely reassured when I got to my conclusion, in which I invoked the human individual and his supposed rights. That day, habit won in the end.

By repeating these pleasant indiscretions, I merely succeeded in disconcerting opinion somewhat. Not in disarming it, least of all in disarming myself. The amazement I generally encountered in my listeners, their rather reticent embarrassment, somewhat like what you are showing – no, don't protest – did not calm me at all. You see, it is not enough to accuse yourself in order to clear yourself; otherwise, I'd be as innocent as a lamb. One must accuse oneself in a certain way, which it took me considerable time to perfect. I did not discover it until I fell into the most utterly forlorn state. Until then, the laughter continued to drift my way, without my random efforts succeeding in divesting it of its benevolent, almost tender quality that hurt me.

But the sea is rising, it seems to me. It won't be long before our boat leaves; the day is ending. Look, the doves are gathering up there. They are crowding against one another, hardly stirring, and the light is waning. Don't you think we should keep silent to enjoy this rather sinister moment? No, I interest you? You are very polite. Moreover, I now run the risk of really interesting you. Before explaining myself on the subject of judges–penitent, I must talk to you of debauchery and of the little-ease.

You are wrong, *cher*, the boat is going at full speed. But the Zuyderzee is a dead sea, or almost. With its flat shores, lost in the fog, there's no knowing where it begins or ends. So we are steaming along without any landmark; we can't gauge our speed. We are making progress and yet nothing is changing. It's not navigation but dreaming.

In the Greek archipelago I had the contrary feeling. Constantly new islands would appear on the horizon. Their treeless backbone marked the limit of the sky and their rocky shore contrasted sharply with the sea. No confusion possible; in the sharp light everything was a landmark. And from one island to another, ceaselessly on our little boat, which was nevertheless dawdling, I felt as if we were scudding along, night and day, on the crest of the short, cool waves in a race full of spray and laughter. Since then, Greece itself drifts somewhere within me, on the edge of my memory, tirelessly . . . Hold on, I too am drifting; I am becoming lyrical! Stop me, *cher*, I beg you.

By the way, do you know Greece? No? So much the better. What should we do there, I ask you? There it requires pure hearts. Do you know that there friends walk along the street in pairs holding hands? Yes, the women stay at home and you often see a middle-aged, respectable man, sporting moustaches, gravely striding along the pavements, his fingers locked in those of his friend. In the Orient likewise, at times? I don't say no. But tell me, would you take my hand in the streets of

Paris? Oh, I'm joking. *We* have a sense of decorum; scum gives us a stilted manner. Before appearing in the Greek islands, we should have to wash at length. There the air is chaste, the sea and sensual enjoyment transparent. And we . . .

Let's sit down on these deck-chairs. What a fog! I interrupted myself, I believe, on the way to the little-ease. Yes, I'll tell you what I mean. After having struggled, after having exhausted all my insolent airs, discouraged by the uselessness of my efforts, I made up my mind to leave the society of men. No, no, I didn't look for a desert island; there are none left. I simply took refuge among women. As you know, they don't really condemn any weakness; they are more inclined to try to humiliate or disarm our strength. This is why woman is the reward, not of the warrior, but of the criminal. She is his harbour, his haven; it is in a woman's bed that he is generally arrested. Is she not all that remains to us of earthly paradise? In distress, I hastened to my natural harbour. But I no longer indulged in pretty speeches. I still gambled a little, out of habit; but invention was lacking. I hesitate to admit it for fear of using a few more forbidden expressions: it seems to me that at that time I felt the need of love. Obscene, isn't it? In any case, I experienced a secret suffering, a sort of privation that made me emptier and allowed me, partly forced to it, and partly just out of curiosity, to make a few commitments. Inasmuch as I needed to love and be loved, I thought I was in love. In other words, I acted the fool.

I often caught myself asking a question which, as a man of experience, I had always previously avoided. I would hear myself asking: 'Do you love me?' You know that it is customary to answer in such cases: 'And you?' If I answered yes, I found myself committed beyond my real feelings. If I dared to say no, I ran the risk of ceasing to be loved, and I would suffer as a result. The greater the threat to the emotion in which I had hoped to find calm, the more I demanded it of my partner. Hence I was led to ever more explicit promises and came to exact an ever vaster emotion from my heart. Thus I developed a deceptive passion for a charming fool who had so thoroughly read the sentimental press that she spoke of love with the assurance and conviction of an intellectual announcing the classless society. Such conviction, as you must know, is contagious. I tried myself out at talking likewise of love and eventually convinced myself. At least until she became my mistress and I realized that the sentimental press, though it taught how to talk of love, did not teach how to make love. After having loved a parrot, I had to go to bed with a serpent. So I looked elsewhere for the love promised by books which I had never encountered in life.

But I lacked practice. For more than thirty years I had been in love with myself exclusively. What hope was there of losing such a habit? I didn't lose it and remained a trifler in passion. I multiplied the promises. I contracted simultaneous loves as, at an earlier period, I had multiple liaisons. In this way I accumulated more misfortunes, for others, than at the time of my fine indifference. Have I told you that my parrot, in despair, wanted to let herself die of hunger? Fortunately I arrived in time and submitted to holding her hand until she met, on his return from a journey to Bali, the engineer with greying temples who had already been described to her by her favourite weekly. In any case, far from finding myself transported and absolved in the eternity, as the saying goes, of passion, I added even more to the weight of my crimes and to my deviation from virtue. As a result, I conceived such a loathing for love that for years I could not hear *La Vie en rose* or the *Liebestod* without gnashing my teeth. I tried accordingly to give up women, in a certain way, and to live in a state of chastity. After all, their friendship ought to satisfy me. But this was tantamount to giving up gambling. Without desire, women bored me beyond all expectation, and obviously I bored them too. No more gambling and no more theatre – I was probably in the realm of truth. But truth, *cher ami*, is a colossal bore.

Despairing of love and of chastity, I at last told myself that there was nothing left but debauchery, a substitute for love, which quiets the laughter, restores silence and, above all, confers immortality. At a certain degree of lucid intoxication, lying late at night between two prostitutes and drained of all desire, hope ceases to be a torture, you see, the mind dominates the whole past, and the pain of living is for ever over. In a sense, I had always lived in debauchery, never having ceased wanting to be immortal. Wasn't this the key to my nature and also a result of the great self-love I have told you about? Yes, I was bursting with a longing to be immortal. I was too much in love with myself not to want the precious object of my love never to disappear. Since, in the waking state and with a little self-knowledge, one can see no reason why immortality should be conferred on a salacious monkey, one has to obtain substitutes for that immortality. Because I longed for eternal life, I went to bed with harlots and drank for nights on end. In the morning, to be sure, my mouth was filled with the bitter taste of the mortal state. But, for hours on end, I had soared in bliss. Dare I admit it to you? I still remember with affection certain nights when I used to go to a sordid night-club to meet a quick-change dancer who honoured me with her favours and for whose reputation I even fought one evening with a bearded braggart. Every night I would strut at the bar, in the red light and dust of that earthly paradise, lying fantastically and drinking at length. I would wait for dawn and at last end up in the always unmade bed of my princess, who would indulge mechanically in sex and then sleep without transition. Day would come softly to throw light on this disaster and I would get up and stand motionless in a dawn of glory.

Alcohol and women provided me, I admit, with the only solace of which I was worthy. I'll reveal this secret to you, *cher ami*, don't be afraid to make use of it. Then you'll see that true debauchery is liberating because it creates no obligations. In it you possess only yourself; hence it remains the favourite pastime of the great lovers of their own person. It is a jungle without past or future, without any promise above all, or any immediate penalty. The places where it is practised are separated from the world. On entering, one leaves behind fear and hope. Conversation is not obligatory there; what one comes for can be had without words, and often indeed without money. Ah, I beg you, let me pay honour to the unknown and forgotten women who helped me then! Even today, my recollection of them contains something resembling respect.

In any case, I freely took advantage of that liberation. I was even seen in a hotel dedicated to what is called sin, living at the same time with a mature prostitute and an unmarried girl of the best society. I played the gallant with the first and gave the second an opportunity to learn a few facts of life. Unfortunately the prostitute had a most middle-class nature; she has since consented to write her memoirs for a confessional paper quite open to modern ideas. The girl, for her part, got married to satisfy her unbridled instincts and make use of her remarkable gifts. I am not a little proud likewise to have been admitted as an equal, at that time, by a masculine guild too often reviled. But I'll not insist on that: you know that even very intelligent people glory in being able to empty one bottle more than the next man. I might ultimately have found peace and release in that happy dissipation. But, there too, I encountered an obstacle in myself. This time it was my liver, and a fatigue so dreadful that it hasn't yet left me. One plays at being immortal and after a few weeks one doesn't even know whether or not one can hang on till the next day.

The sole benefit of that experience, when I had given up my nocturnal exploits, was that life became less painful for me. The fatigue that was gnawing at my body had simultaneously eroded many raw points in me. Each excess decreases vitality, hence suffering. There is nothing frenzied about debauchery, contrary to what is thought. It is but a long sleep. You must have noticed that men who really suffer from jealousy have no more urgent desire than to go to bed with the woman they nevertheless think has betrayed them. Of course they want to assure themselves once more that their dear treasure still belongs to them. They want to possess it, as the saying goes. But there is also the fact that immediately afterwards they are less jealous. Physical jealousy is a result of the imagination at the same time as being a self-judgment. One attributes to the rival the nasty thoughts one had oneself in the same circumstances. Fortunately excess of sensual satisfaction weakens both imagination and judgment. The suffering then lies dormant as long as virility does. For the same reasons adolescents lose their metaphysical unrest with their first mistress; and certain marriages, which are merely formalized debauches, become the monotonous hearses of daring and invention. Yes, *cher ami*, bourgeois marriage has put our country into slippers and will soon lead it to the gates of death.

I am exaggerating? No, but I am straying from the subject. I merely wanted to tell you the advantage I derived from those months of orgy. I lived in a sort of fog in which the laughter became so muffled that eventually I ceased to notice it. The indifference that already filled so much of me now encountered no resistance and extended its sclerosis. No more emotions! An even temper, or rather no temper at all. Tubercular lungs are cured by drying up and gradually asphyxiate their happy owner. So it was with me as I peacefully died of my cure. I was still living on my work although my reputation was seriously damaged by my flights of language, and the regular exercise of my profession compromised by the disorder of my life. It is noteworthy, however, that I aroused less resentment by my nocturnal excesses than by my verbal provocations. The references, purely verbal, that I often made to God in my speeches before the court awakened distrust in my clients. They probably feared that heaven could not represent their interests as well as a lawyer invincible in the code of law. Whence it was but a step to conclude that I invoked the divinity in proportion to my ignorance. My clients took that step and became scarce. Now and then I still argued a case. At times even, forgetting that I no longer believed in what I was saying, I was a good advocate. My own voice would lead me on and I would follow it; without really soaring, as I used to do, I at least got off the ground and did a little hedge-hopping. Outside my profession, I saw but few people and painfully kept alive one or two exhausted liaisons. It even happened that I would spend purely friendly evenings, without any element of desire, yet with this difference that, resigned to boredom, I scarcely listened to what was being said. I became a little fatter and at last was able to believe that the crisis was over. Nothing remained but to grow older.

One day, however, during a trip to which I was treating a friend without telling her I was doing so to celebrate my cure, I was aboard an ocean liner – on the upper deck, of course. Suddenly, far off at sea, I perceived a black speck on the steel-grey ocean. I turned away at once and my heart began to beat wildly. When I forced myself to look, the black speck had disappeared. I was on the point of shouting, of stupidly calling for help, when I saw it again. It was one of those bits of débris that ships leave behind them. Yet I had not been able to endure watching it; for I had thought at once of a drowning person. Then I realized, calmly, just as you resign yourself to an idea the truth of which you have long known, that that cry which had sounded over the Seine behind me years before had never ceased, carried by the river to the waters of the Channel, to travel throughout the world, across the limitless expanse of the ocean, and that it had waited for me there until the day I encountered it. I realized likewise that it would continue to await me on seas and rivers, everywhere in short where lies the bitter water of my baptism. Here too, by the way, aren't we on the water? On this flat, monotonous, interminable water whose limits are indistinguishable from those of the land? Is it credible that we shall ever reach Amsterdam? We shall never get out of this immense stoup of holy water. Listen. Don't you hear the cries of invisible gulls? If they are crying in our direction, to what are they calling us?

But they are the same gulls that were crying, that were already calling over the Atlantic the day I realized once and for all that I was not cured, that I was still cornered and that I had to make do with it as best I could. Ended the glorious life, but ended also the frenzy and the convulsions. I had to submit and admit my guilt. I had to live in the little-ease. To be sure, you are not familiar with that dungeon cell that was called the little-ease in the Middle Ages. More often than not, one was forgotten there for life. That cell was distinguished from others by ingenious dimensions. It was not high enough to stand up in nor yet wide enough to lie down in. One had to take on an awkward manner and live on the diagonal; sleep was a collapse, and waking a squatting. *Mon cher*, there was genius – and I am weighing my words – in that so simple invention. Every day through the unchanging constraint that stiffened his body, the condemned man learned that he was guilty and that innocence consists in stretching joyously. Can you imagine a frequenter of summits and upper decks in that cell? What? One could live in those cells and still be innocent? Improbable. Highly improbable! Or else my reasoning would collapse. That innocence should be reduced to living hunch-backed – not for one second would I entertain such an hypothesis. Moreover, we cannot assert the innocence of anyone, whereas we can state with certainty the guilt of all. Every man testifies to the crime of all the others – that is my faith and my hope.

Believe me, religions are on the wrong track the moment they start to moralize and fulminate commandments. God is not needed to create guilt or to punish. Our fellow-men suffice, aided by ourselves. You were speaking of the Last Judgment. Allow me to laugh respectfully. I shall wait for it resolutely, for I have known what is worse, the judgment of men. For them, no extenuating circumstances; even the good intention is accounted a crime. Have you at least heard of the spitting cell, which a race of people recently thought up to prove itself the greatest on earth? A walled-up box in which the prisoner can stand without moving. The solid door that locks him in his cement shell stops at chin-level. Hence only his face is visible, and every passing jailer spits copiously on it. The prisoner, wedged into his cell, cannot wipe his face, though he is allowed, it is true, to close his eyes. Well, that, *mon cher*, is a human invention. They didn't need God for that little masterpiece.

So what? Well, God's sole usefulness would be to guarantee innocence, and I am inclined to see religion rather as a huge laundering venture – as it was once but briefly, for exactly three years, and it wasn't called religion. Since then, soap has been lacking, our faces are dirty, and we wipe one another's nose. All dunces, all punished, let's all spit on one another and – hurry! to the little-ease! Each tries to spit first, that's all. I'll tell you a big secret, *mon cher*. Don't wait for the Last Judgment. It takes place every day.

No, it's nothing; I'm merely shivering a little in this damned humidity. We're landing anyway. Here we are. After you. But stay a little, I beg you, and walk home with me. I haven't finished; I must go on. Continuing is what is hard. Say, do you know why he was crucified – the one you are perhaps thinking of at this moment? Well, there were heaps of reasons for that. There are always reasons for murdering a man. On the contrary, it is impossible to justify his living. That's why crime always finds lawyers, and innocence only rarely. But, besides the reasons that have been very well explained to us for the past two thousand years, there was a major one for that terrible agony, and I don't know why it has been so carefully hidden. The real reason is that *he* knew he was not altogether innocent. If he did not bear the weight of the crime he was accused of, he had committed others – even though he didn't know which ones. Did he really not know them? He was at the source, after all; he must have heard of a certain slaughter of the innocents. The children of Judea massacred while his parents were taking him to a safe place – why did they die if not because of him? Those blood-spattered soldiers, those infants cut in two filled him with horror. But given the man he was, I am sure he could not forget them. And as for that sadness that can be felt in his every act, wasn't it the incurable melancholy of a man who heard night after night the voice of Rachel weeping for her children and refusing all comfort? The lamentation would rend the night, Rachel would call her children who had been killed for him, and he was still alive!

Knowing what he knew, familiar with everything about man – ah, who would have believed that crime consists less in making others die than in not dying oneself! – brought face to face day and night with his innocent crime, he found it too hard for him to hold on and continue. It was better to have done with it, not to defend himself, to die, in order not to be the only one to live, and to go elsewhere where perhaps he would be upheld. He was not upheld, he complained and, as a last straw, he was censured. Yes, it was the third evangelist, I believe, who first suppressed his complaint. 'Why hast thou forsaken me?' – it was a seditious cry, wasn't it? Well then, the scissors! Mind you, if Luke had suppressed nothing, the matter would hardly have been noticed; in any case, it would not have assumed such importance. Thus the censor shouts aloud what he proscribes. The world's order likewise is ambiguous.

None the less, the censured one was unable to carry on. And I know, *cher*, what I am talking about. There was a time when I didn't have the slightest idea, at any single moment, how I could reach the next one. Yes, one can wage war in this world, ape love, torture one's fellow-man, or merely say evil of one's neighbour while knitting. But, in certain cases, carrying on, merely continuing, is superhuman. And he was not superhuman, you can take my word for it. He cried aloud his agony and that's why I love him, my friend who died without knowing.

The unfortunate thing is that he left us alone, to carry on, whatever happens, even when we are lodged in the little-ease, knowing in turn what he knew but incapable of doing what he did and of dying like him. People naturally tried to get some help from his death. After all, it was a stroke of genius to tell us: 'You're not a very pretty sight, that's certain! Well, we won't go into the details. We'll just liquidate it all at once, on the cross!' But too many people now climb on to the cross merely to be seen from a greater distance, even if they have to trample somewhat on the one who has been there so long. Too many people have decided to do without generosity in order to practise charity. Oh, the injustice, the rank injustice that has been done him! It wrings my heart!

Heavens, how easily one slips into a habit; I'm on the point of making a speech to the court. Forgive me and realize that I have my reasons. Why, a few streets from here there is a museum called 'Our Lord in the attic'. At the time, they had the catacombs in the attic. After all, the cellars are flooded here. But today – set your mind at rest – their Lord is neither in the attic nor in the cellar. They have hoisted him on to a judge's bench, in the secret of their hearts, and they smite, above all they judge, they judge in his name. He spoke softly to the adulteress: 'Neither do I condemn thee!' but that doesn't matter; they condemn without absolving anyone. In the name of the Lord, here is what you deserve. Lord? He, my friend, didn't expect so much. He simply wanted to be loved, nothing more. Of course, there are those who love him, even among Christians. But they are not numerous. He had fore-seen that too; he had a sense of humour. Peter, you know, the funk, Peter denied him: 'I know not the man ... I know not what thou sayest ... etc.' Really, he went too far! And my friend makes a play on words: 'Thou art Peter, and upon this rock I will build my church.' Irony could go no further, don't you think? But no, they still triumph! 'You see, he had said it!' He had said it indeed; he knew the question thoroughly. And then he left for ever, leaving them to judge and condemn, with pardon on their lips and the sentence in their hearts.

For it cannot be said there is no more pity; no, by heaven, we never stop talking of it. It's just that no one is ever acquitted any more. Over the dead body of innocence the judges swarm, the judges of all species, those of Christ and those of the Anti-Christ, who are the same anyway, reconciled in the little-ease. For one mustn't blame everything exclusively on the Christians. The others are involved too. Do you know what has become of one of the houses in this city that lodged Descartes? A lunatic asylum. Yes, it's general delirium, and persecution. We too, naturally, are obliged to come to it. You have had a chance to observe that I spare nothing and, as for you, I know that you think as I do. Wherefore, since we are all judges, we are all guilty before one another, all Christs in our cheap way, one by one crucified, always without knowing. We should be at least, if I, Clamence, had not found a way out, the only solution, truth at last . . .

No, I am stopping, *cher ami*, fear nothing! Besides I'm going to leave you, for we are at my door. In solitude and when fatigued, one is inclined, after all, to take oneself for a prophet. When all is said and done, that's really what I am, having taken refuge in a desert of stones, fogs, and stagnant waters – an empty prophet for shabby times, Elijah without a messiah, stuffed with fever and alcohol, my back up against this mouldy door, my finger raised towards a threatening sky, showering imprecations on lawless men who cannot endure any judgment. For they can't endure it, *très cher*, and that's the whole question. He who clings to a law does not fear the judgment that puts him in his place within an order he believes in. But the keenest of human torments is to be judged without law. Yet we are in that torment. Deprived of their natural curb, the judges, loosed at random, are racing through their job. Hence we have to try to go faster than they, don't we? And it's a real madhouse. Prophets and quacks multiply; they hasten to get there with a good law or a flawless organization before the world is deserted. Fortunately, *I* arrived! I am the end and the beginning; I announce the law. In short, I am a judge-penitent.

Yes, yes, I'll tell you tomorrow what this noble profession consists of. You are leaving the day after tomorrow, so we are in a hurry. Come to my place, will you? Ring three times. You are going back to Paris? Paris is a long way off; Paris is beautiful; I haven't forgotten it. I remember its twilights at this same season, more or less. Evening falls, dry and rasping, over the roofs blue with smoke, the city rumbles, the river seems to flow backward. Then I used to wander in the streets. They wander likewise now, I know! They wander, pretending to hasten towards the tired wife, the strict home ... Ah, *mon ami*, do you know what the solitary creature is like as he wanders in big cities? ...

I'm embarrassed to be in bed when you come. It's nothing, just a little fever that I'm treating with gin. I'm accustomed to these attacks. Malaria, I think, that I caught at the time I was Pope. No, I'm only half joking. I know what you're thinking: it's very hard to disentangle the true from the false in what I'm saying. I admit you are right. I myself ... You see, a person I knew used to divide human beings into three categories: those who prefer having nothing to hide rather than being obliged to lie, those who prefer lying to having nothing to hide, and finally those who like both lying and the hidden. I'll let you choose which case suits me best.

But what do I care? Don't lies eventually lead to the truth? And don't all my stories, true or false, tend towards the same conclusion? Don't they all have the same meaning? So what does it matter whether they are true or false if, in both cases, they are significant of what I have been and of what I am? Sometimes it is easier to see clearly into the liar than into the man who tells the truth. Truth, like light, blinds. Falsehood, on the contrary, is a beautiful twilight that enhances every object. Well, take it how you like, I was named Pope in a prison-camp.

Sit down, please. You are examining this room. Bare, to be sure, but clean. A Vermeer, without furniture or copper pots. Without books either, for I gave up reading some time ago. At one time, my house was full of half-read books. It's just as disgusting as those people who cut a piece off a foie gras and have the rest thrown away. At any rate, I have ceased to like anything but confessions, and authors of confessions write especially to avoid confessing, to tell nothing of what they know. When they claim to get to the painful admissions, you have to watch out, for they are about to dress the corpse. Believe me, I know what I'm talking about. So I put a stop to it. No more books, no more useless objects either; the bare necessities, clean and polished like a coffin. Besides, these Dutch beds, so hard and with their immaculate sheets – one dies in them as if already wrapped in a shroud, embalmed in purity.

You are curious to know my pontifical adventures? Nothing out of the ordinary, you know. Shall I have the strength to tell you of them? Yes, the fever is going down. It was all so long ago. It was in Africa where, thanks to a certain Mr Rommel, war was raging. I wasn't involved in it – no, don't worry. I had already dodged the one in Europe. Mobilized of course, but I never saw action. In a way, I regret it. Maybe that would have changed a great many things? The French army didn't need me on the front; it merely asked me to take part in the retreat. A little later I got back to Paris, and the Germans. I was tempted by the Resistance, about which people were beginning to talk just around the time I discovered that I was patriotic. You are smiling? You are wrong. I made my discovery in the Métro passages, at the Châtelet station. A dog had strayed into the labyrinth. Big, wire-haired, one ear cocked, eyes laughing, he was cavorting and sniffing at the legs of passers-by. I have a very old and very faithful fondness for dogs. I like them because they always forgive. I called this one, who hesitated, obviously won over, wagging his tail enthusiastically a few yards ahead of me. Just then, a young German soldier who was walking briskly along, passed me. Having reached the dog, he caressed the shaggy head. Without hesitating, the animal fell in step with the same enthusiasm and disappeared with him. From the resentment and the sort of rage I felt against the German soldier, it was clear to me that my reaction was patriotic. If the dog had followed a French civilian, I'd not even have thought of it. But, on the contrary, I imagined that friendly dog as the mascot of a German regiment and it made me fly into a rage. Hence the test was convincing.

I reached the Southern Zone with the intention of finding out about the Resistance. But once there and having found out, I hesitated. The undertaking struck me as a little mad and, in a word, romantic. I think especially that underground action suited neither my temperament nor my preference for exposed heights. It seemed to me that I was being asked to do some weaving in a cellar, for days and nights on end, until some brutes should come to haul me from hiding, undo my weaving and then drag me to another cellar to beat me to death. I admired those who indulged in such heroism of the depths but couldn't imitate them.

So I crossed over to North Africa with the vague intention of getting to London. But in Africa the situation was not clear; the opposing parties seemed to be equally right and I stood aloof. I can see from your manner that I am skipping rather fast, in your opinion, over these details which have a certain significance. Well, let's say that, having judged you at your true value, I am skipping over them so that you will notice them the better. In any case, I eventually reached Tunisia where a fond friend gave me work. That friend was a very intelligent woman who was involved in the film-business. I followed her to Tunis and didn't discover her real employment until the days following the Allied landing in Algeria. She was arrested that day by the Germans and I too, but without having intended it. I don't know what became of her. As for me, no harm was done me and I realized, after considerable anguish, that it was chiefly just a security measure. I was interned near Tripoli in a camp where we suffered from thirst and destitution more than from brutality. I'll not describe it to you. We children of this half-century don't need a diagram to imagine such places. A hundred and fifty years ago, people became sentimental about lakes and forests. Today we have the lyricism of the prison-cell. Hence, I'll leave it to you. You need only add a few details: the heat, the vertical sun, the flies, the sand, the lack of water.

There was a young Frenchman with me who had faith. Yes, it's decidedly a fairy-tale! The Duguesclin type, if you will. He had crossed over from France into Spain to go and fight. The Catholic general had interned him and, having seen that in the Franco camps the chick-peas were, if I may say so, blessed by Rome, he had developed a profound melancholy. Neither the sky of Africa, where he had next landed, nor the leisures of the camp had distracted him from that melancholy. But his reflections, and the sun too, had somewhat unhinged him. One day when, under a tent dripping with molten lead, the ten or so of us were panting among the flies, he repeated his diatribes against the Roman, as he called him. He looked at us with a wild stare above his week-old beard. Bare to the waist and covered with sweat, he drummed with his hands on the visible keyboard of his ribs. He declared to us the need for a new Pope who should live among the wretched instead of praying on a throne, and the sooner the better. He stared with wild eyes as he shook his head. 'Yes,' he repeated, 'as soon as possible!' Then he calmed down suddenly and in a dull voice said that we must choose him amongst ourselves, pick a complete man with his vices and virtues and swear allegiance to him, on the sole condition that he should agree to keep alive, in himself and in others, the community of our sufferings. 'Who among us,' he asked, 'has the most failings?' As a joke, I raised my hand and was the only one to do so. 'OK. Jean-Baptiste will do.' No, he didn't say precisely that because I had another name in those days. He declared at least that nominating oneself as I had done presupposed also the greatest virtue and proposed electing me. The others agreed, in fun, but with a trace of seriousness all the same. The truth is that Duguesclin had impressed us. It seems to me that even I was not altogether laughing. To begin with, I considered that my little prophet was right; and then with the sun, the exhausting labour, the struggle for water, we were not at our best. In any case, I exercised my pontificate for several weeks, with increasing seriousness.

Of what did it consist? Well, I was something like a group-leader or the secretary of a cell. The others, in any case, and even those who lacked faith, got into the habit of obeying me. Duguesclin was suffering; I administered his suffering. I discovered then that it was not so easy as I thought to be a Pope, and I remembered this just yesterday after having given you such a scornful speech about judges, our brothers. The big problem in the camp was the water allotment. Other groups, political or sectarian, had formed and each favoured his comrades. I was consequently led to favour mine, and this was a little concession to begin with. Even among us, I could not maintain complete equality. According to my comrades' condition, or the work they had to do, I gave an advantage to this one or to that. Such distinctions are far-reaching, you can take my word for it. But decidedly I am tired and no longer want to think of that period. Let's just say that I closed the circle the day I drank the water of a dying comrade. No, no, it wasn't Duguesclin; he was already dead, I believe, for he stinted himself too much. Besides, had he been there, out of love for him I'd have resisted longer, for I loved him – yes, I loved him, or so it seems to me. But I drank the water, that's certain, while convincing myself that the others needed me more than this fellow who was going to die anyway and that I had a duty to keep myself alive for them. Thus, *cher*, empires and churches are born under the sun of death. And in order to correct somewhat what I said yesterday, I am going to tell you the great idea that has come to me while telling all this, which – I'm not sure now – I may have lived or only dreamed. My great idea is that one must forgive the Pope. To begin with, he needs it more than anyone else. Secondly, that's the only way to set oneself above him . . .

Did you close the door thoroughly? Yes? Make sure, please. Forgive me, I have the bolt-complex. On the point of going to sleep, I can never remember whether or not I shot the bolt. And every night I must get up to make sure. One can be certain of nothing, as I've told you. Don't think that this worry about the bolt is the reaction of a frightened house-holder. In the old days I didn't lock my apartment or my car. I didn't lock up my money; I didn't cling to what I owned. To tell the truth, I was a little ashamed to own anything. Didn't I occasionally, in my general conversations, exclaim with earnestness: 'Property, gentlemen, is murder!' Not being sufficiently big-hearted to share my wealth with a deserving poor man, I left it at the disposal of eventual thieves, hoping thus to correct injustice by chance. Today, moreover, I possess nothing. Hence I am not worried about my safety, but about myself and my presence of mind. I am equally eager to block the door of the closed little universe of which I am the king, the Pope, and the judge.

By the way, will you please open that cupboard? Yes, look at that painting. Don't you recognize it? It is *The Just Judges*. That doesn't make you jump? Can it be that your culture has gaps? Yet if you read the papers, you would recall the theft in 1934 from the Saint-Bavon Cathedral at Ghent, of one of the panels of the famous Van Eyck altarpiece, *The Adoration of the Lamb*. That panel was called *The Just Judges*. It represented judges on horseback coming to adore the sacred animal. It was replaced by an excellent copy, for the original was never found. Well, here it is. No, I had nothing to do with it. A frequenter of *Mexico City* – you had a glimpse of him the other evening – sold it to the gorilla for a bottle, one drunken evening. I first advised our friend to hang it in a place of honour, and for a long time, while they were being looked for throughout the world, our devout judges sat enthroned at *Mexico City* above the drunkards and the pimps. Then the gorilla, at my request, put it in custody here. He baulked a little at doing so, but he got a fright when I explained the matter to him. Since then, these worthy magistrates form my sole company. At *Mexico City*, above the bar, you saw what a void they left.

Why did I not return the panel? Ah! Ah! You have a policeman's reflex, you do! Well, I'll answer you as I would the state's attorney, if it could ever occur to anyone that this painting had come to rest in my room. First, because it belongs not to me but to the proprietor of *Mexico City*, who deserves it as much as the Archbishop of Ghent. Secondly, because among all those who file past *The Adoration of the Lamb* no one could distinguish the copy from the original and hence no one is wronged by my misconduct. Thirdly, because in this way I dominate. False judges are held up to the world's admiration and I alone know the true ones. Fourth, because I thus have a chance of being sent to prison – an attractive idea in a way. Fifth, because those judges are on their way to meet the Lamb, because there is no lamb or innocence any longer, and because the clever rascal who stole the panel was an instrument of the unknown justice that one ought not to thwart. Finally, because this way everything is in harmony. Justice being separated once and for all from innocence – the latter on the cross and the former in the cupboard – I have the way clear to work according to my convictions. With a clear conscience I can practise the difficult profession of judge-penitent, in which I have set myself up after so many blighted hopes and contradictions; and now it is time, since you are leaving, for me to tell you what it is.

Allow me first to sit up so that I can breathe more easily. Oh, how weak I am! Lock up my judges, please. As for the profession of judge-penitent, I am practising it at present. Ordinarily, my offices are at *Mexico City*. But real vocations are carried beyond the place of work. Even in bed, even with a fever, I am functioning. Besides, one doesn't practise this profession, one breathes it constantly. Don't get the idea that I have talked to you at such length for five days just for the fun of it. No, I used to talk through my hat quite enough in the past. Now my words have a purpose. They have the purpose, obviously, of silencing the laughter, of avoiding judgment personally, though there is apparently no escape. Is not the great thing that stands in the way of our escaping it the fact that we are the first to condemn ourselves? Therefore it is essential to begin by extending the condemnation to all, without distinction, in order to thin it out at the start.

No excuses ever, for anyone; that's my principle at the outset. I deny the good intention, the respectable mistake, the indiscretion, the extenuating circumstance. With me there is no giving of absolution or blessing. Everything is simply totted up, and then: 'It comes to so much. You are an evil-doer, a satyr, a congenital liar, a homosexual, an artist, etc.' Just like that. Just as flatly. In philosophy as in politics, I am for any theory that refuses to grant man innocence and for any practice that treats him as guilty. You see in me, *très cher*, an enlightened advocate of slavery.

Without slavery, to tell the truth, there is no definitive solution. I very soon realized that. Once upon a time, I was always talking of freedom. At breakfast I used to spread it on my toast, I used to chew it all day long, and in company my breath was delightfully redolent of freedom. With that key-word I would bludgeon whoever contradicted me; I made it serve my desires and my power. I used to whisper it in bed in the ear of my sleeping partners and it helped me to drop them. I would slip it . . . But steady, I am getting excited and losing all sense of proportion. After all, I did on occasion make a more disinterested use of freedom and even – just imagine my naïveté – defended it two or three times without of course going so far as to die for it, but nevertheless taking a few risks. I must be forgiven such rash acts; I didn't know what I was doing. I didn't know that freedom is not a reward or a decoration that is celebrated with champagne. Nor yet a gift, a box of dainties designed to make you lick your chops. Oh, no! It's a chore, on the contrary, and a long-distance race, quite solitary and very exhausting. No champagne, no friends raising their glasses as they look at you affectionately. Alone in a forbidding room, alone in the prisoner's box before the judges, and alone to decide in face of oneself or in the face of others' judgment. At the end of all freedom is a court-sentence; that's why freedom is too heavy to bear, especially when you're down with a fever, or are distressed, or love nobody.

Ah, *mon cher*, for anyone who is alone, without God and without a master, the weight of days is dreadful. Hence one must choose a master, God being out of fashion. Besides, that word has lost its meaning; it's not worth the risk of shocking anyone. Take our moral philosophers, for instance, so serious, loving their neighbour and all the rest – nothing distinguishes them from Christians, except that they don't preach in churches. What, in your opinion, keeps them from becoming converted? Respect perhaps, respect for men; yes, self-respect. They don't want to start a scandal so they keep their feelings to themselves. I knew, for example, an atheistic novelist who used to pray every night. That didn't stop anything: how he gave it to God in his books! What a dusting-off, as someone or other would say. A militant free-thinker to whom I spoke of this raised his hands – with no evil intention, I assure you – to heaven: 'You're telling me nothing new,' that apostle sighed, 'they are all like that.' According to him, eighty per cent of our writers, if only they could avoid putting their names to it, would write and hail the name of God. But they do sign their names, according to him, because they love themselves and they hail nothing at all because they loathe themselves. Since, nevertheless, they cannot keep themselves from judging, they make up for it by moralizing. In short, their satanism is virtuous. An odd epoch indeed! It's not at all surprising that minds are confused and that one of my friends, an atheist when he was a model husband, was converted when he became an adulterer!

Ah, the little sneaks, play-actors, hypocrites — and yet so touching! Believe me, they all are, even when they set fire to heaven. Whether they are atheists or church-goers, Muscovites or Bostonians, all Christians from father to son. But actually there is no father left, no rule left! They are free and hence have to shift for themselves; and since they don't want freedom or its judgments, they asked to be rapped on the knuckles, they invent dreadful rules, they rush out to build piles of faggots to replace churches. Savonarolas, I tell you. But they believe solely in sin, never in grace. They think of it, to be sure. Grace is what they want — acceptance, surrender, happiness, and maybe, for they are sentimental too, betrothal, the virginal bride, the upright man, the organ music. Take me, for example, and I am not sentimental — do you know what I used to dream of? A total love of the whole heart and body, day and night, in an uninterrupted embrace, sensual enjoyment and mental excitement — all lasting five years and ending in death. Alas!

So, after all, for want of betrothal or uninterrupted love, it will be marriage, brutal marriage, with power and the whip. The essential is that everything should become simple, as for the child, that every act should be ordered, that good and evil should be arbitrarily, hence obviously, pointed out. And I'm all in favour, however Sicilian and Javanese I may be and not at all Christian, though I feel friendship for the first Christian of all. But on the bridges of Paris I too learned that I was afraid of freedom. So hurrah for the master, whoever he may be, to take the place of heaven's law. 'Our Father who art provisionally here . . . Our guides, our delightfully severe masters, O cruel and beloved leaders . . . ' In short, you see, the essential is to cease being free and to obey, in repentance, a greater rogue than oneself. When we are all guilty, that will be democracy. Not to mention the fact, *cher ami*, that we must take revenge for having to die alone. Death is solitary, whereas slavery is collective. The others get theirs too, and at the same time as we – that's what counts. All together at last, but on our knees and heads bowed.

Isn't it a good thing too to live like the rest of the world, and for that doesn't the rest of the world have to be like me? Threat, dishonour, police are the sacraments of that resemblance. Scorned, hunted down, compelled, I can then show what I am worth, enjoy what I am, be natural at last. This is why, *très cher*, after having solemnly paid my respects to freedom, I decided privately that it had to be handed over without delay to anyone who comes along. And every time I can, I preach in my church of *Mexico City*, I invite the good people to submit to authority and humbly to solicit the comforts of slavery, even if I have to present it as true freedom.

But I'm not being crazy; I'm well aware that slavery is not immediately realizable. It will be one of the blessings of the future, that's all. In the meantime, I must get along with the present and seek at least a provisional solution. Hence I had to find another means of extending judgment to everybody in order to make it weigh less heavily on my own shoulders. I found the means. Open the window a little, please; it's frightfully hot. Not too much, I'm cold as well. My idea is both simple and fertile. How to get everyone involved in order to have the right to sit calmly on the outside myself? Should I climb up to the pulpit, like many of my illustrious contemporaries, and curse humanity? Very dangerous, that is! One day, or one night, laughter bursts out without a warning. The judgment you are passing on others eventually snaps back in your face, causing some damage. And so what? you ask. Well, here's the stroke of genius. I discovered that while waiting for the masters with their rods, we should, like Copernicus, reverse the reasoning in order to win the day. Inasmuch as one couldn't condemn others without immediately judging oneself, one had to overwhelm oneself to have the right to judge others. Inasmuch as every judge some day ends up as a penitent, one had to travel the road in the opposite direction and practise the profession of penitent to be able to end up as a judge. You follow me? Good. But to make myself even clearer, I'll tell you how I operate.

First I closed my law-office, left Paris, travelled. I aimed to set up under another name in some place where I shouldn't lack for a practice. There are many in the world, but chance, convenience, irony, and also the necessity for a certain mortification made me choose a capital city of waters and fogs, corseted by canals, particularly crowded, and visited by men from all the corners of the earth. I set up my office in a bar in the sailors' quarter. The clientele of a port is varied. The poor don't go into the luxury districts, whereas eventually the gentlefolk always wind up at least once, as you have seen, in the disreputable places. I lie in wait particularly for the bourgeois, and the straying bourgeois at that; it's with him that I get my best results. Like a virtuoso with a rare violin, I draw my subtlest sounds from him.

So I have been practising my useful profession at *Mexico City* for some time. It consists to begin with, as you know from experience, in indulging in public confession as often as possible. I accuse myself up hill and down dale. It's not hard, for I have now acquired a memory. But let me point out that I don't accuse myself crudely, beating my breast. No, I navigate skilfully, multiplying distinctions and digressions too – in short I adapt my words to my listener and lead him to go me one better. I mingle what concerns me and what concerns others. I choose the features we have in common, the experiences we have endured together, the failings we share – good form, the man of the moment, in fact, such as reigns in me and in others. With all that I construct a portrait which is the image of all and of no one. A mask, in short, rather like those carnival masks which are both lifelike and stylized so that they make people say: 'Why, surely I've met him!' When the portrait is finished, as it is this evening, I show it with great sorrow: 'This, alas, is what I am!' The prosecutor's charge is finished. But at the same time the portrait I hold out to my contemporaries becomes a mirror.

Covered with ashes, tearing my hair, my face scored by clawing, but with piercing eyes, I stand before all humanity recapitulating my shames without losing sight of the effect I am producing and saying: 'I was the lowest of the low.' Then imperceptibly I pass from the 'I' to the 'we'. When I get to 'This is what we are', the game is over and I can tell them off. I am like them, to be sure; we are in the soup together. However, I have a superiority in that I know it and this gives me the right to speak. You see the advantage, I am sure. The more I accuse myself, the more I have a right to judge you. Even better, I provoke you into judging yourself, and this relieves me of that much of the burden. Ah, *mon cher*, we are odd, wretched creatures and, if we merely look back over our lives, there's no lack of occasions to amaze and scandalize ourselves. Just try. I shall listen, you may be sure, to your own confession with a great feeling of fraternity.

Don't laugh! Yes, you are a difficult client; I saw that at once. But you'll come to it inevitably. Most of the others are more sentimental than intelligent; they are disconcerted at once. With the intelligent ones it takes time. It is enough to explain the method fully to them. They don't forget it; they reflect. Sooner or later, half as a game and half out of emotional upset, they give up and tell all. *You* are not only intelligent, you look polished by use. Admit, however, that today you feel less pleased with yourself than you felt five days ago? Now I shall wait for you to write to me or to come back. For you will come back, I am sure! You'll find me unchanged. And why should I change, since I have found the happiness that suits me? I have accepted duplicity instead of being upset about it. On the contrary, I have settled into it and found there the comfort I was looking for throughout life. I was wrong, after all, to tell you that the essential thing was to avoid judgment. The essential thing is to be able to permit oneself everything, even if, from time to time, one has to profess vociferously one's own infamy. I permit myself everything all over again, and without the laughter this time. I haven't changed my way of life; I continue to love myself and to make use of others. Only, the confession of my crimes allows me to begin again lighter in heart and to taste a double enjoyment, first of my nature and secondly of a charming repentance.

Since finding my solution, I yield to everything, to women, to pride, to boredom, to resentment, and even to the fever that I feel delightfully rising at this moment. I dominate at last, but for ever. Once more I have found a height to which I am the only one to climb and from which I can judge everybody. At long intervals, on a really beautiful night I occasionally hear a distant laugh and again I doubt. But quickly I crush everything, people and things, under the weight of my own infirmity and at once I perk up.

So I shall await your respects at *Mexico City* as long as necessary. But take off this blanket; I want to breathe. You will come, won't you? I'll show you the details of my technique, for I feel a sort of affection for you. You will see me teaching them night after night that they are vile. This very evening, moreover, I shall resume. I can't do without it or deny myself those moments when one of them collapses, with the help of alcohol, and beats his breast. Then I grow taller, *très cher*, I grow taller, I breathe freely, I am on the mountain, the plain stretches before my eyes. How intoxicating to feel like God the Father and to hand out definitive testimonials of bad character and habits. I sit enthroned among my bad angels at the summit of the Dutch heaven and I watch ascending towards me, as they issue from the fogs and the water, the multitude of the Last Judgment. They rise slowly; I already see the first of them arriving. On his bewildered face, half hidden by a hand, I read the melancholy of the common condition and the despair of not being able to escape it. And as for me, I pity without absolving, I understand without forgiving and, above all, I feel at last that I am being adored!

Yes, I am moving about. How could I remain in bed like a good patient? I must be higher than you, and my thoughts lift me up. Such nights, or such mornings rather (for the fall occurs at dawn), I go out and walk briskly along the canals. In the livid sky the layers of feathers become thinner, the doves move a little higher, and above the roofs a rosy light announces a new day of my creation. On the Damrak the first tram sounds its bell in the damp air and marks the awakening of life at the extremity of this Europe where, at the same moment, hundreds of millions of men, my subjects, painfully slip out of bed, a bitter taste in their mouths, to go to their joyless work. Then, soaring over this whole continent which is under my sway without knowing it, drinking in the absinthe-coloured light of breaking day, intoxicated with bad words, I am happy – I am happy, I tell you, I won't let you think I'm not happy, I am happy unto death! Oh, sun, beaches, and the islands in the path of the trade-winds, youth whose memory drives one to despair!

I'm going back to bed; forgive me. I fear I got worked up; yet I'm not weeping. At times one wanders, doubting the facts, even when one has discovered the secrets of the good life. To be sure, my solution is not the ideal. But when you don't like your own life, when you know that you must change lives, you don't have any choice, do you? What can one do to become another? Impossible. One would have to cease being anyone, forget oneself for someone else, at least once. But how? Don't be too hard on me. I'm like that old beggar who wouldn't let go of my hand one day on a café terrace: 'Oh, sir,' he said, 'it's not just that I'm no good, but you lose track of the light.' Yes, we have lost track of the light, the mornings, the holy innocence of those who forgive themselves.

Look, it's snowing! Oh, I must go out! Amsterdam asleep in the white night, the dark jade canals under the little snow-covered bridges, the empty streets, my muffled steps – it will be purity, even if fleeting, before tomorrow's mud. See the huge flakes drifting against the window-panes. It must be the doves, surely. They finally make up their minds to come down, the little dears; they are covering the waters and the roofs with a thick layer of feathers; they are fluttering at every window. What an invasion! Let's hope they are bringing good news. Everyone will be saved, eh? – and not only the elect. Possessions and hardships will be shared and you, for example, from today on you will sleep every night on the ground for me. The whole shooting-match, eh! Come now, admit that you would be flabbergasted if a chariot came down from heaven to carry me off, or if the snow suddenly caught fire. You don't believe it? No more do I. But still I must go out.

All right, all right, I'll be quiet; don't get upset! Don't take too seriously my emotional outbursts or my ravings. They are controlled. Why, now that you are going to talk to me about yourself, I shall find out whether or not one of the objectives of my absorbing confession is achieved. I always hope, in fact, that my interlocutor will be a policeman and that he will arrest me for the theft of *The Just Judges*. For the rest – am I right? – no one can arrest me. But as for that theft, it falls within the provisions of the law and I have arranged everything so as to make myself an accomplice: I am harbouring that painting and showing it to whoever wants to see it. You would arrest me then; that would be a good beginning. Perhaps the rest would be taken care of subsequently; I would be decapitated, for instance, and I'd have no more fear of death; I'd be saved. Above the gathered crowd, you would hold up my still warm head, so that they could recognize themselves in it and I could again dominate – an exemplar. All would be consummated; I should have brought to a close, unseen and unknown, my career as a false prophet crying in the wilderness and refusing to come forth.

But of course you are not a policeman; that would be too easy. What? Ah, I suspected as much, you see. So that strange affection I felt for you had sense to it. You practise in Paris the noble profession of lawyer! I sensed that we were of the same species. Are we not all alike, constantly talking and to no one, for ever up against the same questions although we know the answers in advance? Then tell me, please, what happened to you one night on the quays of the Seine and how you managed never to risk your life. You yourself utter the words that for years have never ceased echoing through my nights and that I shall at last say through your mouth: 'O young woman, throw yourself into the water again so that I may a second time have the chance of saving both of us!' A second time, eh, what a risky suggestion! Just suppose, *cher maître*, that we should be taken literally? We'd have to go through with it. Brr . . . ! The water's so cold! But let's not worry! It's too late now. It'll always be too late. Fortunately!

EXILE AND THE KINGDOM

TRANSLATED FROM THE FRENCH BY
JUSTIN O'BRIEN

For Francine

CONTENTS

THE ADULTEROUS WOMAN

A HOUSE-FLY had been circling for the last few minutes in the bus, though the windows were closed. An odd sight here, it had been silently flying back and forth on tired wings. Janine lost track of it, then saw it light on her husband's motionless hand. The weather was cold. The fly shuddered with each gust of sandy wind that scratched against the windows. In the meagre light of the winter morning, with a great fracas of sheet metal and axles, the vehicle was rolling, pitching, and making hardly any progress. Janine looked at her husband. With wisps of greying hair growing low on a narrow forehead, a broad nose, a flabby mouth, Marcel looked like a pouting faun. At each hollow in the roadway she felt him jostle against her. Then his heavy torso would slump back on his widespread legs and he would become inert again and absent, with vacant stare. Nothing about him seemed active but his thick hairless hands, made even shorter by the flannel underwear extending below his cuffs and covering his wrists. His hands were holding so tight to a little canvas suitcase set between his knees that they appeared not to feel the fly's halting progress.

Suddenly the wind was distinctly heard to howl and the gritty fog surrounding the bus became even thicker. The sand now struck the windows in packets as if hurled by invisible hands. The fly shook a chilled wing, flexed its legs, and took flight. The bus slowed and seemed on the point of stopping. But the wind apparently died down, the fog lifted slightly, and the vehicle resumed speed. Gaps of light opened up in the dust-drowned landscape. Two or three frail, whitened palm trees which seemed cut out of metal flashed into sight in the window only to disappear the next moment.

'What a country!' Marcel said.

The bus was full of Arabs pretending to sleep, shrouded in their burnouses. Some had folded their legs on the seat and swayed more than the others in the car's motion. Their silence and impassivity began to weigh upon Janine; it seemed to her as if she had been travelling for days with that mute escort. Yet the bus had left only at dawn from the end of the rail line and for two hours in the cold morning it had been advancing on a stony, desolate plateau which, in the beginning at least, extended its straight lines all the way to reddish horizons. But the wind had risen and gradually swallowed up the vast expanse. From that moment on, the passengers had seen nothing more; one after another, they had ceased talking and were silently progressing in a sort of sleepless night, occasionally wiping their lips and eyes irritated by the sand that filtered into the car.

'Janine!' She gave a start at her husband's call. Once again she thought how ridiculous that name was for someone tall and sturdy like her. Marcel wanted to know where his sample-case was. With her foot she explored the empty space under the seat and encountered an object which she decided must be it. She could not stoop over without gasping somewhat. Yet in school she had won the first prize in gymnastics and hadn't known what it was to be winded. Was that so long ago? Twenty-five years. Twenty-five years were nothing, for it seemed to her only yesterday when she was hesitating between an independent life and marriage, just yesterday when she was thinking anxiously of the time she might be growing old alone. She was not alone and that law student who always wanted to be with her was now at her side. She had eventually accepted him although he was a little shorter than she and she didn't much like his eager, sharp laugh or his black protruding eyes. But she liked his courage in facing up to life, which he shared with all the French of this country. She also liked his crestfallen look when events or men failed to live up to his expectations. Above all, she liked being loved, and he had showered her with attentions. By so often making her aware that she existed for him he made her exist in reality. No, she was not alone. . . .

The bus, with many loud honks, was ploughing its way through invisible obstacles. Inside the car, however, no one stirred. Janine suddenly felt someone staring at her and turned towards the seat across the aisle. He was not an Arab, and she was surprised not to have noticed him from the beginning. He was wearing the uniform of the French regiments of the Sahara and an unbleached linen cap above his tanned face, long and pointed like a jackal's. His grey eyes were examining her with a sort of glum disapproval, in a fixed stare. She suddenly blushed and turned back to her husband, who was still looking straight ahead in the fog and wind. She snuggled down in her coat. But she could still see the French soldier, long and thin, so thin in his fitted tunic that he seemed constructed of a dry, friable material, a mixture of sand and bone. Then it was that she saw the thin hands and burned faces of the Arabs in front of her and noticed that they seemed to have plenty of room, despite their ample garments, on the seat where she and her husband felt wedged in. She pulled her coat around her knees. Yet she wasn't so fat — tall and well-rounded rather, plump and still desirable, as she was well aware when men looked at her, with her rather childish face, her bright, naïve eyes contrasting with this big body she knew to be warm and inviting.

No, nothing had happened as she had expected. When Marcel had wanted to take her along on his trip she had protested. For some time he had been thinking of this trip — since the end of the war, to be precise, when business had returned to normal. Before the war the small dry-goods business he had taken over from his parents on giving up his study of law had provided a fairly good living. On the coast the years of youth can be happy ones. But he didn't much like physical effort and very soon had given up taking her to the beaches. The little car took them out of town solely for the Sunday afternoon ride. The rest of the time he preferred his shop full of multi-coloured piece-goods shaded by the arcades of this half-native, half-European quarter. Above the shop they lived in three rooms furnished with Arab hangings and furniture from the Galerie Barbès. They had not had children. The years had passed in the semi-darkness behind the half-closed shutters. Summer, the beaches, excursions, the mere sight of the sky were things of the past. Nothing seemed to interest Marcel but business. She felt she had discovered his true passion to be money, and, without really knowing why, she didn't like that. After all, it was to her advantage. Far from being miserly, he was generous, especially where she was concerned. 'If something happened to me,' he used to say, 'you'd be provided for.' And, in fact, it is essential to provide for one's needs. But for all the rest, for what is not the most elementary need, how to provide? This is what she felt vaguely, at infrequent intervals. Meanwhile she helped Marcel keep his books and occasionally substituted for him in the shop. Summer was always the hardest, when the heat stifled even the sweet sensation of boredom.

Suddenly, in summer as it happened, the war, Marcel called up then rejected on grounds of health, the scarcity of piece-goods, business at a standstill, the streets empty and hot. If something happened now, she would no longer be provided for. This is why, as soon as piece-goods came back on the market, Marcel had thought of covering the villages of the upper plateaux and of the south himself in order to do without a middle-man and sell directly to the Arab merchants. He had wanted to take her along. She knew that travel was difficult, she had trouble breathing, and she would have preferred staying at home. But he was obstinate and she had accepted because it would have taken too much energy to refuse. Here they were and, truly, nothing was like what she had imagined. She had feared the heat, the swarms of flies, the filthy hotels reeking of aniseed. She had not thought of the cold, of the biting wind, of these semi-polar plateaux cluttered with moraines. She had dreamed too of palm trees and soft sand. Now she saw that the desert was not that at all, but merely stone, stone everywhere, in the sky full of nothing but stone-dust, rasping and cold, as on the ground, where nothing grew among the stones except dry grasses.

The bus stopped abruptly. The driver shouted a few words in that language she had heard all her life without ever understanding it. 'What's the matter?' Marcel asked. The driver, in French this time, said that the sand must have clogged the carburettor, and again Marcel cursed this country. The driver laughed hilariously and asserted that it was nothing, that he would clean the carburettor and they'd be off again. He opened the door and the cold wind blew into the bus, lashing their faces with a myriad grains of sand. All the Arabs silently plunged their noses into their burnouses and huddled up. 'Shut the door,' Marcel shouted. The driver laughed as he came back to the door. Without hurrying, he took some tools from under the dashboard, then, tiny in the fog, again disappeared ahead without closing the door. Marcel sighed. 'You may be sure he's never seen a motor in his life.' 'Oh, be quiet!' said Janine. Suddenly she gave a start. On the shoulder of the road close to the bus, draped forms were standing still. Under the burnous's hood and behind a rampart of veils, only their eyes were visible. Mute, come from nowhere, they were staring at the travellers. 'Shepherds,' Marcel said.

Inside the car there was total silence. All the passengers, heads lowered, seemed to be listening to the voice of the wind loosed across these endless plateaux. Janine was all of a sudden struck by the almost complete absence of luggage. At the end of the railroad line the driver had hoisted their trunk and a few bundles on to the roof. In the racks inside the bus could be seen nothing but gnarled sticks and shopping-baskets.

All these people of the South apparently were travelling empty-handed.

But the driver was coming back, still brisk. His eyes alone were laughing above the veils with which he too had masked his face. He announced that they would soon be under way. He closed the door, the wind became silent, and the rain of sand on the windows could be heard better. The motor coughed and died. After having been urged at great length by the starter, it finally sparked and the driver raced it by pressing on the accelerator. With a big hiccough the bus started off. From the ragged clump of shepherds, still motionless, a hand rose and then faded into the fog behind them. Almost at once the vehicle began to bounce on the road, which had become worse. Shaken up, the Arabs constantly swayed. None the less, Janine was feeling overcome with sleep when there suddenly appeared in front of her a little yellow box filled with lozenges. The jackal-soldier was smiling at her. She hesitated, took one, and thanked him. The jackal pocketed the box and simultaneously swallowed his smile. Now he was staring at the road, straight in front of him. Janine turned towards Marcel and saw only the solid back of his neck. Through the window he was watching the denser fog rising from the crumbly embankment.

They had been travelling for hours and fatigue had extinguished all life in the bus when shouts burst forth outside. Children wearing burnouses, whirling like tops, leaping, clapping their hands, were running around the bus. It was now going down a long street lined with low houses; they were entering the oasis. The wind was still blowing, but the walls intercepted the grains of sand which had previously cut off the light. Yet the sky was still cloudy. Amidst shouts, in a great screeching of brakes, the bus stopped in front of the adobe arcades of a hotel with dirty windows. Janine got out and, once on the pavement, staggered. Above the houses she could see a slim yellow minaret. On her left rose the first palm trees of the oasis, and she would have liked to go towards them. But although it was close to noon, the cold was bitter; the wind made her shiver. She turned towards Marcel and saw the soldier coming towards her. She was expecting him to smile or salute. He passed without looking at her and disappeared. Marcel was busy getting down the trunk of piece-goods, a black foot-locker perched on the bus's roof. It would not be easy. The driver was the only one to take care of the luggage and he had already stopped, standing on the roof, to hold forth to the circle of burnouses gathered around the bus. Janine, surrounded with faces that seemed cut out of bone and leather, besieged by guttural shouts, suddenly became aware of her fatigue. 'I'm going in,' she said to Marcel, who was shouting impatiently at the driver.

She entered the hotel. The manager, a thin, laconic Frenchman, came to meet her. He led her to a second-floor balcony overlooking the street and into a room which seemed to have but an iron bed, a white-enamelled chair, an uncurtained wardrobe, and, behind a rush screen, a washbasin covered with fine sand-dust. When the manager had closed the door, Janine felt the cold coming from the bare, whitewashed walls. She didn't know where to put her bag, where to put herself. She had either to lie down or to remain standing, and to shiver in either case. She remained standing, holding her bag and staring at a sort of window-slit that opened on to the sky near the ceiling. She was waiting, but she didn't know for what. She was aware only of her solitude, and of the penetrating cold, and of a greater weight in the region of her heart. She was in fact dreaming, almost deaf to the sounds rising from the street along with Marcel's vocal outbursts, more aware on the other hand of that sound of a river coming from the window-slit and caused by the wind in the palm trees, so close now, it seemed to her. Then the wind seemed to increase and the gentle ripple of waters became a hissing of waves. She imagined, beyond the walls, a sea of erect, flexible palm trees unfurling in the storm.

Nothing was like what she had expected, but those invisible waves refreshed her tired eyes. She was standing, heavy, with dangling arms, slightly stooped, as the cold climbed her thick legs. She was dreaming of the erect and flexible palm trees and of the girl she had once been.

* * *

After having washed, they went down to the dining-room. On the bare walls had been painted camels and palm trees drowned in a sticky background of pink and lavender. The arcaded windows let in a meagre light. Marcel questioned the hotel manager about the merchants. Then an elderly Arab wearing a military decoration on his tunic served them. Marcel, preoccupied, tore his bread into little pieces. He kept his wife from drinking water. 'It hasn't been boiled. Take wine.' She didn't like that, for wine made her sleepy. Besides, there was pork on the menu. 'They don't eat it because of the Koran. But the Koran didn't know that well-done pork doesn't cause illness. We French know how to cook. What are you thinking about?' Janine was not thinking of anything, or perhaps of that victory of the cooks over the prophets. But she had to hurry. They were to leave the next morning for still farther south; that afternoon they had to see all the important merchants. Marcel urged the elderly Arab to hurry the coffee. He nodded without smiling and pattered out. 'Slowly in the morning, not too fast in the afternoon,' Marcel said, laughing. Yet eventually the coffee came. They barely took time to swallow it and went out into the dusty, cold street. Marcel called a young Arab to help him carry the trunk, but as a matter of principle quibbled about the payment. His opinion, which he once more expressed to Janine, was in fact based on the vague principle that they always asked for twice as much in the hope of settling for a quarter of the amount. Janine, ill at ease, followed the two trunk-bearers. She had put on a wool dress under her heavy coat and would have liked to take up less space. The pork, although well done, and the small quantity of wine she had drunk also bothered her somewhat.

They walked along a diminutive public garden planted with dusty trees. They encountered Arabs who stepped out of their way without seeming to see them, wrapping themselves in their burnouses. Even when they were wearing rags, she felt they had a look of dignity unknown to the Arabs of her town. Janine followed the trunk, which made a way for her through the crowd. They went through the gate in an earthen rampart and emerged on a little square planted with the same mineral trees and bordered on the far side, where it was widest, with arcades and shops. But they stopped in the square itself in front of a small construction shaped like an artillery shell and painted chalky blue. Inside, in the single room lighted solely by the entrance, an old Arab with a white moustache stood behind a shiny plank. He was serving tea, raising and lowering the teapot over three tiny multi-coloured glasses. Before they could make out anything else in the darkness, the cool scent of mint tea greeted Marcel and Janine at the door. Marcel had barely crossed the threshold and dodged the garlands of pewter teapots, cups and trays, and the postcard displays when he was up against the counter. Janine stayed at the door. She stepped a little aside so as not to cut off the light. At that moment she perceived in the darkness behind the old merchant two Arabs smiling at them, seated on the bulging sacks that filled the back of the shop. Red-and-black rugs and embroidered scarves hung on the walls; the floor was cluttered with sacks and little boxes filled with aromatic seeds. On the counter, beside a sparkling pair of brass scales and an old yardstick with figures effaced, stood a row of loaves of sugar. One of them had been unwrapped from its coarse blue paper and cut into on top. The smell of wool and spices in the room became apparent behind the scent of tea when the old merchant set down the teapot and said good day.

Marcel talked rapidly in the low voice he assumed when talking business. Then he opened the trunk, exhibited the wools and silks, pushed back the scale and yardstick to spread out his merchandise in front of the old merchant. He got excited, raised his voice, laughed nervously, like a woman who wants to make an impression and is not sure of herself. Now, with hands spread wide, he was going through the gestures of selling and buying. The old man shook his head, passed the tea-tray to the two Arabs behind him, and said just a few words that seemed to discourage Marcel. He picked up his goods, piled them back into the trunk, then wiped an imaginary sweat from his forehead. He called the little porter and they started off towards the arcades. In the first shop, although the merchant began by exhibiting the same Olympian manner, they were a little luckier. 'They think they're God Almighty,' Marcel said, 'but they're in business too! Life is hard for everyone.'

Janine followed without answering. The wind had almost ceased. The sky was clearing in spots. A cold, harsh light came from the deep holes that opened up in the thickness of the clouds. They had now left the square. They were walking in narrow streets along earthen walls over which hung rotted December roses or, from time to time, a pomegranate, dried and wormy. An odour of dust and coffee, the smoke of a wood fire, the smell of stone and of sheep permeated this quarter. The shops, hollowed out of the walls, were far from one another; Janine felt her feet getting heavier. But her husband was gradually becoming more cheerful. He was beginning to sell and was feeling more kindly; he called Janine 'Baby'; the trip would not be wasted. 'Of course,' Janine said mechanically, 'it's better to deal directly with them.'

They came back by another street, towards the centre. It was late in the afternoon; the sky was now almost completely clear. They stopped in the square. Marcel rubbed his hands and looked affectionately at the trunk in front of them. 'Look,' said

Janine. From the other end of the square was coming a tall Arab, thin, vigorous, wearing a sky-blue burnous, soft brown boots and gloves and bearing his bronzed aquiline face loftily. Nothing but the *chèche* that he was wearing swathed as a turban distinguished him from those French officers in charge of native affairs whom Janine had occasionally admired. He was advancing steadily towards them, but seemed to be looking beyond their group as he slowly removed the glove from one hand. 'Well,' said Marcel as he shrugged his shoulders, 'there's one who thinks he's a general.' Yes, all of them here had that look of pride; but this one, really, was going too far. Although they were surrounded by the empty space of the square, he was walking straight towards the trunk, without seeing it, without seeing them. Then the distance separating them decreased rapidly and the Arab was upon them when Marcel suddenly seized the handle of the foot-locker and pulled it out of the way. The Arab passed without seeming to notice anything and headed with the same regular step towards the ramparts. Janine looked at her husband; he had his crestfallen look. 'They think they can get away with anything now,' he said. Janine did not reply. She loathed that Arab's stupid arrogance and suddenly felt unhappy. She wanted to leave and thought of her little flat. The idea of going back to the hotel, to that icy room, discouraged her. It suddenly occurred to her that the manager had advised her to climb up to the terrace around the fort to see the desert. She said this to Marcel and that he could leave the trunk at the hotel. But he was tired and wanted to sleep a little before dinner. 'Please,' said Janine. He looked at her, suddenly attentive. 'Of course, my dear,' he said.

She waited for him in the street in front of the hotel. The white-robed crowd was becoming larger and larger. Not a single woman could be seen, and it seemed to Janine that she had never seen so many men. Yet none of them looked at her. Some of them, without appearing to see her, slowly turned towards her that thin, tanned face that made them all look alike to her, the face of the French soldier in the bus and that of the gloved Arab, a face both shrewd and proud. They turned that face towards the foreign woman, they didn't see her, and then, light and silent, they walked around her as she stood there with swelling ankles. And her discomfort, her need of getting away increased. 'Why did I come?' But already Marcel was coming back.

When they climbed the stairs to the fort, it was five o'clock. The wind had died down altogether. The sky, completely clear, was now periwinkle blue. The cold, now drier, made their cheeks smart. Half-way up the stairs an old Arab, stretched out against the wall, asked them if they wanted a guide, but didn't budge, as if he had been sure of their refusal in advance. The stairs were long and steep despite several landings of packed earth. As they climbed, the space widened and they rose into an ever broader light, cold and dry, in which every sound from the oasis reached them pure and distinct. The bright air seemed to vibrate around them with a vibration increasing in length as they advanced, as if their progress struck from the crystal of light a sound-wave that kept spreading out. And as soon as they reached the terrace and their gaze was lost in the vast horizon beyond the palm grove, it seemed to Janine that the whole sky rang with a single short and piercing note, whose echoes gradually filled the space above her, then suddenly died and left her silently facing the limitless expanse.

From east to west, in fact, her gaze swept slowly, without encountering a single obstacle, along a perfect curve. Beneath her, the blue-and-white terraces of the Arab town overlapped one another, splattered with the dark-red spots of peppers drying in the sun. Not a soul could be seen, but from the inner courts, together with the aroma of roasting coffee, there rose laughing voices or incomprehensible stamping of feet. Farther off, the palm grove, divided into uneven squares by clay walls, rustled its upper foliage in a wind that could not be felt up on the terrace. Still farther off and all the way to the horizon extended the ochre-and-grey realm of stones, in which no life was visible. At some distance from the oasis, however, near the wadi that bordered the palm grove on the west, could be seen broad black tents. All around them a flock of motionless dromedaries, tiny at that distance, formed against the grey ground the black signs of a strange handwriting, the meaning of which had to be deciphered. Above the desert, the silence was as vast as the space.

Janine, leaning her whole body against the parapet, was speechless, unable to tear herself away from the void opening before her. Beside her, Marcel was getting restless. He was cold; he wanted to go back down. What was there to see, after all? But she could not take her gaze from the horizon. Over yonder, still farther south, at that point where sky and earth met in a pure line – over yonder it suddenly seemed there was awaiting her something of which, though it had always been lacking, she had never been aware until now. In the advancing afternoon the light relaxed and softened; it was passing from the crystalline to the liquid. Simultaneously, in the heart of a woman brought there by pure chance a knot tightened by the years, habit and boredom was slowly loosening. She was looking at the nomads' encampment. She had not even seen the men living in it; nothing was stirring among the black tents, and yet she could think only of them whose existence she had barely known until this day. Homeless, cut off from the world, they were a handful wandering over the vast territory she could see, which however was but a paltry part of an even greater expanse whose dizzying course stopped only thousands of miles farther south, where the first river finally waters the forest. Since the beginning of time, on the dry earth of this limitless land scraped to the bone, a few men had been ceaselessly trudging, possessing nothing but serving no one, poverty-stricken but free lords of a strange kingdom. Janine did not know why this thought filled her with such a sweet, vast melancholy that it closed her eyes. She knew that this kingdom had been eternally promised her and yet that it would never be hers, never again, except in this fleeting moment perhaps when she opened her eyes again on the suddenly motionless sky and on its waves of steady light, while the voices rising from the Arab town suddenly fell silent. It seemed to her that the world's course had just stopped and that, from that moment on, no one would ever age any more or die. Everywhere, henceforth, life was suspended — except in her heart, where, at the same moment, someone was weeping with affliction and wonder.

But the light began to move; the sun, clear and devoid of warmth, went down towards the west, which became slightly pink, while a grey wave took shape in the east ready to roll slowly over the vast expanse. A first dog barked and its distant bark rose in the now even colder air. Janine noticed that her teeth were chattering. 'We are catching our death of cold,' Marcel said. 'You're a fool. Let's go back.' But he took her hand awkwardly. Docile now, she turned away from the parapet and followed him. Without moving, the old Arab on the stairs watched them go down towards the town. She walked along without seeing anyone, bent under a tremendous and sudden fatigue, dragging her body, the weight of which now seemed to her unbearable. Her exaltation had left her. Now she felt too tall, too thick, too white for this world she had just entered. A child, the girl, the dry man, the furtive jackal were the only creatures who could silently walk that earth. What would she do there henceforth except to drag herself towards sleep, towards death?

She dragged herself, in fact, towards the restaurant with a husband suddenly taciturn unless he was telling her how tired he was, while she was struggling weakly against a cold, aware of a fever rising within her. Then she dragged herself towards her bed, where Marcel came to join her and put the light out at once without asking anything of her. The room was frigid. Janine felt the cold creeping up while the fever was increasing. She breathed with difficulty, her blood pumped without warming her; a sort of fear grew within her. She turned over and the old iron bedstead groaned under her weight. No, she didn't want to fall ill. Her husband was already asleep; she too had to sleep; it was essential. The muffled sounds of the town reached her through the window-slit. With a nasal twang old phonographs in the Moorish cafés ground out tunes she recognized vaguely; they reached her borne on the sound of a slow-moving crowd. She must sleep. But she was counting black tents; behind her eyelids motionless camels were grazing; immense solitudes were whirling within her. Yes, why had she come? She fell asleep on that question.

She awoke a little later. The silence around her was absolute. But, on the edges of town, hoarse dogs were howling in the soundless night. Janine shivered. She turned over, felt her husband's hard shoulder against hers, and suddenly, half asleep, huddled against him. She was drifting on the surface of sleep without sinking in and she clung to that shoulder with unconscious eagerness as her safest haven. She was talking, but no sound issued from her mouth. She was talking, but she herself hardly heard what she was saying. She could feel only Marcel's warmth. For more than twenty years every night thus, in his warmth, just the two of them, even when ill, even when travelling, as at present . . . Besides, what would she have done alone at home? No child! Wasn't that what she lacked? She didn't know. She simply followed Marcel, pleased to know that someone needed her. The only joy he gave her was the knowledge that she was necessary. Probably he didn't love her. Love, even when filled with hate, doesn't have that sullen face. But what is his face like? They made love in the dark by feel, without seeing each other. Is there another love than that of darkness, a love that would cry aloud in daylight? She didn't know, but she did know that Marcel needed her and that she needed that need, that she lived on it night and day, at night especially – every night, when he didn't want to be alone, or to age or die, with that set expression he assumed which she occasionally recognized on other men's faces, the only common expression of those madmen hiding under an appearance of wisdom until the madness seizes them and hurls them desperately towards a woman's body to bury in it, without desire, everything terrifying that solitude and night reveals to them.

Marcel stirred as if to move away from her. No, he didn't love her; he was merely afraid of what was not she, and she and he should long ago have separated and slept alone until the end. But who can always sleep alone? Some men do, cut off from others by a vocation or misfortune, who go to bed every night in the same bed as death. Marcel never could do so – he above all, a weak and disarmed child always frightened by suffering, her own child indeed who needed her and who, just at that moment, let out a sort of whimper. She cuddled a little closer and put her hand on his chest. And to herself she called him with the little love-name she had once given him, which they still used from time to time without even thinking of what they were saying.

She called him with all her heart. After all, she too needed him, his strength, his little eccentricities, and she too was afraid of death. 'If I could overcome that fear I'd be happy....' Immediately, a nameless anguish seized her. She drew back from Marcel. No, she was overcoming nothing, she was not happy, she was going to die, in truth, without having been liberated. Her heart pained her; she was stifling under a huge weight that she suddenly discovered she had been dragging about for twenty years. Now she was struggling under it with all her strength. She wanted to be liberated even if Marcel, even if the others, never were! Fully awake, she sat up in bed and listened to a call that seemed very close. But from the edges of night the exhausted and yet indefatigable voices of the dogs of the oasis were all that reached her ears. A slight wind had risen and she heard its light waters flow in the palm grove. It came from the south, where desert and night mingled now under the again unchanging sky, where life stopped, where no one would ever age or die any more. Then the waters of the wind dried up and she was not even sure of having heard anything except a mute call that she could, after all, silence or notice. But never again would she know its meaning unless she responded to it at once. At once – yes, that much was certain at least!

She got up gently and stood motionless beside the bed, listening to her husband's breathing. Marcel was asleep. The next moment, the bed's warmth left her and the cold gripped her. She dressed slowly, feeling for her clothes in the faint light coming through the blinds from the street-lamps. Her shoes in her hand, she reached the door. She waited a moment more in the darkness, then gently opened the door. The knob squeaked and she stood still. Her heart was beating madly. She listened with her body tense and, reassured by the silence, turned her hand a little more. The knob's turning seemed to her interminable. At last she opened the door, slipped outside, and closed the door with the same stealth. Then, with her cheek against the wood, she waited. After a moment she made out, in the distance, Marcel's breathing. She faced about, felt the icy night air against her cheek, and ran the length of the balcony. The outer door was closed. While she was slipping the bolt, the nightwatchman appeared at the top of the stairs, his face blurred with sleep, and spoke to her in Arabic. 'I'll be back,' said Janine as she stepped out into the night.

Garlands of stars hung down from the black sky over the palm trees and houses. She ran along the short avenue, now empty, that led to the fort. The cold, no longer having to struggle against the sun, had invaded the night; the icy air burned her lungs. But she ran, half blind, in the darkness. At the top of the avenue, however, lights appeared, then descended towards her zigzagging. She stopped, caught the whirr of turning sprockets and, behind the enlarging lights, soon saw vast burnouses surmounting fragile bicycle wheels. The burnouses flapped against her; then three red lights sprang out of the black behind her and disappeared at once. She continued running towards the fort. Half-way up the stairs, the air burned her lungs with such cutting effect that she wanted to stop. A final burst of energy hurled her despite herself on to the terrace, against the parapet, which was now pressing her belly. She was panting and everything was hazy before her eyes. Her running had not warmed her and she was still trembling all over. But the cold air she was gulping down soon flowed evenly inside her and a spark of warmth began to glow amidst her shivers. Her eyes opened at last on the expanse of night.

Not a breath, not a sound – except at intervals the muffled crackling of stones that the cold was reducing to sand – disturbed the solitude and silence surrounding Janine. After a moment, however, it seemed to her that the sky above her was moving in a sort of slow gyration. In the vast reaches of the dry, cold night, thousands of stars were constantly appearing, and their sparkling icicles, loosened at once, began to slip gradually towards the horizon. Janine could not tear herself away from contemplating those drifting flares. She was turning with them, and the apparently stationary progress little by little identified her with the core of her being, where cold and desire were now vying with each other. Before her the stars were falling one by one and being snuffed out among the stones of the desert, and each time Janine opened a little more to the night. Breathing deeply, she forgot the cold, the dead weight of others, the craziness or stuffiness of life, the long anguish of living and dying. After so many years of mad, aimless fleeing from fear, she had come to a stop at last. At the same time, she seemed to recover her roots and the sap again rose in her body, which had ceased trembling. Her whole belly pressed against the parapet as she strained towards the moving sky; she was merely waiting for her fluttering heart to calm down and establish silence within her. The last stars of the constellations dropped their clusters a little lower on the desert horizon and became still. Then, with unbearable gentleness, the water of night began to fill Janine, drowned the cold, rose gradually from the hidden core of her being and overflowed in wave after wave, rising up even to her mouth full of moans. The next moment, the whole sky stretched out over her, fallen on her back on the cold earth.

When Janine returned to the room, with the same precautions, Marcel was not awake. But he whimpered as she got back in bed and a few seconds later sat up suddenly. He spoke and she didn't understand what he was saying. He got up, turned on the light, which blinded her. He staggered towards the washbasin and drank a long draught from the bottle of mineral water. He was about to slip between the sheets when, one knee on the bed, he looked at her without understanding. She was weeping copiously, unable to restrain herself. 'It's nothing, dear,' she said, 'it's nothing.'

THE RENEGADE

WHAT A JUMBLE! What a jumble! I must tidy up my mind. Since they cut out my tongue, another tongue, it seems, has been constantly wagging somewhere in my skull, something has been talking, or someone, that suddenly falls silent and then it all begins again – oh, I hear too many things I never utter, what a jumble, and if I open my mouth it's like pebbles rattling together. Order and method, the tongue says, and then goes on talking of other matters simultaneously – yes, I always longed for order. At least one thing is certain, I am waiting for the missionary who is to come and take my place. Here I am on the trail, an hour away from Taghâsa, hidden in a pile of rocks, sitting on my old rifle. Day is breaking over the desert, it's still very cold, soon it will be too hot, this country drives men mad and I've been here I don't know how many years. . . . No, just a little longer. The missionary is to come this morning, or this evening. I've heard he'll come with a guide, perhaps they'll have but one camel between them. I'll wait, I am waiting, it's only the cold making me shiver. Just be patient a little longer, filthy slave!

But I have been patient for so long. When I was home on that high plateau of the Massif Central, my coarse father, my boorish mother, the wine, the pork soup every day, the wine above all, sour and cold, and the long winter, the frigid wind, the snowdrifts, the revolting bracken – oh, I wanted to get away, leave them all at once and begin to live at last, in the sunlight, with fresh water. I believed the priest, he spoke to me of the seminary, he tutored me daily, he had plenty of time in that Protestant region where he used to hug the walls as he crossed the village. He told me of the future and of the sun, Catholicism is the sun, he used to say, and he would get me to read, he beat Latin into my hard head ('The boy's bright but he's pig-headed'), my head was so hard that, despite all my falls, it has never once bled in my life: 'Bull-headed,' my pig of a father used to say. At the seminary they were proud as punch, a recruit from the Protestant region was a victory, they greeted me like the sun at Austerlitz. The sun was pale and feeble, to be sure, because of the alcohol, they have drunk sour wine and the children's teeth are set on edge, *gra gra*, one really ought to kill one's father, but after all there's no danger that *he*'ll hurl himself into missionary work since he's now long dead, the tart wine eventually cut through his stomach, so there's nothing left but to kill the missionary.

I have something to settle with him and with his teachers, with my teachers who deceived me, with the whole of lousy Europe, everybody deceived me. Missionary work, that's all they could say, go out to the savages and tell them: 'Here is my Lord, just look at him, he never strikes or kills, he issues his orders in a low voice, he turns the other cheek, he's the greatest of masters, choose him, just see how much better he's made me, offend me and you will see.' Yes, I believed, *gra gra*, and I felt better, I had put on weight, I was almost handsome, I wanted to be offended. When we would walk out in tight black rows, in summer, under Grenoble's hot sun and would meet girls in cotton dresses, *I* didn't look away, I despised them, I waited for them to offend me, and sometimes they would laugh. At such times I would think: 'Let them strike me and spit in my face', but their laughter, to tell the truth, came to the same thing, bristling with teeth and quips that tore me to shreds, the offence and the suffering were sweet to me! My confessor couldn't understand when I used to heap accusations on myself: 'No, no, there's good in you!' Good! There was nothing but sour wine in me, and that was all for the best, how can a man become better if he's not bad, I had grasped that in everything they taught me. That's the only thing I did grasp, a single idea, and, pig-headed bright boy, I carried it to its logical conclusion, I went out of my way for punishments, I groused at the normal, in short I too wanted to be an example in order to be noticed and so that after noticing me people would give credit to what had made me better, through me praise my Lord.

Fierce sun! It's rising, the desert is changing, it has lost its mountain-cyclamen colour, O my mountain, and the snow, the soft enveloping snow, no, it's a rather greyish yellow, the ugly moment before the great resplendence. Nothing, still nothing from here to the horizon over yonder where the plateau disappears in a circle of still soft colours. Behind me, the trail climbs to the dune hiding Taghâsa, whose iron name has been beating in my head for so many years. The first to mention it to me was the half-blind old priest who had retired to our monastery, but why do I say the first, he was the only one, and it wasn't the city of salt, the white walls under the blinding sun, that struck me in his account but the cruelty of the savage inhabitants and the town closed to all outsiders, only one of those who had tried to get in, one alone, to his knowledge, had lived to relate what he had seen. They had whipped him and driven him out into the desert after having put salt on his wounds and in his mouth, he had met nomads who for once were compassionate, a stroke of luck, and since then I had been dreaming about his tale, about the fire of the salt and the sky, about the House of the Fetish and his slaves, could anything more barbarous, more exciting be imagined, yes, that was my mission and I had to go and reveal to them my Lord.

They all expatiated on the subject at the seminary to discourage me, pointing out the necessity of waiting, that it was not missionary country, that I wasn't ready yet, I had to prepare myself specially, know who I was, and even then I had to go through tests, then they would see! But go on waiting, ah, no!

– yes, if they insisted, for the special preparation and the tryouts because they took place at Algiers and brought me closer, but for all the rest I shook my pig-head and repeated the same thing, to get among the most barbarous and live as they did, to show them at home, and even in the House of the Fetish, through example, that my Lord's truth would prevail. They would offend me, of course, but I was not afraid of offences, they were essential to the demonstration, and as a result of the way I endured them I'd get the upper hand of those savages like a strong sun. Strong, yes, that was the word I constantly had on the tip of my tongue, I dreamed of absolute power, the kind that makes people kneel down, that forces the adversary to capitulate, converts him in short, and the blinder, the crueller he is, the more he's sure of himself, mired in his own conviction, the more his consent establishes the royalty of whoever brought about his collapse. Converting good folk who had strayed somewhat was the shabby ideal of our priests, I despised them for daring so little when they could do so much, they lacked faith and I had it, I wanted to be acknowledged by the torturers themselves, to fling them on their knees and make them say: 'O Lord, here is thy victory,' to rule in short by the sheer force of words over an army of the wicked. Oh, I was sure of reasoning logically on that subject, never quite sure of myself otherwise, but once I get an idea I don't let go of it, that's my strong point, yes the strong point of the fellow they all pitied!

The sun has risen higher, my forehead is beginning to burn. Around me the stones are beginning to crack open with a dull sound, the only cool thing is the rifle's barrel, cool as the fields, as the evening rain long ago when the soup was simmering, they would wait for me, my father and mother who would occasionally smile at me, perhaps I loved them. But that's all in the past, a film of heat is beginning to rise from the trail, come on, missionary, I'm waiting for you, now I know how to answer the message, my new masters taught me, and I know they are right, you have to settle accounts with that question of love. When I fled the seminary in Algiers I had a different idea of the savages and only one detail of my imaginings was true, they are cruel. I had robbed the treasurer's office, cast off my habit, crossed the Atlas, the upper plateaux and the desert, the bus driver of the Trans-Sahara line made fun of me: 'Don't go there,' he too, what had got into them all, and the gusts of sand for hundreds of wind-blown kilometres, progressing and backing in the face of the wind, then the mountains again made up of black peaks and ridges sharp as steel, and after them it took a guide to go out on the endless sea of brown pebbles, screaming with heat, burning with the fires of a thousand mirrors, to the spot on the confines of the white country and the land of the blacks where stands the city of salt. And the money the guide stole from me, ever naïve I had shown it to him, but he left me on the trail – just about here, it so happens – after having struck me: 'Dog, there's the way, the honour's all mine, go ahead, go on, they'll show you,' and they did show me, oh yes, they're like the sun that never stops, except at night, beating sharply and proudly, that is beating me hard at this moment, too hard, with a multitude of lances burst from the ground, oh shelter, yes shelter, under the big rock, before everything gets muddled.

The shade here is good. How can anyone live in the city of salt, in the hollow of that basin full of dazzling heat? On each of the sharp right-angle walls cut out with a pickaxe and coarsely planed, the gashes left by the pickaxe bristle with blinding scales, pale scattered sand yellows them somewhat except when the wind dusts the upright walls and terraces, then everything shines with dazzling whiteness under a sky likewise dusted even to its blue rind. I was going blind during those days when the stationary fire would crackle for hours on the surface of the white terraces that all seemed to meet as if, in the remote past, they had all together tackled a mountain of salt, flattened it first, and then had hollowed out streets, the insides of houses and windows directly in the mass, or as if – yes, this is more like it, they had cut out their white, burning hell with a powerful jet of boiling water just to show that they could live where no one ever could, thirty days' travel from any living thing, in this hollow in the middle of the desert where the heat of day prevents any contact among creatures, separates them by a portcullis of invisible flames and of searing crystals, where without transition the cold of night congeals them individually in their rock-salt shells, nocturnal dwellers in a dried-up ice-flow, black Eskimoes suddenly shivering in their cubical igloos. Black because they wear long black garments, and the salt that collects even under their nails, that they continue tasting bitterly and swallowing during the sleep of those polar nights, the salt they drink in the water from the only spring in the hollow of a dazzling groove, often spots their dark garments with something like the trail of snails after a rain.

Rain, O Lord, just one real rain, long and hard, rain from your heaven! Then at last the hideous city, gradually eaten away, would slowly and irresistibly cave in and, utterly melted in a slimy torrent, would carry off its savage inhabitants to-wards the sands. Just one rain, Lord! But what do I mean, what Lord, they are the lords and masters! They rule over their sterile homes, over their black slaves that they work to death in the mines and each slab of salt that is cut out is worth a man in the region to the south, they pass by, silent, wearing their mourning veils in the mineral whiteness of the streets, and at night, when the whole town looks like a milky phantom, they stoop down and enter the shade of their homes, where the salt walls shine dimly. They sleep with a weightless sleep and, as soon as they wake, they give orders, they strike, they say they are a united people, that their god is the true god, and that one must obey. They are my masters, they are ignorant of pity and, like masters, they want to be alone, to progress alone, to rule alone, because they alone had the daring to build in the salt and the sands a cold torrid city. And I . . .

What a jumble when the heat rises, I'm sweating, they never do, now the shade itself is heating up, I feel the sun on the stone above me, it's striking, striking like a hammer on all the stones and it's the music, the vast music of noon, air and stones vibrating over hundreds of kilometres, *gra*, I hear the silence as I did once before. Yes, it was the same silence, years ago, that greeted me when the guards led me to them, in the sunlight, in the centre of the square, whence the concentric terraces rose gradually towards the lid of hard blue sky sitting on the edge of the basin. There I was, thrown on my knees in the hollow of that white shield, my eyes corroded by the swords of salt and fire issuing from all the walls, pale with fatigue, my ear bleeding from the blow given by my guide, and they, tall and black, looked at me without saying a word. The day was at its mid-course. Under the blows of the iron sun the sky resounded at length, a sheet of white-hot tin, it was the same silence, and they stared at me, time passed, they kept on staring at me, and I couldn't face their stares, I panted more and more violently, eventually I wept, and suddenly they turned their backs on me in silence and all together went off in the same direction. On my knees, all I could see, in the red-and-black sandals, was their feet sparkling with salt as they raised the long black gowns, the tip rising somewhat, the heel striking the ground lightly, and when the square was empty I was dragged to the House of the Fetish.

Squatting, as I am today in the shelter of the rock and the fire above my head pierces the rock's thickness, I spent several days within the dark of the House of the Fetish, somewhat higher than the others, surrounded by a wall of salt, but without windows, full of a sparkling night. Several days, and I was given a basin of brackish water and some grain that was thrown before me the way chickens are fed, I picked it up. By day the door remained closed and yet the darkness became less oppressive, as if the irresistible sun managed to flow through the masses of salt. No lamp, but by feeling my way along the walls I touched garlands of dried palms decorating the walls and, at the end, a small door, coarsely fitted, of which I could make out the bolt with my fingertips. Several days, long after – I couldn't count the days or the hours, but my handful of grain had been thrown me some ten times and I had dug out a hole for my excrements that I covered up in vain, the stench of an animal den hung on anyway – long after, yes, the door opened wide and they came in.

One of them came towards me where I was squatting in a corner. I felt the burning salt against my cheek, I smelled the dusty scent of the palms, I watched him approach. He stopped a yard away from me, he stared at me in silence, a signal, and I stood up, he stared at me with his metallic eyes that shone without expression in his brown horse-face, then he raised his hand. Still impassive, he seized me by the lower lip, which he twisted slowly until he tore my flesh and, without letting go, made me turn around and back up to the centre of the room, he pulled on my lip to make me fall on my knees there, mad with pain and my mouth bleeding, then he turned away to join the others standing against the walls. They watched me moaning in the unbearable heat of the unbroken daylight that came in the wide-open door, and in that light suddenly appeared the Sorcerer with his raffia hair, his chest covered with a breastplate of pearls, his legs bare under a straw skirt, wearing a mask of reeds and wire with two square openings for the eyes. He was followed by musicians and women wearing heavy motley gowns that revealed nothing of their bodies. They danced in front of the door at the end, but a coarse, scarcely rhythmical dance, they just barely moved, and finally the Sorcerer opened the little door behind me, the masters did not stir, they were watching me, I turned around and saw the Fetish, his double-axe head, his iron nose twisted like a snake.

I was carried before him, to the foot of the pedestal, I was made to drink a black, bitter, bitter water, and at once my head began to burn, I was laughing, that's the offence, I have been offended. They undressed me, shaved my head and body, washed me in oil, beat my face with cords dipped in water and salt, and I laughed and turned my head away, but each time two women would take me by the ears and offer my face to the Sorcerer's blows while I could see only his square eyes, I was still laughing, covered with blood. They stopped, no one spoke but me, the jumble was beginning in my head, then they lifted me up and forced me to raise my eyes towards the Fetish, I had ceased laughing. I knew that I was now consecrated to him to serve him, adore him, no, I was not laughing any more, fear and pain stifled me. And there, in that white house, between those walls that the sun was assiduously burning on the outside, my face taut, my memory exhausted, yes, I tried to pray to the Fetish, he was all there was and even his horrible face was less horrible than the rest of the world. Then it was that my ankles were tied with a cord that permitted just one step, they danced again, but this time in front of the Fetish, the masters went out one by one.

The door once closed behind them, the music again, and the Sorcerer lighted a bark fire around which he pranced, his long silhouette broke on the angles of the white walls, fluttered on the flat surfaces, filled the room with dancing shadows. He traced a rectangle in a corner to which the women dragged me, I felt their dry and gentle hands, they set before me a bowl of water and a little pile of grain and pointed to the Fetish, I grasped that I was to keep my eyes fixed on him. Then the Sorcerer called them one after the other over to the fire, he beat some of them who moaned and who then went and prostrated themselves before the Fetish my god, while the Sorcerer kept on dancing and he made them all leave the room until only one was left, quite young, squatting near the musicians and not yet beaten. He held her by a shock of hair which he kept twisting round his wrist, she dropped backward with eyes popping until she finally fell on her back. Dropping her, the Sorcerer screamed, the musicians turned to the wall, while behind the square-eyed mask the scream rose to an impossible pitch, and the woman rolled on the ground in a sort of fit and, at last on all fours, her head hidden in her locked arms, she too screamed, but with a hollow, muffled sound, and in this position, without ceasing to scream and to look at the Fetish, the Sorcerer took her nimbly and nastily, without the woman's face being visible, for it was covered with the heavy folds of her garment. And, wild as a result of the solitude, I screamed too, yes, howled with fright towards the Fetish until a kick hurled me against the wall, biting the salt as I am biting this rock today with my tongueless mouth, while waiting for the man I must kill.

Now the sun has gone a little beyond the middle of the sky. Through the breaks in the rock I can see the hole it makes in the white-hot metal of the sky, a mouth voluble as mine, constantly vomiting rivers of flame over the colourless desert. On the trail in front of me, nothing, no cloud of dust on the horizon, behind me they must be looking for me, no, not yet, it's only in the late afternoon that they opened the door and I could go out a little, after having spent the day cleaning the House of the Fetish, set out fresh offerings, and in the evening the ceremony would begin, in which I was sometimes beaten, at others not, but always I served the Fetish, the Fetish whose image is engraved in iron in my memory and now in my hope also. Never had a god so possessed or enslaved me, my whole life day and night was devoted to him, and pain and the absence of pain, wasn't that joy, were due to him and even, yes, desire, as a result of being present, almost every day, at that impersonal and nasty act which I heard without seeing it inasmuch as I now had to face the wall or else be beaten. But, my face up against the salt, obsessed by the bestial shadows moving on the wall, I listened to the long scream, my throat was dry, a burning sexless desire squeezed my temples and my belly as in a vice. Thus the days followed one another, I barely distinguished them as if they had liquefied in the torrid heat and the treacherous reverberation from the walls of salt, time had become merely a vague lapping of waves in which there would burst out, at regular intervals, screams of pain or possession, a long ageless day in which the Fetish ruled as this fierce sun does over my house of rocks, and now, as I did then, I weep with unhappiness and longing, a wicked hope consumes me, I want to betray, I lick the barrel of my gun and its soul inside, its soul, only guns have souls – oh, yes! the day they cut out my tongue, I learned to adore the immortal soul of hatred!

What a jumble, what a rage, *gra gra*, drunk with heat and wrath, lying prostrate on my gun. Who's panting here? I can't endure this endless heat, this waiting, I must kill him. Not a bird, not a blade of grass, stone, an arid desire, their screams, this tongue within me talking, and, since they mutilated me, the long, flat, deserted suffering deprived even of the water of night, the night of which I would dream, when locked in with the god, in my den of salt. Night alone with its cool stars and dark fountains could save me, carry me off at last from the wicked gods of mankind, but ever locked up I could not contemplate it. If the new-comer tarries more, I shall see it at least rise from the desert and sweep over the sky, a cold golden vine that will hang from the dark zenith and from which I can drink at length, moisten this black dried hole that no muscle of live flexible flesh revives now, forget at last that day when madness took away my tongue.

How hot it was, really hot, the salt was melting or so it seemed to me, the air was corroding my eyes, and the Sorcerer came in without his mask. Almost naked under greyish tatters, a new woman followed him and her face, covered with a tattoo reproducing the mask of the Fetish, expressed only an idol's ugly stupor. The only thing alive about her was her thin flat body that flopped at the foot of the god when the Sorcerer opened the door of the niche. Then he went out without looking at me, the heat rose, I didn't stir, the Fetish looked at me over that motionless body whose muscles stirred gently and the woman's idol-face didn't change when I approached. Only her eyes enlarged as she stared at me, my feet touched hers, the heat then began to shriek, and the idol, without a word, still staring at me with her dilated eyes, gradually slipped on to her back, slowly drew her legs up and raised them as she gently spread her knees. But, immediately afterwards, *gra*, the Sorcerer was lying in wait for me, they all entered and tore me from the woman, beat me dreadfully on the sinful place, what sin, I'm laughing, where is it and where is virtue, they clapped me against a wall, a hand of steel gripped my jaws, another opened my mouth, pulled on my tongue until it bled, was it I screaming with that bestial scream, a cool cutting caress, yes cool at last, went over my tongue. When I came to, I was alone in the night, glued to the wall, covered with hardened blood, a gag of strange-smelling dry grasses filled my mouth, it had stopped bleeding, but it was vacant and in that absence the only living thing was a tormenting pain. I wanted to rise, I fell back, happy, desperately happy to die at last, death too is cool and its shadow hides no god.

I did not die, a new feeling of hatred stood up one day, at the same time I did, walked towards the door of the niche, opened it, closed it behind me, I hated my people, the Fetish was there and from the depths of the hole in which I was I did more than pray to him, I believed in him and denied all I had believed up to then. Hail! he was strength and power, he could be destroyed but not converted, he stared over my head with his empty, rusty eyes. Hail! he was the master, the only lord, whose indisputable attribute was malice, there are no good masters. For the first time, as a result of offences, my whole body crying out a single pain, I surrendered to him and approved his maleficent order, I adored in him the evil principle of the world. A prisoner of his kingdom – the sterile city carved out of a mountain of salt, divorced from nature, deprived of those rare and fleeting flowerings of the desert, preserved from those strokes of chance or marks of affection such as an unexpected cloud or a brief violent downpour that are familiar even to the sun or the sands, the city of order in short, right angles, square rooms, rigid men – I freely became its tortured, hate-filled citizen, I repudiated the long history that had been taught me. I had been misled, solely the reign of malice was devoid of defects, I had been misled, truth is square, heavy, thick, it does not admit distinctions, good is an idle dream, an intention constantly postponed and pursued with exhausting effort, a limit never reached, its reign is impossible. Only evil can reach its limits and reign absolutely, it must be served to establish its visible kingdom, then we shall see, but what does 'then' mean, only evil is present, down with Europe, reason, honour, and the cross. Yes, I was to be converted to the religion of my masters, yes indeed, I was a slave, but if I too become vicious I cease to be a slave, despite my shackled feet and my mute mouth. Oh, this heat is driving me crazy, the desert cries out everywhere under the unbearable light, and he, the Lord of kindness, whose very name revolts me, I disown him, for I know him now. He dreamed and wanted to lie, his tongue was cut out so that his word would no longer be able to deceive the world, he was pierced with nails even in his head, his poor head, like mine now, what a jumble, how weak I am, and the earth didn't tremble, I am sure, it was not a righteous man they had killed, I refuse to believe it, there are no righteous men but only evil masters who bring about the reign of relentless truth. Yes, the Fetish alone has power, he is the sole god of this world, hatred is his commandment, the source of all life, the cool water, cool like mint that chills the mouth and burns the stomach.

Then it was that I changed, they realized it, I would kiss their hands when I met them, I was on their side, never wearying of admiring them, I trusted them, I hoped they would mutilate my people as they had mutilated me. And when I learned that the missionary was to come, I knew what I was to do. That day like all the others, the same blinding daylight that had been going on so long! Late in the afternoon a guard was suddenly seen running along the edge of the basin, and, a few minutes later, I was dragged to the House of the Fetish and the door closed. One of them held me on the ground in the dark, under threat of his cross-shaped sword, and the silence lasted for a long time until a strange sound filled the ordinarily peaceful town, voices that it took me some time to recognize because they were speaking my language, but as soon as they rang out the point of the sword was lowered towards my eyes, my guard stared at me in silence. Then two voices came closer and I can still hear them, one asking why that house was guarded and whether they should break in the door, Lieutenant, the other said: 'No' sharply, then added, after a moment, that an agreement had been reached, that the town accepted a garrison of twenty men on condition that they would camp outside the walls and respect the customs. The private laughed, 'They're knuckling under,' but the officer didn't know, for the first time in any case they were willing to receive someone to take care of the children and that would be the chaplain, later on they would see about the territory. The other said they would cut off the chaplain's you know what if the soldiers were not there. 'Oh, no!' the officer answered. 'In fact, Father Beffort will come before the garrison; he'll be here in two days.' That was all I heard, motionless, lying under the sword, I was in pain, a wheel of needles and knives was whirling in me. They were crazy, they were crazy, they were allowing a hand to be laid on the city, on their invincible power, on the true god, and the fellow who was to come would not have his tongue cut out, he would show off his insolent goodness without paying for it, without enduring any offence. The reign of evil would be postponed, there would be doubt again, again time would be wasted dreaming of the impossible good, wearing oneself out in fruitless efforts instead of hastening the realization of the only possible kingdom and I looked at the sword threatening me, O sole power to rule over the world! O power, and the city gradually emptied of its sounds, the door finally opened, I remained alone, burned and bitter, with the Fetish, and I swore to him to save my new faith, my true masters, my despotic God, to betray well, whatever it might cost me.

Gra, the heat is abating a little, the stone has ceased to vibrate, I can go out of my hole, watch the desert gradually take on yellow and ochre tints that will soon be mauve. Last night I waited until they were asleep, I had blocked the lock on the door, I went out with the same step as usual, measured by the cord, I knew the streets, I knew where to get the old rifle, what gate wasn't guarded, and I reached here just as the night was beginning to fade around a handful of stars while the desert was getting a little darker. And now it seems days and days that I have been crouching in these rocks. Soon, soon, I hope he comes soon! In a moment they'll begin to look for me, they'll speed over the trails in all directions, they won't know that I left for them and to serve them better, my legs are weak, drunk with hunger and hate. Oh! over there, *gra*, at the end of the trail, two camels are growing bigger, ambling along, already multiplied by short shadows, they are running with that lively and dreamy gait they always have. Here they are, here at last!

Quick, the rifle, and I load it quickly. O Fetish, my god over yonder, may your power be preserved, may the offence be multiplied, may hate rule pitilessly over a world of the damned, may the wicked for ever be masters, may the kingdom come, where in a single city of salt and iron black tyrants will enslave and possess without pity! And now, *gra gra*, fire on pity, fire on impotence and its charity, fire on all that postpones the coming of evil, fire twice, and there they are toppling over, falling, and the camels flee towards the horizon, where a geyser of black birds has just risen in the unchanged sky. I laugh, I laugh, the fellow is writhing in his detested habit, he is raising his head a little, he sees me – me his all-powerful shackled master, why does he smile at me, I'll crush that smile! How pleasant is the sound of a rifle butt on the face of goodness, today, today at last, all is consummated and everywhere in the desert, even hours away from here, jackals sniff the non-existent wind, then set out in a patient trot towards the feast of carrion awaiting them. Victory! I raise my arms to a heaven moved to pity, a lavender shadow is just barely suggested on the opposite side, O nights of Europe, home, childhood, why must I weep in the moment of triumph?

He stirred, no the sound comes from somewhere else, and from the other direction here they come rushing like a flight of dark birds, my masters, who fall upon me, seize me, ah yes! strike, they fear their city sacked and howling, they fear the avenging soldiers I called forth, and this is only right, upon the sacred city. Defend yourselves now, strike! strike me first, you possess the truth! O my masters, they will then conquer the soldiers, they'll conquer the word and love, they'll spread over the deserts, cross the seas, fill the light of Europe with their black veils – strike the belly, yes, strike the eyes – sow their salt on the continent, all vegetation, all youth will die out, and dumb crowds with shackled feet will plod beside me in the world-wide desert under the cruel sun of the true faith, I'll not be alone. Ah! the pain, the pain they cause me, their rage is good and on this cross-shaped war-saddle where they are now quartering me, pity! I'm laughing, I love the blow that nails me down crucified.

*   *   *

How silent the desert is! Already night and I am alone. I'm thirsty. Still waiting, where is the city, those sounds in the distance, and the soldiers perhaps the victors, no, it can't be, even if the soldiers are victorious, they're not wicked enough, they won't be able to rule, they'll still say one must become better, and still millions of men between evil and good, torn, bewildered, O Fetish, why hast thou forsaken me? All is over, I'm thirsty, my body is burning, a darker night fills my eyes.

This long, this long dream, I'm awaking, no, I'm going to die, dawn is breaking, the first light, daylight for the living, and for me the inexorable sun, the flies. Who is speaking, no one, the sky is not opening up, no, no, God doesn't speak in the desert, yet whence comes that voice saying: 'If you consent to die for hate and power, who will forgive us?' Is it another tongue in me or still that other fellow refusing to die, at my feet, and repeating: 'Courage! courage! courage!'? Ah! supposing I were wrong again! Once fraternal men, sole recourse, O solitude, forsake me not! Here, here who are you, torn, with bleeding mouth, is it you, Sorcerer, the soldiers defeated you, the salt is burning over there, it's you my beloved master! Cast off that hate-ridden face, be good now, we are mistaken, we'll begin all over again, we'll rebuild the city of mercy, I want to go back home. Yes, help me, that's right, give me your hand. . . .

* * *

A handful of salt fills the mouth of the garrulous slave.

THE SILENT MEN

IT WAS THE dead of winter and yet a radiant sun was rising over the already active city. At the end of the jetty, sea and sky fused in a single dazzling light. But Yvars did not see them. He was cycling slowly along the boulevards above the harbour. On the fixed pedal of his cycle his crippled leg rested stiffly while the other laboured to cope with the slippery road surface still wet with the night's moisture. Without raising his head, a slight figure astride the saddle, he avoided the rails of the former tramline, suddenly turned the handlebars to let cars pass him, and occasionally elbowed back into place the bag in which Fernande had put his lunch. At such moments he would think bitterly of the bag's contents. Between the two slices of coarse bread, instead of the Spanish omelet he liked or the beefsteak fried in oil, there was nothing but cheese.

The ride to the shop had never seemed to him so long. To be sure, he was ageing. At forty, though he had remained as slim as a vine shoot, a man's muscles don't warm up so quickly. At times, reading sports commentaries in which a thirty-year-old athlete was referred to as a veteran, he would shrug his shoulders. 'If he's a veteran,' he would say to Fernande, 'then I'm practically in a wheelchair.' Yet he knew that the reporter wasn't altogether wrong. At thirty a man is already beginning to lose his wind without noticing it. At forty he's not yet in a wheelchair, but he's definitely heading in that direction. Wasn't that just why he now avoided looking towards the sea during the ride to the other end of town where the cooper's shop was? When he was twenty he never got tired of watching it, for it used to hold in store a happy week-end on the beach.

Despite or because of his lameness, he had always liked swimming. Then the years had passed, there had been Fernande, the birth of the boy, and, to make ends meet, the overtime, at the shop on Saturdays and on various odd jobs for others on Sundays. Little by little he had lost the habit of those violent days that used to satiate him. The deep, clear water, the hot sun, the girls, the physical life – there was no other form of happiness in this country. And that happiness disappeared with youth. Yvars continued to love the sea, but only at the end of the day when the water in the bay became a little darker. The moment was pleasant on the terrace beside his house where he would sit down after work, grateful for his clean shirt that Fernande ironed so well and for the glass of anisette all frosted over. Evening would fall, the sky would become all soft and mellow, the neighbours talking with Yvars would suddenly lower their voices. At those times he didn't know whether he was happy or felt like crying. At least he felt in harmony at such moments, he had nothing to do but wait quietly, without quite knowing for what.

In the morning when he went back to work, on the other hand, he didn't like to look at the sea. Though it was always there to greet him, he refused to see it until evening. This morning he was pedalling along with head down, feeling even heavier than usual; his heart too was heavy. When he had come back from the meeting, the night before, and had announced that they were going back to work, Fernande had gaily said: 'Then the boss is giving you all a rise?' The boss was not giving any rise; the strike had failed. They hadn't managed things right, it had to be admitted. An impetuous walk-out, and the union had been right to back it up only half-heartedly. After all, some fifteen workers hardly counted; the union had to consider the other coopers' shops that hadn't joined in. You couldn't really blame the union. Cooperage, threatened by the building of tankers and tank trucks, was not thriving. Fewer and fewer barrels and large casks were being made; work

consisted chiefly in repairing the huge tuns already in existence. Employers saw their business compromised, to be sure,
but even so they wanted to maintain a margin of profit and the
easiest way still seemed to them to block wages despite the rise
in living costs. What can coopers do when cooperage disappears? You don't change trades when you've gone to the
trouble of learning one; this one was hard and called for a
long apprenticeship. The good cooper, the one who fits his
curved staves and tightens them in the fire with an iron hoop,
almost hermetically, without caulking with raffia or oakum,
was rare. Yvars knew this and was proud of it. Changing trades
is nothing, but to give up what you know, your master crafts-
manship, is not easy. A fine craft without employment and
you're stuck, you have to resign yourself. But resignation isn't
easy either. It was hard to have one's mouth shut, not to be able
to discuss really, and to take the same road every morning with
an accumulating fatigue, in order to receive at the end of every
week merely what they were willing to give you, which is less
and less adequate.

So they had got angry. Two or three of them had hesitated,
but the anger had spread to them too after the first discussions
with the boss. He had told them flatly, in fact, that they could
take it or leave it. A man doesn't talk like that. 'What's he
expect of us?' Esposito had said. 'That we'll stoop over and
wait to be kicked?' The boss wasn't a bad sort, however. He
had inherited from his father, had grown up in the shop, and
had known almost all the workers for years. Occasionally he
invited them to have a snack in the shop; they would cook
sardines or sausage meat over fires of shavings and, thanks
partly to the wine, he was really very nice. At New Year he
always gave five bottles of vintage wine to each of the men, and
often, when one of them was ill or celebrated an event like
marriage or first communion, he would make a gift of money.
At the birth of his daughter, there had been sugar-coated
almonds for everyone. Two or three times he had invited

Yvars to shoot on his coastal property. He liked his workmen, no doubt, and often recalled the fact that his father had begun as an apprentice. But he had never gone to their homes; he wasn't aware. He thought only of himself because he knew nothing but himself, and now you could take it or leave it. In other words, he had become obstinate likewise. But, in his position, he could allow himself to be.

He had forced the union's hand, and the shop had closed its doors. 'Don't go to the trouble of picketing,' the boss had said; 'when the shop's not working, I save money.' That wasn't true, but it didn't help matters since he was telling them to their faces that he gave them work out of charity. Esposito was wild with fury and had told him he wasn't a man. The boss was hot-blooded and they had to be separated. But, at the same time, it had made an impression on the workers. Twenty days on strike, the wives sad at home, two or three of them discouraged, and, in the end, the union had advised them to give in on the promise of arbitration and recovery of the lost days through overtime. They had decided to go back to work. Swaggering, of course, and saying that it wasn't all settled, that it would have to be reconsidered. But this morning, with a fatigue that resembled defeat, cheese instead of meat, the illusion was no longer possible. No matter how the sun shone, the sea held forth no more promises. Yvars pressed on his single pedal and with each turn of the wheel it seemed to him he was ageing a little. He couldn't think of the shop, of the fellow-workers and the boss he would soon be seeing again without feeling his heart become a trifle heavier. Fernande had been worried: 'What will you men say to him?' 'Nothing.' Yvars had straddled his bicycle, and had shaken his head. He had clenched his teeth; his small, dark, and wrinkled face with its delicate features had become hard. 'We're going back to work. That's enough.' Now he was cycling along, his teeth still clenched, with a sad, dry anger that darkened even the sky itself.

He left the boulevard, and the sea, to attack the moist streets of the old Spanish quarter. They led to an area occupied solely by sheds, junkyards, and garages, where the shop was – a sort of low shed that was faced with stone up to a half-way point and then glassed in up to the corrugated metal roof. This shop opened on to the former cooperage, a courtyard surrounded by a covered shed that had been abandoned when the business had enlarged and now served only as a storehouse for worn-out machines and old casks. Beyond the courtyard, separated from it by a sort of path covered with old tiles, the boss's garden began, at the end of which his house stood. Big and ugly, it was nevertheless prepossessing because of the Virginia creeper and the straggling honeysuckle surrounding the outside steps.

Yvars saw at once that the doors of the shop were closed. A group of workmen stood silently in front of them. This was the first time since he had been working here that he had found the doors closed when he arrived. The boss had wanted to emphasize that he had the upper hand. Yvars turned towards the left, parked his bicycle under the lean-to that prolonged the shed on that side, and walked towards the door. From a distance he recognized Esposito, a tall, dark, hairy fellow who worked beside him, Marcou, the union delegate, with his tenor's profile, Saïd, the only Arab in the shop, then all the others who silently watched him approach. But before he had joined them, they all suddenly looked in the direction of the shop doors, which had just begun to open. Ballester, the foreman, appeared in the opening. He opened one of the heavy doors and, turning his back to the workmen, pushed it slowly on its iron rail.

Ballester, who was the oldest of all, disapproved of the strike but had kept silent as soon as Esposito had told him that he was serving the boss's interests. Now he stood near the door, broad and short in his navy-blue jersey, already barefoot (he was the only one besides Saïd who worked barefoot), and he watched them go in one by one with his eyes that were so pale they seemed colourless in his old tanned face, his mouth downcast under his thick, drooping moustache. They were silent, humiliated by this return of the defeated, furious at their own silence, but the more it was prolonged the less capable they were of breaking it. They went in without looking at Ballester, for they knew he was carrying out an order in making them go in like that, and his bitter and downcast look told them what he was thinking. Yvars, for one, looked at him. Ballester, who liked him, nodded his head without saying a word.

Now they were all in the little locker-room on the right of the entrance: open stalls separated by unpainted boards to which had been attached, on either side, little locked cupboards; the farthest stall from the entrance, up against the walls of the shed, had been transformed into a shower above a gutter hollowed out of the earthen floor. In the centre of the shop could be seen work in various stages, already finished large casks, loose-hooped, waiting for the forcing in the fire, thick benches with a long slot hollowed out in them (and in some of them had been slipped circular wooden bottoms waiting to be planed to a sharp edge), and finally cold fires. Along the wall, on the left of the entrance, the workbenches extended in a row. In front of them stood piles of staves to be planed. Against the right wall, not far from the dressing-room, two large power saws, thoroughly oiled, strong and silent, gleamed.

Some time ago, the workshop had become too big for the handful of men who worked there. This was an advantage in the hot season, a disadvantage in winter. But today, in this vast space, the work dropped half finished, the casks abandoned in every corner with a single hoop holding the base of the staves spreading at the top like coarse wooden flowers, the sawdust covering the benches, the tool-boxes and machines – everything gave the shop a look of neglect. They looked at it, dressed now in their old sweaters and their faded and patched trousers and they hesitated. Ballester was watching them. 'So,' he said, 'we get started?' One by one, they went to their posts without saying a word. Ballester went from one to another, briefly reminding them of the work to be begun or finished. No one answered. Soon the first hammer resounded against the iron-tipped wedge sinking a hoop over the convex part of a barrel, a plane groaned as it hit a knot, and one of the saws, started up by Esposito, got under way with a great whirring of blade. Saïd would bring staves on request or light fires of shavings on which the casks were placed to make them swell in their corset of iron hoops. When no one called for him, he stood at a workbench riveting the big rusty hoops with heavy hammer blows. The scent of burning shavings began to fill the shop. Yvars, who was planing and fitting the staves cut out by Esposito, recognized the old scent and his heart relaxed some- what. All were working in silence, but a warmth, a life was gradually beginning to reawaken in the shop. Through the broad windows a clean, fresh light began to fill the shed. The smoke rose bluish in the golden sunlight; Yvars even heard an insect buzz close to him.

At that moment the door into the former shop opened in the end wall and M. Lassalle, the boss, stopped on the thresh- old. Thin and dark, he was scarcely more than thirty. His white overall hanging open over a tan gabardine suit, he looked at ease in his body. Despite his very bony face cut like a hatchet, he generally aroused liking, as do most people who exude vitality. Yet he seemed somewhat embarrassed as he came through the door. His greeting was less sonorous than usual; in any case, no one answered it. The sound of the hammers hesitated, lost the beat, and resumed even louder. M. Lassalle took a few hesitant steps, then he headed towards little Valery, who had been working with them for only a year. Near the power saw, a few feet away from Yvars, he was putting a bottom on a big hogshead and the boss watched him. Valery went on working without saying anything. 'Well, my boy,' said M. Lassalle, 'how are things?' The young man suddenly became more awkward in his movements. He glanced at

Esposito, who was close to him, picking up a pile of staves in his huge arms to take them to Yvars. Esposito looked at him too while going on with his work, and Valery peered back into his hogshead without answering the boss. Lassalle, rather nonplussed, remained a moment planted in front of the young man, then he shrugged his shoulders and turned towards Marcou. The latter, astride his bench, was giving the finishing touches, with slow, careful strokes, to sharpening the edge of a bottom. 'Hello, Marcou,' Lassalle said in a flatter voice. Marcou did not answer, entirely occupied with taking very thin shavings off his wood. 'What's got into you?' Lassalle asked in a loud voice as he turned towards the other workmen. 'We didn't agree, to be sure. But that doesn't keep us from having to work together. So what's the use of this?' Marcou got up, raised his bottom piece, verified the circular sharp edge with the palm of his hand, squinted his languorous eyes with a look of satisfaction, and, still silent, went towards another workman who was putting together a hogshead. Throughout the whole shop could be heard nothing but the sound of hammers and of the power saw. 'OK,' Lassalle said. 'When you get over this, let me know through Ballester.' Calmly, he walked out of the shop.

Almost immediately afterwards, above the din of the shop, a bell rang out twice. Ballester, who had just sat down to roll a cigarette, got up slowly and went to the door at the end. After he had left, the hammers resounded with less noise; one of the workmen had even stopped when Ballester came back. From the door he said merely: 'The boss wants you, Marcou and Yvars.' Yvars's first impulse was to go and wash his hands, but Marcou grasped him by the arm as he went by and Yvars limped out behind him.

Outside in the courtyard, the light was so clear, so liquid, that Yvars felt it on his face and bare arms. They went up the outside stairs, under the honeysuckle on which a few blossoms were already visible. When they entered the corridor, whose walls were covered with diplomas, they heard a child crying and M. Lassalle's voice saying: 'Put her to bed after lunch. We'll call the doctor if she doesn't get over it.' Then the boss appeared suddenly in the corridor and showed them into the little office they already knew, furnished with imitation rustic furniture and its walls decorated with sports trophies. 'Sit down,' Lassalle said as he took his place behind the desk. They remained standing. 'I called you in because you, Marcou, are the delegate and you, Yvars, my oldest employee after Ballester. I don't want to get back to the discussions, which are now over. I cannot, absolutely not, give you what you ask. The matter has been settled, and we reached the conclusion that work had to be resumed. I see that you are angry with me, and that hurts me, I'm telling you just as I feel it. I merely want to add this: what I can't do today I may perhaps be able to do when business picks up. And if I can do it, I'll do it even before you ask me. Meanwhile, let's try to work together.' He stopped talking, seemed to reflect, then looked up at them. 'Well?' he said. Marcou was looking out of the window. Yvars, his teeth clenched, wanted to speak but couldn't. 'Listen,' said Lassalle, 'you have all closed your minds. You'll get over it. But when you become reasonable again, don't forget what I've just said to you.' He rose, went towards Marcou, and held out his hand. 'Chao!' he said. Marcou suddenly turned pale, his popular tenor's face hardened and, for a second only, became mean-looking. Then he abruptly turned on his heel and went out. Lassalle, likewise pale, looked at Yvars without holding out his hand. 'Go to hell!' he shouted.

When they went back into the shop, the men were lunching. Ballester had gone out. Marcou simply said: 'Just wind,' and returned to his bench. Esposito stopped biting into his bread to ask what they had answered; Yvars said they hadn't answered anything. Then he went to get his haversack and came back and sat down on his workbench. He was beginning to eat when, not far from him, he noticed Saïd lying on his back in a pile of shavings, his eyes looking vaguely at the windows made blue by a sky that had become less luminous. He asked him if he had already finished. Saïd said he had eaten his figs. Yvars stopped eating. The uneasy feeling that hadn't left him since the interview with Lassalle suddenly disappeared to make room for a pleasant warmth. He broke his bread in two as he got up and, faced with Saïd's refusal, said that everything would be better next week. 'Then it'll be your turn to treat me,' he said. Saïd smiled. Now he bit into the piece of Yvars's sandwich, but in a gingerly way like a man who isn't hungry.

Esposito took an old pot and lighted a little fire of shavings and chips. He heated some coffee that he had brought in a bottle. He said it was a gift to the shop that his grocer had made when he learned of the strike's failure. A mustard jar passed from hand to hand. Each time Esposito poured out the already sugared coffee. Saïd swallowed it with more pleasure than he had taken in eating. Esposito drank the rest of the coffee right from the burning pot, smacking his lips and swearing. At that moment Ballester came in to give the back-to-work signal.

While they were rising and gathering papers and utensils into their haversacks, Ballester came and stood in their midst and said suddenly that it was hard for all, and for him too, but that this was no reason to act like children and that there was no use in sulking. Esposito, the pot in his hand, turned towards him; his long, coarse face had suddenly become flushed. Yvars knew what he was about to say – and what everyone was thinking at the same time – that they were not sulking, that their mouths had been closed, they had to take it or leave it, and that anger and helplessness sometimes hurt so much that you can't even cry out. They were men, after all, and they weren't going to begin smiling and simpering. But Esposito said none of this, his face finally relaxed, and he slapped Ballester's shoulder gently while the others went back to their work. Again the hammers rang out, the big shed filled with the familiar din, with the smell of shavings and of old clothes damp with sweat. The big saw whined and bit into the fresh wood of the stave that Esposito was slowly pushing in front of him. Where the saw bit, damp sawdust spurted out and covered with something like bread-crumbs the big hairy hands firmly gripping the wood on each side of the moaning blade. Once the stave was ripped, you could hear only the sound of the motor.

At present Yvars felt only the strain in his back as he leaned over the plane. Generally the fatigue didn't come until later on. He had got out of training during these weeks of inactivity, it was clear. But he thought also of age, which makes manual labour harder when it's not mere precision work. That strain also foreshadowed old age. Wherever the muscles are involved, work eventually becomes hateful, it precedes death, and on evenings following great physical effort sleep itself is like death. The boy wanted to become a schoolteacher, he was right; those who indulge in clichés about manual work don't know what they're talking about.

When Yvars straightened up to catch his breath and also to drive away these evil thoughts, the bell rang out again. It was insistent, but in such a strange way, with stops and imperious starts, that the men interrupted their work. Ballester listened, surprised, then made up his mind and went slowly to the door. He had disappeared for several seconds when the ringing finally ceased. They resumed work. Again the door was flung open and Ballester ran towards the locker-room. He came out wearing canvas shoes and, slipping on his jacket, said to Yvars as he went by: 'The child has had an attack. I'm off to get Germain,' and ran towards the main door. Dr Germain took care of the shop's health; he lived in this outlying quarter. Yvars repeated the news without commentary. They gathered around him and looked at one another, embarrassed. Nothing could be heard but the motor of the power saw running freely. 'It's perhaps nothing,' one of them said. They went back to their places, the shop filled again with their noises, but they were working slowly, as if waiting for something.

A quarter of an hour later, Ballester came in again, hung up his jacket, and, without saying a word, went out through the little door. On the windows the light was getting dimmer. A little later, in the intervals when the saw was not ripping into the wood, the dull bell of an ambulance could be heard, at first in the distance, then nearer, finally just outside. Then silence. After a moment Ballester came back and everyone went up to him. Esposito had turned off the motor. Ballester said that while undressing in her room the child had suddenly keeled over as if mowed down. 'Did you ever hear anything like it!' Marcou said. Ballester shook his head and gestured vaguely towards the shop; but he looked as if he had had quite a turn. Again the ambulance bell was heard. They were all there, in the silent shop, under the yellow light coming through the glass panels, with their rough, useless hands hanging down along their old sawdust-covered trousers.

The rest of the afternoon dragged. Yvars now felt only his fatigue and his still heavy heart. He would have liked to talk. But he had nothing to say, nor had the others. On their uncommunicative faces could be read merely sorrow and a sort of obstinacy. Sometimes the word 'calamity' took shape in him, but just barely, for it disappeared immediately – as a bubble forms and bursts simultaneously. He wanted to get home, to be with Fernande again, and the boy, on the terrace. As it happened, Ballester announced closing-time. The machines stopped. Without hurrying, they began to put out the fires and to put everything in order on their benches, then they went one by one to the locker-room. Saïd remained behind; he was to clean up the shop and water down the dusty soil. When Yvars reached the locker-room, Esposito, huge and hairy, was already under the shower. His back was turned to them as he soaped himself noisily. Generally, they kidded him about his modesty; the big bear, indeed, obstinately hid his pudenda. But no one seemed to notice on this occasion. Esposito backed out of the shower and wrapped a towel around him like a loincloth. The others took their turns, and Marcou was vigorously slapping his bare sides when they heard the big door roll slowly open on its cast-iron wheel. Lassalle came in.

He was dressed as at the time of his first visit, but his hair was rather dishevelled. He stopped on the threshold, looked at the vast deserted shop, took a few steps, stopped again, and looked towards the locker-room. Esposito, still covered with his loin-cloth, turned towards him. Naked, embarrassed, he teetered from one foot to the other. Yvars thought that it was up to Marcou to say something. But Marcou remained invisible behind the sheet of water that surrounded him. Esposito grabbed a shirt and was nimbly slipping it on when Lassalle said: 'Good night,' in a rather toneless voice and began to walk towards the little door. When it occurred to Yvars that some-one ought to call him, the door had already closed.

Yvars dressed without washing, said good night likewise, but with his whole heart, and they answered with the same warmth. He went out rapidly, got his bicycle, and, when he straddled it, he felt the strain in his back again. He was cycling along now in the late afternoon through the trafficky city. He was going fast because he was eager to get back to the old house and the terrace. He would wash in the wash-house before sitting down to look at the sea, which was already accompanying him, darker than in the morning, above the parapet of the boulevard. But the little girl accompanied him too and he couldn't stop thinking of her.

At home, his boy was back from school and reading the picture papers. Fernande asked Yvars whether everything had gone all right. He said nothing, cleaned up in the wash-house, then sat down on the bench against the low wall of the terrace. Mended washing hung above his head and the sky was becom-ing transparent; over the wall the soft evening sea was visible.

Fernande brought the anisette, two glasses, and the jug of cool water. She sat down beside her husband. He told her everything, holding her hand as in the early days of their marriage. When he had finished, he didn't stir, looking towards the sea where already, from one end of the horizon to the other, the twilight was swiftly falling. 'Ah! it's his own fault!' he said. If only he were young again, and Fernande too, they would have gone away, across the sea.

THE GUEST

THE SCHOOLMASTER WAS watching the two men climb towards him. One was on horseback, the other on foot. They had not yet tackled the abrupt rise leading to the schoolhouse built on the hillside. They were toiling onwards, making slow progress in the snow, among the stones, on the vast expanse of the high, deserted plateau. From time to time the horse stumbled. Without hearing anything yet, he could see the breath issuing from the horse's nostrils. One of the men, at least, knew the region. They were following the trail although it had disappeared days ago under a layer of dirty white snow. The schoolmaster calculated that it would take them half an hour to get on to the hill. It was cold; he went back into the school to get a sweater.

He crossed the empty, frigid classroom. On the blackboard the four rivers of France, drawn with four different coloured chalks, had been flowing towards their estuaries for the past three days. Snow had suddenly fallen in mid-October after eight months of drought without the transition of rain, and the twenty pupils, more or less, who lived in the villages scattered over the plateau had stopped coming. With fair weather they would return. Daru now heated only the single room that was his lodging, adjoining the classroom and giving also on to the plateau to the east. Like the class windows, his window looked to the south too. On that side the school was a few kilometres from the point where the plateau began to slope towards the south. In clear weather could be seen the purple mass of the mountain range where the gap opened on to the desert.

Somewhat warmed, Daru returned to the window from which he had first seen the two men. They were no longer visible. Hence they must have tackled the rise. The sky was not so dark, for the snow had stopped falling during the night. The morning had opened with a dirty light which had scarcely become brighter as the ceiling of clouds lifted. At two in the afternoon it seemed as if the day were merely beginning. But still this was better than those three days when the thick snow was falling amidst unbroken darkness with little gusts of wind that rattled the double door of the classroom. Then Daru had spent long hours in his room, leaving it only to go to the shed and feed the chickens or get some coal. Fortunately the delivery truck from Tadjid, the nearest village to the north, had brought his supplies two days before the blizzard. It would return in forty-eight hours.

Besides, he had enough to resist a siege, for the little room was cluttered with bags of wheat that the administration left as a stock to distribute to those of his pupils whose families had suffered from the drought. Actually they had all been victims because they were all poor. Every day Daru would distribute a ration to the children. They had missed it, he knew, during these bad days. Possibly one of the fathers or big brothers would come this afternoon and he could supply them with grain. It was just a matter of carrying them over to the next harvest. Now shiploads of wheat were arriving from France and the worst was over. But it would be hard to forget that poverty, that army of ragged ghosts wandering in the sunlight, the plateaux burned to a cinder month after month, the earth shrivelled up little by little, literally scorched, every stone bursting into dust under one's foot. The sheep had died then by thousands and even a few men, here and there, sometimes without anyone's knowing.

In contrast with such poverty, he who lived almost like a monk in his remote schoolhouse, none the less satisfied with the little he had and with the rough life, had felt like a lord with his whitewashed walls, his narrow couch, his unpainted shelves, his well, and his weekly provision of water and food. And suddenly this snow, without warning, without the foretaste of rain. This is the way the region was, cruel to live in, even without men – who didn't help matters either. But Daru had been born here. Everywhere else, he felt exiled.

He stepped out on to the terrace in front of the schoolhouse. The two men were now half-way up the slope. He recognized the horseman as Balducci, the old gendarme he had known for a long time. Balducci was holding on the end of a rope an Arab who was walking behind him with hands bound and head lowered. The gendarme waved a greeting to which Daru did not reply, lost as he was in contemplation of the Arab dressed in a faded blue jellaba, his feet in sandals but covered with socks of heavy raw wool, his head surmounted by a narrow, short *chèche*. They were approaching. Balducci was holding back his horse in order not to hurt the Arab, and the group was advancing slowly.

Within earshot, Balducci shouted: 'One hour to do the three kilometres from El Ameur!' Daru did not answer. Short and square in his thick sweater, he watched them climb. Not once had the Arab raised his head. 'Hello,' said Daru when they got up on to the terrace. 'Come in and warm up.' Balducci painfully got down from his horse without letting go the rope. From under his bristling moustache he smiled at the schoolmaster. His little dark eyes, deep-set under a tanned forehead, and his mouth surrounded with wrinkles made him look attentive and studious. Daru took the bridle, led the horse to the shed, and came back to the two men, who were now waiting for him in the school. He led them into his room. 'I am going to heat up the classroom,' he said. 'We'll be more comfortable there.' When he entered the room again, Balducci was on the couch. He had undone the rope tying him to the Arab, who had squatted near the stove. His hands still bound,

413

the *chèche* pushed back on his head, he was looking towards the window. At first Daru noticed only his huge lips, fat, smooth, almost negroid; yet his nose was straight, his eyes were dark and full of fever. The *chèche* revealed an obstinate forehead and, under the weathered skin now rather discoloured by the cold, the whole face had a restless and rebellious look that struck Daru when the Arab, turning his face towards him, looked him straight in the eyes. 'Go into the other room,' said the schoolmaster, 'and I'll make you some mint tea.' 'Thanks,' Balducci said. 'What a nuisance! How I long for retirement.' And addressing his prisoner in Arabic: 'Come on, you.' The Arab got up and, slowly, holding his bound wrists in front of him, went into the classroom.

With the tea, Daru brought a chair. But Balducci was already enthroned on the nearest pupil's desk and the Arab had squatted against the teacher's platform facing the stove, which stood between the desk and the window. When he held out the glass of tea to the prisoner, Daru hesitated at the sight of his bound hands. 'He might perhaps be untied.' 'Certainly,' said Balducci. 'That was for the journey.' He started to get to his feet. But Daru, setting the glass on the floor, had knelt beside the Arab. Without saying anything, the Arab watched him with his feverish eyes. Once his hands were free, he rubbed his swollen wrists against each other, took the glass of tea, and sucked up the burning liquid in swift little sips.

'Good,' said Daru. 'And where are you headed for?'

Balducci withdrew his moustache from the tea. 'Here, my boy.'

'Odd pupils! And you're spending the night?'

'No. I'm going back to El Ameur. And you will deliver this fellow to Tinguit. He is expected at police headquarters.'

Balducci was looking at Daru with a friendly little smile.

'What's this story?' asked the schoolmaster. 'Are you pulling my leg?'

'No, my boy. Those are the orders.'

'The orders? I'm not...' Daru hesitated, not wanting to hurt the old Corsican. 'I mean, that's not my job.'

'What! What's the meaning of that? In wartime people do all kinds of jobs.'

'Then I'll wait for the declaration of war!'

Balducci nodded.

'OK. But the orders exist and they concern you too. Things are brewing, it appears. There is talk of a forthcoming revolt. We are mobilized, in a way.'

Daru still had his obstinate look.

'Listen, my boy,' Balducci said. 'I like you and you must understand. There's only a dozen of us at El Ameur to patrol throughout the whole territory of a small department and I must get back in a hurry. I was told to hand this man over to you and return without delay. He couldn't be kept there. His village was beginning to stir; they wanted to take him back. You must take him to Tinguit tomorrow before the day is over. Twenty kilometres shouldn't worry a husky fellow like you. After that, all will be over. You'll come back to your pupils and your comfortable life.'

Behind the wall the horse could be heard snorting and pawing the earth. Daru was looking out of the window. Decidedly, the weather was clearing and the light was increasing over the snowy plateau. When all the snow was melted, the sun would take over again and once more would burn the fields of stone. For days, still, the unchanging sky would shed its dry light on the solitary expanse where nothing had any connexion with man.

'After all,' he said, turning around towards Balducci, 'what did he do?' And, before the gendarme had opened his mouth, he asked: 'Does he speak French?'

'No, not a word. We had been looking for him for a month, but they were hiding him. He killed his cousin.'

'Is he against us?'

'I don't think so. But you can never be sure.'

'Why did he kill?'

'A family squabble, I think. One owed the other grain, it seems. It's not at all clear. In short, he killed his cousin with a billhook. You know, like a sheep, *kreezk*!'

Balducci made the gesture of drawing a blade across his throat and the Arab, his attention attracted, watched him with a sort of anxiety. Daru felt a sudden wrath against the man, against all men with their rotten spite, their tireless hates, their blood lust.

But the kettle was singing on the stove. He served Balducci more tea, hesitated, then served the Arab again, who, a second time, drank avidly. His raised arms made the jellaba fall open and the schoolmaster saw his thin, muscular chest.

'Thanks, my boy,' Balducci said. 'And now, I'm off.'

He got up and went towards the Arab, taking a small rope from his pocket.

'What are you doing?' Daru asked dryly.

Balducci, disconcerted, showed him the rope.

'Don't bother.'

The old gendarme hesitated. 'It's up to you. Of course, you are armed?'

'I have my shot-gun.'

'Where?'

'In the trunk.'

'You ought to have it near your bed.'

'Why? I have nothing to fear.'

'You're mad. If there's an uprising, no one is safe, we're all in the same boat.'

'I'll defend myself. I'll have time to see them coming.'

Balducci began to laugh, then suddenly the moustache covered the white teeth.

'You'll have time? OK. That's just what I was saying. You have always been a little cracked. That's why I like you, my son was like that.'

At the same time he took out his revolver and put it on the desk.

'Keep it; I don't need two weapons from here to El Ameur.'

The revolver shone against the black paint of the table. When the gendarme turned towards him, the schoolmaster caught the smell of leather and horseflesh.

'Listen, Balducci,' Daru said suddenly, 'every bit of this disgusts me, and most of all your fellow here. But I won't hand him over. Fight, yes, if I have to. But not that.'

The old gendarme stood in front of him and looked at him severely.

'You're being a fool,' he said slowly. 'I don't like it either. You don't get used to putting a rope on a man even after years of it, and you're even ashamed — yes, ashamed. But you can't let them have their way.'

'I won't hand him over,' Daru said again.

'It's an order, my boy, and I repeat it.'

'That's right. Repeat to them what I've said to you: I won't hand him over.'

Balducci made a visible effort to reflect. He looked at the Arab and at Daru. At last he decided.

'No, I won't tell them anything. If you want to drop us, go ahead; I'll not denounce you. I have an order to deliver the prisoner and I'm doing so. And now you'll just sign this paper for me.'

'There's no need. I'll not deny that you left him with me.'

'Don't be mean with me. I know you'll tell the truth. You're from hereabouts and you are a man. But you must sign, that's the rule.'

Daru opened his drawer, took out a little square bottle of purple ink, the red wooden penholder with the 'sergeant-major' pen he used for making models of penmanship, and signed. The gendarme carefully folded the paper and put it into his wallet. Then he moved towards the door.

'I'll see you off,' Daru said.

'No,' said Balducci. 'There's no use being polite. You insulted me.'

He looked at the Arab, motionless in the same spot, sniffed peevishly, and turned away towards the door. 'Good-bye, son,' he said. The door shut behind him. Balducci appeared suddenly outside the window and then disappeared. His footsteps were muffled by the snow. The horse stirred on the other side of the wall and several chickens fluttered in fright. A moment later Balducci reappeared outside the window leading the horse by the bridle. He walked towards the little rise without turning round and disappeared from sight with the horse following him. A big stone could be heard bouncing down. Daru walked back towards the prisoner, who, without stirring, never took his eyes off him. 'Wait,' the schoolmaster said in Arabic and went towards the bedroom. As he was going through the door, he had a second thought, went to the desk, took the revolver, and stuck it in his pocket. Then, without looking back, he went into his room.

For some time he lay on his couch watching the sky gradually close over, listening to the silence. It was this silence that had seemed painful to him during the first days here, after the war. He had requested a post in the little town at the base of the foothills separating the upper plateaux from the desert. There, rocky walls, green and black to the north, pink and lavender to the south, marked the frontier of eternal summer. He had been named to a post farther north, on the plateau itself. In the beginning, the solitude and the silence had been hard for him on these wastelands peopled only by stones. Occasionally, furrows suggested cultivation, but they had been dug to uncover a certain kind of stone good for building. The only ploughing here was to harvest rocks. Elsewhere a thin layer of soil accumulated in the hollows would be scraped out to enrich paltry village gardens. This is the way it was: bare rock covered three-quarters of the region. Towns sprang up, flourished, then disappeared; men came by, loved one another or fought bitterly, then died. No one in this desert, neither he nor his guest, mattered. And yet, outside this desert neither of them, Daru knew, could have really lived.

When he got up, no noise came from the classroom. He was amazed at the unmixed joy he derived from the mere thought that the Arab might have fled and that he would be alone with no decision to make. But the prisoner was there. He had merely stretched out between the stove and the desk. With eyes open, he was staring at the ceiling. In that position, his thick lips were particularly noticeable, giving him a pouting look. 'Come,' said Daru. The Arab got up and followed him. In the bedroom, the schoolmaster pointed to a chair near the table under the window. The Arab sat down without taking his eyes off Daru.

'Are you hungry?'

'Yes,' the prisoner said.

Daru set the table for two. He took flour and oil, shaped a cake in a frying-pan, and lighted the little stove that functioned on bottled gas. While the cake was cooking, he went out to the shed to get cheese, eggs, dates, and condensed milk. When the cake was done he set it on the window-sill to cool, heated some condensed milk diluted with water, and beat up the eggs into an omelet. In one of his motions he knocked against the revolver stuck in his right pocket. He set the bowl down, went into the classroom, and put the revolver in his desk drawer. When he came back to the room, night was falling. He put on the light and served the Arab. 'Eat,' he said. The Arab took a piece of the cake, lifted it eagerly to his mouth, and stopped short.

'And you?' he asked.

'After you. I'll eat too.'

The thick lips opened slightly. The Arab hesitated, then bit into the cake determinedly.

The meal over, the Arab looked at the schoolmaster. 'Are you the judge?'

'No, I'm simply keeping you until tomorrow.'

'Why do you eat with me?'

'I'm hungry.'

The Arab fell silent. Daru got up and went out. He brought back a folding bed from the shed, set it up between the table and the stove, at right angles to his own bed. From a large suitcase which, upright in a corner, served as a shelf for papers, he took two blankets and arranged them on the camp-bed. Then he stopped, felt useless, and sat down on his bed. There was nothing more to do or to get ready. He had to look at this man. He looked at him, therefore, trying to imagine his face bursting with rage. He couldn't do so. He could see nothing but the dark yet shining eyes and the animal mouth.

'Why did you kill him?' he asked in a voice whose hostile tone surprised him.

The Arab looked away.

'He ran away. I ran after him.'

He raised his eyes to Daru again and they were full of a sort of woeful interrogation. 'Now what will they do to me?'

'Are you afraid?'

He stiffened, turning his eyes away.

'Are you sorry?'

The Arab stared at him open-mouthed. Obviously he did not understand. Daru's annoyance was growing. At the same time he felt awkward and self-conscious with his big body wedged between the two beds.

'Lie down there,' he said impatiently. 'That's your bed.'

The Arab didn't move. He called to Daru:

'Tell me!'

The schoolmaster looked at him.

'Is the gendarme coming back tomorrow?'

'I don't know.'

'Are you coming with us?'

'I don't know. Why?'

The prisoner got up and stretched out on top of the blankets, his feet towards the window. The light from the electric bulb shone straight into his eyes and he closed them at once.

'Why?' Daru repeated, standing beside the bed.

The Arab opened his eyes under the blinding light and looked at him, trying not to blink.

'Come with us,' he said.

In the middle of the night, Daru was still not asleep. He had gone to bed after undressing completely; he generally slept naked. But when he suddenly realized that he had nothing on, he hesitated. He felt vulnerable and the temptation came to him to put on his clothes again. Then he shrugged his shoulders; after all, he wasn't a child and, if need be, he could break his adversary in two. From his bed he could observe him, lying on his back, still motionless with his eyes closed under the harsh light. When Daru turned out the light, the darkness seemed to coagulate all of a sudden. Little by little, the night came back to life in the window where the starless sky was stirring gently. The schoolmaster soon made out the body lying at his feet. The Arab still did not move, but his eyes seemed open. A faint wind was prowling around the schoolhouse. Perhaps it would drive away the clouds and the sun would reappear.

During the night the wind increased. The hens fluttered a little and then were silent. The Arab turned over on his side with his back to Daru, who thought he heard him moan. Then he listened for his guest's breathing, become heavier and more regular. He listened to that breath so close to him and mused without being able to go to sleep. In this room where he had been sleeping alone for a year, this presence bothered him. But it bothered him also by imposing on him a sort of brotherhood he knew well but refused to accept in the present circumstances. Men who share the same rooms, soldiers or prisoners, develop a strange alliance as if, having cast off their armour with their clothing, they fraternized every evening, over and above their differences, in the ancient community of dream and fatigue. But Daru shook himself; he didn't like such musings, and it was essential to sleep.

A little later, however, when the Arab stirred slightly, the schoolmaster was still not asleep. When the prisoner made a second move, he stiffened, on the alert. The Arab was lifting himself slowly on his arms with almost the motion of a sleepwalker. Seated upright in bed, he waited motionless without turning his head towards Daru, as if he were listening attentively. Daru did not stir; it had just occurred to him that the revolver was still in the drawer of his desk. It was better to act at once. Yet he continued to observe the prisoner, who, with the same slithery motion, put his feet on the ground, waited again, then began to stand up slowly. Daru was about to call out to him when the Arab began to walk, in a quite natural but extraordinarily silent way. He was heading towards the door at the end of the room that opened into the shed. He lifted the latch with precaution and went out, pushing the door behind him but without shutting it. Daru had not stirred. 'He is running away,' he merely thought. 'Good riddance!' Yet he listened attentively. The hens were not fluttering; the guest must be on the plateau. A faint sound of water reached him, and he didn't know what it was until the Arab again stood framed in the doorway, closed the door carefully, and came back to bed without a sound. Then Daru turned his back on him and fell asleep. Still later he seemed, from the depths of his sleep, to hear furtive steps around the schoolhouse. 'I'm dreaming! I'm dreaming!' he repeated to himself. And he went on sleeping.

When he awoke, the sky was clear; the loose window let in a cold, pure air. The Arab was asleep, hunched up under the blankets now, his mouth open, utterly relaxed. But when Daru shook him, he started dreadfully, staring at Daru with wild eyes as if he had never seen him and such a frightened expression that the schoolmaster stepped back. 'Don't be afraid. It's me.

422

You must eat.' The Arab nodded his head and said yes. Calm had returned to his face, but his expression was vacant and listless.

The coffee was ready. They drank it seated together on the folding bed as they munched their pieces of the cake. Then Daru led the Arab under the shed and showed him the tap where he washed. He went back into the room, folded the blankets and the bed, made his own bed and put the room in order. Then he went through the classroom and out on to the terrace. The sun was already rising in the blue sky; a soft, bright light was bathing the deserted plateau. On the ridge the snow was melting in spots. The stones were about to reappear. Crouched on the edge of the plateau, the schoolmaster looked at the deserted expanse. He thought of Balducci. He had hurt him, for he had sent him off in a way as if he didn't want to be associated with him. He could still hear the gendarme's farewell and, without knowing why, he felt strangely empty and vulnerable. At that moment, from the other side of the schoolhouse, the prisoner coughed. Daru listened to him almost despite himself and then, furious, threw a pebble that whistled through the air before sinking into the snow. That man's stupid crime revolted him, but to hand him over was contrary to honour. Merely thinking of it made him smart with humiliation. And he cursed at one and the same time his own people who had sent him this Arab and the Arab too who had dared to kill and not managed to get away. Daru got up, walked in a circle on the terrace, waited motionless, and then went back into the schoolhouse.

The Arab, leaning over the cement floor of the shed, was washing his teeth with two fingers. Daru looked at him and said: 'Come.' He went back into the room ahead of the prisoner. He slipped a hunting-jacket on over his sweater and put on walking-shoes. Standing, he waited until the Arab had put on his *chèche* and sandals. They went into the classroom and the schoolmaster pointed to the exit, saying:

'Go ahead.' The fellow didn't budge. 'I'm coming,' said Daru. The Arab went out. Daru went back into the room and made a package of pieces of rusk, dates, and sugar. In the classroom, before going out, he hesitated a second in front of his desk, then crossed the threshold and locked the door. 'That's the way,' he said. He started towards the east, followed by the prisoner. But, a short distance from the schoolhouse, he thought he heard a slight sound behind them. He retraced his steps and examined the surroundings of the house; there was no one there. The Arab watched him without seeming to understand. 'Come on,' said Daru.

They walked for an hour and rested beside a sharp peak of limestone. The snow was melting faster and faster and the sun was drinking up the puddles at once, rapidly cleaning the plateau, which gradually dried and vibrated like the air itself. When they resumed walking, the ground rang under their feet. From time to time a bird rent the space in front of them with a joyful cry. Daru breathed in deeply the fresh morning light. He felt a sort of rapture before the vast familiar expanse, now almost entirely yellow under its dome of blue sky. They walked an hour more, descending towards the south. They reached a level height made up of crumbly rocks. From there on, the plateau sloped down, eastward, towards a low plain where there were a few spindly trees and, to the south, towards outcroppings of rock that gave the landscape a chaotic look.

Daru surveyed the two directions. There was nothing but the sky on the horizon. Not a man could be seen. He turned towards the Arab, who was looking at him blankly. Daru held out the package to him. 'Take it,' he said. 'There are dates, bread, and sugar. You can hold out for two days. Here are a thousand francs too.' The Arab took the package and the money but kept his full hands at chest level as if he didn't know what to do with what was being given him. 'Now look,' the schoolmaster said as he pointed in the direction of the east, 'there's the way to Tinguit. You have a two-hour walk. At

Tinguit you'll find the administration and the police. They are expecting you.' The Arab looked towards the east, still holding the package and the money against his chest. Daru took his elbow and turned him rather roughly towards the south. At the foot of the height on which they stood could be seen a faint path. 'That's the trail across the plateau. In a day's walk from here you'll find pasture lands and the first nomads. They'll take you in and shelter you according to their law.' The Arab had now turned towards Daru and a sort of panic was visible in his expression. 'Listen,' he said. Daru shook his head: 'No, be quiet. Now I'm leaving you.' He turned his back on him, took two long steps in the direction of the school, looked hesitantly at the motionless Arab, and started off again. For a few minutes he heard nothing but his own step resounding on the cold ground and did not turn his head. A moment later, however, he turned around. The Arab was still there on the edge of the hill, his arms hanging now, and he was looking at the schoolmaster. Daru felt something rise in his throat. But he swore with impatience, waved vaguely, and started off again. He had already gone some distance when he again stopped and looked. There was no longer anyone on the hill.

Daru hesitated. The sun was now rather high in the sky and was beginning to beat down on his head. The schoolmaster retraced his steps, at first somewhat uncertainly, then with decision. When he reached the little hill, he was bathed in sweat. He climbed it as fast as he could and stopped, out of breath, at the top. The rock-fields to the south stood out sharply against the blue sky, but on the plain to the east a steamy heat was already rising. And in that slight haze, Daru, with heavy heart, made out the Arab walking slowly on the road to prison.

A little later, standing before the window of the classroom, the schoolmaster was watching the clear light bathing the whole surface of the plateau, but he hardly saw it. Behind him on the blackboard, among the winding French rivers, sprawled the clumsily chalked-up words he had just read: 'You handed over our brother. You will pay for this.' Daru looked at the sky, the plateau, and, beyond, the invisible lands stretching all the way to the sea. In this vast landscape he had loved so much, he was alone.

THE ARTIST AT WORK

*Take me up and cast me forth into
the sea . . . for I know that for my
sake this great tempest is upon you.*

JONAH I. 12

GILBERT JONAS, THE painter, believed in his star. Indeed, he believed solely in it, although he felt respect, and even a sort of admiration, for other people's religion. His own faith, however, was not lacking in virtues since it consisted in acknowledging obscurely that he would be granted much without ever deserving anything. Consequently when, about his thirty-fifth year, a dozen critics suddenly disputed as to which had discovered his talent, he showed no surprise. But his serenity, attributed by some to smugness, resulted, on the contrary, from a trusting modesty. Jonas credited everything to his star rather than to his own merits.

He was somewhat more astonished when a picture dealer offered him a monthly remittance that freed him from all care. The architect Rateau, who had loved Jonas and his star since their school days, vainly pointed out to him that the remittance would provide only a bare living and that the dealer was taking no risk. 'All the same . . . ' Jonas said. Rateau – who succeeded, but by dint of hard work, in everything he did – chided his friend. 'What do you mean by "all the same"? You must bargain.' But nothing availed. In his heart Jonas thanked his star. 'Just as you say,' he told the dealer. And he gave up his job in the paternal publishing-house to devote himself altogether to painting. 'What luck!' he said.

In reality he thought: 'It's the same old luck.' As far back as he could remember, he found the same luck at work. He felt, for instance, an affectionate gratitude towards his parents, first because they had brought him up carelessly and this had given free rein to his daydreaming, secondly because they had separated, on grounds of adultery. At least that was the pretext given by his father, who forgot to specify that it was a rather peculiar adultery: he could not endure the good works indulged in by his wife, who, a veritable lay saint, had, without seeing any wrong in it, given herself body and soul to suffering humanity. But the husband intended to be the master of his wife's virtues. 'I'm sick and tired,' that Othello used to say, 'of sharing her with the poor.'

This misunderstanding was profitable to Jonas. His parents, having read or heard about the many cases of sadistic murderers who were children of divorced parents, vied with each other in pampering him with a view to stamping out the spark of such an unfortunate evolution. The less obvious were the effects of the trauma experienced, according to them, by the child's psyche, the more worried they were, for invisible havoc must be deepest. Jonas had merely to announce that he was pleased with himself or his day, for his parents' ordinary anxiety to become panic. Their attentions multiplied and the child wanted for nothing.

His alleged misfortune finally won Jonas a devoted brother in the person of his friend Rateau. Rateau's parents often entertained his little schoolmate because they pitied his hapless state. Their commiserating remarks inspired their strong and athletic son with the desire to take under his protection the child whose nonchalant successes he already admired. Admiration and condescension mixed well to form a friendship that Jonas received, like everything else, with encouraging simplicity.

When without any special effort Jonas had finished his formal studies, he again had the luck to get into his father's publishing-house, to find a job there and, indirectly, his vocation as a painter. As the leading publisher in France, Jonas's father was of the opinion that books, because of the very slump in culture, represented the future. 'History shows,' he would say, 'that the less people read, the more books they buy.' Consequently, he but rarely read the manuscripts submitted to him and decided to publish them solely on the basis of the author's personality or the subject's topical interest (from this point of view, sex being the only subject always topical, the publisher had eventually gone in for specialization) and spent his time looking for unusual formats and free publicity. Hence at the same time as he took over the manuscript-reading department, Jonas also took over considerable leisure time which had to be filled up. Thus it was that he made the acquaintance of painting.

For the first time he discovered in himself an unsuspected and tireless enthusiasm, soon devoted his days to painting, and, still without effort, excelled in that exercise. Nothing else seemed to interest him, and he was barely able to get married at the suitable age, since painting consumed him wholly. For human beings and the ordinary circumstances of life he merely reserved a kindly smile, which dispensed him from paying attention to them. It took a motor-cycle accident when Rateau was riding too exuberantly with his friend on the rear seat, to interest Jonas – bored and with his right hand inert and bandaged – in love. Once again, he was inclined to see in that serious accident the good effects of his star, for without it he wouldn't have taken the time to look at Louise Poulin as she deserved.

According to Rateau, it must be added, Louise did not deserve to be looked at. Short and strapping himself, he liked nothing but tall women. 'I don't know what you find in that insect,' he would say. Louise was in fact small and dark in skin, hair, and eyes, but well built and pretty in the face. Jonas, tall and rugged, was touched at the sight of the insect, especially as she was industrious. Louise's vocation was activity. Such a vocation fitted well with Jonas's preference for inertia and its advantages. Louise dedicated herself first to literature, so long at least as she thought that publishing interested Jonas. She read everything, without order, and in a few weeks became capable of talking about everything. Jonas admired her and considered himself definitely dispensed from reading, since Louise informed him sufficiently and made it possible for him to know the essence of contemporary discoveries. 'You mustn't say,' Louise asserted, 'that so-and-so is wicked or ugly, but that he poses as wicked or ugly.' The distinction was important and might even lead, as Rateau pointed out, to the condemnation of the human race. But Louise settled the question once and for all by showing that since this truth was supported simultaneously by the sentimental press and the philosophical reviews, it was universal and not open to discussion. 'Just as you say,' said Jonas, who immediately forgot that cruel discovery to dream of his star.

Louise deserted literature as soon as she realized that Jonas was interested only in painting. She dedicated herself at once to the visual arts, visited museums and exhibitions, dragged Jonas to them though he didn't quite understand what his contemporaries were painting and felt bothered in his artistic simplicity. Yet he rejoiced to be so well informed about everything that concerned his art. To be sure, the next day he forgot even the name of the painter whose works he had just seen. But Louise was right when she peremptorily reminded him of one of the certainties she had kept from her literary period, namely that in reality one never forgets anything. His star decidedly protected Jonas, who could thus, without suffering in his conscience, combine the certainties of remembering and the comforts of forgetting.

But the treasures of self-sacrifice that Louise showered upon him shone most brilliantly in Jonas's daily life. That angel spared him the purchases of shoes, suits, and shirts that, for the normal man, shorten the days of an already too short life. She resolutely took upon herself the thousand inventions of the machine for killing time, from the hermetic brochures of social security to the constantly changing moods of the internal revenue office. 'OK,' said Rateau, 'but she can't go to the dentist in your place.' She may not have gone, but she telephoned and made the appointments, at the most convenient hours; she took care of changing the oil in the tiny car, of booking rooms in holiday hotels, of the coal for his stove; she herself bought the gifts Jonas wanted to give, chose and sent his flowers, and even found time, on certain evenings, to call in at his house in his absence and open his bed to spare him the trouble when he came home.

With the same enthusiasm, of course, she entered that bed, then took care of the appointment with the mayor, led Jonas to the town hall two years before his talent was at last recognized, and arranged the honeymoon so that they didn't miss a museum. Not without having first found, in the midst of the housing shortage, a three-room flat into which they settled on their return. Then she produced, in rapid succession, two children, a boy and a girl. Her intention of going up to three was realized soon after Jonas had left the publishing-house to devote himself to painting.

As soon as she had become a mother, it must be added, Louise devoted herself solely to her child, and later to her children. She still tried to help her husband, but didn't have time. To be sure, she regretted her neglect of Jonas, but her resolute character kept her from wasting time in such regrets. 'It can't be helped,' she would say, 'each of us has his workbench.' Jonas was, in any case, delighted with this expression, for, like all the artists of his epoch, he wanted to be looked upon as an artisan. Hence the artisan was somewhat neglected and had to buy his shoes himself. However, besides the fact that this was in the nature of things, Jonas was again tempted to rejoice. Of course, he had to make an effort to visit the shops, but that effort was rewarded by one of those hours of solitude that give such value to marital bliss.

The problem of living-space was, however, by far the greatest of their problems, for time and space shrank simultaneously around them. The birth of the children, Jonas's new occupation, their restricted quarters, the modesty of the monthly remittance which prevented them from getting a larger apartment did not leave much room for the double activity of Louise and Jonas. The apartment was on the second floor of what had been a private house in the eighteenth century, in the old section of the capital. Many artists lived in that quarter, faithful to the principle that in art the pursuit of the new can take place only in an old setting. Jonas, who shared that conviction, was delighted to live in that quarter.

There could be no question as to the apartment's being old. But a few very modern arrangements had given it an original appearance resulting chiefly from the fact that it provided a great volume of air while occupying but a limited surface. The rooms, particularly high and graced with magnificent tall windows, had certainly been intended, to judge from their majestic proportions, for receptions and ceremonies. But the necessities of urban congestion and of income from house property had forced the successive owners to cut up those over-large rooms with partitions and thus to multiply the stalls they let at exorbitant prices to their flock of tenants. They none the less sang the praises of what they called 'the considerable cubic space'. No one could deny the advantage. It simply had to be attributed to the impossibility of partitioning the rooms horizontally as well. Otherwise the landlords would certainly not have hesitated to make the necessary sacrifices in order to provide a few more shelters for the rising generation, particularly inclined at that moment to marry and reproduce. Besides, the cubic air-space was not all to the good. It had the inconvenience of making the rooms hard to heat in winter, and this unfortunately forced the landlords to increase the rent supplement for heat. In summer, because of the great window surface, the apartment was literally flooded with light, for there were no blinds. The landlords had neglected to put them in, doubtless discouraged by the height of the windows and the cost of carpentry. After all, thick curtains could perform the same service and presented no problem of cost, since they were the tenants' responsibility. Furthermore, the landlords were not unwilling to help them by furnishing curtains from their own stores at cost price. Real-estate philanthropy, in fact, was merely their avocation. In their regular daily life those new princes sold cotton and velvet.

Jonas had gone into raptures over the apartment's advantages and had accepted its drawbacks without difficulties. 'Just as you say,' he said to the landlord about the supplement for heat. As for the curtains, he agreed with Louise that it was enough to provide them just for the bedroom and to leave the other windows bare. 'We have nothing to hide,' that pure heart said. Jonas had been particularly entranced by the largest room, the ceiling of which was so high that there could be no question of installing a lighting system. The entrance door opened directly into that room, which was joined by a narrow hall to the two others, much smaller and strung in a row. At the end of the hall were the kitchen, the water-closet, and a nook graced with the name of shower-room. Indeed, it might have been a shower if only the fixture had been installed, vertically of course, and one were willing to stand utterly motionless under the spray.

The really extraordinary height of the ceilings and the narrowness of the rooms made of the apartment an odd assortment of parallelepipeds almost entirely glassed in, all doors and windows, with no wall space for the furniture, and with the human beings floating about like bottle imps in a vertical aquarium. Furthermore, all the windows opened on to a court – in other words, on to other windows in the same style just across the way, behind which one could discern the lofty outline of other windows opening on to a second court. 'It's the hall of mirrors,' Jonas said in delight. On Rateau's advice, it was decided to locate the master bedroom in one of the small rooms, the other to be for the already expected baby. The big room served as a studio for Jonas during the day, as a living-room in the evening and at meal-times. They could also at a pinch eat in the kitchen, provided that Jonas or Louise was willing to remain standing. For his part, Rateau had outdone himself in ingenious inventions. By means of sliding doors, retractable shelves, and folding tables, he had managed to make up for the paucity of furniture while emphasizing the jack-in-the-box appearance of that unusual apartment.

But when the rooms were full of paintings and children, they had to think up a new arrangement. Before the birth of the third child, in fact, Jonas worked in the big room, Louise knitted in the bedroom, while the two children occupied the last room, raised a great rumpus there, and also tumbled at will throughout the rest of the flat. They agreed to put the newborn in a corner of the studio, which Jonas walled off by propping up his canvases like a screen; this offered the advantage of having the baby within earshot and being able to answer his calls. Besides, Jonas never needed to bestir himself, for Louise forestalled him. She wouldn't wait until the baby cried before entering the studio, though with every possible precaution and always on tiptoe. Jonas, touched by such discretion, one day assured Louise that he was not so sensitive and could easily go on working despite the noise of her steps. Louise replied that she was also aiming not to waken the baby. Jonas, full of admiration for the workings of the maternal instinct, laughed heartily at his misunderstanding. As a result, he didn't dare confess that Louise's cautious entries bothered him more than an out-and-out invasion. First, because they lasted longer, and secondly because they followed a pantomime in which Louise – her arms outstretched, her shoulders thrown back, and her leg raised high – could not go unnoticed. This method even went against her avowed intentions, since Louise constantly ran the risk of bumping into one of the canvases with which the studio was cluttered. At such moments the noise would waken the baby, who would manifest his displeasure according to his capacities, which were considerable. The father, delighted by his son's pulmonary prowess, would rush to cuddle him and soon be relieved in this by his wife. Then Jonas would pick up his canvases and, brushes in hand, would listen ecstatically to his son's insistent and sovereign voice.

This was just about the time that Jonas's success brought him many friends. Those friends turned up on the telephone or in impromptu visits. The telephone, which, after due deliberation, had been put in the studio, rang often and always to the detriment of the baby's sleep, who would then mingle his cries with the urgent ringing of the phone. If it so happened that Louise was busy caring for the other children, she strove to get to the telephone with them, but most of the time she would find Jonas holding the baby in one arm and in his other hand his brushes and the receiver, which was extending a friendly invitation to lunch. Jonas was always amazed that anyone was willing to lunch with him, for his conversation was dull, but he preferred going out in the evening in order to keep his workday unbroken. Most of the time, unfortunately, the friend would be free only for lunch, and just for this particular lunch; he would insist upon holding it for his dear Jonas. His dear Jonas would accept: 'Just as you say!' and after hanging up would add: 'Isn't he thoughtful!' while handing the baby to Louise. Then he would go back to work, soon interrupted by lunch or dinner. He had to move the canvases out of the way, unfold the special table, and sit down with the children. During the meal Jonas would keep an eye on the painting he was working on and occasionally, in the beginning at least, he would find his children rather slow in chewing and swallowing, so that each meal was excessively long. But he read in his newspaper that it was essential to eat slowly in order to assimilate, and thenceforth each meal provided reasons for rejoicing at length.

On other occasions his new friends would drop in. Rateau, for one, never came until after dinner. He was at his office during the day and, besides, he knew that painters work during the daylight hours. But Jonas's new friends almost all belonged to the species of artists and critics. Some had painted, others were about to paint, and the remainder were concerned with what had been, or would be, painted. All, to be sure, held the labours of art in high esteem and complained of the organization of the modern world that makes so difficult the pursuit of those labours, as well as the exercise of meditation, indispensable to the artist. They complained of this for whole afternoons, begging Jonas to go on working, to behave as if they weren't there, to treat them cavalierly, for they weren't philistines and knew the value of an artist's time. Jonas, pleased to have friends capable of allowing one to go on working in their presence, would go back to his picture without ceasing to answer the questions asked him or to laugh at the anecdotes told him.

Such simplicity put his friends more and more at ease. Their good spirits were so genuine that they forgot the meal hour. But the children had a better memory. They would rush in, mingle with the guests, howl, be cuddled by the visitors, and pass from lap to lap. At last the light would dwindle in the square of sky outlined by the court, and Jonas would lay down his brushes. There was nothing to do but to invite the friends to share pot-luck and to go on talking, late into the night, about art of course, but especially about the untalented painters, plagiarists or self-advertisers, who weren't there. Jonas liked to get up early to take advantage of the first hours of daylight. He knew that this would be difficult, that breakfast wouldn't be ready on time and that he himself would be tired. But on the other hand he rejoiced to learn in an evening so many things that could not fail to be helpful to him, though in an invisible way, in his art. 'In art, as in nature, nothing is ever wasted,' he used to say. 'This is a result of the star.'

To the friends were sometimes added the disciples, for Jonas now had a following. At first he had been surprised, not seeing what anyone could learn from him who still had everything to discover. The artist in him was groping in the darkness; how could he have pointed out the right paths? But he readily realized that a disciple is not necessarily someone who longs to learn something. Most often, on the contrary, one became a disciple for the disinterested pleasure of teaching one's master. Thenceforth he could humbly accept such a surfeit of honours. Jonas's disciples explained to him at length what he had painted, and why. In this way Jonas discovered in his work many intentions that rather surprised him, and a host of things he hadn't put there. He had thought himself poor and, thanks to his pupils, suddenly found himself rich. At times, faced with such hitherto unsuspected wealth, Jonas would feel a tingle of pride. 'None the less it's true,' he would say. 'That face in the background stands out. I don't quite understand what they mean by indirect humanization. Yet, with that effect I've really gone somewhere.' But very soon he would transfer that un-comfortable mastery to his star. 'It's the star,' he would say, 'that's gone somewhere. I'm staying home with Louise and the children.'

In addition, the disciples had another advantage: they forced Jonas to be more severe with himself. They ranked him so high in their conversations, and especially in regard to his conscien-tiousness and energy, that henceforth no weakness was permit-ted him. Thus he lost his old habit of nibbling a piece of sugar or chocolate when he had finished a difficult passage and before he went back to work. If he were alone, he would nevertheless have given in clandestinely to that weakness. But he was helped in his moral progress by the almost con-stant presence of his disciples and friends in whose sight he would have been embarrassed to nibble chocolate and whose interesting conversation he couldn't interrupt anyway for such a petty idiosyncrasy.

Furthermore, his disciples insisted on his remaining faithful to his aesthetic. Jonas, who laboured at length only to get a very occasional fleeting flash in which reality would suddenly appear to him in a new light, had only a very vague idea of his own aesthetic. His disciples, on the other hand, had several ideas, contradictory and categorical, and they would allow no joking on the subject. Jonas would have liked, at times, to resort to his whim, that humble friend of the artist. But his disciples' frowns in the face of certain pictures that strayed from their idea forced him to reflect a little more about his art, and this was all to his advantage.

Finally, the disciples helped Jonas in another way by obliging him to give his opinion about their own production. Not a day went by, in fact, without someone's bringing him a picture barely sketched in, which its author would set between Jonas and the canvas he was working on, in order to take advantage of the best light. An opinion was expected. Until then Jonas had always been secretly ashamed of his fundamental inability to judge a work of art. Except for a handful of pictures that carried him away, and for the obviously coarse daubs, everything seemed to him equally interesting and indifferent. Consequently he was obliged to build up a stock of judgments, which had to be varied because his disciples, like all the artists of the capital, after all had a measure of talent and, when they were around, he had to draw rather fine lines of distinction to satisfy each. Hence that happy obligation forced him to amass a vocabulary and opinions about his art. Yet his natural kindness was not embittered by the effort. He soon realized that his disciples were not asking him for criticisms, for which they had no use, but only for encouragement and, if possible, praise. The praises merely had to be different. Jonas was not satisfied to be his usual agreeable self. He showed ingenuity in his ways of being so.

Thus the time went by for Jonas, who painted amidst friends and pupils seated on chairs that were now arranged in concentric circles around his easel. Often, in addition, neighbours would appear at the windows across the way and swell his public. He would discuss, exchange views, examine the paintings submitted to him, smile as Louise went by, soothe the children, and enthusiastically answer telephone-calls, without ever setting down his brushes with which he would from time to time add a stroke to a half-finished painting. In a way, his life was very full, not an hour was wasted, and he gave thanks to fate that spared him boredom. In another way, it took many brush-strokes to finish a picture and it occasionally occurred to him that boredom had the one advantage that it could be avoided through strenuous work. But Jonas's production slowed down in proportion to his friends' becoming more interesting. Even in the rare moments when he was altogether alone, he felt too tired to catch up. And at such moments he could but dream of a new régime that would reconcile the pleasures of friendship with the virtues of boredom.

He broached the subject to Louise, who was independently beginning to worry about the growth of the two older children and the smallness of their room. She suggested putting them in the big room with their bed hidden by a screen and moving the baby into the small room where he would not be wakened by the telephone. As the baby took up no room, Jonas could turn the little room into his studio. Then the big one would serve for the daytime gatherings, and Jonas could wander back and forth, either chat with his friends or work, since he was sure of being understood in his need for isolation. Furthermore, the necessity for putting the older children to bed would allow them to cut the evenings short. 'Wonderful,' Jonas said after a moment's reflection. 'Besides,' said Louise, 'if your friends leave early, we'll see a little more of each other.' Jonas looked at her. A suggestion of melancholy passed over Louise's face. Touched, he put his arms around her and kissed her in his most affectionate way. She surrendered to him and for a moment they were happy as they had been in the beginning of their marriage. But she shook herself free; the room was perhaps too small for Jonas. Louise got a folding rule and they discovered that because of the congestion caused by his canvases and those of his pupils, by far the more numerous, he generally worked in a space hardly any larger than the one that was about to be assigned to him. Jonas hastened to move the furniture.

Luckily, the less he worked, the more his reputation grew. Each exhibit was eagerly awaited and extolled in advance. To be sure, a small number of critics, among whom were two regular visitors to the studio, tempered the warmth of their reviews with some reservations. But the disciples' indignation more than made up for this little misfortune. Of course, the latter would emphatically assert, they ranked the pictures of the first period above everything else, but the present experiments foreshadowed a real revolution. Jonas would rather reproach himself for the slight annoyance he felt every time his first works were glorified and would thank them effusively. Only Rateau would grumble: 'Weird ones . . . They like you inert, like a statue. And they deny you the right to live!' But Jonas would defend his disciples: 'You can't understand,' he told Rateau, 'because you like everything I do.' Rateau laughed: 'Of course! It's not your pictures I like; it's your painting.'

The pictures continued to be popular in any event and, after an exhibition that was enthusiastically received, the dealer suggested, on his own, an increase in the monthly remittance. Jonas accepted, declaring how grateful he was. 'Anyone who heard you now,' the dealer said, 'would think money meant something to you.' Such goodheartedness disarmed the painter. However, when he asked the dealer's permission to give a canvas to a charity sale, the dealer wanted to know whether or not it was a 'paying charity'. Jonas didn't know. The dealer therefore suggested sticking squarely to the terms of the contract which granted him the exclusive right of sale.

'A contract's a contract,' he said. In theirs, there was no provision for charity. 'Just as you say,' the painter said.

The new arrangement was a source of constant satisfaction to Jonas. He could, in fact, get off by himself often enough to answer the many letters he now received, which his courtesy could not leave unanswered. Some concerned Jonas's art, while others, far more plentiful, concerned the correspondent, who either wanted to be encouraged in his artistic vocation or else needed advice or financial aid. The more Jonas's name appeared in the press, the more he was solicited, like everyone, to take an active part in exposing most revolting injustices. Jonas would reply, write about art, thank people, give his advice, go without a necktie in order to send a small financial contribution, finally sign the just protests that were sent him. 'You're indulging in politics now? Leave that to writers and ugly old maids,' said Rateau. No, he would sign only the protests that insisted they had no connexion with any particular party line. But they all laid claim to such beautiful independence. For weeks on end, Jonas would go about with his pockets stuffed with correspondence, constantly neglected and renewed. He would answer the most urgent, which generally came from unknowns, and keep for a better moment those that called for a more leisurely reply — in other words, his friends' letters. So many obligations at least kept him from dawdling and from yielding to a care-free spirit. He always felt behindhand, and always guilty, even when he was working, as he was from time to time.

Louise was ever more mobilized by the children and wore herself out doing everything that, in other circumstances, he could have done in the home. This made him suffer. After all, *he* was working for his pleasure whereas she had the worst end of the bargain. He became well aware of this when she was out marketing. 'The telephone!' the eldest child would shout, and Jonas would immediately drop his picture, only to return to it, beaming, with another invitation. 'Gasman!' the meter-reader would shout from the door one of the children had opened for him. 'Coming! Coming!' And when Jonas would leave the telephone or the door, a friend or a disciple, sometimes both, would follow him to the little room to finish the interrupted conversation. Gradually they all became regular frequenters of the hallway. They would stand there, chat among themselves, ask Jonas's opinion from a distance, or else overflow briefly into the little room. 'Here at least,' those who entered would exclaim, 'a fellow can see you a bit, and without interruption.' This touched Jonas. 'You're right,' he would say. 'After all, we never get a chance to see each other.' At the same time he was well aware that he disappointed those he didn't see, and this saddened him. Often they were friends he would have preferred to meet. But he didn't have time, he couldn't accept everything. Consequently, his reputation suffered. 'He's become proud,' people said, 'now that he's a success. He doesn't see anyone any more.' Or else: 'He doesn't love anyone, except himself.' No, he loved Louise, and his children, and Rateau, and a few others, and he had a liking for all. But life is short, time races by, and his own energy had limits. It was hard to paint the world and men and, at the same time, to live with them. On the other hand, he couldn't complain, or explain the things that stood in his way. For, if he did, people slapped him on the back, saying: 'Lucky fellow! That's the price of fame!'

Consequently, his mail piled up, the disciples would allow no falling off, and society people now thronged around him. It must be added that Jonas admired them for being interested in painting when, like everyone else, they might have got excited about the English Royal Family or gastronomic tours. In truth, they were mostly society women, all very simple in manner. They didn't buy any pictures themselves and introduced their friends to the artist only in the hope, often groundless, that *they* would buy in their place. On the other hand, they helped Louise, especially in serving tea to the visitors. The cups passed from hand to hand, travelled along the hallway from the kitchen to the big room, and then came back to roost in the little studio, where Jonas, in the centre of a handful of friends and visitors, enough to fill the room, went on painting until he had to lay down his brushes to take, gratefully, the cup that a fascinating lady had poured especially for him.

He would drink his tea, look at the sketch that a disciple had just put on his easel, laugh with his friends, interrupt himself to ask one of them please to post the pile of letters he had written during the night, pick up the second child, who had stumbled over his feet, pose for a photograph, and then at 'Jonas, the telephone!' he would wave his cup in the air, thread his way with many an excuse through the crowd standing in the hall, come back, fill in a corner of the picture, stop to answer the fascinating lady that certainly he would be happy to paint her portrait, and would get back to his easel. He worked, but 'Jonas! A signature!' 'What is it, a registered letter?' 'No, the Kashmir prisoners.' 'Coming! Coming!' Then he would run to the door to receive a young friend of the convicts and listen to his protest, worry briefly whether politics were involved, and sign after receiving complete assurance on that score, together with expostulations about the duties inseparable from his privileges as an artist, and at last he would reappear only to meet, without being able to catch their names, a recently victorious boxer or the greatest dramatist of some foreign country. The dramatist would stand facing him for five minutes, expressing through the emotion in his eyes what his ignorance of French would not allow him to state more clearly, while Jonas would nod his head with a real feeling of brotherhood. Fortunately, he would suddenly be saved from that dead-end situation by the bursting-in of the latest spellbinder of the pulpit who wanted to be introduced to the great painter. Jonas would say that he was delighted, which he was, feel the packet of unanswered letters in his pocket, take up his brushes, get ready to go on with a passage, but would first have to thank someone for the pair of setters that had just been brought him, go and shut them in the master bedroom, come back to accept the lady donor's invitation to lunch, rush out again in answer to Louise's call to see for himself without a shadow of doubt that the setters had not been broken in to apartment life, and lead them into the shower-room, where they would bark so persistently that eventually no one would even hear them. Every once in a while, over the visitors' heads, Jonas would catch a glimpse of the look in Louise's eyes and it seemed to him that that look was sad. Finally the day would end, the visitors would take leave, others would tarry in the big room and wax emotional as they watched Louise put the children to bed, obligingly aided by an elegant, overdressed lady who would complain of having to return to her luxurious home where life, spread out over two floors, was so much less close and homelike than at the Jonases'.

One Saturday afternoon Rateau came to bring an ingenious clothes-drier that could be screwed on to the kitchen ceiling. He found the flat packed and, in the little room, surrounded by art-lovers, Jonas painting the lady who had given the dogs, while he himself was being painted by an official artist. According to Louise, the latter was working on order from the Government. 'It will be called *The Artist at Work*.' Rateau withdrew to a corner of the room to watch his friend, obviously absorbed in his effort. One of the art-lovers, who had never seen Rateau, leaned over towards him and said: 'He looks well, doesn't he?' Rateau didn't reply. 'You paint, I suppose,' he continued. 'So do I. Well, take my word for it, he's on the decline.' 'Already?' Rateau asked. 'Yes. It's success. You can't resist success. He's finished.' 'He's on the decline or he's finished?' 'An artist who is on the decline is finished. Just see, he has nothing in him to paint any more. He's being painted himself and will be hung in a museum.'

Later on, in the middle of the night, Louise, Rateau, and Jonas, the latter standing and the other two seated on a corner of the bed, were silent. The children were asleep, the dogs were boarding in the country, Louise had just washed, and Jonas and Rateau had dried, the many dishes, and their fatigue felt good. 'Why don't you get a servant?' Rateau had asked when he saw the stack of dishes. But Louise had answered sadly: 'Where would we put her?' So they were silent. 'Are you happy?' Rateau had suddenly asked. Jonas smiled, but he looked tired. 'Yes. Everybody is kind to me.' 'No,' said Rateau. 'Watch out. They're not all good.' 'Who isn't?' 'Your painter friends, for instance.' 'I know,' Jonas said. 'But many artists are like that. They're not sure of existing, not even the greatest. So they look for proofs; they judge and condemn. That strengthens them; it's a beginning of existence. They're so lonely!' Rateau shook his head. 'Take my word for it,' Jonas said; 'I know them. You have to love them.' 'And what about you?' Rateau said. 'Do you exist? You never say anything bad about anyone.' Jonas began to laugh. 'Oh, I often think bad of them. But then I forget.' He became serious. 'No, I'm not sure of existing. But some day I'll exist, I'm sure.'

Rateau asked Louise her opinion. Shaking off her fatigue, she said she thought Jonas was right: their visitors' opinion was of no importance. Only Jonas's work mattered. And she was aware that the child got in his way. He was growing anyway, and they would have to buy a couch that would take up space. What could they do until they got a bigger apartment? Jonas looked at the master bedroom. Of course, it was not the ideal; the bed was very wide. But the room was empty all day long. He said this to Louise, who reflected. In the bedroom, at least, Jonas would not be bothered; after all, people wouldn't dare lie down on their bed. 'What do you think of it?' Louise in turn asked Rateau. He looked at Jonas. Jonas was looking at the windows across the way. Then he raised his eyes to the starless sky, and went and pulled the curtains. When he returned, he smiled at Rateau and sat down beside him on the bed without saying a word. Louise, obviously done in, declared that she was going to take her shower. When the two friends were alone, Jonas felt Rateau's shoulder touch his. He didn't look at him, but said: 'I love to paint. I'd like to paint all my life, day and night. Isn't that lucky?' Rateau looked at him affectionately: 'Yes,' he said, 'it's lucky.'

The children were growing and Jonas was glad to see them happy and healthy. They were now at school and came home at four o'clock. Jonas could still enjoy them on Saturday afternoons, or Thursdays, and also for whole days during their frequent and prolonged holidays. They were not yet big enough to play quietly but were hardy enough to fill the apartment with their squabbles and their laughter. He had to quiet them, threaten them, sometimes even pretend to hit them. There was also the laundry to be done, the buttons to be sewn on. Louise couldn't do it all. Since they couldn't house a servant, nor even bring one into the close intimacy in which they lived, Jonas suggested calling on the help of Louise's sister, Rose, who had been left a widow with a grown daughter. 'Yes,' Louise said, 'with Rose we'll not have to stand on ceremony. We can put her out when we want to.' Jonas was delighted with this solution, which would relieve Louise at the same time that it relieved his conscience, embarrassed by his wife's fatigue. The relief was even greater since the sister often brought along her daughter as a reinforcement. Both were as good as gold; virtue and unselfishness predominated in their honest natures. They did everything possible to help out and didn't begrudge their time. They were helped in this by the boredom of their solitary lives and their delight in the easy circumstances prevailing at Louise's. As it was foreseen, no one stood on ceremony and the two relatives, from the very beginning, felt at home. The big room became a common room, at once dining-room, linen-closet, and nursery. The little room, in which the last-born slept, served as a storeroom for the paintings and a folding bed on which Rose sometimes slept, when she happened to come without her daughter.

Jonas occupied the master bedroom and worked in the space separating the bed from the window. He merely had to wait until the room was made up in the morning, after the children's room. From then on, no one came to bother him except to get a sheet or towel, for the only cupboard in the house happened to be in that room. As for the visitors, though rather less numerous, they had developed certain habits and, contrary to Louise's hope, they didn't hesitate to lie down on the double bed to be more comfortable when chatting with Jonas. The children would also come in to greet their father. 'Let's see the picture.' Jonas would show them the picture he was painting and would kiss them affectionately. As he sent them away, he felt that they filled his heart fully, without any reservation. Deprived of them, he would have merely an empty solitude. He loved them as much as his painting because they were the only things in the world as alive as it was.

Nevertheless Jonas was working less, without really knowing why. He was always diligent, but he now had trouble painting, even in the moments of solitude. He would spend such moments looking at the sky. He had always been absent-minded, easily lost in thought, but now he became a dreamer. He would think of painting, of his vocation, instead of painting. 'I love to paint,' he still said to himself, and the hand holding the brush would hang at his side as he listened to a distant radio.

At the same time, his reputation declined. He was brought articles full of reservations, others frankly unfriendly, and some so nasty that they deeply distressed him. But he told himself that he could get some good out of such attacks that would force him to work better. Those who continued to come treated him more familiarly, like an old friend with whom you don't have to put yourself out. When he wanted to go back to his work, they would say: 'Oh, go on! There's plenty of time.' Jonas realized that in a certain way they were already identifying him with their own failure. But, in another way, there was something salutary about this new solidarity. Rateau shrugged his shoulders, saying: 'You're a fool. They don't care about you at all!' 'They love me a little now,' Jonas replied. 'A little love is wonderful. Does it matter how you get it?' He therefore went on talking, writing letters, and painting as best he could. Now and then he really would paint, especially on Sunday afternoons when the children went out with Louise and Rose. In the evening he would rejoice at having made a little progress on the picture under way. At that time he was painting skies.

The day when the dealer told him that, because of the considerable falling-off in sales, he was regretfully obliged to reduce the remittance, Jonas approved, but Louise was worried. It was September and the children had to be outfitted for school. She set to work herself with her customary courage and was soon swamped. Rose, who could mend and sew on buttons, could not make things. But her husband's cousin could; she came to help Louise. From time to time she would settle in Jonas's room on a corner chair, where the silent woman would sit still for hours. So still that Louise suggested to Jonas painting a *Seamstress*. 'Good idea,' Jonas said. He tried, spoiled two canvases, then went back to a half-finished sky. The next day, he walked up and down in the apartment for some time and meditated instead of painting. A disciple, all excited, came to show him a long article he would not have seen otherwise, from which he learned that his painting was not only over-rated but out of date. The dealer phoned him to tell him again how worried he was by the decline in sales. Yet he continued to dream and meditate. He told the disciple that there was some truth in the article, but that he, Jonas, could still count on many good working years. To the dealer he replied that he understood his worry without sharing it. He had a big work, really new, to create; everything was going to begin all over again. As he was talking, he felt that he was telling the truth and that his star was there. All he needed was a good system.

During the ensuing days he tried to work in the hall, two days later in the shower-room with electric light, and the following day in the kitchen. But, for the first time, he was bothered by the people he kept bumping into everywhere, those he hardly knew and his own family, whom he loved. For a little while he stopped working and meditated. He would have painted landscapes out of doors if the weather had been propitious. Unfortunately, it was just the beginning of winter and it was hard to do landscapes before spring. He tried, however, and gave up; the cold pierced him to the marrow. He lived several days with his canvases, most often seated beside them or else planted in front of the window; he didn't paint any more. Then he got into the habit of going out in the morning. He would give himself the assignment of sketching a detail, a tree, a lopsided house, a profile as it went by. At the end of the day, he had done nothing. The least temptation – the newspapers, an encounter, shop windows, the warmth of a café – would lead him astray. Each evening he would keep providing good excuses to a bad conscience that never left him. He was going to paint, that was certain, and paint better, after this period of apparent waste. It was all just working within him, and the star would come out newly washed and sparkling from behind these black clouds. Meanwhile he never left the cafés. He had discovered that alcohol gave him the same exaltation as a day of good productive work at the time when he used to think of his picture with the affection and warmth that he had never felt except towards his children. With the second cognac he recovered that poignant emotion that made him at one and the same time master and servant of the whole world. The only difference was that he enjoyed it in a vacuum, with idle hands, without communicating it to a work. Still, this was closest to the joy for which he lived, and he now spent long hours sitting and dreaming in smoke-filled, noisy places.

Yet he fled the places and sections frequented by artists. Whenever he met an acquaintance who spoke to him of his painting, he would be seized with panic. He wanted to get away, that was obvious, and he did get away. He knew what was said behind his back: 'He thinks he's Rembrandt', and his discomfort increased. In any event, he never smiled any more, and his former friends drew an odd and inevitable conclusion from this: 'If he has given up smiling, this is because he's very satisfied with himself.' Knowing that, he became more and more elusive and skittish. It was enough for him, on entering a café, to have the feeling that someone there recognized him for everything to cloud over within him. For a second, he would stand there, powerless and filled with a strange sadness, his inscrutable face hiding both his uneasiness and his avid and sudden need for friendship. He would think of Rateau's cheering look and would rush out in a hurry. 'Just look at that fellow's hangover!' he heard someone say close to him one day as he was disappearing.

He now frequented only the outlying sections, where no one knew him. There he could talk and smile and his kindliness came back, for no one expected anything of him. He made a few friends, who were not very hard to please. He particularly enjoyed the company of one of them, who used to serve him in a station buffet where he often went. That fellow had asked him 'what he did in life'. 'Painter,' Jonas had replied. 'Picture-painter or house-painter?' 'Picture.' 'Well,' said the fellow, 'that's not easy.' And they had never broached the subject again. No, it was not easy, but Jonas would manage all right, as soon as he had found how to organize his work.

Day after day and drink after drink, he had many encounters, and women helped him. He could talk to them, before or after the love-making, and especially boast a little, for they would understand him even if they weren't convinced. At times it seemed to him that his old strength was returning. One day when he had been encouraged by one of his female acquaintances, he made up his mind. He returned home, tried to work again in the bedroom, the seamstress being absent. But after an hour of it he put his canvas away, smiled at Louise without seeing her, and went out. He drank all day long and spent the night with his acquaintance, though without being in any condition to desire her. In the morning, the image of suffering with its tortured face received him in the person of Louise. She wanted to know if he had taken that woman. Jonas said that, being drunk, he had not, but that he had taken others before. And for the first time, his heart torn within him, he saw that Louise suddenly had the look of a drowned woman, that look that comes from surprise and an excess of pain. It dawned upon him that he had not thought of Louise during this whole time, and he was ashamed. He begged her forgiveness, it was all over, tomorrow everything would begin again as it had been in the past. Louise could not speak and turned away to hide her tears.

The following day Jonas went out very early. It was raining. When he returned, wet to the skin, he was loaded down with boards. At home, two old friends, come to ask after him, were drinking coffee in the big room. 'Jonas is changing his technique. He's going to paint on wood!' they said. Jonas smiled. 'That's not it. But I am beginning something new.' He went into the little hall leading to the shower-room, the lavatory, and the kitchen. In the right angle where the two halls joined, he stopped and studied at length the high walls rising to the dark ceiling. He needed a stepladder, which he went down and got from the concierge.

When he came back, there were several additional people in the apartment, and he had to struggle against the affection of his visitors, delighted to find him again, and against his family's questions, in order to reach the end of the hall. At that moment his wife came out of the kitchen. Setting down his ladder, Jonas hugged her against him. Louise looked at him. 'Please,' she said, 'never do it again.' 'No, no,' Jonas said, 'I'm going to paint. I must paint.' But he seemed to be talking to himself, for he was looking elsewhere. He got to work. Half-way up the walls he built a flooring to get a sort of narrow, but high and deep, loft. By the late afternoon, all was finished. With the help of the ladder, Jonas hung from the floor of the loft and, to test the solidity of his work, chinned himself several times. Then he mingled with the others and everyone was delighted to find him so friendly again. In the evening, when the apartment was relatively empty, Jonas got an oil lamp, a chair, a stool, and a frame. He took them all up into the loft before the puzzled gaze of the three women and the children. 'Now,' he said from his lofty perch, 'I'll be able to work without being in anyone's way.' Louise asked him if he were sure of it. 'Of course,' he replied. 'I don't need much room. I'll be freer. There have been great painters who painted by candlelight, and . . . ' 'Is the floor solid enough?' It was. 'Don't worry,' Jonas said, 'it's a very good solution.' And he came down again.

Very early the next day he climbed into the loft, sat down, set the frame on the stool against the wall, and waited without lighting the lamp. The only direct sounds he heard came from the kitchen or the lavatory. The other noises seemed distant, and the visits, the ringing of the door-bell and the telephone, the comings and goings, the conversations, reached him half muffled, as if they came from out on the street or from the farther court. Besides, although the whole apartment was overflowing with blinding sunlight, the darkness here was restful. From time to time a friend would come and plant himself under the loft. 'What are you doing up there, Jonas?' 'I'm working.' 'Without light?' 'Yes, for the moment.' He was not painting, but he was meditating. In the darkness and this half-silence which, by contrast with what he had known before, seemed to him the silence of the desert or of the tomb, he listened to his own heart. The sounds that reached the loft seemed not to concern him any more, even when addressed to him. He was like those men who die alone at home in their sleep, and in the morning the telephone rings, feverish and insistent, in the deserted house, over a body for ever deaf. But he was alive, he listened to this silence within himself, he was waiting for his star, still hidden but ready to rise again, to burst forth at last, unchanged and unchanging, above the disorder of these empty days. 'Shine, shine,' he said. 'Don't deprive me of your light.' It would shine again, of that he was sure. But he would have to meditate still longer, since at last the chance was given him to be alone without separating from his family. He still had to discover what he had not yet clearly understood, although he had always known it and had always painted as if he knew it. He had to grasp at last that secret which was not merely the secret of art, as he could now see. That is why he didn't light the lamp.

Every day now Jonas would climb back into his loft. The visitors became less numerous because Louise, preoccupied, paid little attention to the conversation. Jonas would come down for meals and then climb back to his perch. He would sit motionless in the darkness all day long. At night he would go to his wife, who was already in bed. After a few days he asked Louise to hand up his lunch, which she did with such pains that Jonas was stirred. In order not to disturb her on other occasions, he suggested her preparing some supplies that he could store in the loft. Little by little he got to the point of not coming down all day long. But he hardly touched his supplies.

One evening he called Louise and asked for some blankets. 'I'll spend the night up here.' Louise looked at him with her head bent backward. She opened her mouth and then said nothing. She was merely scrutinizing Jonas with a worried and sad expression. He suddenly saw how much she had aged and how deeply the trials of their life had marked her too. It occurred to him that he had never really helped her. But before he could say a word, she smiled at him with an affection that wrung his heart. 'Just as you say, dear,' she said.

Henceforth he spent his nights in the loft, scarcely ever coming down any more. As a result, the apartment was emptied of visitors since Jonas was no more to be seen either by day or night. Some were told that he was in the country; others, when lying became an effort, that he had found a studio. Rateau alone came faithfully. He would climb up on the ladder until his big, friendly head was just over the level of the flooring. 'How goes it?' he would ask. 'Wonderfully.' 'Are you working?' 'It comes to the same thing.' 'But you have no canvas!' 'I'm working just the same.' It was hard to prolong this dialogue from ladder to loft. Rateau would shake his head, come down again, help Louise replace fuses or repair a lock, then, without climbing on to the ladder, say good night to Jonas, who would reply in the darkness: 'So long, old boy.' One evening Jonas added thanks to his good night. 'Why thanks?' 'Because you love me.' 'That's really news!' Rateau said as he left.

Another evening Jonas called Rateau, who came running. The lamp was lighted for the first time. Jonas was leaning, with a tense look, out of the loft. 'Hand me a canvas,' he said. 'But what's the matter with you? You're so much thinner; you look like a ghost.' 'I've hardly eaten for the last two days. But that doesn't matter. I must work.' 'Eat first.' 'No, I'm not hungry.' Rateau brought a canvas. On the point of disappearing into the loft, Jonas asked him: 'How are they?' 'Who?' 'Louise and the children.' 'They're all right. They'd be better if you were with them.' 'I'm still with them. Tell them above all that I'm still with them.' And he disappeared. Rateau came and told Louise how worried he was. She admitted that she herself had been anxious for several days. 'What can we do? Oh, if only I could work in his place!' Wretched, she faced Rateau. 'I can't live without him,' she said. She looked like the girl she had been, and this surprised Rateau. He suddenly realized that she had blushed.

The lamp stayed lighted all night and all the next morning. To those who came, Rateau or Louise, Jonas answered merely: 'Forget it, I'm working.' At noon he asked for some kerosene. The lamp, which had been smoking, again shone brightly until evening. Rateau stayed to dinner with Louise and the children. At midnight he went to say good night to Jonas. Under the still lighted loft he waited a moment, then went away without saying a word. On the morning of the second day, when Louise got up, the lamp was still lighted.

A beautiful day was beginning, but Jonas was not aware of it. He had turned the canvas against the wall. Exhausted, he was sitting there waiting, with his hands, palms up, on his knees. He told himself that now he would never again work, he was happy. He heard his children grumbling, water running, and the dishes clinking together. Louise was talking. The huge windows rattled as a truck passed on the boulevard. The world was still there, young and lovable. Jonas listened to the welcome murmur rising from mankind. From such a distance, it did not run counter to that joyful strength within him, his art, these for ever silent thoughts he could not express but which set him above all things, in a free and crisp air. The children were running through the apartment, the little girl was laughing, Louise too now, and he hadn't heard her laugh for so long. He loved them! How he loved them! He put out the lamp and, in the darkness that suddenly returned, right thcrc! wasn't that his star still shining? It was the star, he recognized it with his heart full of gratitude, and he was still watching it when he fell, without a sound.

'It's nothing,' the doctor they had called declared a little later. 'He is working too much. In a week he will be on his feet again.' 'You are sure he will get well?' asked Louise with distorted face. 'He will get well.' In the other room Rateau was looking at the canvas, completely blank, in the centre of which Jonas had merely written in very small letters a word that could be made out, but without any certainty as to whether it should be read *solitary* or *solidary*.

THE GROWING STONE

THE CAR SWUNG clumsily round the curve in the red sand-stone trail, now a mass of mud. The headlights suddenly picked out in the night – first on one side of the road, then on the other – two wooden huts with sheet-metal roofs. On the right near the second one, a tower of coarse beams could be made out in the light fog. From the top of the tower a metal cable, invisible at its starting-point, shone as it sloped down into the light from the car before disappearing behind the embankment that blocked the road. The car slowed down and stopped a few yards from the huts.

The man who emerged from the seat to the right of the driver laboured to extricate himself from the car. As he stood up, his huge, broad frame lurched a little. In the shadow beside the car, solidly planted on the ground and weighed down by fatigue, he seemed to be listening to the idling motor. Then he walked in the direction of the embankment and entered the cone of light from the headlights. He stopped at the top of the slope, his broad back outlined against the darkness. After a moment he turned round. In the light from the dashboard he could see the chauffeur's black face, smiling. The man signalled and the chauffeur turned off the motor. At once a vast cool silence fell over the trail and the forest. Then the sound of the water could be heard.

The man looked at the river below him, visible solely as a broad dark motion, flecked with occasional shimmers. A denser motionless darkness, far beyond, must be the other bank. By looking fixedly, however, one could see on that still bank a yellowish light like an oil lamp in the distance.

The big man turned back towards the car and nodded. The chauffeur switched off the lights, turned them on again, then blinked them regularly. On the embankment the man appeared and disappeared, taller and more massive each time he came back to life. Suddenly, on the other bank of the river, a lantern held up by an invisible arm swung back and forth several times. At a final signal from the look-out, the chauffeur turned off his lights once and for all. The car and the man disappeared into the night. With the lights out, the river was almost visible — or at least a few of its long liquid muscles shining intermittently. On each side of the road, the dark masses of forest foliage stood out against the sky and seemed very near. The fine rain that had soaked the trail an hour earlier was still hovering in the warm air, intensifying the silence and immobility of this broad clearing in the virgin forest. In the black sky misty stars flickered.

But from the other bank rose sounds of chains and muffled plashings. Above the hut on the right of the man still waiting there, the cable stretched taut. A dull creaking began to run along it, just as there rose from the river a faint yet quite audible sound of stirred-up water. The creaking became more regular, the sound of water spread farther and then became localized, as the lantern grew larger. Now its yellowish halo could be clearly seen. The halo gradually expanded and again contracted while the lantern shone through the mist and began to light up from beneath a sort of square roof of dried palms supported by thick bamboos. This crude shelter, around which vague shadows were moving, was slowly approaching the bank. When it was about in the middle of the river, three little men, almost black, were distinctly outlined in the yellow light, naked from the waist up and wearing conical hats. They stood still with feet apart, leaning somewhat to offset the strong drift of the river pressing with all its invisible water against the side of a big crude raft that eventually emerged from the darkness. When the ferry came still closer, the man could see behind the shelter on the downstream side two tall negroes likewise wearing nothing but broad straw hats and cotton trousers. Side by side they weighed with all their might on long poles that sank slowly into the river towards the stern while the negroes, with the same slow motion, bent over the water as far as their balance would allow. In the bow the three mulattoes, still and silent, watched the bank approach without raising their eyes towards the man waiting for them.

The ferry suddenly bumped against something. And the lantern swaying from the shock lighted up a pier jutting into the water. The tall negroes stood still with hands above their heads gripping the ends of the poles, which were barely stuck in the bottom, but their taut muscles rippled constantly with a motion that seemed to come from the very thrust of the water. The other ferrymen looped chains over the posts on the dock, leaped on to the boards, and lowered a sort of gang-plank that covered the bow of the raft with its inclined plane.

The man returned to the car and slid in while the chauffeur stepped on the starter. The car slowly climbed the embankment, pointed its bonnet towards the sky, and then lowered it towards the river as it tackled the downward slope. With brakes on, it rolled forward, slipped somewhat on the mud, stopped, started up again. It rolled on to the pier with a noise of bouncing planks, reached the end, where the mulattoes, still silent, were standing on either side, and plunged slowly towards the raft. The raft ducked its nose in the water as soon as the front wheels struck it and almost immediately bobbed back to receive the car's full weight. Then the chauffeur ran the vehicle to the stern, in front of the square roof where the lantern was hanging. At once the mulattoes swung the inclined plane back on to the pier and jumped simultaneously on to the ferry, pushing it off from the muddy bank. The river strained under the raft and raised it on the surface of the water, where it drifted slowly at the end of the long drawbar running along the cable overhead. The tall negroes relaxed their effort and drew in their poles. The man and the chauffeur got out of the car and came over to stand on the edge of the raft facing upstream. No one had spoken during the manœuvre, and even now each remained in his place, motionless and quiet except for one of the tall negroes who was rolling a cigarette in coarse paper.

The man was looking at the gap through which the river sprang from the vast Brazilian forest and swept down towards them. Several hundred yards wide at that point, the muddy, silky waters of the river pressed against the side of the ferry and then, unimpeded at the two ends of the raft, sheered off and again spread out in a single powerful flood gently flowing through the dark forest towards the sea and the night. A stale smell, come from the water or the spongy sky, hung in the air. Now the slapping of the water under the ferry could be heard, and at intervals the calls of bullfrogs from the two banks or the strange cries of birds. The big man approached the small, thin chauffeur, who was leaning against one of the bamboos with his hands in the pockets of his dungarees, once blue but now covered with the same red dust that had been blowing in their faces all day long. A smile spread over his face, all wrinkled in spite of his youth. Without really seeing them, he was staring at the faint stars still swimming in the damp sky.

But the birds' cries became sharper, unfamiliar chatterings mingled with them, and almost at once the cable began to creak. The tall negroes plunged their poles into the water and groped blindly for the bottom. The man turned round towards the shore they had just left. Now that shore was obscured by the darkness and the water, vast and savage like the continent of trees stretching beyond it for thousands of kilometres. Between the nearby ocean and this sea of vegetation, the handful of men drifting at that moment on a wild river seemed lost. When the raft bumped the new pier it was as if, having cast off all moorings, they were landing on an island in the darkness after days of frightened sailing.

Once on land, the men's voices were at last heard. The chauffeur had just paid them and, with voices that sounded strangely gay in the heavy night, they were saying farewell in Portuguese as the car started up again.

'They said sixty, the kilometres to Iguape. Three hours more and it'll be over. Socrates is happy,' the chauffeur announced.

The man laughed with a warm, hearty laugh that resembled him.

'Me too, Socrates, I'm happy too. The trail is hard.'

'Too heavy, Mr D'Arrast, you too heavy,' and the chauffeur laughed too as if he would never stop.

The car had taken on a little speed. It was advancing between high walls of trees and inextricable vegetation, amidst a soft, sweetish smell. Fireflies on the wing constantly criss-crossed in the darkness of the forest, and every once in a while red-eyed birds would bump against the windshield. At times a strange, savage sound would reach them from the depths of the night and the chauffeur would roll his eyes comically as he looked at his passenger.

The road kept turning and crossed little streams on bridges of wobbly boards. After an hour the fog began to thicken. A fine drizzle began to fall, dimming the car's lights. Despite the jolts, D'Arrast was half asleep. He was no longer riding in the damp forest but on the roads of the Serra that they had taken in the morning as they left São Paulo. From those dirt trails constantly rose the red dust which they could still taste, and on both sides, as far as the eye could see, it covered the sparse vegetation of the plains. The harsh sun, the pale mountains full of ravines, the starved zebus encountered along the roads, with a tired flight of ragged urubus as their only escort, the long, endless crossing of an endless desert... He gave a start. The car had stopped. Now they were in Japan: fragile houses on both sides of the road and, in the houses, furtive kimonos. The chauffeur was talking to a Japanese wearing soiled dungarees and a Brazilian straw hat. Then the car started up again.

'He said only forty kilometres.'

'Where were we? In Tokyo?'

'No. Registro. In Brazil all the Japanese come here.'

'Why?'

'Don't know. They're yellow, you know, Mr D'Arrast.'

But the forest was gradually thinning out, and the road was becoming easier, though slippery. The car was skidding on sand. The window let in a warm, damp breeze that was rather sour.

'You smell it?' the chauffeur asked, smacking his lips. 'That's the good old sea. Soon, Iguape.'

'If we have enough petrol,' D'Arrast said. And he went back to sleep peacefully.

*   *   *

Sitting up in bed early in the morning, D'Arrast looked in amazement at the huge room in which he had just awakened. The lower half of the big walls was newly painted brown. Higher up, they had once been painted white, and patches of yellowish paint covered them up to the ceiling. Two rows of beds faced each other. D'Arrast saw only one bed unmade at the end of his row and that bed was empty. But he heard a noise on his left and turned towards the door, where Socrates, a bottle of mineral water in each hand, stood laughing, 'Happy memory!' he said. D'Arrast shook himself. Yes, the hospital in which the Mayor had lodged them the night before was named 'Happy Memory'. 'Sure memory,' Socrates continued. 'They told me first build hospital, later build water. Meanwhile, happy memory, take fizz water to wash.' He disappeared, laughing and singing, not at all exhausted apparently by the cataclysmic sneezes that had shaken him all night long and kept D'Arrast from closing an eye.

461

Now D'Arrast was completely awake. Through the iron-latticed window he could see a little red-earth courtyard soaked by the rain that was noiselessly pouring down on a clump of tall aloes. A woman passed holding a yellow scarf over her head. D'Arrast lay back in bed, then sat up at once and got out of the bed, which creaked under his weight. Socrates came in at that moment: 'For you, Mr D'Arrast. The Mayor is waiting outside.' But, seeing the look on D'Arrast's face, he added: 'Don't worry; he never in a hurry.'

After shaving with the mineral water, D'Arrast went out under the portico of the building. The Mayor – who had the proportions and, under his gold-rimmed glasses, the look of a nice little weasel – seemed lost in dull contemplation of the rain. But a charming smile transfigured him as soon as he saw D'Arrast. Holding his little body erect, he rushed up and tried to stretch his arms round the engineer. At that moment an automobile drove up in front of them on the other side of the low wall, skidded in the wet clay, and came to a stop at an angle. 'The Judge!' said the Mayor. Like the Mayor, the Judge was dressed in navy blue. But he was much younger, or at least seemed so because of his elegant figure and his look of a startled adolescent. Now he was crossing the courtyard in their direction, gracefully avoiding the puddles. A few steps from D'Arrast, he was already holding out his arms and welcoming him. He was proud to greet the noble engineer who was honouring their poor village; he was delighted by the priceless service the noble engineer was going to do Iguape by building that little jetty to prevent the periodic flooding of the lower quarters of town. What a noble profession, to command the waters and dominate rivers! Ah, surely the poor people of Iguape would long remember the noble engineer's name and many years from now would still mention it in their prayers. D'Arrast, captivated by such charm and eloquence, thanked him and didn't dare wonder what possible connexion a judge could have with a jetty. Besides, according to the Mayor, it was time to go to the club, where the leading citizens wanted to receive the noble engineer appropriately before going to inspect the poorer quarters. Who were the leading citizens?

'Well,' the Mayor said, 'myself as Mayor, Mr Carvalho here, the Harbour Captain, and a few others less important. Besides, you won't have to pay much attention to them, for they don't speak French.'

D'Arrast called Socrates and told him he would meet him when the morning was over.

'All right,' Socrates said, 'I'll go to the Garden of the Fountain.'

'The Garden?'

'Yes, everybody knows. Have no fear, Mr D'Arrast.'

The hospital, D'Arrast noticed as he left it, was built on the edge of the forest, and the heavy foliage almost hung over the roofs. Over the whole surface of the trees was falling a sheet of fine rain which the dense forest was noiselessly absorbing like a huge sponge. The town, some hundred houses roofed with faded tiles, extended between the forest and the river, and the water's distant murmur reached the hospital. The car entered drenched streets and almost at once came out on a rather large rectangular square which showed, among numerous puddles in its red clay, the marks of tyres, iron wheels, and horseshoes. All around, brightly plastered low houses closed off the square, behind which could be seen the two round towers of a blue-and-white church of colonial style. A smell of salt water coming from the estuary dominated this bare setting. In the centre of the square a few wet silhouettes were wandering. Along the houses a motley crowd of gauchos, Japanese, half-breed Indians, and elegant leading citizens, whose dark suits looked exotic here, were sauntering with slow gestures. They stepped aside with dignity to make way for the car, then stopped and watched it. When the car stopped in front of one of the houses on the square, a circle of wet gauchos silently formed round it.

At the club – a sort of small bar on the second floor furnished with a bamboo counter and iron café tables – the leading citizens were numerous. Sugar-cane alcohol was drunk in honour of D'Arrast after the Mayor, glass in hand, had wished him welcome and all the happiness in the world. But while D'Arrast was drinking near the window, a huge lout of a fellow in riding-breeches and leggings came over and, staggering somewhat, delivered himself of a rapid and obscure speech in which the engineer recognized solely the word 'passport'. He hesitated and then took out the document, which the fellow seized greedily. After having thumbed through the passport, he manifested obvious displeasure. He resumed his speech, shaking the document under the nose of the engineer, who, without getting excited, merely looked at the angry man. Whereupon the Judge, with a smile, came over and asked what was the matter. For a moment the drunk scrutinized the frail creature who dared to interrupt him and then, staggering even more dangerously, shook the passport in the face of his new interlocutor. D'Arrast sat peacefully beside a café table and waited. The dialogue became very lively, and suddenly the Judge broke out in a deafening voice that one would never have suspected in him. Without any forewarning, the lout suddenly backed down like a child caught in the act. At a final order from the Judge, he sidled towards the door like a punished schoolboy and disappeared.

The Judge immediately came over to explain to D'Arrast, in a voice that had become harmonious again, that the uncouth individual who had just left was the Chief of Police, that he dared to claim the passport was not in order, and that he would be punished for his outburst. Judge Carvalho then addressed himself to the leading citizens, who stood in a circle round him, and seemed to be questioning them. After a brief discussion, the Judge expressed solemn excuses to D'Arrast, asked him to agree that nothing but drunkenness could explain such forgetfulness of the sentiments of respect and gratitude that the whole town of Iguape owed him, and, finally, asked him to decide himself on the punishment to be inflicted on the wretched individual. D'Arrast said that he didn't want any punishment, that it was a trivial incident, and that he was particularly eager to go to the river. Then the Mayor spoke up to assert with much simple good humour that a punishment was really mandatory, that the guilty man would remain incarcerated, and that they would all wait until their distinguished visitor decided on his fate. No protest could soften that smiling severity, and D'Arrast had to promise that he would think the matter over. Then they agreed to visit the poorer quarters of the town.

The river was already spreading its yellowish waters over the low, slippery banks. They had left behind them the last houses of Iguape and stood between the river and a high, steep embankment to which clung huts made of clay and branches. In front of them, at the end of the embankment, the forest began again abruptly, as on the other bank. But the gap made by the water rapidly widened between the trees until reaching a vague greyish line that marked the beginning of the sea. Without saying a word, D'Arrast walked towards the slope, where the various flood levels had left marks that were still fresh. A muddy path climbed towards the huts. In front of them, negroes stood silently staring at the newcomers. Several couples were holding hands, and on the edge of the mound, in front of the adults, a row of black children with bulging bellies and spindly legs were gaping with round eyes.

When he arrived in front of the huts, D'Arrast beckoned to the Harbour Captain. He was a fat, laughing negro wearing a white uniform. D'Arrast asked him in Spanish if it were possible to visit a hut. The Captain was sure it was, he even thought it a good idea, and the noble engineer would see very interesting things. He harangued the negroes at length, pointing to D'Arrast and to the river. They listened without saying a word. When the Captain had finished, no one stirred. He spoke again impatiently. Then he called upon one of the men, who shook his head. Whereupon the Captain said a few brief words in a tone of command. The man stepped forth from the group, faced D'Arrast, and with a gesture showed him the way. But his look was hostile. He was an elderly man with short, greying hair and a thin, wizened face; yet his body was still young, with hard wiry shoulders and muscles visible through his cotton trousers and torn shirt. They went ahead, followed by the Captain and the crowd of negroes, and climbed a new, steeper embankment where the huts made of clay, tin, and reeds clung to the ground with such difficulty that they had to be strengthened at the base with heavy stones. They met a woman going down the path, sometimes slipping in her bare feet, who was carrying on her head an iron drum full of water. Then they reached a small irregular square bordered by three huts. The man walked towards one of them and pushed open a bamboo door on hinges made of tropical liana. He stood aside without saying a word, staring at the engineer with the same impassive look. In the hut, D'Arrast saw nothing at first but a dying fire built right on the ground in the exact centre of the room. Then in a back corner he made out a brass bed with a bare, broken mattress, a table in the other corner covered with earthenware dishes, and, between the two, a sort of stand supporting a colour print representing St George. Nothing else but a pile of rags to the right of the entrance and, hanging from the ceiling, a few loincloths of various colours drying over the fire. Standing still, D'Arrast breathed in the smell of smoke and poverty that rose from the ground and choked him. Behind him, the Captain clapped his hands. The engineer turned round and, against the light, saw the graceful silhouette of a black girl approach and hold out something to him. He took a glass and drank the thick sugar-cane alcohol. The girl held out her tray to receive the empty glass and went out with such a supple motion that D'Arrast suddenly wanted to hold her back.

But on following her out he didn't recognize her in the crowd of negroes and leading citizens gathered round the hut. He thanked the old man, who bowed without a word. Then he left. The Captain, behind him, resumed his explanations and asked when the French company from Rio could begin work and whether or not the jetty could be built before the rainy season. D'Arrast didn't know; to tell the truth, he wasn't thinking of that. He went down towards the cool river under the fine mist. He was still listening to that great pervasive sound he had been hearing continually since his arrival, which might have been made by the rustling of either the water or the trees, he could not tell. Having reached the bank, he looked out in the distance at the vague line of the sea, the thousands of kilometres of solitary waters leading to Africa and, beyond, his native Europe.

'Captain,' he asked, 'what do these people we have just seen live on?'

'They work when they're needed,' the Captain said. 'We are poor.'

'Are they the poorest?'

'They are the poorest.'

The Judge, who arrived at that moment, slipping somewhat in his best shoes, said they already loved the noble engineer who was going to give them work.

'And, you know, they dance and sing every day.'

Then, without transition, he asked D'Arrast if he had thought of the punishment.

'What punishment?'

'Why, our Chief of Police.'

'Let him go.' The Judge said that this was not possible; there had to be a punishment. D'Arrast was already walking towards Iguape.

*   *   *

467

In the little Garden of the Fountain, mysterious and pleasant under the fine rain, clusters of exotic flowers hung down along the lianas among the banana trees and pandanus. Piles of wet stones marked the intersection of paths on which a motley crowd was strolling. Half-breeds, mulattoes, a few gauchos were chatting in low voices or sauntering along the bamboo paths to the point where groves and bush became thicker and more impenetrable. There, the forest began abruptly.

D'Arrast was looking for Socrates in the crowd when Socrates suddenly bumped him from behind.

'It's holiday,' he said, laughing, and clung to D'Arrast's tall shoulders to jump up and down.

'What holiday?'

'Why, you not know?' Socrates said in surprise as he faced D'Arrast. 'The feast of good Jesus. Each year they all come to the grotto with a hammer.'

Socrates pointed out, not a grotto, but a group that seemed to be waiting in a corner of the garden.

'You see? One day the good statue of Jesus, it came upstream from the sea. Some fishermen found it. How beautiful! How beautiful! Then they washed it here in the grotto. And now a stone grew up in the grotto. Every year it's the feast. With the hammer you break, you break off pieces for blessed happiness. And then it keeps growing and you keep breaking. It's the miracle!'

They had reached the grotto and could see its low entrance beyond the waiting men. Inside, in the darkness studded with the flickering flames of candles, a squatting figure was pounding with a hammer. The man, a thin gaucho with a long moustache, got up and came out holding in his open palm, so that all might see, a small piece of moist schist, over which he soon closed his hand carefully before going away. Another man then stooped down and entered the grotto.

D'Arrast turned round. On all sides pilgrims were waiting, without looking at him, impassive under the water dripping from the trees in thin sheets. He too was waiting in front of the grotto under the same film of water, and he didn't know for what. He had been waiting constantly, to tell the truth, for a month since he had arrived in this country. He had been waiting – in the red heat of humid days, under the little stars of night, despite the tasks to be accomplished, the jetties to be built, the roads to be cut through – as if the work he had come to do here were merely a pretext for a surprise or for an encounter he did not even imagine but which had been waiting patiently for him at the end of the world. He shook himself, walked away without anyone in the little group paying attention to him, and went towards the exit. He had to go back to the river and go to work.

But Socrates was waiting for him at the gate, lost in voluble conversation with a short, fat, strapping man whose skin was yellow rather than black. His head, completely shaved, gave even more sweep to a considerable forehead. On the other hand, his broad, smooth face was adorned with a very black beard, trimmed square.

'He's champion!' Socrates said by way of introduction. 'Tomorrow he's in the procession.'

The man, wearing a sailor's outfit of heavy serge, a blue-and-white jersey under the pea jacket, was examining D'Arrast attentively with his calm black eyes. At the same time he was smiling, showing all his very white teeth between his full, shiny lips.

'He speaks Spanish,' Socrates said and, turning towards the stranger, added: 'Tell Mr D'Arrast.' Then he danced off towards another group. The man ceased to smile and looked at D'Arrast with outright curiosity.

'You are interested, Captain?'

'I'm not a captain,' D'Arrast said.

'That doesn't matter. But you're a noble. Socrates told me.'

'Not I. But my grandfather was. His father too and all those before his father. Now there is no more nobility in our country.'

'Ah!' the negro said, laughing. 'I understand; everybody is a noble.'

'No, that's not it. There are neither noblemen nor common people.'

The fellow reflected; then he made up his mind.

'No one works? No one suffers?'

'Yes, millions of men.'

'Then that's the common people.'

'In that way, yes, there is a common people. But the masters are policemen or merchants.'

The mulatto's kindly face closed in a frown. Then he grumbled: 'Humph! Buying and selling, eh! What filth! And with the police, dogs command.'

Suddenly, he burst out laughing.

'You, you don't sell?'

'Hardly at all. I make bridges, roads.'

'That's good. Me, I'm a ship's cook. If you wish, I'll make you our dish of black beans.'

'All right.'

The cook came closer to D'Arrast and took his arm.

'Listen, I like what you tell. I'm going to tell you too. Maybe you will like.'

He drew him over near the gate to a damp wooden bench beneath a clump of bamboos.

'I was at sea, off Iguape, on a small coastwise tanker that supplies the harbours along here. It caught fire on board. Not by my fault! I know my job! No, just bad luck. We were able to launch the lifeboats. During the night, the sea got rough; it capsized the boat and I went down. When I came up, I hit the boat with my head. I drifted. The night was dark, the waters are vast, and, besides, I don't swim well; I was afraid. Just then I saw a light in the distance and recognized the church of the good Jesus in Iguape. So I told the good Jesus that at his procession I would carry a hundred-pound stone on my head if he saved me. You don't have to believe me, but the waters became calm and my heart too. I swam slowly, I was happy, and I reached the shore. Tomorrow I'll keep my promise.'

He looked at D'Arrast in a suddenly suspicious manner.

'You're not laughing?'

'No, I'm not laughing. A man has to do what he has promised.'

The fellow clapped him on the back.

'Now, come to my brother's, near the river. I'll cook you some beans.'

'No,' D'Arrast said, 'I have things to do. This evening, if you wish.'

'Good. But tonight there's dancing and praying in the big hut. It's the feast for Saint George.' D'Arrast asked him if he danced too. The cook's face hardened suddenly; for the first time his eyes became shifty.

'No, no, I won't dance. Tomorrow I must carry the stone. It is heavy. I'll go this evening to celebrate the saint. And then I'll leave early.'

'Does it last long?'

'All night and a little into the morning.'

He looked at D'Arrast with a vaguely shameful look.

'Come to the dance. You can take me home afterwards. Otherwise, I'll stay and dance. I probably won't be able to keep from it.'

'You like to dance?'

'Oh, yes! I like. Besides, there are cigars, saints, women. You forget everything and you don't obey any more.'

'There are women too? All the women of the town?'

'Not of the town, but of the huts.'

The ship's cook resumed his smile. 'Come. The Captain I'll obey. And you will help me keep my promise tomorrow.'

D'Arrast felt slightly annoyed. What did that absurd promise mean to him? But he looked at the handsome frank face smiling trustingly at him, its dark skin gleaming with health and vitality.

'I'll come,' he said. 'Now I'll walk along with you a little.'

Without knowing why, he had a vision at the same time of the black girl offering him the drink of welcome.

They went out of the garden, walked along several muddy streets, and reached the bumpy square, which looked even larger because of the low structures surrounding it. The humidity was now dripping down the plastered walls, although the rain had not increased. Through the spongy expanse of the sky, the sound of the river and of the trees reached them somewhat muted. They were walking in step, D'Arrast heavily and the cook with elastic tread. From time to time the latter would raise his head and smile at his companion. They went in the direction of the church, which could be seen above the houses, reached the end of the square, walked along other muddy streets now filled with aggressive smells of cooking. From time to time a woman, holding a plate or kitchen utensil, would peer out inquisitively from one of the doors and then disappear at once. They passed in front of the church, plunged into an old section of similar low houses, and suddenly came out on the sound of the invisible river behind the area of the huts that D'Arrast recognized.

'Good. I'll leave you. See you this evening,' he said.

'Yes, in front of the church.'

But the cook did not let go of D'Arrast's hand. He hesitated. Finally he made up his mind.

'And you, have you never called out, made a promise?'

'Yes, once, I believe.'

'In a shipwreck?'

'If you wish.' And D'Arrast pulled his hand away roughly. But as he was about to turn on his heels, he met the cook's eyes. He hesitated, and then smiled.

'I can tell you, although it was unimportant. Someone was about to die through my fault. It seems to me that I called out.'

'Did you promise?'

'No. I should have liked to promise.'

'Long ago?'

'Not long before coming here.'

The cook seized his beard with both hands. His eyes were shining.

'You are a captain,' he said. 'My house is yours. Besides, you are going to help me keep my promise, and it's as if you had made it yourself. That will help you too.'

D'Arrast smiled, saying: 'I don't think so.'

'You are proud, Captain.'

'I used to be proud; now I'm alone. But just tell me: has your good Jesus always answered you?'

'Always . . . no, Captain!'

'Well, then?'

The cook burst out with a gay, childlike laugh.

'Well,' he said, 'he's free, isn't he?'

At the club, where D'Arrast lunched with the leading citizens, the Mayor told him he must sign the town's guest-book so that some trace would remain of the great event of his coming to Iguape. The Judge found two or three new expressions to praise, besides their guest's virtues and talents, the simplicity with which he represented among them the great country to which he had the honour to belong. D'Arrast simply said that it was indeed an honour to him and an advantage to his firm to have been awarded the allocation of this long construction job. Whereupon the Judge expressed his admiration for such humility. 'By the way,' he asked, 'have you thought of what should be done to the Chief of Police?' D'Arrast smiled at him and said: 'Yes, I have a solution.' He would consider it a personal favour and an exceptional grace if the foolish man could be forgiven in his name so that his stay here in Iguape, where he so much enjoyed knowing the beautiful town and generous inhabitants, could begin in a climate of peace and friendship. The Judge, attentive and smiling, nodded his head. For a moment he meditated on the wording as an expert, then called on those present to applaud the magnanimous traditions of the great French nation and, turning again towards D'Arrast, declared himself satisfied. 'Since that's the way it is,' he concluded, 'we shall dine this evening with the Chief.' But D'Arrast said that he was invited by friends to the ceremony of the dances in the huts. 'Ah, yes!' said the Judge. 'I am glad you are going. You'll see, one can't resist loving our people.'

* * *

That evening, D'Arrast, the ship's cook, and his brother were seated round the ashes of a fire in the centre of the hut the engineer had already visited in the morning. The brother had not seemed surprised to see him return. He spoke Spanish hardly at all and most of the time merely nodded his head. As for the cook, he had shown interest in cathedrals and then had expatiated at length on the black bean soup. Now night had almost fallen and, although D'Arrast could still see the cook and his brother, he could scarcely make out in the back of the hut the squatting figures of an old woman and of the same girl who had served him. Down below, he could hear the monotonous river.

The cook rose, saying: 'It's time.' They got up, but the women did not stir. The men went out alone. D'Arrast hesitated, then joined the others. Night had now fallen and the rain had stopped. The pale-black sky still seemed liquid. In its transparent dark water, stars began to light up, low on the horizon. Almost at once they flickered out, falling one by one into the river as if the last lights were trickling from the sky. The heavy air smelled of water and smoke. Near by the sound of the huge forest could be heard too, though it was motionless. Suddenly drums and singing broke out in the distance, at first muffled and then distinct, approaching closer and closer and finally stopping. Soon after, one could see a procession of black girls wearing low-waisted white dresses of coarse silk. In a tight-fitting red jacket adorned with a necklace of varicoloured teeth, a tall negro followed them and, behind him, a disorderly crowd of men in white pyjamas and musicians carrying triangles and broad, short drums. The cook said they should follow the men.

The hut, which they reached by following the river a few hundred yards beyond the last huts, was large, empty, and relatively comfortable, with plastered walls. It had a dirt floor, a roof of thatch and reeds supported by a central pole, and bare walls. On a little palm-clad altar at the end, covered with candles that scarcely lighted half the hall, there was a magnificent coloured print in which St George, with alluring grace, was getting the better of a bewhiskered dragon. Under the altar a sort of niche decorated with rococo paper sheltered a little statue of red-painted clay representing a horned god, standing between a candle and a bowl of water. With a fierce look the god was brandishing an oversized knife made of silver paper.

The cook led D'Arrast to a corner, where they stood against the wall near the door. 'This way,' he whispered, 'we can leave without disturbing.' Indeed, the hut was packed tight with men and women. Already the heat was rising. The musicians took their places on both sides of the little altar. The men and women dancers separated into two concentric circles with the men inside. In the very centre the black leader in the red jacket took his stand. D'Arrast leaned against the wall, folding his arms.

But the leader, elbowing his way through the circle of dancers, came towards them and, in a solemn way, said a few words to the cook. 'Unfold your arms, Captain,' the cook said. 'You are hugging yourself and keeping the saint's spirit from descending.' Obediently D'Arrast let his arms fall to his sides. Still leaning against the wall, with his long, heavy limbs and his big face already shiny with sweat, D'Arrast himself looked like some benevolent animal deity. The tall negro looked at them and, satisfied, went back to his place. At once, in a resounding voice, he intoned the opening notes of a song that all picked up in chorus, accompanied by the drums. Then the circles began to turn in opposite directions in a sort of heavy, insistent dance rather like stamping, slightly emphasized by the double line of swaying hips.

The heat had increased. Yet the pauses gradually diminished, the stops became less frequent, and the dance speeded up. Without any slowing of the others' rhythm, without ceasing to dance himself, the tall negro again elbowed his way through the circles to go towards the altar. He came back with a glass of water and a lighted candle that he stuck in the ground in the centre of the hut. He poured the water around the candle in two concentric circles and, again erect, turned maddened eyes towards the roof. His whole body taut and still, he was waiting. 'St George is coming. Look! Look!' whispered the cook, whose eyes were popping.

Indeed, some dancers now showed signs of being in a trance, but a rigid trance with hands on hips, step stiff, eyes staring and vacant. Others quickened their rhythm, bent convulsively backward, and began to utter inarticulate cries. The cries gradually rose higher, and when they fused in a collective shriek, the leader, with eyes still raised, uttered a long, barely phrased outcry at the top of his lungs. In it the same words kept recurring. 'You see,' said the cook, 'he says he is the god's field of battle.' Struck by the change in his voice, D'Arrast looked at the cook, who, leaning forward with fists clenched and eyes staring, was mimicking the others' measured stamping without moving from his place. Then he noticed that he himself, though without moving his feet, had for some little time been dancing with his whole weight.

But all at once the drums began to beat violently and suddenly the big devil in red broke loose. His eyes flashing, his four limbs whirling around him, he hopped with bent knee on one leg after the other, speeding up his rhythm until it seemed that he must eventually fly to pieces. But abruptly he stopped on the verge of one leap to stare at those around him with a proud and terrible look while the drums thundered on. Immediately a dancer sprang from a dark corner, knelt down, and held out a short sabre to the man possessed of the spirit. The tall negro took the sabre without ceasing to look around him and then whirled it above his head. At that moment D'Arrast noticed the cook dancing among the others. The engineer had not seen him leave his side.

In the reddish, uncertain light a stifling dust rose from the ground, making the air even thicker and sticking to one's skin. D'Arrast felt gradually overcome by fatigue and breathed with ever greater difficulty. He did not even see how the dancers had got hold of the huge cigars they were now smoking while still dancing; their strange smell filled the hut and rather made his head swim. He merely saw the cook passing near him, still dancing and puffing at a cigar. 'Don't smoke,' he said. The cook grunted without losing the beat, staring at the central pole with the expression of a boxer about to collapse, his spine constantly twitching in a long shudder. Beside him a heavy negress, rolling her animal face from side to side, kept barking. But the young negresses especially went into the most frightful trance, their feet glued to the floor and their bodies shaken from feet to head by convulsive motions that became more violent upon reaching the shoulders. Their heads would wag backwards and forwards, as though separated from a decapitated body. At the same time all began to howl incessantly with a long collective and toneless howl, apparently not pausing to breathe or to introduce modulations – as if the bodies were tightly knotted, muscles and nerves, in a single exhausting outburst, at last giving voice in each of them to a creature that had until then been absolutely silent. And, still howling, the women began to fall one by one. The black leader knelt by each one and quickly and convulsively pressed her temples with his huge, black-muscled hand. Then they would get up, staggering, return to the dance, and resume their howls, at first feebly and then louder and faster, before falling again, and getting up again, and beginning over again, and for a long time more, until the general howl decreased, changed, and degenerated into a sort of coarse barking which shook them with gasps. D'Arrast, exhausted, his muscles taut from his long dance as he stood still, choked by his own silence, felt himself stagger. The heat, the dust, the smoke of the cigars, the smell of bodies now made the air almost unbreathable. He looked for the cook, who had disappeared. D'Arrast let himself slide down along the wall and squatted, holding back his nausea.

When he opened his eyes, the air was still as stifling but the noise had stopped. The drums alone were beating out a figured bass, and groups in every corner of the hut, covered with whitish cloths, were marking time by stamping. But in the centre of the room, from which the glass and candle had now been removed, a group of black girls in a semi-hypnotic state were dancing slowly, always on the point of letting the beat get ahead of them. Their eyes closed and yet standing erect, they were swaying lightly on their toes, almost in the same spot. Two of them, fat ones, had their faces covered with a curtain of raffia. They surrounded another girl, tall, thin, and wearing a fancy costume. D'Arrast suddenly recognized her as the daughter of his host. In a green dress and a huntress's hat of blue gauze turned up in front and adorned with plumes, she held in her hand a green-and-yellow bow with an arrow on the tip of which was spitted a multicoloured bird. On her slim body her pretty head swayed slowly, tipped backward a little, and her sleeping face reflected an innocent melancholy. At the pauses in the music she staggered as if only half awake. Yet the intensified beat of the drums provided her with a sort of invisible support around which to entwine her languid arabesques until, stopping again together with the music, tottering on the edge of equilibrium, she uttered a strange bird cry, shrill and yet melodious.

D'Arrast, bewitched by the slow dance, was watching the black Diana when the cook suddenly loomed up before him, his smooth face now distorted. The kindness had disappeared from his eyes, revealing nothing but a sort of unsuspected avidity. Coldly, as if speaking to a stranger, he said: 'It's late, Captain. They are going to dance all night long, but they don't want you to stay now.' With head heavy, D'Arrast got up and followed the cook, who went along the wall towards the door. On the threshold the cook stood aside, holding the bamboo door, and D'Arrast went out. He turned back and looked at the cook, who had not moved. 'Come. In a little while you'll have to carry the stone.'

'I'm staying,' the cook said with a set expression.

'And your promise?'

Without replying, the cook gradually pushed against the door that D'Arrast was holding open with one hand. They remained this way for a second until D'Arrast gave in, shrugging his shoulders. He went away.

The night was full of fresh aromatic scents. Above the forest the few stars in the austral sky, blurred by an invisible haze, were shining dimly. The humid air was heavy. Yet it seemed delightfully cool on coming out of the hut. D'Arrast climbed the slippery slope, staggering like a drunken man in the pot-holes. The forest, near-by, rumbled slightly. The sound of the river increased. The whole continent was emerging from the night, and loathing overcame D'Arrast. It seemed to him that he would have liked to spew forth this whole country, the melancholy of its vast expanses, the glaucous light of its forests, and the nocturnal lapping of its big deserted rivers. This land was too vast, blood and seasons mingled here, and time lique-fied. Life here was flush with the soil, and, to identify with it, one had to lie down and sleep for years on the muddy or dried-up ground itself. Yonder, in Europe, there was shame and wrath. Here, exile or solitude, among these listless and con-vulsive madmen who danced to die. But through the humid

479

night, heavy with vegetable scents, the wounded bird's out-
landish cry, uttered by the beautiful sleeping girl, still reached
his ears.

*   *   *

When D'Arrast, his head in the vice of a crushing migraine,
had awakened after a bad sleep, a humid heat was weighing
upon the town and the still forest. He was waiting now under
the hospital portico, looking at his watch, which had stopped,
uncertain of the time, surprised by the broad daylight and the
silence of the town. The almost clear blue sky hung low over
the first dull roofs. Yellowish urubus, transfixed by the heat,
were sleeping on the house across from the hospital. One of
them suddenly fluttered, opened his beak, ostensibly got ready
to fly away, flapped his dusty wings twice against his body, rose
a few inches above the roof, fell back, and went to sleep almost
at once.

The engineer went down towards the town. The main
square was empty, like the streets through which he had just
walked. In the distance, and on both sides of the river, a low
mist hung over the forest. The heat fell vertically, and D'Arrast
looked for a shady spot. At that moment, under the overhang
on one of the houses, he saw a little man gesturing to him. As
he came closer, he recognized Socrates.

'Well, Mr D'Arrast, you like the ceremony?'

D'Arrast said that it was too hot in the hut and that he
preferred the sky and the night air.

'Yes,' Socrates said, 'in your country there's only the Mass.
No one dances.' He rubbed his hands, jumped on one foot,
whirled about, laughed uproariously. 'Not possible, they're
not possible.' Then he looked at D'Arrast inquisitively. 'And
you, are you going to Mass?'

'No.'

'Then, where are you going?'

'Nowhere. I don't know.'

Socrates laughed again. 'Not possible! A noble without a church, without anything!'

D'Arrast laughed likewise. 'Yes, you see, I never found my place. So I left.'

'Stay with us, Mr D'Arrast, I love you.'

'I'd like to, Socrates, but I don't know how to dance.' Their laughter echoed in the silence of the empty town.

'Ah,' Socrates said, 'I forget. The Mayor wants to see you. He is lunching at the club.' And without warning he started off in the direction of the hospital.

'Where are you going?' D'Arrast shouted.

Socrates imitated a snore. 'Sleep. Soon the procession.' And, half running, he resumed his snores.

The Mayor simply wanted to give D'Arrast a place of honour to see the procession. He explained it to the engineer while sharing with him a dish of meat and rice such as would miraculously cure a paralytic. First they would take their places on a balcony of the Judge's house, opposite the church, to see the procession come out. Then they would go to the town hall in the main street leading to the church, which the penitents would take on their way back. The Judge and the Chief of Police would accompany D'Arrast, the Mayor being obliged to take part in the ceremony. The Chief of Police was in fact in the clubroom and kept paying court to D'Arrast with an indefatigable smile, lavishing upon him incomprehensible but obviously well-meaning speeches. When D'Arrast left, the Chief of Police hastened to make a way for him, holding all the doors open before him.

Under the burning sun, in the still empty town, the two men walked towards the Judge's house. Their steps were the only sound heard in the silence. But all of a sudden a firecracker exploded in a neighbouring street and flushed on every roof the heavy, awkward flocks of bald-necked urubus. Almost at once dozens of firecrackers went off in all directions, doors opened, and people began to emerge from the houses and fill the narrow streets.

The Judge told D'Arrast how proud he was to receive him in his unworthy house and led him up a handsome baroque staircase painted chalky-blue. On the landing, as D'Arrast passed, doors opened and children's dark heads popped out and disappeared at once with smothered laughter. The main room, beautiful in architecture, contained nothing but rattan furniture and large cages filled with squawking birds. The balcony on which the Judge and D'Arrast settled overlooked the little square in front of the church. The crowd was now beginning to fill it, strangely silent, motionless under the heat that came down from the sky in almost visible waves. Only the children ran about in the square, stopping abruptly to light firecrackers, and sharp reports followed one another in rapid succession. Seen from the balcony, the church with its plaster walls, its dozen blue steps, its blue-and-gold towers, looked smaller.

Suddenly the organ burst forth within the church. The crowd, turned towards the portico, drew over to the sides of the square. The men took off their hats and the women knelt down. The distant organ played at length something like marches. Then an odd sound of wings came from the forest. A tiny aeroplane with transparent wings and frail fuselage, out of place in this ageless world, came in sight over the trees, swooped a little above the square, and, with the clacking of a big rattle, passed over the heads raised towards it. Then the plane turned and disappeared in the direction of the estuary.

But in the shadow of the church a vague bustle again attracted attention. The organ had stopped, replaced now by brasses and drums, invisible under the portico. Black-surpliced penitents came out of the church one by one, formed groups outside the doors, and began to descend the steps. Behind them came white penitents bearing red-and-blue banners, then a little group of boys dressed up as angels, sodalities of

Children of Mary with little black and serious faces. Finally, on a multicoloured shrine borne by leading citizens sweating in their dark suits, came the effigy of the good Jesus himself, a reed in his hand and his head crowned with thorns, bleeding and tottering above the crowd that lined the steps.

When the shrine reached the bottom of the steps, there was a pause during which the penitents tried to line up in a semblance of order. Then it was that D'Arrast saw the ship's cook. Bare from the waist up, he had just come out under the portico carrying on his bearded head an enormous rectangular block set on a cork mat. With steady tread he came down the church steps, the stone perfectly balanced in the arch formed by his short, muscular arms. As soon as he fell in behind the shrine, the procession moved. From the portico burst the musicians, wearing bright-coloured coats and blowing into beribboned brasses. To the beat of a quick march, the penitents hastened their step and reached one of the streets opening off the square. When the shrine had disappeared behind them, nothing could be seen but the cook and the last of the musicians. Behind them, the crowd got in motion amidst exploding firecrackers, while the plane, with a great rattle of its engine, flew back over the groups trailing behind. D'Arrast was looking exclusively at the cook, who was disappearing into the street now and whose shoulders he suddenly thought he saw sag. But at that distance he couldn't see well.

Through the empty streets, between closed shops and bolted doors, the Judge, the Chief of Police, and D'Arrast reached the town hall. As they got away from the band and the firecrackers, silence again enveloped the town and already a few urubus returned to the places on the roofs that they seemed to have occupied for all time. The town hall stood in a long, narrow street leading from one of the outlying sections to the church square. For the moment, the street was empty. From the balcony could be seen, as far as the eye could reach, nothing but a pavement full of pot-holes, in which the recent rain had left puddles. The sun, now slightly lower, was still nibbling at the windowless façades of the houses across the street.

They waited a long time, so long that D'Arrast, from staring at the reverberation of the sun on the opposite wall, felt his fatigue and dizziness returning. The empty street with its deserted houses attracted and repelled him at one and the same time. Once again he wanted to get away from this country; at the same time he thought of that huge stone; he would have liked that trial to be over. He was about to suggest going down to find out something when the church-bells began to peal forth loudly. Simultaneously, from the other end of the street on their left, a clamour burst out and a seething crowd appeared. From a distance the people could be seen swarming round the shrine, pilgrims and penitents mingled, and they were advancing, amidst firecrackers and shouts of joy, along the narrow street. In a few seconds they filled it to the edges, advancing towards the town hall in an indescribable disorder – ages, races, and costumes fused in a motley mass full of gaping eyes and yelling mouths. From the crowd emerged an army of tapers like lances with flames fading into the burning sunlight. But when they were close and the crowd was so thick under the balcony that it seemed to rise up along the walls, D'Arrast saw that the ship's cook was not there.

Quick as lightning, without excusing himself, he left the balcony and the room, dashed down the staircase, and stood in the street under the deafening sound of the bells and fire-crackers. There he had to struggle against the crowds of merrymakers, the taper-bearers, the shocked penitents. But, bucking the human tide with all his weight, he cut a path in such an impetuous way that he staggered and almost fell when he was eventually free, beyond the crowd, at the end of the street. Leaning against the burning-hot wall, he waited until he had caught his breath. Then he resumed his way. At that moment a group of men emerged into the street. The ones in front were walking backwards, and D'Arrast saw that they surrounded the cook.

He was obviously dead tired. He would stop, then, bent under the huge stone, run a little with the hasty step of stevedores and coolies – the rapid, flat-footed trot of drudgery. Gathered about him, penitents in surplices soiled with dust and candle-drippings encouraged him when he stopped. On his left his brother was walking or running in silence. It seemed to D'Arrast that they took an interminable time to cover the space separating them from him. Having almost reached him, the cook stopped again and glanced around with dull eyes. When he saw D'Arrast – yet without appearing to recognize him – he stood still, turned towards him. An oily, dirty sweat covered his face, which had gone grey; his beard was full of threads of saliva; and a brown, dry froth glued his lips together. He tried to smile. But, motionless under his load, his whole body was trembling except for the shoulders, where the muscles were obviously caught in a sort of cramp. The brother, who had recognized D'Arrast, said to him simply: 'He already fell.' And Socrates, popping up from nowhere, whispered in his ear: 'Dance too much, Mr D'Arrast, all night long. He's tired.'

The cook advanced again with his jerky trot, not like a man who wants to progress but as if he were fleeing the crushing load, as if he hoped to lighten it through motion. Without knowing how, D'Arrast found himself at his right. He laid his hand lightly on the cook's back and walked beside him with hasty, heavy steps. At the other end of the street the shrine had disappeared, and the crowd, which probably now filled the square, did not seem to advance any more. For several seconds, the cook, between his brother and D'Arrast, made progress. Soon a mere space of some twenty yards separated him from the group gathered in front of the town hall to see him pass. Again, however, he stopped. D'Arrast's hand became heavier. 'Come on, cook, just a little more,' he said. The man trembled;

the saliva began to trickle from his mouth again, while the sweat literally spurted from all over his body. He tried to breathe deeply and stopped short. He started off again, took three steps, and tottered. And suddenly the stone slipped on to his shoulder, gashing it, and then forward on to the ground, while the cook, losing his balance, toppled over on his side. Those who were preceding him and urging him on jumped back with loud shouts. One of them seized the cork mat while the others took hold of the stone to load it on him again.

Leaning over him, D'Arrast with his bare hand wiped the blood and dust from his shoulder, while the little man, his face against the ground, panted. He heard nothing and did not stir. His mouth opened avidly as if each breath were his last. D'Arrast grasped him round the waist and raised him up as easily as if he had been a child. Holding him upright in a tight clasp with his full height leaning over him, D'Arrast spoke into his face as if to breathe his own strength into him. After a moment, the cook, bloody and caked with earth, detached himself with a haggard expression on his face. He staggered towards the stone, which the others were raising a little. But he stopped, looked at the stone with a vacant stare, and shook his head. Then he let his arms fall at his sides and turned towards D'Arrast. Huge tears flowed silently down his ravaged face. He wanted to speak, he was speaking, but his mouth hardly formed the syllables. 'I promised,' he was saying. And then: 'Oh, Captain! Oh, Captain!' and the tears drowned his voice. His brother suddenly appeared behind him, threw his arms around him, and the cook, weeping, collapsed against him, defeated, with his head thrown back.

D'Arrast looked at him, not knowing what to say. He turned towards the crowd in the distance, now shouting again. Suddenly he tore the cork mat from the hands holding it and walked towards the stone. He gestured to the others to hold it up and then he loaded it almost effortlessly. His head pressed down under the weight of the stone, his shoulders hunched, and breathing rather hard, he looked down at his feet as he listened to the cook's sobs. Then with vigorous tread he started off on his own, without flagging covered the space separating him from the crowd at the end of the street, and energetically forced his way through the first rows, which stood aside as he approached. In the hubbub of bells and firecrackers he entered the square between two solid masses of onlookers, suddenly silent and gaping at him in amazement. He advanced with the same impetuous pace, and the crowd opened a path for him to the church. Despite the weight which was beginning to crush his head and neck, he saw the church and the shrine, which seemed to be waiting for him at the door. He had already gone beyond the centre of the square in that direction when brutally, without knowing why, he veered off to the left and turned away from the church, forcing the pilgrims to face him. Behind him, he heard someone running. In front of him mouths opened on all sides. He didn't understand what they were shouting, although he seemed to recognize the one Portuguese word that was being constantly hurled at him. Suddenly Socrates appeared before him, rolling startled eyes, speaking incoherently and pointing out the way to the church behind him. 'To the church! To the church!' was what Socrates and the crowd were shouting at him. Yet D'Arrast continued in the direction in which he was launched. And Socrates stood aside, his arms raised in the air comically, while the crowd gradually fell silent. When D'Arrast entered the first street, which he had already taken with the cook and therefore knew it led to the river, the square had become but a confused murmur behind him.

The stone weighed painfully on his head now and he needed all the strength of his long arms to lighten it. His shoulders were already stiffening when he reached the first streets on the slippery slope. He stopped and listened. He was alone. He settled the stone firmly on its cork base and went down with a cautious but still steady tread towards the huts.

When he reached them, his breath was beginning to fail, his arms were trembling under the stone. He hastened his pace, finally reached the little square where the cook's hut stood, ran to it, kicked the door open, and brusquely hurled the stone on to the still glowing fire in the centre of the room. And there, straightening up until he was suddenly enormous, drinking in with desperate gulps the familiar smell of poverty and ashes, he felt rising within him a surge of obscure and panting joy that he was powerless to name.

When the inhabitants of the hut arrived, they found D'Arrast standing with his shoulders against the back wall and eyes closed. In the centre of the room, in the place of the hearth, the stone was half buried in ashes and earth. They stood in the doorway without advancing and looked at D'Arrast in silence as if questioning him. But he didn't speak. Whereupon the brother led the cook up to the stone, where he dropped on the ground. The brother sat down too, beckoning to the others. The old woman joined him, then the girl of the night before, but no one looked at D'Arrast. They were squatting in a silent circle around the stone. No sound but the murmur of the river reached them through the heavy air. Standing in the darkness, D'Arrast listened without seeing anything, and the sound of the waters filled him with a tumultuous happiness. With eyes closed, he joyfully acclaimed his own strength; he acclaimed, once again, a fresh beginning in life. At that moment, a firecracker went off that seemed very close. The brother moved a little away from the cook and, half turning towards D'Arrast but without looking at him, pointed to the empty place and said: 'Sit down with us.'

THE MYTH OF SISYPHUS

TRANSLATED FROM THE FRENCH BY
JUSTIN O'BRIEN

For PASCAL PIA

CONTENTS

O my soul, do not aspire to immortal life,
but exhaust the limits of the possible.

PINDAR, PYTHIAN III

The pages that follow deal with an absurd sensitivity that can be found widespread in the age – and not with an absurd philosophy which our time, properly speaking, has not known. It is therefore simply fair to point out, at the outset, what these pages owe to certain contemporary thinkers. It is so far from my intention to hide this that they will be found cited and commented upon throughout this work.

But it is useful to note at the same time that the absurd, hitherto taken as a conclusion, is considered in this essay as a starting-point. In this sense it may be said that there is something provisional in my commentary: one cannot pre-judge the position it entails. There will be found here merely the description, in the pure state, of an intellectual malady. No metaphysic, no belief is involved in it for the moment. These are the limits and the only bias of this book. Certain personal experiences urge me to make this clear.

AN ABSURD REASONING

Absurdity and Suicide

THERE IS BUT one truly serious philosophical problem, and that is suicide. Judging whether life is or is not worth living amounts to answering the fundamental question of philosophy. All the rest — whether or not the world has three dimensions, whether the mind has nine or twelve categories — comes afterwards. These are games; one must first answer. And if it is true, as Nietzsche claims, that a philosopher, to deserve our respect, must preach by example, you can appreciate the importance of that reply, for it will precede the definitive act. These are facts the heart can feel; yet they call for careful study before they become clear to the intellect.

If I ask myself how to judge that this question is more urgent than that, I reply that one judges by the actions it entails. I have never seen anyone die for the ontological argument. Galileo, who held a scientific truth of great importance, abjured it with the greatest ease as soon as it endangered his life. In a certain sense, he did right.[1] That truth was not worth the stake. Whether the earth or the sun revolves around the other is a matter of profound indifference. To tell the truth, it is a futile question. On the other hand, I see many people die because they judge that life is not worth living. I see others paradoxically getting killed for the ideas or illusions that give them a reason for living (what is called a reason for living is also an excellent reason for dying). I therefore conclude

---

1 From the point of view of the relative value of truth. On the other hand, from the point of view of virile behaviour, this scholar's fragility may well make us smile.

that the meaning of life is the most urgent of questions. How to answer it? On all essential problems (I mean thereby those that run the risk of leading to death or those that intensify the passion of living) there are probably but two methods of thought: the method of La Palisse and the method of Don Quixote. Solely the balance between evidence and lyricism can allow us to achieve simultaneously emotion and lucidity. In a subject at once so humble and so heavy with emotion, the learned and classical dialectic must yield, one can see, to a more modest attitude of mind deriving at one and the same time from common sense and understanding.

Suicide has never been dealt with except as a social phenomenon. On the contrary, we are concerned here, at the outset, with the relationship between individual thought and suicide. An act like this is prepared within the silence of the heart, as is a great work of art. The man himself is ignorant of it. One evening he pulls the trigger or jumps. Of an apartment-building manager who had killed himself I was told that he had lost his daughter five years before, that he had changed greatly since, and that that experience had 'undermined' him. A more exact word cannot be imagined. Beginning to think is beginning to be undermined. Society has but little connection with such beginnings. The worm is in man's heart. That is where it must be sought. One must follow and understand this fatal game that leads from lucidity in the face of existence to flight from light.

There are many causes for a suicide, and generally the most obvious ones were not the most powerful. Rarely is suicide committed (yet the hypothesis is not excluded) through reflection. What sets off the crisis is almost always unverifiable. Newspapers often speak of 'personal sorrows' or of 'incurable illness'. These explanations are plausible. But one would have to know whether a friend of the desperate man had not that very day addressed him indifferently. He is the guilty one. For that is enough to precipitate all the rancours and all the boredom still in suspension.[2]

But if it is hard to fix the precise instant, the subtle step when the mind opted for death, it is easier to deduce from the act itself the consequences it implies. In a sense, and as in melodrama, killing yourself amounts to confessing. It is confessing that life is too much for you or that you do not understand it. Let's not go too far in such analogies, however, but rather return to everyday words. It is merely confessing that that 'is not worth the trouble'. Living, naturally, is never easy. You continue making the gestures commanded by existence for many reasons, the first of which is habit. Dying voluntarily implies that you have recognized, even instinctively, the ridiculous character of that habit, the absence of any profound reason for living, the insane character of that daily agitation, and the uselessness of suffering.

What, then, is that incalculable feeling that deprives the mind of the sleep necessary to life? A world that can be explained even with bad reasons is a familiar world. But, on the other hand, in a universe suddenly divested of illusions and lights, man feels an alien, a stranger. His exile is without remedy since he is deprived of the memory of a lost home or the hope of a promised land. This divorce between man and his life, the actor and his setting, is properly the feeling of absurdity. All healthy men having thought of their own suicide, it can be seen, without further explanation, that there is a direct connection between this feeling and the longing for death.

The subject of this essay is precisely this relationship between the absurd and suicide, the exact degree to which suicide is a solution to the absurd. The principle can be

---

2 Let us not miss this opportunity to point out the relative character of this essay. Suicide may indeed be related to much more honourable considerations – for example, the political suicides of protest, as they were called, during the Chinese revolution.

established that for a man who does not cheat, what he believes to be true must determine his action. Belief in the absurdity of existence must then dictate his conduct. It is legitimate to wonder, clearly and without false pathos, whether a conclusion of this importance requires forsaking as rapidly as possible an incomprehensible condition. I am speaking, of course, of men inclined to be in harmony with themselves.

Stated clearly, this problem may seem both simple and insoluble. But it is wrongly assumed that simple questions involve answers that are no less simple and that evidence implies evidence. *A priori* and reversing the terms of the problem, just as one does or does not kill oneself, it seems that there are but two philosophical solutions, either yes or no. This would be too easy. But allowance must be made for those who, without concluding, continue questioning. Here I am only slightly indulging in irony: this is the majority. I notice also that those who answer 'no' act as if they thought 'yes'. As a matter of fact, if I accept the Nietzschean criterion, they think 'yes' in one way or another. On the other hand, it often happens that those who commit suicide were assured of the meaning of life. These contradictions are constant. It may even be said that they have never been so keen as on this point where, on the contrary, logic seems so desirable. It is a commonplace to compare philosophical theories and the behaviour of those who profess them. But it must be said that of the thinkers who refused a meaning to life none except Kirilov who belongs to literature, Peregrinos who is born of legend,[3] and Jules Lequier who belongs to hypothesis, admitted his logic to the point of refusing that life. Schopenhauer is often cited, as a fit subject for laughter, because he praised suicide while seated at a well-set table. This is no subject for joking.

---

3 I have heard of an emulator of Peregrinos, a post-war writer who, after having finished his first book, committed suicide to attract attention to his work. Attention was in fact attracted, but the book was judged no good.

That way of not taking the tragic seriously is not so grievous, but it helps to judge a man.

In the face of such contradictions and obscurities must we conclude that there is no relationship between the opinion one has about life and the act one commits to leave it? Let us not exaggerate in this direction. In a man's attachment to life there is something stronger than all the ills in the world. The body's judgment is as good as the mind's, and the body shrinks from annihilation. We get into the habit of living before acquiring the habit of thinking. In that race which daily hastens us towards death, the body maintains its irreparable lead. In short, the essence of that contradiction lies in what I shall call the act of eluding because it is both less and more than diversion in the Pascalian sense. Eluding is the invariable game. The typical act of eluding, the fatal evasion that constitutes the third theme of this essay, is hope. Hope of another life one must 'deserve' or trickery of those who live not for life itself but for some great idea that will transcend it, refine it, give it a meaning, and betray it.

Thus everything contributes to spreading confusion. Hitherto, and it has not been wasted effort, people have played on words and pretended to believe that refusing to grant a meaning to life necessarily leads to declaring that it is not worth living. In truth, there is no necessary common measure between these two judgments. One merely has to refuse to be misled by the confusions, divorces, and inconsistencies previously pointed out. One must brush everything aside and go straight to the real problem. One kills oneself because life is not worth living, that is certainly a truth – yet an unfruitful one because it is a truism. But does that insult to existence, that flat denial in which it is plunged come from the fact that it has no meaning? Does its absurdity require one to escape it through hope or suicide – this is what must be clarified, hunted down, and elucidated while brushing aside all the rest. Does the Absurd dictate death? This problem must be given priority over others, outside all methods of thought and all exercises of the disinterested mind. Shades of meaning, contradictions, the psychology that an 'objective' mind can always introduce into all problems have no place in this pursuit and this passion. It calls simply for an unjust – in other words, logical – thought. That is not easy. It is always easy to be logical. It is almost impossible to be logical to the bitter end. Men who die by their own hand consequently follow to its conclusion their emotional inclination. Reflection on suicide gives me an opportunity to raise the only problem to interest me: is there a logic to the point of death? I cannot know unless I pursue, without reckless passion, in the sole light of evidence, the reasoning of which I am here suggesting the source. This is what I call an absurd reasoning. Many have begun it. I do not yet know whether or not they kept to it.

When Karl Jaspers, revealing the impossibility of constituting the world as a unity, exclaims: 'This limitation leads me to myself, where I can no longer withdraw behind an objective point of view that I am merely representing, where neither I myself nor the existence of others can any longer become an object for me,' he is evoking after many others those waterless deserts where thought reaches its confines. After many others, yes indeed, but how eager they were to get out of them! At that last crossroad where thought hesitates, many men have arrived and even some of the humblest. They then abdicated what was most precious to them, their life. Others, princes of the mind, abdicated likewise, but they initiated the suicide of their thought in its purest revolt. The real effort is to stay there, rather, in so far as that is possible, and to examine closely the odd vegetation of those distant regions. Tenacity and acumen are privileged spectators of this inhuman show in which absurdity, hope, and death carry on their dialogue. The mind can then analyse the figures of that elementary yet subtle dance before illustrating them and reliving them itself.

Absurd Walls

LIKE GREAT WORKS, deep feelings always mean more than they are conscious of saying. The regularity of an impulse or a repulsion in a soul is encountered again in habits of doing or thinking, is reproduced in consequences of which the soul itself knows nothing. Great feelings take with them their own universe, splendid or abject. They light up with their passion an exclusive world in which they recognize their climate. There is a universe of jealousy, of ambition, of selfishness, or of generosity. A universe – in other words, a metaphysic and an attitude of mind. What is true of already specialized feelings will be even more so of emotions basically as indeterminate, simultaneously as vague and as 'definite', as remote and as 'present' as those furnished us by beauty or aroused by absurdity.

At any street-corner the feeling of absurdity can strike any man in the face. As it is, in its distressing nudity, in its light without effulgence, it is elusive. But that very difficulty deserves reflection. It is probably true that a man remains for ever unknown to us and that there is in him something irreducible that escapes us. But *practically* I know men and recognize them by their behaviour, by the totality of their deeds, by the consequences caused in life by their presence. Likewise, all those irrational feelings which offer no purchase to analysis. I can define them *practically*, appreciate them *practically*, by gathering together the sum of their consequences in the domain of the intelligence, by seizing and noting all their aspects, by outlining their universe. It is certain that apparently, though I have seen the same actor a hundred times, I shall not for that reason know him any better personally. Yet if I add up the heroes he has personified and if I say that I know him a little better at the hundredth character counted off, this will be felt to contain an element of truth. For this apparent paradox is also an apologue. There is a moral to it. It teaches that a man defines himself by his make-believe as well as by his sincere impulses. There is thus a lower key of feelings, inaccessible in the heart but partially disclosed by the acts they imply and the attitudes of mind they assume. It is clear that in this way I am defining a method. But it is also evident that that method is one of analysis and not of knowledge. For methods imply metaphysics; unconsciously they disclose conclusions that they often claim not to know yet. Similarly, the last pages of a book are already contained in the first pages. Such a link is inevitable. The method defined here acknowledges the feeling that all true knowledge is impossible. Solely appearances can be enumerated and the climate make itself felt.

Perhaps we shall be able to overtake that elusive feeling of absurdity in the different but closely related worlds of intelligence, of the art of living, or of art itself. The climate of absurdity is in the beginning. The end is the absurd universe and that attitude of mind which lights the world with its true colours to bring out the privileged and implacable visage which that attitude has discerned in it.

* * *

All great deeds and all great thoughts have a ridiculous beginning. Great works are often born on a street-corner or in a restaurant's revolving door. So it is with absurdity. The absurd world more than others derives its nobility from that abject birth. In certain situations, replying 'nothing' when asked what one is thinking about may be pretence in a man. Those who are loved are well aware of this. But if that reply is sincere, if it symbolizes that odd state of soul in which the void becomes eloquent, in which the chain of daily gestures is broken, in which the heart vainly seeks the link that will connect it again, then it is as it were the first sign of absurdity.

It happens that the stage sets collapse. Rising, streetcar, four hours in the office or the factory, meal, streetcar, four hours of work, meal, sleep, and Monday Tuesday Wednesday Thursday Friday and Saturday according to the same rhythm – this path is easily followed most of the time. But one day the 'why' arises and everything begins in that weariness tinged with amazement. 'Begins' – this is important. Weariness comes at the end of the acts of a mechanical life, but at the same time it inaugurates the impulse of consciousness. It awakens consciousness and provokes what follows. What follows is the gradual return into the chain or it is the definitive awakening. At the end of the awakening comes, in time, the consequence: suicide or recovery. In itself weariness has something sickening about it. Here, I must conclude that it is good. For everything begins with consciousness and nothing is worth anything except through it. There is nothing original about these remarks. But they are obvious; that is enough for a while, during a sketchy reconnaissance in the origins of the absurd. Mere 'anxiety', as Heidegger says, is at the source of everything.

Likewise and during every day of an unillustrious life, time carries us. But a moment always comes when we have to carry it. We live on the future: 'tomorrow', 'later on', 'when you have made your way', 'you will understand when you are old enough'. Such irrelevancies are wonderful, for, after all, it's a matter of dying. Yet a day comes when a man notices or says that he is thirty. Thus he asserts his youth. But simultaneously he situates himself in relation to time. He takes his place in it. He admits that he stands at a certain point on a curve that he acknowledges having to travel to its end. He belongs to time, and by the horror that seizes him, he recognizes his worst enemy. Tomorrow, he was longing for tomorrow, whereas everything in him ought to reject it. That revolt of the flesh is the absurd.[4]

---

4 But not in the proper sense. This is not a definition, but rather an *enumeration* of the feelings that may admit of the absurd. Still, the enumeration finished, the absurd has nevertheless not been exhausted.

A step lower and strangeness creeps in: perceiving that the world is 'dense', sensing to what a degree a stone is foreign and irreducible to us, with what intensity nature or a landscape can negate us. At the heart of all beauty lies something inhuman, and these hills, the softness of the sky, the outline of these trees at this very minute lose the illusory meaning with which we had clothed them, henceforth more remote than a lost paradise. The primitive hostility of the world rises up to face us across millennia. For a second we cease to understand it because for centuries we have understood in it solely the images and designs that we had attributed to it beforehand, because henceforth we lack the power to make use of that artifice. The world evades us because it becomes itself again. That stage scenery masked by habit becomes again what it is. It withdraws at a distance from us. Just as there are days when under the familiar face of a woman, we see as a stranger her we had loved months or years ago, perhaps we shall come even to desire what suddenly leaves us so alone. But the time has not yet come. Just one thing: that denseness and that strangeness of the world is the absurd.

Men, too, secrete the inhuman. At certain moments of lucidity, the mechanical aspect of their gestures, their meaningless pantomime makes silly everything that surrounds them. A man is talking on the telephone behind a glass partition; you cannot hear him, but you see his incomprehensible dumb show: you wonder why he is alive. This discomfort in the face of man's own inhumanity, this incalculable tumble before the image of what we are, this 'nausea', as a writer of today calls it, is also the absurd. Likewise the stranger who at certain seconds comes to meet us in a mirror, the familiar and yet alarming brother we encounter in our own photographs is also the absurd.

I come at last to death and to the attitude we have towards it. On this point everything has been said and it is only proper to avoid pathos. Yet one will never be sufficiently surprised that everyone lives as if no one 'knew'. This is because in reality there is no experience of death. Properly speaking, nothing has been experienced but what has been lived and made conscious. Here, it is barely possible to speak of the experience of others' deaths. It is a substitute, an illusion, and it never quite convinces us. That melancholy convention cannot be persuasive. The horror comes in reality from the mathematical aspect of the event. If time frightens us, this is because it works out the problem and the solution comes afterwards. All the pretty speeches about the soul will have their contrary convincingly proved, at least for a time. From this inert body on which a slap makes no mark the soul has disappeared. This elementary and definitive aspect of the adventure constitutes the absurd feeling. Under the fatal lighting of that destiny, its uselessness becomes evident. No code of ethics and no effort are justifiable *a priori* in the face of the cruel mathematics that command our condition.

Let me repeat: all this has been said over and over. I am limiting myself here to making a rapid classification and to pointing out these obvious themes. They run through all literatures and all philosophies. Everyday conversation feeds on them. There is no question of reinventing them. But it is essential to be sure of these facts in order to be able to question oneself subsequently on the primordial question. I am interested – let me repeat again – not so much in absurd discoveries as in their consequences. If one is assured of these facts, what is one to conclude, how far is one to go to elude nothing? Is one to die voluntarily or to hope in spite of everything? Beforehand, it is necessary to take the same rapid inventory on the plane of the intelligence.

* * *

The mind's first step is to distinguish what is true from what is false. However, as soon as thought reflects on itself, what it first discovers is a contradiction. Useless to strive to be convincing in this case. Over the centuries no one has furnished a clearer and more elegant demonstration of the business than Aristotle: 'The often ridiculed consequence of these opinions is that they destroy themselves. For by asserting that all is true we assert the truth of the contrary assertion and consequently the falsity of our own thesis (for the contrary assertion does not admit that it can be true). And if one says that all is false, that assertion is itself false. If we declare that solely the assertion opposed to ours is false or else that solely ours is not false, we are nevertheless forced to admit an infinite number of true or false judgments. For the one who expresses a true assertion proclaims simultaneously that it is true, and so on *ad infinitum.*'

This vicious circle is but the first of a series in which the mind that studies itself gets lost in a giddy whirling. The very simplicity of these paradoxes makes them irreducible. Whatever may be the plays on words and the acrobatics of logic, to understand is, above all, to unify. The mind's deepest desire, even in its most elaborate operations, parallels man's unconscious feeling in the face of his universe: it is an insistence upon familiarity, an appetite for clarity. Understanding the world for a man is reducing it to the human, stamping it with his seal. The cat's universe is not the universe of the anthill. The truism 'All thought is anthropomorphic' has no other meaning. Likewise, the mind that aims to understand reality can consider itself satisfied only by reducing it to terms of thought. If man realized that the universe like him can love and suffer, he would be reconciled. If thought discovered in the shimmering mirrors of phenomena eternal relations capable of summing them up and summing themselves up in a single principle, then would be seen an intellectual joy of which the myth of the blessed would be but a ridiculous imitation. That nostalgia for unity, that appetite for the absolute illustrates the essential impulse of the human drama. But the fact of that nostalgia's existence does not imply that it is to be immediately satisfied.

For if, bridging the gulf that separates desire from conquest, we assert with Parmenides the reality of the One (whatever it may be), we fall into the ridiculous contradiction of a mind that asserts total unity and proves by its very assertion its own difference and the diversity it claimed to resolve. This other vicious circle is enough to stifle our hopes.

These are again truisms. I shall again repeat that they are not interesting in themselves but in the consequences that can be deduced from them. I know another truism: it tells me that man is mortal. One can nevertheless count the minds that have deduced the extreme conclusions from it. It is essential to consider as a constant point of reference in this essay the regular hiatus between what we fancy we know and what we really know, practical assent and simulated ignorance which allows us to live with ideas which, if we truly put them to the test, ought to upset our whole life. Faced with this inextricable contradiction of the mind, we shall fully grasp the divorce separating us from our own creations. So long as the mind keeps silent in the motionless world of its hopes, everything is reflected and arranged in the unity of its nostalgia. But with its first move this world cracks and tumbles: an infinite number of shimmering fragments is offered to the understanding. We must despair of ever reconstructing the familiar, calm surface which would give us peace of heart. After so many centuries of inquiries, so many abdications among thinkers, we are well aware that this is true for all our knowledge. With the exception of professional rationalists, today people despair of true knowledge. If the only significant history of human thought were to be written, it would have to be the history of its successive regrets and its impotences.

Of whom and of what indeed can I say: 'I know that!' This heart within me I can feel, and I judge that it exists. This world I can touch, and I likewise judge that it exists. There ends all my knowledge, and the rest is construction. For if I try to seize this self of which I feel sure, if I try to define and to summarize it, it is nothing but water slipping through my fingers. I can sketch one by one all the aspects it is able to assume, all those likewise that have been attributed to it, this upbringing, this origin, this ardour or these silences, this nobility or this vileness. But aspects cannot be added up. This very heart which is mine will for ever remain indefinable to me. Between the certainty I have of my existence and the content I try to give to that assurance, the gap will never be filled. For ever I shall be a stranger to myself. In psychology as in logic, there are truths but no truth. Socrates' 'Know thyself' has as much value as the 'Be virtuous' of our confessionals. They reveal a nostalgia at the same time as an ignorance. They are sterile exercises on great subjects. They are legitimate only in precisely so far as they are approximate.

And here are trees and I know their gnarled surface, water and I feel its taste. These scents of grass and stars at night, certain evenings when the heart relaxes – how shall I negate this world whose power and strength I feel? Yet all the knowledge on earth will give me nothing to assure me that this world is mine. You describe it to me and you teach me to classify it. You enumerate its laws and in my thirst for knowledge I admit that they are true. You take apart its mechanism and my hope increases. At the final stage you teach me that this wondrous and multicoloured universe can be reduced to the atom and that the atom itself can be reduced to the electron. All this is good and I wait for you to continue. But you tell me of an invisible planetary system in which electrons gravitate around a nucleus. You explain this world to me with an image. I realize then that you have been reduced to poetry: I shall never know. Have I the time to become indignant? You have already changed theories. So that science that was to teach me everything ends up in a hypothesis, that lucidity founders in metaphor, that uncertainty is resolved in a work of art. What need had I of so many efforts? The soft lines of these hills and the hand of evening on this troubled heart teach me much more. I have returned to my beginning. I realize that if through science I can seize phenomena and enumerate them, I cannot, for all that, apprehend the world. Were I to trace its entire relief with my finger, I should not know any more. And you give me the choice between a description that is sure but that teaches me nothing and hypotheses that claim to teach me but that are not sure. A stranger to myself and to the world, armed solely with a thought that negates itself as soon as it asserts, what is this condition in which I can have peace only by refusing to know and to live, in which the appetite for conquest bumps into walls that defy its assaults? To will is to stir up paradoxes. Everything is ordered in such a way as to bring into being that poisoned peace produced by thoughtlessness, lack of heart, or fatal renunciations.

Hence the intelligence, too, tells me in its way that this world is absurd. Its contrary, blind reason, may well claim that all is clear; I was waiting for proof and longing for it to be right. But despite so many pretentious centuries and over the heads of so many eloquent and persuasive men, I know that is false. On this plane, at least, there is no happiness if I cannot know. That universal reason, practical or ethical, that determinism, those categories that explain everything are enough to make a decent man laugh. They have nothing to do with the mind. They negate its profound truth, which is to be enchained. In this unintelligible and limited universe, man's fate henceforth assumes its meaning. A horde of irrationals has sprung up and surrounds him until his ultimate end. In this recovered and now studied lucidity, the feeling of the absurd becomes clear and definite. I said that the world is absurd, but I was too hasty. This world in itself is not reasonable, that is all that can be said. But what is absurd is the confrontation of this irrational and the wild longing for clarity whose call echoes in the human heart. The absurd depends as much on man as on the world. For the moment it is all that links them together. It binds them one to the other as only hatred can weld two creatures together. This is all I can discern clearly in this measureless universe where my adventure takes place. Let us pause here. If I hold to be true that absurdity that determines my relationship with life, if I become thoroughly imbued with that sentiment that seizes me in face of the world's scenes, with that lucidity imposed on me by the pursuit of a science, I must sacrifice everything to these certainties and I must see them squarely to be able to maintain them. Above all, I must adapt my behaviour to them and pursue them in all their consequences. I am speaking here of decency. But I want to know beforehand if thought can live in those deserts.

* * *

I already know that thought has at least entered those deserts. There it found its bread. There it realized that it had previously been feeding on phantoms. It justified some of the most urgent themes of human reflection.

From the moment absurdity is recognized, it becomes a passion, the most harrowing of all. But whether or not one can live with one's passions, whether or not one can accept their law, which is to burn the heart they simultaneously exalt – that is the whole question. It is not, however, the one we shall ask just yet. It stands at the centre of this experience. There will be time to come back to it. Let us recognize rather those themes and those impulses born of the desert. It will suffice to enumerate them. They, too, are known to all today. There have always been men to defend the rights of the irrational. The tradition of what may be called humiliated thought has never ceased to exist. The criticism of rationalism has been made so often that it seems unnecessary to begin again. Yet our epoch is marked by the rebirth of those paradoxical systems that strive to trip up the reason as if truly it had always forged ahead. But that is not so much a proof of the efficacy of the reason as of the intensity of its hopes. On the plane of history, such a constancy of two attitudes illustrates the essential passion of man torn between his urge towards unity and the clear vision he may have of the walls enclosing him.

But never perhaps at any time has the attack on reason been more violent than in ours. Since Zarathustra's great outburst: 'By chance it is the oldest nobility in the world. I conferred it upon all things when I proclaimed that above them no eternal will was exercised,' since Kierkegaard's fatal illness, 'that malady that leads to death with nothing else following it', the significant and tormenting themes of absurd thought have followed one another. Or at least, and this proviso is of capital importance, the themes of irrational and religious thought. From Jaspers to Heidegger, from Kierkegaard to Chestov, from the phenomenologists to Scheler, on the logical plane and on the moral plane, a whole family of minds related by their nostalgia but opposed by their methods or their aims, have persisted in blocking the royal road of reason and in recovering the direct paths of truth. Here I assume these thoughts to be known and lived. Whatever may be or have been their ambitions, all started out from that indescribable universe where contradiction, antinomy, anguish, or impotence reigns. And what they have in common is precisely the themes so far disclosed. For them, too, it must be said that what matters above all is the conclusions they have managed to draw from those discoveries. That matters so much that they must be examined separately. But for the moment we are concerned solely with their discoveries and their initial experiments. We are concerned solely with noting their agreement. If it would be presumptuous to try to deal with their philosophies, it is possible and sufficient in any case to bring out the climate that is common to them.

Heidegger considers the human condition coldly and announces that that existence is humiliated. The only reality is 'anxiety' in the whole chain of beings. To the man lost in the world and its diversions this anxiety is a brief, fleeting fear. But if that fear becomes conscious of itself, it becomes anguish, the perpetual climate of the lucid man 'in whom existence is concentrated'. This professor of philosophy writes without trembling and in the most abstract language in the world that 'the finite and limited character of human existence is more primordial than man himself'. His interest in Kant extends only to recognizing the restricted character of his 'pure Reason'. This is to conclude at the end of his analyses that 'the world can no longer offer anything to the man filled with anguish'. This anxiety seems to him so much more important than all the categories in the world that he thinks and talks only of it. He enumerates its aspects: boredom when the ordinary man strives to quash it in him and benumb it; terror when the mind contemplates death. He too does not separate consciousness from the absurd. The consciousness of death is the call of anxiety and 'existence then delivers itself its own summons through the intermediary of consciousness'. It is the very voice of anguish and it adjures existence 'to return from its loss in the anonymous They'. For him, too, one must not sleep, but must keep alert until the consummation. He stands in this absurd world and points out its ephemeral character. He seeks his way amid these ruins.

Jaspers despairs of any ontology because he claims that we have lost 'naïveté'. He knows that we can achieve nothing that will transcend the fatal game of appearances. He knows that the end of the mind is failure. He tarries over the spiritual adventures revealed by history and pitilessly discloses the flaw in each system, the illusion that saved everything, the preaching that hid nothing. In this ravaged world in which the impossibility of knowledge is established, in which everlasting nothingness seems the only reality and irremediable despair seems the only attitude, he tries to recover the Ariadne's thread that leads to divine secrets.

Chestov, for his part, throughout a wonderfully monotonous work, constantly straining towards the same truths,

tirelessly demonstrates that the tightest system, the most universal rationalism always stumbles eventually on the irrational
of human thought. None of the ironic facts or ridiculous
contradictions that depreciate the reason escapes him. One
thing only interests him, and that is the exception, whether
in the domain of the heart or of the mind. Through the
Dostoevskian experiences of the condemned man, the exacerbated adventures of the Nietzschean mind, Hamlet's imprecations, or the bitter aristocracy of an Ibsen, he tracks down,
illuminates, and magnifies the human revolt against the irremediable. He refuses the reason its reasons and begins to
advance with some decision only in the middle of that
colourless desert where all certainties have become stones.

Of all perhaps the most engaging, Kierkegaard, for a part of
his existence at least, does more than discover the absurd, he
lives it. The man who writes: 'The surest of stubborn silences is
not to hold one's tongue but to talk' makes sure in the beginning that no truth is absolute or can render satisfactory an
existence that is impossible in itself. Don Juan of the understanding, he multiplies pseudonyms and contradictions, writes
his *Discourses of Edification* at the same time as that manual of
cynical spiritualism, *The Diary of the Seducer*. He refuses consolations, ethics, reliable principles. As for that thorn he feels in
his heart, he is careful not to quiet its pain. On the contrary, he
awakens it and, in the desperate joy of a man crucified and
happy to be so, he builds up piece by piece – lucidity, refusal,
make-believe – a category of the man possessed. That face both
tender and sneering, those pirouettes followed by a cry from
the heart are the absurd spirit itself grappling with a reality
beyond its comprehension. And the spiritual adventure that
leads Kierkegaard to his beloved scandals begins likewise in the
chaos of an experience divested of its setting and relegated to its
original incoherence.

On quite a different plane, that of method, Husserl and
the phenomenologists, by their very extravagances, reinstate

the world in its diversity and deny the transcendent power of the reason. The spiritual universe becomes incalculably enriched through them. The rose petal, the milestone, or the human hand are as important as love, desire, or the laws of gravity. Thinking ceases to be unifying or making a semblance familiar in the guise of a major principle. Thinking is learning all over again to see, to be attentive, to focus consciousness; it is turning every idea and every image, in the manner of Proust, into a privileged moment. What justifies thought is its extreme consciousness. Though more positive than Kierkegaard's or Chestov's, Husserl's manner of proceeding, in the beginning, nevertheless negates the classic method of the reason, disappoints hope, opens to intuition and to the heart a whole proliferation of phenomena, the wealth of which has about it something inhuman. These paths lead to all sciences or to none. This amounts to saying that in this case the means are more important than the end. All that is involved is 'an attitude for understanding' and not a consolation. Let me repeat: in the beginning, at very least.

How can one fail to feel the basic relationship of these minds! How can one fail to see that they take their stand around a privileged and bitter moment in which hope has no further place? I want everything to be explained to me or nothing. And the reason is impotent when it hears this cry from the heart. The mind aroused by this insistence seeks and finds nothing but contradictions and nonsense. What I fail to understand is nonsense. The world is peopled with such irrationals. The world itself, whose single meaning I do not understand, is but a vast irrational. If one could only say just once: 'This is clear,' all would be saved. But these men vie with one another in proclaiming that nothing is clear, all is chaos, that all man has is his lucidity and his definite knowledge of the walls surrounding him.

All these experiences agree and confirm one another. The mind, when it reaches its limits, must make a judgment and choose its conclusions. This is where suicide and the reply stand. But I wish to reverse the order of the inquiry and start out from the intelligent adventure and come back to daily acts. The experiences called to mind here were born in the desert that we must not leave behind. At least it is essential to know how far they went. At this point of his effort man stands face to face with the irrational. He feels within him his longing for happiness and for reason. The absurd is born of this confrontation between the human need and the unreasonable silence of the world. This must not be forgotten. This must be clung to because the whole consequence of a life can depend on it. The irrational, the human nostalgia, and the absurd that is born of their encounter – these are the three characters in the drama that must necessarily end with all the logic of which an existence is capable.

Philosophical Suicide

THE FEELING OF the absurd is not, for all that, the notion of the absurd. It lays the foundations for it, and that is all. It is not limited to that notion, except in the brief moment when it passes judgment on the universe. Subsequently it has a chance of going further. It is alive; in other words, it must die or else reverberate. So it is with the themes we have gathered together. But there again what interests me is not works or minds, criticism of which would call for another form and another place, but the discovery of what their conclusions have in common. Never, perhaps, have minds been so different. And yet we recognize as identical the spiritual landscapes in which they get under way. Likewise, despite such dissimilar zones of knowledge, the cry that terminates their itinerary rings out in the same way. It is evident that the thinkers we have just recalled have a common climate. To say that that climate is deadly scarcely amounts to playing on words. Living under that stifling sky forces one to get away or to stay. The important thing is to find out how people get away in the first case and why people stay in the second case. This is how I define the problem of suicide and the possible interest in the conclusions of existential philosophy.

But first I want to detour from the direct path. Up to now we have managed to circumscribe the absurd from the outside. One can, however, wonder how much is clear in that notion and by direct analysis try to discover its meaning on the one hand and, on the other, the consequences it involves.

If I accuse an innocent man of a monstrous crime, if I tell a virtuous man that he has coveted his own sister, he will reply that this is absurd. His indignation has its comical aspect. But it also has its fundamental reason. The virtuous man illustrates by that reply the definitive antinomy existing between the deed I am attributing to him and his lifelong principles. 'It's absurd' means 'It's impossible' but also 'It's contradictory'. If I see a man armed only with a sword attack a group of machine guns, I shall consider his act to be absurd. But it is so solely by virtue of the disproportion between his intention and the reality he will encounter, of the contradiction I notice between his true strength and the aim he has in view. Likewise we shall deem a verdict absurd when we contrast it with the verdict the facts apparently dictated. And, similarly, a demonstration by the absurd is achieved by comparing the consequences of such a reasoning with the logical reality one wants to set up. In all these cases, from the simplest to the most complex, the magnitude of the absurdity will be in direct ratio to the distance between the two terms of my comparison. There are absurd marriages, challenges, rancours, silences, wars, and even peace treaties. For each of them the absurdity springs from a comparison. I am thus justified in saying that the feeling of absurdity does not spring from the mere scrutiny of a fact or an impression, but that it bursts from the comparison between a bare fact and a certain reality, between an action and the world that transcends it. The absurd is essentially a divorce. It lies in neither of the elements compared; it is born of their confrontation.

In this particular case and on the plane of intelligence, I can therefore say that the Absurd is not in man (if such a metaphor could have a meaning) nor in the world, but in their presence together. For the moment it is the only bond uniting them. If I wish to limit myself to facts, I know what man wants, I know what the world offers him, and now I can say that I also know what links them. I have no need to dig deeper. A single certainty is enough for the seeker. He simply has to derive all the consequences from it.

The immediate consequence is also a rule of method. The odd trinity brought to light in this way is certainly not a startling discovery. But it resembles the data of experience in that it is both infinitely simple and infinitely complicated. Its first distinguishing feature in this regard is that it cannot be divided. To destroy one of its terms is to destroy the whole. There can be no absurd outside the human mind. Thus, like everything else, the absurd ends with death. But there can be no absurd outside this world either. And it is by this elementary criterion that I judge the notion of the absurd to be essential and consider that it can stand as the first of my truths. The rule of method alluded to above appears here. If I judge that a thing is true, I must preserve it. If I attempt to solve a problem, at least I must not by that very solution conjure away one of the terms of the problem. For me the sole datum is the absurd. The first and, after all, the only condition of my inquiry is to preserve the very thing that crushes me, consequently to respect what I consider essential in it. I have just defined it as a confrontation and an unceasing struggle.

And carrying this absurd logic to its conclusion, I must admit that that struggle implies a total absence of hope (which has nothing to do with despair), a continual rejection (which must not be confused with renunciation), and a conscious dissatisfaction (which must not be compared to immature unrest). Everything that destroys, conjures away, or exorcises these requirements (and, to begin with, consent which overthrows divorce) ruins the absurd and devaluates the attitude that may then be proposed. The absurd has meaning only in so far as it is not agreed to.

* * *

There exists an obvious fact that seems utterly moral: namely, that a man is always a prey to his truths. Once he has admitted them, he cannot free himself from them. One has to pay something. A man who has become conscious of the absurd is for ever bound to it. A man devoid of hope and conscious of being so has ceased to belong to the future. That is natural. But it is just as natural that he should strive to escape the universe of which he is the creator. All the foregoing has significance only on account of this paradox. Certain men, starting from a critique of rationalism, have admitted the absurd climate. Nothing is more instructive in this regard than to scrutinize the way in which they have elaborated their consequences.

Now, to limit myself to existential philosophies, I see that all of them without exception suggest escape. Through an odd reasoning, starting out from the absurd over the ruins of reason, in a closed universe limited to the human, they deify what crushes them and find reason to hope in what impoverishes them. That forced hope is religious in all of them. It deserves attention.

I shall merely analyse here as examples a few themes dear to Chestov and Kierkegaard. But Jaspers will provide us, in caricatural form, a typical example of this attitude. As a result the rest will be clearer. He is left powerless to realize the transcendent, incapable of plumbing the depth of experience, and conscious of that universe upset by failure. Will he advance or at least draw the conclusions from that failure? He contributes nothing new. He has found nothing in experience but the confession of his own impotence and no occasion to infer any satisfactory principle. Yet without justification, as he says to himself, he suddenly asserts all at once the transcendent, the essence of experience, and the superhuman significance of life when he writes: 'Does not the failure reveal, beyond any possible explanation and interpretation, not the absence but the existence of transcendence?' That existence which, suddenly and through a blind act of human confidence, explains everything, he defines as 'the unthinkable unity of the general and the particular'. Thus the absurd becomes god (in the broadest meaning of this word) and that inability to understand becomes the existence that illuminates everything. Nothing logically prepares this reasoning. I can call it a leap. And paradoxically can be understood Jaspers's insistence, his infinite patience devoted to making the experience of the transcendent impossible to realize. For the more fleeting that approximation is, the more empty that definition proves to be, and the more real that transcendent is to him; for the passion he devotes to asserting it is in direct proportion to the gap between his powers of explanation and the irrationality of the world and of experience. It thus appears that the more bitterly Jaspers destroys the reason's preconceptions, the more radically he will explain the world. That apostle of humiliated thought will find at the very end of humiliation the means of regenerating being to its very depth.

Mystical thought has familiarized us with such devices. They are just as legitimate as any attitude of mind. But for the moment I am acting as if I took a certain problem seriously. Without judging beforehand the general value of this attitude or its educative power, I mean simply to consider whether it answers the conditions I set myself, whether it is worthy of the conflict that concerns me. Thus I return to Chestov. A commentator relates a remark of his that deserves interest: 'The only true solution,' he said, 'is precisely where human judgment sees no solution. Otherwise, what need would we have of God? We turn towards God only to obtain the impossible. As for the possible, men suffice.' If there is a Chestovian philosophy, I can say that it is altogether summed up in this way. For when, at the conclusion of his passionate analyses, Chestov discovers the fundamental absurdity of all existence, he does not say: 'This is the absurd,' but rather: 'This is God: we must rely on him even if he does not correspond to any of our rational categories.' So that confusion may not be possible, the Russian philosopher even hints that this God is perhaps full of hatred and hateful, incomprehensible and con-tradictory; but the more hideous is his face, the more he asserts his power. His greatness is his incoherence. His proof is his inhumanity. One must spring into him and by this leap free oneself from rational illusions. Thus, for Chestov acceptance of the absurd is contemporaneous with the absurd itself. Being aware of it amounts to accepting it, and the whole logical effort of his thought is to bring it out so that at the same time the tremendous hope it involves may burst forth. Let me repeat that this attitude is legitimate. But I am persisting here in considering a single problem and all its consequences. I do not have to examine the emotion of a thought or of an act of faith. I have a whole lifetime to do that. I know that the rationalist finds Chestov's attitude annoying. But I also feel that Chestov is right rather than the rationalist, and I merely want to know if he remains faithful to the commandments of the absurd.

Now, if it is admitted that the absurd is the contrary of hope, it is seen that existential thought for Chestov presupposes the absurd but proves it only to dispel it. Such subtlety of thought is a conjuror's emotional trick. When Chestov elsewhere sets his absurd in opposition to current morality and reason, he calls it truth and redemption. Hence, there is basically in that definition of the absurd an approbation that Chestov grants it. If it is admitted that all the power of that notion lies in the way it runs counter to our elementary hopes, if it is felt that to remain, the absurd requires not to be consented to, then it can be clearly seen that it has lost its true aspect, its human and relative character in order to enter an eternity that is both incomprehensible and satisfying. If there is an absurd, it is in man's universe. The moment the notion transforms itself into eternity's springboard, it ceases to be linked to human lucidity. The absurd is no longer that evidence that man ascertains without consenting to it. The struggle is eluded. Man integrates the absurd and in that communion causes to disappear its essential character, which is opposition, laceration, and divorce. This leap is an escape. Chestov, who is so fond of quoting Hamlet's remark: 'The time is out of joint,' writes it down with a sort of savage hope that seems to belong to him in particular. For it is not in this sense that Hamlet says it or Shakespeare writes it. The intoxication of the irrational and the vocation of rapture turn a lucid mind away from the absurd. To Chestov reason is useless but there is something beyond reason. To an absurd mind reason is useless and there is nothing beyond reason.

This leap can at least enlighten us a little more as to the true nature of the absurd. We know that it is worthless except in an equilibrium, that it is, above all, in the comparison and not in the terms of that comparison. But it so happens that Chestov puts all the emphasis on one of the terms and destroys the equilibrium. Our appetite for understanding, our nostalgia for the absolute are explicable only in so far, precisely, as we can understand and explain many things. It is useless to negate the reason absolutely. It has its order in which it is efficacious. It is properly that of human experience. Whence we wanted to make everything clear. If we cannot do so, if the absurd is born on that occasion, it is born precisely at the very meeting-point of that efficacious but limited reason with the ever resurgent irrational. Now, when Chestov rises up against a Hegelian proposition such as 'the motion of the solar system takes place in conformity with immutable laws and those laws are its reason', when he devotes all his passion to upsetting Spinoza's rationalism, he concludes, in effect, in favour of the vanity of all reason. Whence, by a natural and illegitimate reversal, to the pre-eminence of the irrational.[5] But the transition is not evident. For here may intervene the notion of limit and the notion of level. The laws of nature may be operative up to a certain limit, beyond which they turn against themselves to give birth to the absurd. Or else, they may justify themselves on the level of description without for that reason being true on the level of explanation. Everything is sacrificed here to the irrational, and, the demand for clarity being conjured away, the absurd disappears with one of the terms of its comparison. The absurd man, on the other hand, does not undertake such a levelling process. He recognizes the struggle, does not absolutely scorn reason, and admits the irrational. Thus he again embraces in a single glance all the data of experience and he is little inclined to leap before knowing. He knows simply that in that alert awareness there is no further place for hope.

What is perceptible in Leo Chestov will be perhaps even more so in Kierkegaard. To be sure, it is hard to outline clear propositions in so elusive a writer. But, despite apparently opposed writings, beyond the pseudonyms, the tricks, and the smiles, can be felt throughout that work, as it were, the presentiment (at the same time as the apprehension) of a truth which eventually bursts forth in the last works: Kierkegaard likewise takes the leap. His childhood having been so frightened by Christianity, he ultimately returns to its harshest aspect. For him, too, antinomy and paradox become criteria of the religious. Thus, the very thing that led to despair of the

---

5 Apropos of the notion of exception particularly and against Aristotle.

meaning and depth of this life now gives it its truth and its clarity. Christianity is the scandal, and what Kierkegaard calls for quite plainly is the third sacrifice required by Ignatius Loyola, the one in which God most rejoices: 'The sacrifice of the intellect.'[6] This effect of the 'leap' is odd, but must not surprise us any longer. He makes of the absurd the criterion of the other world, whereas it is simply a residue of the experience of this world. 'In his failure,' says Kierkegaard, 'the believer finds his triumph.'

It is not for me to wonder to what stirring preaching this attitude is linked. I merely have to wonder if the spectacle of the absurd and its own character justifies it. On this point, I know that it is not so. Upon considering again the content of the absurd, one understands better the method that inspired Kierkegaard. Between the irrational of the world and the insurgent nostalgia of the absurd, he does not maintain the equilibrium. He does not respect the relationship that constitutes, properly speaking, the feeling of absurdity. Sure of being unable to escape the irrational, he wants at least to save himself from that desperate nostalgia that seems to him sterile and devoid of implication. But if he may be right on this point in his judgment, he could not be in his negation. If he substitutes for his cry of revolt a frantic adherence, at once he is led to blind himself to the absurd which hitherto enlightened him and to deify the only certainty he henceforth possesses, the irrational. The important thing, as Abbé Galiani said to Mme d'Epinay, is not to be cured, but to live with one's ailments. Kierkegaard wants to be cured. To be cured is his frenzied wish, and it runs throughout his whole journal. The entire effort of

---

6 It may be thought that I am neglecting here the essential problem, that of faith. But I am not examining the philosophy of Kierkegaard or of Chestov or, later on, of Husserl (this would call for a different place and a different attitude of mind); I am simply borrowing a theme from them and examining whether its consequences can fit the already established rules. It is merely a matter of persistence.

his intelligence is to escape the antinomy of the human condition. An all the more desperate effort since he intermittently perceives its vanity when he speaks of himself, as if neither fear of God nor piety were capable of bringing him to peace. Thus it is that, through a strained subterfuge, he gives the irrational the appearance and God the attributes of the absurd: unjust, incoherent, and incomprehensible. Intelligence alone in him strives to stifle the underlying demands of the human heart. Since nothing is proved, everything can be proved.

Indeed, Kierkegaard himself shows us the path taken. I do not want to suggest anything here, but how can one fail to read in his works the signs of an almost intentional mutilation of the soul to balance the mutilation accepted in regard to the absurd? It is the leitmotiv of the *Journal*. 'What I lacked was the animal which *also* belongs to human destiny. . . . But give me a body then.' And further on: 'Oh! especially in my early youth what should I not have given to be a man, even for six months . . . what I lack, basically, is a body and the physical conditions of existence.' Elsewhere, the same man nevertheless adopts the great cry of hope that has come down through so many centuries and quickened so many hearts, except that of the absurd man. 'But for the Christian death is certainly not the end of everything and it implies infinitely more hope than life implies for us, even when that life is overflowing with health and vigour.' Reconciliation through scandal is still reconciliation. It allows one perhaps, as can be seen, to derive hope of its contrary, which is death. But even if fellow-feeling inclines one towards that attitude, still it must be said that excess justifies nothing. That transcends, as the saying goes, the human scale; therefore it must be superhuman. But this 'therefore' is superfluous. There is no logical certainty here. There is no experimental probability either. All I can say is that, in fact, that transcends my scale. If I do not draw a negation from it, at least I do not want to found anything on the incomprehensible. I want to know whether I can live with what I know and with that alone. I am told again that here the intelligence must sacrifice its pride and the reason bow down. But if I recognize the limits of the reason, I do not therefore negate it, recognizing its relative powers. I merely want to remain in this middle path where the intelligence can remain clear. If that is its pride, I see no sufficient reason for giving it up. Nothing more profound, for example, than Kierkegaard's view according to which despair is not a fact but a state: the very state of sin. For sin is what alienates from God. The absurd, which is the metaphysical state of the conscious man, does not lead to God.[7] Perhaps this notion will become clearer if I risk this shocking statement: the absurd is sin without God.

It is a matter of living in that state of the absurd. I know on what it is founded, this mind and this world straining against each other without being able to embrace each other. I ask for the rule of life of that state, and what I am offered neglects its basis, negates one of the terms of the painful opposition, demands of me a resignation. I ask what is involved in the condition I recognize as mine; I know it implies obscurity and ignorance; and I am assured that this ignorance explains everything and that this darkness is my light. But there is no reply here to my intent, and this stirring lyricism cannot hide the paradox from me. One must therefore turn away. Kierkegaard may shout in warning: 'If man had no eternal consciousness, if, at the bottom of everything, there were merely a wild, seething force producing everything, both large and trifling, in the storm of dark passions, if the bottomless void that nothing can fill underlay all things, what would life be but despair?' This cry is not likely to stop the absurd man. Seeking what is true is not seeking what is desirable. If in order to elude the anxious question: 'What would life be?' one must, like the donkey, feed on the roses of illusion, then the absurd mind, rather than resigning itself to falsehood, prefers to

7 I did not say 'excludes God', which would still amount to asserting.

adopt fearlessly Kierkegaard's reply: 'despair'. Everything considered, a determined soul will always manage.

* * *

I am taking the liberty at this point of calling the existential attitude philosophical suicide. But this does not imply a judgment. It is a convenient way of indicating the movement by which a thought negates itself and tends to transcend itself in its very negation. For the existentials negation is their God. To be precise, that god is maintained only through the negation of human reason.[8] But, like suicides, gods change with men. There are many ways of leaping, the essential being to leap. Those redeeming negations, those ultimate contradictions which negate the obstacle that has not yet been leaped over, may spring just as well (this is the paradox at which this reasoning aims) from a certain religious inspiration as from the rational order. They always lay claim to the eternal, and it is solely in this that they take the leap.

It must be repeated that the reasoning developed in this essay leaves out altogether the most widespread spiritual attitude of our enlightened age: the one, based on the principle that all is reason, which aims to explain the world. It is natural to give a clear view of the world after accepting the idea that it must be clear. That is even legitimate, but does not concern the reasoning we are following out here. In fact, our aim is to shed light upon the step taken by the mind when, starting from a philosophy of the world's lack of meaning, it ends up by finding a meaning and depth in it. The most touching of those steps is religious in essence; it becomes obvious in the theme of the irrational. But the most paradoxical and most significant is certainly the one that attributes rational reasons to

8 Let me assert again: it is not the affirmation of God that is questioned here, but rather the logic leading to that affirmation.

a world it originally imagined as devoid of any guiding principle. It is impossible in any case to reach the consequences that concern us without having given an idea of this new attainment of the spirit of nostalgia.

I shall examine merely the theme of 'the Intention' made fashionable by Husserl and the phenomenologists. I have already alluded to it. Originally Husserl's method negates the classic procedure of the reason. Let me repeat. Thinking is not unifying or making the appearance familiar under the guise of a great principle. Thinking is learning all over again how to see, directing one's consciousness, making of every image a privileged place. In other words, phenomenology declines to explain the world, it wants to be merely a description of actual experience. It confirms absurd thought in its initial assertion that there is no truth, but merely truths. From the evening breeze to this hand on my shoulder, everything has its truth. Consciousness illuminates it by paying attention to it. Consciousness does not form the object of its understanding, it merely focuses, it is the act of attention, and, to borrow a Bergsonian image, it resembles the projector that suddenly focuses on an image. The difference is that there is no scenario, but a successive and incoherent illustration. In that magic lantern all the pictures are privileged. Consciousness suspends in experience the objects of its attention. Through its miracle it isolates them. Henceforth they are beyond all judgments. This is the 'intention' that characterizes consciousness. But the word does not imply any idea of finality; it is taken in its sense of 'direction': its only value is topographical.

At first sight, it certainly seems that in this way nothing contradicts the absurd spirit. That apparent modesty of thought that limits itself to describing what it declines to explain, that intentional discipline whence result paradoxically a profound enrichment of experience and the rebirth of the world in its prolixity are absurd procedures. At least at first sight. For methods of thought, in this case as elsewhere, always assume two aspects, one psychological and the other metaphysical.[9] Thereby they harbour two truths. If the theme of the intentional claims to illustrate merely a psychological attitude, by which reality is drained instead of being explained, nothing in fact separates it from the absurd spirit. It aims to enumerate what it cannot transcend. It affirms solely that without any unifying principle thought can still take delight in describing and understanding every aspect of experience. The truth involved then for each of those aspects is psychological in nature. It simply testifies to the 'interest' that reality can offer. It is a way of awaking a sleeping world and of making it vivid to the mind. But if one attempts to extend and give a rational basis to that notion of truth, if one claims to discover in this way the 'essence' of each object of knowledge, one restores its depth to experience. For an absurd mind that is incomprehensible. Now, it is this wavering between modesty and assurance that is noticeable in the intentional attitude, and this shimmering of phenomenological thought will illustrate the absurd reasoning better than anything else.

For Husserl speaks likewise of 'extra-temporal essences' brought to light by the intention, and he sounds like Plato. All things are not explained by one thing but by all things. I see no difference. To be sure, those ideas or those essences that consciousness 'effectuates' at the end of every description are not yet to be considered perfect models. But it is asserted that they are directly present in each datum of perception. There is no longer a single idea explaining everything, but an infinite number of essences giving a meaning to an infinite number of essences giving a meaning to an infinite number of objects. The world comes to a stop, but also lights up. Platonic realism becomes intuitive, but it is still realism. Kierkegaard was swallowed up in his God; Parmenides plunged thought into the

---

9 Even the most rigorous epistemologies imply metaphysics. And to such a degree that the metaphysic of many contemporary thinkers consists in having nothing but an epistemology.

One. But here thought hurls itself into an abstract polytheism. But this is not all: hallucinations and fictions likewise belong to 'extra-temporal essences'. In the new world of ideas, the species of centaurs collaborates with the more modest species of metropolitan man.

For the absurd man, there was a truth as well as a bitterness in that purely psychological opinion that all aspects of the world are privileged. To say that everything is privileged is tantamount to saying that everything is equivalent. But the metaphysical aspect of that truth is so far-reaching that through an elementary reaction he feels closer perhaps to Plato. He is taught, in fact, that every image presupposes an equally privileged essence. In this ideal world without hierarchy, the formal army is composed solely of generals. To be sure, transcendency had been eliminated. But a sudden shift in thought brings back into the world a sort of fragmentary immanence which restores to the universe its depth.

Am I to fear having carried too far a theme handled with greater circumspection by its creators? I read merely these assertions of Husserl, apparently paradoxical yet rigorously logical if what precedes is accepted: 'That which is true is true absolutely, in itself; truth is one, identical with itself, however different the creatures who perceive it, men, monsters, angels or gods.' Reason triumphs and trumpets forth with that voice, I cannot deny. What can its assertions mean in the absurd world? The perception of an angel or a god has no meaning for me. That geometrical spot where divine reason ratifies mine will always be incomprehensible to me. There, too, I discern a leap, and though performed in the abstract, it none the less means for me forgetting just what I do not want to forget. When farther on Husserl exclaims: 'If all masses subject to attraction were to disappear, the law of attraction would not be destroyed but would simply remain without any possible application,' I know that I am faced with a metaphysic of consolation. And if I want to discover the point where thought leaves the path of evidence, I have only to reread the parallel reasoning that Husserl voices regarding the mind: 'If we could contemplate clearly the exact laws of psychic processes, they would be seen to be likewise eternal and invariable, like the basic laws of theoretical natural science. Hence they would be valid even if there were no psychic process.' Even if the mind were not, its laws would be! I see then that of a psychological truth Husserl aims to make a rational rule: after having denied the integrating power of human reason, he leaps by this expedient to eternal Reason.

Husserl's theme of the 'concrete universe' cannot then surprise me. If I am told that all essences are not formal but that some are material, that the first are the object of logic and the second of science, this is merely a question of definition. The abstract, I am told, indicates but a part, without consistency in itself, of a concrete universal. But the wavering already noted allows me to throw light on the confusion of these terms. For that may mean that the concrete object of my attention, this sky, the reflection of that water on this coat, alone preserve the prestige of the real that my interest isolates in the world. And I shall not deny it. But that may mean also that this coat itself is universal, has its particular and sufficient essence, belongs to the world of forms. I then realize that merely the order of the procession has been changed. This world has ceased to have its reflection in a higher universe, but the heaven of forms is figured in the host of images of this earth. This changes nothing for me. Rather than encountering here a taste for the concrete, the meaning of the human condition, I find an intellectualism sufficiently unbridled to generalize the concrete itself.

* * *

It is futile to be amazed by the apparent paradox that leads thought to its own negation by the opposite paths of humiliated reason and triumphal reason. From the abstract god of Husserl to the dazzling god of Kierkegaard the distance is not so great. Reason and the irrational lead to the same preaching. In truth the way matters but little; the will to arrive suffices. The abstract philosopher and the religious philosopher start out from the same disorder and support each other in the same anxiety. But the essential is to explain. Nostalgia is stronger here than knowledge. It is significant that the thought of the epoch is at once one of the most deeply imbued with a philosophy of the non-significance of the world and one of the most divided in its conclusions. It is constantly oscillating between extreme rationalization of reality which tends to break up that thought into standard reasons and its extreme irrationalization which tends to deify it. But this divorce is only apparent. It is a matter of reconciliation, and, in both cases, the leap suffices. It is always wrongly thought that the notion of reason is a one-way notion. To tell the truth, however rigorous it may be in its ambition, this concept is none the less just as unstable as others. Reason bears a quite human aspect, but it also is able to turn towards the divine. Since Plotinus, who was the first to reconcile it with the eternal climate, it has learned to turn away from the most cherished of its principles, which is contradiction, in order to integrate into it the strangest, the quite magic one of participation.[10] It is an instrument of thought and not thought itself. Above all, a man's thought is his nostalgia.

Just as reason was able to soothe the melancholy of Plotinus, it provides modern anguish the means of calming itself in the familiar setting of the eternal. The absurd mind has less luck. For it the world is neither so rational nor so irrational. It is

10 A. – At that time reason had to adapt itself or die. It adapts itself. With Plotinus, after being logical it becomes æsthetic. Metaphor takes the place of the syllogism.

B. – Moreover, this is not Plotinus' only contribution to phenomenology. This whole attitude is already contained in the concept so dear to the Alexandrian thinker that there is not only an idea of man but also an idea of Socrates.

unreasonable and only that. With Husserl the reason eventually has no limits at all. The absurd, on the contrary, establishes its limits since it is powerless to calm its anguish. Kierkegaard independently asserts that a single limit is enough to negate that anguish. But the absurd does not go so far. For it that limit is directed solely at the reason's ambitions. The theme of the irrational, as it is conceived by the existentials, is reason becoming confused and escaping by negating itself. The absurd is lucid reason noting its limits.

Only at the end of this difficult path does the absurd man recognize his true motives. Upon comparing his inner exigence and what is then offered him, he suddenly feels he is going to turn away. In the universe of Husserl the world becomes clear and that longing for familiarity that man's heart harbours becomes useless. In Kierkegaard's apocalypse that desire for clarity must be given up if it wants to be satisfied. Sin is not so much knowing (if it were, everybody would be innocent) as wanting to know. Indeed, it is the only sin of which the absurd man can feel that it constitutes both his guilt and his innocence. He is offered a solution in which all the past contradictions have become merely polemical games. But this is not the way he experienced them. Their truth must be preserved, which consists in not being satisfied. He does not want preaching.

My reasoning wants to be faithful to the evidence that aroused it. That evidence is the absurd. It is that divorce between the mind that desires and the world that disappoints, my nostalgia for unity, this fragmented universe and the contradiction that binds them together. Kierkegaard suppresses my nostalgia and Husserl gathers together that universe. That is not what I was expecting. It was a matter of living and thinking with those dislocations, of knowing whether one had to accept or refuse. There can be no question of masking the evidence, of suppressing the absurd by denying one of the terms of its equation. It is essential to know whether one can live with it or whether, on the other hand, logic commands one to die of it. I am not interested in philosophical suicide, but rather in plain suicide. I merely wish to purge it of its emotional content and know its logic and its integrity. Any other position implies for the absurd mind deceit and the mind's retreat before what the mind itself has brought to light. Husserl claims to obey the desire to escape 'the inveterate habit of living and thinking in certain well-known and convenient conditions of existence', but the final leap restores in him the eternal and its comfort. The leap does not represent an extreme danger as Kierkegaard would like it to do. The danger, on the contrary, lies in the subtle instant that precedes the leap. Being able to remain on that dizzying crest – that is integrity and the rest is subterfuge. I know also that never has helplessness inspired such striking harmonies as those of Kierkegaard. But if helplessness has its place in the indifferent landscapes of history, it has none in a reasoning whose exigence is now known.

Absurd Freedom

NOW THE MAIN thing is done, I hold certain facts from which I cannot separate. What I know, what is certain, what I cannot deny, what I cannot reject – this is what counts. I can negate everything of that part of me that lives on vague nostalgias, except this desire for unity, this longing to solve, this need for clarity and cohesion. I can refute everything in this world surrounding me that offends or enraptures me, except this chaos, this sovereign chance and this divine equivalence which springs from anarchy. I don't know whether this world has a meaning that transcends it. But I know that I do not know that meaning and that it is impossible for me just now to know it. What can a meaning outside my condition mean to me? I can understand only in human terms. What

I touch, what resists me – that is what I understand. And these two certainties – my appetite for the absolute and for unity and the impossibility of reducing this world to a rational and reasonable principle – I also know that I cannot reconcile them. What other truth can I admit without lying, without bringing in a hope I lack and which means nothing within the limits of my condition?

If I were a tree among trees, a cat among animals, this life would have a meaning, or rather this problem would not arise, for I should belong to this world. I should *be* this world to which I am now opposed by my whole consciousness and my whole insistence upon familiarity. This ridiculous reason is what sets me in opposition to all creation. I cannot cross it out with a stroke of the pen. What I believe to be true I must therefore preserve. What seems to me so obvious, even against me, I must support. And what constitutes the basis of that conflict, of that break between the world and my mind, but the awareness of it? If therefore I want to preserve it, I can through a constant awareness, ever revived, ever alert. This is what, for the moment, I must remember. At this moment the absurd, so obvious and yet so hard to win, returns to a man's life and finds its home there. At this moment, too, the mind can leave the arid, dried-up path of lucid effort. That path now emerges in daily life. It encounters the world of the anonymous impersonal pronoun 'one', but henceforth man enters in with his revolt and his lucidity. He has forgotten how to hope. This hell of the present is his Kingdom at last. All problems recover their sharp edge. Abstract evidence retreats before the poetry of forms and colours. Spiritual conflicts become embodied and return to the abject and magnificent shelter of man's heart. None of them is settled. But all are transfigured. Is one going to die, escape by the leap, rebuild a mansion of ideas and forms to one's own scale? Is one, on the contrary, going to take up the heart-rending and marvellous wager of the absurd? Let's make a final effort in this regard and draw all our conclusions. The body, affection, creation, action, human nobility will then resume their places in this mad world. At last man will again find there the wine of the absurd and the bread of indifference on which he feeds his greatness.

Let us insist again on the method: it is a matter of persisting. At a certain point on his path the absurd man is tempted. History is not lacking in either religions or prophets, even without gods. He is asked to leap. All he can reply is that he doesn't fully understand, that it is not obvious. Indeed, he does not want to do anything but what he fully understands. He is assured that this is the sin of pride, but he does not understand the notion of sin; that perhaps hell is in store, but he has not enough imagination to visualize that strange future; that he is losing immortal life, but that seems to him an idle consideration. An attempt is made to get him to admit his guilt. He feels innocent. To tell the truth, that is all he feels – his irreparable innocence. This is what allows him everything. Hence, what he demands of himself is to live *solely* with what he knows, to accommodate himself to what is, and to bring in nothing that is not certain. He is told that nothing is. But this at least is a certainty. And it is with this that he is concerned: he wants to find out if it is possible to live *without appeal*.

* * *

Now I can broach the notion of suicide. It has already been felt what solution might be given. At this point the problem is reversed. It was previously a question of finding out whether or not life had to have a meaning to be lived. It now becomes clear, on the contrary, that it will be lived all the better if it has no meaning. Living an experience, a particular fate, is accepting it fully. Now, no one will live this fate, knowing it to be absurd, unless he does everything to keep before him that absurd brought to light by consciousness. Negating one of the terms of the opposition on which he lives amounts to escaping it. To abolish conscious revolt is to elude the problem. The theme of permanent revolution is thus carried into individual experience. Living is keeping the absurd alive. Keeping it alive is, above all, contemplating it. Unlike Eurydice, the absurd dies only when we turn away from it. One of the only coherent philosophical positions is thus revolt. It is a constant confrontation between man and his own obscurity. It is an insistence upon an impossible transparency. It challenges the world anew every second. Just as danger provided man the unique opportunity of seizing awareness, so metaphysical revolt extends awareness to the whole of experience. It is that constant presence of man in his own eyes. It is not aspiration, for it is devoid of hope. That revolt is the certainty of a crushing fate, without the resignation that ought to accompany it.

This is where it is seen to what a degree absurd experience is remote from suicide. It may be thought that suicide follows revolt – but wrongly. For it does not represent the logical outcome of revolt. It is just the contrary by the consent it presupposes. Suicide, like the leap, is acceptance at its extreme. Everything is over and man returns to his essential history. His future, his unique and dreadful future – he sees and rushes towards it. In its way, suicide settles the absurd. It engulfs the absurd in the same death. But I know that in order to keep alive, the absurd cannot be settled. It escapes suicide to the extent that it is simultaneously awareness and rejection of death. It is, at the extreme limit of the condemned man's last thought, that shoelace that despite everything he sees a few yards away, on the very brink of his dizzying fall. The contrary of suicide, in fact, is the man condemned to death.

That revolt gives life its value. Spread out over the whole length of a life, it restores its majesty to that life. To a man devoid of blinkers, there is no finer sight than that of the intelligence at grips with a reality that transcends it. The sight of human pride is unequalled. No disparagement is of any use. That discipline that the mind imposes on itself, that will conjured up out of nothing, that face-to-face struggle have something exceptional about them. To impoverish that reality whose inhumanity constitutes man's majesty is tantamount to impoverishing him himself. I understand then why the doctrines that explain everything to me also debilitate me at the same time. They relieve me of the weight of my own life, and yet I must carry it alone. At this juncture, I cannot conceive that a sceptical metaphysics can be joined to an ethics of renunciation.

Consciousness and revolt, these rejections are the contrary of renunciation. Everything that is indomitable and passionate in a human heart quickens them, on the contrary, with its own life. It is essential to die unreconciled and not of one's own free will. Suicide is a repudiation. The absurd man can only drain everything to the bitter end, and deplete himself. The absurd is his extreme tension, which he maintains constantly by solitary effort, for he knows that in that consciousness and in that day-to-day revolt he gives proof of his only truth, which is defiance. This is a first consequence.

* * *

If I remain in that prearranged position which consists in drawing all the conclusions (and nothing else) involved in a newly discovered notion, I am faced with a second paradox. In order to remain faithful to that method, I have nothing to do with the problem of metaphysical liberty. Knowing whether or not man is free doesn't interest me. I can experience only my own freedom. As to it, I can have no general notions, but merely a few clear insights. The problem of 'freedom as such' has no meaning. For it is linked in quite a different way with the problem of God. Knowing whether or not man is free involves knowing whether he can have a master. The absurdity peculiar to this problem comes from the fact that the very notion that makes the problem of freedom possible also takes away all its meaning. For in the presence of God there is less a problem of freedom than a problem of evil. You know the alternative: either we are not free and God the all-powerful is responsible for evil. Or we are free and responsible but God is not all-powerful. All the scholastic subtleties have neither added anything to nor subtracted anything from the acuteness of this paradox.

This is why I cannot get lost in the glorification or the mere definition of a notion which eludes me and loses its meaning as soon as it goes beyond the frame of reference of my individual experience. I cannot understand what kind of freedom would be given me by a higher being. I have lost the sense of hierarchy. The only conception of freedom I can have is that of the prisoner or the individual in the midst of the State. The only one I know is freedom of thought and action. Now if the absurd cancels all my chances of eternal freedom, it restores and magnifies, on the other hand, my freedom of action. That privation of hope and future means an increase in man's availability.

Before encountering the absurd, the everyday man lives with aims, a concern for the future or for justification (with regard to whom or what is not the question). He weighs his chances, he counts on 'someday', his retirement or the labour of his sons. He still thinks that something in his life can be directed. In truth, he acts as if he were free, even if all the facts make a point of contradicting that liberty. But after the absurd, everything is upset. That idea that 'I am', my way of acting as if everything has a meaning (even if, on occasion, I said that nothing has) – all that is given the lie in vertiginous fashion by the absurdity of a possible death. Thinking of the future, establishing aims for oneself, having preferences – all this presupposes a belief in freedom, even if one occasionally ascertains that one doesn't feel it. But at that moment I am well aware that that higher liberty, that freedom *to be*, which alone can serve as basis for a truth, does not exist. Death is there as the only reality. After death the chips are down. I am not even free, either, to perpetuate myself, but a slave, and, above all, a slave without hope of an eternal revolution, without recourse to contempt. And who without revolution and without contempt can remain a slave? What freedom can exist in the fullest sense without assurance of eternity?

But at the same time the absurd man realizes that hitherto he was bound to that postulate of freedom on the illusion of which he was living. In a certain sense, that hampered him. To the extent to which he imagined a purpose to his life, he adapted himself to the demands of a purpose to be achieved and became the slave of his liberty. Thus I could not act otherwise than as the father (or the engineer or the leader of a nation, or the post-office sub-clerk) that I am preparing to be. I think I can choose to be that rather than something else. I think so unconsciously, to be sure. But at the same time I strengthen my postulate with the beliefs of those around me, with the presumptions of my human environment (others are so sure of being free, and that cheerful mood is so contagious!). However far one may remain from any presumption, moral or social, one is partly influenced by them and even, for the best among them (there are good and bad presumptions), one adapts one's life to them. Thus the absurd man realizes that he was not really free. To speak clearly, to the extent to which I hope, to which I worry about a truth that might be individual to me, about a way of being or creating, to the extent to which I arrange my life and prove thereby that I accept its having a meaning, I create for myself barriers between which I confine my life. I do like so many bureaucrats of the mind and heart who only fill me with disgust and whose only vice, I now see clearly, is to take man's freedom seriously.

The absurd enlightens me on this point: there is no future. Henceforth this is the reason for my inner freedom. I shall use two comparisons here. Mystics, to begin with, find freedom in giving themselves. By losing themselves in their god, by accepting his rules, they become secretly free. In spontaneously accepted slavery they recover a deeper independence. But what does that freedom mean? It may be said, above all, that they *feel* free with regard to themselves, and not so much free as liberated. Likewise, completely turned towards death (taken here as the most obvious absurdity), the absurd man feels released from everything outside that passionate attention crystallizing in him. He enjoys a freedom with regard to common rules. It can be seen at this point that the initial themes of existential philosophy keep their entire value. The return to consciousness, the escape from everyday sleep represent the first steps of absurd freedom. But it is existential *preaching* that is alluded to, and with it that spiritual leap which basically escapes consciousness. In the same way (this is my second comparison) the slaves of antiquity did not belong to themselves. But they knew that freedom which consists in not feeling responsible.[11] Death, too, has patrician hands which, while crushing, also liberate.

Losing oneself in that bottomless certainty, feeling henceforth sufficiently remote from one's own life to increase it and take a broad view of it – this involves the principle of a liberation. Such new independence has a definite time limit, like any freedom of action. It does not write a cheque on eternity. But it takes the place of the illusions of *freedom*, which all stopped with death. The divine availability of the condemned man before whom the prison doors open in a certain early dawn, that unbelievable disinterestedness with regard to everything except for the pure flame of life – it is clear that death and the absurd are here the principles of the only reasonable freedom: that which a human heart can experience and live. This is a second consequence. The absurd man thus catches sight of a burning and frigid, transparent and

---

11 I am concerned here with a factual comparison, not with an apology of humility. The absurd man is the contrary of the reconciled man.

limited universe in which nothing is possible but everything is given, and beyond which all is collapse and nothingness. He can then decide to accept such a universe and draw from it his strength, his refusal to hope, and the unyielding evidence of a life without consolation.

* * *

But what does life mean in such a universe? Nothing else for the moment but indifference to the future and a desire to use up everything that is given. Belief in the meaning of life always implies a scale of values, a choice, our preferences. Belief in the absurd, according to our definitions, teaches the contrary. But this is worth examining.

Knowing whether or not one can live *without appeal* is all that interests me. I do not want to get out of my depth. This aspect of life being given me, can I adapt myself to it? Now, faced with this particular concern, belief in the absurd is tantamount to substituting the quantity of experiences for the quality. If I convince myself that this life has no other aspect than that of the absurd, if I feel that its whole equilibrium depends on that perpetual opposition between my conscious revolt and the darkness in which it struggles, if I admit that my freedom has no meaning except in relation to its limited fate, then I must say that what counts is not the best living but the most living. It is not up to me to wonder if this is vulgar or revolting, elegant or deplorable. Once and for all, value judgments are discarded here in favour of factual judgments. I have merely to draw the conclusions from what I can see and to risk nothing that is hypothetical. Supposing that living in this way were not honourable, then true propriety would command me to be dishonourable.

The most living; in the broadest sense, that rule means nothing. It calls for definition. It seems to begin with the fact that the notion of quantity has not been sufficiently explored.

For it can account for a large share of human experience. A man's rule of conduct and his scale of values have no meaning except through the quantity and variety of experiences he has been in a position to accumulate. Now, the conditions of modern life impose on the majority of men the same quantity of experiences and consequently the same profound experience. To be sure, there must also be taken into consideration the individual's spontaneous contribution, the 'given' element in him. But I cannot judge of that, and let me repeat that my rule here is to get along with the immediate evidence. I see, then, that the individual character of a common code of ethics lies not so much in the ideal importance of its basic principles as in the norm of an experience that it is possible to measure. To stretch a point somewhat, the Greeks had the code of their leisure just as we have the code of our eight-hour day. But already many men among the most tragic cause us to foresee that a longer experience changes this table of values. They make us imagine that adventurer of the everyday who through mere quantity of experiences would break all records (I am purposely using this sports expression) and would thus win his own code of ethics.[12] Yet let's avoid romanticism and just ask ourselves what such an attitude may mean to a man with his mind made up to take up his bet and to observe strictly what he takes to be the rules of the game.

Breaking all the records is first and foremost being faced with the world as often as possible. How can that be done without contradictions and without playing on words? For on the one hand the absurd teaches that all experiences are unimportant, and on the other it urges towards the greatest quantity of experiences. How, then, can one fail to do as so many of those men I was speaking of earlier – choose the form of life

---

12 Quantity sometimes constitutes quality. If I can believe the latest restatements of scientific theory, all matter is constituted by centres of energy. Their greater or lesser quantity makes its specificity more or less remarkable. A billion ions and one ion differ not only in quantity but also in quality. It is easy to find an analogy in human experience.

that brings us the most possible of that human matter, thereby introducing a scale of values that on the other hand one claims to reject?

But again it is the absurd and its contradictory life that teaches us. For the mistake is thinking that that quantity of experiences depends on the circumstances of our life when it depends solely on us. Here we have to be over-simple. To two men living the same number of years, the world always provides the same sum of experiences. It is up to us to be conscious of them. Being aware of one's life, one's revolt, one's freedom, and to the maximum, is living, and to the maximum. Where lucidity dominates, the scale of values becomes useless. Let's be even more simple. Let us say that the sole obstacle, the sole deficiency to be made good, is constituted by premature death. Thus it is that no depth, no emotion, no passion, and no sacrifice could render equal in the eyes of the absurd man (even if he wished it so) a conscious life of forty years and a lucidity spread over sixty years.[13] Madness and death are his irreparables. Man does not choose. The absurd and the extra life it involves *therefore do not depend on man's will*, but on its contrary, which is death.[14] Weighing words carefully, it is altogether a question of luck. One just has to be able to consent to this. There will never be any substitute for twenty years of life and experience.

By what is an odd inconsistency in such an alert race, the Greeks claimed that those who died young were beloved of the gods. And that is true only if you are willing to believe that entering the ridiculous world of the gods is for ever losing the purest of joys, which is feeling, and feeling on this earth.

13 Same reflection on a notion as different as the idea of eternal nothingness. It neither adds anything to nor subtracts anything from reality. In psychological experience of nothingness, it is by the consideration of what will happen in two thousand years that our own nothingness truly takes on meaning. In one of its aspects, eternal nothingness is made up precisely of the sum of lives to come which will not be ours.

14 The will is only the agent here: it tends to maintain consciousness. It provides a discipline of life, and that is appreciable.

The present and the succession of presents before a constantly conscious soul is the ideal of the absurd man. But the word 'ideal' rings false in this connection. It is not even his vocation, but merely the third consequence of his reasoning. Having started from an anguished awareness of the inhuman, the meditation on the absurd returns at the end of its itinerary to the very heart of the passionate flames of human revolt.[15]

* * *

Thus I draw from the absurd three consequences, which are my revolt, my freedom, and my passion. By the mere activity of consciousness I transform into a rule of life what was an invitation to death – and I refuse suicide. I know, to be sure, the dull resonance that vibrates throughout these days. Yet I have but a word to say: that it is necessary. When Nietzsche writes: 'It clearly seems that the chief thing in heaven and on earth is to *obey* at length and in a single direction: in the long run there results something for which it is worth the trouble of living on this earth as, for example, virtue, art, music, the dance, reason, the mind – something that transfigures, something delicate, mad, or divine,' he elucidates the rule of a really distinguished code of ethics. But he also points the way of the absurd man. Obeying the flame is both the easiest and the hardest thing to do. However, it is good for man to judge himself occasionally. He is alone in being able to do so.

'Prayer,' says Alain, 'is when night descends over thought.' 'But the mind must meet the night,' reply the mystics and the existentials. Yes, indeed, but not that night that is born under

15 What matters is coherence. We start out here from acceptance of the world. But Oriental thought teaches that one can indulge in the same effort of logic by choosing *against* the world. That is just as legitimate and gives this essay its perspectives and its limits. But when the negation of the world is pursued just as rigorously, one often achieves (in certain Vedantic schools) similar results regarding, for instance, the indifference of works. In a book of great importance, *Le Choix*, Jean Grenier establishes in this way a veritable 'philosophy of indifference'.

closed eyelids and through the mere will of man – dark, impenetrable night that the mind calls up in order to plunge into it. If it must encounter a night, let it be rather that of despair, which remains lucid – polar night, vigil of the mind, whence will arise perhaps that white and virginal brightness which outlines every object in the light of the intelligence. At that degree, equivalence encounters passionate understanding. Then it is no longer even a question of judging the existential leap. It resumes its place amid the age-old fresco of human attitudes. For the spectator, if he is conscious, that leap is still absurd. In so far as it thinks it solves the paradox, it reinstates it intact. On this score, it is stirring. On this score, everything resumes its place and the absurd world is reborn in all its splendour and diversity.

But it is bad to stop, hard to be satisfied with a single way of seeing, to go without contradiction, perhaps the most subtle of all spiritual forces. The preceding merely defines a way of thinking. But the point is to live.

THE ABSURD MAN

If Stavrogin believes, he does not think he believes. If he does not believe, he does not think he does not believe.

— *The Possessed*

'MY FIELD,' SAID Goethe, 'is time.' That is indeed the absurd speech. What, in fact, is the absurd man? He who, without negating it, does nothing for the eternal. Not that nostalgia is foreign to him. But he prefers his courage and his reasoning. The first teaches him to live *without appeal* and to get along with what he has; the second informs him of his limits. Assured of his temporally limited freedom, of his revolt devoid of future, and of his mortal consciousness, he lives out his adventure within the span of his lifetime. That is his field, that is his action, which he shields from any judgment but his own. A greater life cannot mean for him another life. That would be unfair. I am not even speaking here of that paltry eternity that is called posterity. Mme Roland relied on herself. That rashness was taught a lesson. Posterity is glad to quote her remark, but forgets to judge it. Mme Roland is indifferent to posterity.

There can be no question of holding forth on ethics. I have seen people behave badly with great morality and I note every day that integrity has no need of rules. There is but one moral code that the absurd man can accept, the one that is not separated from God: the one that is dictated. But it so happens that he lives outside that God. As for the others (I mean also immoralism), the absurd man sees nothing in them but justifications and he has nothing to justify. I start out here from the principle of his innocence.

That innocence is to be feared. 'Everything is permitted,' exclaims Ivan Karamazov. That, too, smacks of the absurd. But on condition that it not be taken in the vulgar sense. I don't know whether or not it has been sufficiently pointed out that it is not an outburst of relief or of joy, but rather a bitter acknowledgement of a fact. The certainty of a God giving a meaning to life far surpasses in attractiveness the ability to behave badly with impunity. The choice would not be hard to make. But there is no choice, and that is where the bitterness comes in. The absurd does not liberate; it binds. It does not authorize all actions. 'Everything is permitted' does not mean that nothing is forbidden. The absurd merely confers an equivalence on the consequences of those actions. It does not recommend crime, for this would be childish, but it restores to remorse its futility. Likewise, if all experiences are indifferent, that of duty is as legitimate as any other. One can be virtuous through a whim.

All systems of morality are based on the idea that an action has consequences that legitimize or cancel it. A mind imbued with the absurd merely judges that those consequences must be considered calmly. It is ready to pay up. In other words, there may be responsible persons, but there are no guilty ones, in its opinion. At very most, such a mind will consent to use past experience as a basis for its future actions. Time will prolong time, and life will serve life. In this field that is both limited and bulging with possibilities, everything in himself, except his lucidity, seems unforeseeable to him. What rule, then, could emanate from that unreasonable order? The only truth that might seem instructive to him is not formal: it comes to life and unfolds in men. The absurd mind cannot so much expect ethical rules at the end of its reasoning as, rather, illustrations and the breath of human lives. The few following images are of this type. They prolong the absurd reasoning by giving it a specific attitude and their warmth.

Do I need to develop the idea that an example is not necessarily an example to be followed (even less so, if possible, in the absurd world) and that these illustrations are not therefore models? Besides the fact that a certain vocation is required for this, one becomes ridiculous, with all due allowance, when drawing from Rousseau the conclusion that one must walk on all fours and from Nietzsche that one must maltreat one's mother. 'It is essential to be absurd,' writes a modern author, 'it is not essential to be a dupe.' The attitudes of which I shall treat can assume their whole meaning only through consideration of their contraries. A sub-clerk in the post office is the equal of a conqueror if consciousness is common to them. All experiences are indifferent in this regard. There are some that do either a service or a disservice to man. They do him a service if he is conscious. Otherwise, that has no importance: a man's failures imply judgment, not of circumstances, but of himself.

I am choosing solely men who aim only to expend themselves or whom I see to be expending themselves. That has no further implications. For the moment I want to speak only of a world in which thoughts, like lives, are devoid of future. Everything that makes man work and get excited utilizes hope. The sole thought that is not mendacious is therefore a sterile thought. In the absurd world the value of a notion or of a life is measured by its sterility.

Don Juanism

IF IT WERE sufficient to love, things would be too easy. The more one loves, the stronger the absurd grows. It is not through lack of love that Don Juan goes from woman to woman. It is ridiculous to represent him as a mystic in quest of total love. But it is indeed because he loves them with the same passion and each time with his whole self that he must repeat his gift and his profound quest. Whence each woman hopes to give him what no one has ever given him. Each time they are utterly wrong and merely manage to make him feel the need of that repetition. 'At last,' exclaims one of them, 'I have given you love.' Can we be surprised that Don Juan laughs at this? 'At last? No,' he says, 'but once more.' Why should it be essential to love rarely in order to love much?

* * *

Is Don Juan melancholy? This is not likely. I shall barely have recourse to the legend. That laugh, the conquering insolence, that playfulness and love of the theatre are all clear and joyous. Every healthy creature tends to multiply himself. So it is with Don Juan. But, furthermore, melancholy people have two reasons for being so: they don't know or they hope. Don Juan knows and does not hope. He reminds one of those artists who know their limits, never go beyond them, and in that precarious interval in which they take their spiritual stand enjoy all the wonderful ease of masters. And that is indeed genius: the intelligence that knows its frontiers. Up to the frontier of physical death Don Juan is ignorant of melancholy. The moment he knows, his laugh bursts forth and makes one forgive everything. He was melancholy at the time when he hoped. Today, on the mouth of that woman he recognizes the bitter and comforting taste of the only knowledge. Bitter? Barely: that necessary imperfection that makes happiness perceptible!

It is quite false to try to see in Don Juan a man brought up on Ecclesiastes. For nothing is vanity to him except the hope of another life. He proves this because he gambles that other life against heaven itself. Longing for desire killed by satisfaction, that commonplace of the impotent man, does not belong to him. That is all right for Faust, who believed in God enough to sell himself to the devil. For Don Juan the thing is simpler.

Molina's *Burlador* ever replies to the threats of hell: 'What a long respite you give me!' What comes after death is futile, and what a long succession of days for whoever knows how to be alive! Faust craved worldly goods; the poor man had only to stretch out his hand. It already amounted to selling his soul when he was unable to gladden it. As for satiety, Don Juan insists upon it, on the contrary. If he leaves a woman it is not absolutely because he has ceased to desire her. A beautiful woman is always desirable. But he desires another, and no, this is not the same thing.

This life gratifies his every wish, and nothing is worse than losing it. This madman is a great wise man. But men who live on hope do not thrive in this universe where kindness yields to generosity, affection to virile silence, and communion to solitary courage. And all hasten to say: 'He was a weakling, an idealist or a saint.' One has to disparage the greatness that insults.

* * *

People are sufficiently annoyed (or that smile of complicity that debases what it admires) by Don Juan's speeches and by that same remark that he uses on all women. But to anyone who seeks quantity in his joys, the only thing that matters is efficacy. What is the use of complicating the passwords that have stood the test? No one, neither the woman nor the man, listens to them, but rather to the voice that pronounces them. They are the rule, the convention, and the courtesy. After they are spoken the most important still remains to be done. Don Juan is already getting ready for it. Why should he give himself a problem in morality? He is not like Milosz's Mañara, who damns himself through a desire to be a saint. Hell for him is a thing to be provoked. He has but one reply to divine wrath, and that is human honour: 'I have honour,' he says to the Commander, 'and I am keeping my promise because I am a knight.' But it would be just as great an error to make an immoralist of him. In this regard, he is 'like everyone else': he has the moral code of his likes and dislikes. Don Juan can be properly understood only by constant reference to what he commonly symbolizes: the ordinary seducer and the sexual athlete. He *is* an ordinary seducer.[16] Except for the difference that he is conscious, and that is why he is absurd. A seducer who has become lucid will not change for all that. Seducing is his condition in life. Only in novels does one change condition or become better. Yet it can be said that at the same time nothing is changed and everything is transformed. What Don Juan realizes in action is an ethic of quantity, whereas the saint, on the contrary, tends towards quality. Not to believe in the profound meaning of things belongs to the absurd man. As for those cordial or wonder-struck faces, he eyes them, stores them up, and does not pause over them. Time keeps up with him. The absurd man is he who is not apart from time. Don Juan does not think of 'collecting' women. He exhausts their number and with them his chances of life. 'Collecting' amounts to being capable of living off one's past. But he rejects regret, that other form of hope. He is incapable of looking at portraits.

* * *

Is he selfish for all that? In his way, probably. But here, too, it is essential to understand one another. There are those who are made for living and those who are made for loving. At least Don Juan would be inclined to say so. But he would do so in a very few words such as he is capable of choosing. For the love we are speaking of here is clothed in illusions of the eternal. As all the specialists in passion teach us, there is no eternal love but what is thwarted. There is scarcely any passion without

---

16 In the fullest sense and with his faults. A healthy attitude *also* includes faults.

struggle. Such a love culminates only in the ultimate contra-diction of death. One must be Werther or nothing. There, too, there are several ways of committing suicide, one of which is the total gift and forgetfulness of self. Don Juan, as well as anyone else, knows that this can be stirring. But he is one of the very few who know that this is not the important thing. He knows just as well that those who turn away from all personal life through a great love enrich themselves perhaps but certainly impoverish those their love has chosen. A mother or a passionate wife necessarily has a closed heart, for it is turned away from the world. A single emotion, a single creature, a single face, but all is devoured. Quite a different love disturbs Don Juan, and this one is liberating. It brings with it all the faces in the world, and its tremor comes from the fact that it knows itself to be mortal. Don Juan has chosen to be nothing.

For him it is a matter of seeing clearly. We call love what binds us to certain creatures only by reference to a collective way of seeing for which books and legends are responsible. But of love I know only that mixture of desire, affection, and intelligence that binds me to this or that creature. That compound is not the same for another person. I do not have the right to cover all these experiences with the same name. This exempts one from conducting them with the same gestures. The absurd man multiplies here again what he cannot unify. Thus he discovers a new way of being which liberates him at least as much as it liberates those who approach him. There is no noble love but that which recognizes itself to be both short-lived and exceptional. All those deaths and all those rebirths gathered together as in a sheaf make up for Don Juan the flowering of his life. It is his way of giving and of vivifying. I let it be decided whether or not one can speak of selfishness.

* * *

I think at this point of all those who absolutely insist that Don Juan be punished. Not only in another life, but even in this one. I think of all those tales, legends, and laughs about the aged Don Juan. But Don Juan is already ready. To a conscious man old age and what it portends are not a surprise. Indeed, he is conscious only in so far as he does not conceal its horror from himself. There was in Athens a temple dedicated to old age. Children were taken there. As for Don Juan, the more people laugh at him, the more his figure stands out. Thereby he rejects the one the romantics lent him. No one wants to laugh at that tormented, pitiful Don Juan. He is pitied; heaven itself will redeem him? But that's not it. In the universe of which Don Juan has a glimpse, ridicule *too* is included. He would consider it normal to be chastised. That is the rule of the game. And, indeed, it is typical of his nobility to have accepted all the rules of the game. Yet he knows he is right and that there can be no question of punishment. A fate is not a punishment.

That is his crime, and how easy it is to understand why the men of God call down punishment on his head. He achieves a knowledge without illusions which negates everything they profess. Loving and possessing, conquering and consuming – that is his way of knowing. (There is significance in that favourite Scriptural word that calls the carnal act 'knowing'.) He is their worst enemy to the extent that he is ignorant of them. A chronicler relates that the true *Burlador* died assassinated by Franciscans who wanted 'to put an end to the excesses and blasphemies of Don Juan, whose birth assured him impunity'. Then they proclaimed that heaven had struck him down. No one has proved that strange end. Nor has anyone proved the contrary. But without wondering if it is probable, I can say that it is logical. I want merely to single out at this point the word 'birth' and to play on words: it was the fact of living that assured his innocence. It was from death alone that he derived a guilt now become legendary.

What else does that stone Commander signify, that cold statue set in motion to punish the blood and courage that dared to think? All the powers of eternal Reason, of order, of universal morality, all the foreign grandeur of a God open to wrath are summed up in him. That gigantic and soulless stone merely symbolizes the forces that Don Juan negated for ever. But the Commander's mission stops there. The thunder and lightning can return to the imitation heaven whence they were called forth. The real tragedy takes place quite apart from them. No, it was not under a stone hand that Don Juan met his death. I am inclined to believe in the legendary bravado, in that mad laughter of the healthy man provoking a non-existent God. But, above all, I believe that on that evening when Don Juan was waiting at Anna's the Commander didn't come, and that after midnight the blasphemer must have felt the dreadful bitterness of those who have been right. I accept even more readily the account of his life that has him eventually burying himself in a monastery. Not that the edifying aspect of the story can be considered probable. What refuge can he ask of God? But this symbolizes rather the logical outcome of a life completely imbued with the absurd, the grim ending of an existence turned towards short-lived joys. At this point sensual pleasure winds up in asceticism. It is essential to realize that they may be, as it were, the two aspects of the same destitution. What more ghastly image can be called up than that of a man betrayed by his body who, simply because he did not die in time, lives out the comedy while awaiting the end, face to face with that God he does not adore, serving him as he served life, kneeling before a void and arms outstretched towards a heaven without eloquence that he knows to be also without depth?

I see Don Juan in a cell of one of those Spanish monasteries lost on a hilltop. And if he contemplates anything at all, it is not the ghosts of past loves, but perhaps, through a narrow slit in the sun-baked wall, some silent Spanish plain, a noble, soulless land in which he recognizes himself. Yes, it is on this melancholy and radiant image that the curtain must be rung down. The ultimate end, awaited but never desired, the ultimate end is negligible.

Drama

'THE PLAY'S THE thing,' says Hamlet, 'wherein I'll catch the conscience of the king.' 'Catch' is indeed the word. For conscience moves swiftly or withdraws within itself. It has to be caught on the wing, at that barely perceptible moment when it glances fleetingly at itself. The everyday man does not enjoy tarrying. Everything, on the contrary, hurries him onwards. But at the same time nothing interests him more than himself, especially his potentialities. Whence his interest in the theatre, in the show, where so many fates are offered him, where he can accept the poetry without feeling the sorrow. There at least can be recognized the thoughtless man, and he continues to hasten towards some hope or other. The absurd man begins where that one leaves off, where, ceasing to admire the play, the mind wants to enter in. Entering into all these lives, experiencing them in their diversity, amounts to acting them out. I am not saying that actors in general obey that impulse, that they are absurd men, but that their fate is an absurd fate which might charm and attract a lucid heart. It is necessary to establish this in order to grasp without misunderstanding what will follow.

The actor's realm is that of the fleeting. Of all kinds of fame, it is known, his is the most ephemeral. At least, this is said in conversation. But all kinds of fame are ephemeral. From the point of view of Sirius, Goethe's works in ten thousand years will be dust and his name forgotten. Perhaps a handful of archæologists will look for 'evidence' as to our era. That idea has always contained a lesson. Seriously meditated upon, it reduces our perturbations to the profound nobility that is found in indifference. Above all, it directs our concerns towards what is most certain – that is, towards the immediate. Of all kinds of fame the least deceptive is the one that is lived.

Hence the actor has chosen multiple fame, the fame that is hallowed and tested. From the fact that everything is to die someday he draws the best conclusion. An actor succeeds or does not succeed. A writer has some hope even if he is not appreciated. He assumes that his works will bear witness to what he was. At best the actor will leave us a photograph, and nothing of what he was himself, his gestures and his silences, his gasping or his panting with love, will come down to us. For him, not to be known is not to act, and not acting is dying a hundred times with all the creatures he would have brought to life or resuscitated.

* * *

Why should we be surprised to find a fleeting fame built upon the most ephemeral of creations? The actor has three hours to be Iago or Alceste, Phèdre or Gloucester. In that short space of time he makes them come to life and die on fifty square yards of boards. Never has the absurd been so well illustrated or at such length. What more revelatory epitome can be imagined than those marvellous lives, those exceptional and total destinies unfolding for a few hours within a stage set? Off the stage, Sigismundo ceases to count. Two hours later he is seen dining out. Then it is, perhaps, that life is a dream. But after Sigismundo comes another. The hero suffering from uncertainty takes the place of the man roaring for his revenge. By thus sweeping over centuries and minds, by miming man as he can be and as he is, the actor has much in common with that other absurd individual, the traveller. Like him, he drains something and is constantly on the move. He is a traveller in time and, for the best, the hunted traveller, pursued by souls. If ever the ethics of quantity could find sustenance, it is indeed on that strange stage. To what degree the actor benefits from the characters is hard to say. But that is not the important thing. It is merely a matter of knowing how far he identifies himself with those irreplaceable lives. It often happens that he carries them with him, that they somewhat overflow the time and place in which they were born. They accompany the actor, who cannot very readily separate himself from what he has been. Occasionally when reaching for his glass he resumes Hamlet's gesture of raising his cup. No, the distance separating him from the creatures into whom he infuses life is not so great. He abundantly illustrates every month or every day that so suggestive truth that there is no frontier between what a man wants to be and what he is. Always concerned with better representing, he demonstrates to what a degree appearing creates being. For that is his art — to simulate absolutely, to project himself as deeply as possible into lives that are not his own. At the end of his effort his vocation becomes clear: to apply himself wholeheartedly to being nothing or to being several. The narrower the limits allotted him for creating his character, the more necessary his talent. He will die in three hours under the mask he has assumed today. Within three hours he must experience and express a whole exceptional life. That is called losing oneself to find oneself. In those three hours he travels the whole course of the dead-end path that the man in the audience takes a lifetime to cover.

* * *

A mime of the ephemeral, the actor trains and perfects himself only in appearances. The theatrical convention is that the heart expresses itself and communicates itself only through gestures and in the body — or through the voice, which is as much of the soul as of the body. The rule of that art insists that everything be magnified and translated into flesh. If it were essential on the stage to love as people really love, to employ that irreplaceable voice of the heart, to look as people contemplate in life, our speech would be in code. But here silences must make themselves heard. Love speaks up louder, and immobility itself becomes spectacular. The body is king. Not everyone can be 'theatrical', and this unjustly maligned word covers a whole æsthetic and a whole ethic. Half a man's life is spent in implying, in turning away, and in keeping silent. Here the actor is the intruder. He breaks the spell chaining that soul, and at last the passions can rush on to their stage. They speak in every gesture; they live only through shouts and cries. Thus the actor creates his characters for display. He outlines or sculptures them and slips into their imaginary form, transfusing his blood into their phantoms. I am of course speaking of great drama, the kind that gives the actor an *opportunity* to fulfil his wholly physical fate. Take Shakespeare, for instance. In that impulsive drama the physical passions lead the dance. They explain everything. Without them all would collapse. Never would King Lear keep the appointment set by madness without the brutal gesture that exiles Cordelia and condemns Edgar. It is just that the unfolding of that tragedy should thenceforth be dominated by madness. Souls are given over to the demons and their saraband. No fewer than four madmen: one by trade, another by intention, and the last two through suffering – four disordered bodies, four unutterable aspects of a single condition.

The very scale of the human body is inadequate. The mask and the buskin, the make-up that reduces and accentuates the face in its essential elements, the costume that exaggerates and simplifies – that universe sacrifices everything to appearance and is made solely for the eye. Through an absurd miracle, it is the body that also brings knowledge. I should never really understand Iago unless I played his part. It is not enough to hear him, for I grasp him only at the moment when I see him. Of the absurd character the actor consequently has the monotony, that single, oppressive silhouette, simultaneously strange and familiar, that he carries about from hero to hero. There, too, the great dramatic work contributes to this unity of tone.[17] This is where the actor contradicts himself: the same and yet so various, so many souls summed up in a single body. Yet it is the absurd contradiction itself, that individual who wants to achieve everything and live everything, that useless attempt, that ineffectual persistence. What always contradicts itself nevertheless joins in him. He is at that point where body and mind converge, where the mind, tired of its defeats, turns towards its most faithful ally. 'And blest are those,' says Hamlet, 'whose blood and judgment are so well commingled that they are not a pipe for fortune's finger to sound what stop she please.'

* * *

How could the Church have failed to condemn such a practice on the part of the actor? She repudiated in that art the heretical multiplication of souls, the emotional debauch, the scandalous presumption of a mind that objects to living but one life and hurls itself into all forms of excess. She proscribed in them that preference for the present and that triumph of Proteus which are the negation of everything she teaches. Eternity is not a game. A mind foolish enough to prefer a comedy to eternity has lost its salvation. Between 'everywhere' and 'for ever' there is no compromise. Whence that much maligned profession can give rise to a tremendous spiritual conflict. 'What matters,' said Nietzsche, 'is not eternal life but eternal vivacity.' All drama is, in fact, in this choice.

Adrienne Lecouvreur on her death-bed was willing to confess and receive communion, but refused to abjure her

---

17 At this point I am thinking of Molière's Alceste. Everything is so simple, so obvious and so coarse. Alceste against Philinte, Célimène against Elianthe, the whole subject in the absurd consequence of a nature carried to its extreme, and the verse itself, the 'bad verse', barely accented like the monotony of the character's nature.

profession. She thereby lost the benefit of the confession. Did this not amount, in effect, to choosing her absorbing passion in preference to God? And that woman in the death-throes refusing in tears to repudiate what she called her art gave evidence of a greatness that she never achieved behind the footlights. This was her finest role and the hardest one to play. Choosing between heaven and a ridiculous fidelity, preferring oneself to eternity or losing oneself in God is the age-old tragedy in which each must play his part.

The actors of the era knew they were excommunicated. Entering the profession amounted to choosing Hell. And the Church discerned in them her worst enemies. A few men of letters protest: 'What! Refuse the last rites to Molière!' But that was just, and especially in one who died onstage and finished under the actor's make-up a life entirely devoted to dispersion. In his case genius is invoked, which excuses everything. But genius excuses nothing, just because it refuses to do so.

The actor knew at that time what punishment was in store for him. But what significance could such vague threats have compared to the final punishment that life itself was reserving for him? This was the one that he felt in advance and accepted wholly. To the actor as to the absurd man, a premature death is irreparable. Nothing can make up for the sum of faces and centuries he would otherwise have traversed. But in any case, one has to die. For the actor is doubtless everywhere, but time sweeps him along, too, and makes its impression with him.

It requires but a little imagination to feel what an actor's fate means. It is in time that he makes up and enumerates his characters. It is in time likewise that he learns to dominate them. The greater number of different lives he has lived, the more aloof he can be from them. The time comes when he must die to the stage and for the world. What he has lived faces him. He sees clearly. He feels the harrowing and irreplaceable quality of that adventure. He knows and can now die. There are homes for aged actors.

Conquest

'NO,' SAYS THE conqueror, 'don't assume that because I love action I have had to forget how to think. On the contrary I can thoroughly define what I believe. For I believe it firmly and I see it surely and clearly. Beware of those who say: "I know this too well to be able to express it." For if they cannot do so, this is because they don't know it or because out of laziness they stopped at the outer crust.

'I have not many opinions. At the end of a life man notices that he has spent years becoming sure of a single truth. But a single truth, if it is obvious, is enough to guide an existence. As for me, I decidedly have something to say about the individual. One must speak of him bluntly and, if need be, with the appropriate contempt.

'A man is more a man through the things he keeps to himself than through those he says. There are many that I shall keep to myself. But I firmly believe that all those who have judged the individual have done so with much less experience than we on which to base their judgment. The intelligence, the stirring intelligence perhaps foresaw what it was essential to note. But the era, its ruins, and its blood overwhelm us with facts. It was possible for ancient nations, and even for more recent ones down to our machine age, to weigh one against the other the virtues of society and of the individual, to try to find out which was to serve the other. To begin with, that was possible by virtue of that stubborn aberration in man's heart according to which human beings were created to serve or be served. In the second place, it was possible because neither society nor the individual had yet revealed all their ability.

'I have seen bright minds express astonishment at the masterpieces of Dutch painters born at the height of the bloody wars in Flanders, be amazed by the prayers of Silesian mystics brought up during the frightful Thirty Years' War. Eternal values survive secular turmoils before their astonished eyes. But there has been progress since. The painters of today are deprived of such serenity. Even if they have basically the heart the creator needs – I mean the closed heart – it is of no use; for everyone, including the saint himself, is mobilized. This is perhaps what I have felt most deeply. At every form that miscarries in the trenches, at every outline, metaphor, or prayer crushed under steel, the eternal loses a round. Conscious that I cannot stand aloof from my time, I have decided to be an integral part of it. This is why I esteem the individual only because he strikes me as ridiculous and humiliated. Knowing that there are no victorious causes, I have a liking for lost causes: they require an uncontaminated soul, equal to its defeat as to its temporary victories. For anyone who feels bound up with this world's fate, the clash of civilizations has something agonizing about it. I have made that anguish mine at the same time that I wanted to join in. Between history and the eternal I have chosen history because I like certainties. Of it, at least, I am certain, and how can I deny this force crushing me?

'There always comes a time when one must choose between contemplation and action. This is called becoming a man. Such wrenches are dreadful. But for a proud heart there can be no compromise. There is God or time, that cross or this sword. This world has a higher meaning that transcends its worries, or nothing is true but those worries. One must live with time and die with it, or else elude it for a greater life. I know that one can compromise and live in the world while believing in the eternal. That is called accepting. But I loathe this term and want all or nothing. If I choose action, don't think that contemplation is like an unknown country to me. But it cannot give me everything, and, deprived of the eternal, I want to ally myself with time. I do not want to put down to my account either nostalgia or bitterness, and I merely want to see clearly. I tell you, tomorrow you will be mobilized. For you and for me that is a liberation. The individual can do nothing and yet he can do everything. In that wonderful unattached state you understand why I exalt and crush him at one and the same time. It is the world that pulverizes him and I who liberate him. I provide him with all his rights.

* * *

'Conquerors know that action is in itself useless. There is but one useful action, that of remaking man and the earth. I shall never remake men. But one must do "as if". For the path of struggle leads me to the flesh. Even humiliated, the flesh is my only certainty. I can live only on it. The creature is my native land. This is why I have chosen this absurd and ineffectual effort. This is why I am on the side of the struggle. The epoch lends itself to this, as I have said. Hitherto the greatness of a conqueror was geographical. It was measured by the extent of the conquered territories. There is a reason why the word has changed in meaning and has ceased to signify the victorious general. The greatness has changed camp. It lies in protest and the blind-alley sacrifice. There, too, it is not through a preference for defeat. Victory would be desirable. But there is but one victory, and it is eternal. That is the one I shall never have. That is where I stumble and cling. A revolution is always accomplished against the gods, beginning with the revolution of Prometheus, the first of modern conquerors. It is man's demands made against his fate; the demands of the poor are but a pretext. Yet I can seize that spirit only in its historical act, and that is where I make contact with it. Don't assume, however, that I take pleasure in it: opposite the essential contradiction, I maintain my human contradiction. I establish my lucidity in the midst of what negates it. I exalt man before what crushes him, and my freedom, my revolt, and my passion come together then in that tension, that lucidity, and that vast repetition.

'Yes, man is his own end. And he is his only end. If he aims to be something, it is in this life. Now I know it only too well. Conquerors sometimes talk of vanquishing and overcoming. But it is always "overcoming oneself" that they mean. You are well aware of what that means. Every man has felt himself to be the equal of a god at certain moments. At least, this is the way it is expressed. But this comes from the fact that in a flash he felt the amazing grandeur of the human mind. The conquerors are merely those among men who are conscious enough of their strength to be sure of living constantly on those heights and fully aware of that grandeur. It is a question of arithmetic, of more or less. The conquerors are capable of the more. But they are capable of no more than man himself when he wants. This is why they never leave the human crucible, plunging into the seething soul of revolutions.

'There they find the creature mutilated, but they also encounter there the only values they like and admire, man and his silence. This is both their destitution and their wealth. There is but one luxury for them – that of human relations. How can one fail to realize that in this vulnerable universe everything that is human and solely human assumes a more vivid meaning? Taut faces, threatened fraternity, such strong and chaste friendship among men – these are the true riches because they are transitory. In their midst the mind is most aware of its powers and limitations. That is to say, its efficacity. Some have spoken of genius. But genius is easy to say; I prefer the intelligence. It must be said that it can be magnificent then. It lights up this desert and dominates it. It knows its obligations and illustrates them. It will die at the same time as this body. But knowing this constitutes its freedom.

* * *

'We are not ignorant of the fact that all churches are against us. A heart so keyed up eludes the eternal, and all churches, divine or political, lay claim to the eternal. Happiness and courage, retribution or justice are secondary ends for them. It is a doctrine they bring, and one must subscribe to it. But I have no concern with ideas or with the eternal. The truths that come within my scope can be touched with the hand. I cannot separate from them. This is why you cannot base anything on me: nothing of the conqueror lasts, not even his doctrines.

'At the end of all that, despite everything, is death. We know also that it ends everything. This is why those cemeteries all over Europe, which obsess some among us, are hideous. People beautify only what they love, and death repels us and tires our patience. It, too, is to be conquered. The last Carrara, a prisoner in Padua emptied by the plague and besieged by the Venetians, ran screaming through the halls of his deserted palace: he was calling on the devil and asking him for death. This was a way of overcoming it. And it is likewise a mark of courage characteristic of the Occident to have made so ugly the places where death thinks itself honoured. In the rebel's universe, death exalts injustice. It is the supreme abuse.

'Others, without compromising either, have chosen the eternal and denounced the illusion of this world. Their cemeteries smile amid numerous flowers and birds. That suits the conqueror and gives him a clear image of what he has rejected. He has chosen, on the contrary, the black iron fence or the potter's field. The best among the men of God occasionally are seized with fright mingled with consideration and pity for minds that can live with such an image of their death. Yet those minds derive their strength and justification from this. Our fate stands before us and we provoke him. Less out of pride than out of awareness of our ineffectual condition. We, too, sometimes feel pity for ourselves. It is the only compassion that seems acceptable to us: a feeling that perhaps you hardly understand and that seems to you scarcely virile. Yet the most daring among us are the ones who feel it. But we call the lucid ones virile and we do not want a strength that is apart from lucidity.'

* * *

Let me repeat that these images do not propose moral codes and involve no judgments: they are sketches. They merely represent a style of life. The lover, the actor, or the adventurer plays the absurd. But equally well, if he wishes, the chaste man, the civil servant, or the president of the Republic. It is enough to know and to mask nothing. In Italian museums are sometimes found little painted screens that the priest used to hold in front of the face of condemned men to hide the scaffold from them. The leap in all its forms, rushing into the divine or the eternal, surrendering to the illusions of the everyday or of the idea – all these screens hide the absurd. But there are civil servants without screens, and they are the ones of whom I mean to speak.

I have chosen the most extreme ones. At this level the absurd gives them a royal power. It is true that those princes are without a kingdom. But they have this advantage over others: they know that all royalties are illusory. They know that is their whole nobility, and it is useless to speak in relation to them of hidden misfortune or the ashes of disillusion. Being deprived of hope is not despairing. The flames of earth are surely worth celestial perfumes. Neither I nor anyone can judge them here. They are not striving to be better; they are attempting to be consistent. If the term 'wise man' can be applied to the man who lives on what he has without speculating on what he has not, then they are wise men. One of them, a conqueror but in the realm of mind, a Don Juan but of knowledge, an actor but of the intelligence, knows this better than anyone: 'You nowise deserve a privilege on earth and in heaven for having brought to perfection your dear little meek sheep; you none the less continue to be at best a ridiculous dear little sheep with horns and nothing more – even supposing that you do not burst with vanity and do not create a scandal by posing as a judge.'

In any case, it was essential to restore to the absurd reasoning more cordial examples. The imagination can add many others, inseparable from time and exile, who likewise know how to live in harmony with a universe without future and without weakness. This absurd, godless world is, then, peopled with men who think clearly and have ceased to hope. And I have not yet spoken of the most absurd character, who is the creator.

ABSURD CREATION

Philosophy and Fiction

ALL THOSE LIVES maintained in the rarefied air of the absurd could not persevere without some profound and constant thought to infuse its strength into them. Right here, it can be only a strange feeling of fidelity. Conscious men have been seen to fulfil their task amid the most stupid of wars without considering themselves in contradiction. This is because it was essential to elude nothing. There is thus a metaphysical honour in enduring the world's absurdity. Conquest or play-acting, multiple loves, absurd revolt are tributes that man pays to his dignity in a campaign in which he is defeated in advance.

It is merely a matter of being faithful to the rule of the battle. That thought may suffice to sustain a mind; it has supported and still supports whole civilizations. War cannot be negated. One must live it or die of it. So it is with the absurd: it is a question of breathing with it, of recognizing its lessons and recovering their flesh. In this regard the absurd joy par excellence is creation. 'Art and nothing but art,' said Nietzsche; 'we have art in order not to die of the truth.'

In the experience that I am attempting to describe and to stress on several modes, it is certain that a new torment arises wherever another dies. The childish chasing after forgetfulness, the appeal of satisfaction are now devoid of echo. But the constant tension that keeps man face to face with the world, the ordered delirium that urges him to be receptive to everything leave him another fever. In this universe the work of art is then the sole chance of keeping his consciousness and of fixing its adventures. Creating is living doubly. The groping, anxious quest of a Proust, his meticulous collecting of flowers, of wallpapers, and of anxieties, signifies nothing else. At the same time, it has no more significance than the continual and imperceptible creation in which the actor, the conqueror, and all absurd men indulge every day of their lives. All try their hands at miming, at repeating, and at re-creating the reality that is theirs. We always end up by having the appearance of our truths. All existence for a man turned away from the eternal is but a vast mime under the mask of the absurd. Creation is the great mime.

Such men know to begin with, and then their whole effort is to examine, to enlarge, and to enrich the ephemeral island on which they have just landed. But first they must know. For the absurd discovery coincides with a pause in which future passions are prepared and justified. Even men without a gospel have their Mount of Olives. And one must not fall asleep on theirs either. For the absurd man it is not a matter of explaining and solving, but of experiencing and describing. Everything begins with lucid indifference.

Describing – that is the last ambition of an absurd thought. Science likewise, having reached the end of its paradoxes, ceases to propound and stops to contemplate and sketch the ever virgin landscape of phenomena. The heart learns thus that the emotion delighting us when we see the world's aspects comes to us not from its depth but from their diversity. Explanation is useless, but the sensation remains and, with it, the constant attractions of a universe inexhaustible in quantity. The place of the work of art can be understood at this point.

It marks both the death of an experience and its multiplication. It is a sort of monotonous and passionate repetition of the themes already orchestrated by the world: the body, inexhaustible image on the pediment of temples, forms or colours, number or grief. It is therefore not indifferent, as a conclusion, to encounter once again the principal themes of this essay in the wonderful and childish world of the creator.

It would be wrong to see a symbol in it and to think that the work of art can be considered at last as a refuge for the absurd. It is itself an absurd phenomenon, and we are concerned merely with its description. It does not offer an escape for the intellectual ailment. Rather, it is one of the symptoms of that ailment which reflects it throughout a man's whole thought. But for the first time it makes the mind get outside of itself and places it in opposition to others, not for it to get lost but to show it clearly the blind path that all have entered upon. In the time of the absurd reasoning, creation follows indifference and discovery. It marks the point from which absurd passions spring and where the reasoning stops. Its place in this essay is justified in this way.

It will suffice to bring to light a few themes common to the creator and the thinker in order to find in the work of art all the contradictions of thought involved in the absurd. Indeed, it is not so much identical conclusions that prove minds to be related as the contradictions that are common to them. So it is with thought and creation. I hardly need to say that the same anguish urges man to these two attitudes. This is where they coincide in the beginning. But among all the thoughts that start from the absurd, I have seen that very few remain within it. And through their deviations or infidelities I have best been able to measure what belonged to the absurd. Similarly I must wonder: is an absurd work of art possible?

* * *

It would be impossible to insist too much on the arbitrary nature of the former opposition between art and philosophy. If you insist on taking it in too limited a sense, it is certainly false. If you mean merely that these two disciplines each have their peculiar climate, that is probably true but remains vague. The only acceptable argument used to lie in the contradiction brought up between the philosopher enclosed *within* his system and the artist placed *before* his work. But this was pertinent for a certain form of art and of philosophy which we consider secondary here. The idea of an art detached from its creator is not only outmoded; it is false. In opposition to the artist, it is pointed out that no philosopher ever created several systems. But that is true in so far, indeed, as no artist ever expressed more than one thing under different aspects. The instantaneous perfection of art, the necessity for its renewal – this is true only through a preconceived notion. For the work of art likewise is a construction and everyone knows how monotonous the great creators can be. For the same reason as the thinker, the artist commits himself and becomes himself in his work. That osmosis raises the most important of æsthetic problems. Moreover, to anyone who is convinced of the mind's singleness of purpose, nothing is more futile than these distinctions based on methods and objects. There are no frontiers between the disciplines that man sets himself for understanding and loving. They interlock, and the same anxiety merges them.

It is necessary to state this to begin with. For an absurd work of art to be possible, thought in its most lucid form must be involved in it. But at the same time thought must not be apparent except as the regulating intelligence. This paradox can be explained according to the absurd. The work of art is born of the intelligence's refusal to reason the concrete. It marks the triumph of the carnal. It is lucid thought that provokes it, but in that very act that thought repudiates itself. It will not yield to the temptation of adding to what is described a deeper meaning that it knows to be illegitimate. The work of art embodies a drama of the intelligence, but it proves this only indirectly. The absurd work requires an artist conscious of these limitations and an art in which the concrete signifies nothing more than itself. It cannot be the end, the meaning, and the consolation of a life. Creating or not creating changes nothing. The absurd creator does not prize his work. He could repudiate it. He does sometimes repudiate it. An Abyssinia suffices for this, as in the case of Rimbaud.

At the same time a rule of æsthetics can be seen in this. The true work of art is always on the human scale. It is essentially the one that says 'less'. There is a certain relationship between the global experience of the artist and the work that reflects that experience, between *Wilhelm Meister* and Goethe's maturity. That relationship is bad when the work aims to give the whole experience in the lace-paper of an explanatory literature. That relationship is good when the work is but a piece cut out of experience, a facet of the diamond in which the inner lustre is epitomized without being limited. In the first case there is overloading and pretension to the eternal. In the second, a fecund work because of a whole implied experience, the wealth of which is suspected. The problem for the absurd artist is to acquire this *savoir-vivre* which transcends *savoir-faire*. And in the end, the great artist under this climate is, above all, a great living being, it being understood that living in this case is just as much experiencing as reflecting. The work then embodies an intellectual drama. The absurd work illustrates thought's renouncing of its prestige and its resignation to being no more than the intelligence that works up appearances and covers with images what has no reason. If the world were clear, art would not exist.

I am not speaking here of the arts of form or colour in which description alone prevails in its splendid modesty.[18] Expression begins where thought ends. Those adolescents with empty eyesockets who people temples and museums –

---

18 It is curious to note that the most intellectual kind of painting, the one that tries to reduce reality to its essential elements, is ultimately but a visual delight. All it has kept of the world is its colour. (This is apparent particularly in Léger.)

their philosophy has been expressed in gestures. For an absurd man it is more educative than all libraries. Under another aspect the same is true for music. If any art is devoid of lessons, it is certainly music. It is too closely related to mathematics not to have borrowed their gratuitousness. That game the mind plays with itself according to set and measured laws takes place in the sonorous compass that belongs to us and beyond which the vibrations nevertheless meet in an inhuman universe. There is no purer sensation. These examples are too easy. The absurd man recognizes as his own these harmonies and these forms.

But I should like to speak here of a work in which the temptation to explain remains greatest, in which illusion offers itself automatically, in which conclusion is almost inevitable. I mean fictional creation. I propose to inquire whether or not the absurd can hold its own there.

* * *

To think is first of all to create a world (or to limit one's own world, which comes to the same thing). It is starting out from the basic disagreement that separates man from his experience in order to find a common ground according to one's nostalgia, a universe hedged with reasons or lighted up with analogies but which, in any case, gives an opportunity to rescind the unbearable divorce. The philosopher, even if he is Kant, is a creator. He has his characters, his symbols, and his secret action. He has his plot endings. On the contrary, the lead taken by the novel over poetry and the essay merely represents, despite appearances, a greater intellectualization of the art. Let there be no mistake about it; I am speaking of the greatest. The fecundity and the importance of a literary form are often measured by the trash it contains. The number of bad novels must not make us forget the value of the best. These, indeed, carry with them their universe. The novel has its logic, its reasonings, its intuition, and its postulates. It also has its requirements of clarity.[19]

The classical opposition of which I was speaking above is even less justified in this particular case. It held in the time when it was easy to separate philosophy from its authors. Today when thought has ceased to lay claim to the universal, when its best history would be that of its repentances, we know that the system, when it is worth while, cannot be separated from its author. The *Ethics* itself, in one of its aspects, is but a long and reasoned personal confession. Abstract thought at last returns to its prop of flesh. And, likewise, the fictional activities of the body and of the passions are regulated a little more according to the requirements of a vision of the world. The writer has given up telling 'stories' and creates his universe. The great novelists are philosophical novelists – that is, the contrary of thesis-writers. For instance, Balzac, Sade, Melville, Stendhal, Dostoevsky, Proust, Malraux, Kafka, to cite but a few.

But in fact the preference they have shown for writing in images rather than in reasoned arguments is revelatory of a certain thought that is common to them all, convinced of the uselessness of any principle of explanation and sure of the educative message of perceptible appearance. They consider the work of art both as an end and a beginning. It is the outcome of an often unexpressed philosophy, its illustration and its consummation. But it is complete only through the implications of that philosophy. It justifies at last that variant of an old theme that a little thought estranges from life whereas much thought reconciles to life. Incapable

---

19 If you stop to think of it, this explains the worst novels. Almost everybody considers himself capable of thinking and, to a certain degree, whether right or wrong, really does think. Very few, on the contrary, can fancy themselves poets or artists in words. But from the moment when thought won out over style, the mob invaded the novel.

That is not such a great evil as is said. The best are led to make greater demands upon themselves. As for those who succumb, they did not deserve to survive.

of refining the real, thought pauses to mimic it. The novel in question is the instrument of that simultaneously relative and inexhaustible knowledge, so like that of love. Of love, fictional creation has the initial wonder and the fecund rumination.

* * *

These at least are the charms I see in it at the outset. But I saw them likewise in those princes of humiliated thought whose suicides I was later able to witness. What interests me, indeed, is knowing and describing the force that leads them back towards the common path of illusion. The same method will consequently help me here. The fact of having already utilized it will allow me to shorten my argument and to sum it up without delay in a particular example. I want to know whether, accepting a life *without appeal*, one can also agree to work and create *without appeal* and what is the way leading to these liberties. I want to liberate my universe of its phantoms and to people it solely with flesh-and-blood truths whose presence I cannot deny. I can perform absurd work, choose the creative attitude rather than another. But an absurd attitude, if it is to remain so, must remain aware of its gratuitousness. So it is with the work of art. If the commandments of the absurd are not respected, if the work does not illustrate divorce and revolt, if it sacrifices to illusions and arouses hope, it ceases to be gratuitous. I can no longer detach myself from it. My life may find a meaning in it, but that is trifling. It ceases to be that exercise in detachment and passion which crowns the splendour and futility of a man's life.

In the creation in which the temptation to explain is the strongest, can one overcome that temptation? In the fictional world in which awareness of the real world is keenest, can I remain faithful to the absurd without sacrificing to the desire to judge? So many questions to be taken into consideration in a last effort. It must be already clear what they signify. They are the last scruples of an awareness that fears to forsake its initial and difficult lesson in favour of a final illusion. What holds for creation, looked upon as *one* of the possible attitudes for the man conscious of the absurd, holds for all the styles of life open to him. The conqueror or the actor, the creator or Don Juan may forget that their exercise in living could not do without awareness of its mad character. One becomes accustomed so quickly. A man wants to earn money in order to be happy, and his whole effort and the best of a life are devoted to the earning of that money. Happiness is forgotten; the means are taken for the end. Likewise, the whole effort of this conqueror will be diverted to ambition, which was but a way towards a greater life. Don Juan in turn will likewise yield to his fate, be satisfied with that existence whose nobility is of value only through revolt. For one it is awareness and for the other, revolt; in both cases the absurd has disappeared. There is so much stubborn hope in the human heart. The most destitute men often end up by accepting illusion. That approval prompted by the need for peace inwardly parallels the existential consent. There are thus gods of light and idols of mud. But it is essential to find the middle path leading to the faces of man.

So far, the failures of the absurd exigence have best informed us as to what it is. In the same way, if we are to be informed, it will suffice to notice that fictional creation can present the same ambiguity as certain philosophies. Hence I can choose as illustration a work comprising everything that denotes awareness of the absurd, having a clear starting-point and a lucid climate. Its consequences will enlighten us. If the absurd is not respected in it, we shall know by what expedient illusion enters in. A particular example, a theme, a creator's fidelity will suffice, then. This involves the same analysis that has already been made at greater length.

I shall examine a favourite theme of Dostoevsky. I might just as well have studied other works.[20] But in this work the problem is treated directly, in the sense of nobility and emotion, as for the existential philosophies already discussed. This parallelism serves my purpose.

Kirilov

ALL OF DOSTOEVSKY's heroes question themselves as to the meaning of life. In this they are modern: they do not fear ridicule. What distinguishes modern sensibility from classical sensibility is that the latter thrives on moral problems and the former on metaphysical problems. In Dostoevsky's novels the question is propounded with such intensity that it can only invite extreme solutions. Existence is illusory *or* it is eternal. If Dostoevsky were satisfied with this inquiry, he would be a philosopher. But he illustrates the consequences that such intellectual pastimes may have in a man's life, and in this regard he is an artist. Among those consequences, his attention is arrested particularly by the last one, which he himself calls logical suicide in his *Diary of a Writer*. In the instalments for December 1876, indeed, he imagines the reasoning of 'logical suicide'. Convinced that human existence is an utter absurdity for anyone without faith in immortality, the desperate man comes to the following conclusions:

'Since in reply to my questions about happiness, I am told, through the intermediary of my consciousness, that I cannot be happy except in harmony with the great all, which I cannot conceive and shall never be in a position to conceive, it is evident . . . '

20 Malraux's work, for instance. But it would have been necessary to deal at the same time with the social question which in fact cannot be avoided by absurd thought (even though that thought may put forward several solutions, very different from one another). One must, however, limit oneself.

'Since, finally, in this connection, I assume both the role of the plaintiff and that of the defendant, of the accused and of the judge, and since I consider this comedy perpetrated by nature altogether stupid, and since I even deem it humiliating for me to deign to play it . . .'

'In my indisputable capacity of plaintiff and defendant, of judge and accused, I condemn that nature which, with such impudent nerve, brought me into being in order to suffer – I condemn it to be annihilated with me.'

There remains a little humour in that position. This suicide kills himself because, on the metaphysical plane, he is *vexed*. In a certain sense he is taking his revenge. This is his way of proving that he 'will not be had'. It is known, however, that the same theme is embodied, but with the most wonderful generality, in Kirilov of *The Possessed*, likewise an advocate of logical suicide. Kirilov the engineer declares somewhere that he wants to take his own life because it 'is his idea'. Obviously the word must be taken in its proper sense. It is for an idea, a thought, that he is getting ready for death. This is the superior suicide. Progressively, in a series of scenes in which Kirilov's mask is gradually illuminated, the fatal thought driving him is revealed to us. The engineer, in fact, goes back to the arguments of the *Diary*. He feels that God is necessary and that he must exist. But he knows that he does not and cannot exist. 'Why do you not realize,' he exclaims, 'that this is sufficient reason for killing oneself?' That attitude involves likewise for him some of the absurd consequences. Through indifference he accepts letting his suicide be used to the advantage of a cause he despises. 'I decided last night that I didn't care.' And finally he prepares his deed with a mixed feeling of revolt and freedom. 'I shall kill myself in order to assert my insubordination, my new and dreadful liberty.' It is no longer a question of revenge, but of revolt. Kirilov is consequently an absurd character – yet with this essential reservation: he kills himself. But he himself explains this contradiction, and in such a way that at the same time he reveals the absurd secret in all its purity. In truth, he adds to his fatal logic an extraordinary ambition which gives the character its full perspective: he wants to kill himself to become god.

The reasoning is classic in its clarity. If God does not exist, Kirilov is god. If God does not exist, Kirilov must kill himself. Kirilov must therefore kill himself to become god. That logic is absurd, but it is what is needed. The interesting thing, however, is to give a meaning to that divinity brought to earth. That amounts to clarifying the premise: 'If God does not exist, I am god,' which still remains rather obscure. It is important to note at the outset that the man who flaunts that mad claim is indeed of this world. He performs his gymnastics every morning to preserve his health. He is stirred by the joy of Chatov recovering his wife. On a sheet of paper to be found after his death he wants to draw a face sticking out his tongue at 'them'. He is childish and irascible, passionate, methodical, and sensitive. Of the superman he has nothing but the logic and the obsession, whereas of man he has the whole catalogue. Yet it is he who speaks calmly of his divinity. He is not mad, or else Dostoevsky is. Consequently it is not a megalomaniac's illusion that excites him. And taking the words in their specific sense would, in this instance, be ridiculous.

Kirilov himself helps us to understand. In reply to a question from Stavrogin, he makes clear that he is not talking of a god-man. It might be thought that this springs from concern to distinguish himself from Christ. But in reality it is a matter of annexing Christ. Kirilov in fact fancies for a moment that Jesus at his death *did not find himself in Paradise*. He found out then that his torture had been useless. 'The laws of nature,' says the engineer, 'made Christ live in the midst of falsehood and die for a falsehood.' Solely in this sense Jesus indeed personifies the whole human drama. He is the complete man, being the one who realized the most absurd condition. He is not the God-man but the man-god. And, like him, each of us can be crucified and victimized – and is to a certain degree.

The divinity in question is therefore altogether terrestrial. 'For three years,' says Kirilov, 'I sought the attribute of my divinity and I have found it. The attribute of my divinity is independence.' Now can be seen the meaning of Kirilov's premise: 'If God does not exist, I am god.' To become god is merely to be free on this earth, not to serve an immortal being. Above all, of course, it is drawing all the inferences from that painful independence. If God exists, all depends on him and we can do nothing against his will. If he does not exist, everything depends on us. For Kirilov, as for Nietzsche, to kill God is to become god oneself; it is to realize on this earth the eternal life of which the Gospel speaks.[21]

But if this metaphysical crime is enough for man's fulfilment, why add suicide? Why kill oneself and leave this world after having won freedom? That is contradictory. Kirilov is well aware of this, for he adds: 'If you feel *that*, you are a tsar and, far from killing yourself, you will live covered with glory.' But men in general do not know it. They do not feel 'that'. As in the time of Prometheus, they entertain blind hopes.[22] They need to be shown the way and cannot do without preaching. Consequently, Kirilov must kill himself out of love for humanity. He must show his brothers a royal and difficult path on which he will be the first. It is a pedagogical suicide. Kirilov sacrifices himself, then. But if he is crucified, he will not be victimized. He remains the man–god, convinced of a death without future, imbued with evangelical melancholy. 'I,' he says, 'am unhappy because I am *obliged* to assert my freedom.' But once he is dead and men are at last enlightened, this earth will be peopled with tsars and lighted up with human glory.

21 'Stavrogin: "Do you believe in eternal life in the other world?" Kirilov: "No, but in eternal life in this world."'
22 'Man simply invented God in order not to kill himself. That is the summary of universal history down to this moment.'

Kirilov's pistol shot will be the signal for the last revolution. Thus, it is not despair that urges him to death, but love of his neighbour for his own sake. Before terminating in blood an indescribable spiritual adventure, Kirilov makes a remark as old as human suffering: 'All is well.'

This theme of suicide in Dostoevsky, then, is indeed an absurd theme. Let us merely note before going on that Kirilov reappears in other characters who themselves set in motion additional absurd themes. Stavrogin and Ivan Karamazov try out the absurd truths in practical life. They are the ones liberated by Kirilov's death. They try their skill at being tsars. Stavrogin leads an 'ironic' life, and it is well known in what regard. He arouses hatred around him. And yet the key to the character is found in his farewell letter: 'I have not been able to detest anything.' He is a tsar in indifference. Ivan is likewise by refusing to surrender the royal powers of the mind. To those who, like his brother, prove by their lives that it is essential to humiliate oneself in order to believe, he might reply that the condition is shameful. His key word is: 'Everything is permitted,' with the appropriate shade of melancholy. Of course, like Nietzsche, the most famous of God's assassins, he ends in madness. But this is a risk worth running, and, faced with such tragic ends, the essential impulse of the absurd mind is to ask: 'What does that prove?'

* * *

Thus the novels, like the *Diary*, propound the absurd question. They establish logic unto death, exaltation, 'dreadful' freedom, the glory of the tsars become human. All is well, everything is permitted, and nothing is hateful – these are absurd judgments. But what an amazing creation in which those creatures of fire and ice seem so familiar to us. The passionate world of indifference that rumbles in their hearts does not seem at all monstrous to us. We recognize in it our everyday anxieties. And probably no one so much as Dostoevsky has managed to give the absurd world such familiar and tormenting charms.

Yet what is his conclusion? Two quotations will show the complete metaphysical reversal that leads the writer to other revelations. The argument of the one who commits logical suicide having provoked protests from the critics, Dostoevsky in the following instalments of the *Diary* amplifies his position and concludes thus: 'If faith in immortality is so necessary to the human being (that without it he comes to the point of killing himself), it must therefore be the normal state of humanity. Since this is the case, the immortality of the human soul exists without any doubt.' Then again in the last pages of his last novel, at the conclusion of that gigantic combat with God, some children ask Aliocha: 'Karamazov, is it true what religion says, that we shall rise from the dead, that we shall see one another again?' And Aliocha answers: 'Certainly, we shall see one another again, we shall joyfully tell one another everything that has happened.'

Thus Kirilov, Stavrogin, and Ivan are defeated. *The Brothers Karamazov* replies to *The Possessed*. And it is indeed a conclusion. Aliocha's case is not ambiguous, as is that of Prince Muichkin. Ill, the latter lives in a perpetual present, tinged with smiles and indifference, and that blissful state might be the eternal life of which the Prince speaks. On the contrary, Aliocha clearly says: 'We shall meet again.' There is no longer any question of suicide and of madness. What is the use, for anyone who is sure of immortality and of its joys? Man exchanges his divinity for happiness. 'We shall joyfully tell one another everything that has happened.' Thus again Kirilov's pistol rang out somewhere in Russia, but the world continued to cherish its blind hopes. Men did not understand 'that'.

Consequently, it is not an absurd novelist addressing us, but an existential novelist. Here, too, the leap is touching and gives its nobility to the art that inspires it. It is a stirring acquiescence, riddled with doubts, uncertain and ardent. Speaking of *The Brothers Karamazov*, Dostoevsky wrote: 'The chief question that will be pursued throughout this book is the very one from which I have suffered consciously or unconsciously all life long: the existence of God.' It is hard to believe that a novel sufficed to transform into joyful certainty the suffering of a lifetime. One commentator[23] correctly pointed out that Dostoevsky is on Ivan's side and that the affirmative chapters took three months of effort whereas what he called 'the blasphemies' were written in three weeks in a state of excitement. There is not one of his characters who does not have that thorn in the flesh, who does not aggravate it or seek a remedy for it in sensation or immortality.[24] In any case, let us remain with this doubt. Here is a work which, in a chiaroscuro more gripping than the light of day, permits us to seize man's struggle against his hopes. Having reached the end, the creator makes his choice against his characters. That contradiction thus allows us to make a distinction. It is not an absurd work that is involved here, but a work that propounds the absurd problem.

Dostoevsky's reply is humiliation, 'shame' according to Stavrogin. An absurd work, on the contrary, does not provide a reply; that is the whole difference. Let us note this carefully in conclusion: what contradicts the absurd in that work is not its Christian character, but rather its announcing a future life. It is possible to be Christian and absurd. There are examples of Christians who do not believe in a future life. In regard to the work of art, it should therefore be possible to define one of the directions of the absurd analysis that could have been anticipated in the preceding pages. It leads to propounding 'the absurdity of the Gospel'. It throws light upon this idea, fertile in repercussions, that convictions do not prevent incredulity. On the contrary, it is easy to see that the author of

23 Boris de Schloezer.
24 Gide's curious and penetrating remark: almost all Dostoevsky's heroes are polygamous.

The Possessed, familiar with these paths, in conclusion took a quite different way. The surprising reply of the creator to his characters, of Dostoevsky to Kirilov, can indeed be summed up thus: existence is illusory *and* it is eternal.

Ephemeral Creation

AT THIS POINT I perceive, therefore, that hope cannot be eluded for ever and that it can beset even those who wanted to be free of it. This is the interest I find in the works discussed up to this point. I could, at least in the realm of creation, list some truly absurd works.[25] But everything must have a beginning. The object of this quest is a certain fidelity. The Church has been so harsh with heretics only because she deemed that there is no worse enemy than a child who has gone astray. But the record of Gnostic effronteries and the persistence of Manichaean currents have contributed more to the construction of orthodox dogma than all the prayers. With due allowance, the same is true of the absurd. One recognizes one's course by discovering the paths that stray from it. At the very conclusion of the absurd reasoning, in one of the attitudes dictated by its logic, it is not a matter of indifference to find hope coming back in under one of its most touching guises. That shows the difficulty of the absurd *ascesis*. Above all, it shows the necessity of unfailing altertness and thus confirms the general plan of this essay.

But if it is still too early to list absurd works, at least a conclusion can be reached as to the creative attitude, one of those which can complete absurd existence. Art can never be so well served as by a negative thought. Its dark and humiliated proceedings are as necessary to the understanding of a great

25 Melville's *Moby Dick*, for instance.

work as black is to white. To work and create 'for nothing', to sculpture in clay, to know that one's creation has no future, to see one's work destroyed in a day while being aware that fundamentally this has no more importance than building for centuries – this is the difficult wisdom that absurd thought sanctions. Performing these two tasks simultaneously, negating on the one hand and magnifying on the other, is the way open to the absurd creator. He must give the void its colours.

This leads to a special conception of the work of art. Too often the work of a creator is looked upon as a series of isolated testimonies. Thus, artist and man of letters are confused. A profound thought is in a constant state of becoming; it adopts the experience of a life and assumes its shape. Likewise, a man's sole creation is strengthened in its successive and multiple aspects: his works. One after another, they comple-ment one another, correct or overtake one another, contradict one another too. If something brings creation to an end, it is not the victorious and illusory cry of the blinded artist: 'I have said everything,' but the death of the creator which closes his experience and the book of his genius.

That effort, that superhuman consciousness are not necessarily apparent to the reader. There is no mystery in human creation. Will performs this miracle. But at least there is no true creation without a secret. To be sure, a succession of works can be but a series of approximations of the same thought. But it is possible to conceive of another type of creator proceeding by juxtaposition. Their works may seem to be devoid of interrelations. To a certain degree, they are contradictory. But viewed all together, they resume their natural grouping. From death, for instance, they derive their definitive significance. They receive their most obvious light from the very life of their author. At the moment of death, the succession of his works is but a collection of failures. But if those failures all have the same resonance, the creator has managed to repeat the image of his own condition, to make the air echo with the sterile secret he possesses.

The effort to dominate is considerable here. But human intelligence is up to much more. It will merely indicate clearly the voluntary aspect of creation. Elsewhere I have brought out the fact that human will had no other purpose than to maintain awareness. But that could not do without discipline. Of all the schools of patience and lucidity, creation is the most effective. It is also the staggering evidence of man's sole dignity: the dogged revolt against his condition, perseverance in an effort considered sterile. It calls for a daily effort, self-mastery, a precise estimate of the limits of truth, measure, and strength. It constitutes an *ascesis*. All that 'for nothing', in order to repeat and mark time. But perhaps the great work of art has less importance in itself than in the ordeal it demands of a man and the opportunity it provides him of overcoming his phantoms and approaching a little closer to his naked reality.

* * *

Let there be no mistake in æsthetics. It is not patient inquiry, the unceasing, sterile illustration of a thesis that I am calling for here. Quite the contrary, if I have made myself clearly understood. The thesis-novel, the work that proves, the most hateful of all, is the one that most often is inspired by a *smug* thought. You demonstrate the truth you feel sure of possessing. But those are ideas one launches, and ideas are the contrary of thought. Those creators are philosophers, ashamed of themselves. Those I am speaking of or whom I imagine are, on the contrary, lucid thinkers. At a certain point where thought turns back on itself, they raise up the images of their works like the obvious symbols of a limited, mortal, and rebellious thought.

They perhaps prove something. But those proofs are ones that the novelists provide for themselves rather than for the world in general. The essential is that the novelists should triumph in the concrete and that this constitute their nobility. This wholly carnal triumph has been prepared for them by a thought in which abstract powers have been humiliated. When they are completely so, at the same time the flesh makes the creation shine forth in all its absurd lustre. After all, ironic philosophies produce passionate works.

Any thought that abandons unity glorifies diversity. And diversity is the home of art. The only thought to liberate the mind is that which leaves it alone, certain of its limits and of its impending end. No doctrine tempts it. It awaits the ripening of the work and of life. Detached from it, the work will once more give a barely muffled voice to a soul for ever freed from hope. Or it will give voice to nothing if the creator, tired of his activity, intends to turn away. That is equivalent.

* * *

Thus, I ask of absurd creation what I required from thought – revolt, freedom, and diversity. Later on it will manifest its utter futility. In that daily effort in which intelligence and passion mingle and delight each other, the absurd man discovers a discipline that will make up the greatest of his strengths. The required diligence, the doggedness and lucidity thus resemble the conqueror's attitude. To create is likewise to give a shape to one's fate. For all these characters, their work defines them at least as much as it is defined by them. The actor taught us this: there is no frontier between being and appearing.

Let me repeat. None of all this has any real meaning. On the way to that liberty, there is still a progress to be made. The final effort for these related minds, creator or conqueror, is to manage to free themselves also from their undertakings: succeed in granting that the very work, whether it be conquest, love, or creation, may well not be; consummate thus the utter futility of any individual life. Indeed, that gives them more freedom in the realization of that work, just as becoming aware of the absurdity of life authorized them to plunge into it with every excess.

All that remains is a fate whose outcome alone is fatal. Outside of that single fatality of death, everything, joy or happiness, is liberty. A world remains of which man is the sole master. What bound him was the illusion of another world. The outcome of his thought, ceasing to be renunciatory, flowers in images. It frolics – in myths, to be sure, but myths with no other depth than that of human suffering and, like it, inexhaustible. Not the divine fable that amuses and blinds, but the terrestrial face, gesture, and drama in which are summed up a difficult wisdom and an ephemeral passion.

THE MYTH OF SISYPHUS

THE GODS HAD condemned Sisyphus to ceaselessly rolling a rock to the top of a mountain, whence the stone would fall back of its own weight. They had thought with some reason that there is no more dreadful punishment than futile and hopeless labour.

If one believes Homer, Sisyphus was the wisest and most prudent of mortals. According to another tradition, however, he was disposed to practise the profession of highwayman. I see no contradiction in this. Opinions differ as to the reasons why he became the futile labourer of the underworld. To begin with, he is accused of a certain levity in regard to the gods. He stole their secrets. Ægina, the daughter of Æsopus, was carried off by Jupiter. The father was shocked by that disappearance and complained to Sisyphus. He, who knew of the abduction, offered to tell about it on condition that Æsopus would give water to the citadel of Corinth. To the celestial thunderbolts he preferred the benediction of water. He was punished for this in the underworld. Homer tells us also that Sisyphus had put Death in chains. Pluto could not endure the sight of his deserted, silent empire. He dispatched the god of war, who liberated Death from the hands of her conqueror.

It is said also that Sisyphus, being near to death, rashly wanted to test his wife's love. He ordered her to cast his unburied body into the middle of the public square. Sisyphus woke up in the underworld. And there, annoyed by an obedience so contrary to human love, he obtained from Pluto permission to return to earth in order to chastise his wife.

But when he had seen again the face of this world, enjoyed water and sun, warm stones and the sea, he no longer wanted to go back to the infernal darkness. Recalls, signs of anger, warnings were of no avail. Many years more he lived facing the curve of the gulf, the sparkling sea, and the smiles of earth. A decree of the gods was necessary. Mercury came and seized the impudent man by the collar and, snatching him from his joys, led him forcibly back to the underworld, where his rock was ready for him.

You have already grasped that Sisyphus is the absurd hero. He *is*, as much through his passions as through his torture. His scorn of the gods, his hatred of death, and his passion for life won him that unspeakable penalty in which the whole being is exerted towards accomplishing nothing. This is the price that must be paid for the passions of this earth. Nothing is told us about Sisyphus in the underworld. Myths are made for the imagination to breathe life into them. As for this myth, one sees merely the whole effort of a body straining to raise the huge stone, to roll it and push it up a slope a hundred times over; one sees the face screwed up, the cheek tight against the stone, the shoulder bracing the clay-covered mass, the foot wedging it, the fresh start with arms outstretched, the wholly human security of two earth-clotted hands. At the very end of his long effort measured by skyless space and time without depth, the purpose is achieved. Then Sisyphus watches the stone rush down in a few moments towards that lower world whence he will have to push it up again towards the summit. He goes back down to the plain.

It is during that return, that pause, that Sisyphus interests me. A face that toils so close to stones is already stone itself! I see that man going back down with a heavy yet measured step towards the torment of which he will never know the end. That hour like a breathing-space which returns as surely as his suffering, that is the hour of consciousness. At each of those moments when he leaves the heights and gradually sinks towards the lairs of the gods, he is superior to his fate. He is stronger than his rock.

If this myth is tragic, that is because its hero is conscious. Where would his torture be, indeed, if at every step the hope of succeeding upheld him? The workman of today works every day in his life at the same tasks, and this fate is no less absurd. But it is tragic only at the rare moments when it becomes conscious. Sisyphus, proletarian of the gods, powerless and rebellious, knows the whole extent of his wretched condition: it is what he thinks of during his descent. The lucidity that was to constitute his torture at the same time crowns his victory. There is no fate that cannot be surmounted by scorn.

* * *

If the descent is thus sometimes performed in sorrow, it can also take place in joy. This word is not too much. Again I fancy Sisyphus returning towards his rock, and the sorrow was in the beginning. When the images of earth cling too tightly to memory, when the call of happiness becomes too insistent, it happens that melancholy rises in man's heart: this is the rock's victory, this is the rock itself. The boundless grief is too heavy to bear. These are our nights of Gethsemane. But crushing truths perish from being acknowledged. Thus, Œdipus at the outset obeys fate without knowing it. But from the moment he knows, his tragedy begins. Yet at the same moment, blind and desperate, he realizes that the only bond linking him to the world is the cool hand of a girl. Then a tremendous remark rings out: 'Despite so many ordeals, my advanced age and the nobility of my soul make me conclude that all is well.' Sophocles' Œdipus, like Dostoevsky's Kirilov, thus gives the recipe for the absurd victory. Ancient wisdom confirms modern heroism.

One does not discover the absurd without being tempted to write a manual of happiness. 'What! by such narrow ways — ?' There is but one world, however. Happiness and the absurd are two sons of the same earth. They are inseparable. It would be a mistake to say that happiness necessarily springs from the absurd discovery. It happens as well that the feeling of the absurd springs from happiness. 'I conclude that all is well,' says Œdipus, and that remark is sacred. It echoes in the wild and limited universe of man. It teaches that all is not, has not been, exhausted. It drives out of this world a god who had come into it with dissatisfaction and a preference for futile sufferings. It makes of fate a human matter, which must be settled among men.

All Sisyphus' silent joy is contained therein. His fate belongs to him. His rock is his thing. Likewise, the absurd man, when he contemplates his torment, silences all the idols. In the universe suddenly restored to its silence, the myriad wondering little voices of the earth rise up. Unconscious, secret calls, invitations from all the faces, they are the necessary reverse and price of victory. There is no sun without shadow, and it is essential to know the night. The absurd man says yes and his effort will henceforth be unceasing. If there is a personal fate, there is no higher destiny, or at least there is but one which he concludes is inevitable and despicable. For the rest, he knows himself to be the master of his days. At that subtle moment when man glances backwards over his life, Sisyphus returning towards his rock, in that slight pivoting he contemplates that series of unrelated actions which becomes his fate, created by him, combined under his memory's eye and soon sealed by his death. Thus, convinced of the wholly human origin of all that is human, a blind man eager to see who knows that the night has no end, he is still on the go. The rock is still rolling.

I leave Sisyphus at the foot of the mountain! One always finds one's burden again. But Sisyphus teaches the higher fidelity that negates the gods and raises rocks. He too concludes that all is well. This universe henceforth without a master seems to him neither sterile nor futile. Each atom of that stone, each mineral flake of that night-filled mountain, in itself forms a world. The struggle itself towards the heights is enough to fill a man's heart. One must imagine Sisyphus happy.

Hope and the Absurd in the Work of Franz Kafka

THE WHOLE ART of Kafka consists in forcing the reader to reread. His endings, or his absence of endings, suggest explanations which, however, are not revealed in clear language but, before they seem justified, require that the story be reread from another point of view. Sometimes there is a double possibility of interpretation, whence appears the necessity for two readings. This is what the author wanted. But it would be wrong to try to interpret everything in Kafka in detail. A symbol is always in general and, however precise its translation, an artist can restore to it only its movement: there is no word-for-word rendering. Moreover, nothing is harder to understand than a symbolic work. A symbol always transcends the one who makes use of it and makes him say in reality more than he is aware of expressing. In this regard, the surest means of getting hold of it is not to provoke it, to begin the work without a preconceived attitude and not to look for its hidden currents. For Kafka in particular it is fair to agree to his rules, to approach the drama through its externals and the novel through its form.

At first glance and for a casual reader, they are disturbing adventures that carry off quaking and dogged characters into pursuit of problems they never formulate. In *The Trial*, Joseph K. is accused. But he doesn't know of what. He is doubtless eager to defend himself, but he doesn't know why. The lawyers find his case difficult. Meanwhile, he does not neglect to love, to eat, or to read his paper. Then he is judged. But the courtroom is very dark. He doesn't understand much. He merely assumes that he is condemned, but to what he barely wonders. At times he suspects just the same, and he continues living. Some time later two well-dressed and polite gentlemen come to get him and invite him to follow them. Most courteously they lead him into a wretched suburb, put his head on a stone, and slit his throat. Before dying the condemned man says merely: 'Like a dog.'

You see that it is hard to speak of a symbol in a tale whose most obvious quality just happens to be naturalness. But naturalness is a hard category to understand. There are works in which the event seems natural to the reader. But there are others (rarer, to be sure) in which the character considers natural what happens to him. By an odd but obvious paradox, the more extraordinary the character's adventures are, the more noticeable will be the naturalness of the story: it is in proportion to the divergence we feel between the strangeness of a man's life and the simplicity with which that man accepts it. It seems that this naturalness is Kafka's. And, precisely, one is well aware what *The Trial* means. People have spoken of an image of the human condition. To be sure. Yet it is both simpler and more complex. I mean that the significance of the novel is more particular and more personal to Kafka. To a certain degree, he is the one who does the talking, even though it is me he confesses. He lives and he is condemned. He learns this on the first pages of the novel he is pursuing in this world, and if he tries to cope with this, he none the less does so without surprise. He will never show sufficient astonishment at this lack of astonishment. It is by such contradictions that the first signs of the absurd work are recognized. The mind projects into the concrete its spiritual tragedy. And it can do so solely by means of a perpetual paradox which confers on colours the power to express the void and on daily gestures the strength to translate eternal ambitions.

Likewise, *The Castle* is perhaps a theology in action, but it is first of all the individual adventure of a soul in quest of its grace, of a man who asks of this world's objects their royal secret and of women the signs of the god that sleeps in them. *Metamorphosis*, in turn, certainly represents the horrible imagery of an ethic of lucidity. But it is also the product of that incalculable amazement man feels at being conscious of the beast he becomes effortlessly. In this fundamental ambiguity lies Kafka's secret. These perpetual oscillations between the natural and the extraordinary, the individual and the universal, the tragic and the everyday, the absurd and the logical, are found throughout his work and give it both its resonance and its meaning. These are the paradoxes that must be enumerated, the contradictions that must be strengthened, in order to understand the absurd work.

A symbol, indeed, assumes two planes, two worlds of ideas and sensations, and a dictionary of correspondences between them. This lexicon is the hardest thing to draw up. But awaking to the two worlds brought face to face is tantamount to getting on the trail of their secret relationships. In Kafka these two worlds are that of everyday life on the one hand and, on the other, that of supernatural anxiety.[26] It seems that we are witnessing here an interminable exploitation of Nietzsche's remark: 'Great problems are in the street.'

There is in the human condition (and this is a commonplace of all literatures) a basic absurdity as well as an implacable nobility. The two coincide, as is natural. Both of them are represented, let me repeat, in the ridiculous divorce separating our spiritual excesses and the ephemeral joys of the body. The absurd thing is that it should be the soul of this body which it transcends so inordinately. Whoever would like to represent this absurdity must give it life in a series of parallel contrasts.

---

26 It is worth noting that the works of Kafka can quite as legitimately be interpreted in the sense of a social criticism (for instance in *The Trial*). It is probable, moreover, that there is no need to choose. Both interpretations are good. In absurd terms, as we have seen, revolt against men is *also* directed against God: great revolutions are always metaphysical.

Thus it is that Kafka expresses tragedy by the everyday and the absurd by the logical.

An actor lends more force to a tragic character the more careful he is not to exaggerate it. If he is moderate, the horror he inspires will be immoderate. In this regard Greek tragedy is rich in lessons. In a tragic work fate always makes itself felt better in the guise of logic and naturalness. Œdipus's fate is announced in advance. It is decided supernaturally that he will commit the murder and the incest. The drama's whole effort is to show the logical system which, from deduction to deduction, will crown the hero's misfortune. Merely to announce to us that uncommon fate is scarcely horrible, because it is improbable. But if its necessity is demonstrated to us in the framework of everyday life, society, state, familiar emotion, then the horror is hallowed. In that revolt that shakes man and makes him say: 'That is not possible,' there is an element of desperate certainty that 'that' can be.

This is the whole secret of Greek tragedy, or at least of one of its aspects. For there is another which, by a reverse method, would help us to understand Kafka better. The human heart has a tiresome tendency to label as fate only what crushes it. But happiness likewise, in its way, is without reason, since it is inevitable. Modern man, however, takes the credit for it himself, when he doesn't fail to recognize it. Much could be said, on the contrary, about the privileged fates of Greek tragedy and those favoured in legend who, like Ulysses, in the midst of the worst adventures are saved from themselves. It was not so easy to return to Ithaca.

What must be remembered in any case is that secret complicity that joins the logical and the everyday to the tragic. This is why Samsa, the hero of *Metamorphosis*, is a travelling salesman. This is why the only thing that disturbs him in the strange adventure that makes a vermin of him is that his boss will be angry at his absence. Legs and feelers grow out on him, his spine arches up, white spots appear on his belly and – I shall not say that this does not astonish him, for the effect would be spoiled – but it causes him a 'slight annoyance'. The whole art of Kafka is in that distinction. In his central work, *The Castle*, the details of everyday life stand out, and yet in that strange novel in which nothing concludes and everything begins over again, it is the essential adventure of a soul in quest of its grace that is represented. That translation of the problem into action, that coincidence of the general and the particular are recognized likewise in the little artifices that belong to every great creator. In *The Trial* the hero might have been named Schmidt or Franz Kafka. But he is named Joseph K. He is not Kafka and yet he is Kafka. He is an average European. He is like everybody else. But he is also the entity K. who is the x of this flesh–and–blood equation.

Likewise, if Kafka wants to express the absurd, he will make use of consistency. You know the story of the crazy man who was fishing in a bathtub. A doctor with ideas as to psychiatric treatments asked him 'if they were biting', to which he received the harsh reply: 'Of course not, you fool, since this is a bathtub.' That story belongs to the baroque type. But in it can be grasped quite clearly to what a degree the absurd effect is linked to an excess of logic. Kafka's world is in truth an indescribable universe in which man allows himself the tormenting luxury of fishing in a bathtub, knowing that nothing will come of it.

Consequently, I recognize here a work that is absurd in its principles. As for *The Trial*, for instance, I can indeed say that it is a complete success. Flesh wins out. Nothing is lacking, neither the unexpressed revolt (but *it* is what is writing), nor lucid and mute despair (but *it* is what is creating), nor that amazing freedom of manner which the characters of the novel exemplify until their ultimate death.

* * *

Yet this world is not so closed as it seems. Into this universe devoid of progress, Kafka is going to introduce hope in a strange form. In this regard *The Trial* and *The Castle* do not follow the same direction. They complement each other. The barely perceptible progression from one to the other represents a tremendous conquest in the realm of evasion. *The Trial* propounds a problem which *The Castle*, to a certain degree, solves. The first describes according to a quasi-scientific method and without concluding. The second, to a certain degree, explains. *The Trial* diagnoses, and *The Castle* imagines a treatment. But the remedy proposed here does not cure. It merely brings the malady back into normal life. It helps to accept it. In a certain sense (let us think of Kierkegaard), it makes people cherish it. The Land Surveyor K. cannot imagine another anxiety than the one that is tormenting him. The very people around him become attached to that void and that nameless pain, as if suffering assumed in this case a privileged aspect. 'How I need you,' Frieda says to K. 'How forsaken I feel, since knowing you, when you are not with me.' This subtle remedy that makes us love what crushes us and makes hope spring up in a world without issue, this sudden 'leap' through which everything is changed, is the secret of the existential revolution and of *The Castle* itself.

Few works are more rigorous in their development than *The Castle*. K. is named Land Surveyor to the Castle and he arrives in the village. But from the village to the Castle it is impossible to communicate. For hundreds of pages K. persists in seeking his way, makes every advance, uses trickery and expedients, never gets angry, and with disconcerting goodwill tries to assume the duties entrusted to him. Each chapter is a new frustration. And also a new beginning. It is not logic, but consistent method. The scope of that insistence constitutes the work's tragic quality. When K. telephones to the Castle, he hears confused, mingled voices, vague laughs, distant invitations. That is enough to feed his hope, like those few signs appearing in summer skies or those evening anticipations which make up our reason for living. Here is found the secret of the melancholy peculiar to Kafka. The same, in truth, that is found in Proust's work or in the landscape of Plotinus: a nostalgia for a lost paradise. 'I become very sad,' says Olga, 'when Barnabas tells me in the morning that he is going to the Castle: that probably futile trip, that probably wasted day, that probably empty hope.' 'Probably' – on this implication Kafka gambles his entire work. But nothing avails; the quest of the eternal here is meticulous. And those inspired automata, Kafka's characters, provide us with a precise image of what we should be if we were deprived of our distractions[27] and utterly consigned to the humiliations of the divine.

In *The Castle* that surrender to the everyday becomes an ethic. The great hope of K. is to get the Castle to adopt him. Unable to achieve this alone, his whole effort is to deserve this favour by becoming an inhabitant of the village, by losing the status of foreigner that everyone makes him feel. What he wants is an occupation, a home, the life of a healthy, normal man. He can't stand his madness any longer. He wants to be reasonable. He wants to cast off the peculiar curse that makes him a stranger to the village. The episode of Frieda is signifi-cant in this regard. If he takes as his mistress this woman who has known one of the Castle's officials, this is because of her past. He derives from her something that transcends him – while being aware of what makes her for ever unworthy of the Castle. This makes one think of Kierkegaard's strange love for Regina Olsen. In certain men, the fire of eternity consuming them is great enough for them to burn in it the very heart of those closest to them. The fatal mistake that consists in giving to God what is not God's is likewise the subject of this episode

---

27 In *The Castle* it seems that 'distractions' in the Pascalian sense are represented by the assistants who 'distract' K. from his anxiety. If Frieda eventually becomes the mistress of one of the assistants, this is because she prefers the stage setting to truth, everyday life to shared anguish.

of *The Castle*. But for Kafka it seems that this is not a mistake. It is a doctrine and a 'leap'. There is nothing that is not God's.

Even more significant is the fact that the Land Surveyor breaks with Frieda in order to go towards the Barnabas sisters. For the Barnabas family is the only one in the village that is utterly forsaken by the Castle and by the village itself. Amalia, the elder sister, has rejected the shameful propositions made her by one of the Castle's officials. The immoral curse that followed has for ever cast her out from the love of God. Being incapable of losing one's honour for God amounts to making oneself unworthy of his grace. You recognize a theme familiar to existential philosophy: truth contrary to morality. At this point things are far-reaching. For the path pursued by Kafka's hero from Frieda to the Barnabas sisters is the very one that leads from trusting love to the deification of the absurd. Here again Kafka's thought runs parallel to Kierkegaard. It is not surprising that the 'Barnabas story' is placed at the end of the book. The Land Surveyor's last attempt is to recapture God through what negates him, to recognize him, not according to our categories of goodness and beauty, but behind the empty and hideous aspects of his indifference, of his injustice, and of his hatred. That stranger who asks the Castle to adopt him is at the end of his voyage a little more exiled because this time he is unfaithful to himself, forsaking morality, logic, and intellectual truths in order to try to enter, endowed solely with his mad hope, the desert of divine grace.[28]

* * *

The word 'hope' used here is not ridiculous. On the contrary, the more tragic the condition described by Kafka, the firmer and more aggressive that hope becomes. The more truly absurd *The Trial* is, the more moving and illegitimate the

28 This is obviously true only of the unfinished version of *The Castle* that Kafka left us. But it is doubtful that the writer would have destroyed in the last chapters his novel's unity of tone.

impassioned 'leap' of *The Castle* seems. But we find here again in a pure state the paradox of existential thought as it is expressed, for instance, by Kierkegaard: 'Earthly hope must be killed; only then can one be saved by true hope,'[29] which can be translated: 'One has to have written *The Trial* to undertake *The Castle.*'

Most of those who have spoken of Kafka have indeed defined his work as a desperate cry with no recourse left to man. But this calls for review. There is hope and hope. To me the optimistic work of Henri Bordeaux seems peculiarly discouraging. This is because it has nothing for the discriminating. Malraux's thought, on the other hand, is always bracing. But in these two cases neither the same hope nor the same despair is at issue. I see merely that the absurd work itself may lead to the infidelity I want to avoid. The work which was but an ineffectual repetition of a sterile condition, a lucid glorification of the ephemeral, becomes here a cradle of illusions. It explains, it gives a shape to hope. The creator can no longer divorce himself from it. It is not the tragic game it was to be. It gives a meaning to the author's life.

It is strange in any case that works of related inspiration like those of Kafka, Kierkegaard, or Chestov – those, in short, of existential novelists and philosophers completely oriented towards the Absurd and its consequences – should in the long run lead to that tremendous cry of hope.

They embrace the God that consumes them. It is through humility that hope enters in. For the absurd of this existence assures them a little more of supernatural reality. If the course of this life leads to God, there is an outcome after all. And the perseverance, the insistence with which Kierkegaard, Chestov, and Kafka's heroes repeat their itineraries are a special warrant of the uplifting power of that certainty.[30]

---

29 Purity of heart.

30 The only character without hope in *The Castle* is Amalia. She is the one with whom the Land Surveyor is most violently contrasted.

Kafka refuses his god moral nobility, evidence, virtue, co-herence, but only the better to fall into his arms. The absurd is recognized, accepted, and man is resigned to it, but from then on we know that it has ceased to be the absurd. Within the limits of the human condition, what greater hope than the hope that allows an escape from that condition? As I see once more, existential thought in this regard (and contrary to current opinion) is steeped in a vast hope. The very hope which at the time of early Christianity and the spreading of the good news inflamed the ancient world. But in that leap that characterizes all existential thought, in that insistence, in that surveying of a divinity devoid of surface, how can one fail to see the mark of a lucidity that repudiates itself? It is merely claimed that this is pride abdicating to save itself. Such a repudiation would be fecund. But this does not change that. The moral value of lucidity cannot be diminished in my eyes by calling it sterile like all pride. For a truth also, by its very definition, is sterile. All facts are. In a world where everything is given and nothing is explained, the fecundity of a value or of a metaphysic is a notion devoid of meaning.

In any case, you see here in what tradition of thought Kafka's work takes its place. It would indeed be intelligent to consider as inevitable the progression leading from *The Trial* to *The Castle*. Joseph K. and the Land Surveyor K. are merely two poles that attract Kafka.[31] I shall speak like him and say that his work is probably not absurd. But that should not deter us from seeing its nobility and universality. They come from the fact that he managed to represent so fully the everyday passage from hope to grief and from desperate wisdom to intentional blind-ness. His work is universal (a really absurd work is not univer-sal) to the extent to which it represents the emotionally

---

31 On the two aspects of Kafka's thought, compare 'In the Penal Colony', published by the *Cahiers du Sud* (and in America by *Partisan Review* – translator's note): 'Guilt ["of man" is understood] is never doubtful' and a fragment of *The Castle* (Momus's report): 'The guilt of the Land Surveyor K. is hard to establish.'

moving face of man fleeing humanity, deriving from his contradictions reasons for believing, reasons for hoping from his fecund despairs, and calling life his terrifying apprenticeship in death. It is universal because its inspiration is religious. As in all religions, man is freed of the weight of his own life. But if I know that, if I can even admire it, I also know that I am not seeking what is universal, but what is true. The two may well not coincide.

This particular view will be better understood if I say that truly hopeless thought just happens to be defined by the opposite criteria and that the tragic work might be the work that, after all future hope is exiled, describes the life of a happy man. The more exciting life is, the more absurd is the idea of losing it. This is perhaps the secret of that proud aridity felt in Nietzsche's work. In this connection, Nietzsche appears to be the only artist to have derived the extreme consequences of an æsthetic of the Absurd, inasmuch as his final message lies in a sterile and conquering lucidity and an obstinate negation of any supernatural consolation.

The preceding should nevertheless suffice to bring out the capital importance of Kafka in the framework of this essay. Here we are carried to the confines of human thought. In the fullest sense of the word, it can be said that everything in that work is essential. In any case, it propounds the absurd problem altogether. If one wants to compare these conclusions with our initial remarks, the content with the form, the secret meaning of *The Castle* with the natural art in which it is moulded, K.'s passionate, proud quest with the everyday setting against which it takes place, then one will realize what may be its greatness. For if nostalgia is the mark of the human, perhaps no one has given such flesh and volume to these phantoms of regret. But at the same time will be sensed what exceptional nobility the absurd work calls for, which is perhaps not found here. If the nature of art is to bind the general to the particular, ephemeral eternity of a drop of water to the play of its lights, it is even truer to judge the greatness of the absurd writer by the distance he is able to introduce between these two worlds. His secret consists in being able to find the exact point where they meet in their greatest disproportion.

And, to tell the truth, this geometrical locus of man and the inhuman is seen everywhere by the pure in heart. If Faust and Don Quixote are eminent creations of art, this is because of the immeasurable nobilities they point out to us with their earthly hands. Yet a moment always comes when the mind negates the truths that those hands can touch. A moment comes when the creation ceases to be taken tragically; it is merely taken seriously. Then man is concerned with hope. But that is not his business. His business is to turn away from subterfuge. Yet this is just what I find at the conclusion of the vehement proceedings Kafka institutes against the whole universe. His unbelievable verdict is this hideous and upsetting world in which the very moles dare to hope.[32]

32 What is offered above is obviously an interpretation of Kafka's work. But it is only fair to add that nothing prevents its being considered, aside from any interpretation, from a purely æsthetic point of view. For instance, B. Groethuysen in his remarkable preface to *The Trial* limits himself, more wisely than we, to following merely the painful fancies of what he calls, most strikingly, a daydreamer. It is the fate and perhaps the greatness of that work that it offers everything and confirms nothing.

REFLECTIONS ON THE GUILLOTINE

TRANSLATED BY JUSTIN O'BRIEN

SHORTLY BEFORE THE war of 1914, an assassin whose crime was particularly repulsive (he had slaughtered a family of farmers, including the children) was condemned to death in Algiers. He was a farm worker who had killed in a sort of bloodthirsty frenzy but had aggravated his case by robbing his victims. The affair created a great stir. It was generally thought that decapitation was too mild a punishment for such a monster. This was the opinion, I have been told, of my father, who was especially aroused by the murder of the children. One of the few things I know about him, in any case, is that he wanted to witness the execution, for the first time in his life. He got up in the dark to go to the place of execution at the other end of town amid a great crowd of people. What he saw that morning he never told anyone. My mother relates merely that he came rushing home, his face distorted, refused to talk, lay down for a moment on the bed, and suddenly began to vomit. He had just discovered the reality hidden under the noble phrases with which it was masked. Instead of thinking of the slaughtered children, he could think of nothing but that quivering body that had just been dropped on to a board to have its head cut off.

Presumably that ritual act is horrible indeed if it manages to overcome the indignation of a simple, straightforward man and if a punishment he considered richly deserved had no other effect in the end than to nauseate him. When the extreme penalty simply causes vomiting on the part of the respectable citizen it is supposed to protect, how can anyone maintain that it is likely, as it ought to be, to bring more peace and order into the community? Rather, it is obviously no less repulsive than the crime, and this new murder, far from making amends for the harm done to the social body, adds a new blot to the first one. Indeed, no one dares speak directly of the ceremony. Officials and journalists who have to talk about it, as if they were aware of both its provocative and its shameful aspects, have made up a sort of ritual language, reduced to stereotyped phrases. Hence we read at breakfast time in a corner of the newspaper that the condemned 'has paid his debt to society' or that he has 'atoned' or that 'at five a.m. justice was done'. The officials call the condemned man 'the interested party' or 'the patient' or refer to him by a number. People write of capital punishment as if they were whispering. In our well-policed society we recognize that an illness is serious from the fact that we don't dare speak of it directly. For a long time, in middle-class families people said no more than that the elder daughter had a 'suspicious cough' or that the father had a 'growth' because tuberculosis and cancer were looked upon as some-what shameful maladies. This is probably even truer of capital punishment since everyone strives to refer to it only through euphemisms. It is to the body politic what cancer is to the individual body, with this difference: no one has ever spoken of the necessity of cancer. There is no hesitation, on the other hand, about presenting capital punishment as a regrettable necessity, a necessity that justifies killing because it is necessary, and let's not talk about it because it is regrettable.

But it is my intention to talk about it crudely. Not because I like scandal, nor, I believe, because of an unhealthy streak in my nature. As a writer, I have always loathed avoiding the issue; as a man, I believe that the repulsive aspects of our condition, if they are inevitable, must merely be faced in silence. But when silence or tricks of language contribute to maintaining an abuse that must be reformed or a suffering that can be relieved, then there is no other solution but to speak out and show the obscenity hidden under the verbal cloak. France shares with England and Spain the honour of being one of the last countries this side of the iron curtain to keep capital punishment in its arsenal of repression. The survival of such a primitive rite has been made possible among us only by the thoughtlessness or ignorance of the public, which reacts only with the ceremonial phrases that have been drilled into it. When the imagination sleeps, words are emptied of their meaning: a deaf population absent-mindedly registers the condemnation of a man. But if people are shown the machine, made to touch the wood and steel and to hear the sound of a head falling, then public imagination, suddenly awakened, will repudiate both the vocabulary and the penalty.

When the Nazis in Poland indulged in public executions of hostages, to keep those hostages from shouting words of revolt and liberty they muzzled them with a plaster-coated gag. It would be shocking to compare the fate of those innocent victims with that of condemned criminals. But, aside from the fact that criminals are not the only ones to be guillotined in our country, the method is the same. We smother under padded words a penalty whose legitimacy we could assert only after we had examined the penalty in reality. Instead of saying that the death penalty is first of all necessary and then adding that it is better not to talk about it, it is essential to say what it really is and then say whether, being what it is, it is to be considered as necessary.

So far as I am concerned, I consider it not only useless but definitely harmful, and I must record my opinion here before getting to the subject itself. It would not be fair to imply that I reached this conclusion as a result of the weeks of investigation and research I have just devoted to this question. But it would be just as unfair to attribute my conviction to mere mawkishness. I am far from indulging in the flabby pity characteristic of humanitarians, in which values and responsibilities fuse, crimes are balanced against one another, and innocence finally loses its rights. Unlike many of my well-known contemporaries, I do not think that man is by nature a social animal. To tell the truth, I think just the reverse. But I believe, and this is quite different, that he cannot live henceforth outside of society, whose laws are necessary to his physical survival. Hence the responsibilities must be established by society itself according to a reasonable and workable scale. But the law's final justification is in the good it does or fails to do to the society of a given place and time. For years I have been unable to see anything in capital punishment but a penalty the imagination could not endure and a lazy disorder that my reason condemned. Yet I was ready to think that my imagination was influencing my judgment. But, to tell the truth, I found during my recent research nothing that did not strengthen my conviction, nothing that modified my arguments. On the contrary, to the arguments I already had others were added. Today I share absolutely Koestler's conviction: the death penalty besmirches our society, and its upholders cannot reasonably defend it. Without repeating his decisive defence, without piling up facts and figures that would only duplicate others (and Jean Bloch-Michel's make them useless), I shall merely state reasons to be added to Koestler's; like his, they argue for an immediate abolition of the death penalty.

We all know that the great argument of those who defend capital punishment is the exemplary value of the punishment. Heads are cut off not only to punish but to intimidate, by a frightening example, any who might be tempted to imitate the guilty. Society is not taking revenge; it merely wants to forestall. It waves the head in the air so that potential murderers will see their fate and recoil from it.

This argument would be impressive if we were not obliged to note:

1) that society itself does not believe in the exemplary value it talks about;

2) that there is no proof that the death penalty ever made a single murderer recoil when he had made up his mind,

whereas clearly it had no effect but one of fascination on thousands of criminals;

3) that, in other regards, it constitutes a repulsive example, the consequences of which cannot be foreseen.

To begin with, society does not believe in what it says. If it really believed what it says, it would exhibit the heads. Society would give executions the benefit of the publicity it generally uses for national bond issues or new brands of drinks. But we know that executions in our country, instead of taking place publicly, are now perpetrated in prison courtyards before a limited number of specialists. We are less likely to know why and since when. This is a relatively recent measure. The last public execution, which took place in 1939, beheaded Weidmann, the author of several murders, who was notorious for his crimes. That morning a large crowd gathered at Versailles, including a large number of photographers. Between the moment when Weidmann was shown to the crowd and the moment when he was decapitated, photographs could be taken. A few hours later *Paris-Soir* published a page of illustrations of that appetizing event. Thus the good people of Paris could see that the light precision instrument used by the executioner was as different from the historical scaffold as a Jaguar is from one of our old Pierce-Arrows. The administration and the government, contrary to all hope, took such excellent publicity very badly and protested that the press had tried to satisfy the sadistic instincts of its readers. Consequently, it was decided that executions would no longer take place publicly, an arrangement that, soon after, facilitated the work of the occupation authorities. Logic, in that affair, was not on the side of the lawmaker.

On the contrary, a special decoration should have been awarded to the editor of *Paris-Soir*, thereby encouraging him to do better the next time. If the penalty is intended to be exemplary, then, not only should the photographs be multiplied, but the machine should even be set on a platform in Place de la Concorde at two p.m., the entire population should be invited, and the ceremony should be put on television for those who couldn't attend. Either this must be done or else there must be no more talk of exemplary value. How can a furtive assassination committed at night in a prison courtyard be exemplary? At most, it serves the purpose of periodically informing the citizens that they will die if they happen to kill – a future that can be promised even to those who do not kill. For the penalty to be truly exemplary it must be frightening. Tuaut de La Bouverie, representative of the people in 1791 and a partisan of public executions, was more logical when he declared to the National Assembly: 'It takes a terrifying spectacle to hold the people in check.'

Today there is no spectacle, but only a penalty known to all by hearsay and, from time to time, the news of an execution dressed up in soothing phrases. How could a future criminal keep in mind, at the moment of his crime, a sanction that everyone strives to make more and more abstract? And if it is really desired that he constantly keep that sanction in mind so that it will first balance and later reverse a frenzied decision, should there not be an effort to engrave that sanction and its dreadful reality in the sensitivity of all by every visual and verbal means?

Instead of vaguely evoking a debt that someone this very morning paid society, would it not be a more effective example to remind each taxpayer in detail of what he may expect? Instead of saying: 'If you kill, you will atone for it on the scaffold,' wouldn't it be better to tell him, for purposes of example: 'If you kill, you will be imprisoned for months or years, torn between an impossible despair and a constantly renewed terror, until one morning we shall slip into your cell after removing our shoes the better to take you by surprise while you are sound asleep after the night's anguish. We shall fall on you, tie your hands behind your back, cut with scissors your shirt collar and your hair if need be. Perfectionists that we are, we shall bind your arms with a strap so that you are forced to stoop and your neck will be more accessible. Then we shall carry you, an assistant on each side supporting you by the arm, with your feet dragging behind through the corridors. Then, under a night sky, one of the executioners will finally seize you by the seat of your pants and throw you horizontally on a board while another will steady your head in the lunette and a third will let fall from a height of seven feet a hundred-and-twenty-pound blade that will slice off your head like a razor.'

For the example to be even better, for the terror to impress each of us sufficiently to outweigh at the right moment an irresistible desire for murder, it would be essential to go still further. Instead of boasting, with the pretentious thoughtlessness characteristic of us, of having invented this rapid and humane[1] method of killing condemned men, we should publish thousands of copies of the eyewitness accounts and medical reports describing the state of the body after the execution, to be read in schools and universities. Particularly suitable for this purpose is the recent report to the Academy of Medicine made by Doctors Piedelièvre and Fournier. Those courageous doctors, invited in the interest of science to examine the bodies of the guillotined after the execution, considered it their duty to sum up their dreadful observations: 'If we may be permitted to give our opinion, such sights are frightfully painful. The blood flows from the blood vessels at the speed of the severed carotids, then it coagulates. The muscles contract and their fibrillation is stupefying; the intestines ripple and the heart moves irregularly, incompletely, fascinatingly. The mouth puckers at certain moments in a terrible pout. It is true that in that severed head the eyes are motionless with dilated pupils; fortunately they look at nothing and, if they are devoid of the

---

[1] According to the optimistic Dr Guillotin, the condemned was not to feel anything. At most a 'slight sensation of coldness on his neck'.

cloudiness and opalescence of the corpse, they have no motion; their transparence belongs to life, but their fixity belongs to death. All this can last minutes, even hours, in sound specimens: death is not immediate.... Thus, every vital element survives decapitation. The doctor is left with this impression of a horrible experience, of a murderous vivisection, followed by a premature burial.'[2]

I doubt that there are many readers who can read that terrifying report without blanching. Consequently, its exemplary power and its capacity to intimidate can be counted on. There is no reason not to add to it eyewitness accounts that confirm the doctors' observations. Charlotte Corday's severed head blushed, it is said, under the executioner's slap. This will not shock anyone who listens to more recent observers. An executioner's assistant (hence hardly suspect of indulging in romanticizing and sentimentality) describes in these terms what he was forced to see: 'It was a madman undergoing a real attack of *delirium tremens* that we dropped under the blade. The head dies at once. But the body literally jumps about in the basket, straining on the cords. Twenty minutes later, at the cemetery, it is still quivering.'[3] The present chaplain of the Santé prison, Father Devoyod (who does not seem opposed to capital punishment), gives in his book, *Les Délinquants*,[4] an account that goes rather far and renews the story of Languille, whose decapitated head answered the call of his name:[5] 'The morning of the execution, the condemned man was in a very bad mood and refused the consolations of religion. Knowing his heart of hearts and the affection he had for his wife, who was very devout, we said to him: "Come now, out of love for your wife, commune with yourself a moment before dying," and the condemned man accepted. He communed at length

2 *Justice sans bourreau,* No. 2 (June 1956).
3 Published by Roger Grenier in *Les Monstres* (Gallimard). These declarations are authentic.
4 Editions Matot-Braine, Reims.
5 In 1905 in the Loiret.

before the crucifix, then he seemed to pay no further attention to our presence. When he was executed, we were a short distance from him. His head fell into the trough in front of the guillotine and the body was immediately put into the basket; but, by some mistake, the basket was closed before the head was put in. The assistant who was carrying the head had to wait a moment until the basket was opened again; now, during that brief space of time we could see the condemned man's eyes fixed on me with a look of supplication, as if to ask forgiveness. Instinctively we made the sign of the cross to bless the head, and then the lids blinked, the expression of the eyes softened, and finally the look, that had remained full of expression, became vague . . . .' The reader may or may not, according to his faith, accept the explanation provided by the priest. At least those eyes that 'had remained full of expression' need no interpretation.

I could adduce other first-hand accounts that would be just as hallucinating. But I, for one, could not go on. After all, I do not claim that capital punishment is exemplary, and the penalty seems to me just what it is, a crude surgery practised under conditions that leave nothing edifying about it. Society, on the other hand, and the State, which is not so impressionable, can very well put up with such details and, since they extol an example, ought to try to get everyone to put up with them so that no one will be ignorant of them and the population, terrorized once and for all, will become Franciscan one and all. Whom do they hope to intimidate, otherwise, by that example for ever hidden, by the threat of a punishment described as easy and swift and easier to bear, after all, than cancer, by a penalty submerged in the flowers of rhetoric? Certainly not those who are considered respectable (some of them are) because they are sleeping at that hour, and the great example has not been announced to them, and they will be eating their toast and marmalade at the time of the premature burial, and they will be informed of the work of justice, if perchance they read the newspapers, by an insipid news item that will melt like sugar in their memory. And, yet, those peaceful creatures are the ones who provide the largest percentage of homicides. Many such respectable people are potential criminals. According to a magistrate, the vast majority of murderers he had known did not know when shaving in the morning that they were going to kill later in the day. As an example and for the sake of security, it would be wiser, instead of hiding the execution, to hold up the severed head in front of all who are shaving in the morning.

Nothing of the sort happens. The State disguises executions and keeps silent about these statements and eyewitness accounts. Hence it doesn't believe in the exemplary value of the penalty, except by tradition and because it has never bothered to think about the matter. The criminal is killed because this has been done for centuries and, besides, he is killed in a way that was set at the end of the eighteenth century. Out of habit, people will turn to arguments that were used centuries ago, even though these arguments must be contradicted by measures that the evolution of public sensitivity has made inevitable. A law is applied without being thought out and the condemned die in the name of a theory in which the executioners do not believe. If they believed in it, this would be obvious to all. But publicity not only arouses sadistic instincts with incalculable repercussions eventually leading to another murder; it also runs the risk of provoking revolt and disgust in the public opinion. It would become harder to execute men one after another, as is done in our country today, if those executions were translated into vivid images in the popular imagination. The man who enjoys his coffee while reading that justice has been done would spit it out at the least detail. And the texts I have quoted might seem to vindicate certain professors of criminal law who, in their obvious inability to justify that anachronistic penalty, console themselves by declaring, with the sociologist Tarde, that it is better to cause death without causing suffering than it is to cause suffering without causing death. This is why we must approve the position of Gambetta, who, as an adversary of the death penalty, voted against a bill involving suppression of publicity for executions, declaring: 'If you suppress the horror of the spectacle, if you execute inside prisons, you will smother the public outburst of revolt that has taken place of late and you will strengthen the death penalty.'

Indeed, one must kill publicly or confess that one does not feel authorized to kill. If society justifies the death penalty by the necessity of the example, it must justify itself by making the publicity necessary. It must show the executioner's hands each time and force everyone to look at them – the over-delicate citizens and all those who had any responsibility in bringing the executioner into being. Otherwise, society admits that it kills without knowing what it is saying or doing. Or else it admits that such revolting ceremonies can only excite crime or completely upset opinion. Who could better state this than a magistrate at the end of his career, Judge Falco, whose brave confession deserves serious reflection: 'The only time in my life when I decided against a commutation of penalty and in favour of execution, I thought that, despite my position, I could attend the execution and remain utterly impassive. Moreover, the criminal was not very interesting: he had tormented his daughter and finally thrown her into a well. But, after his execution, for weeks and even months, my nights were haunted by that recollection.... Like everyone else, I served in the war and saw an innocent generation die, but I can state that nothing gave me the sort of bad conscience I felt in the face of the kind of administrative murder that is called capital punishment.'[6]

But, after all, why should society believe in that example when it does not stop crime, when its effects, if they exist, are

6 *Réalités*, No. 105 (October 1954).

invisible? To begin with, capital punishment could not intimidate the man who doesn't know that he is going to kill, who makes up his mind to it in a flash and commits his crime in a state of frenzy or obsession, nor the man who, going to an appointment to have it out with someone, takes along a weapon to frighten the faithless one or the opponent and uses it although he didn't want to or didn't think he wanted to. In other words, it could not intimidate the man who is hurled into crime as if into a calamity. This is tantamount to saying that it is powerless in the majority of cases. It is only fair to point out that in our country capital punishment is rarely applied in such cases. But the word 'rarely' itself makes one shudder.

Does it frighten at least that race of criminals on whom it claims to operate and who live off crime? Nothing is less certain. We can read in Koestler that at a time when pickpockets were executed in England, other pickpockets exercised their talents in the crowd surrounding the scaffold where their colleague was being hanged. Statistics drawn up at the beginning of the century in England show that out of 250 who were hanged, 170 had previously attended one or more executions. And in 1886, out of 167 condemned men who had gone through the Bristol prison, 164 had witnessed at least one execution. Such statistics are no longer possible to gather in France because of the secrecy surrounding executions. But they give cause to think that around my father, the day of that execution, there must have been a rather large number of future criminals, who did not vomit. The power of intimidation reaches only the quiet individuals who are not drawn towards crime and has no effect on the hardened ones who need to be softened. In Koestler's essay and in the detailed studies will be found the most convincing facts and figures on this aspect of the subject.

It cannot be denied, however, that men fear death. The privation of life is indeed the supreme penalty and ought to excite in them a decisive fear. The fear of death, arising from the most obscure depths of the individual, ravages him; the instinct to live, when it is threatened, panics and struggles in agony. Therefore the legislator was right in thinking that his law was based upon one of the most mysterious and most powerful incentives of human nature. But law is always simpler than nature. When law ventures, in the hope of dominating, into the dark regions of consciousness, it has little chance of being able to simplify the complexity it wants to codify.

If fear of death is, indeed, a fact, another fact is that such fear, however great it may be, has never sufficed to quell human passions. Bacon is right in saying that there is no passion so weak that it cannot confront and overpower fear of death. Revenge, love, honour, pain, another fear manage to overcome it. How could cupidity, hatred, jealousy fail to do what love of a person or a country, what a passion for freedom manage to do? For centuries the death penalty, often accompanied by barbarous refinements, has been trying to hold crime in check; yet crime persists. Why? Because the instincts that are warring in man are not, as the law claims, constant forces in a state of equilibrium. They are variable forces constantly waxing and waning, and their repeated lapses from equilibrium nourish the life of the mind as electrical oscillations, when close enough, set up a current. Just imagine the series of oscillations, from desire to lack of appetite, from decision to renunciation, through which each of us passes in a single day, multiply these variations infinitely, and you will have an idea of psychological proliferation. Such lapses from equilibrium are generally too fleeting to allow a single force to dominate the whole being. But it may happen that one of the soul's forces breaks loose until it fills the whole field of consciousness; at such a moment no instinct, not even that of life, can oppose the tyranny of that irresistible force. For capital punishment to be really intimidating, human nature would have to be different; it would have to be as stable and serene as the law itself. But then human nature would be dead.

It is not dead. This is why, however surprising this may seem to anyone who has never observed or directly experienced human complexity, the murderer, most of the time, feels innocent when he kills. Every criminal acquits himself before he is judged. He considers himself, if not within his right, at least excused by circumstances. He does not think or foresee; when he thinks, it is to foresee that he will be forgiven altogether or in part. How could he fear what he considers highly improbable? He will fear death after the verdict but not before the crime. Hence the law, to be intimidating, should leave the murderer no chance, should be implacable in advance and particularly admit no extenuating circumstance. But who among us would dare ask this?

If anyone did, it would still be necessary to take into account another paradox of human nature. If the instinct to live is fundamental, it is no more so than another instinct of which the academic psychologists do not speak: the death instinct, which at certain moments calls for the destruction of oneself and of others. It is probable that the desire to kill often coincides with the desire to die or to annihilate oneself.[7] Thus, the instinct for self-preservation is matched, in variable proportions, by the instinct for destruction. The latter is the only way of explaining altogether the various perversions which, from alcoholism to drugs, lead an individual to his death while he knows full well what is happening. Man wants to live, but it is useless to hope that this desire will dictate all his actions. He also wants to be nothing; he wants the irreparable, and death for its own sake. So it happens that the criminal wants not only the crime but the suffering that goes with it, even (one might say, especially) if that suffering is exceptional. When that odd desire grows and becomes dominant, the prospect of being put to death not only fails to stop the criminal, but probably even

---

7 It is possible to read every week in the papers of criminals who originally hesitated between killing themselves and killing others.

adds to the vertigo in which he swoons. Thus, in a way, he kills in order to die.

Such peculiarities suffice to explain why a penalty that seems calculated to frighten normal minds is in reality altogether unrelated to ordinary psychology. All statistics without exception, those concerning countries that have abolished execution as well as the others, show that there is no connection between the abolition of the death penalty and criminality.[8] Criminal statistics neither increase nor decrease. The guillotine exists, and so does crime; between the two there is no other apparent connection than that of the law. All we can conclude from the figures, set down at length in statistical tables, is this: for centuries crimes other than murder were punished with death, and the supreme punishment, repeated over and over again, did not do away with any of those crimes. For centuries now, those crimes have no longer been punished with death. Yet they have not increased; in fact, some of them have decreased. Similarly, murder has been punished with execution for centuries and yet the race of Cain has not disappeared. Finally, in the thirty-three nations that have abolished the death penalty or no longer use it, the number of murders has not increased. Who could deduce from this that capital punishment is really intimidating?

Conservatives cannot deny these facts or these figures. Their only and final reply is significant. They explain the paradoxical attitude of a society that so carefully hides the executions it claims to be exemplary. 'Nothing proves, indeed,' say the conservatives, 'that the death penalty is exemplary; as a matter of fact, it is certain that thousands of murderers have not been intimidated by it. But there is no way of knowing those it has intimidated; consequently, nothing proves that it is not exemplary.' Thus, the greatest of punishments, the one that

8 Report of the English Select Committee of 1930 and of the English Royal Commission that recently resumed the study: 'All the statistics we have examined confirm the fact that abolition of the death penalty has not provoked an increase in the number of crimes.'

involves the last dishonour for the condemned and grants the supreme privilege to society, rests on nothing but an unverifiable possibility. Death, on the other hand, does not involve degrees or probabilities. It solidifies all things, culpability and the body, in a definitive rigidity. Yet it is administered among us in the name of chance and a calculation. Even if that calculation were reasonable, should there not be a certainty to authorize the most certain of deaths? However, the condemned is cut in two, not so much for the crime he committed but by virtue of all the crimes that might have been and were not committed, that can be and will not be committed. The most sweeping uncertainty in this case authorizes the most implacable certainty.

I am not the only one to be amazed by such a dangerous contradiction. Even the State condemns it, and such bad conscience explains in turn the contradiction of its own attitude. The State divests its executions of all publicity because it cannot assert, in the face of facts, that they ever served to intimidate criminals. The State cannot escape the dilemma Beccaria described when he wrote: 'If it is important to give the people proofs of power often, then executions must be frequent; but crimes will have to be frequent too, and this will prove that the death penalty does not make the complete impression that it should, whence it results that it is both useless and necessary.' What can the State do with a penalty that is useless and necessary, except to hide it without abolishing it? The State will keep it then, a little out of the way, not without embarrassment, in the blind hope that one man at least, one day at least, will be stopped from his murderous gesture by thought of the punishment and, without anyone's ever knowing it, will justify a law that has neither reason nor experience in its favour. In order to continue claiming that the guillotine is exemplary, the State is consequently led to multiply very real murders in the hope of avoiding a possible murder which, as far as it knows or ever will know, may never be perpetrated.

An odd law, to be sure, which knows the murder it commits and will never know the one it prevents.

What will be left of that power of example if it is proved that capital punishment has another power, and a very real one, which degrades men to the point of shame, madness, and murder?

It is already possible to follow the exemplary effects of such ceremonies on public opinion, the manifestations of sadism they arouse, the hideous vainglory they excite in certain criminals. No nobility in the vicinity of the gallows, but disgust, contempt, or the vilest indulgence of the senses. These effects are well known. Decency forced the guillotine to emigrate from Place de l'Hotel de Ville to the city gates, then into the prisons. We are less informed as to the feelings of those whose job it is to attend such spectacles. Just listen then to the warden of an English prison who confesses to 'a keen sense of personal shame' and to the chaplain who speaks of 'horror, shame, and humiliation'.[9] Just imagine the feelings of the man who kills under orders – I mean the executioner. What can we think of those officials who call the guillotine 'the shunting engine', the condemned man 'the client' or 'the parcel'? The priest Bela Just, who accompanied more than thirty condemned men, writes: 'The slang of the administrators of justice is quite as cynical and vulgar as that of the criminals.'[10] And here are the remarks of one of our assistant executioners on his journeys to the provinces: 'When we would start on a trip, it was always a lark, with taxis and the best restaurants part of the spree!'[11] The same one says, boasting of the executioner's skill in releasing the blade: 'You could *allow yourself the fun* of pulling the client's hair.' The dissoluteness expressed here has other, deeper aspects. The clothing of the condemned belongs in principle

---

9 Report of the Select Committee, 1930.
10 *La Potence et la Croix* (Fasquelle).
11 Roger Grenier: *Les Monstres* (Gallimard).

to the executioner. The elder Deibler used to hang all such articles of clothing in a shed and *now and then would go and look at them*. But there are more serious aspects. Here is what our assistant executioner declares: 'The new executioner is batty about the guillotine. He sometimes spends days on end at home sitting on a chair, ready with hat and coat on, waiting for a summons from the Ministry.'[12]

Yes, this is the man of whom Joseph de Maistre said that, for him to exist, there had to be a special decree from the divine power and that, without him, 'order yields to chaos, thrones collapse, and society disappears'. This is the man through whom society rids itself altogether of the guilty man, for the executioner signs the prison release and takes charge of a free man. The fine and solemn example, thought up by our legislators, at least produces one sure effect – to depreciate or to destroy all humanity and reason in those who take part in it directly. But, it will be said, these are exceptional creatures who find a vocation in such dishonour. They seem less exceptional when we learn that hundreds of persons offer to serve as executioners without pay. The men of our generation, who have lived through the history of recent years, will not be astonished by this bit of information. They know that behind the most peaceful and familiar faces slumbers the impulse to torture and murder. The punishment that aims to intimidate an unknown murderer certainly confers a vocation of killer on many another monster about whom there is no doubt. And since we are busy justifying our cruellest laws with probable considerations, let there be no doubt that out of those hundreds of men whose services were declined, one at least must have satisfied otherwise the bloodthirsty instincts the guillotine excited in him.

If, therefore, there is a desire to maintain the death penalty, let us at least be spared the hypocrisy of a justification

12 Ibid.

by example. Let us be frank about that penalty which can have no publicity, that intimidation which works only on respectable people, so long as they are respectable, which fascinates those who have ceased to be respectable and debases or deranges those who take part in it. It is a penalty, to be sure, a frightful torture, both physical and moral, but it provides no sure example except a demoralizing one. It punishes, but it forestalls nothing; indeed, it may even arouse the impulse to murder. It hardly seems to exist, except for the man who suffers it – in his soul for months and years, in his body during the desperate and violent hour when he is cut in two without suppressing his life. Let us call it by the name which, for lack of any other nobility, will at least give the nobility of truth, and let us recognize it for what it is essentially: a revenge.

A punishment that penalizes without forestalling is indeed called revenge. It is a quasi-arithmetical reply made by society to whoever breaks its primordial law. That reply is as old as man; it is called the law of retaliation. Whoever has done me harm must suffer harm; whoever has put out my eye must lose an eye; and whoever has killed must die. This is an emotion, and a particularly violent one, not a principle. Retaliation is related to nature and instinct, not to law. Law, by definition, cannot obey the same rules as nature. If murder is in the nature of man, the law is not intended to imitate or reproduce that nature. It is intended to correct it. Now, retaliation does no more than ratify and confer the status of a law on a pure impulse of nature. We have all known that impulse, often to our shame, and we know its power, for it comes down to us from the primitive forests. In this regard, we French, who are properly indignant upon seeing the oil king in Saudi Arabia preach international democracy and call in a butcher to cut off a thief's hand with a cleaver, live also in a sort of Middle Ages without even the consolations of faith. We still define justice according to the rules of a crude arithmetic.[13] Can it be said at least that that arithmetic is exact and that justice, even when elementary, even when limited to legal revenge, is safeguarded by the death penalty? The answer must be no.

Let us leave aside the fact that the law of retaliation is inapplicable and that it would seem just as excessive to punish the incendiary by setting fire to his house as it would be insufficient to punish the thief by deducting from his bank account a sum equal to his theft. Let us admit that it is just and necessary to compensate for the murder of the victim by the death of the murderer. But beheading is not simply death. It is just as different, in essence, from the privation of life as a concentration camp is from prison. It is a murder, to be sure, and one that arithmetically pays for the murder committed. But it adds to death a rule, a public premeditation known to the future victim, an organization, in short, which is in itself a source of moral sufferings more terrible than death. Hence there is no equivalence. Many laws consider a premeditated crime more serious than a crime of pure violence. But what then is capital punishment but the most premeditated of murders, to which no criminal's deed, however calculated it may be, can be compared? For there to be equivalence, the death penalty would have to punish a criminal who had warned his victim of the date at which he would inflict a horrible death on him and who, from that moment onwards, had confined him at his mercy for months. Such a monster is not encountered in private life.

There, too, when our official jurists talk of putting to death without causing suffering, they don't know what they are

13 A few years ago I asked for the reprieve of six Tunisians who had been condemned to death for the murder, in a riot, of three French policemen. The circumstances in which the murder had taken place made difficult any division of responsibilities. A note from the executive office of the President of the Republic informed me that my appeal was being considered by the appropriate organization. Unfortunately, when that note was addressed to me I had already read two weeks earlier that the sentence had been carried out. Three of the condemned men had been put to death and the three others reprieved. The reasons for reprieving some rather than the others were not convincing. But probably it was essential to carry out three executions where there had been three victims.

talking about and, above all, they lack imagination. The devastating, degrading fear that is imposed on the condemned for months or years[14] is a punishment more terrible than death, and one that was not imposed on the victim. Even in the fright caused by the mortal violence being done to him, most of the time the victim is hastened to his death without knowing what is happening to him. The period of horror is counted out with his life, and hope of escaping the madness that has swept down upon that life probably never leaves him. On the other hand, the horror is parcelled out to the man who is condemned to death. Torture through hope alternates with the pangs of animal despair. The lawyer and chaplain, out of mere humanity, and the jailers, so that the condemned man will keep quiet, are unanimous in assuring him that he will be reprieved. He believes this with all his being and then he ceases to believe it. He hopes by day and despairs of it by night.[15] As the wecks pass, hope and despair increase and become equally unbearable. According to all accounts, the colour of the skin changes, fear acting like an acid. 'Knowing that you are going to die is nothing,' said a condemned man in Fresnes. 'But not knowing whether or not you are going to live, that's terror and anguish.' Cartouche said of the supreme punishment: 'Why, it's just a few minutes that have to be lived through.' But it is a matter of months, not of minutes. Long in advance the condemned man knows that he is going to be killed and that the only thing that can save him is a reprieve, rather similar, for him, to the decrees of heaven. In any case, he cannot intervene, make a plea himself, or convince. Everything goes on outside of him.

14 Roemen, condemned to death at the Liberation of France, remained seven hundred days in chains before being executed, and this is scandalous. Those condemned under common law, as a general rule, wait from three to six months for the morning of their death. And it is difficult, if one wants to maintain their chances of survival, to shorten that period. I can bear witness, moreover, to the fact that the examination of appeals for mercy is conducted in France with a seriousness that does not exclude the visible inclination to pardon, in so far as the law and customs permit.

15 Sunday not being a day of execution, Saturday night is always better in the cell blocks reserved for those condemned to death.

He is no longer a man but a thing waiting to be handled by the executioners. He is kept as if he were inert matter, but he still has a consciousness which is his chief enemy.

When the officials whose job it is to kill that man call him a parcel, they know what they are saying. To be unable to do anything against the hand that moves you from one place to another, holds you or rejects you, is this not indeed being a parcel, or a thing, or, better, a hobbled animal? Even then an animal can refuse to eat. The condemned man cannot. He is given the benefit of a special diet (at Fresnes, Diet No. 4 with extra milk, wine, sugar, jam, butter); they see to it that he nourishes himself. If need be, he is forced to do so. The animal that is going to be killed must be in the best condition. The thing or the animal has a right only to those debased freedoms that are called whims. 'They are very touchy,' a top-sergeant at Fresnes says without the least irony of those condemned to death. Of course, but how else can they have contact with freedom and the dignity of the will that man cannot do without? Touchy or not, the moment the sentence has been pronounced the condemned man enters an imperturbable machine. For a certain number of weeks he travels along in the intricate machinery that determines his every gesture and eventually hands him over to those who will lay him down on the killing machine. The parcel is no longer subject to the laws of chance that hang over the living creature but to mechanical laws that allow him to foresee accurately the day of his beheading.

That day his being an object comes to an end. During the three-quarters of an hour separating him from the end, the certainty of a powerless death stifles everything else; the animal, tied down and amenable, knows a hell that makes the hell he is threatened with seem ridiculous. The Greeks, after all, were more humane with their hemlock. They left their condemned a relative freedom, the possibility of putting off or hastening the hour of his death. They gave him a choice between suicide and execution. On the other hand, in order to be doubly sure, we deal with the culprit ourselves. But there could not really be any justice unless the condemned, after making known his decision months in advance, had approached his victim, bound him firmly, informed him that he would be put to death in an hour, and had finally used that hour to set up the apparatus of death. What criminal ever reduced his victim to such a desperate and powerless condition?

This doubtless explains the odd submissiveness that is customary in the condemned at the moment of their execution. These men who have nothing more to lose could play their last card, choose to die of a chance bullet or be guillotined in the kind of frantic struggle that dulls all the faculties. In a way, this would amount to dying freely. And yet, with but few exceptions, the rule is for the condemned to walk towards death passively in a sort of dreary despondency. That is probably what our journalists mean when they say that the condemned died courageously. We must read between the lines that the condemned made no noise, accepted his status as a parcel, and that everyone is grateful to him for this. In such a degrading business, the interested party shows a praiseworthy sense of propriety by keeping the degradation from lasting too long. But the compliments and the certificates of courage belong to the general mystification surrounding the death penalty. For the condemned will often be seemly in proportion to the fear he feels. He will deserve the praise of the press only if his fear or his feeling of isolation is great enough to sterilize him completely. Let there be no misunderstanding. Some among the condemned, whether political or not, die heroically, and they must be granted the proper admiration and respect. But the majority of them know only the silence of fear, only the impassivity of fright, and it seems to me that such terrified silence deserves even greater respect. When the priest Bela Just offers to write to the family of a young condemned man a few moments before he is hanged and hears the reply: 'I have no courage, even for that,' how can a priest, hearing that confession of weakness, fail to honour the most wretched and most sacred thing in man? Those who say nothing but leave a little pool on the spot from which they are taken – who would dare say they died as cowards? And how can we describe the men who reduced them to such cowardice? After all, every murderer when he kills runs the risk of the most dreadful of deaths, whereas those who kill him risk nothing except advancement.

No, what man experiences at such times is beyond all morality. Not virtue, nor courage, nor intelligence, nor even innocence has anything to do with it. Society is suddenly reduced to a state of primitive terrors where nothing can be judged. All equity and all dignity have disappeared. 'The conviction of innocence does not immunize against brutal treatment . . . . I have seen authentic bandits die courageously whereas innocent men went to their deaths trembling in every muscle.'[16] When the same man adds that, according to his experience, intellectuals show more weakness, he is not implying that such men have less courage than others but merely that they have more imagination. Having to face an inevitable death, any man, whatever his convictions, is torn asunder from head to toe.[17] The feeling of powerlessness and solitude of the condemned man, bound and up against the public coalition that demands his death, is in itself an unimaginable punishment. From this point of view, too, it would be better for the execution to be public. The actor in every man could then come to the aid of the terrified animal and help him cut a figure, even in his own eyes. But darkness and secrecy offer no recourse. In such a disaster, courage, strength of soul, even faith may be disadvantages. As a general rule, a man is undone by waiting for capital punishment well before he dies. Two deaths

16 Bela Just: op. cit.
17 A great surgeon, a Catholic himself, told me that as a result of his experience he did not even inform believers when they had an incurable cancer. According to him, the shock might destroy even their faith.

are inflicted on him, the first being worse than the second, whereas he killed but once. Compared to such torture, the penalty of retaliation seems like a civilized law. It never claimed that the man who gouged out one of his brother's eyes should be totally blinded.

Such a basic injustice has repercussions, besides, on the relatives of the executed man. The victim has his family, whose sufferings are generally very great and who, most often, want to be avenged. They are, but the relatives of the condemned man then discover an excess of suffering that punishes them beyond all justice. A mother's or a father's long months of waiting, the visiting-room, the artificial conversations filling up the brief moments spent with the condemned man, the visions of the execution are all tortures that were not imposed on the relatives of the victim. Whatever may be the feelings of the latter, they cannot want the revenge to extend so far beyond the crime and to torture people who share their own grief. 'I have been reprieved, Father,' writes a condemned man, 'I can't yet realize the good fortune that has come my way. My reprieve was signed on April 30 and I was told Wednesday as I came back from the visiting-room. I immediately informed Papa and Mama, who had not yet left the prison. You can imagine their happiness.'[18] We can indeed imagine it, but only in so far as we can imagine their uninterrupted suffering until the moment of the reprieve, and the final despair of those who receive the other notification, which punishes, in iniquity, their innocence and their misfortune.

To cut short this question of the law of retaliation, we must note that even in its primitive form it can operate only between two individuals of whom one is absolutely innocent and the

18 Father Devoyod: op. cit. Equally impossible to read calmly the petitions for reprieve presented by a father or a mother who obviously does not understand such sudden misfortune.

other absolutely guilty. The victim, to be sure, is innocent. But can the society that is supposed to represent the victim lay claim to innocence? Is it not responsible, at least in part, for the crime it punishes so severely? This theme has often been developed, and I shall not repeat the arguments that all sorts of thinkers have brought forth since the eighteenth century. They can be summed up anyway by saying that every society has the criminals it deserves. But in so far as France is concerned, it is impossible not to point out the circumstances that ought to make our legislators more modest. Answering an inquiry of the *Figaro* in 1952 on the death penalty, a colonel asserted that establishing hard labour for life as the most severe penalty would amount to setting up schools of crime. That high-ranking officer seemed to be ignorant, and I can only congratulate him, of the fact that we already have our schools of crime, which differ from our federal prisons in this notable regard: it is possible to leave them at any hour of the day or night; they are the taverns and slums, the glory of our Republic. On this point it is impossible to express oneself moderately.

Statistics show 64,000 overcrowded dwellings (from three to five persons per room) in the city of Paris alone. To be sure, the killer of children is a particularly vile creature who scarcely arouses pity. It is probable, too (I say probable), that none of my readers, forced to live in the same conditions, would go so far as to kill children. Hence there is no question of reducing the culpability of certain monsters. But those monsters, in decent dwellings, would perhaps have had no occasion to go so far. The least that can be said is that they are not alone guilty, and it seems strange that the right to punish them should be granted to the very people who subsidize, not housing, but the growing of beets for the production of alcohol.[19]

But alcohol makes this scandal even more shocking. It is known that the French nation is systematically intoxicated by

19 France ranks first among countries for its consumption of alcohol and fifteenth in building.

its parliamentary majority, for generally vile reasons. Now, the proportion of alcohol's responsibility in the cause of blood-thirsty crimes is shocking. A lawyer (Maître Guillon) estimated it at 60 per cent. For Dr Lagriffe the proportion extends from 41.7 to 72 per cent. An investigation carried out in 1951 in the clearing-centre of the Fresnes prison, among the common-law criminals, showed 29 per cent to be chronic alcoholics and 24 per cent to have an alcoholic inheritance. Finally, 95 per cent of the killers of children are alcoholics. These are impressive figures. We can balance them with an even more magnificent figure: the tax report of a firm producing *apéritifs*, which in 1953 showed a profit of 410 million francs. Comparison of these figures justifies informing the stockholders of that firm and the Deputies with a financial interest in alcohol that they have certainly killed more children than they think. As an opponent of capital punishment, I am far from asking that they be condemned to death. But, to begin with, it strikes me as indispensable and urgent to take them under military escort to the next execution of a murderer of children and to hand them on their way out a statistical report including the figures I have given.

The State that sows alcohol cannot be surprised to reap crime.[20] Instead of showing surprise, it simply goes on cutting off heads into which it has poured so much alcohol. It metes out justice imperturbably and poses as a creditor: its good conscience does not suffer at all. Witness the alcohol salesman who, in answer to the *Figaro*'s inquiry, exclaimed: 'I know just what the staunchest enemy of the death penalty would do if, having a weapon within reach, he suddenly saw assassins on the point of killing his father, his mother, his children, or his best friend. Well!' That 'well' in itself seems somewhat alcoholized.

---

20 The partisans of the death penalty made considerable publicity at the end of the last century about an increase in criminality beginning in 1880, which seemed to parallel a decrease in application of the penalty. But in 1880 a law was promulgated that permitted bars to be opened without any prior authorization. After that, just try to interpret statistics!

Naturally, the staunchest enemy of capital punishment would shoot those murderers, and rightly so, without thereby losing any of his reasons for staunchly defending abolition of the death penalty. But if he were to follow through his thinking and the aforementioned assassins reeked of alcohol, he would then go and take care of those whose vocation is to intoxicate future criminals. It is even quite surprising that the relatives of victims of alcoholic crimes have never thought of getting some enlightenment from the Parliament. Yet nothing of the sort takes place, and the State, enjoying general confidence, even supported by public opinion, goes on chastising assassins (particularly the alcoholics) somewhat in the way the pimp chastises the hard-working creatures who assure his livelihood. But the pimp at least does no moralizing. The State does. Although jurisprudence admits that drunkenness sometimes constitutes an extenuating circumstance, the State is ignorant of chronic alcoholism. Drunkenness, however, accompanies only crimes of violence, which are not punished with death, whereas the chronic alcoholic is capable also of premeditated crimes, which will bring about his death. Consequently, the State reserves the right to punish in the only case in which it has a real responsibility.

Does this amount to saying that every alcoholic must be declared irresponsible by a State that will beat its breast until the nation drinks nothing but fruit juice? Certainly not. No more than that the reasons based on heredity should cancel all culpability. The real responsibility of an offender cannot be precisely measured. We know that arithmetic is incapable of adding up the number of our antecedents, whether alcoholic or not. Going back to the beginning of time, the figure would be twenty-two times, raised to the tenth power, greater than the number of present inhabitants of the earth. The number of bad or morbid predispositions our antecedents have been able to transmit to us is, thus, incalculable. We come into the world laden with the weight of an infinite necessity. One would have to grant us, therefore, a general irresponsibility. Logic would demand that neither punishment nor reward should ever be meted out, and, by the same token, all society would become impossible. The instinct of preservation of societies, and hence of individuals, requires instead that individual responsibility be postulated and accepted without dreaming of an absolute indulgence that would amount to the death of all society. But the same reasoning must lead us to conclude that there never exists any total responsibility or, consequently, any absolute punishment or reward. No one can be rewarded completely, not even the winners of Nobel Prizes. But no one should be punished absolutely if he is thought guilty, and certainly not if there is a chance of his being innocent. The death penalty, which really neither provides an example nor assures distributive justice, simply usurps an exorbitant privilege by claiming to punish an always relative culpability by a definitive and irreparable punishment.

If indeed capital punishment represents a doubtful example and an unsatisfactory justice, we must agree with its defenders that it is eliminative. The death penalty definitively eliminates the condemned man. That alone, to tell the truth, ought to exclude, for its partisans especially, the repetition of risky arguments which, as we have just seen, can always be contested. Instead, one might frankly say that it is definitive because it must be, and affirm that certain men are irremediable in society, that they constitute a permanent danger for every citizen and for the social order, and that therefore, before anything else, they must be suppressed. No one, in any case, can refute the existence in society of certain wild animals whose energy and brutality nothing seems capable of breaking. The death penalty, to be sure, does not solve the problem they create. Let us agree, at least, that it suppresses the problem.

I shall come back to such men. But is capital punishment applied only to them? Is there any assurance that none of those executed is remediable? Can it even be asserted that none of them is innocent? In both cases, must it not be admitted that capital punishment is eliminative only in so far as it is irreparable? The 15th of March 1957, Burton Abbott was executed in California, condemned to death for having murdered a little girl of fourteen. Men who commit such a heinous crime are, I believe, classified among the irremediable. Although Abbott continually protested his innocence, he was condemned. His execution had been set for the 15th of March at ten o'clock. At 9:10 a delay was granted to allow his attorneys to make a final appeal.[21] At eleven o'clock the appeal was refused. At 11:15 Abbott entered the gas chamber. At 11:18 he breathed in the first whiffs of gas. At 11:20 the secretary of the Committee on Reprieves called on the telephone. The Committee had changed its mind. They had tried to reach the Governor, who was out sailing; then they had phoned the prison directly. Abbott was taken from the gas chamber. It was too late. If only it had been cloudy over California that day, the Governor would not have gone out sailing. He would have telephoned two minutes earlier; today Abbott would be alive and would perhaps see his innocence proved. Any other penalty, even the harshest, would have left him that chance. The death penalty left him none.

This case is exceptional, some will say. Our lives are exceptional, too, and yet, in the fleeting existence that is ours, this takes place near us, at some ten hours' distance by air. Abbott's misfortune is less an exception than a news item like so many others, a mistake that is not isolated if we can believe our newspapers (see the Deshays case, to cite but the most recent one). The jurist Olivecroix, applying the law of probability to the chance of judicial error, around 1860, concluded that perhaps one innocent man was condemned in every two

---

21 It must be noted that the custom in American prisons is to move the condemned man into another cell on the eve of his execution while announcing to him the ceremony in store for him.

hundred and fifty-seven cases. The proportion is small? It is small in relation to average penalties. It is infinite in relation to capital punishment. When Hugo writes that to him the name of the guillotine is Lesurques,[22] he does not mean that all those who are decapitated are Lesurques, but that one Lesurques is enough for the guillotine to be permanently dishonoured. It is understandable that Belgium gave up once and for all pronouncing the death penalty after a judicial error and that England raised the question of abolition after the Hayes case. It is also possible to understand the conclusions of the Attorney General who, when consulted as to the appeal of a very probably guilty criminal whose victim had not been found, wrote: 'The survival of X . . . gives the authorities the possibility of examining at leisure any new clue that might eventually be brought in as to the existence of his wife.[23] . . . On the other hand, the execution, by cancelling that hypothetical possibility of examination, would, I fear, give to the slightest clue a theoretical value, a power of regret that I think it inopportune to create.' A love of justice and truth is expressed here in a most moving way, and it would be appropriate to quote often in our courts that 'power of regret' which so vividly sums up the danger that faces every juror. Once the innocent man is dead, no one can do anything for him, in fact, but to rehabilitate him, if there is still someone to ask for this. Then he is given back his innocence, which, to tell the truth, he had never lost. But the persecution of which he was a victim, his dreadful sufferings, his horrible death have been given him for ever. It remains only to think of the innocent men of the future, so that these tortures may be spared them. This was done in Belgium. In France consciences are apparently untroubled.

Probably the French take comfort from the idea that justice has progressed hand in hand with science. When the learned

---

22 This is the name of the innocent man guillotined in the case of the *Courrier de Lyon*.
23 The condemned man was accused of having killed his wife. But her body had not been found.

expert holds forth in court, it seems as if a priest has spoken, and the jury, raised in the religion of science, expresses its opinion. However, recent cases, chief among them the Besnard case, have shown us what a comedy of experts is like. Culpability is no better established for having been established in a test tube, even a graduated one. A second test tube will tell a different story, and the personal equation loses none of its importance in such dangerous mathematics. The proportion of learned men who are really experts is the same as that of judges who are psychologists, hardly any greater than that of serious and objective juries. Today, as yesterday, the chance of error remains. Tomorrow another expert testimony will declare the innocence of some Abbott or other. But Abbott will be dead, scientifically dead, and the science that claims to prove innocence as well as guilt has not yet reached the point of resuscitating those it kills.

Among the guilty themselves, is there any assurance that none but the irretrievable have been killed? All those who, like me, have at a period of their lives necessarily followed the assize courts know that a large element of chance enters into any sentence. The look of the accused, his antecedents (adultery is often looked upon as an aggravating circumstance by jurors who may or may not all have been always faithful), his manner (which is in his favour only if it is conventional – in other words, play-acting most of the time), his very elocution (the old hands know that one must neither stammer nor be too eloquent), the mishaps of the trial enjoyed in a sentimental key (and the truth, alas, is not always emotionally effective): so many flukes that influence the final decision of the jury. At the moment of the death verdict, one may be sure that to arrive at the most definite of penalties, an extraordinary combination of uncertainties was necessary. When it is known that the supreme verdict depends on the jury's evaluation of the extenuating circumstances, when it is known, above all, that the reform of 1832 gave our juries the power of granting *indeterminate* extenuating circumstances, it is possible to imagine the latitude left to the passing mood of the jurors. The law no longer foresees precisely the cases in which death is to be the outcome; so the jury decides after the event by guesswork. Inasmuch as there are never two comparable juries, the man who is executed might well not have been. Beyond reclaim in the eyes of the respectable people of Ille-et-Vilaine, he would have been granted a semblance of excuse by the good citizens of the Var. Unfortunately, the same blade falls in the two Départements. And it makes no distinction.

The temporal risks are added to the geographical risks to increase the general absurdity. The French Communist workman who has just been guillotined in Algeria for having put a bomb (discovered before it went off) in a factory locker-room was condemned as much because of the general climate as because of what he did. In the present state of mind in Algeria, there was a desire at one and the same time to prove to the Arab opinion that the guillotine was designed for Frenchmen too and to satisfy the French opinion wrought up by the crimes of terrorism. At the same moment, however, the Minister who approved the execution was accepting Communist votes in his electoral district. If the circumstances had been different, the accused would have got off easy and his only risk, once he had become a Deputy of the party, would be finding himself having a drink at the same bar as the Minister someday. Such thoughts are bitter, and one would like them to remain alive in the minds of our leaders. They must know that times and customs change; a day comes when the guilty man, too rapidly executed, does not seem so black. But it is too late and there is no alternative but to repent or to forget. Of course, people forget. None the less, society is no less affected. The unpunished crime, according to the Greeks, infected the whole city. But innocence condemned or crime too severely punished, in the long run, soils the city just as much. We know this, in France.

Such, it will be said, is human justice, and, despite its imperfections, it is better than arbitrariness. But that sad evaluation is bearable only in connection with ordinary penalties. It is scandalous in the face of verdicts of death. A classic treatise on French law, in order to excuse the death penalty for not involving degrees, states this: 'Human justice has not the slightest desire to assure such a proportion. Why? Because it knows it is frail.' Must we therefore conclude that such frailty authorizes us to pronounce an absolute judgment and that, uncertain of ever achieving pure justice, society must rush headlong, through the greatest risks, towards supreme injustice? If justice admits that it is frail, would it not be better for justice to be modest and to allow its judgments sufficient latitude so that a mistake can be corrected?[24] Could not justice concede to the criminal the same weakness in which society finds a sort of permanent extenuating circumstance for itself? Can the jury decently say: 'If I kill you by mistake, you will forgive me when you consider the weaknesses of our common nature. But I am condemning you to death without considering those weaknesses or that nature'? There is a solidarity of all men in error and aberration. Must that solidarity operate for the tribunal and be denied the accused? No, and if justice has any meaning in this world, it means nothing but the recognition of that solidarity; it cannot, by its very essence, divorce itself from compassion. Compassion, of course, can in this instance be but awareness of a common suffering and not a frivolous indulgence paying no attention to the sufferings and rights of the victim. Compassion does not exclude punishment, but it suspends the final condemnation. Compassion loathes the definitive, irreparable measure that does an injustice to mankind as a whole because of failing to take into account the wretchedness of the common condition.

---

24 We congratulated ourselves on having reprieved Sillon, who recently killed his four-year-old daughter in order not to give her to her mother, who wanted a divorce. It was discovered, in fact, during his imprisonment that Sillon was suffering from a brain tumour that might explain the madness of his deed.

To tell the truth, certain juries are well aware of this, for they often admit extenuating circumstances in a crime that nothing can extenuate. This is because the death penalty seems excessive to them in such cases and they prefer not punishing enough to punishing too much. The extreme severity of the penalty then favours crime instead of penalizing it. There is not a court session during which we do not read in the press that a verdict is incoherent and that, in view of the facts, it seems either insufficient or excessive. But the jurors are not ignorant of this. However, faced with the enormity of capital punishment, they prefer, as we too should prefer, to look like fools rather than to compromise their nights to come. Knowing themselves to be fallible, they at least draw the appropriate consequences. And true justice is on their side precisely in so far as logic is not.

There are, however, major criminals whom all juries would condemn at any time and in any place whatever. Their crimes are not open to doubt, and the evidence brought by the accusation is confirmed by the confessions of the defence. Most likely, everything that is abnormal and monstrous in them is enough to classify them as pathological. But the psychiatric experts, in the majority of cases, affirm their responsibility. Recently in Paris a young man, somewhat weak in character but kind and affectionate, devoted to his family, was, according to his own admission, annoyed by a remark his father made about his coming home late. The father was sitting reading at the dining-room table. The young man seized an axe and dealt his father several blows from behind. Then in the same way he struck down his mother, who was in the kitchen. He undressed, hid his bloodstained trousers in the closet, went to make a call on the family of his fiancée, without showing any signs, then returned home and notified the police that he had just found his parents murdered. The police immediately discovered the bloodstained trousers and, without difficulty, got a calm confession from the parricide.

The psychiatrists decided that this man who murdered through annoyance was responsible. His odd indifference, of which he was to give other indications in prison (showing pleasure because his parents' funeral had attracted so many people – 'They were much loved,' he told his lawyer), cannot, however, be considered as normal. But his reasoning power was apparently untouched.

Many 'monsters' offer equally impenetrable exteriors. They are eliminated on the mere consideration of the facts. Apparently the nature or the magnitude of their crimes allows no room for imagining that they can ever repent or reform. They must merely be kept from doing it again, and there is no other solution but to eliminate them. On this frontier, and on it alone, discussion about the death penalty is legitimate. In all other cases the arguments for capital punishment do not stand up to the criticisms of the abolitionists. But in extreme cases, and in our state of ignorance, we make a wager. No fact, no reasoning can bring together those who think that a chance must always be left to the vilest of men and those who consider that chance illusory. But it is perhaps possible, on that final frontier, to go beyond the long opposition between partisans and adversaries of the death penalty by weighing the advisability of that penalty today, and in Europe. With much less competence, I shall try to reply to the wish expressed by a Swiss jurist, Professor Jean Graven, who wrote in 1952 in his remarkable study on the problem of the death penalty: 'Faced with the problem that is once more confronting our conscience and our reason, we think that a solution must be sought, not through the conceptions, problems, and arguments of the past, nor through the hopes and theoretical promises of the future, but through the ideas, recognized facts, and necessities of the present.'[25] It is possible, indeed, to debate endlessly as to the benefits or harm attributable to the death penalty

25 *Revue de Criminologie et de Police Technique* (Geneva), special issue, 1952.

through the ages or in an intellectual vacuum. But it plays a role here and now, and we must take our stand here and now in relation to the modern executioner. What does the death penalty mean to the men of the mid-century?

To simplify matters, let us say that our civilization has lost the only values that, in a certain way, can justify that penalty and, on the other hand, suffers from evils that necessitate its suppression. In other words, the abolition of the death penalty ought to be asked for by all thinking members of our society, for reasons both of logic and of realism.

Of logic, to begin with. Deciding that a man must have the definitive punishment imposed on him is tantamount to deciding that that man has no chance of making amends. This is the point, to repeat ourselves, where the arguments clash blindly and crystallize in a sterile opposition. But it so happens that none among us can settle the question, for we are all both judges and interested parties. Whence our uncertainty as to our right to kill and our inability to convince each other. Without absolute innocence, there is no supreme judge. Now, we have all done wrong in our lives even if that wrong, without falling within the jurisdiction of the laws, went as far as the unknown crime. There are no just people – merely hearts more or less lacking in justice. Living at least allows us to discover this and to add to the sum of our actions a little of the good that will make up in part for the evil we have added to the world. Such a right to live, which allows a chance to make amends, is the natural right of every man, even the worst man. The lowest of criminals and the most upright of judges meet side by side, equally wretched in their solidarity. Without that right, moral life is utterly impossible. None among us is authorized to despair of a single man, except after his death, which transforms his life into destiny and then permits a definitive judgment. But pronouncing the definitive judgment before his death, decreeing the closing of accounts when the creditor is still alive, is no man's right. On this limit, at least, whoever judges absolutely condemns himself absolutely.

Bernard Fallot of the Masuy gang, working for the Gestapo, was condemned to death after admitting the many terrible crimes of which he was guilty, and declared himself that he could not be pardoned. 'My hands are too red with blood,' he told a prison mate.[26] Public opinion and the opinion of his judges certainly classed him among the irremediable, and I should have been tempted to agree if I had not read a surprising testimony. This is what Fallot said to the same companion after declaring that he wanted to die courageously: 'Shall I tell you my greatest regret? Well, it is not having known the Bible I now have here. I assure you that I wouldn't be where I now am.' There is no question of giving in to some conventional set of sentimental pictures and calling to mind Victor Hugo's good convicts. The age of enlightenment, as people say, wanted to suppress the death penalty on the pretext that man was naturally good. Of course he is not (he is worse or better). After twenty years of our magnificent history we are well aware of this. But precisely because he is not absolutely good, no one among us can pose as an absolute judge and pronounce the definitive elimination of the worst among the guilty, because no one of us can lay claim to absolute innocence. Capital judgment upsets the only indisputable human solidarity – our solidarity against death – and it can be legitimized only by a truth or a principle that is superior to man.

In fact, the supreme punishment has always been, throughout the ages, a religious penalty. Inflicted in the name of the king, God's representative on earth, or by priests or in the name of society considered as a sacred body, it denies, not human solidarity, but the guilty man's membership in the divine community, the only thing that can give him life. Life

---

26 Jean Bocognano: *Quartier des fauves, prison de Fresnes* (Editions du Fuseau).

on earth is taken from him, to be sure, but his chance of making amends is left him. The real judgment is not pronounced; it will be in the other world. Only religious values, and especially belief in eternal life, can therefore serve as a basis for the supreme punishment because, according to their own logic, they keep it from being definitive and irreparable. Consequently, it is justified only in so far as it is not supreme.

The Catholic Church, for example, has always accepted the necessity of the death penalty. It inflicted that penalty itself, and without stint, in other periods. Even today it justifies it and grants the State the right to apply it. The Church's position, however subtle, contains a very deep feeling that was expressed directly in 1937 by a Swiss National Councillor from Fribourg during a discussion in the National Council. According to M. Grand, the lowest of criminals when faced with execution withdraws into himself. 'He repents and his preparation for death is thereby facilitated. The Church has saved one of its members and fulfilled its divine mission. This is why it has always accepted the death penalty, not only as a means of self-defence, but *as a powerful means of salvation.*[27] . . . Without trying to make of it a thing of the Church, the death penalty can point proudly to its almost divine efficacy, like war.'

By virtue of the same reasoning, probably, there could be read on the sword of the Fribourg executioner the words: 'Lord Jesus, thou art the judge.' Hence the executioner is invested with a sacred function. He is the man who destroys the body in order to deliver the soul to the divine sentence, which no one can judge beforehand. Some may think that such words imply rather scandalous confusions. And, to be sure, whoever clings to the teaching of Jesus will look upon that handsome sword as one more outrage to the person of Christ. In the light of this, it is possible to understand the dreadful remark of the Russian condemned man about to be

27 My italics.

hanged by the Tsar's executioners in 1905 who said firmly to the priest who had come to console him with the image of Christ: 'Go away and commit no sacrilege.' The unbeliever cannot keep from thinking that men who have set at the centre of their faith the staggering victim of a judicial error ought at least to hesitate before committing legal murder. Believers might also be reminded that Emperor Julian, before his conversion, did not want to give official offices to Christians because they systematically refused to pronounce death sentences or to have anything to do with them. For five centuries Christians therefore believed that the strict moral teaching of their master forbade killing. But Catholic faith is not nourished solely by the personal teaching of Christ. It also feeds on the Old Testament, on St Paul, and on the Church Fathers. In particular, the immortality of the soul and the universal resurrection of bodies are articles of dogma. As a result, capital punishment is for the believer a temporary penalty that leaves the final sentence in suspense, an arrangement necessary only for terrestrial order, an administrative measure which, far from signifying the end for the guilty man, may instead favour his redemption. I am not saying that all believers agree with this, and I can readily imagine that some Catholics may stand closer to Christ than to Moses or St Paul. I am simply saying that faith in the immortality of the soul allowed Catholicism to see the problem of capital punishment in very different terms and to justify it.

But what is the value of such a justification in the society we live in, which in its institutions and its customs has lost all contact with the sacred? When an atheistic or sceptical or agnostic judge inflicts the death penalty on an unbelieving criminal, he is pronouncing a definitive punishment that cannot be reconsidered. He takes his place on the throne of God,[28]

28 As everyone knows, the jury's decision is preceded by the words: 'Before God and my conscience . . . .'

without having the same powers and even without believing in God. He kills, in short, because his ancestors believed in eternal life. But the society that he claims to represent is in reality pronouncing a simple measure of elimination, doing violence to the human community united against death, and taking a stand as an absolute value because society is laying claim to absolute power. To be sure, it delegates a priest to the condemned man, through tradition. The priest may legitimately hope that fear of punishment will help the guilty man's conversion. Who can accept, however, that such a calculation should justify a penalty most often inflicted and received in a quite different spirit? It is one thing to believe before being afraid and another to find faith after fear. Conversion through fire or the guillotine will always be suspect, and it may seem surprising that the Church has not given up conquering infidels through terror. In any case, society that has lost all contact with the sacred can find no advantage in a conversion in which it professes to have no interest. Society decrees a sacred punishment and at the same time divests it both of excuse and of usefulness. Society proceeds sovereignly to eliminate the evil ones from her midst as if she were virtue itself. Like an honourable man killing his wayward son and remarking: 'Really, I didn't know what to do with him.' She assumes the right to select as if she were nature herself and to add great sufferings to the elimination as if she were a redeeming god.

To assert, in any case, that a man must be absolutely cut off from society because he is absolutely evil amounts to saying that society is absolutely good, and no one in his right mind will believe this today. Instead of believing this, people will more readily think the reverse. Our society has become so bad and so criminal only because she has respected nothing but her own preservation or a good reputation in history. Society has indeed lost all contact with the sacred. But society began in the nineteenth century to find a substitute for religion by proposing herself as an object of adoration. The doctrines of evolution and the notions of selection that accompany them have made of the future of society a final end. The political utopias that were grafted on to those doctrines placed at the end of time a golden age that justified in advance any enterprises whatever. Society became accustomed to legitimizing what might serve her future and, consequently, to making use of the supreme punishment in an absolute way. From then on, society considered as a crime and a sacrilege anything that stood in the way of her plan and her temporal dogmas. In other words, after being a priest, the executioner became a government official. The result is here all around us. The situation is such that this mid-century society which has lost the right, in all logic, to decree capital punishment ought now to suppress it for reasons of realism.

In relation to crime, how can our civilization be defined? The reply is easy: for thirty years now, State crimes have been far more numerous than individual crimes. I am not even speaking of wars, general or localized, although bloodshed too is an alcohol that eventually intoxicates like the headiest of wines. But the number of individuals killed directly by the State has assumed astronomical proportions and infinitely outnumbers private murders. There are fewer and fewer condemned by common law and more and more condemned for political reasons. The proof is that each of us, however honourable he may be, can foresee the possibility of being someday condemned to death, whereas that eventuality would have seemed ridiculous at the beginning of the century. Alphonse Karr's witty remark: 'Let the noble assassins begin' has no meaning now. Those who cause the most blood to flow are the same ones who believe they have right, logic, and history on their side.

Hence our society must now defend herself not so much against the individual as against the State. It may be that the proportions will be reversed in another thirty years. But, for the moment, our self-defence must be aimed at the State first and foremost. Justice and expediency command the law to protect the individual against a State given over to the follies of sectarianism or of pride. 'Let the State begin and abolish the death penalty' ought to be our rallying cry today.

Bloodthirsty laws, it has been said, make bloodthirsty customs. But any society eventually reaches a state of ignominy in which, despite every disorder, the customs never manage to be as bloodthirsty as the laws. Half of Europe knows that condition. We French knew it in the past and may again know it. Those executed during the Occupation led to those executed at the time of the Liberation, whose friends now dream of revenge. Elsewhere States laden with too many crimes are getting ready to drown their guilt in even greater massacres. One kills for a nation or a class that has been granted divine status. One kills for a future society that has likewise been given divine status. Whoever thinks he has omniscience imagines he has omnipotence. Temporal idols demanding an absolute faith tirelessly decree absolute punishments. And religions devoid of transcendence kill great numbers of condemned men devoid of hope.

How can European society of the mid-century survive unless it decides to defend individuals by every means against the State's oppression? Forbidding a man's execution would amount to proclaiming publicly that society and the State are not absolute values, that nothing authorizes them to legislate definitively or to bring about the irreparable. Without the death penalty, Gabriel Péri and Brasillach would perhaps be among us. We could then judge them according to our opinion and proudly proclaim our judgment, whereas now they judge us and we keep silent. Without the death penalty Rajk's corpse would not poison Hungary; Germany, with less guilt on her conscience, would be more favourably looked upon by Europe; the Russian Revolution would not be agonizing in shame; and Algerian blood would weigh less heavily on our consciences. Without the death penalty, Europe would not be infected by the corpses accumulated for the last twenty years in its tired soil. On our continent, all values are upset by fear and hatred between individuals and between nations. In the conflict of ideas the weapons are the cord and the guillotine. A natural and human society exercising her right of repression has given way to a dominant ideology that requires human sacrifices. 'The example of the gallows,' it has been written,[29] 'is that a man's life ceases to be sacred when it is thought useful to kill him.' Apparently it is becoming ever more useful; the example is being copied; the contagion is spreading everywhere. And together with it, the disorder of nihilism. Hence we must call a spectacular halt and proclaim, in our principles and institutions, that the individual is above the State. And any measure that decreases the pressure of social forces upon the individual will help to relieve the congestion of a Europe suffering from a rush of blood, allowing us to think more clearly and to start on the way towards health. Europe's malady consists in believing nothing and claiming to know everything. But Europe is far from knowing everything, and, judging from the revolt and hope we feel, she believes in something: she believes that the extreme of man's wretchedness, on some mysterious limit, borders on the extreme of his greatness. For the majority of Europeans, faith is lost. And with it, the justifications faith provided in the domain of punishment. But the majority of Europeans also reject the State idolatry that aimed to take the place of faith. Henceforth in mid-course, both certain and uncertain, having made up our minds never to submit and never to oppress, we should admit at one and the same time our hope and our ignorance, we should refuse absolute law and the irreparable judgment. We know enough to say that this or that major criminal deserves hard labour for life. But we don't

29 By Francart.

know enough to decree that he be shorn of his future – in other words, of the chance we all have of making amends. Because of what I have just said, in the unified Europe of the future the solemn abolition of the death penalty ought to be the first article of the European Code we all hope for.

From the humanitarian idylls of the eighteenth century to the bloodstained gallows the way leads directly, and the executioners of today, as everyone knows, are humanists. Hence we cannot be too wary of the humanitarian ideology in dealing with a problem such as the death penalty. On the point of concluding, I should like therefore to repeat that neither an illusion as to the natural goodness of the human being nor faith in a golden age to come motivates my opposition to the death penalty. On the contrary, its abolition seems to me necessary because of reasoned pessimism, of logic, and of realism. Not that the heart has no share in what I have said. Anyone who has spent weeks with texts, recollections, and men having any contact, whether close or not, with the gallows could not possibly remain untouched by that experience. But, let me repeat, I do not believe, none the less, that there is no responsibility in this world and that we must give way to that modern tendency to absolve everything, victim and murderer, in the same confusion. Such purely sentimental confusion is made up of cowardice rather than of generosity and eventually justifies whatever is worst in this world. If you keep on excusing, you eventually give your blessing to the slave camp, to cowardly force, to organized executioners, to the cynicism of great political monsters; you finally hand over your brothers. This can be seen around us. But it so happens, in the present state of the world, that the man of today wants laws and institutions suitable to a convalescent, which will curb him without breaking him and lead him without crushing him. Hurled into the unchecked dynamic movement of history, he needs a natural philosophy and a few laws of equilibrium. He needs, in short, a society based on reason and not the anarchy into which he has been plunged by his own pride and the excessive powers of the State.

I am convinced that abolition of the death penalty would help us progress towards that society. After taking such an initiative, France could offer to extend it to the non-abolitionist countries on both sides of the iron curtain. But, in any case, she should set the example. Capital punishment would then be replaced by hard labour − for life in the case of criminals considered irremediable and for a fixed period in the case of the others. To any who feel that such a penalty is harsher than capital punishment we can only express our amazement that they did not suggest, in this case, reserving it for such as Landru and applying capital punishment to minor criminals. We might remind them, too, that hard labour leaves the condemned man the possibility of choosing death, whereas the guillotine offers no alternative. To any who feel, on the other hand, that hard labour is too mild a penalty, we can answer first that they lack imagination and secondly that privation of freedom seems to them a slight punishment only in so far as contemporary society has taught us to despise freedom.[30]

The fact that Cain is not killed but bears a mark of reprobation in the eyes of men is the lesson we must draw from the Old Testament, to say nothing of the Gospels, instead of looking back to the cruel examples of the Mosaic law. In any case, nothing keeps us from trying out an experiment, limited in duration (ten years, for instance), if our Parliament is still incapable of making up for its votes in favour of alcohol by such a great civilizing step as complete abolition of the penalty.

---

30 See the report on the death penalty by Representative Dupont in the National Assembly on 31 May 1791: 'A sharp and burning mood consumes the assassin; the thing he fears most is inactivity; it leaves him to himself, and to get away from it he continually braves death and tries to cause death in others; solitude and his own conscience are his real torture. Does this not suggest to you what kind of punishment should be inflicted on him, what is the kind to which he will be most sensitive? *Is it not in the nature of the malady that the remedy is to be found?*' I have italicized the last sentence, for it makes of that little-known Representative a true precursor of our modern psychology.

And if, really, public opinion and its representatives cannot give up the law of laziness which simply eliminates what it cannot reform, let us at least – while hoping for a new day of truth – not make of it the 'solemn slaughterhouse'[31] that befouls our society. The death penalty as it is now applied, and however rarely it may be, is a revolting butchery, an outrage inflicted on the person and body of man. That truncation, that living and yet uprooted head, those spurts of blood date from a barbarous period that aimed to impress the masses with degrading sights. Today when such vile death is administered on the sly, what is the meaning of this torture? The truth is that in the nuclear age we kill as we did in the age of the spring balance. And there is not a man of normal sensitivity who, at the mere thought of such crude surgery, does not feel nauseated. If the French State is incapable of overcoming habit and giving Europe one of the remedies it needs, let France begin by reforming the manner of administering capital punishment. The science that serves to kill so many could at least serve to kill decently. An anaesthetic that would allow the condemned man to slip from sleep to death (which would be left within his reach for at least a day so that he could use it freely and would be administered to him in another form if he were unwilling or weak of will) would assure his elimination, if you insist, but would put a little decency into what is at present but a sordid and obscene exhibition.

I suggest such compromises only in so far as one must occasionally despair of seeing wisdom and true civilization influence those responsible for our future. For certain men, more numerous than we think, it is physically unbearable to know what the death penalty really is and not to be able to prevent its application. In their way, they suffer that penalty themselves, and without any justice. If only the weight of filthy images weighing upon them were reduced, society would lose

---

31 Tarde.

nothing. But even that, in the long run, will be inadequate. There will be no lasting peace either in the heart of individuals or in social customs until death is outlawed.

CHINUA ACHEBE
Things Fall Apart

AESCHYLUS
The Oresteia

ISABEL ALLENDE
The House of the Spirits

THE ARABIAN NIGHTS
(in 2 vols, tr. Husain Haddawy)

MARGARET ATWOOD
The Handmaid's Tale

JOHN JAMES AUDUBON
The Audubon Reader

AUGUSTINE
The Confessions

JANE AUSTEN
Emma
Mansfield Park
Northanger Abbey
Persuasion
Pride and Prejudice
Sanditon and Other Stories
Sense and Sensibility

HONORÉ DE BALZAC
Cousin Bette
Eugénie Grandet
Old Goriot

GIORGIO BASSANI
The Garden of the Finzi-Continis

SIMONE DE BEAUVOIR
The Second Sex

SAMUEL BECKETT
Molloy, Malone Dies,
The Unnamable
(US only)

SAUL BELLOW
The Adventures of Augie March

HECTOR BERLIOZ
The Memoirs of Hector Berlioz

THE BIBLE
(King James Version)
The Old Testament
The New Testament

WILLIAM BLAKE
Poems and Prophecies

GIOVANNI BOCCACCIO
Decameron

JORGE LUIS BORGES
Ficciones

JAMES BOSWELL
The Life of Samuel Johnson
The Journal of a Tour to
the Hebrides

JEAN ANTHELME
BRILLAT-SAVARIN
The Physiology of Taste

CHARLOTTE BRONTË
Jane Eyre
Villette
Shirley and The Professor

EMILY BRONTË
Wuthering Heights

MIKHAIL BULGAKOV
The Master and Margarita

SAMUEL BUTLER
The Way of all Flesh

JAMES M. CAIN
The Postman Always Rings Twice
Double Indemnity
Mildred Pierce
Selected Stories
(in 1 vol. US only)

ITALO CALVINO
If on a winter's night a traveler

ALBERT CAMUS
The Outsider (UK)
The Stranger (US)
The Plague, The Fall,
Exile and the Kingdom,
and Selected Essays
(in 1 vol.)

GIACOMO CASANOVA
History of My Life

WILLA CATHER
Death Comes for the Archbishop
My Ántonia

MIGUEL DE CERVANTES
Don Quixote

ALEXANDER SOLZHENITSYN
One Day in the Life of
Ivan Denisovich

SOPHOCLES
The Theban Plays

MURIEL SPARK
The Prime of Miss Jean Brodie,
The Girls of Slender Means, The
Driver's Seat, The Only Problem
(in 1 vol.)

CHRISTINA STEAD
The Man Who Loved Children

JOHN STEINBECK
The Grapes of Wrath

STENDHAL
The Charterhouse of Parma
Scarlet and Black

LAURENCE STERNE
Tristram Shandy

ROBERT LOUIS STEVENSON
The Master of Ballantrae and
Weir of Hermiston
Dr Jekyll and Mr Hyde
and Other Stories

HARRIET BEECHER STOWE
Uncle Tom's Cabin

ITALO SVEVO
Zeno's Conscience

JONATHAN SWIFT
Gulliver's Travels

TACITUS
Annals and Histories

JUNICHIRŌ TANIZAKI
The Makioka Sisters

W. M. THACKERAY
Vanity Fair

HENRY DAVID THOREAU
Walden

ALEXIS DE TOCQUEVILLE
Democracy in America

LEO TOLSTOY
Collected Shorter Fiction (in 2 vols)
Anna Karenina
Childhood, Boyhood and Youth
The Cossacks
War and Peace

ANTHONY TROLLOPE
Barchester Towers
Can You Forgive Her?
Doctor Thorne
The Eustace Diamonds
Framley Parsonage
The Last Chronicle of Barset
Phineas Finn
The Small House at Allington
The Warden

IVAN TURGENEV
Fathers and Children
First Love and Other Stories
A Sportsman's Notebook

MARK TWAIN
Tom Sawyer
and Huckleberry Finn

JOHN UPDIKE
The Complete Henry Bech
Rabbit Angstrom

GIORGIO VASARI
Lives of the Painters, Sculptors and
Architects (in 2 vols)

VIRGIL
The Aeneid

VOLTAIRE
Candide and Other Stories

EVELYN WAUGH
The Complete Short Stories
Black Mischief, Scoop, The Loved
One, The Ordeal of Gilbert
Pinfold (in 1 vol.)
Brideshead Revisited
Decline and Fall (US)
Decline and Fall, Vile Bodies,
Put Out More Flags (UK)
A Handful of Dust
The Sword of Honour Trilogy
Waugh Abroad: Collected Travel
Writing

EDITH WHARTON
The Age of Innocence
The Custom of the Country
Ethan Frome, Summer,
Bunner Sisters
(in 1 vol.)
The House of Mirth
The Reef

This book is set in BEMBO which was cut
by the punch-cutter Francesco Griffo
for the Venetian printer-publisher
Aldus Manutius in early 1495
and first used in a pamphlet
by a young scholar
named Pietro
Bembo.